There is the realm of Fairie where elves enjoy immortal life and equally immortal passions . . . And there is the other realm, the mortal realm, where lives are lived in violence and misery. And there is the Veil between them, a Veil through which only elven men can pass. It has been this way since the dawn of time . . .

Or so elven Jerlayne was taught by her mother, the redoubtable Elmeene. And for unexplained reasons, Elmeene had warned Jerlayne not to marry the handsome elf, Aulaudin, but Jerlayne, who inherited her mother's stubbornness, if not her wisdom, refused to listen. Now, a century after her wedding day, Jerlayne's marriage is in shambles: None of her children have matured into elves like their parents. Her last daughter turned out to be a siren who leveled their home and killed half their household.

And now Jerlayne wants answers—she demands to know why Elmeene opposed her marriage. And Elmeene will give her those answers, but in doing so, these two elven women will confront an issue that will rock both realms to their very foundations. For they will open a secret door behind which every secret of faerie is revealed, every taboo is shattered, and elves and mortals will find themselves united against an unsuspected enemy.

JERLAYNE

LYNN ABBEY

DAW BOOKS, INC.

DONALD A. WOLLHEIM, FOUNDER

375 Hudson Street, New York, NY 10014

www.dawbooks.com

ELIZABETH R. WOLLHEIM

SHEILA E. GILBERT

PUBLISHERS

First Printing, April 1999
1   2   3   4   5   6   7   8   9

To My Parents

Chapter 1

"Shape a chain," Elmeene said, handing Jerlayne an iron bar three-fingers thick and as long as her forearm. "Twenty links, all the same, and nothing left over."

Jerlayne ran her fingers over the iron, expecting the worst and finding it beneath the rust: cracks, impurities, a hollow place the size of a rice grain. All that and Elmeene expected her to shape a twenty-link chain. No, that wasn't quite true: Elmeene expected Jerlayne to admit she wasn't ready for the challenge.

Elmeene was the best shaper in the heartland, possibly the best in all of Fairie. She was legend itself. Jerlayne had watched her mother make a twenty-link chain in a single day; and when Elmeene sharpened a knife between her thumb and forefinger, the blade kept its edge. Other mothers brought their daughters to Stonewell to learn that perfection *was* attainable.

Jerlayne was the youngest of Elmeene's six daughters. All her lessons had been learned in front of a chain-draped wall: a suffocating reminder that a Stonewell daughter didn't need to visit another homestead to learn perfection.

"Second thoughts?" Elmeene asked. "You wanted to know. You wanted to see for yourself. Now you have. Your father brought that iron home directly after you were born. It's waited all these years; it will wait a few more, if you're not ready."

"I'm ready," Jerlayne replied, swallowing a sigh. Not that a sigh, however dramatic, would fluster Elmeene. Nothing Jerlayne had ever said or done had raised more than her mother's exquisitely shaped eyebrows.

"You're certain? There's no shame in waiting another year, in waiting another ten years. You're young yet. Your sisters—"

"How old were you, Mother?"

That, at least, made Elmeene's eyes widen. Her dark chestnut eyebrows rose like crescent moons on her tawny forehead and for a moment it seemed Elmeene would admit what Jerlayne already knew. Then Elmeene reclaimed her serenity.

"What a strange question! I'm sure I don't remember how old I was. Why would anyone care? I was a daughter when I began, a woman when I finished. It will be the same for you whenever you shape your chain. Age doesn't matter. The chain is all that matters, all that has ever mattered."

Liar.

Jerlayne swallowed the accusation as she'd swallowed her sigh, but she couldn't banish it from her thoughts. How could Elmeene pretend she'd forgotten the day she shaped her first chain and reshaped Fairie in the process?

When Elmeene had been a girl—a daughter—Fairie had been in eclipse. The Veil between the realms was tattered because mortals had discovered how to work iron and elves had discovered that the merest touch of iron was poison. Elfin healers had named the poison *blooddeath* because it lurked in blood and was invariably fatal. The best a woman could do was ease a victim's suffering. By Elmeene's time, some two thousand years ago, every grown elf had the 'death: men because they had to forage beyond the Veil, women because they loved their sons and husbands.

And because of the chains.

Shaping a twenty-link chain was a daughter's rite of passage: without it, she couldn't bargain with the shadow-skinned goblins; without goblins willing to keep the fields safe from ogres, she couldn't found a homestead. If she couldn't found a homestead, then she'd never find a husband, and with neither homestead nor husband in her future, she might just as well remain a daughter with her parents—which most elfin daughters were doing when Elmeene was young because most mothers weren't sharing what little they knew about the deadly metal the goblins craved.

Except Elmeene's dying mother, Alseyne.

It hadn't been easy. Through four decades Jerlayne had compounded eavesdropping, unwary remarks, and an occasional pointed question to Jereige, her father, who was sometimes willing to talk about the past, into an imperfect understanding of Elmeene's history. Glaring holes remained, but Jerlayne knew she'd come by her contrariness honestly: Elmeene had badgered Alseyne mercilessly until, on her deathbed, Jerlayne's grandmother had agreed to share what little she knew about iron.

When those few lessons had ended, Elmeene had promptly gone off to shape her perfect chain: her doubly perfect chain, because not only were the links strong enough to satisfy the most demanding goblins, Elmeene had shaped it without catching 'death. Once elfin women knew how to avoid the 'death, it had only been a matter of time before they learned how to shape the poison out of their own blood, then out of their husbands' and sons' blood. Shaping those miracles hadn't saved Alseyne or a thousand others in whom 'death's roots plunged too deep, but they saved the elfin sons and daughters and, through them, Fairie itself.

Elmeene's chain, shaped in the winter of her fifty-first year and still hanging on her workroom wall, had been the first stitch that sewed Fairie together again.

If anyone had asked, Jerlayne would have said that she was proud of her mother and proud to be her mother's daughter. But in Fairie, while it was respectable to be first in shaping traditional chains or foraging beyond the Veil it was not at all respectable to be the first to make a change, even when that change had kept Fairie from certain doom.

If Jerlayne could have talked to her mother when questions first formed in her mind, she was certain she wouldn't have grown to resent Elmeene's every suggestion, every statement. But Elmeene rebuffed every question with blithe, unwavering disinterest.

Jereige had said ten thousand times: *Your mother has suffered enough. Be patient. Try to understand; try to forgive.*

Jerlayne had tried, but how could she forgive what she couldn't understand and how could she understand what was wrapped in denials? In ordinary conversation, elves might misplace a few years, even a few decades after they'd lived, as Elmeene had lived, for more than two millennia, but the truth was carved into each homestead's foundation stone, and the stones weren't all that hard to read: Elmeene had been not merely the first to shape a perfect chain, she was, and remained, the youngest.

Jerlayne could never be the first, but if she shaped her chain now, she'd become the youngest, by two seasons.

Age mattered to mortals beyond the Veil. Age, as Elmeene had said, wasn't *supposed* to matter in Fairie. Elves were children until a son learned to forage on his own beyond the Veil or a daughter shaped her chain. After childhood came maturity, which could last forever unless accident or apathy intervened. The elfin sages of Fairie's forests with their pointed ears looked different, but not older. *Old* was a mortal phenomenon. Men saw it as they foraged, but for women, who never parted the Veil, *old* happened only to animals.

No elf would admit that age mattered, but everyone knew who was older, who'd done what and when—especially Elmeene with her chain-decorated workroom

Of course, it wouldn't matter if Jerlayne waited another year before shaping her twenty-link chain. No shame at all; by then she'd be a year older and Elmeene's never-discussed accomplishment would remain unequaled, unchallenged, at least at Stonewell.

Especially at Stonewell.

Jerlayne made fists around the iron. A tingling like fine, wind-blown snow or stinging gnats swirled around her arms: a reminder that although iron had yielded its secrets, it remained deadly. Blooddeath was curable now, but make a false move while shaping the metal and a woman could find her soul trapped inside a crystal prison. Chains, with their twisted, continuous links, were especially treacherous. A daughter needed just the right amount of confidence; too much could be worse than too little.

Some daughters never tried. They lived out their lives on the homesteads where they'd been born. They weren't scyldrin; they lived in the great house with their parents, not in outlying cottages with gnomes or dwarves. Jerlayne knew a few immortal daughters, forever content to play their mothers' handmaidens. They seemed happy enough, but it wasn't accident or coincidence that all of Jerlayne's sisters—even timid Maialene—had made their chains, married, and founded their own homesteads before they turned seventy.

Jerlayne believed she'd go mad if she waited even another year.

"I'm ready, Mother," she answered when Elmeene repeated her question, then added, acidly: "As ready as you were."

"If you are no readier than that, daughter, then by the nameless powers that wove the Veil, I should take that iron from you and bury it beneath the biggest oak tree in the forest."

For a heartbeat Jerlayne saw her mothers's passion, strong,

like the iron she shaped, and brittle, too, for reasons that remained mysteries. Then, with her next heartbeat, Elmeene's imperturbable face returned and Jerlayne, feeling unaccountably ashamed, lowered her eyes before whispering, "I am ready."

"Look at me. Meet my eyes when you tell me you're ready to shape a twenty-link chain. This isn't another lesson. I'll be here. I won't leave this room until you're finished, but my hands won't be above yours and by the time I know you're in trouble, you'll have gone too far. I won't be able to pull you out. You've never seen a woman die in iron, but I have—" Elmeene paused, giving Jerlayne a moment to wonder: *How and when, exactly,* had *Alseyne died?*—"And I do not want to see it again. Look at me!"

Jerlayne did, regretting—not for the first time—that they couldn't make peace.

What would it matter if she became the youngest to shape a twenty-link chain without catching 'death? She knew the shaping could be done and that the 'death could be vanquished; Elmeene hadn't known. Elmeene had risked everything to save her mother's life; Jerlayne wanted only to be judged a woman and escape Stonewell.

"Mother, do you think I'm ready?"

Elmeene smiled and patted Jerlayne's arm. "If I did not, you would not have that iron in your hands."

"Twenty links."

"Twenty *perfect* links. I'll be here, beside you, when it's done."

Jerlayne closed her eyes. The tingling intensified, then subsided as she merged her soul with the iron. There were no words for what women did when they shaped. Men brought words back from the mortal realm and shared the images of their meanings when they joined with their wives; but women together, mothers teaching daughters, needed spoken words. They could shape metal, wood, and living flesh, but they couldn't pass a notion directly between minds as men did. Daughters learned shaping from their mothers' fingertips and in whispered exchanges of *Which way? . . . This way. Where? . . . Here. Like that? . . . No, like this . . .* and the most important questions of all: *Did you feel? Did you feel?*

Jerlayne did feel. From the first crooked stick she'd shaped arrow-straight, Jerlayne had felt the structure of things as fast as Elmeene revealed them to her. She could shape the grass as it grew, but metals were her passion: silver, tin, copper, and especially iron. In the beginning, Elmeene had tried to stifle Jerlayne's fascination with the treacherous metal. She'd sealed her workroom with locks that were too intricate, too heavy for a child to manipulate until the Stonewell dwarves complained that the mistress' daughter was shaping their tools into beautiful, but useless, toys.

After that the workroom door was never locked and Jerlayne had spent more time curled up among pillows, entranced with shaping, than she spent anywhere else, including her own bed.

She told herself, as she settled into the cushions, that this day was no different from any other day. It wasn't quite a lie. Jerlayne had made twenty-link chains many times before, from whatever she could find: wood, brass, even iron, and usually without Elmeene's permission. She *was* ready.

With deft and thoughtful prodding, the iron bar revealed its secrets until it filled Jerlayne's mind. The hardest part was dividing the bar into twenty equal sections, because after she'd divided it in half, and then half again—each a tedious, but not particularly difficult process—Jerlayne had to divide each of the quarters into fifths.

Jerlayne had practiced her fifths until she could divide her dreams into five equal parts. Here among the cushions, she'd had practiced sevenths and elevenths, either of which made fifths seem as easy as halves. She could have made a thirty-five link chain, if her mother had asked for it, but according to Elmeene, five was the largest number a shaping woman needed to know. Five was a natural number: a body had five fingers, five toes on each side, twenty digits in all: twenty, just like a goblin chain. Nothing except days came naturally in a group of seven, and eleven was unnecessary because twelve was more convenient and easier.

It wasn't that Jerlayne objected to convenience or ease. She'd rather divide a thing into halves or quarters instead of thirds, but seven, eleven, and even thirteen were as natural as five, no matter what Elmeene said.

Jerlayne knew better than let her thoughts wander when she had iron in her hands, but knowing was sometimes easier than doing. Her mind echoed with imaginary conversations until, despite knowing, Jerlayne had grown angry; and with anger came carelessness. Deep in the fourth quarter of iron, Jerlayne pushed when she should have pulled and found herself tumbling through cold, dark crystals.

Her mind's voice cried out: *Drop it. Let go!* Separation, fast and without regard for flesh left behind, was the surest way to escape from iron. A moment's delay and 'death would find her blood. More than a moment and motes of metal would seize her thoughts; she'd lose her soul to iron and die. But separation would end the shaping and destroy the metal, too. Elmeene would have to ask Jereige to forage another bar and that might take years.

There was another way, if Jerlayne could think fast enough, clearly enough to remember precisely where on the iron she'd been before she made her mistake. She'd practiced that, too, but in copper and tin, never iron, never while she was truly falling through metal crystals. Jerlayne recalled a pattern of rust. Her descent slowed; the iron fought back: crystals glowed hungrily at the edge of her thoughts.

She needed more than rust.

Blooddeath had pricked her before Jerlayne recalled an odd angle in the iron itself. She'd decided, at the time, it wasn't a flaw, and decided as well that she would leave it alone, but as she remembered its place amid the rust, she remembered enough to make the leap back to herself. Trembling from cold and shock, Jerlayne almost lost her grip on the bar, almost opened her eyes, almost saw the worried frown on her mother's face.

There would be no punishment if she abandoned her shaping, no limit to the number of times a daughter could try to shape her twenty-link chain. But Jerlayne would know, and her mother would know. Someday Elmeene would pat another daughter on the wrist and confide, as she'd once confided to Jerlayne: Your sister, Maialene, tried four times before she succeeded. And then Elmeene might add: your sister, Jerlayne, tried—

I tried once! Jerlayne shouted into her traitorous imagination. *And I will succeed or I'll die! I won't fail. I can't! I won't go back to being my mother's daughter . . . I'm done with lies and secrets and questions no one will answer.*

Jerlayne emptied her mind of everything that wasn't a twenty-link chain. She dove into the iron, straight back to the place where she'd made her mistake. She expected a mess, a tangle of iron and rust that might take a day to restore; she found a shimmering streak of her own blood locked into the metal. Her body had begun to merge with iron. Her escape had been by the narrowest of margins, yet she had escaped. She hadn't been transformed and though she'd almost certainly caught 'death, she knew the cure.

Still, only a raving fool would try to release her own blood from an iron prison.

Perfection had become impossible and, by rights, Jerlayne knew she should abandon the shaping. But it was a tiny streak and, studying it, she felt the way to shape the link quite thoroughly around it. There'd be a flaw in her chain, true, but she'd found larger flaws in every chain on the workroom wall, including three in Elmeene's "perfect" chain.

How important was perfection?

Could anyone truly achieve it?

Should she even try, when every chain on the wall was better than it needed to be?

Jerlayne balanced her questions. On one side: even if Elmeene couldn't perceive the flaw or didn't say anything about it, Jerlayne would know it was there. Worse, she'd have to spend the rest of her life lying about it. For an elf, a life could be a very long time. On the other hand: if Elmeene challenged the flaw, Jerlayne could challenge every chain on the wall. It would be a terrible fight and it would expand to include her father, which would upset him, but Jerlayne believed that she'd prevail because her mother had more to lose.

She began shaping links.

*　　*　　*

Time trudged uphill in a shaping trance. Two days could feel like ten and a twenty-link chain usually took three days to shape. Jerlayne had prepared for four, but she hadn't prepared for foolish mistakes and she'd never before been burdened with blooddeath. 'Death was an ache at the back of her thoughts, ignorable, but not forgettable: a constant drain on her strength.

Tears of pain and exhaustion were crusted on Jerlayne's cheeks as she released the last link and opened her eyes.

Elmeene was there, as she'd promised, with a cool towel and a cup of warm lemon-grass tea.

"Relax, Jerlayne. It's over. Drink this before you try to talk."

Jerlayne never took her mother's advice without testing it.

She wanted to see her chain and learn how long she'd been entranced. "Where is—?" she began, but her throat had swollen while she shaped and she began to choke.

Elmeene hugged her until the spasms passed, then offered the tea a second time. "Slowly, Jerlayne. Slowly. Let it cool on your tongue before you swallow. You've scarcely moved for two days."

"Two—?" Jerlayne was certain the shaping had taken four days, or even five.

"A bit more. It's evening now, but it's not yet midnight and you began in the afternoon."

A twenty-link chain shaped in just two days? It never took less than three . . . unless, in her weariness, she'd miscounted. "Where is it, Mother?" Jerlayne pushed the teacup aside. She was stronger than she'd been ten heartbeats earlier, but not strong enough to wrestle past her mother's arm. "Let me see my chain. How many links?"

"Twenty. Twenty iron links in two days! You faltered once, near the beginning: I thought you were going to let go, but you held on and, after that, I couldn't see your fingers for the fire and steam."

"Let me see it."

Elmeene picked it up from the floor. Jerlayne's eyes played tricks when she tried to count the links. She reached for the chain. Her mother jerked it out of reach.

"I need to know it's all there."

"I can count. You've shaped yourself proud." Elmeene dragged the links across her palm. "You've shaped Stonewell proud, Jerlayne. I'll study them in the morning, but you know what I'll find. Twenty links, two days, and two seasons younger. You've made your mark Jerlayne. You did what you set out to do."

Jerlayne slumped against the pillows. She sipped tea in silence until the cup was empty, then she kept it pressed against her lips, wondering if she'd kept any secrets from her cat-smiling mother. "I told you I was ready," she said weakly.

"Of course you were. Your mind's been filled with nothing but iron and chains since you first opened your eyes. Now that it's done, you can turn your mind to other things. There's more to life than shaping iron, Jerlayne."

They agreed on that, but for different reasons and to different ends. Jerlayne tried to return her mother's smile and leave the arguments for another day. Shaping a twenty-first link would have been easier.

"I'm not a child any longer. I'm a woman, now, an elf, the same as you and Father. I'm leaving Stonewell."

"Leaving? What are you—? A dwarf going walkabout? Where would you go, anyway?" Elmeene's breath caught in her throat. "No. No, Jerlayne. You can't be thinking *that*. You're not ready. Why . . . you've been so wrapped up in shaping, you don't have any friends. You've hardly trysted. You need time to explore, to enjoy yourself—"

"I know who I'm going to marry, Mother. I've known since the first time I saw him."

"Who?" Elmeene demanded then shook her head vigorously. "No, don't tell me. I don't want to know. This isn't the time for this discussion, Jerlayne. We're both too tired. We'll talk when we're rested."

"I'm not going to waver. Father will listen."

"Don't rush to your father!"

"I'm going to have my own homestead. I'm going shape the world."

The chain slipped through Elmeene's fingers, clattering to the floor. "Don't say such a thing, Jerlayne. Don't even think it. You frighten me, daughter. The world is as it is: two realms, Fairie with a homestead when you're ready for it, and theirs, with the Veil brought down between them. Don't meddle with the Veil! You're young yet. You may have learned everything I can teach you about shaping, but you haven't learned everything there is to know about elves and Fairie, or being a woman. Believe me in this, if you believe nothing else I say. Life isn't shaping. You're waiting for the sun to rise, but you're facing west! You're not ready."

"I'm not a child, Elmeene!"

That was the first time Jerlayne had used her mother's given-name, the way her sisters did when they came visiting from their homesteads. As a declaration of equality, it filled the workroom with a stagnant silence. Elmeene strode from shelf to table, extinguishing the lamps until only one remained. She carried that one to the door.

"You'll always be my daughter, Jerlayne. I will always tell you when I think you're facing the wrong way. I always have, but you never listen. You delight in not listening to me."

Suddenly, unexpectedly, the knowledge that she *could* leave brought caution to the front of Jerlayne's mind. "I do listen," she insisted softly. "But I have to leave. I have to."

Elmeene shook her head. She put her finger on the lamp's shutter.

"Why can't you understand me, Mother? You changed Fairie when you shaped your chain and Fairie survived. Father survived. We're all here because of you. Of all elves, you should know it isn't wrong to shape the world."

The workroom fell into darkness. "I've never said it was *wrong,* Jerlayne. I said you shouldn't do it . . . unless you have no other choice. You've made yourself blind to all the other choices. You remind me so much of your father . . ."

Jerlayne was speechless, trying to wring some meaning from her mother's remark. Jereige said she reminded him of Elmeene, and so did everyone who knew Elmeene well enough to have an opinion, but Jereige himself was slow to voice an opinion, slower to anger: the precise opposite of his wife and youngest daughter.

While Jerlayne pondered, Elmeene picked up the twenty-link chain.

"Rest well, daughter. Dream of what you've done and the choices that lie before you. We'll talk in the morning."

She closed the door. The room went dark.

Chapter 2

Jerlayne didn't dream of her chain or anything else. Concentrating on the ache of 'death, she kept herself awake until long after the rest of Stonewell had gone to bed. She didn't need a lamp to wander the tangle that was her parents' home, the only home she knew, though the corridors suddenly felt strange to her. Her destination was her private room, deep in an old quarter of the sprawling great house. There were at least ten ways to get there from the workroom, only one of which took her past Elmeene and Jereige's bedroom where, when she was still a daughter, she'd often stood for hours with her ear pressed against the wooden door. The door was partly open; the dark room within, entirely silent.

Married elves didn't need voices to talk to each other. They were joined and could share whole thoughts and memories. Men said joining was different—richer and deeper—than the kinship links they shared with other men. Women, of course, had nothing to compare joining with, although Jerlayne's sisters, all older and married before she was born, whispered that joining by itself was better than sex and joining *with* sex was indescribable.

Elmeene might think that her youngest daughter was a shy, studious recluse, but Jerlayne had discovered trysting several decades ago, about the same time as her shaping lessons had begun in earnest. She'd studied it thoroughly with the elfin sons she saw at Fairie festivals and at home with the younger gnomes and dwarves who were, if not exactly friends, the folk she knew best. Jerlayne hadn't trysted with the elf she intended to marry, hadn't so much as taken his hand or stolen a kiss as they walked, though she'd sought and accepted his gifts. Some might say that he'd already declared his interest, others might claim he tolerated her as a pesky, younger sister.

Still, neither joining nor sex were the driving forces behind

Jerlayne's determination to escape from Stonewell. Whatever her mother had told her father, however she'd told him, Jereige would understand that two women couldn't live under one roof, no matter how sprawling, not if their names were Elmeene and Jerlayne.

If she'd truly been able to change the world, Jerlayne would have skipped the traditional wedding. She didn't like fuss or festivities, but her mother did. Jerlayne knew there were battles not worth fighting. Her sisters' weddings were the stuff of Fairie legend; hers would be, too.

She tiptoed down the corridor to her room. The wall lamp, when lit with the matches that hung beside it, revealed a chamber that was considerably neater than she'd left it. How typical of Elmeene to take advantage of her chain-making to send a bevy of gnomes into a sweeping, dusting, cleaning frenzy. A thick carpet of fresh rushes sweetened the air and there were fresh linens on the bed. Standing beside the mattress, Jerlayne realized the linens weren't merely fresh, they were brand new.

The snow-white fabric was luminous in the moonlight, cool, and flawlessly smooth to the touch. Nothing like Fairie's homespun; Jereige must have foraged the cloth from the mortal realm. Elmeene had worked cascades of fairy-lace along the hems and selvedges.

Jerlayne ran her hand beneath the gossamer fringe. Instead of flowers or butterflies, the design was interlocking chains, twenty-link chains, knotted from white thread so fine no individual strands were evident.

Elmeene told the truth when she said there were homestead skills Jerlayne hadn't learned. Her lace-work, when she begrudged the time to do it, quickly devolved into a snarl of loops and knots best suited for the rag-bin. More than that, even if her thread-bending was as fine as her metal-shaping, Jerlayne knew—with sudden shame—that she'd never have made special bed linens for a daughter as troublesome as she knew herself to be.

She smoothed the lace, careful to make it appear untouched, careful to leave it unstained by her unexpected tears. Then she knelt in a corner and pried up one of the floorboards. A small metal box from the mortal realm nestled in the hole.

The box had a tight-fitting, hinged lid with a painted picture of oddly round-faced, winged children. Inside it held a handful of small, musty, and nearly black bryony berries. Elmeene kept a wax-sealed jar many times the size of Jerlayne's tin box on a shelf in her workroom, but Jerlayne's once-older sister Maialene, the one who'd needed four tries to shape the chain that freed her from Stonewell, had suggested she gather and dry her own berries.

Even you *might make a mistake someday and you might not want to tell Elmeene that you'd taken bryony from her jar. If you slip a handful in your sleeve every gathering-time, you can dry them yourself and keep them tucked away safe. Hidden. She'd never know.*

Staring at her never-touched hoard, Jerlayne had wondered how many times Maialene had resorted to a bryony cache. Maialene was Stonewell's least-accomplished daughter and the sister from whom Jerlayne had learned the most about the subjects their mother would never discuss. Maialene had a dazzling, but pompous, husband; a prosperous homestead not too far from Stonewell; and a tendency to lapse into liquid-eyed silence when she came visiting.

Between them, Maialene and Elmeene lived the lives Jerlayne intended to avoid.

In over two centuries of married life, Maialene had given birth to three elfin sons. She'd never borne a daughter and just last spring, at a wedding where the goblin wine had flowed too freely, Maialene had confided that she never would.

What if I couldn't teach her all that she needed to know? What if I made a mistake and lost her? The scyldrin are enough for me . . . and sons. My sons are my joy. I won't allow myself to shape a daughter.

Until that conversation Jerlayne's vision of her future had gotten no farther than escape from Stonewell. Her imagination stopped short of children because children meant daughters, sooner or later, and daughters meant she could find herself in Elmeene's unenviable, unimaginable place. That prospect and it alone had kept her from demanding her twenty-link test a decade ago. But Maialene had implied that an elfin woman had control over her children's shapes.

Once the notion had broached Jerlayne's imagination, it seemed, not merely possible, but inevitable. Stonewell, with its equal number of sons and daughters was unusual; most homesteads raised two or three sons for every daughter. Anyone who'd ever spent a cold, spring night in the birth-byre with the cows and ewes should have known that such a great disparity couldn't happen by accident. When Jerlayne thought of an elfin daughter as an accident in need of healing—healing was, after all, just another sort of shaping—then myriad possibilities had opened up in her mind. If Maialene had managed to shape herself three sons, Jerlayne was confident she could do it, too.

The six dark berries Jerlayne counted into her ice-cold palm were scarcely wrinkled and breathtakingly bitter on her tongue as she chewed them. After a nearly three-day fast, they struck her stomach like arrowheads. Within moments she was on her knees with her teeth clenched.

She'd swallowed bryony before—one berry, once a year—since she'd learned the cure during her twenty-fifth summer. The berries always nauseated her—no surprise considering how they worked—but memory was no preparation for the violent retching that squeezed her stomach into shapes best left unimagined. Jerlayne thought of the grayish must on the berries and concluded, between gasps, that six berries had been five too many.

The metal box tumbled loudly from fingers that suddenly, unexpectedly, grew numb and turned mottled, almost goblin-dark shades of blue. Berries bounced everywhere; she'd never collect them all.

Jerlayne had a vision of herself dead on her bedroom floor: blue-fingered, black-tongued, and surrounded by incriminating berries. The vision was stronger than the poison ripping her gut and gave her the strength to enter a shaping trance wherein she mated motes of the two poisons, iron and bryony, until the iron was gone. Rising from the trance, she retched what was left of the bryony into the chamber pot. The sun was rising, too, and her fingers showed blue in the dawn light. Hands trembling, Jerlayne shoved the hinged box into its hole and clumsily replaced the floorboard.

Anyone entering the room would see that the board had been moved and she had no strength to search for the scattered berries. The bryony would betray her and every risk she'd taken would be exposed, but Jerlayne was too weary to care. She blew out the lamp and had barely stretched between the lace-edged sheets before she fell asleep.

When Jerlayne opened her eyes again, she was ravenous, but refreshed—until she noticed that she was wearing a favorite nightgown, which she hadn't been wearing when she'd fallen asleep. Sitting up quickly, Jerlayne confirmed her other sudden fears: there wasn't a scattered berry on the floor and the loosened board had been hammered back into place. She checked beneath the board. The tin box held a handful of bryony berries.

Jerlayne cursed softly, invoking the name a mortal god in whom she did not believe, except at moments like this when she had to guess whether her reputation had been saved by one of the scyldrin, or if she owed her nightgown and more to Elmeene. If her savior were her mother, Elmeene might wait for days, even months or years, before collecting her debt. Jerlayne expressed her frustration with her fist, pounding the floorboard back into place.

"Secrets," she muttered, pulling off her nightgown. "Secrets everywhere. Secrets to keep the peace, one way or another and if you don't *want* to keep a secret, you've got to keep *that* a secret. I don't care where the sages send me, so long as there are no secrets."

The room was lit with afternoon light, but by the taste in her mouth, Jerlayne guessed she'd been asleep for several days. The mortal gods knew what else her mother might have done. Jerlayne washed quickly with cold water from a basin, then dressed in a warm shirt with mortal-realm buttons and a Fairie-woven skirt. The skirt was long enough to keep out drafts, short enough to walk the autumn meadows where she hoped to find her father and, with luck, salvage her escape from Stonewell. But, first things first; Jerlayne stopped in the kitchen on her way out to quell her rumbling stomach.

In mid-afternoon, Stonewell's large kitchen was a quiet place with only a few young gnomes sitting in a circle, gossiping as they peeled vegetables into a cauldron. They greeted Jerlayne politely and she returned the favor. No names were exchanged, though certainly they knew hers as she knew theirs. Jerlayne made a point of learning all the scyldrin names. Elmeene said itinerant scyldrin came and went too fast for remembering names and that Jerlayne would change her habits when she had her own homestead.

As usual, there was a bit of truth in Elmeene's remarks: the scyldrin rarely settled at the homestead where they'd been born. Once scyldrin—especially dwarves—were grown, they wandered from homestead to homestead until they found one they liked, one where no one recognized or remembered their faces. Like everyone else in Fairie, scyldrin cherished their secrets.

Only one of the young women in the kitchen had been born at Stonewell and none had declared an intention to settle there. Somewhere between guests and household, itinerant scyldrin pitched in, kept to themselves while keeping a close watch on everyone else, and, more often than not, moved on after a season or two. It was the watching that Elmeene objected to, and the silences.

Attitudes changed once a scyld declared an intention to settle. Settled scyldrin were part of Stonewell's family; young gnomes and dwarves were adopted by settled scyldrin of the same ilk, raised, and loved until they were ready to go off on their own. There were no tests for scyldrin, no twenty-link chains. They went where they wished until they found what they wanted.

Jerlayne envied their freedom until she counted its cost. Scyldrin weren't orphans. They knew exactly who their parents were: only joined elves had homesteads and only joined elves had children. If scyldrin said where they'd been born, they named their mothers and fathers as well. But the Elmeenes of Fairie, and the Jereiges, too, paid scant attention to their scyldrin and the scyldrin, once they started traveling, would tell an elf only where they'd been, never where they'd begun.

Jerlayne had to remind herself that Milia, who'd fallen silent with the other gnomes, was her sister—her older sister—and the others might be cousins. Wherever there were secrets, there had to be lies.

Head down, not meeting their silver, gnomish eyes, Jerlayne busied herself in the pantry. The food was all Fairie-fresh but her meal—cold meat, cheese, and a slathering of vinegary spice-sauce layered between slices of fresh bread—was a mortal inspiration. Beyond the Veil, folk often ate while walking, or so Jereige said.

From the kitchen Jerlayne walked across the fallow fields to the stream where, if her father was in Fairie, as he almost certainly was, and if Elmeene had talked to him, as she almost certainly had, Jereige would be waiting for her. Jerlayne finished her sandwich with three fields still to cross and found herself hoping that her father was not only warned and waiting, but that he had the makings of another sandwich with him.

Jereige was where she'd hoped to find him; not waiting, but hip-deep in the stream with the tip of a fishing pole waggling over his head and the late afternoon light glinting off a silk-and-feather lure. It would have been easier to catch fish with worms or dragonflies, or in the weir beside the mill, which was how the gnomes caught the fish that the kitchen cooked. Jereige wasn't interested in ease; he wasn't particularly fond of fish for supper, either.

Fishing, he said, soothed his mind after foraging in the mortal realm. A fisherman—or woman—couldn't waste a thought on anything but the lure while it was swirling overhead or he'd find himself with the hook in his hair and the silk line draped over his nose. The longer Jereige fished and the harder he concentrated on moving the lure, the better he claimed to feel when the setting sun sent him home.

Jereige had tried to teach Jerlayne the art of making the lure dance above the water; he'd taught all his other elfin children. Maialene was as enthusiastic about fishing as she was about anything. Jerlayne had declined the lessons. She wasn't enthralled by the notion of standing hip-deep in cold water and by the time her daily shaping lessons were over, she hadn't been interested in learning anything else, despite her father's assurances that fishing would ease the frustrations she felt after hours in Elmeene's workroom.

Jerlayne often wondered if her father had developed his fondness for fishing before or after he'd joined with Elmeene. She'd never been bold enough to ask.

He saw her coming through the willow trees and reeled in his whirling lure as gracefully as he reeled it out. A quilt and cushions waited on the bank; a basket of food, also. Jerlayne's stomach growled eagerly. The rest of her remembered that her father had already heard Elmeene's side of everything.

"Your mother said you'd likely wake up this afternoon," Jereige said, shedding his oilskin waders and setting his pole carefully against a tree. "Help yourself to whatever's in the basket. She said you'd be hungry when you got here. She packed it herself."

Everything, Jerlayne repeated to herself. She opened the basket, half-expecting to find it filled with reproachful bryony berries, but there was only bread, fruit, and a carefully covered bowl of her favorite pudding. Conflicting emotions, the same as she'd felt when she beheld the lace-trimmed bed linens, froze her where she sat.

"She showed me the chain you shaped. A fine piece of work, by all I could determine."

What could a man determine about shaped iron? What *had* Elmeene determined about her chain and the berries scattered across her floor, and what she told Jereige?

Jerlayne thought: *It's flawed, Father. There's a streak of my blood sealed in one of the links, so much blood that I caught the 'death and had to take bryony—and Mother caught me. Did she tell you already? I'm ashamed, but I don't see a way out.* She said: "I did my best."

"You were taught by the best, and now your lessons are behind you."

Her father had the kindest smile, the gentlest eyes of any man in Fairie. Had Elmeene told him what to say? Probably not; she didn't need to. Jereige, the fisherman, was expert at luring things to the surface, whether things were fish or a daughter's most inmost thoughts.

Jerlayne looked away from those eyes. "I'm ready to leave Stonewell, Jereige." She used his name, as she'd used Elmeene's. The shape was uncomfortable on her tongue. "I'm ready to marry and found a homestead."

"I'm not surprised that you're ready to leave Stonewell, but ready for marriage and a homestead? Can I be as certain of that? Can you?"

She stared at the stream. "I am."

"You're young—"

"I'm not!" She spun around to glare at him. Her anger melted instantly, but not her frustration. "Why does everyone say I'm young? I'm scarcely two years younger than Moth—than *Elmeene* was when the two of you founded Stonewell."

"Refounded," Jereige corrected, fisherman-calm. "That was a long time ago."

"Which means what? That what was right for you and Moth—*Elmeene* isn't right for me?"

"I mean only that what was necessary then might not be necessary now. Fairie had withered when your mother and I joined. Everywhere homesteads lay fallow and the Veil might have unraveled if those of us who'd survived hadn't settled quickly. Your mother and I settled at Stonewell, but on land that had long been part of Fairie. The fields were already cleared and there was a great house standing ready for us. Our first years together weren't spent living in the wilderness! Now there's very little old land left. I'd never say this is a bad thing, but lately the sages have been pushing the mists back and making Fairie grow as it hasn't grown since before I was born. Life is very hard against the Veil—and you only get one chance. You have so much promise, Jerlayne . . . let someone else settle along the Veil; you wait until some of the older elves decide it's time to retreat into the forest. Brookside has stood since before the 'death. Eydelen rarely parts the Veil for foraging and half their fields are fallow already . . ."

Jerlayne had no intention of settling herself in someone else's homestead, especially a homestead like Brookside which was one of Stonewell's neighbors. She'd expected better from her father. "I want my own homestead."

"You want to leave Stonewell. You're weary of your mother's lessons and you believe the only way to leave is to found your own homestead."

Jerlayne's heart skipped a beat. "Is there another way that no one's seen fit to tell me about?" she asked, bitterness intermixed with hope.

"You have five sisters, two married brothers. You could visit them, live with your brothers and sisters, see the sun rise over a different horizon. You never fostered. Almost every time I came home, I expected one or the other of you to say that you were going to live and learn somewhere else—"

"She *is* the best," Jerlayne interrupted, explaining why she, at least, had never suggested fosterage.

"And she wanted no one else to be your teacher, but that's over now. The mortals take *holidays,* a resting time when they let their lives lie fallow. It's not a bad notion. You could take a holiday with your sister."

"A *holiday* with Maialene at Brightwings?" Jerlayne blurted, and felt no need to apologize. "I'd choke on the boredom or the furniture!"

"Don't be so quick to judge, Jerlayne. You have other sisters, and your brothers married well—"

"I know what I want, Father and I won't find it living here or with anyone else except my own husband on my own homestead. I want to marry, I want to be my own mistress and I'm ready. I told Elmeene."

"Indeed you did, and she agrees with you—"

Jerlayne's eyes widened and her father's chin dipped decisively.

"Surprised? I would rather that you waited, but your mother tells me I must bring about this marriage you desire, with whomever you desire, and that I must ask no question beside 'What is his name?'"

"Aulaudin," Jerlayne interjected. Both her parents were skilled at controlling conversation by controlling which questions were asked and, more importantly, which answers were heard. Elmeene had done it two nights past, now her father had resorted to the same trick: they didn't *want* to know who she'd chosen. "I have chosen Aulaudin."

Her father's eyes widened. He stared at her as if she'd become a stranger. "Aulaudin of Briary?"

Elves weren't like the gnomes and dwarves, changing names or reusing them. Among Fairie's elves, there was only one Aulaudin, and Jereige knew it.

Aulaudin had been visiting Stonewell regularly since before Jerlayne had been born—since before Maialene had been born. He came with his brothers and their father, Maun, because Maun and Jereige were both blooddeath orphans and they remained kin-close.

Maun was not Jerlayne's favorite elf in Fairie. He held outrageous opinions, especially about goblins and ogres, and held them loudly. His sense of humor was atrocious: he played tricks on everyone and teased her mercilessly simply because she'd once asked him not to. He could be downright cruel when Jereige wasn't there to keep an eye on him . . . Jereige or Aulaudin.

Aulaudin was everything his father wasn't: kind, quiet, a listener rather than a talker, just like her father. In her earliest memories, Jerlayne saw Aulaudin sitting in the courtyard, saying little while her brothers swapped tales of daring adventure in the mortal realm. She'd been fascinated by his rust-colored hair; in truth, she'd wanted strands for shaping and, after a year of pleading that brought a blush to her cheeks when she recalled it, he'd given her a lock bound up in a black velvet ribbon.

Looking back, there was no denying that she'd been a strange, troublesome child, but Aulaudin hadn't been repelled by her questions or her determination to shape anything she could get her fingers around. By childhood's end, he'd become her friend and though he seemed to enjoy the courtyard boasting with the men, Aulaudin visited her when he came to Stonewell.

At least, Jerlayne thought he did. Her treasure box bulged with oddments Aulaudin had brought her from the mortal realm and they exhausted themselves with all-night conversation, but they'd never progressed beyond talk and trinkets. They'd never so much as kissed or walked together, arm-in-arm. Their paths never crossed at Fairie gatherings where he passed his time with the older men and avoided both dancing and trysting.

She'd never told Aulaudin what she'd just told her father and she watched, appalled, as frown lines formed on Jereige's face.

"Am I too late?" she demanded. Aulaudin *was* considerably older. She'd never understood why he'd never joined and founded a homestead with his wife. "Has someone spoken up for him?"

Jerlayne had heard no rumors, and she listened hard for them at every Fairie gathering she attended. As far as she'd been able to determine, none of the other elfin girls and unmarried women noticed him at all. She'd assumed he was waiting for her, and the thought that she'd assumed incorrectly threw cold water at her heart.

Jereige face stiffened. "No. Not recently."

"What do you mean, 'Not recently'?"

Her father cast a longing glace at his fishing pole before answering: "Aulaudin's not—he's not *suitable*. His time came and passed before you were born. He'll stay with his parents at Briary, as Joren, Nereige, and Brel stay with your mother and I."

Secrets. Things remembered, but not discussed, even in rumors. "I don't understand. Maun is your oldest friend, your dearest friend; you've said so yourself. I thought you'd be *happy* that I'd chosen Aulaudin. What's wrong with Aulaudin? What's not *suitable* about him? I've heard you say that Maun's the best forager in Fairie. Whenever a man needs help or advice beyond the Veil, you say he should turn to Maun of Briary. And Aulaudin's his right hand. I'll be the best-provided-for woman in all Fairie."

Another glance at the fishing pole, then, softly, with a frown: "You don't know."

"Know what? What can I know when no one tells me anything!" Jerlayne tried to laugh, but bitterness sharpened the sound and her father's frown deepened. She knew then what it had to be: "Tatterfall."

In Fairie, where nothing was supposed to change, nightmares could never be forgotten. Homesteads didn't always prosper, even on the old land. Sometimes, foraging, shaping, and goblin protection weren't enough: a hard winter or two, a flood, a fire, or other disaster could consume a young homestead. A few scyldrin might show up somewhere else, shocked and battered, to tell the final tale, but the elves never did. There was no starting over for elves. Joining was forever and so was their homestead.

If a homestead survived its first score of years, usually it was safe. Usually. Every once in a while—not since Jerlayne had been born—a more mature homestead vanished overnight. That fate had befallen Tatterfall, where Aulaudin's elder brother, Boraudin, had been the master.

The Veil protected all of Fairie from its mortal-realm enemies but, within Fairie, the elfin homesteads lived in dread of another enemy: ogres. The mortal descendants of gnomes and dwarves, ogres haunted the forests, reminding all the scyldrin why only elfin women bore Fairie's children. Ogres went naked in the coldest weather, or so Jerlayne had heard. She'd never seen a living ogre. Few had, and survived to tell their tale.

Ogres lived without fire; they ate their meat raw, and their favorite meat was torn from an elf, a dwarf, or a gnome. Armed with stone weapons, a horde of ogres might emerge, without warning, from Fairie's quiet forests to obliterate a homestead, elves, scyldrin, and goblins together, in a night.

"Aulaudin wasn't there," Jerlayne protested. "It wasn't his fault. It wasn't anyone's fault. Ogres destroyed Tatterfall."

"Did they?" Jereige asked.

Jereige's friend, Maun, claimed that Tatterfall's goblins hadn't honored their bargain, that they were responsible for his son's death. Maun's relentless arguing against the obvious had isolated all Briary from the rest of Fairie. Jerlayne knew her beloved was troubled by his father's unreasoning behavior but, as discussion didn't seem to ease Aulaudin's mind, she carefully avoided the subject—which was not to say she'd never thought about Tatterfall's end. Maialene said Maun's rust-haired son had been handfasted before Tatterfall, but not after. Jerlayne had asked as many questions as she'd dared without revealing the reasons for her curiosity, but her sister claimed not to remember the other woman's name, and no one else admitted remembering even that much.

"All the goblins were killed, weren't they?" Jerlayne countered her father's question, knowing that he'd been among the men who'd gone to witness the carnage afterward. "It wasn't that they didn't honor the bargain to protect Tatterfall, but that there were too many ogres and they were overwhelmed. I've heard *you* say that. I've heard you say that to Maun—not that Maun listens." Then Jerlayne posed a question of her own: "Why else would we give the goblins everything they ask for, if ogres weren't our greatest enemy?"

Ogres were as real and more dangerous than mortals beyond the Veil. Every spring, after the snow had melted but before the forest turned green, ogres grew desperate. No homestead was safe, even in Fairie's heartland. Jerlayne had never seen a living ogre because she'd always done what every right-thinking elf did when the great gong was struck: retreated into windowless rooms, behind locked doors, and stayed there while the goblins earned their keep.

When she was fifteen, when Stonewell had been attacked for the first time in her lifetime, Jerlayne had emerged as soon as the all-clear rang. She's seen the goblins hauling corpses into shadow. That had been enough; since then she waited indoors until Elmeene called her to help with the healing. She'd laid her hands on the damage an ogre mace did to dark-blue goblin flesh. She'd felt their pain and felt one of them die. They were a strange folk—cold, hard, even menacing—but without them, she'd have wound up in an ogre's stomach.

Jerlayne was thinking about the day—dreading it—when she'd have to bargain with a goblin for her homestead's protection when Jereige offered an unexpected answer to her question.

"Salt," he said seriously. "Your brothers and I would be hard-pressed to keep Stonewell in salt, and that's foraging in today's mortal realm. In old times, salt was as precious beyond the Veil as it is here. Mortals fought wars for salt and sometimes we traded them gold for salt because we could always take the gold back and we always needed more salt than we got from the goblins."

Jerlayne thought of the locked chest in the Stonewell pantry where the white salt was kept and the other caches, all metal-locked, where coarse salt was kept for pickling, dyeing, and everything else that called for salt. She'd never deny that salt was essential to a well-run homestead. And it was part of the bargain married women made with the goblins: iron for protection *and* so many rock-hard hives of salt.

But to say that salt was more important than protection, *that* was foolishness.

"It's not the old times," Jerlayne reminded her father. "And hard-pressed isn't the same as impossible. When I bargain with goblins, it will be for protection. We've trapped ourselves, Father, between the goblins and the ogres. Without goblins, the ogres would destroy us. Without ogres, there *would* be no reason to bargain. We'd need nothing . . ."

She caught her breath on an insight she'd never had before: "We need nothing now. We have the cure for 'death. You could forage enough salt and the scyldrin could learn to protect us from the ogres . . . the dwarves could, anyway."

Elves didn't fight. They argued, as she and her mother argued, but never to the point of physical violence. And they never killed, even when the stock was slaughtered for winter— Jerlayne's least favorite day of the entire year—elves stood apart.

"They would," she concluded. "The homesteads are their homes as well as ours; and they're responsible for the ogres."

She thought of Milia, sitting in the Stonewell kitchen. Jerlayne had been a young child when Milia came to the workroom for the shaping that guaranteed she'd never bear an ogre or any other child. No wonder that the scyldrin didn't remain at the homestead where they'd been born. The long life of an elfin woman was marked by child-bearing as much as it was by anything else, and it was possible that Elmeene truly didn't know how many scyldrin she'd borne. Child-bearing was not a future that Jerlayne feared, but not one that she chose to dwell on, either. Fairie needed scyldrin, homesteads needed sons and, when she was ready, she'd shape herself a daughter.

Jerlayne saw her face reflected in her father's eyes, heard the stream and watched the subtle flare of his nostrils as he breathed deeply, and said nothing. Silently, Jerlayne cursed the perversities of magic that gave her the talent to shape iron and heal flesh but left her isolated, dependent on her eyes and ears when she desperately wanted to know what a man was thinking.

She wanted to get past the secrets, questions, and lies; the things not said or simply unsayable. She wanted Aulaudin. She wanted joining, the goblins and their bargains be damned.

"Please, Father? Isn't it time for Fairie to forget Tatterfall? Whatever happened, there was no one left afterward. Everyone died, goblins, elves, and scyldrin together." She paused, not for drama but to pry unfamiliar words from the depths of her memory. "If there were *heroes* or *villains,* Aulaudin of Briary wasn't among them. Tatterfall wasn't his fault. I'm ready to take my chances against ogres and goblins, so long as I can take them with Aulaudin. Please, Father. Please say it's not impossible? Please say you'll go to Briary?"

Jereige's eyes glazed; Jerlayne quickly looked across the stream lest she witness him blinking back a tear and ruin what her heart said was the brink of victory.

"I will leave before supper. I will return . . . when I return. Do me this favor: don't tell your mother where I've gone. She had a notion you were fastened on Listogan of Singletree."

Against her better judgment, Jerlayne gasped. "Listogan of Singletree? Dust from the Veil, Father, he's loud and thinks too much of himself! No woman would ever join with Listogan!"

Jereige cracked a faint smile. "But every woman notices him, you have to admit that," he said and Jerlayne returned his smile. "*You've* noticed him. Your mother couldn't think of anyone else you have noticed."

Jerlayne's smile faded. "Aulaudin comes here every season! How can she think so little of him!"

Another moment of awkward silence and words not spoken before Jereige asked: "Tell me, Jerlayne, have you spoken to Aulaudin? Is he—? Does Briary expect me?"

"No. Nobody will be expecting you. I haven't talked to anyone, until now. It's not right, Father. It's not Aulaudin's fault that his father's not truly welcome anywhere in Fairie except Stonewell. Maun's the elf who won't let anyone forget Tatterfall. Aulaudin never talks about Tatterfall. He doesn't care—"

A look crossed Jereige's eyes, as if he knew that she'd lied: Aulaudin *cared* about Tatterfall; he simply didn't talk about it. But there was more to Jereige's expression. As dark as the stone well at midnight, his eyes held guilt, anger, and above all else, secret knowledge. Then he blinked and everything was gone before he retrieved his fishing pole.

"Are you sure that you want me to do this thing, daughter?

At the very least, you could come with me and speak to Aulaudin yourself. I can't remember a time when this came as a surprise."

Jerlayne's confidence had fallen somewhere below her knees, below her ankles. That midnight look was burnt behind her eyes now. She wished she'd never come to the stream, wished she'd had her argument with Elmeene. She wished for Aulaudin and for the first time in her life, she was afraid of wishing.

"I trust him, Father. I trust him as if we were already joined; there's no need for words between Aulaudin and me."

Her father's face said he didn't believe her, but he collected his box of bright-colored lures and, with the pole set against his shoulder like a goblin's spear, started back toward the house.

"I will do what I can," he said when Jerlayne caught up with him, both stools tucked under her arm. "But for your own sake, say nothing to your mother. The outcome is by no means certain. There's no need to borrow trouble."

Chapter 3

"**Y**ou're a strange one, Auden," the mortal woman said, smiling nervously. "You show up, right as rain, when it's time to harvest the fields. Every year since Himself, God rest him, took sick. You keep the peace and do the work of three men together and when it's time for me to pay you, all you want is a ruby glass."

"I've no need for money, ma'am," Aulaudin of Briary answered, matching her dialect and accent. A man of Fairie could easily pass among mortals, if he paid proper attention to their fast-changing fashions and language.

The woman stood on her toes and stretched to the utmost reaching for one of the etched ruby-crystal goblets. Her blind fingers brushed one of the stems. The goblet wobbled; Aulaudin swallowed his breath before she got it safely in her grasp.

"Five years, five goblets." She blew softly across the goblet's bell, banishing no dust. The goblets, like everything else in the modest, rough-hewn house, were shining spotless. "There are seven left . . ."

"I know."

"We brought them from Home, packed inside a barrel of flour, to keep them whole. We had dreams, Himself and I. . . ."

Her voice trailed a second time; Aulaudin waited patiently, as men could wait when they had all the time under the sun. He guessed she was barely thirty, a child by Fairie's measure, but a mature woman in the mortal realm; a widowed woman with three small children sleeping in the upper loft and indelible weariness smudged beneath her eyes.

Aulaudin reached for the goblet. She pulled it close against the bodice of an unnecessarily fine dress that smelt of herbs and cedar.

"You'll come back next year?"

"Yes," Aulaudin answered, lowering his arm.

"And the next after that, and after that, until they're gone?"

"That is my intention."

He wanted the goblets as a gift for his mother, because they were more intricate than anything the women could shape from the broken glass that men usually foraged and because the fate of this mortal homestead fascinated him.

"And then? When the year is 1887, will you appear on my porch like an—"

"Seven years is too long a time for questions."

It wasn't of course, not for Fairie, but for the fast-living, faster-dying mortals seven—even five—years might well be eternity. Earlier, he'd thought she'd remarry. Marriage was different on their side of the Veil. They exchanged vows, but they didn't—couldn't—join. When one died, the other often remarried. A widow with young children faced a hard life if she didn't. Aulaudin had thought he'd regret not taking all twelve goblets that first autumn.

The widow offered the goblet, her fingers lightly wrapped around its bell. Aulaudin took it by the stem. Her hand slid over his. It was cool and faintly trembling.

"There is—" she began, before her breath failed.

Aulaudin met her anxious eyes calmly. He'd been foraging the mortal realm, collecting their castoffs, stealing from their cupboards, and deceiving them in their ordinary lives for centuries. He'd been this close, and closer, to a mortal woman before.

"There is work to be done." She lowered her eyes. "There's always work that wants doing."

"I am here at harvest," Aulaudin said as he began to withdraw his hand and the goblet. He enjoyed the company of mortals and he would stay, if she asked.

Her hand closed over his again and she invited Aulaudin to stay, on his terms, which he did. He left a month later, with one carefully wrapped goblet in his pack. He'd heard his name in the morning air; his father wanted him home. She'd stood dry-eyed as she'd asked if he'd return for the harvest. He'd nodded. Once he'd heard his father out, Aulaudin could return. His heart was willing and men sometimes lingered for years in the mortal realm, if they were sons without prospect of a Fairie wife or homestead.

When Aulaudin thought of wives and homesteads, he thought not of Briary, but Tatterfall.

That name with all its memories clamored in his mind as he walked a rutted cart-path away from the mortal woman and her homestead. A sleety mist hung down from a heavy sky. He could shiver, even shed a tear, without asking himself why.

Fenced-in fields yielded to scrub meadow; the path became a hunter's trail leading into unbroken land, much as it would at any newly founded Fairie homestead, though in Fairie, a cold fog between the trees would have been the Veil. In the mortal realm, fog was only weather—numbing, raw, and damp—that matched Aulaudin's mood as he veered off the trail, seeking solitude.

A man didn't need solitude to part the Veil. He could part it anywhere, on either side, though it was necessary to know precisely where on the opposite side he wished to end his journey. Aulaudin could have sat in the widow's parlor, opened his mind, and shifted himself directly into Briary's dining room. Could have, if he'd been willing to risk the sanity of any innocent eyes that might witness the two realms overlaid or risk the secrets that preserved Fairie. Aulaudin hadn't been willing to take those risks two centuries ago when Tatterfall died; he wouldn't take them now.

Unslinging his pack and cradling it in his arms, Aulaudin settled against a oak tree whose stubborn, gold leaves offered some protection from the weather. Eyes closed, he entered the shifting trance. His mind held a handful of Fairie touchstones, some of them in easy walking distance of Briary, one of them far to the west, in the ruins of Tatterfall. Aulaudin would have gone to Tatterfall regardless: it was the place where he cached ungiven gifts, but the weather and his mood made the ruins irresistible.

Boraudin's face filled Aulaudin's mind as palpable as the fog. A mere five years had separated them, rather than the century or more that commonly separated elfin siblings. They'd been inseparable, learning together, competing, and fighting with each other, to the consternation of their elders, which had made the bruises worthwhile. They discovered the delights of trysting the same summer. The discovery strengthened rather than threatened the bond between them—until the day when Glanrer of Mossbank arrived at Briary to negotiate a marriage between his daughter, Diera, and Boraudin.

The brothers laughed at first, even suggested that Diera would have to marry them both, but in less than a season, Boraudin had made his choice. He was thoroughly in love when he and Diera joined. The newlyweds welcomed Aulaudin at Tatterfall: there was more than enough work to be done, but their bachelor days were over. What the brothers had shared since childhood vanished long before Tatterfall.

Aulaudin unclenched his fists. He tilted his head against the tree's trunk until the cold drips from its branches struck him in the face. Slowly, Boraudin's face drained into memory. His mind was empty and he began again to construct the ruins in his mind.

Five recollections, each perfectly textured, were sufficient for a man to shift himself from one realm to the other. A wise man over-learned his touchstone places. Aulaudin knew Tatterfall from its broken walls to the lichens adhering to its most ancient trees. If anything changed between visits, he had a score of other recollections to fall back upon: Boraudin's homestead would not be swallowed by the mist, would not be forgotten, not while his brother lived.

The Veil parting, when it came, was effortless. One breath filled Aulaudin's lungs with mortal realm air, the next had him completely within Fairie. He relaxed and released himself from the shifting trance. The air around him was colder than it had been a moment earlier, darker, too, because it was night at Tatterfall and the ruins, when Aulaudin opened his eyes, were bathed in a full moon's light.

A mortal man had explained it to Aulaudin once: Their vast realm was stretched over the surface of a sphere they called the World. The moon circled the World in a stately way, but the World also itself spun around the sun and tilted like a top. Half the World knew daylight while the other half knew night; half knew summer, half knew winter. Aulaudin had nodded, as if he'd understood.

Fairie was brightened by the same sun, the same moon as the mortal's World. The stars overhead formed the same patterns, season by season. But Fairie was a tiny place where every homestead marched through the hours and seasons together. Aulaudin had wondered if Fairie were a burr on the World's skin, but though he dwelt comfortably among mortals, he never shed his deceptions and his questions went unasked.

Before he stood, Aulaudin took the measure of Tatterfall's

changes since his last visit at high summer. A tree had fallen, crushing what little had remained of the kitchen wall. An animal had dug its winter den under the threshold steps. When the ruins were as raw as his grief, Aulaudin would have filled in the den and attacked the tree with a dwarf's axe. He'd fought the forest for decades, until he'd accepted that he couldn't bring Tatterfall back and understood that remembering it with its gaping wounds was worse than forgetting it altogether.

The forest would win, anyway. He couldn't uproot every vagrant weed. The land *wanted* to heal. Aulaudin had witnessed the steady changes for nearly two hundred years. All the outbuildings were gone; anything that had been built from wood was gone, eaten by bugs and fungus. The brick chimney had crumbled a century ago; the bricks themselves were little more than ruddy splotches in the moss. A time would come when only the foundation stones remained; bones protruding from the ground.

Aulaudin's heart ached when he imagined that day, but it was the uncomplicated ache of tasks completed and decisions well-made. He stood up, shaking mortal-realm mud from his sleeves and boots, and retrieved his pack which—like his clothes and everything else that was in close contact with a man as he shifted, including a layer of mud and wet leaves—had accompanied Aulaudin through the Veil.

However smooth the shift had felt, Aulaudin knew his arrival would have been heralded by ghostly breezes and will-o'-the-wisp light, either of which was enough to scare any Fairie predator, including a stray ogre. He walked confidently through the ruins, adding the ruby goblet to the trove of ungiven gifts he kept in the hive-shaped bread oven. Then he checked the other hiding places where he kept extra knives, an axe, clothes, and boots.

The mist, dispelled by his passage through the Veil, reasserted itself. The dimmer stars were already lost in silver. Aulaudin hacked a bough off a nearby evergreen and used it to sweep a season's debris from what had been Tatterfall's inner courtyard. Then he sat cross-legged on the slate and recalled his brother's face.

"Boraudin?" he whispered, mind and voice together.

When Boraudin was alive, Aulaudin had rarely called him by name. They were so close, so attuned, he'd needed only to loose a stray thought and their minds were linked. Sometimes it had been difficult to know where his own notions ended and his brother's had begun. Now and forever there was emptiness—loneliness—where his brother had been.

"Boraudin? Are you here? Can you hear me?"

Mortals entreated a myriad of gods when confronted with fate. The scyldrin worshipped fate itself; and the goblins—so far as anyone not a goblin could tell—had two gods, one for men, the other for women. Elves had no gods, only sages who said the spirits of their dead returned to Fairie's forest. The sages said the dead were at peace with their particular fate and were unconcerned about the living. There was no need for the living to concern themselves with the dead: an unmarked grave was sufficient when there was a body to bury—which there hadn't been here at Tatterfall.

Aulaudin had tried to be comforted by what the sages said. He wanted to believe that his brother was beyond suffering, but believing wasn't enough; he needed proof. The sages laughed when he'd asked them to carry a message to Boraudin. When he'd lived a millennium or three, if he wanted to become a sage himself, then he could send a message to the dead.

Aulaudin couldn't wait that long. «Boraudin?»

The years after Tatterfall had been hard years at Briary. Despite the hard, gruesome evidence of goblin limbs scattered through the carnage, Maun blamed the goblins for his son's death. He tried to banish them from Briary, saying no hope was better than false hope. But goblins bargained with a homestead's mistress, not its master. Aglaidia gave them extra iron and bid them stay.

All Fairie witnessed the spectacle of a joined husband and wife at odds with each other and living apart. For Aulaudin, already raw from by Boraudin's death, the scrutiny was intolerable. He'd withdrawn, cultivated a mask of jovial indifference, pretended not to notice, and brought his misery to the ruins.

Time healed the breach between his parents and if time had not restored Briary's luster among the homesteads, it had wrought a sort of grudging tolerance. In the last few decades, it had become possible to attend at a gathering without inciting gossip—so long as no one mentioned Tatterfall to Maun.

Time had healed Aulaudin as well, little as he wished to admit it. He'd grown accustomed to the emptiness where Boraudin had been. It was habit that brought him back to Tatterfall and, although the grief was real whenever he saw the ruins, he no longer strained his inner senses when he searched. Indifference had ceased to be a mask. He dwelt in Fairie, abiding by its customs, but he cared more for the woman he'd left in the mortal realm than he did for any elf, living or dead.

Aulaudin called his brother for the fourth time. The mist had thickened and the slate was hard beneath his rump. He thought of home, of Briary, warm food, and a hot bath. It would be midnight before he got there: The shortest route involved shifting to a mortal realm touchstone, then back to Fairie.

Without changing position, Aulaudin cleared his mind for the mortal-realm parting. He'd imagined a stark horizon—naked rocks, arid sand, and a cloudless sky—when a whistling wind blew against his face and back. Breaking the trance, he opened his eyes and saw light flickering within the mist.

"Boraudin?"

No answer, though the wind blew harder.

Stiff-legged, Aulaudin scrambled from the courtyard's center to the darkest shadows along its ruined walls. He made himself small as the wind ebbed suddenly and the light intensified: whoever was coming knew his way. Aulaudin shielded his eyes with an upraised arm, hoping to recognize a silhouette as the Veil burst open, but the parting blinded him. He was blinking in darkness when he heard a familiar voice.

"Aulaudin—Son, didn't I teach you *not* to look?"

Feeling foolish as well as blind, Aulaudin stood and faced his father. "The very first thing," he admitted. "I wasn't expecting you."

"All the more reason not to look!" Aulaudin heard the scuff of Maun's boots on the slate and braced himself for a hearty clout somewhere on his body. "You could do yourself lasting harm."

The blow came on his upper arm, half earnest, half jest.

"I'll remember next time."

"See to it, and if you're going to hide, son, do a better job. Crouching down like that . . . blinded . . . if I were a goblin . . ."

A blow to the arm was one thing—Maun had always framed his lessons and advice with his hands—but a screed about goblins, that wasn't the father Aulaudin wanted to be around, especially at Tatterfall. He turned away.

"You don't like hearing it. You want to believe what you've been told: They've got no magic. They can't shape or shift. They *need* us, so they protect us. It's lies, Aulaudin, lies. They

can part the Veil, nice as you please, and they kill what they
don't need."

Aulaudin shook his head. He could see again, enough to see
that Maun's fists were cocked in front of him and his lips were
pulled back in an angry grimace.

"Goblins died here," he said softly, reluctantly. Aulaudin
didn't like or trust goblins any more than his father did; he just
didn't talk about it.

"So it's said."

"And true!" Aulaudin snarled, twice as angry to find himself
defending the shadow-folk. "Viljuen weeps, Father—I was
here. I was too late, but I was here before anyone else and there
were goblins among the dead."

"But who killed them?"

"Ogres, Father. Ogres."

"Not ogres."

"They were torn apart, like the rest. I couldn't tell a gnome
from a dwarf from an elf, but a goblin's arm, Maun, can only be
a goblin's arm. Even you must concede that."

"A token."

"Viljuen weeps. Why can't you believe the truth?" Aulaudin
backed away.

"Why don't you? What haunts you, my son? You come here
often enough."

Aulaudin stopped short, stung by the realization that Maun
knew about his sanctuary here—had apparently known for
some time and said nothing about it. It fell together: Maun had
parted the Veil with the confidence of one who'd visited the ruins frequently and Aulaudin had cached his ungiven gifts for
safety, not secrecy.

"I come to remember Boraudin," he said wearily. "Why do
you come?"

"Tonight, I've come for you. You've taken your time answering my call—trysting with that mortal woman again?
When you weren't beyond at sunset and you didn't show up for
supper, I guessed you'd be here."

Aulaudin opened his mouth for a sharp retort and closed it
again, feeling more foolish than he'd felt when the Veil-light
blinded him. Behind the foolishness, a wave of panic was
swelling. "What I heard wasn't a rush or hurry. What's wrong?
Where—Briary?"

Maun stared at him a moment, letting Aulaudin imagine the

worst, which in this place was easy to do, then Maun succumbed to laughter.

"You worry too much, son," he said, striding forward and clapping Aulaudin's arm again. "Why would I waste time looking for you in the flesh, if I were the bearer of bad tidings?"

Aulaudin wanted to say: *I don't know, Father. I don't know why you do anything. I haven't known you since—since Boraudin died*—but those words would only provoke another tirade. He shook his head and winced as Maun clapped him a third time in the same aching place.

"I've had a visit from my old friend, Jereige of Stonewell."

Aulaudin fought the puzzled scowl that was trying to form on his face. The battle, which he lost, brought another gust of laughter from his father.

"Jereige of Stonewell, Aulaudin! Jereige's daughter—the one who thinks you hung the moon. She's done it! She's shaped her chain—done it faster than her mother, too. Just as you said she would. And she's not letting it collect dust under her bed."

It was Aulaudin's night for feeling foolish. "Jerlayne?" he asked, then straightened as the likely truth struck him. "No."

"No? You'd say 'no' to a Stonewell daughter? Have you lost your wits? What else have you been trying to accomplish all these years?"

"Not joining!" Aulaudin sputtered, even as he asked himself the same question. How many times had she told him, *You're my only friend?* Could he honestly say to himself that he'd never considered this very consequence? "What did you tell Jereige?"

"That you were off foraging."

"You didn't tell him I'd accept?"

"I'd thought you would," Maun said, his pale blue eyes boring into Aulaudin's. "But, naturally, I made no commitments on your behalf."

Aulaudin met his father's stare. Maun's presence bore against his thoughts, offering a more intense, but not necessarily more truthful, sharing than spoken words. Aulaudin rejected the offering, then looked away. "Jerlayne doesn't know. She hadn't been born when it happened, and she pays no heed to gossip."

"Nonsense, son. Elmeene's dragged that child to every gathering Jereige got wind of and a few more beside. They'll need

a new roof over the bedchamber when she finds out who her
daughter's set her heart on. My poor friend didn't dare face his
wife before he let Stonewell . . . ah! But maybe Jereige knew
your mind in this already?"

Aulaudin shook his head. "No, he and I never talked. *Jerlayne* and I never talked about this. I'd have told her . . . somehow. I won't . . . can't. Jerlayne doesn't know the truth. No one
does, not all of it."

"I believe you might be right about Jerlayne, she lives with
herself. But Jereige damn well knows everything that happened, because I damn well told him. He's ridden hard from
Stonewell to see me, and waited three days now to see you."

Aulaudin wrestled with rage that his father had confided his
secrets and shame to Jereige, and with a greater rage that envied a friendship that had stood for millennia. He'd made himself into a man with many acquaintances, and no friends
whatsoever. Except Jerlayne? "What exactly did Jereige say?"

"He said, 'Maun, my friend, my daughter's heart-set on your
son, Aulaudin.' "

"I meant about the other."

"What's to say, Aulaudin? The matter wasn't broached. He
knows; he knew before I talked to him. Before Jerlayne talked
to him. It's no great secret that you and Betisane were handfast
when . . . when *this*—" Maun opened his arms to the Tatterfall
ruins, "happened and she pulled her little hand back so fast all
Fairie felt the wind of it."

Aulaudin was open-mouthed between anger and embarrassment. "Because of you!" he spat. "You and your goblins. You
and Mother. Viljuen weeps. You'd made your mark. Do you
have any notion what it's been like—"

"Having a madman for a father?" Maun interrupted and concluded, more succinct than the notions in Aulaudin's mind, but
essentially the same. "I'm right, Aulaudin; it's that simple. I'd
sooner have twenty ogre lairs on Briary's verge than a single
goblin. I not a fool, and if I were, your mother would enlighten
me. All Briary has suffered—you, your brothers, the scyldrin,
and your mother most of all—but I'm right; there's no changing that. Still, don't go blaming Betisane on me. She'd turned
her back on you before I'd taken it into my head to be the one
voice against many. I know why I stopped visiting the homesteads of the witless. Why did you? For shame of me or shame
of yourself?"

"Father, I'm not listening to this. There's nothing more to be said," Aulaudin warned, aware that his threat was hollow: his mind was too filled with rage to attempt the Veil and he wouldn't roam the tame forest near Briary by moonlight, much less the wilderness here at Tatterfall.

"You courted Betisane because Boraudin had courted Diera and she was Diera's closest friend. It may be that you even loved her, but that love was rooted in your brother, Aulaudin. I had no liking for her, I'll tell you that, but she was right to turn away. Your joining was doomed; one of you would not have survived the first time—probably you. You've licked your wounds and kept them raw for two hundred years! Damn my eyes if I didn't think, when Jerlayne fastened on you and you didn't run away, that you were ready to put this place behind you."

"Are you?" Aulaudin shouted back, not the words either of them expected to hear, yet once they were in the air, Aulaudin had no wish to call them back. "Are you?" he repeated more soberly. "Can you walk away from the *truths* you think you found here?"

"She suits you, Aulaudin, and she's Jereige's daughter. It would please me but, more, I think it would please you, though it's a dull life you'll be leading, all sober conversation, and damned hard work. Think about it: all the times we've ridden together to Stonewell—don't tell me it was for the pleasure of *my* company, or Jereige's, or his sons'. Has your blood all gone to dust and mold with Tatterfall?"

For the first time since Maun arrived, Aulaudin imagined Jerlayne, not as a child, but as the woman she'd become. His blood hadn't turned to dust or mold in the mortal realm, but it had come close in Fairie.

"I'm too old. I've been living the bachelor life for too long."

"I'd lived it far longer, son—over a thousand years before Aglaidia walked in front of me. *She* may have a regret or two, but I certainly don't. You're never too old, if it's true love."

"If—*if* I agreed, there'd be goblins at the wedding . . ."

"If you agreed, I'd dance with their damned high priestess. If I got sufficiently drunk, I might take her to bed and make my own bargain for good measure."

Aulaudin suppressed a smile. "I have to think about it."

"Take your time, son. Take all night, if you want. But if you truly don't know your answer right now, I'll go home and tell my friend to steer his daughter toward some other man, because my son's joined to the dead."

"A homestead," Aulaudin murmured. Like Tatterfall? He shook his head, but the notion, *not like Tatterfall,* remained.

"Think of this: no more living under the same roof as a madman," Maun offered with a trace of the sly humor that had been his hallmark when he taught his sons the ways of Fairie and foraging.

The notions were all tempting but, "I'm not ready."

"No one ever is, including Jerlayne. You can try to persuade her to move slowly. . . ."

Aulaudin gave his father a sidelong glance and thumped *him* soundly between the shoulders. "You don't know Jerlayne. You can't 'persuade' Jerlayne of anything. She's like water; she always finds a way to what she wants."

"Well, then: what she wants is you, son. Let's go home. We'll talk to Jereige and send you off with him tomorrow."

Maun's presence beckoned again, bearing the notion of Briary's hearth-room. Aulaudin added the notion of a hot meal and they began the journey home.

Chapter 4

An autumn sunset reflected in the blessing bowl, rippling in harmony with the brass chime Jereige had just struck. Jerlayne drew a breath and held it, lest she awaken—as she had so many times in the past year—from her wedding dream. Elmeene struck the second chime. Jerlayne let her breath out: this wasn't a dream. This was her wedding, with Aulaudin beside her, dressed in stiff finery and looking as nervous as she felt.

As the second chime faded, Jerlayne swirled her fingers through the bowl's sun-warmed water. She moved gently, so the water didn't splash, yet thoroughly, because the magic of joining was in the water, placed there by the three sages, who now stood behind them, each holding a chime.

There was a third note, identical to the first, and a fourth, which was Aulaudin's signal to dip his hand in the bowl. Then the fifth chime was struck and everything else succumbed to silence. Time itself seemed stopped as Jerlayne raised her hand to meet Aulaudin's. Their fingertips touched and joining began.

Aulaudin smiled.

Jerlayne swallowed her relief before it became an audible sigh. Most of her dreams had ended before she reached this moment; in the few that hadn't, her beloved pulled away, shaking his head before he vanished. The nightmares had been caused, no doubt, by Aulaudin's reticence during the first months of their bethrothal. By winter's end, if he'd asked to postpone the rite one more time, Jerlayne might have agreed, might have given back the gold ring and every other gift he'd given her. But with the coming of spring he'd conquered his misgivings.

Summer had been an idyll of long walks through the Stonewell fields and longer conversations in the courtyard until two sages arrived. The interviews were tradition; they were supposed to help the sages find the right place for their homestead. The sages—Gudwal, whom Jerlayne knew and loved as a many-times great-grandfather; and Claideris, a northern stranger who'd had little to say and none of it friendly—had stayed for only an afternoon before declaring themselves ready to begin the homestead search.

If it had been only Gudwal, or Gudwal and Arlesken, the round-faced sage who usually traveled with him, Jerlayne wouldn't have worried, but she hadn't been able, then or now, to get Claideris' bitter eyes out of her mind. She expected that they'd find themselves 'steading in a swamp or clinging to the windward side of a mountain. Right after the sages left, Aulaudin had striven to reassure her, but Claideris had unnerved him, too, and worse: they'd exchanged words when the black-haired, pipe-smoking woman intimated that Tatterfall's ruin was the result of its elves not being up to the challenge of a Veil-side homestead.

Then to make a bad day worse, Elmeene had returned home from a day at the bedside of a gravely injured dwarf. At first, Jerlayne had thought her mother had been offended that the sages hadn't stayed long enough to enjoy Stonewell's fabled hospitality, but Elmeene's anger ran deeper—

That woman! That WOMAN under my roof, questioning MY daughter! Since when does SHE have THAT right!

Not even Jereige had understood what riled Elmeene so, nor had he been able to ease her temper.

Tradition decreed it was an ill omen if a betrothed couple saw their homestead land before they were joined, but ten days later there was nothing to stop the bride's mother from answering the Vigilance call for help in clearing the new homestead's land. She'd wanted, she'd said, to see for herself where "that woman" had settled her daughter.

Elmeene had followed a score of shapers and three-times that many dwarves from homesteads all around Fairie. She'd been gone a month—which had left a grateful Jerlayne in charge of her own wedding—and come back with her hair trimmed close around her ears, but the cleared land, she said triumphantly, was good land.

Gudwal prevailed. That woman would have set you in a filthy swamp, or worse, but Gudwal set you above a valley. In a century or two, when the mists lift, you'll be the first in Fairie to see the sun rise.

Jerlayne had thought that she should have been elated. A Veil-side homestead, a homestead that expanded Fairie, was an honor, a sign that the sages foresaw great events in her future, Aulaudin's future. And her new home would be far away from Stonewell, farther than any of her sisters' homesteads were from Elmeene's workroom. Much too far for casual visits.

For her mother's sake, for Aulaudin's, and her own, Jerlayne had pretended to be elated. She'd submerged herself in hectic last-moment preparations and told herself that everything would be just like her fondest dreams. . . .

With joining magic wrapped around her wrist, Jerlayne stopped pretending and succumbed to true terror. Her fingers slipped away from Aulaudin's: an ill omen, if ever one were imagined. She panicked; her hand trembled but the gap widened until Aulaudin reached and caught and held her tight. Magic flowed swiftly after that. Jerlayne closed her eyes when it reached her heart and carried Aulaudin's smile into the darkness.

It was no secret that joining had its dangerous moment. Just as Tatterfall was a name all elves knew but few spoke, there was ample whispering about weddings that had ended with a pair of funerals. Elmeene had warned Jerlayne not to lose heart when every good thing faded from her mind, leaving only bleak despair. But warnings didn't prepare her for an endless fall through frigid, black *nothing*.

Then just before she was irretrievably lost, Jerlayne felt warmth all around her.

«I will love you, Jerlayne, forever.»

Aulaudin's voice, not as his tongue shaped it, but its perfect essence, flowing from his mind directly into hers.

When Elmeene had warned her that joining progressed faster in men, Jerlayne's pride had been severely pricked. She'd made her chain fast, and she swore to herself that she'd be the one waiting in the light. But when the moment came, she rejoiced that her beloved was there to welcome her. As she returned his smile, the mystery of joining—the sharing of thought, so natural to men and unknown among daughters—unfolded in her mind.

«I've already loved you forever.»

*   *   *

An elfin wedding lasted three days, two nights.

The first day and night were set aside for the rituals that had culminated with the sunset joining. The second night and day were for family. Not close-kin—their parents, brothers, and sisters—they'd been at Stonewell from the start; but elves from all over Fairie, because all elves were kin. Call them aunts and uncles if they were older, cousins if they weren't. By the pair and household, hundreds of them entered the reception garden before Jerlayne and Aulaudin opened their newly joined eyes. More of them arrived as twilight was lost to the bright flashes of men bringing their families through the Veil.

Still flushed from joining and too excited to think of sleep, Jerlayne spent the second evening of her wedding greeting elves she'd known all her life and elves she'd never seen before—a reminder, as if she'd needed one, that her parents held a rare measure of renown in Fairie and that the homestead of the daughter who'd bested Elmeene of Stonewell was expected to prosper.

The last elf to approach the vine-wrapped bower where she and Aulaudin sat with the blessing bowl between them was Gudwal; not as the sage-of-sages or interrogator, but as the living root of their bloodlines. There were elves in Fairie who weren't descended from Gudwal, but neither Jerlayne nor Aulaudin were among them, though Jerlayne's straight descent through Jereige was shorter than Aulaudin's collateral descent through his mother by three generations.

Gudwal appeared no older than any other elf, except for his ears, which parted his iron-colored hair and arched above his head like a half-formed crown. Only sages let their ears grow. Younger elves—no matter their accomplishments—kept theirs hidden out of respect.

Gudwal blessed them with water from the bowl and held their hands between his. For a brief moment, Jerlayne had a sense of all the elves who'd ever lived in Fairie smiling warmly at her. It was a special blessing, Gudwal whispered, from all their kin who longer spoke for themselves. When Gudwal had released their hands, Jerlayne glanced at Aulaudin, expecting to see the same joy on his face that she felt in her heart, but her husband stared straight ahead with clouded empty eyes.

Since she'd completed her twenty-link chain and announced her intention to marry, Jerlayne had dismissed any suggestion that she was too young to marry. She came to the end of laughter when she touched Aulaudin's hand and joined the shadows in his thoughts. In her lifetime no elf had died: all the elves whose blessing Gudwal bestowed on her were strangers whose living laughter she'd never heard. Aulaudin had seen death, not in the blooddeath times, as their parents and the sages had seen it, but the death of a brother at Tatterfall. In the midst of Gudwal's blessing, his heart turned bleak as a winter's night.

Jerlayne wanted to leave the bower then, to be by herself until she'd made peace with the understanding that she didn't—couldn't—entirely know her husband. But leaving her wedding was unthinkable. After Gudwal's blessing, they visited with their guests, listened to tales of weddings long forgotten. She was lucky to catch a nap in the bower after midnight because with dawn came the scyldrin: gnomes and dwarves from the homesteads; sprites, pixies, nixies, and brownies from the forest: all the festival-loving lks of Fairie.

They came throughout the day, in groups small and large. Bachelor sons grew weary escorting them from the homesteads where they dwelt or gathered. Weddings were scyldrin celebrations and, more than that, chances to examine Fairie's newest elfin pair, to consider whether their as-yet-unnamed homestead might be a better place to live. Jerlayne was gracious until her cheeks ached from smiling.

It was nearly midnight before the last sprite had laid her jewel-toned leaves at the newlyweds' feet. Jereige and Elmeene summoned the guests to a cold feast laid out at the garden's other end. Jerlayne escaped to the great house to change her clothes quickly: Aulaudin's heart had thawed as the scyldrin made their offerings and she no longer wanted to be alone.

Gudwal was already seated on a great mound of cushions when Jerlayne returned to the bower. She gratefully took the plate of food Aulaudin offered her, but refused the wine as Gudwal cleared his throat.

"Long before I was born, when time was already old and the Veil had already fallen, the Ten dwelt in Fairie . . ."

The Ten were the first elves, a band of brothers and sisters so thoroughly joined that the sisters shared with each other and all their brothers equally. They all walked through the misty Veil and explored the realm beyond Fairie where mortals lived feral lives and were dangerous only in the way of bears and wolves. The sisters, who hadn't yet begun to shape, unraveled the secrets of plants; they gathered the useful seeds, brought them into Fairie, and planted gardens. The brothers hunted at first, then captured and tamed the most useful beasts.

"The beasts they tamed," Gudwal explained, "the ancestors of the horses and cows, pigs and chickens, cats, dogs, and every other creature we see in Fairie today had all been born beyond the Veil. That made them mortal, and mortal they remain, even now. The plants, too, grow and die naturally, though I have seen trees in the forest that are as old as Fairie itself and still growing.

"As they established their gardens, their fields, their orchards, their flocks, and their herds, the Ten founded the first homestead. They lived differently, not in wedded pairs as elves live now, because they were joined together. In due time the five sisters gave birth to elfin children.

"The sons and daughters of the Ten joined with one another, not according to the great sharing of the Ten but in the pairs we know today. The sons shared notions among themselves and with all their fathers, but their sisters shared nothing until they chose one man to be their husband. They shared only with him afterward."

For elfin women of the second generation, the great silence had begun, but in that silence, the young women taught themselves to shape and heal. Their children—the grandchildren of the Ten—could neither part the Veil nor share their thoughts with anyone, but they were immortal and had shaping in their blood and bones. They shaped themselves as they grew, becoming the scyldrin ilks: gnomes and dwarves and all the others, even night-dwelling trolls and giants three times the height of their parents.

And it was a good time for trolls and giants because, by then, mortals no longer lived as beasts in caves and earthen dens.

Mortals had always been more numerous and clever in ways that elves couldn't comprehend. The men of Fairie had approached them in friendship, willing to trade knowledge for knowledge. But mortals weren't interested in trade, not with immortals. They stole what they wanted and would have stripped Fairie bare, if trolls and giants had not shaped themselves from the third generation.

Fairie grew and elves had all they could do to shape and forage for the scyldrin who quickly came to outnumber them. They gave over their crops and animals to the gnomes and dwarves; an arrangement which endured with few modifications. Those ilks whose shapes or temperaments proved ill-suited to domestic life retreated into the forest.

With trolls and giants as guardians, there was peace, after a fashion, as much peace as there could be when mortals dreamed that Fairie was their rightful paradise. The elfin children of the Ten dispersed through the Fairie forest, founding new homesteads. They made Fairie larger, but making Fairie larger served only to enrage the mortals, who, no longer content with raiding, began to torture and murder the immortals they captured.

The elves and scyldrin learned an unwelcome lesson: Fairie shrank as readily as it grew. Whenever an elf died—especially an elf who'd founded a homestead—the mist reclaimed the land. Little by little, the children and grandchildren fell back to the first homestead, the homestead where the Ten still dwelt.

"They asked one another: What can we do?" Gudwal said with proper drama. "What *can* we do? If we become like them to save ourselves, what will we have saved?"

Murder was, ever and always, unconscionable in Fairie. Voices could be raised, but not hands, never weapons. A dwarf would have fought back against mortal violence. Dwarves *did* fight back when mortals stumbled out of the mist. But dwarves sickened if they strayed far or long from Fairie, as did the giants and the trolls. The trolls and giants *hunted*, but that wasn't enough, not against packs of vengeful mortals.

Fairie again seemed doomed, but just when the danger grew greatest, the scyldrin found new shapes: fierce dragons and griffins who would slay each other or an elf or scyld as readily as they slew a mortal interloper. They replaced the giants and trolls and established domains within the mists. And for a time nothing that ventured into the mists came out again.

Fairie grew, protected by its mist-dwelling guardians. The elves recovered and the gnomes and dwarves, though they could not join any more than they could shape or share, found love among themselves. They paired off to found their own homesteads, which did not push back the Veil. They had children of their own, but the great-grandchildren of the Ten were mortal, and wilder than the mortals who dwelt beyond the Veil. The dwarves and gnomes were ashamed of what they'd borne; many vowed abstinence and tried to hide their children. And because they'd separated themselves from the elfin homesteads, because they were not joined and could not share with one another they were able to keep their secrets for a long time.

No one knew until too late that the ogres—as the mortal scyldrin were called—were cleverer than their parents suspected. No one heard the terror-filled screams of dwarves and gnomes as their children banded together to murder them; to devour them as beasts devoured prey. No one suspected anything until an ogre horde took aim at Fairie's heart, at the homestead of the Ten. Then pain and panic echoed among the folds of the Veil.

Immortal elves and scyldrin were too stunned to defend themselves, even if they had weapons or the skill to use them. Some few fled ahead of the horde or found lucky places in which to hide. The men among them shared notions of blood, chaos, and a desperate, futile hope that the dragons and griffins who laired in the mist would emerge to save them.

Fairie learned another hard lesson that day: the guardians cared only for their misty domains. They'd forgotten their birthplaces. The death-cries of their kin, if they heard them at all, did not touch their hearts.

When the carnage ended—when the ogres had sated themselves on immortal flesh and vanished into the forest—seven of the Ten were gone and countless scyldrin with them. The survivors were drawn back to the killing ground. They wondered why they had been spared only to wait in fear for the ogres to return and finish what they'd begun.

Of the Ten, only the sisters Legarra and Reberi were left and with them their brother, Viljuen. While his sisters mourned with their children, Viljuen wept with rage. If the dragons would not come to Fairie's aid, then he'd find a path through the Veil and allies among the enemy. Viljuen took up an ogre's wooden spear—he was the only elf ever said to arm himself— and began his quest in a burst of light: the first true parting of the Veil.

He'd warned those he left behind that he would not return quickly, might not return at all, but he was back before the next new moon. A strange woman stood at his side.

"No woman before or since was like her," Gudwal explained, using precisely the words he'd used every other time Jerlayne had heard him tell the *Tale of the Ten*, precisely the same words other sages used when they told it.

The rest of the wedding story was subject to changes, a bit

more detail or a bit less, if the weather turned bad, but the appearance of the goblin priestess never varied. In silhouette, she resembled an elf, as both mortals and ogres resembled elves. But her skin was a deep, bluish gray, like a bruise or a stormy sky. Her hair was as dark and elusive as the new moon. Her eyes were brightly black and showed no white at the rim. Viljuen said she was a goblin, and though her ilk had never been seen in Fairie before, he said they'd been there from the beginning. Goblins had woven the Veil, and now goblins would protect all the elves and peaceful ilks from the rampaging ogres.

Gudwal straightened atop his cushions. "There were questions, of course. Reberi and Legarra were not fools. They asked questions and the goblin priestess showed them an answer: the shadows moved and a score of goblin warriors separated from the night. They carried spears and clubs, as the ogres had carried, but the goblins' weapons were leather-wrapped, fire-hardened, and tipped with beaten stone that held a fearsome edge. They could not enter the mists where the dragons and griffins prowled, but the forests and plains belonged to them."

Jerlayne didn't need a sage or a goblin to tell her that Viljuen was hardly in a position to refuse the priestess' offer. If elves and scyldrin had stood little chance against ogres, they stood none at all against the goblin warriors. She imagined the thoughts Viljuen and his sisters shared before he asked the priestess what the elves might do in return.

The bargaining between elves and goblins had begun: The priestess confessed that her folk had exhausted their magic when they wove the Veil. They couldn't shape or share, nor pass through the Veil they had created. Such things weren't important to them, but there were things beyond the Veil that they did crave and other things that elfin women might shape for them—all in exchange for protection.

"A fair bargain," the sage said at the conclusion of his tale. "A bargain we honor to this day, to this very night."

And so Gudwal's tale ended, as it ended at every wedding.

Tonight, before sunrise, a goblin would come to Stonewell. He might be a goblin Jerlayne knew; that is, a goblin she had seen before. No one *knew* the goblins. The warriors were as alike as hawks from the same hatching. At least twenty of them lived within Stonewell's boundary stones. On an unlucky day,

Jerlayne might catch a glimpse of an iron-armed pair patrolling the forest fringe, but the only time she came close to them was after an ogre raid, when their wounded came for healing.

Or at a wedding.

Jerlayne had attended a score of weddings. The first was still clear in her mind: she'd been no more than eight or nine and afraid to let go of her mother's hand when the goblin appeared. He'd stood, arms all outstretched, waiting for the bride to offer her masterpiece, a twenty-link chain shaped from the metal goblins prized above all others: copper, in the beginning, then bronze, now iron. If the goblin accepted the chain, he and his band accepted the obligation to protect the new homestead. If he didn't, no other goblins would step into the breach.

No wonder, then, that mothers drilled their daughters mercilessly. The stakes were survival, for her daughter, a new homestead, and, perhaps, Fairie itself. It was true that no bridal gift had ever failed to please the goblins, but that only increased a daughter's dread . . . though not Jerlayne's.

It seemed to Jerlayne that most elves did believe the sages, but most elves never asked question about anything that couldn't be proven with their own senses. She'd asked Elmeene once—just once, at that first wedding, with elves and scyldrin and goblins all around them—*if the Ten were brothers and sisters, then where were their parents?* Children, she'd announced boldly, didn't simply appear out of nowhere, and certainly not ten brothers and sisters all at once.

Elmeene's reaction had been more memorable than the goblin's appearance. Her normal, cedary complexion had turned a frightening shade of yellow. Her hands had formed fists; her arms had crossed and locked tight over her breasts. She'd been stunned, struck speechless and paralyzed by what Jerlayne eventually had understood was near-fatal embarrassment. Jereige had come running—something Jerlayne hadn't seen him do before or since. He'd carried Elmeene into the great house, where goblins wouldn't follow, then he'd come back for his daughter.

Jereige *could* get very angry. He didn't yell or flail his arms; he got quieter and calmer and his words took the edge of the finest mortal-made steel.

You mustn't ever again ask foolish questions where sensible folk can overhear them.

He didn't specifically state what Jerlayne's fate would be if she disobeyed. That, she'd guessed quickly enough, was a question beyond foolish.

Even in private, every question she'd ever asked about goblins had been too foolish to merit an answer.

Chapter 5

The banquet tables were empty and more than a few of the guests had fallen asleep before the goblin appeared on the garden path. Jerlayne hadn't seen him emerge from the forest or walk across the night-shadowed grass, but no one ever saw the goblins at first. They said it wasn't magic. They had no magic; they were merely warriors who'd mastered the art of stealth.

Clothed in black cloth and leather, and black as well from hair to fingertips, eyes, and teeth (though *that* blackness was a moonlight illusion: their skin was blue, the darkest blue imaginable) the goblin went directly to the bridal table where an iron twenty-link chain and an unfinished knife were waiting for him. The chain was new, shaped from iron that Aulaudin had foraged; the knife had also been rough-shaped from his iron.

Jerlayne calmly left the bower, went to the table, and took up the dull knife. She moistened her fingertips then squeezed them down the blade. Acrid smoke curled around her hand and the fresh edge glowed as she sharpened the iron. The smoke and glow were gone when she presented it for the goblin's inspection.

He held it up in the lantern light, sighted along its single edge, flipped it once, point over hilt to test its balance, then drew it lightly across his thumb. Goblin blood was as red as any elf's. He blotted the blood on his sleeve, where the stain disappeared, and slid the knife into a sheath Jerlayne supposed had been left deliberately empty. She had, after all, been told—though Elmeene and Arhon, Elmeene's goblin—that a knife would be welcomed, in addition to the twenty-link chain.

No words had been exchanged before Jerlayne offered her chain to the goblin. The goblin snapped his cloak over his shoulder. The sound of iron sliding over iron was the loudest sound in earshot as the goblin passed the chain from one hand to the other. Aulaudin came down from the bower, settling an arm around Jerlayne's shoulder as if to protect her, or share her fate in goblin judgement. He needn't have worried: she was Elmeene's daughter and no goblin would reject her chain.

A second goblin emerged from the night shadows. The first goblin gave the chain to his companion, then, baring his dark and glistening teeth, spoke for the first time.

"The same on each midwinter's eve, dear lady, and again each midsummer night, each in exchange for our protection," he indicated himself and his companion, "and a hive of salt. The shadows at your gate will never be empty and your names will not be spoken on the plains."

Jerlayne had never seen the plains. There were none in Fairie. Men said there were plains in the mortal realm: expanses of grass as expressive and changeable as an ocean. Jerlayne had never seen an ocean, either, though Fairie had abutted an ocean for nearly four centuries now, at Wavehome, in the southwest, where a siren sang and the mists were still lifting. And the shadows at a homestead's gate were always empty: Jerlayne had checked many times as a child. But the words were ritual; what mattered was that two goblins had attached themselves to her unbuilt homestead and, of course, the salt. A hive was a sprite-sized cake of salt, and they'd need every grain of it to salt their meat and pickle their vegetables.

The goblin—*her* goblin—had offered a fair trade: protection, provided by himself and his companion, and more than enough salt for a foundling homestead in exchange for two knives, two chains. Aulaudin had shown her his Tatterfall stockpiles. They had more than enough iron for ten midsummers, ten midwinters.

Elmeene bargained for forty hives each year and twenty goblins, enough to defend Stonewell against an ogre horde, should one ever reappear. Jerlayne wasn't Elmeene . . . yet. Goblin bargains weren't forever, like joining and homesteads. She'd get better terms as time passed. Until then . . .

She turned to Aulaudin, seeking his thoughts, his approval through joining. He gave nothing away. Men's work lay beyond the Veil; they had nothing to do with goblins. Women's work was shaping, and bargaining with goblins. The decision was hers and hers alone. Aulaudin would forage whatever she needed.

Absently, Jerlayne thought of Maun, who was nowhere to be seen. She tried to imagine Briary when Maun and Aglaidia had been estranged because of Tatterfall, because of goblins. How had Aglaidia met her twice-yearly obligations? Had Aulaudin foraged for his mother? Sons were vital to a homestead's prosperity, more so than daughters. Daughters, if they were able, married and left, but most sons stayed where they'd been born. *My sons are my joy,* Maialene had said.

Two nights ago, Aglaidia had been the only elf who'd cried when her son joined his new wife.

A shiver raced down Jerlayne's spine as she pulled her thoughts away from idle questions and met the goblin's eyes. Her hand was steady when she extended it to accept the goblin's bargain.

"Goro," he said, giving Jerlayne the name by which she'd henceforth know him, but not his proper name. The goblins who dwelt in Fairie's forests, protecting the homesteads, kept their proper names to themselves.

"Jerlayne," she replied. Elves had no secret names.

She touched Goro's hand as she'd touched Aulaudin's two nights' earlier. There was a joining between them; not an elfin joining, but honorable and binding all the same.

Goro's nod was a signal to Arhon and nineteen Stonewell goblins who emerged from the night bearing pole-slung hides, each bursting with honey-colored wine. The hides were pierced and goblets filled. The dignified melodies of elfin harps gave way to the wild rhythms of goblin pipes and tambourines.

In the hours that followed, as night gave way to dawn and morning, Jerlayne danced with Goro and the other goblins. She danced with her father, with her brothers, her mother, her sisters. She danced with all her kin and with Aulaudin's kin, too—even with Maun, who'd gulped down so much wine that he'd danced twice with a goblin, to everyone's open-mouthed astonishment.

Jerlayne danced with everyone except her husband.

Aulaudin was there. She saw him constantly on the far side of a wall of cousins. At other weddings, Jerlayne had been part of that wall. Keeping the newly joined husband and wife apart had been the greatest sport a wedding offered: Whirl them close, then whirl them apart, laughing all the time. Jerlayne tried to laugh as Aulaudin was whisked away, but the sound was hollow.

By noon, she wanted to escape, with or without Aulaudin, but weddings lasted until the end of the third day. Anything less defied tradition and invited disaster. She drained another goblet of potent goblin wine and gave herself back to the celebration with an unvoiced prayer that the sun set soon.

And, for all Jerlayne knew, her prayer was answered. Elves acknowledged mortal gods without quite worshiping them and she never clearly remembered much of her that afternoon, until suddenly the sky was washed in golds and reds and she stood at the Stonewell gate in traveling clothes. Her hands were between Elmeene's and there were tears—tears!—in her mother's amber eyes.

Elmeene embraced her tightly and whispered: "You're so young. There's so much you don't know. So many questions you've not begun to ask."

Jerlayne freed herself from the awkward hug. Tears were so unexpected at a wedding, so ill-omened. She couldn't believe her mother, the paragon of propriety, would be caught shedding them. She retreated a step, and found Elmeene clinging to her wrists.

"When questions cloud your mind, Jerlayne, come home. You can always come to me when you need answers."

What questions? Jerlayne thought. Elmeene had never been eager to answer her questions before. And what answers? She had all the answers a woman needed. She knew how to shape, to heal and mend, and to manage a homestead while her husband foraged beyond the Veil. What else was there? Raising sons and daughters? She'd hardly turn to Elmeene for advice about daughters.

Elmeene's tears dried between one blink and the next. Concern and confession vanished as if they'd never existed, leaving Jerlayne—already wobbling on her feet—convinced she'd been dreaming. Then Aulaudin was coming to the gate with Maun beside him.

The sight of her husband in traveling clothes banished Jerlayne's idle worries.

Stonewell hostlers led four horses behind Aulaudin. Two were saddled: her own mare and Aulaudin's stallion. The other two horses, also mares, were laden with packs of gifts and food for the journey and afterward. A man could only forage so much, and in the first months of his marriage, he might not forage at all. They'd need everything they'd been given, hard work, and luck besides.

The gnome who'd led Jerlayne's mare cupped his hands to boost her into the saddle. Any other day, she'd have done without, but she was wearier than she'd ever imagined being. The mare shied as she landed heavily. For an instant, there was a danger that the animal would bolt, but Goro appeared in the mare's shadow, sudden and silent. He clamped his black-gloved hand over the reins and pulled the mare's nose toward her chest to keep her still.

When the mare was steady again, Goro whispered, "I will never be far away." He spoke Fairie's language as if it were foreign to him, which it was; goblins had their own language and kept it secret.

For any dangers that didn't require goblins, Gudwal had a blessing that he bestowed on them with wild herbs and sparkling powders. Their parents blessed then, too—mothers first, then fathers, Maun after Jereige. With his red-rimmed eyes and redder cheeks, Aulaudin's father would regret all the wine he'd drunk, but he hadn't succumbed to one of his goblin-baiting rages.

Wisdom said to look to your beloved's parents if you wished to see your future. Aulaudin was nothing like Maun. Jerlayne had never seen Aulaudin truly angry; she didn't believe anger, much less blind rage, was a part of his nature. Maun was, by any honest measure, a man on the verge of ugly. His shoulders were as broad as a dwarf's; his chest was barrel-shaped. His eyes, skin, and hair were bleached and colorless like a gnome's. But Maun, when he smiled, could melt winter and brighten the darkest day.

Maun wished them health and happiness with proper decorum and then—where a wish for children would have been traditional—he slapped a burr against the stallion's rump. Goro and Jerlayne together kept her mare's hooves on the ground, but the pack mares followed the stallion, raising dust on the Stonewell road.

"Chase him, woman," Maun advised his son's wife, and after a moment's hesitation, Jerlayne agreed.

She caught Aulaudin easily, but not before her only home had disappeared behind hills and trees. The sound of goblin music—a wedding's celebration lasted longer than the wedding itself—was barely audible above the horses' blowing. Then, that too was gone.

They rode in silence, stirrups nearly touching as their horses ambled east, from the short Stonewell road to the cart-road that connected the neighborhood homesteads. Taking the reins in her right hand, Jerlayne laid her left in the crook of Aulaudin's arm. He freed a hand for her. As it had three sunsets past, joining seeped between their fingers.

Jerlayne heard nervous laughter. She saw a twilight stranger—a woman she scarcely recognized—and watched that stranger's cheeks darken with embarrassment as she realized her husband was staring at her.

"Are you tired, my love?" Aulaudin asked. "Ready to stop for the night?"

She nodded, not trusting her voice, not wanting to hear how it sounded to Aulaudin's ears.

While he tended the horses, Jerlayne unpacked pots and cleared leaves for a hearth. Fire was not her favorite shaping, though Elmeene had kept her at it until she could coax a flame out of wet wood in the rain. Cooking was another of her lesser skills, and all her lessons in that discipline had come in Stonewell's high-vaulted kitchen. She was scowling at the pots when Aulaudin knelt beside her.

His breath was warm and moist on her neck when he brushed her hair aside.

"Forget supper, beloved," he advised.

"A wife—" Jerlayne began, and lost her though as his lips moved across her cheek. "I should . . . *cook*—" Another distraction: Aulaudin's fingers were unbraiding her hair. Another lost thought. "Aren't you—?"

"Not for *supper*."

They had a tent, sewn from bright cloth, but Aulaudin hadn't raised it. The night, he said, was warm enough for lovers. He spread their blankets beneath a cloudless sky. The stars would protect them from storms; the goblins and Gudwal's blessing would protect them from everything else.

Her husband was sweeter than goblin wine and equally potent. Jerlayne lost her way in joining and, with no notion of what was real or what was dream, wrapped herself around him. When dawn opened her eyes, she found she couldn't remember the moment when she'd become a truly joined wife, but

there were a thousand new colors in the light and all were reflected in Aulaudin's hair.

They needn't hurry, Aulaudin assured her when he awoke.
Scyldrin weren't waiting for them and they'd be too busy once
they came to the end of their journey to think of lovemaking.
Jerlayne agreed with a kiss.

This time, she remembered everything.

Her sisters had told the truth about the difference between
trysting and joining.

*   *   *

They traveled east, toward their sage-chosen homestead.
They traveled slowly both by choice and because the cart-road
had decayed into a narrow hunter's trail. When they neared the
misty border forest, there was no trail at all. Painted blazings,
chalk-white by day and shimmering at night, guided them
through the gnarled and towering trees, so very different from
the trees Jerlayne had climbed at Stonewell.

Each evening, as sunset became twilight, Aulaudin let his
thoughts drift until they met and merged with other men's
thoughts. Vigilance, men called it. Most nights, a man touched
only the most familiar minds: father; brothers; sons; a true uncle, perhaps, if he were close by. Men threw their nets farther
when the moon was dark, touching the thoughts of everyone
within their lineage. And once a year, at midsummer, there was
a grand Vigilance, when all men met at midnight.

Jerlayne held Aulaudin's hand as his thoughts wandered.
Through joining she felt the ebb and flow of his conversations,
but they were without words, like the wind. She waited, barely
patient, until his eyes reopened.

"We're still on the proper path." His hand tightened around
hers; she shared his confidence.

"How long?"

"Three days, maybe two if we don't dally."

His hand tightened a second time and an entirely different
feeling flooded her perceptions.

They could easily dally. Less than a week after their wedding, they hadn't nearly had their fill of each other. Yet, Jerlayne withdrew her hand and stared east, where the sky—what
could be seen of it through the trees—was darkest and where
their homestead waited. She drew her hand into her sleeve.

That afternoon, they'd ridden past an ogre lair: filthy, and

stinking of fresh offal. The goblins would have driven the
ogres further away. Should have. Goro had taken iron from her
hands; he'd sworn to protect her and Aulaudin.

Somewhere, ahead or behind, but certainly nearby, two goblins were also traveling east. They couldn't go back to the
plains, not after taking her iron. Those goblins who dwelled in
Stonewell's shadows said it was better to live in shadows on
homestead largesse than stay on the plains no elf had seen but
where food was scarce and war incessant.

East was a good direction, Jerlayne told herself. Not like
north, where the Veil concealed mountains and dragons did
Fairie's guarding. In the east the guardians were mostly
griffins; much smaller and less dangerous.

"You're sad, my love?" Aulaudin asked, though surely, with
his men's talent, he already knew the answer.

And knew, as well, that Jerlayne lied—her first wedded
lie—when she shook her head. A small lie, and, maybe not a lie
at all. There was no single word for what she felt in the thickening twilight, as western clouds promised a rainy day tomorrow. She gave her head a more vigorous shake to loosen her
thoughts.

"It's so far, Aulaudin . . ."

"You were at the clearing for Darkhollow—that was as far
west as we're to go east. A lot farther—" Aulaudin took her
hand. "I *know* where we're going. I haven't *seen* it, not with
my eyes, so we must travel the long way. But I know where it
is, and we're not lost."

"How?"

Aulaudin's eyebrows knotted across the bridge of his nose.
"How?" he repeated. "I—I know, that's all. It is what men
do, what they can do. Women shape. How do you make
iron move? You see," Aulaudin said before she'd sorted her
thoughts into questions and answers. "You can't tell me and I
can't tell you. It simply *is*. And the place the sages chose for us,
and that was cleared for us, is no more than three days away—
even if it rains hard."

"I went to Darkhollow. It was not so far from Stonewell,
even with—" Jerlayne recalled the time when they had not
been riding and wanton distraction threatened her thoughts.

"It might *seem* farther, but it's not—not if you'd had to ride
the entire distance."

Not if Jereige hadn't made the air shimmer sometimes as father and daughter had ridden together. There were pass-throughs scattered about Fairie: places where men had parted the Veil so many times that it was thinner than elsewhere. Places where a man could skirt the mortal realm with a daughter, or his whole household, beside him. Places, too, where mortals sometimes found themselves drawn into Fairie, but not for long. If the ogres didn't find them, the goblins would.

"I'm sorry," she said, kissing his cheek.

"You'll feel better once you've seen the land for yourself."

He returned the kiss on her lips. Jerlayne knew what he wanted and wanted it too—but not quite at that moment. "What if it's too far?" she asked, unable to stifle the questions before they escaped. "What if no one wants to come so far from the road? What if they can't find us, if the blazings wash away? What if no one wants to? What if we're left all alone?"

"Have you ever heard of that happening?"

Jerlayne shook her head. She hadn't; she didn't imagine that anyone had. Fairie didn't remember failure. Tatterfall was the exception; all Fairie knew Tatterfall was gone because Maun kept its memory alive.

"They'll come, my love." Aulaudin knelt behind her and draped himself around her like a soft, warm cloak. "The scyldrin will come. You'll shape, I'll forage, and we'll make ourselves a homestead that no dwarf or gnome can resist. We might even lure ourselves a sylph or two."

"But—" Jerlayne swivelled about until she could see his face, all luminous eyes in the twilight. "What if—?"

Aulaudin put an end to her questions with a breath-stealing embrace. "They have. They will," he insisted when they both needed air. "It has always been that way and it won't change just because you and I are the first along this path."

The night was chilly, too chilly for arguments. She wanted a fire, blankets, and Aulaudin's arms around her. The rain would hold off until midnight; they could put the tent up then.

* * *

They were dirty and weary when they reached the top of a rock-strew hill four days later and saw for the first time the place the sages had chosen for them. It was a shallow valley with a year-round stream meandering north to south. Tree stumps from the clearing had been dragged into the stream bed to partially dam it. There'd be a fish pond by spring and green life growing in the cleared fields, but for now there was only the frost-kissed promise of a marsh behind the seeping dam. Jerlayne imagined she could see clouds of stinging insects.

Beyond the dam, there was naked brown dirt, etched and eroded by heavy rain, and the promise of more at any moment in the low-hanging clouds. Beyond the dirt, the Veil mists billowed. That fog might not lift for a century, until the sages laid out neighbor homesteads or Aulaudin and Jerlayne together created such prosperity that the sky turned blue by itself.

Today, there was no prosperity and rain clouds combined with the Veil mist to give everything a haunted, ominous air. Jerlayne thought of Stonewell's tidy fields, its carefully groomed forests. Her breath caught in her throat and her mare, sensing her hesitation, refused to set a hoof on the sloppy slope. The mare finally followed Aulaudin's stallion, though, snorting at every stride and shaking each hoof as she raised it, like a cat coming in through the mud.

Midway down the slope they came to a cleared and level plot where the sages had raised the foundation stone. Its sides were raw and smooth, except for the glyphs that symbolized her name and Aulaudin's. The space between the names would remain empty until they found their homestead's name—which would have been Muddybottom, if Jerlayne had known the glyphs or been audacious enough to shape them into the stone. Further down the slope, but still above the muddy bottom, posts marked the square the sages had chosen for the first room of their homestead. A flat sill-stone lay midway along the eastern wall, where it would catch a first glimpse of the sun when it rose above the mists, exactly as Elmeene had promised.

Jerlayne's room at Stonewell had faced west. Sunset, not sunrise, was her special time of day.

She considered dismounting and dragging the stone through the mud to the western wall—her traveling clothes were so fouled by the weather that no amount of new dirt would show among their stains. But it wasn't a newly wedded woman's place to question the sages and, even if it were, the door would open onto a rising slope. Jerlayne would never see the sunsets she'd seen as a daughter.

It was the right place—the sages had chosen it for her and Aulaudin—but it was nothing like the place she'd dreamt about since childhood. And though she'd known nothing could match those dreams, Jerlayne found herself fighting back tears.

"Our gifts."

Aulaudin's voice broke Jerlayne's morose reverie. She followed his pointing finger downslope to the brook where house-building materials waited: wood and stone from Fairie, metal and glass foraged from the mortal realm. There were also barrels of grains, oil, and salted meat. They had more than enough of everything they'd need to see them through their first building and to the day when Aulaudin returned to foraging.

Jerlayne knew the theory of house-building and much of the practice. She was confident that Aulaudin knew what she knew. Fairie had no *schools,* not as Jereige described the places where mortals passed their knowledge from one short-lived generation to the next. Fairie had tradition, and elfin parents spent decades imparting that tradition to each son and daughter they raised.

There was a difference, perhaps, between knowing and doing, especially if there were only herself and Aulaudin to turn their wedding gifts into a home. Truly, Jerlayne didn't think it could be done without help. She heard her mother's parting words: *When questions cloud your mind . . . come home.* None of her sisters, not even Maialene, had come home.

Jerlayne was thinking of shame and how two elves might raise the huge roof-beam, when she noticed movement on the far side of the brook.

"I told you," Aulaudin said, as the movement became a man and woman hurrying down a narrow path. "Gnomes were here first." He chuckled softly. "I'll wager they've been worried."

Nodding and blinking back relieved tears, Jerlayne tidied her hair and tried not to notice that the gnomes were neater and cleaner than she'd been since leaving Stonewell. She and Aulaudin tied their horses to the shaped end of the roof-beam and were waiting with outstretched arms as the gnomes forded the stream.

Age was always chancy in Fairie. Jerlayne had quietly hoped that they'd attract older scyldrin, wiser in the ways of homesteading than they were. But the silver-haired, silver-eyed couple who took their hands seemed no older or wiser than she felt.

"We followed the blazes," the man explained quickly, anx-

iously. "And found the 'steading gifts. We made our place
yonder and took the delicates in with us. A man from Darkhollow came with pigs and chickens." He wrinkled his nose, as if
Darkhollow weren't among his favorite places in Fairie. "We
penned the chickens and set the pigs loose in the woods."

Among the scyldrin, gnomes were renowned for their dili-
gence, but also for generally dour dispositions. It was said that
a gnome would rather mourn at a funeral than dance at a wedding, and by all appearances, this pair wouldn't have enjoyed a
wedding. There was a moment—an overly long moment—of
silence, then the woman unknotted her apron and offered them
a gift of ripe apples.

"A welcome gift—from this land. We found the tree growing just over the hill. The sun's right, and the soil, too. Your
sages went a long way to find this place, but it's a *good* place
for 'steading."

When they'd all eaten apples together, the gnomes announced their intention to plant an orchard around the wild tree.

"We'll gather seeds from that tree and mix them with the
seeds we brought with us," the man declared, slicing the air
with his hands, "but we need more, and hooks for pruning and
harvesting. Tempered hooks and a crank for the press, if you'll
be wanting cider." His tone said only a fool wouldn't want
cider, and that he hoped his elves weren't as foolish as their di-
sheveled clothes hinted. "You can forage these things?"

Aulaudin bit his lower lip. Jerlayne shared his sober realization: they were elves, they were married, and this would be
their lives. Scyldrin would come to their homestead to live and
depend on them. There were no cities, no towns, no villages on
the immortal side of the Veil—the words themselves roused no
images from Jerlayne's memory. She caught echoes of strangeness, though, through Aulaudin who knew the mortal side as
well as he knew Fairie.

They were joined. Theirs was a passion and ecstasy the
scyldrin could only imagine, but joining was responsibility
more than passion. The homestead would rise or fall on their
talents.

"A crank," Aulaudin repeated.

"Aye, and a metal one, if you please." The gnome met
Aulaudin's eyes. "Wood's best for the plates, the screw and
staves. We've brought fine, aged wood—we're the first; there

are no dwarves here, not yet. Our wood awaits the mistress' shaping. But iron's best for the crank. There's a good press where we come from, if you're not familiar—"

"I know cider presses. At Briary." Aulaudin's voice took the edge of pride even as his presence faded from Jerlayne's mind.

Men could hide their thoughts when they willed. It was necessary, on the other side of the Veil, where a few mortals were said to be sensitive to elves. Jerlayne understood. Both her parents had warned her that Aulaudin—older and long accustomed to a solitary life—could isolate himself without warning. Still, it was the first time Aulaudin had done what men could do: dampening his presence until she knew his thoughts only by the expression on his face, the way she'd known them before joining.

"When there's a roof over *our* heads—" Aulaudin pointed at the roof-beam where their horses were tied. Elves took the risks: foraging, shaping, bargaining with goblins; they made the decisions. "Then, you'll have your crank and whatever else you need."

"Petrin," the man said, accepting Aulaudin as the homestead's master. He extended his hand. "Banda," he added, cocking his head toward the woman beside him. "From Singingstones, inward, south and west."

"I know it. A fine homestead." Aulaudin took Petrin's hand.

His thoughts remained faint in Jerlayne's mind. Those she sensed were thick with doubt and indecipherable memory. Jerlayne wanted to share the thought that she sympathized with his doubts, wanted more to know exactly what his doubts were. She wanted so much that she missed Banda surging toward her until the woman had seized her hand.

"I will nurse your children. However they grow and change, I'll care for the scyldrin of this homestead. The first gnome will be ours, to raise beneath our roof."

Chapter 6

Despite worsening weather, Jerlayne, Aulaudin, and the gnomes built a one-room "great-house" and a two-room cottage that autumn. Though Elmeene and other women had rough-shaped the stones and timbers, it was Jerlayne's hands that throbbed each night after a day of measuring, fitting, and final shaping. She could have made it easier for herself, but this would be *her* homestead, hers and Aulaudin's, forever. Every beam had to be straight. Each corner had to be as square as she could make it, whether it was destined for the great house or the gnome's cottage.

Frost rimmed the last thatch bundles they tied onto the great house's roof and it was snowing when Aulaudin dressed for his first foraging since the wedding. The mortal realm was a dangerous place, but not so dangerous that a quick-witted man couldn't provide his homestead with all it needed and many luxuries beside—or so Jereige had said to Jerlayne and Elmeene each time he left Stonewell. Jerlayne had never doubted her father. She'd watched him leave and, more important, return countless times. He'd never come to serious harm, and neither had any of her brothers.

Aulaudin said much the same thing as they walked, hand-in-hand, through the snow to the wooden posts that would be their homestead's gate come spring.

"I know the dangers, my love. My father taught me well. I was foraging long before you were born."

They were alone. The gnomes weren't there to hear his faintly teasing tone, or witness his fingers tracing the curves of her face, tilting her chin upward. Aulaudin had inherited a gentle measure of his father's mischief, and in the last month Jerlayne had come to love him in ways her daughter's dreams had never envisioned. Exhausting as house construction had been, the time had been precious because they'd been inseparable.

"Would Jereige have spoken to Maun if he didn't think I could forage for you?"

Jerlayne lowered her eyes as she shook her head. They'd never talked about those conversations, about her father's reluctance which hadn't, at any rate, involved foraging. If Aulaudin guessed Jereige's reservations through their joined thoughts, he said nothing.

"I'll be gone two days, less if I can find Petrin's crank early on. I have a notion where a piece of tempered iron might be ripening."

She neither spoke nor moved, and Aulaudin wrapped both hands around the one he held. Though calloused by house-shaping, Jerlayne's hands remained exquisitely sensitive to joining. Her vision blurred with mortal-realm images: a *city* with brooding towers and hard, straight paths cornering between them. The paths were lit by ruddy globes that threw sharp-edged shadows across shapes her husband named: *carriage, trolley, train,* and, and the end, *wash tub* an ominous hulk with circular teeth, a basin large enough to drown a half-grown pig, and—very prominently on one side—a bar of tempered iron.

"Mortals wash themselves in *that?*" she asked as dread yielded to fascination.

"No, most have *bathtubs.* A few have *showers.* The tubs are only for their linen."

Aulaudin squeezed her fingers, but offered no other image so Jerlayne imagined mortal men and women naked in gentle rain showers, flinging soap bubbles off their fingers.

"Nothing so lovely," Aulaudin corrected with words only. "It will be all right, my love. I will be all right."

Jerlayne strove for courage and serenity, but the subtleties of deception within joining, which her husband and all men mastered before they married, remained out of reach.

"It is less dangerous than shaping iron."

He didn't add that he would never interfere with her shaping and Jerlayne didn't counter that shaping iron was different. She could release the iron if it began to threaten or burn. What could he do if he were injured or, worse, if mortals trapped him away from Fairie? It happened. Men didn't always return. Sometimes their mangled bodies were found and carried home, but more often they were lost . . . forever. In her life-time, Jerlayne hadn't lost anyone, but a cousin had vanished the winter before her birth and she'd heard whispers at her own wedding that Fairie was overdue for deaths, droughts, and punishing winters. She imagined the bitter smells of mourning.

"I will be back in two days," Aulaudin said, as sharply as he'd ever said anything. He released her hand and put an empty arm's length between them. "Foraging is what I *do*, what men do—me, your father, your brothers, and mine: all the men of Fairie. We cannot shape, so we forage."

He turned away, slow as ice. The words to restore peace and trust hovered just beyond Jerlayne's tongue. Petrin came down the slope of the far side of the stream, leading two mares; one saddled for riding, the other as a packhorse. Aulaudin said he'd found a good touchstone—a place with distinctive rocks and a good view of the mistless western horizon—a few hilltops away.

A man could come to harm in the forest, too, especially the wild forest around a new homestead. In her heart, Jerlayne wanted to banish the gnomes and the horses to Stonewell or Briary. Anywhere was safer than their raw homestead.

In her mind, she knew her heart was wrong.

"May luck and shadows surround you," she called when her mind had won its battle.

The words were the very words that Elmeene uttered each day and every time Jereige left Stonewell. For a moment Jerlayne thought Aulaudin hadn't heard her, then he stopped, turned, and grinned.

"Less than two days! Tomorrow by sunset! I'll find you a present. What would you like?"

Even at a distance, the thrill of joining raced up Jerlayne's spine to ground itself in her heart. *You—and only you—safe again beside me,* that was what she wanted, but she asked for a rose, a blooming rose, because there'd be no flowers in Fairie until spring, no flower garden outside her window for years to come.

"A rose as beautiful as you," Aulaudin promised before he swung into the saddle.

Joining burnt so hot within her that Jerlayne stood sightless until he was gone.

"How does a woman endure this?" she whispered, pressing her hands against her belly where, not ten days ago, she'd felt the first stirring of life. "Mother laughed when Father went foraging. How? How does she endure this?"

When questions cloud your mind . . . come home.

Jerlayne couldn't go to Stonewell, not with winter threatening, and even if it had been summer, without a man to slip her along the pass-throughs, there wasn't enough time, not if she wanted to be waiting at tomorrow's sunset.

In all Fairie's history, how many brides might have stood beside their unfinished gates, waiting forever for a husband who never returned? Unseemly, unelfin tears flowed as Jerlayne reminded herself that Aulaudin was older; he'd been foraging for centuries, not decades. But her fears, once roused, could not be quelled and she ran into their one-room home, seeking its darkest corner where she sank to the dirt floor. With her arms wrapped around her knees, Jerlayne cried until long after sunset, when Banda approached with a bowl of soup.

She ate, tasting nothing, and curled up under warm blankets in the feather bed where she felt nothing but her husband's absence.

Aulaudin returned the next day, early—as he'd promised. An iron crank, half-wrapped in paper and cloth, protruded from one bulging pack. His clothes were dirty and his shirt was torn beyond mending. Beneath the shirt he was torn as well: a nasty gouge the length of his left forearm. He'd cut himself, he said, on a piece of glass.

Jerlayne knew as soon as she touched him that he hadn't caught the 'death, but judged the cut too serious to leave for nature's healing. She tended it by lamplight. Her hands trembled despite her resolve to be calm and the healing was painful for them both, though neither she nor he would admit it. Nor would Aulaudin admit how he'd gotten hurt, even after supper when they joined in the privacy of the feather bed.

"You've seen worse."

She had, of course. Jereige and her brothers had come home bleeding and, by itself, a homestead was a dangerous place. Scarcely a month went by that a scyld wasn't injured seriously enough to warrant the mistress' attention and there'd been those times—the worst times—when she healed battered goblins. Jerlayne could mend almost any wound that wasn't fatal, and a few that would have been, if she hadn't got to them quickly enough. The inescapable fear that gripped her as she lay beside her husband was that she wouldn't be there when he needed her.

"Next time, take me with you," she murmured, squeezing him tight.

"You'll break me in two," Aulaudin chided as his ribs popped, but he made no attempt to free himself and said nothing about Jerlayne's request until she'd released him. "The mortal realm's no place for women."

It was that simple. Men didn't shape; women didn't part the Veil. The Veil men parted wasn't the same as the mists that crept over the roof each night. Women couldn't even sense where the men's Veil was. Jerlayne had followed Jereige once. Hiding in the underbrush, with a slotted spoon held up to block the parting light, she'd watched her father simply fade out of Fairie as he sat beneath a tree. She'd sat in his place all afternoon and never felt anything.

"But you *could* take me." She sat up, hugging her knees. "When we traveled, Father would part the Veil for everyone. I've breathed mortal air; it's no different than Fairie air. I wouldn't sicken, not like the scyldrin."

Aulaudin sat up with a sigh. "A pass-through isn't foraging. The Veil is parted open all the while you're passing through. If anything happened—" he paused, letting her imagine an appropriate catastrophe, "you could all get back into Fairie. So could anything that was troubling you, but that's another matter. If you were with me on a midden field, and I knew you could not return to Fairie without me, my attention would be divided and I might make the very mistake you fear most."

Jerlayne couldn't argue with him, so she said nothing. Aulaudin threw the blankets aside. He stood and dressed in clean, Fairie-made clothes. He favored his arm, but not unduly.

"Let me show you what I've brought back."

He lit the lamp with an ember from the hearth and pulled treasures from the sacks they'd left by the door: a wood-handled cleaver with a tempered blade no woman, not Elmeene nor any of her daughters, could match, shards of jewel-colored glass and a coil of leading for a window; a sack of sugar for luxury, spices for their stew, and a copper-bottom pot to simmer it in; a silvered mirror for vanity; five ruby-red goblets for festivals; and at the very bottom of the last pack, a box of nails to spare Jerlayne the tedium of shaping them.

Jerlayne's spirits lifted; they could hardly do otherwise, but there were writhing shadows across the thoughts they shared until Aulaudin brought forth his final treasure.

"For you, beloved."

The gift was two hand-spans high, half that in width and

depth. It was hard and heavy and wrapped in a length of emerald silk that would have been gift enough to soothe Jerlayne's heart. Within the silk, Jerlayne found a polished wooden box with a brass clasp.

"Open it."

The box was lined with crimson velvet and cunningly padded to cushion a clear glass dome, a polished wooden pedestal and, within the dome, attached to the pedestal, a single rose painted in sunrise colors. The rose wasn't real— mortal magic was mostly artifice—yet it was beautiful, as beautiful as any of the treasures Jereige had collected for Elmeene.

Jerlayne held her fingers away from the glass, afraid it was too fragile for touch. Aulaudin laid his hand over hers, pressing down until she felt the dome's unnatural smoothness. At Aulaudin's insistence, she removed the dome and stroked the petals.

«Porcelain,» he told her in joining's silent way.

Aulaudin slid his hand beneath the pedestal. She heard a *click* and from somewhere within the wood music played. It was strange, metallic music—nothing like the pure notes of elfin chimes—but beautiful, like the porcelain rose.

"Mortals name their flowers. They call this rose *Sunrise*. I like Sunrise for the name of our homestead."

Jerlayne agreed.

* * *

Gudwal came in the middle of a snow squall to carve the empty space between their names on the foundation stone. How he knew when to come was and remained a mystery but the rhythm of Jerlayne's life changed with Sunrise's naming. The idyll of newly wedded bliss yielded to the bustle of a growing homestead. More gnomes appeared at their door— disgruntled because they weren't the first, but content to establish themselves across the stream with Petrin and Banda. A trio of rock-working dwarves arrived between two storms. They chipped themselves a cellar out of the ground the day they arrived and vowed they'd chisel sill stones until spring, a half-session away.

Midwinter approached. A week before the bargain gifts were due, Jerlayne asked for iron and Aulaudin brought scrap from his Tatterfall cache, and a length of chain, too.

"They'll neither know, nor care," he said, laying the cloth-wrapped links in Jerlayne's hands.

The assurance was valid. Just last summer, with wedding preparations at a fever pitch, Elmeene had paid Arhon with iron forged in the mortal realm and if Arhon suspected, he'd said nothing. The time had long since passed when Fairie metal was indisputably finer than mortal work. Mortals alloyed and tempered their iron in ways elfin women couldn't duplicate.

The danger, then, in giving mortal-made metal to the goblins was not that they wouldn't accept it, but that they'd decide they preferred it to what they'd been getting. Jerlayne had probed the chain from Aulaudin's cache and determined that it wasn't as pure or strong as one she might make herself. But it would satisfy a goblin and that, when she was tired and pregnant, was nothing to disdain. She shaped the knife in an afternoon, scrubbed the chain in vinegar to brighten it, and turned her attention to making a midwinter banquet for her tiny household.

Trying not to remember the scents of Stonewell before the longest night of the year, Jerlayne prepared for a day in the cook-shed while Aulaudin foraged wine and savories. Sunrise had ample flour for their bread oven and ingredients for their open-hearth stew pots.

She'd gone down to the stream for a bucket of water when she heard what sounded like a man screaming. Before she could scramble up the stream's half-mud, half-ice banks, the scream became a growl and something huge and shaggy burst out of the trees on the far side of the stream. A spear-wielding goblin followed.

A bear, Jerlayne told herself, ogres went naked, even in the depth of winter. The bear spun around and threatened the goblin with a stone-headed club she hadn't noticed at first. Ogres, then, draped themselves in fur; and could swing their brutal weapons with sufficient force and accuracy to shatter the spear the goblin carried. He drew his sword, but to use it he'd have to get closer.

The ogre bellowed, and the goblin replied with a shrill wail as he lunged forward. The action went too fast for Jerlayne. When the goblin sprang back, his sword still in his hand, there was a spear sticking out of the ogre's side.

Jerlayne hadn't seen the spear strike its target, couldn't see the other goblin, who must have thrown it. She was reassured, though, to know that Sunrise's two goblins were alive and working together.

Blood ran down the ogre's filthy leg and stained the snow where he stood, though to Jerlayne's healing-trained eye, the spear hadn't struck anything vital.

Common sense said *get away from here,* and Jerlayne tried. She tried too hard, too fast, and wound up on her rump. Her foot slipped between two stones as she shoved herself upright and she sprained her ankle, not seriously, but bad enough that once she was standing, she stood with her weight off her heel and watched as the goblin thrust his sword straight for the ogre's heart.

It seemed a foolish attack, but the goblin knew what he was about. He dodged and ducked and rammed the sword between the ogre's short ribs then held on, enlarging the wound, while it smashed his ribs with its club. Jerlayne was overwhelmed by the display of sheer bravery that she didn't notice the second goblin until a second sword struck deep into the ogre's neck.

Horrified, she covered her eyes. When she opened them again, the ogre was dead and the second goblin was helping the first to his feet. Sprained ankle notwithstanding, Jerlayne knew her responsibilities: if a goblin was hurt protecting her homestead, it was her obligation to heal him.

"Over here!" she shouted.

Both goblins looked straight at her. Goro, she thought, was the first and injured goblin; a suspicion that seemed proved when, after a moment's conference, the second goblin back-tracked into the trees and the first approached her alone.

"You're hurt. I'll heal your wounds—"

"Bruised," he corrected, and jumped lightly down from the opposite bank to the stream bed. "Nothing that warrants healing. And you?"

The stream was barely a half-foot deep, three times that in width. Either one of them could have met the other on the opposite side, but neither did. Instead, the goblin pulled off his gloves, went on one knee, and splashed icy water against his face. While he gasped and drank, Jerlayne noticed that Goro— if the goblin was Goro—looked less impressive than he had at her wedding. His armor—squares of thick leather, bound tightly together and embossed with steel scraps—had seen better days. The shirt he wore beneath the armor, his breeches, and leggings, all had been carefully but repeatedly patched. His boots were clearly mismatched.

Perhaps he'd borrowed his wedding clothes from Arhon and the Stonewell goblins.

Novice goblins for a novice homestead?

He lowered his hands and met her stare. "Is something amiss?"

She gulped and thanked the mortal gods when she noticed blood weeping from his scalp.

"You're more than bruised. You're bleeding."

He seemed puzzled, then swiped the blood from his fore-head. "It's nothing."

"I'll tend it at the house."

"I do not go between walls or beneath roofs."

"Of course," Jerlayne chided herself for not remembering. "Beside the cooking shed, then? I'll need water, and a place for you to sit."

"It's an old wound. Not yours to heal."

Not hers to heal? A wound not received while defending Sunrise? At Stonewell, Arhon admitted there was always fighting in the plains, but goblins who swore to protect a homestead were exiled from their homeland. Then Jerlayne understood. He must have fallen on the ice, struck his head, and was too proud to seek her help. Pride was the goblins' greatest weakness.

"I don't mind—" Jerlayne began and was stunned by the anger flaring in the goblin's all-black eyes, but she held her ground. "I'll feel better," she told him calmly, "knowing that our protectors are whole."

"I am quite whole," the goblin assured her, pulling on his gauntlets. "More so, I think, than you, standing with all your weight on one foot."

Jerlayne successfully fought a blush, but stayed balanced on one foot. "You are Goro, aren't you?"

Another stare, barely less angry than the prior one. "You can't tell us apart, can you?"

Again, she matched his temper. "I've been awake for two days. I'll remember you clearly enough now, whether, you're Goro or some other goblin."

He blinked once, but said nothing and Jerlayne picked up her bucket. "I offered; remember that. I'll heal your wounds. It doesn't matter to me where or how you got them. I don't want injured goblins protecting my homestead."

The ankle held Jerlayne's weight readily enough, but she'd have to put the bucket down on the grass and use both hands to get herself up the bank. A leathered hand closed beside hers on the bucket's handle.

"I'll take your offer."

It was an odd angle, looking up toward that dark face with the sun shining behind him. Everything was in silhouette. She let go of the bucket; he offered her his other hand. Jerlayne pulled hers back.

"I *am* Goro. My second doesn't speak your language," he said, as if that should have reassured her. Then, with her bucket in his hand, Goro strode from the stream-side mud to the frozen grass with one easy stride. Setting the bucket down, he held out both gloved hands, palms-up.

Jerlayne wished that it were her husband standing on the bank and knew, in a wordless way, that if Aulaudin were at Sunrise, Goro wouldn't have accepted her offer. Still, dealing with goblins was women's work and she was up to the task. She grasped his hands at the wrists and raised her aching foot.

"Other one."

She hesitated.

"Unless you want me to lift you, lead with your good foot."

Duly warned, Jerlayne switched feet and one breathtaking moment later, was standing toe-to-toe in front of him. Goro, she realized, was shorter than Aulaudin. And goblin eyes weren't featureless; they had pupils, irises, and sclera like an elf's, only in shades of black. Goro's widened until she thought to release his wrists.

"For your sake, and your child's, Sunrise needs a well closer to your walls," Goro said, reclaiming the bucket before starting up the slick path. "I can't protect a homestead that's lost its mistress."

Jerlayne stood still a moment before following him. Though Goro and his second hadn't shown their faces the day Gudwal carved the homestead's name on the foundation stone, she wasn't surprised that he knew Sunrise's name. But she hadn't told anyone except Aulaudin that she was pregnant.

"We all have our tasks," he said over his shoulder. "You shape, your husband forages, and I watch you, very closely. This is not a good time for tumbling down hills or shaping iron."

Gritting her teeth, Jerlayne caught up with him. "You'll have your iron, a hand-knife and a twenty-link chain!"

"Perhaps I should reconsider—"

Jerlayne bridled. "You'll take what you bargained for, and so will we." Protection was important, but they also needed the salt, or would need it to preserve food for *next* winter.

"Of course. But we need only so many knives, so many chains. . ." Goro paused and smiled broadly, which made her nervous.

They reached the shed. The goblin wouldn't sit within its three open walls or beneath its partial roof, but he did consent to sit on a stump just beyond its limited shelter. Jerlayne ladled water from a pot she'd left simmering into the stream-filled bucket and dampened a clean bread towel with the resulting warm water. Goro's scalp wound was a straight-line cut a bit longer than her index finger. It was warm to the touch and festered. The wounds of cows and pigs and horses festered easily, but immortal flesh did not.

"You were struck with poison," she said as she wrung out the cloth. When Goro said nothing, she added, "and not by that ogre."

"Not by that ogre," Goro agreed, mimicking her tone precisely, something she'd never heard Arhon do with Elmeene.

Jerlayne added hot water to the bucket, a bit more than necessary, and re-immersed the cloth. "Are there ogres threatening Sunrise?"

"None that live."

She pressed harder, swiping away the last of the festered clot. Steam rose from the goblin's scalp.

"Ogres are not poisonous and their weapons, striking unarmored flesh, make holes about this large—" Goro used his thumb and forefingers to frame a goose-egg emptiness.

"I've seen ogre wounds," Jerlayne snapped.

"Then you know I don't have one."

"You didn't get this falling on the ice."

"I didn't say I had."

Jerlayne laid her palm over the wound. She thought about poison as she would have thought about blooddeath except, instead of bryony berries with motes of iron, she made heat through her hand to sear the festering wound. The poison was entrenched; Jerlayne needed three healing passes before she was confident that the wound was clean and could be sealed.

Goro's scalp had shrunk a little, too, the consequence of a long-open cut. She shuddered to think how long he'd had the wound before she pulled the edges together.

Her patient never once flinched.

"It will be tender and there may be a thickening, until your body remembers itself." She smoothed his hair over the pale blue flesh, but left it unbound.

He stood up slowly. Jerlayne knew from Stonewell that healing a goblin after he'd defended the homestead was simply good sense. She knew better, also, than to expect gratitude from a goblin and was perplexed when Goro lingered outside the shed.

"You can leave."

"We should revisit our bargain."

Jerlayne abandoned her ladles. "I said you would have your knife and chain."

"I would rather have mail, a shirt such as Arhon wears—"

"In one day! I'll keep to the bargain we have, thank you. A knife and chain for protection and salt. You *do* have the salt?"

"As surely as you have the chain," Goro replied quickly. "I mean for next midwinter, skipping midsummer entirely."

"We need midsummer salt and year-round protection."

"You'll have it, and two extra hives, one advanced at midsummer."

The new offer was tempting. Though there were few things as tedious as interlocking the thousands upon thousands of links in a chain-mail shirt, it was ultimately, easier than making a seamless chain or even a knife. Jerlayne knew that for a fact, having made ten of the metal garments Elmeene had given to Arhon over the years. "If there are ogres around, I'd like more goblins protecting my homestead," she continued.

"So would I. With the promise of mail, I might be able to swear another one or two."

"One hive tomorrow and two every half-season starting next midsummer?"

"I did not say—"

"I made the shirt that Arhon wears."

Goro bared his obsidian teeth. "I thought as much. Shall we agree: One hive tomorrow, then, and two each half-season thereafter, for mail shirts delivered at midwinter?"

"We can agree." Jerlayne held out her hand.

She'd touched him before—healed him moments ago—and

felt nothing more than she'd have felt bandaging a dwarf's swollen thumb. But now, through the patched leather of his gauntlets, Jerlayne sensed—

Sensed what?

Nothing she had words for except, perhaps, pride, though it was more than the animal stubbornness she associated with goblins and, by everything she knew of elves and goblins, she shouldn't have sensed anything at all.

"I will bring salt tomorrow," he said, lowering his hand.

"How did you get that wound?" Jerlayne called after him, before he reached the trees.

But her questions came too late. Goro had disappeared among the trees, as any man might when the sunlight was winter-weak and there were deep shadows everywhere. Jerlayne was tempted to follow the trail the goblin had left in the snow—to see if his footprints simply stopped between one stride and the next. But her ankle was throbbing and she had the unnerving thought that Goro had *wanted* her to follow him. Together that thought and her ankle were enough to quell temptation.

Chapter 7

Throughout that first Sunrise winter, Aulaudin spent more nights beyond the Veil than he did in his own bed. Even so, the young homestead needed more than one man could provide. Aulaudin shared his thoughts with his brothers and Maun, and with Jerlayne's brothers, too; collecting a century of debts and incurring obligations as he led expeditions after food, brick, lumber, and pipe for the spring construction.

Jerlayne put Goro and midwinter out of her mind as she scrambled to keep everyone fed, warm, and dressed in dry clothes. The last provided impossible once the thaw arrived. Their hastily thatched roof leaked and there was no straw for patching it. The threshold had become a boot-eating mire. Tempers were short by the time the ground was dry and Jereige surprised them with a visit. Her father led a party of Stonewell gnomes and pack animals loaded down with fresh fruit, honeybread, and other welcome luxuries.

In return, Jerlayne gave him a message for Elmeene.

"Tell her we're better off than we appear. Tell her my first child will be born before midsummer."

Elmeene sent Nereige, the youngest of Jerlayne's bachelor brothers, with more food and a reply. "I'll come when it's time, if you need me, if you have questions."

But difficult pregnancies were rare among women who could shape iron, and Banda insisted that she knew everything there was to know about midwifery. As for questions, Jerlayne had no time at all for questions.

A steady stream of mules and horses, men and scyldrin flowed between Stonewell and Sunrise throughout the spring. In addition to barrels of pickled eels and salt pork, which no one particularly liked but everyone ate for strength, Elmeene sent wax-sealed cheeses, flour for bread, and leather for shoes and gloves. All were ordinary stock the homestead could have provided for itself or Aulaudin could have foraged, but Stonewell's largesse freed the Sunrisers for planting and building.

Everything was a gift, except the salt, which had to be returned. Jerlayne evaporated the barrel brine, reclaiming as much as she could, but careful as she was, her wedding hives were gone completely and the midwinter hive would scarcely last until midsummer. Goro's proposal had become a necessity, as perhaps he'd known it would. She told Aulaudin how much iron she'd need to shape a mail shirt. After a frown and a sigh, he promised to find what she needed to display her good intentions at the midsummer exchange.

Their baby was born just after midsummer. Aulaudin was beside his wife, Banda, too, with boiled water, piles of clean cloth and a sharp, shiny knife that Aulaudin had foraged to Banda's specifications.

They needed the water and the cloth.

"A daughter," Banda announced with the swaddled newborn snug in her arms. "Full-formed and ready to be born."

The infant's eyes were gray, her skin shone with a healthy blush, and the tiny hand she waved showed a proper number of fingers, each in its proper place—exactly as Jerlayne had expected.

"An elfin daughter—" she sighed with satisfaction, taking the swaddled infant from Banda. Until she saw her daughter's face, Jerlayne hadn't been certain she was ready for the challenge. "What name shall we give her?"

Aulaudin reached for his firstborn and held her without hesitation, but his smile was more awkward than proud. "We'll see."

"But I'm sure she is," Jerlayne protested. "Look at her!"

Aulaudin didn't look and, later in the day, when Jerlayne was thinking clearly again, she was ashamed that she'd spoken with such ill-found confidence. It was much too soon to think about elfin names for an elfin daughter. It was easier with sons. If a son hadn't changed by his sixth winter, his father could safely take him beyond the Veil, but a daughter might not change until she was twenty, or as late as thirty.

And Jerlayne's daughter did change. Her head, hands and feet outgrew the rest of her. By her third birthday it was clear to anyone with open eyes that she belonged with the dwarves.

The stone-working trio, senior among the ten dwarves then living at Sunrise, came to claim their own.

It was Sunrise's first adoption and though all future adoptions would be celebrated by the scyldrin alone, the first was an elfin celebration marked on the foundation stone. Almost as many folk made the trek to Sunrise as had come to Stonewell for Jerlayne and Aulaudin's wedding—as much to establish the homestead in the minds of the Veil-parting men as to partake of a feast that was sparse and rustic by wedding standards.

Goro made an appearance, flanked by not one, but three companions, each wearing mail. Goro himself still wore patched and mended garments, but Jerlayne had learned to recognize him by the shape of his eyes and the slight, downward cast of his lips when he listened to her.

The goblins brought a hide of their potent wine and in short order the only sad face in sight belonged to Banda. Tears slipped down her pale cheeks whenever she looked at Frunzit—the little girl had a dwarven name now—in the arms of her adoring uncles. Jerlayne beckoned Banda inside, away from the laughter and celebration.

Sunrise's great house had grown to four rooms and a detached kitchen since Frunzit's birth and almost deserved its name. There were doors that could be shut and curtains on the windows. The ways of homesteading had come easily to Jerlayne. Often the mistress of Sunrise had only to remember the sound of her own mother's voice or her shadow against a wall to know how to handle a crisis, such as the one Banda presented. Thinking of Elmeene as she hugged Banda, Jerlayne could feel the gnome's sorrow as if it were her own, though she, herself, felt nothing. After her first misguided moments, Jerlayne had never let Frunzit near her heart.

"How do you survive?" Banda asked between sobs, then answered her own questions. "Elves are strong. Elves are stronger than all their scyldrin together. You are the trees. Without elves, Fairie would be nothing. It would vanish."

Jerlayne said nothing. She wasn't strong, not as strong as Banda, who'd given her heart as well as her breast to Frunzit from the start and would do the same with every child born at Sunrise . . . to *her* children, Jerlayne reminded herself, expecting the notion to spark a twinge of regret or anger. But elfin women didn't raise children; they merely bore them.

Then Jerlayne thought of her own childhood, and how she remembered no time when she hadn't known her elfin name.

When questions cloud your mind.

Jerlayne heard Elmeene's voice as clearly as if her mother were in the other room, which she was. A storm had blown up while Jerlayne had comforted Banda, and the celebration—as much of it as could squeeze through the doorway—had moved inside. Thunder crashed and, in the silence afterward, the sound of glass breaking. Fearing for her home's survival, Jerlayne opened the bedroom door. Guests swarmed boisterously around her and she was trapped in a corner for hours between a wardrobe chest and a dwarf who thought it was time to erect a mill above the pond. Every now and again, she heard something break, but her confinement offered a good view of the shelf beside the front door where the porcelain rose and five ruby-red goblets remained untouched.

The danger ended at midnight, when the goblins, and what was left of their wine, retreated into the rising fog. Aulaudin departed, too, leading all the elfin men on a grand foraging. Sunrise, he'd said with laughter and wine lighting up his face, was too small.

Jerlayne caught her mother's eye. Elmeene arched her eyebrows and pointed at the open front door. Jerlayne shook her head. The rain hadn't let up and Jerlayne was exhausted: questions and answers could wait until morning. But morning brought the men and great piles of lumber. Every question in Jerlayne's mind dealt with breakfast and the room her husband was determined to raise before noon.

Four days passed before Jerlayne recalled the conversation she hadn't had with her mother. By then Elmeene had been gone for two days. She and Aulaudin had Sunrise to themselves. The discrepancies between what she remembered of her childhood and the traditions that defined her adulthood seemed quite unimportant.

*   *   *

With the celebration of Frunzit's adoption, Jerlayne and Aulaudin declared that Sunrise had survived its own hard infancy beside the mists. The dwarves built their mill with local stone and wood and beams of steel that Aulaudin wrestled through the Veil. The new mill's shafts could turn the grindstones that Jerlayne shaped from Fairie boulders, pump the bellows for a mending forge, or drive a great cross-cut blade for sawing timber. The saw, in particular, was a much-welcomed device. Jerlayne didn't mind making horseshoes, nails, and the other wrought-iron implements that the dwarves could now hammer without her, but she'd be pleased if she never again splintered her hands on raw lumber.

Her responsibilities had changed. She shaped fewer necessities, more gifts and luxuries: fancy glass for all the scyldrin windows and tables, chimes for calling seventeen scyldrin to supper in the great house. Every morning, she eased the aching muscles that active life bestowed on scyldrin muscles and tended the more serious injuries whenever, wherever they occurred. She finally learned to weave both plain cloth and colored tapestries. Her needlework was scarcely improved, not that she ever tried very hard to shape thread.

Itinerant scyldrin began appear at Sunrise's fancy iron gate. (Why bother with thread when she could make lace with metal?) Most of them moved on after a season or two, but each year added a few more dwarves and gnomes to their family. Aulaudin grew a reputation as a skilled and generous forager; Jerlayne was, as she'd always been, Elmeene's daughter.

Twenty-five years after its founding, there were a score of scyldrin cottages on the far bank. Petrin's orchards had matured, and new fields were plowed every autumn. The mists retreated and most days the sky was blue by noon. Every few months Jerlayne glimpsed the sunrise for which she and Aulaudin had named their homestead.

That winter Goro offered a third bargain: he and his now-four companions would settle among the scyldrin, working with them and providing better protection—quicker protection—in exchange for food and clothes and swords, twelve a year, to be sent back to the plains where war raged among the goblin lineages.

It was an unusual—although not unprecedented—offer with obvious advantages. Goro's goblins were never far away, but Sunrise had buried two gnomes all the same, and didn't turn the pigs loose until they were full-grown. She'd feel safer—in some ways—if the goblins pitched their black tents in plain sight. In other ways, Jerlayne was never comfortable in Goro's company. His smile, which he flashed when she said she needed a few days to think before accepting this new bargain, was filled with unshared secrets.

"Sunrise has come to a dangerous moment," Goro said through that feral grin. "You're prosperous yet new. Your fields push back the mists; you grow more grain than you need—which you need because you must trade with other homesteads. But who knows what else your byres might attract? Fairie's grown; sooner or later the guardians must adjust their domains to accommodate the bulge. Perhaps Fairie needs more than an adjustment, a new guardian.

"If a griffin came, I believe we could drive it off with arrows and fire breaks, but if there are mountains behind those mists," the goblin shook his head dramatically without shedding his smile. "A dragon would be worse than a griffin. We'd need luck to drive off a dragon."

Jerlayne stifled her shivering before the goblin saw it. Elmeene told a frightening tale of her mother's sister who'd given birth to a boy, only to have that boy-child transform into a dragon six days later. It consumed every soul, every stick along a path from her aunt's homestead north to the misty mountains where, so far as anyone knew, it still dwelt.

And who knew what created or attracted a guardian? Looking into Goro's fathomless eyes, Jerlayne almost believed the goblin did.

After talking privately with Aulaudin and gathering opinions from the scyldrin, Jerlayne accepted Goro's third bargain. His goblins pitched their tents outside Petrin's orchard, which didn't please the dour gnome until Jerlayne convinced him that the goblins would protect his trees better than they protected anything else.

Jerlayne could see the orchard verge quite clearly from her new workroom window. See and, perhaps, be seen, though she never caught Goro spying on her as she spied on the goblins. It often seemed that there were more than five blue-skinned goblins living beside the apple orchard. Certainly there were different goblins from one month to the next: Jerlayne knew her mail shirts and knew when they hung from different, frequently wounded, shoulders.

Goro, though, was always at Sunrise. Jerlayne decided he, the only goblin who'd revealed his name, was also the only one who never left. She would have healed Goro's guests, if he'd asked her to. While they were at Sunrise they were Sunrise's protection and she considered their health part of her bargain responsibility. But Goro never asked and she never volunteered.

Another fifteen years after the goblins raised their tents, she and Aulaudin had another child, a son born in the middle of a bitterly cold winter. By the next summer, he'd grown all that he'd grow, turned nut-brown, and vanished into the trees. All Sunrise hoped he'd found brownie kin this close to the Veil, but he'd come and gone to fast for even Banda to mourn his passing.

Some thirty years after her brownie, Jerlayne birthed another daughter, the image of Aulaudin until her eighth summer when the sun bleached her from hair to toes. Banda and Petrin adopted their yearned-for child.

To everyone's surprise, including her own, Jerlayne mourned the loss of her gnome daughter with a passion that frightened her and her husband alike. Days darkened around her and she didn't fight back. Retreating to her workroom, Jerlayne closed the windows and drapes, lest she see or hear the child who would not be hers. When closed doors proved insufficient to deter her household's constant, irritating concern, Jerlayne fused the bolts. That stymied the scyldrin, but not Aulaudin.

He parted the Veil in the middle of her workroom and tempted her with the oddest bits of metal he could find in the mortal realm. Jerlayne thanked him dutifully, even sincerely, and left the gifts untouched. There was no way she could shape metal when her heart was an open wound.

"Give me time," she pleaded. "Just leave me alone for now. My heart will heal in its own time."

Aulaudin took his wife in his arms. "My heart aches, beloved. We could heal together."

He opened himself to her, but joining could not be forced, even if that had been Aulaudin's intention. In body and spirit together, Jerlayne turned silently away from the man she loved.

"We cannot go on like this, beloved. The scyldrin are worried; all Sunrise is off its feet. Tonight, at Vigilance, I will seek your father—"

Jerlayne reacted with force and anger: "No! You can't shame us . . . *me* that way. Another week. A month, at most.

That's all I ask, Aulaudin. Don't share this with Jereige or anyone, please. I ask you . . . ?"

"Open the door, then, and the windows. Go for a walk in the
sun. Your garden is a sight; none of us can make the flowers
bloom the way you do."

She thought of the sun and her garden which was, surely,
in worse shape than Aulaudin admitted. She thought of the
old cooking shed where she kept her gardening tools. She
thought of the view from its open side: the terraced path from
the house to the stream, the field and orchards stretching from
the opposite hillside, the clusters of tidy cottages, a little girl
with silver hair and eyes. Jerlayne's tears flowed with a will of
their own.

Aulaudin rushed to her and held her, but even with joining,
Jerlayne remained apart from her own life.

To please him and give herself peace, Jerlayne tended her
garden after that and kept her workroom door open, for all the
good that did. The fog within had become a part of her, lifting
into anger whenever Aulaudin suggested seeking help through
Vigilance.

A hot, dry summer settled over Fairie. The fields ripened
early with a poor harvest. Jerlayne bestirred herself to help the
scyldrin gather what they could, but months of lethargy had
sapped her strength. She retreated to the cool shadows of the
great house feeling worse than ever.

Aulaudin stayed close, and not only because he worried
about her. The forests were tinder-box dry and the rain, when it
did fall, fell with bolts of lightening. After a new moon Vigilance, he told Jerlayne that wildfire had swept across Ivycroft
in the southwest. Goblins couldn't protect a homestead from
fire, but the Ivycroft men got everyone and much of the livestock through the Veil, ahead of the flames, and back again after the fires had burned out.

Stale, breathless nights found Aulaudin pacing the roof,
keeping an eye peeled for lightning while the rest of Sunrise
slept. The unyielding weather matched Jerlayne's gloomy
mood. She brought a chair up to the roof and watched with him.

"There, in the north," she said. "I saw a flash."

Aulaudin sighted along her arm. "No clouds," he observed.
"But it could have come from the Veil—" His voice trailed. He

straightened, stiffened, then took her hand. "Your brother, Nereige, is coming."

There was no joining in Aulaudin's touch. That, as much as his tone, told Jerlayne something was wrong, terribly wrong. They paused to light two bull's-eye lanterns, then hurried toward the gate. Halfway there, Jerlayne sensed movement in the trees and directed her lantern toward the trees. She saw darkness in the shadows: Goro, in armor, despite the hour and heat. Jerlayne was about to call and tell him that it was only her brother, come for an unexpected visit, when the light from a third lantern became visible across the stream. Goro vanished into the shadows as Nereige emerged from them.

"M'lene's consented to a search. We rally at Brightwings at sun up."

M'lene was Maialene, Brightwings was her homestead, and a search meant Redis, her husband, was missing beyond the Veil. Jerlayne found Aulaudin's hand. His thoughts were torn between joining the search—he and Redis haunted the same parts of the mortal realm, which Jerlayne had not suspected until that moment—and the danger to Sunrise if he left.

"Aglaun will come here," Nereige assured his brother-by-marriage.

Aglaun was the youngest of Aulaudin's bachelor brothers. The Sunrise scyldrin knew and trusted Aglaun. He spent almost as much time at Sunrise as he did at Briary . . . because Aulaudin didn't have a son. *She* hadn't had any elfin children—

«Not now, beloved.»

Aulaudin's thoughts whispered through hers and, belatedly, Jerlayne realized Nereige hadn't said Aglaun's name aloud. She'd blundered into men's ordinary sharing—it could happen, sometimes, never predictably—when everyone was raw-nerved.

"Is M'lene— How is she?" Jerlayne asked aloud.

"Locked herself in a bedroom." Nereige said with a shrug. "Elmeene's been at Brightwings for days already. It hasn't been easy."

Jerlayne glanced at her husband, who must have known there was disaster brewing at Brightwings and who hadn't told her . . . lest it spread to Sunrise? She didn't blame him but faced with circumstances more dire than her own, the fog burnt out of Jerlayne's mind. She tightened her grip on

Aulaudin's hand, hoping to reassure him as she shared the thought.

«I need to be there at Brightwings. Elmeene is *not* the right woman to be with M'lene.»

Aulaudin's thoughts were already reaching across the horizon to Aglaun; the bond between brothers was the strongest of men's sharing bonds. Jerlayne felt the echo of an exchange that was, as men said, simply different than joining. Aulaudin blinked, the sharing ended.

"He'll be here before dawn. Nereige, tell them we're both coming; we'll be there in time."

"Maybe she'll listen to you," Nereige agreed. "Elmeene's not doing herself or M'lene any good." Then he turned and headed back into the trees. Moments later there was a flash of light.

"I'll wake Petrin and saddle the horses," Aulaudin said when they were alone. "Gather what you need quickly. We've got a hard ride ahead of us. The worst is from here to the first pass-through. There won't be time for rest, except for the horses; no time at all for sleep. You're sure you want to go?"

Jerlayne nodded. "I can ride. Elmeene's all strength; M'lene needs someone who understands being weak."

"Hurry, then," Aulaudin advised and headed for the foot-bridge that would take him to the stables.

Jerlayne thought of Goro as she tied a casual armful of summer clothes into a mortal-realm shawl. There wasn't time to stand by the foundation stone, waiting for him to notice her: a woman's typical way to attract her goblin's attention. But he'd been in the woods, he'd know where she'd gone and why. Probably he was saddling his own horse and would follow her as far as the first pass-through. Mortal air affected goblins worse than it affected the scyldrin. When Ivycroft burnt, its goblins had burnt with it.

She wasn't surprised that she heard another horse once or twice as she and Aulaudin rode west on the Sunrise trail, nor that she heard nothing but the night after Aulaudin called a mist down from the hazy, midnight sky. It was raining in the mortal realm where Aulaudin skirted the Veil just enough for the two of them to walk their horses. After Fairie's drought, rain was a disconcerting sensation: a few strides wet, a few more dry. The horses liked it not at all; Jerlayne kept a careful grip on the reins and didn't notice the softer, pass-through flash when Aulaudin left the Veil behind them.

There were more pass-throughs, mostly through the same gentle rain, though the last was an every-shade-of-red sunset viewed across an expanse of grass that had to be larger than all Fairie together.

«Plains?» she asked, wishing they could stop for the handful of moments the sun yet needed to sink away. «The goblin plains?»

«The great plains,» Aulaudin corrected without slowing down. «Mortal plains. There are no goblin plains, except in the lies they tell. They're here—in Fairie—hiding from us as they hid from the Ten.»

They reached Brightwings as the eastern horizon prepared for what would be a considerably less spectacular sunrise. Men had gathered in sight of the foundation stone, their grim silence a marked contrast to the eccentric domes and curves of a great house Jerlayne had never liked. An anxious gnome met them on the cobblestones. The mistress' mother, he said, was waiting for Jerlayne inside; Redis' close-kin were waiting for Aulaudin by the store. Dismounting, Jerlayne shared a last moment with her husband.

«Do you have any hope of finding him?»

«Very little,» Aulaudin admitted. «We ranged together, but he haunted places I never thought were wise.»

«You'll be careful—if you have to look for him in those places?»

His mind shrugged. «This isn't about finding Redis, it's making certain he hasn't been found. The mortals have discovered something called *science*. It used to be our secrets died with us. Mortals looked at our corpses to see if we had wings or horns or cloven hooves before they burnt us of threw us in a slaking pit. Now men like my father think they could learn more from a man's dead body than we know ourselves.»

Questions exploded in Jerlayne's mind. All went unanswered as Aulaudin shut himself away from her with a kiss and a whispered good-bye.

"Don't worry about me, beloved; I promise I'll come back safe. Comfort your sister. Help her make the right decision."

He held Jerlayne at arm's length in the dawn light, memorizing her face as she memorized his. Then there was movement to her right; another gnome with her hands clenched tightly. It was the wrong place to say anything cheerful. They let go of each other and Jerlayne followed the gnome through the overly large, overly red front door.

Chapter 8

Every homestead developed its own style: Stonewell was dignified; Briary was comfortable; Sunrise was a bit of both, but also simple and growing. Brightwings was like nothing else in Fairie. On a sultry morning, it sent an unwelcome shiver down Jerlayne's spine. Her sister's great house was bad enough when she and Redis hosted a festival. At least then the huge, ornately asymmetric rooms, each one a different—bright—color seemed to have a purpose. Today, with Redis gone and probably dead, the colors were offensive.

Jerlayne paused in the aqua foyer with its four curving staircases and turned slowly. No matter how many times she visited, she never remembered which stairway went where.

"Where are they?" she asked the gnome who'd guided her this far. "My brother said my mother and sister were already here."

The gnome pointed to one of the staircases. "Up those stairs, Mistress Jerlayne, and to the left. They're all in the upstairs sitting room, waiting on the mistress. There's not enough air left for breathing."

"There'll be enough for one more," Jerlayne decided, heading for a swooping stairway Maialene had shaped out of Fairie wood and mortal metal.

Women crowded a florally furnished room that was probably inspired by something Redis had seen in the mortal realm. The gathering was very much what Nereige had described: Elmeene and a score of women hovering near a painted door with charred jambs where Maialene had fused the lock and hinges. Jerlayne needed only to think of her own workroom to know how beseiged by good intentions her sister must feel. She said her hellos, ignored the obvious, empty, *fuchsia* chair at her mother's side, and dropped her shawl-wrapped bundle in the middle medallion of the way-too-colorful carpet.

"This isn't working. You all want to help my sister and you want her out here, with you, so you can comfort her . . . comfort her the way you think she should be comforted. But she's in there because she doesn't need what you want to give her, and she won't come out while you're all here ready to pounce on her with your kindness. She doesn't want your kindness and she doesn't want to come out of that room she shares with Redis, so you might just as well go downstairs, have breakfast, and get some rest. The men have left; they're going to be gone awhile."

Perhaps, if she'd stripped naked and painted herself dark blue, Jerlayne could have caused the room's collective eyes to open wider, its jaws to gape lower, but she'd simply said the words someone should have said at Sunrise a month ago. And, having said them, Jerlayne found herself stranded in the center of a stuffy, crowded room.

Rescue came from the last place she expected it: her mother.

"I do believe you might be correct, Jerlayne. It has been several long days and longer nights. We're all tired. Adala! Ferri! Roda!" Elmeene called gnomish names and silver-eyed faces appeared quickly in the doorway. "Where does my daughter keep the guest-goods? We've got twenty-five women here and we'll need to find beds and linen for them all."

With one sweeping gesture Elmeene sent her daughters after the gnomes and the other women after her daughters. Jerlayne almost followed them: Elmeene had that effect, especially on the daughters who knew her best. She braced herself as her mother approached.

"Brush your hair. You look like you've ridden all night."

That remark Jerlayne could almost have predicted. It was the hug that followed which caught her off guard, along with whispered advice: "Finish what you've started, daughter. I know that you can."

Before Jerlayne caught her breath, she was alone in an empty room. She'd forgotten her brush, of course, not that M'lene would care. Jerlayne knocked softly on the bolted door.

"It's me—Jery," she used the child-name she despised because M'lene had never managed to outgrow hers. "I've sent them all away. I'll stay out here for a little while—if you want to talk—then I'll go away."

There was no sound on the door's other side, no reason, really, to think M'lene was listening or awake. Jerlayne could have unshaped the bolt. Any of them could have unshaped the bolt. But that was the last thing Jerlayne would have wanted if she were in her sister's place; the last thing, therefore, that she would do. She settled in the high-backed chair where Elmeene had been sitting. The heat and her own weariness left her napping.

She awoke when the chair beside her creaked.

Maialene was hollow-cheeked and pale. Her voice was thick as she said: "I don't know what to do."

"I understand—"

"No. You don't. You can't." She curled her legs beneath her and pulled a tattered sweater around her shoulders. "You love Aulaudin."

The sisters stared at each other until Jerlayne had sorted through the implications. She couldn't imagine living with Redis or loving him or joining with him—especially joining with him. Then again, she never deliberately imagined any part of Maialene's life. She'd believed Maialene was happy with her pompous, frivolous husband. She'd thought that they were well-suited for each other. The thought wasn't a compliment, but it was sincere.

"You were the one who told me how wonderful joining was . . . I never thought once that you didn't love Redis." The words had come too quick, without thought. "I'm sorry. I shouldn't have said that."

Maialene shrugged and managed a weak smile. "I'm glad someone believed; I've been so sure everyone saw right through me."

"You must have loved each other at the beginning?"

Another shrug. "We needed each other and we didn't dislike each other. That was enough to get us through our first joining. I needed to be the woman I expected myself to be. Redis needed someone who could shape his dreams. He was very . . . he was everything mother admired in a bachelor; I was her daughter. We were each what the other needed so, of course— joining is . . . *joining*. Who can resist at first? But we never loved. We had other loves."

Jerlayne thought of her own early trysts with the Stonewell scyldrin and kept those thoughts to herself, saying, instead: "And now you're alone and you don't know what to do."

"Alone—but not lonely. I'm by myself and it's quiet again. Nothing jumps or tingles. I'm not watching the door, waiting for him to return, wondering what's filled his mind this time. What *invasion* awaits. I don't have to share everything he thinks! My mind is my own. I should cry. I *do* cry because he's gone. Everyone liked him. They'll mourn him. Redis was witty and confident—around others. It was different when we were just the two of us. Nothing was ever enough. He blamed me. It was like living with Mother, only worse. Much worse. If you can imagine that."

"I can't," Jerlayne insisted, though she could, in a backwards way. She didn't know about his confidence, but Redis wasn't witty. He was a suffocatingly dull man who wanted others to think he was witty. So, out of politeness, others laughed, for M'lene's sake, and because it was the only way to quiet Redis. "I do love Aulaudin. If we could share everything, I would only love him more. But I can't imagine feeling one thing when everyone expects you to feel something else."

Maialene stared at the farthest wall. "They're expecting me to die for him."

Jerlayne didn't disagree. If anything happened to Aulaudin, she'd shape a fist around her heart and squeeze it shut—not because she wanted to die, but because she couldn't bear the thought of living without him. Even if Aulaudin weren't the touchstone of her life, the silence that Maialene seemed to welcome was too brutal for Jerlayne to contemplate without another shiver. Joining was a once-and-forever ritual. Men might go on, sustained by their fraternal sharing, but a widow's life was bleak.

Claideris was a widow.

Death was preferable to becoming another Claideris. Fairie life revolved around its homesteads and its homesteads revolved around joined elves. The scyldrin wouldn't stay with a widow or widower. Whatever Maialene decided, Brightwings was finished.

"You can't stay here," Jerlayne whispered, once she understood her sister's dilemma. "Nobody can live alone. And, even if you could, Brightwings is in the heartland. The sages will want the land back."

"I don't want to stay," Maialene agreed quickly. "Brightwings can't burn quickly enough for me. I'll light the blaze myself. Viljuen weeps, Brightwings was Redis' homestead: all that he imagined. Let the land take it back. Let it lie fallow unil no one remembers it, then let someone else begin again. I *hate* it."

Jerlayne sat back in her chair: hate was such a strong word. Men used it, sometimes, to describe mortals: *They hate each other, it's to be expected that they hate us, too.* Yet, listening to Maialene, there could be no doubt that she hated this room and everything attached to it.

"In your heart," Jerlayne said cautiously, "there must be a place where you've gone for peace—"

Maialene laughed bitterly. "Oh, I've thought of *that* a thousand times since my sons were born, but I'm not touched."

Privately, Jerlayne thought that being touched—touched by iron—was precisely her sister's problem: Maialene had lost some small, but vital, part of herself while shaping. Maialene's chain hanging on Elmeene's wall had been her fourth attempt and she was the sister who suggested a secret bryony cache, the sister who wouldn't raise a daughter.

But Jerlayne had come to Brightwings to comfort her sister. "Is there nowhere that calls to you? Stonewell, perhaps?"

Another bitter laugh. "You know better than that! I'm *here* because I didn't want to be *there!*" A moment of silence, then, "The Veil calls me to a cottage—not a homestead—of my own where the mist comes down to my roof each night. Help me, Jery."

Claideris. Maialene wanted to become another Claideris, and she wanted Jerlayne to make her dreams happen. Aulaudin had said to help M'lene make the right decision, but he couldn't have been thinking of this. "You only came that once, for the adoption," Jerlayne said, trying to hide her discomfort. "Sunrise is bigger now. The mists are a half-day's ride away, but we're still on the frontier. We live a simple life, M'lene. Nothing like this. Aulaudin has all he can do—" It became Jerlayne's turn to stare at the wall. Her own despair was still close at hand. "My children have all changed."

"Medis and Relene will find other 'steads, but Dalan's young. He'll come with me. We'd be a boon, not a burden. And when my last son is born, Aulaudin can teach him. Good practice for when he has sons of his own."

In the glass chimney of an unlit lamp, Jerlayne watched her face freeze into the arched-eyebrows look of disbelief she'd seen so often on Elmeene's face, a look she'd sworn she'd never wear herself. She forced her eyebrows down. "Your last son?"

"I can hardly have any more, can I?"

"No." She'd thought about by then and imagined herself in M'lene's position: one last chance for a child—Aulaudin's son—who wouldn't change. A chance she wouldn't have if something happened to Aulaudin before he returned. Guilt and other emotions set Jerlayne's gut churning. "I didn't think. I'm sorry; forgive me. A child could be such a comfort to you. I'll talk to Aulaudin. When—when he and the men come back. I'm sure he'll agree. He understands—" she sought the right word—*"difficulties."*

Maialene nodded. "He changed after Boraudin, after Tatterfall. If I'd known what he'd become—no, he was just Boraudin's brother when I joined with Redis. The three of them: him, Boraudin, and Maun. I didn't want any part of that."

Jerlayne watched a stranger smile as she rose from the other chair.

"Will you tell Elmeene and the rest?" Maialene asked from the bedroom door. "I can't face them, not yet. Tell them it was your idea?"

"M'lene!"

"No one will question you, Jerlayne. Even Elmeene whispers your name. You can do it. Please? For me?"

Afterward, when she'd found moonlight peace in Maialene's neglected herb yard, Jerlayne told herself that she'd had no choice: her sister was iron-touched and no good would come from pushing her uphill. But it was also true that none of the women in Brightwings' kitchen—including Elmeene—had uttered a word against her plan to settle Maialene and Dalan in a Sunrise cottage. She neglected to mention M'lene's "last son"; that scandal could wait until winter when everyone was snowed-in and men were solely responsible for gossip.

The next morning, a pale Maialene emerged from her bedroom, reconciled—or so she said—to her younger sister's advice: Dalan was too inexperienced to face life with neither mother nor father to guide him.

It wasn't what Jerlayne had described in the kitchen the previous night, but she couldn't bring herself to argue with her sister, despite Elmeene's critical glances. Later, when she was staring in a mirror—Brightwings was cluttered with them;

Sunrise had only one hanging from its walls—Elmeene walked up behind her.

"What made you two think it was wise for you to tell one story while she told another?"

Jerlayne shrugged. "*We* didn't think it was wise, but the end's the same. She's coming to Sunrise."

"Is it what she wants? Was it her idea or yours?"

Jerlayne could answer honestly: "Hers. A cottage near the mists. She's never been happy here."

"And whose fault was that, I wonder?"

"I don't know," Jerlayne replied, ending the conversation.

Rain came that afternoon, out of black cloud that rumbled in from the east. It lashed Brightwings with winds that knocked down trees, broke windows, and lifted the roof off the kitchen. The scyldrin saw the hands of fate. They began packing their most precious possessions, breaking and burying the rest in mud, as drought gave way to four days of relentless rain.

When the weather lightened, a taller-than-average goblin waited for Maialene at the foundation stone. In a light rain, they bargained for an hour or more.

Maialene was smiling grimly when she returned. "It's done," she confided to Jerlayne. "They will stay until Brightwings burns, then I'll be rid of them, too: I told them not to follow me to Sunrise. I'm done with their *protection*. No more looking over my shoulder. I live for myself, now. Myself and my last son."

Jerlayne pitied the yet-to-be-born boy, but said nothing.

Another ten days passed before the sages Gudwal and Rintidas led the ragged, dirty men back to Brightwings' foundation stone.

"I have seen my grandson's shadow in the misty trees," Gudwal said to the assembled women. Sages referred to everyone as a grandchild, but Redis, whatever his flaws as a husband, was truly Gudwal's many-times-great-grandson, as Maialene was his granddaughter. His quavering voice owed nothing to ritual. "I have heard his voice in the morning air. He—"

Gudwal covered his face with a trembling hand. His fingers were gnarled, his knuckles, swollen. He and all the silent men with him had *aged*. Jerlayne had heard of aging, knew that it was often the price of too many partings with too little rest in between. Her shaping touch could undo the damage. But knowing couldn't blunt the sight of crinkled flesh around Aulaudin's eyes or the white stubble on his chin. She hadn't recognized him until their eyes met. Her husband's thoughts were weary, but not as weary as Gudwal's, which Aulaudin echoed:

«My grandson does not know how his life ended. My grandson has returned to the air and sunlight. He is at peace.»

Gudwal sighed and lowered his hands. Jerlayne imagined it was different for men. They could hear each other; they'd never know the emptiness, the isolation every married woman dreaded—except Maialene who stood between Redis' mother and Elmeene. M'lene hid her face behind black gauze: a strong elfin woman confronting fate.

Or so she seemed.

Standing somewhat behind her sister, listening to her recite the traditional request that the foundation stone be broken, Jerlayne knew M'lene intended to be on her way to Sunrise before nightfall. Jerlayne had already shared that secret with Aulaudin and felt his resignation.

«None of her sons has married yet,» he reflected, a complication which Jerlayne had not considered. «There's really no better place for her to come—if she's determined to live without Redis.» Aulaudin didn't seem too surprised that Redis' ghost was destined to wander Fairie's forests alone. «Beware the goblins, though. They'll bargain hard for your compassion.»

Jerlayne hadn't considered that, either. She wondered if she should try to find M'lene's goblins before they left. She wondered what happened to a goblin like Goro, who'd bargained with an elfin woman, when the bargaining ended.

«Never worry about goblins, beloved,» Aulaudin advised, sounding like his father and she stifled her thoughts.

They followed Gudwal to the foundation stone and watched dwarves hammer it apart. Everyone thought there'd be a final, somber feast—to empty the larder, if nothing more. The men were tired, thinking of baths and beds. But they'd reckoned without Maialene.

She shaped fire from her hands and set Brightwings ablaze without reclaiming anything more than the clothes she wore. Her sons were astounded and loudly displeased. They raced the flames to rescue their personal treasures. Elmeene and the other women who'd been living in the brightly painted rooms did likewise. Jerlayne, however, had guessed what was coming and had thrown her shawl-wrapped bundle from a window the moment the sky began to sparkle with the men's return.

Aulaudin caught up with her in the garden where the bundle had landed.

"Is she iron-touched?"

"A little," Jerlayne replied, recalling the long-past days when she'd sworn there'd be no secrets in her life.

If she shaped a wall within her mind and kept a few secrets now, it was a mercy. Aulaudin was exhausted and fighting to keep his most recent memories hidden. A few images slipped through: A mortal man running through what seemed to be a cave. A spear of white, unnatural light burnt from the mortal's hand. A *flashlight;* Jerlayne knew the devices. Aulaudin had been foraging them and their *batteries* for several years. Goro and his goblins attached them in pairs to their scabbards. But something about the mortal and his flashlight had frightened Aulaudin. Jerlayne's heart raced as she shared the memory.

Saying nothing, Jerlayne slid her arms around her husband and drew him into a close embrace. His head came to rest heavily on her shoulder. She worked her fingers against the muscles of his neck, finding knots of tension, shaping them away with gentle heat.

Aulaudin sighed, a mix of relief and pain. «I have missed you so much, beloved.»

Jerlayne replied with love and joy that needed no words, then asked: «Is Fairie safe from mortal *science?*»

«We looked and we listened. We think he was *mugged* in an *ellay*. It's not uncommon there. They'll wait and bury him in a year or so. There'd be more trouble if we'd tried to bring him back. As it is, Redis is just another victim and they won't bother with an *autopsy*.»

Sometimes when Aulaudin spoke of the mortal realm—especially when he kept his memories to himself—his words were not quite sensible. She could have asked for meanings, but she really didn't want to know the meaning of *mugged, ellay,* or *autopsy*.

«It will be good to have this behind us.» She caressed his temples. It would be a year or more until all the gray was gone. «We'll sleep by a stream tonight: cool water and stars overhead.»

Aulaudin nodded against her, but his thoughts were filled with sleep, not romance. Jerlayne shared a gentle laugh and held him tighter. They tried to ignore the scyldrin who rushed around them, gathering their possessions before flames leapt from the great house to their cottages. Several of them muttered curses against fate, a few muttered curses against Brightwings' mistress. Jerlayne heard one say: "Sunrise will rue *this* day!"

Since the rains began, only three of Brightwings' scyldrin, all gnomes, had approached her about settling at Sunrise. A frightened and frightening thought sprang up in her mind. «My sister will drive our scyldrin away!»

Aulaudin roused quickly from his standing dreams. «Sunrise is *our* homestead, beloved. Your sister may have her cottage by the Veil, but no more than that. When the scyldrin learn that nothing has changed, they'll be reassured."

Jerlayne wanted to believe him, but before she could, Nereige came running up. "The sylph!" he shouted. "She's panicked!"

Together, they raced behind him.

Redis had persuaded one of the Fairie's gentlest scyldrin to dwell at his homestead. Her name was Olleta and Redis had built for her—had had others build for her—a rainbow-tiled grotto with fountains and a waterfall. Sylphs breathed air, they were the daughters of elves, not fish, but they'd die if their skin parched. Their teeth were sharp and they'd eat their meat cooked or raw without complaint. Perhaps a sylph could have survived on her own in a lake or stream, but in practice all eight of them lived in homestead grottos.

Though she was older than Gudwal, Olleta had the face and mind of a child. Her laughter had made Jerlayne's visits to Brightwings bearable. And like everything else associated with Redis and her homestead, Maialene had turned her back on Olleta without even saying good-bye.

Jereige, his sons, and his sons-by-marriage worked frantically to calm the frightened sylph. Among the women, the plan had been that Olleta would go to Stonewell but Elmeene had said nothing, waiting for Jereige: sylphs fastened their affections on men, not women. Olleta had adored Redis; she'd thrashed her grotto into foam once she knew he was dead.

Jerlayne watched her father strip to the waist and wade into the water. He held Olleta in his arms until her tantrums subsided and the child-sized storm was sobbing softly into his shoulder. Jereige whispered in Olleta's ear then—probably telling her that he would take her to Stonewell. He looked surprised when she unwound herself, but not as surprised as Jerlayne and Aulaudin when Olleta swam to their feet.

"Sunrise," she proclaimed in her strange, lyric way. "I want Sunrise!"

Ancient child that she was, Olleta was a scyld; she had the unchallengeable right to settle wherever she wished.

Two dwarves immediately announced their intention to settle at Sunrise also. They'd been Olleta's companions for millennia. He said his name was Funder, his mate was Grezel, and they'd need a cottage near Olleta's grotto. Jerlayne and Aulaudin welcomed them without hesitation: they knew how to drive a wagon with a water-filled barrel behind the driver's bench. Maialene grimaced when she saw the dwarves and wagon.

Brightwings was near a significant crossroads. Elves and scyldrin were soon heading in different directions. Maialene asked about pass-throughs and riding by moonlight. Dalan, the son who couldn't live without her, grumbled that he was much too tired to do anything but make camp as soon as they'd ridden beyond the smell of smoke.

Jerlayne decided she'd reserve judgement about the youth— an elf in his sixth decade—until she'd gotten to know him better.

The gnomes had rescued food from the Brightwings larder. No one suggested a fire and they ate a cold, quiet supper as twilight deepened around them. Olleta leaned over the edge of her barrel and sang a sweet, melancholy song. Aulaudin fell asleep with his plate half-full on his lap and his head pillowed on Jerlayne's leg. She caressed his face, shaping away the least of his ill-gained wrinkles, praying to nameless gods that she'd never find herself walking Maialene's path.

After a good night's sleep, Dalan and Aulaudin worked together, herding their little group into the pass-throughs and out of them again. They'd have been home in a day were it not for the sylph and her wagon. By the time they did get to Sunrise, four days later, Olleta had fallen in love with Aulaudin. She sang for him, splashed water on him, and pouted when she thought he was ignoring her. It was all innocent, Jerlayne reminded herself: sylphs were sylphs. But she remembered M'lene saying that she and Redis had found "other loves."

«She's a child.» Aulaudin laughed in his wife's mind when

he caught wind of her irritation. «A charming child who's older than the sages, but still a child, and you are the beautiful woman who holds my heart in her hands.»

Goro, too, was gracious about the sylph. He'd never met one before. Olleta splashed him soundly when he walked onto the millpond dam to get a better look. He laughed and warned her that she was lucky he was wearing his armor. Goro always wore armor, but Jerlayne hadn't guessed that he would flirt like a bachelor.

He was less gracious about Maialene.

"While she lives, Efan is responsible for her protection."

Jerlayne was surprised that Goro knew the Brightwings' goblin's name. "Redis is dead in the mortal realm. Brightwings has burnt to the ground. There's nothing left of M'lene's bargain: no homestead left to protect. Does the sage Claideris still have a goblin watching over her?"

Goro scowled. Angry that she'd asked the question? Or, angry at himself for letting her ask it?

"No," Goro replied too quickly to be entirely honest. "Your sister has a son with her. Efan should not have agreed."

"M'lene probably lied to him about Dalan," Jerlayne suggested, wondering what excuse Goro would come up with next.

The goblin scratched his beardless chin. "If she deceived Efan, then I ask myself, who else has she deceived, with what knowledge and why?" He lowered his hand. In that moment, Jerlayne knew what the beasts saw the moment before he slew them. "Let her shape her cottage beyond the boundary stones. We will not protect her or her sons."

"She's iron-touched," Jerlayne protested. "It's not her fault—"

But Goro was already walking away.

Chapter 9

The millpond needed to become a grotto for Olleta to sleep half-in, half-out of the water and where she could shelter in the winter. She'd never freeze—sylphs shaped their own heat—but she needed open water and most winters the Sunrise pond froze thick enough for skating. Olleta's Brightwings grotto had been lined with blue-and-white tiles. She wanted green this time, a foggy green to match the trees in the morning mist.

Aulaudin pulled on his gloves, slung a pack over his shoulders, and went foraging.

Maialene wanted a cottage near the mists. Dalan announced that he'd forage for his mother. He knew everything he needed to know about the fast-changing mortal realm where centuries of experience only blinded a man to opportunity.

"He's worse than Redis and he haunts the same dangerous places," Aulaudin complained to Jerlayne. "I've followed him. He thinks we're cleverer than they are."

"Aren't we?"

Aulaudin shook his head. "There are so many of them it wouldn't matter if they were no cleverer than sheep, but they aren't sheep. They're the same as us, only mortal; they expect to die. That alone makes them dangerous."

Jerlayne didn't understand what her husband had meant until a beautiful afternoon, later that same summer, when Aulaudin burst the Veil in a corn field, in full sight of the scyldrin who were harvesting there. The image of his arrival filled Jerlayne's mind and made her drop the vase she was shaping for Funder and Grezel.

«He got *mugged*,» Aulaudin shouted into Jerlayne's mind, conveying great urgency and *blood*.

Jerlayne met them in the water room behind the kitchen where there was ample hot water and easily washed snow-white tile. She could have wished for foggy green tile such as lined the sylph's grotto or, better still, dark red. *Mugged* meant puncture wounds deeper than her fingers were long: one near Dalan's heart and another in his gut.

"Get Banda," she commanded as soon as she'd laid her hands on the youth and felt the extent of his bleeding. "Get my sister, too—I need *help!*"

Petrin had been in the cornfield; Banda arrived before anyone could have fetched her. Goro appeared moments later; so concerned that he had one foot across the threshold before he remembered that goblins didn't stand beneath roofs or between walls. Jerlayne heard him ask Aulaudin which realm Dalan had been in when he was attacked and what weapon had made the wounds.

Aulaudin answered, "Knives in *ellay,*" just as another vein gave way in Dalan's gut.

Jerlayne needed all her attention and skills to keep Maialene's son from bleeding to death. "Get my sister! Get my mother! Get *someone* here fast," she shouted before closing her eyes and losing herself in Dalan's flesh as if he were a bar of iron becoming a twenty-link—no, a thirty-five-link—chain.

Had the youth been mortal, Jerlayne couldn't have saved him, but the immortality of Fairie was rooted in the smallest part of every elf, scyld, or goblin. As Aulaudin had explained it: Dalan's flesh did not expect to die. It bent to Jerlayne's gentle shaping.

Her greater attention was on the gut wound, but she spared an occasional thought to shape health and life into the wound near his heart which had caused less damage. She was still fighting through Dalan's torn intestines when she felt a presence not her own enter the battle. It was lesson-time all over again, imperfect in every way. Jerlayne and Maialene assisted each other with words and good intentions. They got in each other's way more than once, but by evening Dalan's bleeding had been stanched, his pierced organs repaired.

The two women shrank back from the pallet. Jerlayne shuddered as her awareness became fully her own again and she encountered aches in her own body. Night had fallen. Lantern light dulled and distorted color. She took a few calm, satisfied breaths before noticing how dark and damp the pallet was, how pale and waxen the young man remained.

She raised her eyes to meet Maialene's. They said nothing. Some thoughts were so powerful and transparent that even women could share them: Her sister had noticed the same grim contrast.

"What have I done?"

Neither Jerlayne nor Aulaudin nor the gnomes who'd stood by through the long hours had an answer. Dalan's breath came slow and shallow. His skin was warm but his eyes didn't open. When Jerlayne applied her thumb to lift one eyelid she didn't like what she saw: a huge black pupil staring emptily back at her.

Maialene refused to leave her son's side. She held his hand and whispered his name, over and over, until Jerlayne retreated from the water room to the courtyard.

"He lost so much blood," she said to Aulaudin, who waited for her there with a warm shawl and a cup of tea fortified with brandy. "I didn't think he'd lost so much."

Aulaudin put his arm around her but said nothing.

"Do Medis and Relene know?" she asked when the brandy had warmed her throat.

"I laid low at sunset. I'm not sure they're in Fairie or if I could find them if they were. I haven't thought of them as close-kin. I should have. Should I try to find them?"

This time Jerlayne said nothing and, sighing deeply, Aulaudin walked away. Jerlayne returned to the water room. She took Dalan's other hand but there was nothing more that shaping could do.

The youth's breaths slowed. They became shallower and ceased altogether before dawn. He'd never awakened; never opened his eyes or responded to his mother's presence. Jerlayne gently eased her hand free of his. She'd expected a final battle, but, in a sense, the battle had been lost before she'd become a part of it.

Maialene whispered his name.

"He's gone," Jerlayne explained, reaching across to free her sister's hand. "It's over."

For a moment, as shock twisted M'lene's face into a fright-mask, Jerlayne thought her sister would blame her; *she* did. But Maialene repeated the question she'd asked earlier: "What have I done?" even as Jerlayne hugged her.

Scyldrin buried their own in quiet ceremonies that acknowledged the ultimate power of fate. There were fewer elves, fewer elfin deaths, and fewer still that left a peacefully reposed body in a homestead's water room.

Jerlayne wondered what should be done. Sunrise wasn't Dalan's homestead and he was a bachelor. There was no question of summoning a sage to shatter the foundation stone. A bachelor's death was a private matter. The buzzing of a solitary fly reminded her that she'd have to decide quickly. Aulaudin hadn't yet returned from his vigil. If he'd found Dalan's older brothers, he could find them again and ask what they wanted.

Jerlayne had allowed her thoughts to slip into the comfortably numb patterns of guest goods and food. Moments passed before she realized that her sister had emerged from the first wave of disbelief and had begun to cry.

"If I had loved Redis," she mumbled, "if I had mourned him, Dalan would still be alive."

Jerlayne considered Aulaudin's opinion of Redis and Dalan together and was grateful there was no way M'lene could share her thoughts. "It was an accident. A terrible accident, like lightning."

"It wasn't lightning," M'lene moaned. "I saw his wounds; they weren't lightning."

"No," Jerlayne agreed cautiously. She didn't know what anyone had told Maialene about Dalan's wounds. "He was hurt in the mortal realm, not by lightning."

Maialene swayed weakly. "I wanted him with me and I didn't want anything for myself. I didn't want him foraging. It's too dangerous, Jery. We must learn to live without, or we'll all live alone."

It did not seem a good time to mention that, at least in Aulaudin's opinion, it wasn't that the mortal realm was so dangerous but that Redis was over-bold, over-brash, and he'd taught his sons the same flawed foraging.

"You won't be alone for long," Jerlayne countered instead. "Aulaudin will find Medis and Relene. They'll be here soon. You need to make yourself ready. Your clothes—*our* clothes are stained. We can wash in the kitchen."

Arm in arm, Jerlayne led her dazed sister into the morning light. Banda caught her eye before they entered the kitchen. Jerlayne left M'lene standing like a statue.

"Shall we wash him and wrap him as one of our own?" the gnome asked kindly.

"Yes. I think that will be best. And who among the dwarves should I talk to about a grave?"

"Never you mind, I'll take care of that."

Banda started to walk away but Jerlayne called her back. "I don't want to ask my sister—she's fragile. But dig the grave near the cottage. We'll carry him there."

"Begging my mistress' pardon," Banda countered, using the formal tone she reserved for disagreements. "But she'll stay fragile if you do that. We'll give him a good lie at the top of the hill. Let your sister mourn where you can watch her."

Jerlayne didn't argue. She helped M'lene wash the blood from her hands and got her dressed in borrowed clothes: one of the loose gowns she wore when she was pregnant. Though Elmeene's daughters looked no more like each other than they looked like their mother, Jerlayne hadn't ever noticed how much smaller she was than M'lene.

Dalan's brothers arrived midway through the afternoon. They'd needed Aulaudin's help to find Sunrise through the Veil, but they'd known of his death before he found them.

"The sharing between brothers is the strongest bond," Aulaudin said, and he, of course, would know.

The gnomes had swaddled Dalan in bleached cloth like an infant. They cast a wax-and-plaster mask over his face. One of the itinerant gnomes painted a more life-like semblance on the smooth white surface as it dried. The grave was ready, too. A "good lie" was at the top of a hill in clear sight of the foundation stone.

Jerlayne had the sense that Maialene wished the grave were somewhere else, but then, Maialene surely wished her son was still alive. The grief she hadn't felt for Redis had overwhelmed her. She needed the support of her living sons to walk up the hill. Jerlayne, following them with Aulaudin, had never been so grateful for the presence of other elves around her. Although there were only five of them at Sunrise, through Aulaudin she felt the shadows of his close-kin and hers. There was even a distant sense of Elmeene sharing a mournful thought for her grandson.

But nothing from Maialene and nothing for her. M'lene's hands were white-knuckled on the arms of her living sons, but all she'd ever feel was their pulse.

Four dwarves waited on the hilltop, one at each corner of the bier where Dalan lay. They were dressed in bleached linen that covered their faces, though Jerlayne recognized them all and was pleased that Funder was the dwarf who presented Dalan's death mask to her sister. M'lene clutched it, cross-armed, against her heart and seemed not to move, even to breathe, as the dwarves lowered Dalan into his grave.

Birds sang, breezes rustled through the trees. Near the millpond two dogs barked and chased each other, but the rest of Sunrise was silent. The other scyldrin, including Olleta, and even the goblins in their tents had hidden themselves and would remain out of sight until the grave was covered. There were shovels for everyone on the hilltop. The grave filled quickly, with the dwarves doing most of the work and Maialene doing none at all.

Close-kin arrived throughout the evening as Fairie traditions adapted to the awkwardness of a shattered family mourning its second great loss in a season, and at a homestead where all of them were guests. Jerlayne, who hadn't rested since before Aulaudin brought Dalan through the Veil, excused herself early. But she couldn't find sleep and was sitting in the dark beside an open window when Aulaudin soundlessly opened the door.

"I'm awake," she said as he oh-so-carefully closed the door behind him.

"I expected you to be asleep without a dream."

Tendrils of concern brushed Jerlayne's thoughts. She pushed them away, knowing she'd confirmed Aulaudin's suspicions as she did.

"Dalan's death isn't your fault, beloved. Don't blame yourself."

"I failed." Jerlayne let the words escape; they'd been inside her since she'd seen all that blood. She hadn't had the strength to say them until she was in the dark with her husband. "I've never failed. If I wanted to do something, I did it. If I couldn't do it right the first time, there was always another time, or a way to cover up the mistake—even with my first twenty-link chain. I knew I wasn't perfect, but I didn't think I'd ever *fail*.

"I knew he'd lost blood, but I thought I moved quickly enough. I thought I'd gotten everything back to rights. He was dying, little by little, the whole time I thought I was healing him. I thought I was so clever, so in command and I was killing him. *Killing* him, Aulaudin, I *killed* another elf."

Jerlayne hadn't known what to expect when she uttered the worst of her secrets, but Aulaudin's silence in her ears and in her mind served only to convince her that she had, indeed, done the unforgiveable. For one eternal moment she was falling through herself, then Aulaudin's hands massaged her shoulders. She hadn't sensed him moving through the room.

"If there's blame," he whispered coldly, "then let me take it. I followed him. I saw the mortals coming and I hid—without warning him. There were two of them and, as they would say: Dalan never had a chance, one against two. But, if it had been two against two, if someone had come to his aid, or even made a distracting noise—the kind that attacked him aren't brave and don't like to be seen. If I had picked up the length of wood that lay beside me—"

Jerlayne seized her husband's arm. "You could have been attacked yourself. You could have died beyond the Veil—"

Aulaudin wrenched away. "I could have saved him. Viljuen weeps: a damned goblin would have saved him. *Goro* would have killed *them*. But me—I had the wood right beside me. I'd started to stand and raise my arm and . . ."

She couldn't see her husband, the room was dark and he remained behind her. She began to raise a hand to touch his, and was frozen by the terror he shared.

«I couldn't move. Not even to breathe. It was as if I were joined to fire and the fire controlled me. In my thoughts I was ready to fight, but the rest of me didn't belong to me—until the attackers had run away and Dalan was on the ground.»

The paralysis passed for Jerlayne as it had passed for her husband. She rested her hand on his.

«We're not meant for fighting or violence. That's what we have the goblins for.»

She didn't quite believe her own words, but hoped they would comfort Aulaudin. He pulled away instead.

"I lived with Maun too long, beloved. I don't know why the goblins do what they do in Fairie, but I know there are no goblins beyond the Veil."

Aulaudin fell silent as he relived the attack: not-quite-grown mortal men who had taunted Dalan before they struck him down with knives. In Aulaudin's mind the mortal realm smelled of rot and decay and standing water. The time was night, the stars were hidden, and such light, as there was, came from a flame-colored, unflickering globe some distance away.

"Why?" she asked. "Why would Dalan go to such a place? What was there to forage?"

"He said he was looking for a place he'd gone with Redis. That's the last he said."

"Dalan was conscious when you reached him?"

"He was afraid that he was dying. I told him not to worry; I'd get him back to Fairie. I lied."

Jerlayne rose and put her arms around her husband. "You didn't lie: you got him back to Fairie. Dalan didn't die alone in the mortal realm . . . the way his father did."

Aulaudin's hair moved like rustling silk over his shirt as he shook his head. "It's not enough, beloved. I didn't warm to him; he wasn't my son. I wasn't going to patch the holes in an orphan's education. If I was going to teach someone the men's trade, it would be my own sons. I've been judged for my pride."

"Judged by whom, by what? Do you believe in a god, Aulaudin?" Decades of marriage and she'd never asked him that.

More rustling. "Not a god. Gods forgive and answer prayers. I've been watched, judged, and held wanting, but not by a god. By myself. I'm no god; I don't answer prayers."

She listened to the undercurrents of his mind: the wordless ebb and flow of joining that remained after Aulaudin had ended his thoughts. Her husband would go on; he'd gone on after his brother's death and married her. Healing was rooted deep in Aulaudin's nature. He'd laugh and continue to forage, but he wouldn't begin to forgive himself until he shared his knowledge with a son.

Loosening his Fairie-made shirt, Jerlayne urged him toward the bed they hadn't shared last night.

"I'm weary," he whispered.

And so was she, but not *too* weary. They joined with the subtlest of passions, with slow, gentle kisses and sighs. Jerlayne fell asleep with her body wrapped around his. She awoke with her head on his shoulder with her arm wound beneath his waist. They joined again with vigor and laughter. Jerlayne reached within herself to release a mote of life, but it had flown by itself; sometimes the body knew before the mind thought. She gathered the mote, already changing, against herself and held it fast.

*   *   *

M'lene's two living sons remained a month a Sunrise. The eldest, Relene, wanted his mother to follow him to Amblea, where he hoped to court a bride. Maialene was not sunk so deep in her grief as to agree to that. She rallied her spirits and shooed her grown sons back into their proper lives.

Besides, another four weeks and they'd surely have noticed their mother's changing shape. Aulaudin certainly did.

"A son?" he sputtered when Jerlayne admitted what she'd known since Brightwings. "An elfin son? She can't be certain."

"She says she is."

"Who will teach him the men's trade? Relene? Medis? She's sent them away!"

"When the time comes, she'll turn to you."

They stood at the wrought-iron gate. Aulaudin wore his foraging clothes, all leather and heavy cotton, riveted together with copper disks and interlocking bands of metal that shone like silver but were mostly tin. Their tiny teeth caught the fringe of Jerlayne's shawl as she slid her arms beneath his outer layer for an embrace. She hadn't yet told him that she'd begun to carry another child. In her sister's shadow, this wasn't the time.

"I do not like this latest mortal fashion," she said instead, pulling strands of sky-blue silk from his jacket. "It's like goblin mail."

"Then I'll find something else for foraging. I don't want to be mistaken when I come home."

His words were light, but his voice wasn't. This parting, the first since Dalan had died, was for Jerlayne, as bad as the very first time she'd watched him walk away. Her husband's heart was troubled. He doubted himself and would not forgive himself for Dalan's death. She tasted fear on his lips as they kissed farewell.

An elf, Jerlayne prayed. *Let this child—*

The prayer died. Redis was with the gods, if elves had gods, Dalan, too. At peace, Gudwal had said, and alone, because Maialene had chosen to live for herself, and for her sons. Jerlayne wanted an elf-child, but not at any price, not if she might have to choose between a child and Aulaudin.

Three days later, Aulaudin returned with everything the homestead had asked for and another rose besides—a living rose, a Sunrise rose with blossoms identical to the porcelain rose, still sitting under the glass dome. At least, he swore he'd brought back a Sunrise rose. The thing he pulled out of his pack was thorns, canes, and bare, scraggly roots.

"We will end our days together, my love," he promised when they'd planted the rose beside their gate. "I'm never so foolish beyond the Veil as Redis was, nor bold as my father still is. I forage the midden fields and bring back what mortals have already discarded."

Joined with her husband, Jerlayne could see the dark places and instinctively recoiled from them. Such middens could truly be the source of Sunrise's lumber and bricks, and of the stench that sometimes clung when Aulaudin returned from the mortal realm. But middens couldn't be the source of either Sunrise rose. There had to be more and, as if to confirm her suspicion, Aulaudin's presence appeared suddenly between her and his memories.

«I love you, my love, and you alone.»

His passion swept over her with uncommon intensity. He was hiding something—succumbing to the elfin habit of keeping secrets as he often did when their joined thoughts veered beyond the Veil. The habit disturbed Jerlayne, but not enough for complaints, certainly not tonight. They were alone after having been apart and although elfin couples were restrained, even aloof, in public, it was different when they were alone.

Husband and wife ignored the supper chimes and were not sated of each other until dawn fingers stole through their bedroom draperies.

Chapter 10

Winter came to Sunrise that year, the same as it had come every year, without regard for mourning, guilt, or the raw path between M'lene's cottage and the great house. Wolf tracks were seen in the earliest snows. Goro wouldn't reconsider his vow to ignore Jerlayne's sister, but three scyldrin, a bachelor dwarf and a older gnome couple who'd quarreled with Banda and Petrin about the proper care of the Sunrise orchards, said they'd winter over at the cottage.

"The sad mistress shouldn't be alone," Trenz, the dwarf, said when he and the other two announced their intentions.

M'lene complained that she wanted to be left alone. Then snow piled up in crusty layers that supported the wolves, but not a man or woman. When Trenz killed a wolf with his axe while she and the gnomes were fetching firewood, M'lene decided a small household might be a good idea after all and Jerlayne, in the great house, saw much less of her sister.

Judging by the depth of the snow on the ground and the ice on Olleta's pond, that winter was the hardest since Sunrise's founding. Though he had summery haunts in the mortal realm, Aulaudin judged Fairie's weather too chancy for parting the Veil. He remained at Sunrise for days on end, bored and restless, until Jerlayne shared her secret: come summer, they'd be welcoming a child, and this one would be different.

Jerlayne told the truth, at least part of it: the unborn infant sapped her energy as none of the others had. She ached from the endless tumbling in her belly and suffered nausea, which had never happened to her before. As different as this pregnancy was, she was sure the child would grow to be an elf; and, remembering what Maialene had said about sons and daughters, Jerlayne was tempted to shape a change within herself. But her conscience fought temptation and won decisively: this child would remain a daughter, not become the son who filled Aulaudin's winter dreams.

That spring was a war between ice and mud. When it was over, Frunzit came to say she was leaving Sunrise. It was an inevitable parting; dwarves were wanderers at heart, especially while they were young.

"A part of me wants to stay," she explained through a tear-dampened handkerchief. "I've grown up with Sunrise. I want to see what happens next."

"You can always come back."

They both knew that was unlikely, but not impossible. Jerlayne made a careful memory of Frunzit's strong-boned, attractive features. If she'd learned to recognize Goro by the ridge between his eyes and the corners of his mouth, then surely she could shape an enduring memory of her firstborn's face. A memory that would be stronger than names, because if she did come back it would not be as Frunzit.

The dwarf drew her handkerchief through her fingers and stared at the floor. "I need the shaping, Mis—" Frunzit did not complete the request.

Of all the shapings a woman learned, only one was more important than iron, more important than healing. Jerlayne had learned it from Elmeene and practiced it on Stonewell's cow-calves and ewe-lambs, on the calves and lambs of Sunrise, too, preparing herself for this moment. She led the way into her workroom, shaping the door's metal lock behind her.

Frunzit shed her clothes. Thick-waisted and brawnier than any elf, the young dwarf was, nevertheless, a woman in every significant way.

"Is there anything I should know?" Jerlayne asked, as Elmeene had taught her to: *Don't waste time with chatter. She doesn't want to talk, and neither do you. You both know why she's come and what's to be done. Do it quick.*

"I've kept count of the days, Jerlayne. The time is right."

Jerlayne. Not "Mistress," never "Mother," but Jerlayne, the same way Elmeene had become "Elmeene" when Jerlayne had shaped her first twenty-link chain.

"You can expect to be sore," Jerlayne explained as she shook a blanket across a piled-pillow mattress. "And you may grieve more deeply than you imagine—"

"I know. I've talked to Lenis."

She doesn't want to talk.

Jerlayne knelt on the blanket's edge. She laid her hands on Frunzit's flesh. It wasn't so very different: shape a scyld so she'd never bear an ogre; shape a daughter so she'd be born a son. A cup of steaming tea would not have cooled before she was finished.

"That's all?" Frunzit asked.

Jerlayne nodded and rocked to her feet. By the time she'd un-shaped the workroom door's lock, Frunzit had shrugged into her tunic. She left with her shoes in one hand and not another word.

The scyldrin celebrated Frunzit's departure. They feasted and sang, gave her gifts and, perhaps, exchanged secrets. In her heart Jerlayne did not believe the scyldrin deceived one another. They knew who was related to whom and where every-one had been born. She saw the truth of her suspicions in the way Sunrise's cottages had begun to form clumps and court-yards, but there was a limit to her curiosity: decades after Sun-rise's founding, she'd embraced secrets.

Frunzit left without saying good-bye, not out of rudeness or spite, but simply because it was tradition for the scyldrin to leave that way. Banda said she'd headed west—there was no other direction away from Sunrise—and that two older dwarves, both itinerants, were traveling with her—

"And goblins."

Jerlayne head rose from her tapestry loom. "Goblins? Goblins don't travel."

Banda shrugged. "They protect Sunrise until it's not Sunrise anymore. The scyldrin go on; the goblins come back. Nothing more."

Nothing more that the gnome would say.

Jerlayne promised herself she'd ask Goro when he came to confirm the midsummer bargain which she'd paid in cloth the last several years: yards and yards of woollen cloth, plus a twenty-link chain. She'd have time to make the chain after her child was born.

Maialene bore her son in her mist-side cottage and sent Trenz to Sunrise with the news.

"She's named him Ombrio," the dwarf said, unable to keep disapproval from his voice, "and she won't give him to the gnome."

"She's sure her last son will be an elf," Jerlayne said, virtually repeating what her sister had said before Brightwings burnt.

"But she keeps him in her own bed!" Trenz protested.

Even when they were *sure,* elfin women didn't nurse their infants; it interfered with shaping. Jerlayne was *sure* herself, but she'd turn her daughter over to Banda; and she'd never give a son or daughter a name that wasn't built from hers and Aulaudin's.

"My sister has lost everything," Jerlayne told herself and Trenz. "She doesn't see Fairie the way the rest of us do. Do you want to come back to your cottages?" she asked, realizing as she did that she hoped M'lene would stay where she was.

But once he'd unburdened himself of his disapproval, Trenz was content. He hadn't been gone long when Aulaudin knocked on the workroom door.

"Ombrio!"

Trenz, it seemed, had stopped at the mill where Aulaudin and the dwarves conferred about what around Sunrise needed repairs and what Aulaudin needed to forage.

"I can understand disregarding Redis, but *Ombrio!* How can she be sure and name him Ombrio? Viljuen weeps, beloved— if she's right, who will teach this Ombrio the men's trade?"

"You," Jerlayne replied, letting her annoyance leak. Whatever else Maialene was, she was *sure:* M'lene had borne other elfin children, other sons; she *knew* what Jerlayne had only imagined until this pregnancy.

"Me?"

"He'll learn what he needs to know, won't he, if you're the one who teaches him?"

She'd meant that as a compliment, but the words turned harsh as their daughter thrashed and kicked.

Aulaudin took a silent moment before asking: "Another man's son? Before we raise our own?"

Jerlayne folded her arms across her swollen belly. She should have shaped a son when she'd had the chance; it was way too late now. "There will be sons, I promise," she assured her husband, taking his hand, gauging his mood as only a joined wife could.

He warmed to her thoughts, contemplating brotherhood as he'd known it with Boraudin. It was the clearest memory of his long-dead brother than Aulaudin had yet shared and it surprised Jerlayne: if memory served, they must have been as similar in appearance as two gnomes.

«So Maun always said, though, of course, we looked nothing like him.»

«Of course not,» Jerlayne agreed, casually, yet carefully making strong walls around her certainty that their daughter would be an elf. Daughters took a long time to raise and she'd make sure she'd have no other children, elf or scyld, while she was raising hers. There'd be no brother for Ombrio.

Aulaudin seemed not to notice her secret as they managed an awkward embrace. «Our dwarves have more plans for the mill. More *metal* plans. They want a bucket of copper as wide as I'm tall and twice as long. Viljuen weeps. I'll never find a copper bucket half that size that isn't surrounded by locks and living guards. Mortals make everything out of a new metal now: aluminium. Shall I bring some back for you?»

To keep her secrets safe and because she was genuinely interested in the new metal, Jerlayne answered with enthusiasm that endured until Aulaudin left Sunrise the next morning. He promised he'd be back, with or without the metal, in less than three days. Jerlayne told him not to worry: Their daughter wasn't due until after the next new moon. Aulaudin pointed to the orchards where the blossoms had set early and the gnomes had a bumper harvest to fret over.

"Children aren't apples!" Jerlayne laughed as she sent her husband on his way.

Of course they weren't. Jerlayne awoke before the next dawn with unmistakable spasms in her gut. False labor was uncommon but not unheard of. She retreated into herself, intending to calm the riled muscles with a shaping thought. What she found instead was a daughter more than ready to born. By midmorning, when an itinerant gnome came to her workroom to discuss the day's chores, she'd gotten her birthing stool down from the rafters.

"Tell Banda that today's the day," she calmly told the dumbfounded gnome whose name she'd lost between contractions.

Banda appeared in the bedroom not long after with her cloths, buckets, and black leather scalpel-case they'd never needed.

"You should have called me at once," the gnome complained as she rearranged everything to her liking. "It's my place to be with you when your children are born."

Jerlayne was in no mood to argue. After its sudden, powerful start, her labor had stagnated. Stiff and grim, she paced the length of her workroom, pausing now and again to clutch the back of the sturdy chair. Banda had a wealth of suggestions gleaned from her years at Singingstones and countless spring nights in the birth-byres. Jerlayne dutifully tried them all: yawning, singing, warm cloths, cold cloths, lying still, and dancing awkwardly. Nothing had effect until Banda said:

"The child's got to be born now; you can't wait for Aulaudin. The master will return when he returns. There's no one near who can summon him. Fate knows Sunrise needs a son or two."

Jerlayne froze, suddenly conscious that there'd be no great rejoicing when her daughter was born. She felt sadness and shame and the first useful contraction since Banda's arrival. Even so, her labor was hard. This daughter, this *elfin* daughter, was larger than Jerlayne's other children had been and fought every contraction. Jerlayne triumphed, giving birth long after the sun had set, but her throat was raw from screaming.

"Elves are strong from the beginning," Banda murmured as she swaddled the infant. "They're strong, so they fight being born: that's what the mistress of Singingstones always said, and I've believed her. This one fought all the way. She's yours. Mark my words, Mistress Jerlayne: You've borne your own first child: a daughter. You and Aulaudin will need to settle a name on her."

Jerlayne, of course, needed no persuading. She'd been sure from the beginning, though she'd resisted the name temptation. A shaping touch could tell a mother much about her unborn child, but it took ordinary eyes and ears to sense an infant's personality. When she saw that her daughter had been born with a cloud of rusty red hair, Jerlayne knew that Aulaudin's name should take precedence, and because she was the first, the simplest forms were available.

Aulayne, she thought to herself. *Are you Aulayne? Is that your name?*

All her children had been born with gray eyes, but this daughter's eyes were almost black. By candlelight, it was difficult to see where her pupils ended and the irises began. They were angry, as well. Everything about her was angry: little legs thrashing within the light blanket; tight, tiny fists; a birth-flattened face that turned dark red as she prepared to squall.

Not Aulayne, then. You want a name that's all your own.

The notion might not have occurred to Jerlayne if her sister hadn't led the way with Ombrio. Why should an elfin name be so predictable? Why not give each child a name like no other?

Banda held out her arms to reclaim the infant she would nurse. Jerlayne hesitated, reconsidering that tradition, too: It took shaping to bring milk to the gnome's breasts, shaping to remove it from her own. Why not nurse her daughter? Then Jerlayne saw the unshaped iron sitting on her worktable and surrendered her daughter just as her first tantrum erupted.

The infant was settled in the not-quite-finished nursery before Jerlayne had recovered enough to rise from the birthing stool. She thought of all the finishing touches she'd hoped to add before her daughter was born and realized that she would never apply them, not for lack of opportunity, but because the raw room suited her daughter better.

"Evoni," Jerlayne said aloud, speaking the name that had come into her mind like a dream.

"Your pardon, mistress?"

"Evoni. My daughter's name is Evoni."

Banda said nothing, a sure sign of gnomish disapproval.

"Why not?" Jerlayne demanded. "Evoni. When I say it, I think of her eyes. Why shouldn't she have her own name?"

"It's odd, mistress, that's all. Different."

"Aulaudin says the mortal realm is different every time he parts the Veil. Fairie can risk being a little different every century or so, don't you think?"

Banda wouldn't say what she thought, but Aulaudin did when she met him at the gate the next afternoon. Through joining's touch, Jerlayne had felt his emotions glide from concern to surprise to joy as she told him of her labor and delivery, only to feel them swing back to concern again when she mentioned the name she'd chosen.

"When you see her, you'll understand."

Aulaudin left his swag at the door and followed his wife to the nursery. Evoni awoke when Jerlayne lifted her out of the cradle. Her little fists and face tightened and she let out a mighty wail as offered the bundle to Aulaudin.

"Her lungs are strong," he said, taking his daughter warily, but not reluctantly, into his hands.

Evoni calmed at once, which Jerlayne took as a good omen.

"I couldn't wait until you'd returned," she explained nervously, unnecessarily. "It began so quickly. There was no turning back . . . and no way to reach you." She felt her own disappointment then, her guilt that she had a daughter to teach while her husband remained alone.

Jerlayne was too filled with her own thoughts to spare much attention for her husband's. He was, at any rate, more comfortable with infants, having lived long enough at Briary to watch Aglaidia give birth do a dozen or more scyldrin and three elves. He tucked Evoni competently into the crook of his arm and tickled her chin with a single finger. Evoni seized the finger as if it were the branch of a tree. She began to giggle and Jerlayne thought all was perfect until Aulaudin pulled his hand away with a single word:

"No."

Aulaudin laid his daughter into her cradle. He stared at his hands as if they'd been fouled.

"Accidents happen," Jerlayne said quickly, offering a towel, but Aulaudin ignored her.

"I know it's unusual. I thought about Aulayne. I wanted to name her Aulayne, but she isn't an Aulayne—"

"She isn't ours," Aulaudin countered in a whisper. "She isn't elfin."

He could not have hurt Jerlayne more with his fists. "Of course Evoni's ours! I've been certain since the start. I know, Aulaudin. Women *know*."

"You can't be certain," he protested, still whispering. "Scyldrin change."

"Dwarves, and gnomes, and the other ilks, yes; elves, no. Evoni's elfin. Elmeene, my sisters, all the women, they say: *you'll know,* but it's like shaping—women can't share what they know. We all have to discover it for ourselves. Evoni was different from the moment I first sensed her heart beating."

"Different—" Aulaudin fastened on the word. "Different."

"Yes, *different!*" Jerlayne fought a wave of anger and frustration such as she hadn't felt since leaving Stonewell. "Different because she's ours! Our daughter: Evoni."

He took a backward step from the cradle. "No."

Jerlayne grabbed his arm. As always, touch strengthened the bond between them: her husband was cold, dark, and filled with something best described as fear.

"Aulaudin, open your heart."

She tried to pull him to the cradle, but he'd become a tree rooted in the nursery floor. She released him with a shove. "Think of your younger brothers and sisters. Did Maun and Aglaidia send them to live with gnomes until they came of age? Did they send you?"

Aulaudin shook his head, as if blowing dust from his memories. "No." He worried his lip between his teeth. "Aglaidia said she always knew . . ."

"*I* know. Mothers know. Your mother. My mother. Me. Evoni took shape inside me and I know that she is truly our daughter! Ours. An elf, like you and me."

"But—"

Jerlayne had grown too angry, too indignant for arguments, "Our daughter, my love," she insisted. "Open your heart to her."

"I can't. I don't dare."

He shared an image then, not intentionally: the brooding ruins she knew as Tatterfall and the sad, haunted face of Boraudin. "You wanted a son," she conceded. "We didn't make a son this time—" Jerlayne's breath caught in her throat. Had he expected her to shape their child to fit his wishes? "Next time," she promised, swallowing guilt which instantly turned to acid in her stomach. "This time, open your heart to your daughter. Let there be no more discussions."

Jerlayne scooped Evoni out of the cradle and held her against Aulaudin's chest. "Take her, my love." She could feel her husband's anguish and, perhaps, Evoni felt it too: the infant once again began to squall. "Take her and comfort her, and be comforted yourself."

Aulaudin would not bend his arms around his daughter. "I dare not."

"Why ever not? A daughter needs her father as much as any son. Evoni is your daughter. Take her!"

Aulaudin retreated and spoke in distant tones: "When I part the Veil, with every step I take, I ask myself, is this right? Is this safe? The answers don't come to me in words, but I've learned to trust them with my life and if the answers are no, then, no matter what's behind me or what I'm facing, I find another direction. When I look at this daughter of ours, beloved, the answers come to me: find another direction."

"The only answer is to take your daughter in your arms and open your heart to her." Jerlayne thrust the squalling bundle against his chest. "Take her, my love. Let there be no more foolish discussion."

But Aulaudin, hitherto the most serene and adaptable of men, said no even when his wife called him cruel and heartless. When anger had failed, she pleaded with him, for the sake of *their* love, to love their daughter. And when that failed, Jerlayne raised the specter of Briary after Tatterfall, when his own parents had made mockery of their joining.

Shame and memory drove Aulaudin back to the nursery where he tried—Jerlayne conceded that he made the effort—to conquer his misgivings, but he would not open his heart. Evoni sensed her father's inner conflict and thereafter greeted his presence with wails that could be heard in the cottages across the stream. After a few months of Evoni's tantrums, Jerlayne's despair, and the inner conflict that Aulaudin could not resolve, a palpable tension resided in the rooms of Sunrise.

In a desperate, clumsy attempt to restore tranquility, Aulaudin built himself a new room, far from the bedroom and nursery, but still under a single roof. That bought a measure of peace until Evoni learned to walk. The child, headstrong from birth, craved her father's attention and got it, too, in the worst way.

"Be kind to her," Jerlayne pleaded, collecting the shreds of the shirt Evoni had torn from her father's back. She had nearly to shout to be heard over the toddler's wailing, four rooms away.

"I am not unkind," Aulaudin replied simply, and honestly: he never yelled at her, even when she attacked him in addition to his clothes. He brought her gifts from the mortal realm and never complained when she destroyed them.

"Let her into your heart, Aulaudin, while there's still time."

He shook his head slowly. "I dare not."

"Evoni is your daughter. Your *elfin* daughter."

Aulaudin said nothing, shared nothing, but Jerlayne knew his thought precisely. *Evoni will change. She is not an elf.* He'd admitted he could not defend his position, no more than his father was able to defend his conviction that goblins were responsible for the destruction of Tatterfall; and he was equally incapable of abandoning it.

When she was four, Evoni sank a fork into her father's thigh while he was sleeping beside Jerlayne. The wound was deep and potentially dangerous because she'd slathered the tines with filth from chicken coop, but her truly ominous act was the ruin she made of the simple latch on their bedroom door afterward. At first Jerlayne had hidden the damage, then, in a burst of ill-fated inspiration, she'd used it to convince her husband that their daughter was, in truth and deed, an elf.

"It has gone too far," he said and carried his belongings out of the great house.

As his father had done after Boraudin's death, Aulaudin began living among the scyldrin, in the loft above the mill. Olleta, the sylph, was delighted; the rest of Sunrise, whispering the tales of Briary and Tatterfall, held its collective breath, expecting the worst. But the tension that had clouded Sunrise since Evoni's birth lifted once father and daughter no longer cast shadows across each other's path.

Aulaudin minded his duties as Sunrise's master, spending most of his time in the mortal realm. He was never gone more than a few days at a time—at least Petrin claimed to see the master of Sunrise every few days and a word in Petrin's ear never failed to produce the proper swag beside the foundation stone. But weeks, even months, might pass with no one else seeing Aulaudin's face.

As long as no other man appeared at the gate to say Aulaudin hadn't been heard at sunset, Jerlayne was secretly relieved by her husband's absences. She folded her life around her daughter. Evoni became the moon, bathed in the sunlight of a mother's devotion. No secrets or self-taught lessons for her daughter. Whatever roused Evoni's curiosity was a fit subject for a mother's teaching. She praised Evoni's progress and encouraged her imagination. By her twelfth summer, Evoni was making chains—short chains, imperfect chains, but iron chains nonetheless. Her passion, though, wasn't metal; it was rock, dirt, and, above all, water.

Evoni made lakes in the gardens as Jerlayne had once drawn wings out of the dwarves' tools. When lakes bored her, she filled them in and started over again. Jerlayne was mystified by her daughter's pastimes, but once Aulaudin had removed himself from her life, Evoni had been transformed into a radiantly happy child who rarely balked when Jerlayne called her away from her unfinished waterways.

Husband and wife could not entirely avoid each other. Though they admitted neither gods nor priests, homestead life was bound by rituals that a homestead's elfin master and mistress were expected to perform. They planted the first seeds of every crop, they harvested the first fruits, and separated the culls from the flocks each autumn. Perhaps Sunrise would have survived unharmed if Jerlayne and Aulaudin had shirked their responsibilities, but neither they nor the scyldrin were eager to find out.

And there were the festivals.

Mindful of the disgrace and shame his feuding parents had brought to Briary, Aulaudin sought reconciliation before each gathering. The Sunrise estrangement might have been an open secret throughout Fairie, but it was never witnessed, and neither was their daughter. Once she was old enough to make her preferences known, Evoni wouldn't leave the homestead without a ferocious tantrum. When, at first, they brought her along anyway, she succumbed to fits in the pass-throughs: bloody, shaking fits that left her weak as a newborn kitten and terrified her mother. Aulaudin was the first to say it was cruelty to haul her away from Sunrise and, because the idea came from him, Jerlayne resisted it until she found herself arguing with husband and daughter alike.

When it was time to travel, she and Aulaudin traveled with Ombrio, her sister's son, who'd begun learning the men's trade from his uncle and who welcomed any chance to escape his mother's mournful cottage. They made a strange trio: a prickly, sad couple and half-orphan nephew. Jerlayne knew Fairie swirled with gossip, if only because folk rarely asked about her daughter or her sister, but she went to all the festivals they couldn't avoid and a good many more besides. Once they were away from Sunrise—from their daughter—she'd fall back in love with Aulaudin and for a few perfect days, under the open sky or in someone else's guest rooms, they'd both believe their affection could surmount any challenge.

But festivals didn't last forever. They learned the hard way not to make rash promises on their way home. Jerlayne believed in their daughter; Aulaudin didn't, or couldn't, and the longer any reconciliation lasted, the bitterer the explosion that ended it. In time they learned to say good-bye with a chaste kiss at the wrought-iron gate and go their separate ways.

Routine—awkward but stable—returned to Sunrise: seasons came and went, scyldrin, too, a few more departing than arriving. Goro accepted the oath of another goblin and needed the advantage an extra sword provided when a band of six ogres was spotted in the fallow meadows. Two goblins died exterminating them, one instantly, when a spear shattered his skull; the other when Jerlayne had faced a terrible choice: two mortally wounded goblins lying the grass. When she asked which one she should heal, Goro wouldn't choose for her.

When he was at home, Aulaudin dwelt in the mill loft. Jerlayne and Evoni shared the great house with the scyldrin and the rare—very rare—guests. Maialene kept to herself in her mist-side cottage. A year might pass, or even two, without the sisters setting eyes on each other, but Ombrio was everywhere. As a lad he followed Aulaudin. By the age of twenty he'd mastered the men's trade well enough to forage on his own. After that he made friends with Evoni, courting her unconsciously, as Aulaudin had courted Jerlayne.

For her part, Evoni was not her mother. Like a purring cat, she enjoyed Ombrio's attention, but she had no need of him or any other friend. She mastered everything Jerlayne knew how to teach, and in record time. She could have explored the mysteries of the new metals Aulaudin dutifully brought back from the mortal realm; that's what Jerlayne wanted her to do. She could have called for an iron bar and her rite of passage; that's what Ombrio wanted. But Evoni held them off with unkept promises.

Watching her swim in the millpond with Ombrio and the sylph (Aulaudin had been gone for days and wasn't expected back any time soon) Jerlayne conceded to herself that for all her efforts, she understood her daughter no better than Elmeene had understood her. Evoni had outgrown her tantrums, though not the odd fits that kept her bound to Sunrise. Jerlayne judged Evoni's isolation a loss for all Fairie. She had her grandfather Maun's wit, her father's charm, her mother's shaping talent, and her grandmother Elmeene's ability to live her life exactly as she wished.

Father and daughter regarded each other with remarkable indifference. Evoni simply didn't care, while Aulaudin continued to believe that she would change. Jerlayne had come to pity her husband's stubbornness and marveled that she hadn't noticed that Maun-like trait in him earlier.

The years for transformation were over. Evoni wasn't a sprite, a dwarf, a gnome, nor even a sylph—though she could swim circles around Olleta when she chose. Evoni was from birth an elf, an inescapable fact which would ultimately conquer Aulaudin's stubbornness. Jerlayne imagined the moment when the rifts would all be repaired.

"Thirty years, give or take a few, and she's ready to become her own woman."

Goro's voice, utterly unexpected and coming from behind her back, from the courtyard between the kitchen and the herb garden which she would have sworn was both unoccupied and inaccessible to a wall-shunning goblin. Jerlayne started at the sound and lost her grip on the heavy basket which held the morning's failed experiments. Ruined metal clattered loudly on the flagstone path.

"Your mind was elsewhere; I should have made more noise as I came up the path," Goro apologized with that slight, sly grin of his. Despite the summertime warmth, Goro wore armor from toes to fingertips and a cloak which he shrugged off his shoulders as he stooped to collect the scattered lumps.

He hadn't come *up* the path, Jerlayne would have sworn that, too, but she had been preoccupied, watching her daughter enjoying herself in the millpond, thinking of different choices she'd made at a similar age. It never paid to challenge a goblin.

"I wasn't expecting you," she said instead.

The mysterious smile faded. "I would have been here sooner if you were."

Goro selected one rust-covered lump. Jerlayne recognized her daughter's work: Evoni had drawn two well-shaped links from the metal before its structure had broken down. The failed third link crumbled as the goblin examined it.

"A sword made from this wouldn't be worth wielding," he commented as he brushed the burnt powder from his hands.

"My husband says mortal men no longer fight with swords, except for sport, and they forge their steel in furnaces as hot as the sun, and as big as the millpond."

"You still talk to your husband?"

By its tone, Goro's question might have been offhand, but a flicker of doubt led Jerlayne to meet his black-shaded eyes.

"We travel together," she replied, defensive because, beyond doubt, the question had *not* been offhand. "You know that."

"Other than that. Surely he sees your daughter for what she is. Has peace returned between you?"

"It will." Jerlayne quickly collected the last of the ruined steel including a lump which she plucked from his gloved hand.

"But it hasn't, yet."

Jerlayne stood up. "No, not yet," she said while looking down. In an association governed entirely by bargaining, any question was risky, but sometimes irresistible. "What does it matter to you?"

Goro rose, remarkably silent for a man encased in metal links and stiff leather. "There has been drought in the plains. The lineages must chose between feeding themselves or their herds. They will, in the end, choose their herds. I might swear exiles, if Sunrise were at peace with itself."

Jerlayne wondered if other homesteads were swearing exiles, if other homesteads would ever know of the plains drought. She doubted it. Elmeene didn't know where Stonewell's goblins made their camp, but at Sunrise, once they'd pitched their black tents in sight of the great house, they'd never pulled up stakes. Just then, the kitchen blocked Jerlayne's view of Goro's camp, still, she'd memorized the precise features of the goblins who dwelled there.

They were no friendlier than rocks or trees, but even the gnomes conceded that they worked their share. And though Sunrise prospered, it no longer grew as it once had: there were newer homesteads now, two refoundings in the heartland that attracted scyldrin more readily than the misty frontier. Sunrise could easily welcome a few exiles.

"In exchange for what?" she asked flatly.

Black eyebrows rose on a wrinkling, deep blue forehead; she'd surprised him, a moment worth remembering.

"In exchange for nothing, Jerlayne, since you tell me Sunrise is not at peace with itself."

"My husband and I are and will always be joined. Nothing else need concern you about the peace of Sunrise. What do you want in exchange for welcoming your exiles?"

Eyebrows fell and he studied her through slitted eyes. Jerlayne had the sense she'd given him exactly what he'd wanted.

"That knoll there," Goro pointed at a wooded rise beyond the mill, "for our camp and clearing beyond it for fields and pasture."

She couldn't hide her surprise. "How many exiles do you intend to welcome?"

"I think we would number twenty."

Twenty! That was more than Arhon had a Stonewell, and Stonewell was easily twice the size of Sunrise. "I think we would be well protected," Jerlayne responded striving to match the goblin's off-stride tone and syntax.

Her irony had no impact as Goro frowned and said: "We can only hope that twenty will be enough. I will tell my companions. We will move our tents today."

Goro had what he wanted. He started down the flagstone path—definitely *not* the way he'd come. Jerlayne wouldn't have been surprised if the goblin had simply vanished, but he gave her an even greater surprise when he stopped after a few strides and turned around.

"Thank you, Jerlayne. Men will live because of you."

When he was walking again, she shivered despite the summer's warmth and hurried into the great house, not bothering to see if the goblin walked all the way to his camp.

That summer ebbed into a brilliant autumn. An early frost sweetened Petrin's cider and brought vibrant beauty to every tree, every leaf. After the frost, the air warmed with a last breath of summer: weather meant for joy and reflection.

The goblins had moved their camp. There were more of them than before, but whether there were twenty Jerlayne couldn't have said. Trees weren't walls, branches weren't roofs and, except at night when their fire winked through across the valley, the black tents were invisible. Aulaudin hadn't reconciled himself to Evoni's inevitable elfiness, but the thought was in his mind. Jerlayne had felt it the week before when they celebrated the Briary harvest.

This winter, she told herself. When storms kept Aulaudin in Fairie, as they almost certainly would, she'd find a way to lure him out of the mill loft. Whatever her inner thoughts, Evoni didn't hold a grudge. She wouldn't care if her father moved back into the great house. The healing could begin. Until then, Aulaudin was beyond the Veil. He'd been gone a day, or three, and might be back tomorrow, the day after, or the day after that. He made no promises.

She'd spent the morning with Evoni, working together to unlock the secrets of a new, lightweight metal that Aulaudin had found on one of his middens. They'd lunched together, apart from everyone else, as was their custom. Jerlayne anticipated a quiet afternoon at her tapestry loom.

Evoni had another notion. "Come swimming with me?" She began to braid up her hair.

Jerlayne didn't share her daughter's love of water. Swimming was pleasant enough in high summer, but come autumn, the mucky bottom of the fish pond was all too noticeable between her toes, and she'd much rather weave at the upright loom the dwarves had built for her. She was already sitting there surrounded by an array of muted Fairie wools and bright mortal silks.

"Not today," Jerlayne replied, picking up a silken strand, pausing a moment to marvel at its brilliant color. Aulaudin had foraged it for her. He'd never stopped bringing her gifts; their estrangement hadn't widened that far, though—predictably— he'd say nothing about the pictures she wove of her life with her daughter.

Evoni persisted. "You've got all winter to play with your threads, Mother!" Her eyes were bright and her smile was pure mischief. She was her father's daughter to the bone, if only he would open his eyes and heart to her.

"If it's that important to you." Jerlayne heaved a dramatic sigh and began returning her many-colored threads to their proper baskets.

"Catch me!" Evoni challenged, once Jerlayne was in her shift and standing at the top of the flagstone path.

She laughed as she ran toward the pond, auburn braids and russet hems flared out behind her. It was a scene Jerlayne observed countless times since Evoni had discovered that swimming was like walking, only freer.

Today, for no good reason, her heart skipped a beat as she watched.

Premonition and prophecy were as rare in Fairie as shaping and sharing were beyond the Veil, and nothing to ignore. Jerlayne shouted Evoni's name, but not loud enough to halt her headlong rush to the pond.

Evoni had heard nothing—or had heard and chosen not to listen. Running a race with herself, the young woman kicked off her sandals without missing a stride, stretched her arms above her head, and dove from the grassy bank.

The pond was deep and safe. Today was different. That dive had been different, though Jerlayne could not have said how she knew. Just then, she could not have said anything at all. Her tongue was frozen in her mouth. Her whole body was as rigid as stone, except for her heart which pounded against her ribs.

She was a woman, a shaper. She could shape iron. She could force air into her lungs— "No! Evoni! Come out!"

Freeing her body from paralysis, Jerlayne began to run. She stopped at the bank where Evoni had leapt into the water. Dropping to her knees, she thrust her open hands into the water and shouted her daughter's name.

"Evoni! Evoni!"

Ripples spread out from her submerged wrists. Across the pond, the sylph stuck her head up, her pale-green skin unmistakable in the sunlight, likewise her panic as she clawed the bank.

"Evoni!"

Nothing. Nothing at all. The sylph had slipped back beneath the water which became as smooth as black glass beneath a suddenly ominous sky. Out of nowhere, a pond-sized storm brewed overhead. Jerlayne screamed as she'd screamed the day Evoni was born. Banda emerged from her cottage, followed by her grown daughter. The gnomes added their hysteria to Jerlayne's, but it was the dark cloud, billowing magically between the pond and the sun, that summoned all Sunrise to the pond.

"Evoni!"

Jerlayne threw herself into the water, fighting a wind-whipped froth all the way to the center.

She found Evoni, seized her arm, and turned her own shaping talent against her daughter, to keep Evoni within an elfin shape. Shaping wasn't enough. There was nothing left of Evoni when she beat free and shoved her mother face down against the muck.

Defeated and drowning, Jerlayne readily surrendered, only to be snatched to safety by goblin hands. They wiped her face and pounded the muck out of her mouth and throat even as the froth became a dark-water pillar to darker clouds. The pillar swelled. It put forth arms and eyes. It began to sing.

Someone shouted, "Siren!" Others added, "Break the dam!"

and "Open the weir!" but Jerlayne's voice was not among them. She'd looked up into those terrible eyes and, finding nothing there that recognized her, collapsed with one hand over her heart.

Chapter 11

Aulaudin approached the mortal-realm midden in the bright light of afternoon, walking down the middle of a littered street. All the while, he kept a wary eye out for movement in the dead buildings on either side.

The mortal realm had changed remarkably since Aulaudin had learned the men's trade from his father. It had always been more changeable than Fairie but recently, since his marriage and especially since Evoni's birth, the changes had come with dizzying speed. Fifty years ago, the street Aulaudin walked had been the only straight passage through a warren of tree-tall storehouses between a railyard and a river. Thirty years ago, the mortals had torn up the railyard, built a concrete bridge over the river, and begun abandoning their storehouses. By last year, every storehouse had been emptied and most had been burnt as well. The whole warren was scarcely worth a visit unless Sunrise needed bricks for a chimney or oven.

Yesterday Aulaudin had discovered half the warren was gone, reduced to dusty rubble, and a herd of mortal machines waited silently beneath the bridge, poised to destroy the rest.

Aulaudin thought the constant turmoil had something to do with sheer number of mortals crowded into their realm. Their population had exploded the way rabbits and deer exploded after a mild winter. In Fairie there were wolves, but mortals had no enemies except themselves.

Mortals never had mist-shrouded borders where a homestead could be built without taking anything away from another homestead. They'd had emptiness, instead, to absorb their excesses, but in Aulaudin's lifetime the emptiness had shrunk. These days in the mortal realm, everything had to be built on known land, on land that other mortals had already claimed.

The men of Fairie had watched mortal men make war on one

another since the Ten. Once, wars had had beginnings and ends and were fought within areas that a man could avoid, if he chose. That was no longer true. With the end of mortal emptiness came wars that ebbed and flowed like their oceans. Since Evoni's birth, the mortal realm had seethed with war and the weapons that mortals turned on one another beggared an elf's imagination.

There was a temptation in the mind of a man estranged from his family to find links between his own misery and mortal misery. Mostly, Aulaudin resisted the temptation.

However unpleasant life at Sunrise had become, when he was at home in Fairie, Aulaudin didn't have to worry about being mistaken for someone else's enemy; a fate which had become a constant threat in the mortal realm and the reason he approached each midden with practiced caution. With the spread of war, all mortals, it seemed, had enemies or were enemies. Where once it had been possible to approach a tradesman with an offer of labor in exchange for some desirable piece of metal or cloth, now even the simplest barter provoked suspicious demands for identification that Aulaudin couldn't meet.

The changes weren't necessarily for the worse. Aulaudin's father said the foraging had never been better: between *science* and war, mortals distrusted one another so much that they'd forgotten elves. If men were reduced to scouring middens, well, what bountiful middens they were! If a man couldn't find whatever his homestead needed lying by the side of an endless road, he could search the ruins that sprouted in the middle of every bustling city.

That was Maun. Maun also boasted that he'd learned to drive not only an automobile, but an airplane. He'd mastered the twin mysteries of writing and identification, and carried a score of slippery *licenses* to prove it.

Aulaudin admired his father's audacity; he never felt the need to imitate it, at least not when they weren't together. Which they weren't. As far as his son knew, Maun was rollicking at a Fairie harvest festival that he hadn't mentioned to his wife.

The master of Sunrise could walk the mortal streets musing about his irascible father, even about his disconcerting daughter without compromising his wariness, but the least thought of Jerlayne sent a blinding surge of despair through his mind.

Soon, he counseled himself. *Soon.*

The word was old, with many meanings. Soon Aulaudin would approach the metal-mesh fence that separated the midden from the street. Soon he'd have, if he'd spied it correctly from the deck of a nearby bridge, the steel pipe the Sunrise dwarves wanted for a new watermill shaft. Soon he'd be looking for a secluded spot where he could shift the over-long pipe through the Veil. Soon he'd be home, such as home was. And soon the estrangement between him and Jerlayne would have to end.

There were five men and a woman already on the midden, all shuffling through the rubble. The woman, of course, was mortal. Aulaudin assumed the men were, too; at least there was no one he recognized by sight or shared thought.

When Maun had taught Aulaudin how to forage, men routinely approached mortals with their minds wide open. Partly the openness was a courtesy: as large as the mortal realm was, there was always a chance that foraging men might surprise one another. But openness served another purpose, too: a few mortals were sensitive to shared thoughts and, if they didn't panic or turn instantly hostile, they could befriend a man, showing him things he'd never find on his own.

There were still sensitive mortals and the chance of surprising a fellow forager, but mostly there was noise. Through *science,* mortals had learned to make sounds that they couldn't hear directly. At first the ambient noises had been an annoyance but, like so many other aspects of the mortal realm since Evoni's birth, this annoyance had become constant and oppressive. The air, especially in mortal cities, vibrated with words, sometimes images, and a nauseating array of shrieks, chirps, and whistles.

Aulaudin let his mind open long enough to assure himself that he was the only elf in the area, then he isolated himself as best he could. After six days in the mortal realm, his head throbbed from the constant pressure of *science.* It was definitely time to return to Fairie.

The midden-gleaners gave Aulaudin the once-over as he eased through a tear in the metal-mesh fence. They reminded him of winter-starved vermin scratching at a homestead's clay-sealed granaries: desperate in the face of danger, none of them wanted to be the first to run from a predator. Not that he should have appeared dangerous. Aulaudin had carefully disguised himself in clothes that were as ragged and filthy as theirs. But he was still a stranger and midden-dwellers weren't likely to welcome a stranger, not if they thought they could drive him off.

Aulaudin didn't meet anyone's eyes as he walked across the cracked concrete. Glass shards popped beneath his boots; transparent, green, and amber.

"Some as kills you for them boots," a boozy mortal had told him just the other night, in another city, another midden, no different than this one. "Mighty fine boots."

He'd wear reeking, castoff clothes, even smear his face and hair with dirt, but Aulaudin wouldn't surrender his boots. There were iron scraps scattered amid the glass and other trash. Blooddeath wasn't the threat it had once been. The worst that happened now was that a man might get a little bit embedded in his flesh and not know it until the 'death had spread throughout his body.

Jerlayne could cure the 'death no matter where it hid. She'd shaped it out of him twice, the last time a scant ten years ago: he'd been careless going over a barbed wire fence, careless and unlucky. But since then she'd taught the cure to Evoni, and Aulaudin knew, in the darkest depths of his heart, that if he returned to Sunrise with 'death in his blood, his wife would want his daughter to shape it out of him.

No man was more careful in his foraging these days than the master of Sunrise. He carried two pairs of gloves; one spun from silk, the other cut from leather almost as tough as his boots. He pulled both pairs on as he crossed the midden, even though among mortals the act of donning gloves was sometimes perceived as the start of *war*.

Aulaudin was halfway from the fence to the pipe when he became aware of mortal eyes watching him. He kept walking at a steady pace and judged the situation without turning his head. The mortal, a head taller than himself, brawny as a dwarf, drunk, and angry, probably had been sensitive to the open thoughts he'd shared a few moments earlier. They didn't make eye contact, but the mortal started walking an invisible path that would cross Aulaudin's near the pipe.

Elves didn't fight, not with each other or the scyldrin, not with goblins nor ogres, and certainly not with mortals. It was a lesson every son and daughter learned early and, as a rule, easily. For most young elves, there was no one to fight with:

except at festivals, elfin children never saw anyone their own age and their elders had already learned the lesson.

Aulaudin himself had been an exception. His brother Boraudin had been a mere five years older than him and they'd given each other ample opportunity for brawling. All Briary had conspired to shame them out of their unseemly behavior and the homestead had, in a sense, been successful. From an early age, no matter how enraged they were at each other, he and Boraudin had taken care to keep their bruises hidden.

They'd hidden their brawling so well that they'd never completely outgrown it. A month before he died, a married Boraudin had challenged his brother to defend himself with a shepherd's crook in the mortal realm, where no one else would witness his defeat. For his life, Aulaudin couldn't remember what had started the argument, only that Boraudin had, indeed, knocked him senseless. He hadn't brawled since: hadn't so much as made a fist until Evoni came into his life.

Skills could rust but instincts were immortal. Aulaudin wrested the pipe from the rubble. The exposed end was capped with metal, the other was raw and jagged. Holding the pipe in an over-hand, under-hand grasp, he brought the jagged end in line with the mortal's heart. The mortal hesitated.

"You got no business here," he snarled, adding an oath Aulaudin had never heard before and was too overwrought to remember.

Drawing breath through his mouth, Aulaudin answered, "I'm taking this home," but he spoke in a language the mortal in front of him had likely never heard. Some mortals would walk away from a threatening foreigner: some, of course, would fly into a rage. Aulaudin waited an immortal moment to see which kind faced him.

"Begone!" the mortal said, or something similar. He was drunk and his speech was thick. Aulaudin heard the intent more clearly than he heard the word itself.

With the pipe safely in his hands, Aulaudin had no objection to obedience. He walked backward until the mortal turned away. He kept his pace slow, even after he'd threaded the pipe through the tear in the metal-mesh fence and begun his retreat down the empty street.

When Aulaudin had parted the Veil into this city he'd been a good hour's walk across the river. Getting here unnoticed had been simple—most mortals didn't notice a ragged, dirty man walking alone, but a ragged man carrying a length of pipe would attract attention. The dead buildings, separated by alleys, offered the seclusion a man needed to part the Veil while the afternoon sun remained bright enough to hide the parting flash.

Seclusion was less important than it had ever been. As Maun gleefully explained: *Science* made a fool of any mortal who claimed to have met an elf from Fairie, especially any ragged mortal who drank bitter wine and haunted the same middens where elves foraged. But, for all his brashness, not even Maun would part the Veil before witnesses.

Entering one of the alleys, Aulaudin listened with his ears and opened his mind to the mortal realm's invisible chaos, hoping to separate danger from din. It was a hopeless, futile task which he quickly abandoned.

A crash in the midnight depths stopped him cold and set his heart racing, but the sound wasn't repeated. Cats, Aulaudin told himself, or rats. His eyes adjusted to the alley shadows. Collapsed crates and barrels spilled fetid lumps of what might once have been food. A liquid that might once have been rainwater sloshed beneath his boots. Movement caught his attention: a rat, definitely a rat, making a meal of something he'd rather not recognize.

One of the filthy crates looked strong enough to bear a man's weight. Aulaudin swept it clear of garbage with a double-gloved hand. There was nothing he could do about the damp. Moisture wicked through his trousers. It was just as well that he hadn't eaten in over a day. The moisture against his skin was worse than iron.

Almost as bad as he felt when he looked into his youngest daughter's eyes.

Evoni harbored darkness within her—he'd felt it the first time he'd touched her, looking into her stormy eyes. Aulaudin blamed the darkness on himself, on those fights with Boraudin that had nurtured instincts which had no place in Fairie. He'd passed his failings, the flaws of Tatterfall, onto the child his wife said was theirs.

He feared what Evoni was and what she might become. With each passing year Aulaudin had found himself more frightened, more trapped. Evoni hadn't changed at the age when gnomes or dwarves changed. There were no simple changes left; after nearly thirty winters, even green-skinned sylphs had grown unlikely.

Either Evoni was an elf and her father had been wrong about her—cruel to her—since her birth. Aulaudin shuddered, contemplating the consequences of that cruelty.

Or Evoni was going to shape herself into a guardian.

Considering the fate of most homesteads that reared a guardian, Aulaudin had begun to hope his daughter was an elf. He was prepared to admit his errors and atone for them; confession, his erstwhile mortal companions had said, salved a man's conscience. For the last year or so, he'd rehearsed an apology each time he returned to Fairie. The artful words would, indeed, salve his conscience until he saw Evoni. No matter how much he wanted to be wrong about her, his heart wouldn't be swayed.

«Guardian rising!»

The notion struck the back of Aulaudin's mind. A perfect counterpart to his melancholy, he thought it had been born in his own imagination, but it struck again—

«Guardian rising!»

This time the notion rode a wild tide of echoes as every man beyond the Veil picked it up and flung it blindly to the horizons. Without thought, Aulaudin added his mind's voice to the chorus. Men couldn't drown the mortal din, but the sensitive he'd left on the midden was going to have headache and nightmare to remember.

«Guardian rising!»

With his mind open as for a midsummer Vigilance, Aulaudin felt the notion's truth. The Veil, which was everywhere in the mortal realm as it was in Fairie, trembled as an elf-born child underwent a cataclysmic shaping. Fear's cold hand gripped his heart, but, in the alley there was no way to guess which one of Fairie's homesteads had been struck. All he could do was hold himself calm and begin the shifting trance.

«Aulaudin. Aulaudin of Briary . . . Brother! Come home!»

He recognized the mind of Aglaun, his youngest brother. The fraternal sharing between them strengthened rapidly. In heartbeats, Aulaudin knew that Aglaun had come to the mortal realm to find him and that his mind seethed with images of catastrophe.

«Briary?» he asked. There were no children at Briary nor at any of its neighboring homesteads, but Aglaun's thoughts were full of Briary and, though it shamed him, Aulaudin would rather think of Briary in peril than Sunrise.

Aglaun cut through Aulaudin's hopes. «Sunrise. The guardian has risen at Sunrise. Evoni. Come home.»

«You don't know!» Aulaudin countered, furiously amending Aglaun's notions of Sunrise. «You *can't* know. There's no man there!»

But there was. «Ombrio made the alarm.»

Aulaudin threw up a wall of denial; Aglaun battered it down with two words and an image: «She fought.»

The image was darkness, rain, and howling wind. Aulaudin didn't recognize the shape.

«A siren, Aulaudin. A guardian of the seas. The men of Wavehome named it even as Jerlayne fought. And it *was* Jerlayne, brother. Ombrio is hiding—» Or dead, Aglaun didn't share those words, but the thought was in his mind. «But I have kenned your wife within you too many times not to know what I felt . . . what we all felt. Your daughter rose at Sunrise and your wife fought until she could fight no more. Come to the cornered stones—» the place was the anchor for one of Fairie's pass-throughs, «we'll go back together.»

The pipe fell from Aulaudin's hands, striking his legs. He gasped as the iron burned his flesh, but physical pain meant nothing.

«Come to Briary. Father will be here soon. We'll go to Sunrise together.»

"No!" Aulaudin shouted aloud. When they were already sharing thoughts, men could hear one another's voices. «Stay away! Find Maun and keep him away from Sunrise, I don't want to see him or you! I go alone.»

He imagined Jerlayne, proud and strong, setting herself against Evoni's transformation. He couldn't easily imagine her defeated, but against a guardian she couldn't have been victorious.

«Come to Briary!» Aglaun pleaded.

Done properly, wherever Aulaudin went, whether he abandoned the pipe or not, it would be night before he'd be through the Veil and walked the distance his resting place to Sunrise—dawn, if he followed Aglaun's advice. There was another way home, not a proper way, though every elfin father taught it to every elfin son. It demanded strong emotions, such as elves rarely suffered: the panic of pursuit, the pain of injury . . . the loss of everything that mattered.

Aulaudin cut himself off from his brother. He stilled his heart and parted the Veil with a scream, then he thought of Sunrise. Wild winds erupted in the alley. Cold rain fell from a clear, mortal sky. His mind focused on the clearing between the great house and iron gate where a neglected rose struggled to survive. He'd thought that nothing would change an already empty place, but the Veil parted reluctantly into a storm-wracked tangle of tree limbs and fence posts.

Chapter 12

Aulaudin had come to Sunrise, but not near the gate. He lunged forward, not caring how or where he landed. The grass was slick and he was on his knees when the hole he'd punched between the realms sealed behind him. The parting wind slackened and the storm ebbed into a heavy, death-smelling mist.

He shouted, "Jerlayne," and "Banda," and other names, any name but his daughter's. No one answered. He heard sobbing and made his way through the mist toward the sound. A woman crouched beside a fallen tree.

"What happened here?" He felt foolish for the question, guilty for the anger still thick on his tongue.

The woman looked up, tears and mist shining on her cheeks. He recognized the daughter that Petrin and Banda had adopted . . . recognized Banda, too, crushed beneath the tree. Words failed until the living gnome whispered—

"Evoni."

No other words were necessary.

Aulaudin left her to her grief. He went up hill, toward the great house, expecting the worst.

"Aulaudin! Master!"

The voice came from behind, followed by a haggard, bloody face he didn't recognize.

"The mistress, my wife Jer—" Aulaudin couldn't say her name. He just shook his head and continued up the hill.

The dwarf seized his sleeve. "Below. Follow me."

"Alive?" Aulaudin asked, too softly for his companion to hear.

He followed, one numb foot after the other. Outlines of destruction emerged as they descended: trees uprooted and trees snapped in two, cottages without roofs or walls, and scyldrin everywhere, all in shock. The weir was gone; the pond, too. Aulaudin thought of Olleta.

"Master Aulaudin!"

More dwarves joined them, the ones who'd wanted the pipe. He looked around: the mill had gone with the pond and the weir.

One dwarf said, "Evoni." Another added, *"Siren."*

A siren wasn't as bad as a dragon. A dragon transformed with fire and stone and destroyed everything in its path. But a siren was bad enough; he remembered the backlash when the first—and until today, Fairie's only—siren had risen. Evoni would shape herself a path to the sea, was, in all likelihood, still shaping it: Fairie's seacoast lay in the south. All night and through tomorrow, pieces of Fairie would die.

As pieces had already died.

"Jerlayne?" Aulaudin asked.

The dwarves led him to the stream. The mist became a dirty-gray cloud barely an arm's length above Aulaudin's head. In the unnatural twilight, he saw the vanished pond and the dark gathering on its bank.

Protectors, that's what Jerlayne called them. They were always armed. Goblins always bristled with iron weapons the women shaped for them, just as they were always hidden in blackened armor and blacker cloaks.

Jerlayne had said that Sunrise's goblins were honorable.

And Jerlayne had said that Evoni was an elf.

In fairness, Aulaudin knew nothing could have protected Sunrise from Evoni's transformation, no more than Jerlayne had been able to stop it. He was not in a mood to be fair. Stalking toward them, he wished for the pipe he'd left in the mortal-realm alley and picked up a wind-downed branch instead.

A goblin heard the sound and spun around: they *were* wary. Black eyes narrowed, as if the sight of a man holding a stick were more troublesome than a siren rising from the homestead he'd been sworn to protect. The goblin tugged another black sleeve and, one by one, a score of blue-skinned faces turned toward Sunrise's master.

They were protecting something—hiding it—behind their cloaks and armor.

"Begone!"

They parted into two groups, giving Aulaudin a clear view of one more goblin, kneeling in the flood-flattened grass beside Jerlayne. Goro, he guessed, though the goblins looked pretty much the same to him and no one knew their true names.

"Begone," he repeated, striding forward, leading with his branch.

Goro—if he'd guessed correctly—lowered Jerlayne gently before pivoting on one knee. His face might have been a painted mask for all the expression it revealed. His hair and clothes were wet; everyone's hair and clothes were wet, but there was mud on Goro's sleeve as well and algae clinging to his hair.

"She . . . lives."

Aulaudin recognized the voice he heard no more than twice a year. Goro spoke slowly, as if he were fumbling for words, or speaking to a simple-witted brownie. "Her body is unharmed. Her mind—" the goblin shook his head.

Aulaudin already knew. He and Jerlayne were joined but the bond between them had turned as empty and desolate as ever his daughter's eyes had been. The emptiness called Aulaudin's name, tempting him to follow his wife. He slipped toward darkness.

"Evoni—"

Goro's voice brought Aulaudin abruptly back to Sunrise. The goblin had risen to his feet while Aulaudin's thoughts were elsewhere. They stood close together, an arm's reach closer than Aulaudin had ever been to one of Fairie's shadowy protectors. He didn't like the view and didn't want to be the one who retreated.

"I know," he snarled, hoping to forestall whatever else the goblin had intended to say.

Black eyes widened until there was, for the briefest moment, a ring of white around them. Aulaudin reconsidered his resolve to stand firm, but before he'd taken a backward step, Goro retreated, giving Aulaudin his clearest view yet of the muddy crater that had been their fish pond. Near the ruined mill, where the pond had been deepest, Aulaudin saw Olleta, face down, her leaf-green hair splayed around her.

Though she had a child's face and mind, the sylph been alive when Gudwal was born. She'd survived iron, ogres, and a dragon or two, but not Evoni.

Aulaudin thought angrily of his daughter, then saw her body, halfway onto the bank, as if, at the end, she'd tried to escape.

She hadn't succeeded. A bloodless gash ran the length of her spine, exposing the bone.

"What does she think now?" he wondered. "What does a guardian remember after its shaping?"

"Nothing, I hope," Goro replied. "Hard enough to have been scyldrin. She thought she was an elf—like you and her mother; a shaping woman with a homestead and husband awaiting her. Let her go to the sea and never remember this place. I wouldn't want to remember anything. Would you?"

Aulaudin hadn't meant to ask his questions aloud, hadn't considered that a goblin might be the only one who could hear, hadn't imagined one would answer. He had no intention of answering a goblin's question, except it blazed through his thoughts. Evoni had thought she was an elf; so had he, growing up at Briary. It wasn't just that sons changed sooner than daughters. Aulaudin had always believed he was an elf. Maun had believed what his son had rejected: *This child is an elf. Take him into your heart, because he will not change.*

The young scyldrin, raised by gnomes, knew they would change. They might not welcome the transformation; Aulaudin had never considered the possibility before: could anyone *want* to be a gnome or dwarf? Perhaps they resented it, or feared it, but certainly they'd known what waited for them. Except for Evoni, raised in the great house, rejected by her father, but taught to shape iron by her mother.

Far better indeed that Evoni not remember anything of her past when she got to the sea. Better for her. Definitely better for all the elves of Fairie—especially the foolish elves of Sunrise.

"I asked, what shall be done with her?"

Goro again, obviously repeating himself. Aulaudin realized he was staring at Evoni's shattered, abandoned corpse, and that the goblin was staring at him.

Why ask, he wondered; why answer? Sunrise had buried Dalan with honor. The youth's death, though largely his own fault, hadn't harmed anyone but himself. Sunrise wouldn't honor a murderer. Let the goblins take his daughter, then, as they took their own dead into the shadows after ogre raids, after Tatterfall. Aulaudin couldn't think of a worse fate than eternity among goblins.

"Shall we take her with us?" Goro persisted.

Aulaudin was about to snarl, Of course! when it struck him:

Evoni wasn't dead. Her body was, but she wasn't. Goblins might well hesitate before taking a guardian's husk into their shadows.

"Bury her," he decided quickly. "There. Now."

Dark blue nostrils flared with evident distaste, disapproval.

"You asked. I've answered. Bury her in the mud where she *died*."

Goro let out a stream of clicks, trills, and warbles that passed for language among goblins. One of them responded with a quick burst of what seemed to be disbelief, but they filed off without argument. Beyond doubt, every one of them understood what Aulaudin had said. But no one born on an elfin homestead recognized a word the goblins spoke.

When Aulaudin and Goro were alone—no gnome or dwarf would come within ten paces of the bank where Jerlayne lay— the goblin knelt again and slid an arm beneath Jerlayne's shoulders.

"No—" Aulaudin feinted the raw end of his branch at Goro's head.

The goblin calmly seized the wood. Before Aulaudin blinked, his puny weapon was pointed into the grass.

"Set it down. The ground is treacherous. We'll carry her together."

Aulaudin shook his head.

With a sigh and a gesture, Goro twisted the branch and Aulaudin found his wrists bent at awkward angles. "She cannot remain here in the damp and cold. Set it down and carry her yourself, if you won't let me."

It was a struggle to keep his grip, but Aulaudin managed. "Get away from her."

Another sigh, another gesture, and the branch belonged to Goro, who threw it into the mud as he stood and put two steps between them. "I'm not your enemy, Aulaudin."

It was, Aulaudin thought, the first time he'd heard a goblin say any man's name. There was more than a hint of threat in Goro's voice, as if to say *if I were your enemy, you'd be in the mud beside your feeble stick.* Aulaudin was wise enough to take his victories where and how he found them. Kneeling, he got his arms beneath Jerlayne and lifted her up.

He'd carried his wife many times before, in love and laughter. With her arms around his neck and tucked against his shoulder, she'd never been a burden, not the way she was now.

Aulaudin wanted—needed—another pair of arms to support Jerlayne's head and keep her dangling hands away from his legs as he turned around.

Goro was right there, face like a statue and arms folded in front of him. All Aulaudin had to do was ask. He'd cut out his tongue first. A man had the strength to carry his wife to her bed without a goblin's help.

The goblin followed, though; a dark presence in the mist that thickened around them as they began the climb to the great house. Twice Goro cleared his throat, alerting Aulaudin to mud and loose stones. Once, he called out, "Branch!" and Aulaudin walked safely around it. Aulaudin was grateful for the help, but breathing too hard to say thank you, even if he'd been willing to. Goro opened the wrought-iron gate for Sunrise's master and mistress, then, three steps short of the covered porch, walked into the mist, leaving Aulaudin to wrestle with the high door.

How like a goblin to vanish just when he could have been useful.

Aulaudin's shoulders throbbed once Jerlayne slipped from his arms to the mattress of their bed. Moments passed before Aulaudin had the strength to fetch water from the water room and stir the hearth ashes for embers—moments when he could only watch the slight movements of her ribs and measure the emptiness of life without her. He cut through the seams of her dress, washed the mud from her face, dried her and warmed her in layers of silk and wool. He talked to his wife as he worked—meaningless chatter: nothing about today, or yesterday, or tomorrow; but tales of the mortal realm, tales mortals told each other about the Fairie they believed existed, tales that would make her laugh, even though she'd heard them many times before.

The weather—if the unnaturalness swirling around the homestead could be called weather—worsened. Winds came up and lightning flashed as if every man were coming through the Veil to visit. They weren't. Within the sharing parts of Aulaudin's mind everything was silent. It was as if his homestead had been sequestered. If he'd had nothing better to do, Aulaudin might have settled back against a dry wall and stretched his mind to the limit, but he had Jerlayne to worry about and closed the shutters instead.

Aulaudin thought, as he lit lamps and candles, that Jerlayne was coming around. She'd opened her eyes and it seemed that they followed him as he walked. He sat in a chair beside the bed, her hand in his, letting the magic that was joining pass between them.

Tatterfall had taught Aulaudin about grief and futility; he neither expected forgiveness nor offered it. They couldn't undo the past, might never be able to discuss it, but they had sadness in common now, and regret. It was, he thought, a worthy place to start, but Jerlayne was as elusive as snow in summer. Joining couldn't find her thoughts.

The storm battered already weakened trees and walls. In the dark, it was difficult to guess whether a crash was thunder, wood, or stone. Aulaudin guessed it was halfway to midnight when someone banged the homestead's alarm, a man-high plate of metal he'd wrestled through the Veil decades earlier. All they needed now was a plague of ogres but Aulaudin didn't bother to crack a shutter or bolt the door. With Jerlayne lost to him, Sunrise was dead.

Let Goro and his goblins protect Sunrise, if they could. Aulaudin had stopped caring.

He made his mind as empty and still as Jerlayne's—or tried to. Absorbed by the storm, he waited for the roof to rip away from the walls or for the door to blast from its hinges. Aulaudin didn't notice when he began to hear the singing. It emerged faintly from the silence and might have been there from the beginning. Not the lyric songs the scyldrin sang as they worked or played, nor the rhythmic chants that goblins sang with their drums, but something wild and formless: a song of madness.

A siren's song.

Evoni hadn't followed a path to the sea. She'd abandoned her body without abandoning her home. She watched in the lightning, listened in the wind; Aulaudin—recalling the questions he'd exchanged with Goro—thought himself small. As the storm finally quieted, anger seeped in to fill the void in his heart and thoughts. Leaving Jerlayne, he carried a lamp from one room to the next of the house that hadn't been his home for more than two decades.

What did a guardian remember? The ability to create memory was as immortal as the mind that shaped it, but memories themselves were mortal. They changed unless they were carefully renewed. They needed touchstones—sights, sounds, tastes, all manner of things—or they would fade completely.

Sunrise was Evoni's touchstone. It held her memory; his wife had seen to that.

After feeding Jerlayne's stained, sodden dress to the fire, Aulaudin's attention fell on the tapestries framing the room. Evoni shaping iron, Evoni playing with a spotted dog, Evoni running through the snow. Evoni on every wall of the home he and Jerlayne were meant to share forever. Aulaudin could have stopped his anger before it burst out of control. He could have found something else to look at or think about; he wasn't compelled to tote the lamp from room to room, casting ruddy light on Jerlayne's fantasies—or perhaps he was compelled to journey through his siren daughter's life until he came, at the last, to the room that had been hers: an old room at the center of Sunrise, a room where his own memories were thick and the walls were covered by murals of Evoni swimming beside Olleta.

Aulaudin hurled a chair at one offending scene and followed it with an unlit lamp. Oil blurred the image, but his aim had been off and, once again, it was the sylph who paid the greatest price. Wadding one of Evoni's gowns around his fist, Aulaudin smeared his daughter's portrait then stalked out of the room. He attacked the other murals similarly, then took a knife to the tapestries, hacking them down and hurling them into the nearest hearth.

The singing, still audible in the depths of his mind, neither strengthened nor faded.

At the end, shaking and beyond reason, Aulaudin stood beside Jerlayne's loom which held her last, unfinished, artwork: Evoni in autumn. He slashed the warp threads, then sat on the floor, picking out the wefts until it was hours past midnight and the picture had been reduced to spider knots.

Aulaudin's anger played out before he'd finished his destruction. In its aftermath he found his own emptiness. His arms lay across his lap, too heavy to move. He knocked his head hard against the plastered wall, too numb to feel an ache or pain. A tempter's voice in Aulaudin's conscience chided him for being a fool, and tormented him with the almost-real sounds of doors opening and footsteps coming closer.

In his mind's eye, Aulaudin saw Evoni wearing the torn body she'd left behind. Then Goro stood over him, a chiseled smile on his mask-face; but in all the days and nights of Fairie, no goblin had ever set foot inside a homestead house. Then Jerlayne appeared to him, or so Aulaudin's tortured conscience suggested. He thought he knew her well enough, even now, to know that she'd understand and might be the tiniest bit grateful for his tantrum.

But outside his imagination, except for the siren's wild, faint song, Aulaudin had nothing but an eerie calm for companionship and, as darkness deepened toward dawn, the only face he wished to see belonged to his father.

Maun would know the precise words, like stars at twilight, to mark a path out of the corner he'd wedged himself into. But Aglaun had obeyed his brother's wishes: he'd steered their father away from Sunrise and throughout the night not one stray thought, even comforting or merely curious, had brushed Aulaudin's mind.

The lamp burnt dry.

«Father!» He called the mind he known longer than any other.

Maun was asleep, but that was no obstacle. Aulaudin hurled a nightmare into his father's dreams and shivered as Maun awoke.

«Be damned! You're still alive.»

«So far,» Aulaudin agreed, adding more images of destruction and Jerlayne wrapped in blankets. «I couldn't bring her back. She melted away when I tried. I'm trapped, Father. Can't go forward or back. We're trapped.»

«You should have come here. You shouldn't have gone to Sunrise alone. You knew what you'd find; a part of you wanted this.»

These weren't the starlight words Aulaudin had hoped for. He lashed back with his memories of Tatterfall and another man who'd buried his grief within a mountain of rage. Maun accepted everything, gave nothing back in reply. Aulaudin thought he'd driven Maun away; his conscience roared with bitter laughter, but Maun had learned, had changed.

«Jerlayne could have died, Aulaudin. Anyone can die, anytime. It's simply a choice. She's loved you longer and deeper; and you love her the same. Be patient with her and yourself. It hasn't been a day yet and this is the worst time . . . right before daybreak. It will be easier by sunlight.»

Aulaudin shook his head. «Not here. Evoni's everywhere . . . on the walls . . . in the cloth. In the air. She's grounded by her memories: a siren locked away from the sea.» An idea came unexpectedly. «I've got to take Jerlayne away. They're bound to each other. Jerlayne can't heal herself and Evoni won't go to the sea until they've been broken free of each other. I'll bring her to Briary. With your blessing . . . of course, and Aglaidia's. She knows?»

Aglaidia's face as she learned what had happened at Sunrise echoed in Aulaudin's mind. He heard the memory of her words. *It's certain then? All these years . . . Jerlayne said she knew for certain . . . for certain.* That image faded, replaced by his mother, cross-grained from sleep and rubbing her eyes. Her lips moved, but Aulaudin heard only one word, «*No,*» before everything froze, as if Jerlayne had painted it on one of the walls.

Men could get into one another's thoughts. Long before he became a man, every son learned a thousand ways to defend his innermost privacy and keep his secrets safe. Sharing was as honest as spoken conversation, not more, not less, and utterly dependent on the personalties involved. Aulaudin knew his father was a skilled deceiver—simply shutting him out, leaving him with the unsubtle knowledge that he wasn't party to a private conversation, was more candor than Maun usually admitted.

«She says no,» Maun shared a bit later. «Taking your wife away from there is a good idea, but not to bring her here. Aglaidia says she doesn't know Jerlayne well enough. This is a matter for blood mothers—»

«What is?» Aulaudin demanded. There were no images, no tactile sensations to accompany the Maun's words. His father might well have been talking through a keyhole for all the insight gleaned from his sharing.

«I don't know. She won't say, Aulaudin; she simply won't say—except that if you go anywhere, you must go to Stonewell, to Elmeene, and . . . and . . .» Something very like embarrassment slipped through the featureless wall Maun had erected around his thoughts. «She says you must join with her . . . the sooner the better. Now, if you can, but certainly before you see Elmeene.»

Empty moments slipped away before Aulaudin composed a coherent thought. «Join with her? Join with her! This is a poor jest, Father. Jerlayne's asleep . . . no, worse than asleep, she's unconscious, beneath unconscious.»

A shrug rippled through the void that connected one man's

thoughts to another. «I have said the same to Aglaidia and she is, I tell you, unmoved. Her words—her precise words: They must join and before either of them sees Elmeene.» Another shrug. «They are healers. They will arouse a man to bring him back, if that's the only way. What she suggests—it is only the reverse.»

Aulaudin had never been injured into unconsciousness nor healed by arousal and didn't think tonight was a particularly good time to tinker with the notion but Maun, prodded no doubt by Agaliadia, gave him no peace. He could have dissembled—he'd learned that dubious art from a master. It was one thing to caress his wife's cheek as he'd bathed her, but quite another—an unpleasant other—to spur himself alone into joining's passion.

Yet, if joining would kindle a healing spark. . . ? Would joining sever the bond between Jerlayne and their siren daughter?

The pre-dawn light had grown strong enough to see shapes and hints of color when Aulaudin withdrew again from his wife and their bed. The joining had been worse than he'd imagined—a nausea of the spirit—except that Aglaidia had been right and Jerlayne had awoken. She'd known him and known herself. She remembered everything. For horrifying heartbeats, Aulaudin had been with his wife, in the muck, struggling to separate an elf who'd never been from a siren who could not be denied. Then there were walls everywhere, as impenetrable as any a man could raise around himself.

"My love," Aulaudin whispered desperately from the foot of the bed. "I understand. I swear—"

Jerlayne stared at him, through him, and shook her head. She wouldn't talk, but she was back. She'd severed herself from Evoni, for all the good it had done.

The storm had reawakened while they were joined. The very ground groaned in protest. With each shudder, Aulaudin told himself—

That's the last. She'll leave now. She'll begin to forget.

And the next heartbeat, Evoni would prove him wrong.

By morning's light the mists were thick as swamp smoke and heavy with the smells of raw earth. Evoni wouldn't leave Sunrise for the sea; she was shaping a sea for Sunrise. Jerlayne had taught her how.

For nine terrible days the land moved at Sunrise. Aulaudin gathered those scyldrin he could find in the kitchen, since it seemed that the siren would not directly harm the great house. There was no hope of sending someone to Maialene's cottage. Its part of the forest was already gone.

Aulaudin searched for Ombrio with his mind and found nothing, but then again, he found no other men at all. With the siren shaping a sea around them, Sunrise might well have been in a realm of its own.

Throughout those nine days, Jerlayne refused to leave the bedroom—and refused again on the tenth day, when Aulaudin told her that the skies had cleared. There was a salt-water sea lapping against cliffs that hadn't existed eleven days ago. There were great rocks rising off the shore: the Stones of Sunrise, near, perhaps, where M'lene's cottage had stood. The clouds were charcoal colored and a siren could be heard singing to the wind.

Aulaudin told himself and everyone that, despite everything, the Stones and the sea and even the siren were good omens. There was, after all, no point in believing otherwise. He told his father the same thing: once the mist had lifted, he'd easily found his father and brothers, everyone he sought, except for Ombrio.

He was atop the cliffs, with his hands cupped against his eyes, scanning the sea for more omens. Mortals had such things as telescopes and binoculars. He'd forage for them the next time he parted the Veil, though he wouldn't part the Veil until he'd seen a good omen in his wife's eyes.

"Come to the shore," he'd told her this morning and received no response beyond an empty stare. "What's done is done. It could have been worse; it wasn't Tatterfall. We've survived. Come to the shore. It will give you peace, my love."

Something must have gotten through. Aulaudin heard a sound behind him. Ashen and frail, Jerlayne had dressed carelessly. Her tunic hung loose and open at the shoulder; her unbound hair whipped around her in the onshore breeze that had been constant since the mist had lifted. Taking no chance, Aulaudin held her firmly at the wrist and waist. She wouldn't blow away, but she might jump.

"Out there, beneath the clouds. Do you see the stones rising from the water? We think she dwells there. The gnomes, a few of them are quite sharp-sighted. They say they can see a woman with red hair. We have a guardian . . . and our lives. We've paid too much not to be grateful."

Jerlayne looked across the sparkling waves.

"I want to go to Stonewell," she said, as if she were picking up the threads of a neglected conversation. "I have questions. I need answers."

Chapter 13

"Stay close, my love."

Aulaudin's voice jolted Jerlayne out of the thoughtless haze which had, in the dread, empty days since Evoni's transformation, become her favored armor. They were skirting the Veil: riding through the dense, mortal-realm fog. Behind them and around them were twenty-odd scyldrin who'd survived the Sunrise cataclysm and resolved to live at a less exciting homestead.

Jerlayne hardly blamed them. If an elf had a similar choice, she'd have seized it firmly. But elves had no such choice. Though she was leaving Sunrise, headed for Stonewell and, she hoped, answers to a knot of haunting questions, she and Aulaudin would have to return . . . and would have to make peace between themselves.

Aulaudin seemed willing—more than willing. He hadn't once raised his voice, asked a rude question, or offered a justified recrimination. She could almost hate him for his reasonableness: if *he'd* gotten angry, then *she* could have gotten angry and, perhaps, purged some of the venom that festered in her heart. Anger wasn't likely to help. They'd survived Evoni's rising and the creation of a sea where fields and forests had formerly ruled.

Jerlayne remembered how Evoni had shaped lakes beside the millpond stream. What if she had interfered? What if she had directed her daughter's curiosity down different paths? What if she hadn't made the greatest mistake of her life the day that Evoni had been born?

"Please, my love, stay close. There is always danger here and more right now: the Veil has not completely recovered from . . . please, stay close." Aulaudin carefully, although not easily, avoided mentioning their daughter's name.

They were some five feet apart; far enough that Aulaudin's auburn hair was misty-gray like his shirt. It was a comfortable distance for Jerlayne: she didn't want to see anything clearly. If Jerlayne could see her husband vaguely, she thought that she should be close enough for him to see her clearly, no matter how thoroughly Evoni's transformation had torn the Veil. She let her mare pick their path.

Who knew what the horses saw? Fog? A pair of suns in a clear blue sky?

"Please—"

Jerlayne heard the frustration in Aulaudin's voice and shifted her arms and legs into the positions both she and the mare had been taught meant: move to the left . . . eventually. Aulaudin was a more experienced rider with quicker, more confident moves. Jerlayne tucked her chin and avoided her husband's eyes as his hand took the mare's rein near the bit.

When the mare was walking where Aulaudin wanted her, he loosened his grip. His hand slid backward along the braided leather—a gesture that could have been casual, but wasn't. Jerlayne felt a tingling pressure as their hands touched: an invitation to joining, an invitation she'd denied even before she'd pulled her hand away. He sighed and his hand disappeared from Jerlayne's determinedly narrow view.

She held her breath, waiting for—hoping for—a flash of masculine anger. But Aulaudin said nothing; not to her, not to the scyldrin riding with them, not to himself. Aulaudin's patience stirred an unhealed rage within her. While he retreated silently, Jerlayne wanted to scream, pound his ribs with her fists, and countless other acts of petty violence so shameful to her elfin upbringing that she was certain she'd gone mad.

A tear escaped the corner of Jerlayne's right eye. She didn't know if it flowed for her daughter, her husband, or herself, but she made no effort to blot it on her sleeve. Aulaudin rode on her left. He couldn't see the tear and what he couldn't see she could ignore.

They left the fog and rode through the waning light of an autumn afternoon. The air chilled as soon as the sun slipped below the leaf-laced treetops. Aulaudin brought them to a halt in a mossy clearing.

"We'll make camp here," he said. The scyldrin swung down from their ponies.

Jerlayne stayed in the saddle. Aulaudin offered his arms.

"How much farther?" she asked, refusing his assistance with a nervous shake of her head. Skirting could cut great chunks out of a journey, but a woman rarely knew how far she'd come, how far was left to travel.

"We'll be at Stonewell tomorrow, by midday. No more fog, my love, I promise."

He reached again. Jerlayne cringed and his arms dropped heavily to his sides.

"Couldn't we ride through the evening? The sky's clear; there'll be moonlight."

Aulaudin said nothing and Jerlayne dared a glance at his weary face. He probably had a headache. It was easier to part the Veil than skirt it. She could have eased his pain and restored his energy . . . if she could have borne the thought of touching him.

The sooner they got to Stonewell, the better, for all of them. Jerlayne couldn't make peace with Aulaudin—couldn't accept the peace she knew waited for her in his arms—until she understood how and why she'd been so wrong about her daughter. Could she bear elfin children? Did she dare conceive again? Did she deserve to?

"Beloved, you're . . . you're not strong enough to ride into the night and I do not wish to carry you into your parents' home."

He tried to make light of a legitimate concern. Jerlayne didn't know what Elmeene and Jereige thought about events past, present, or future. She knew only what Aulaudin told her each night after his Vigilance, and he knew only what Jereige shared with him. Perhaps her father and husband were being honest with each other. Possibly Elmeene was being honest with Jereige. At that moment, Jerlayne took nothing for granted.

And she couldn't face another open-air night with her questions unanswered.

A victory, then, for Elmeene. Despite all her wedding-day vows, Jerlayne had become a master of secrets. She could stare at Aulaudin without seeing him, listen to him tell the scyldrin to remount, and not feel guilt, not feel anything.

Cold night air seeped through Jerlayne's cloak and gown. It lay on her skin and touched her bones. She shivered so badly that the reins fell from her hands and she nearly toppled out of the saddle trying to regain them. Aulaudin was there at her side before she was in any danger. His movements as he wove her reins in with his fairly roared with concern, but he kept his opinions to himself, saying only "Two hours, at the outside. Jereige knows we're close; they'll be ready for us. Tuck your hands in and pull up your cowl. There will be hearth blankets and warm cider waiting."

Hours grew long in autumn. There wasn't enough warmth left in Jerlayne's body no matter how tightly she held her cloak or where she tucked her hands, and her feet might have fallen off miles back for all she could feel them when the lights of Stonewell finally came into view. Jereige was at the boundary stone with torch-bearing scyldrin and blankets that had been racked beside the hearth all evening.

Jerlayne tried to tell her father that the she didn't want to be touched, that she'd arrange the very welcome blankets across the saddle herself, but her tongue was as numb as the rest of her. Moments later, when they reached the great house, Jereige didn't ask if she needed help dismounting or offer his open arms; he simply pulled her off the mare's back and passed her into Aulaudin's arms like a great, ungainly sack.

They must have been in each other's thoughts all evening.

It wasn't fair, but Jerlayne didn't truly want to know what her father and husband had shared. Aulaudin carried her across a threshold and beneath a roof that, even after a century's growth and shaping, put Sunrise to shame. Jerlayne began to think of cider and a sandwich piled high with meat and slathered with spiced sauce: her insistence that they travel on to Stonewell had robbed them all of supper.

Then Jerlayne caught sight of her mother sitting in a huge, uncomfortable chair beside the hearth and her appetite vanished. She struggled free of blankets, cloak, and Aulaudin.

"Elmeene?"

Elmeene unwound from the chair, letting a lap robe fall to the floor as her indigo wool gown arranged itself around her.

"I—I have questions."

"I feared you might," Elmeene replied, though there wasn't a hint of fear anywhere about her.

In absolute measure, Elmeene was taller than any of her daughters. Her shoulders were as broad as a man's. Her hands were simply huge. Yet, Jerlayne always felt grossly awkward around her mother.

"I've come for answers. I want to know—"

"Not *now!*"

Women couldn't share thoughts; sometimes they didn't need to: the shape of an eyebrow was sufficient to take Jerlayne back to her earliest shaping lessons when her mother's word could never be challenged. She raged, but didn't argue.

"Not now," Elmeene said with abrupt pleasantness. "Not while you're blue from cold. Come, sit by the fire. Evandi! Neer!" Elmeene shouted gnomish names Jerlayne had known since girlhood. "More blankets, if you please. We'll make my daughter a bed right here by the hearth."

Meaning—among other, more hospitable things—that Elmeene didn't want Jerlayne wandering through Stonewell, looking for answers . . . as if she had the wit or strength to find them. There was something in the steaming cider she'd been handed, something bitter beneath the apple sweetness: bryony and a hint of pine bark. Jerlayne drank it down: if her mother had gone to such lengths, then perhaps there *were* answers.

The scyldrin had made their way to the cottages. Aulaudin, at least as tired, hungry and cold as Jerlayne herself, had disappeared with Jereige. Stonewell gnomes bustled about, fluffing feather mattresses and an abundance of pillows. Jerlayne watched them from the far end of a fast-lengthening corridor: bryony and pine bark weren't the only herbs in the cider; there was a soporific as well. If she weren't so weary, she might have been able to guess which one.

Her eyelids had become unbearably heavy by the time her mother appeared in front of her.

"You'll sleep until noon, at least, Jerlayne. A good sleep, I promise you. You need your rest before we talk."

"I won't."

"Won't what? Won't talk to me tomorrow after you're rested? You've come all this way and we *need* to talk, Jerlayne. We need more than talk. I worried so much in the beginning, then the years passed. I never dreamt you, of all the daughters in Fairie, hadn't put the pieces together."

"Won't sleep."

"Of course you will. I put a whole grain of corn rose in that cider. You'll sleep sound until noon."

And Jerlayne did, but not soundly. A spark of consciousness had escaped Elmeene's herb-laced cider and churned up vivid dreams. She was lost in unending fog, weighted down by wet garments, and unable to cry out because her throat was clogged with mud. Not that it mattered: she couldn't remember any names.

Jerlayne had the wit to mark the passage of time within her drugged sleep, how night deepened and became morning. She knew when the sun had risen above the roof, but the dream-fog, like the mud of the millpond, was stronger than her will. By sleeves and hems, it dragged her down.

Forgetting why she fought, Jerlayne surrendered.

* * *

"Jerlayne! Sixth of my daughters!"

A stinging blow freed Jerlayne from her dreams. She was in Elmeene's workroom, where she'd learned her shaping. A lesson had gone badly, she thought; she'd lost herself in some other substance—lost herself badly: afternoon light slanted through the windows and lesson time was in the morning. She was shamed; she looked down at her hands, and failed to recognize them.

"Jerlayne! Look at me. Talk to me."

Another big-fingered slap.

"Mother . . ." her voice was as wrong as her hands: not a young daughter's voice.

Jerlayne raised her head. She was in Elmeene's workroom, that was true enough, but it wasn't a shaping lesson that had gone awry. There was another face in her mind and, at last, she had the name that had eluded her all night: Evoni.

As Jerlayne whispered her siren-daughter's name, she became naked and defenseless to her memories. The workroom was chill; she began to shiver.

"Tell me everything. Say it out whole, leave nothing to fester," Elmeene suggested from the floor where she knelt beside Jerlayne's chair.

The workroom was silver with moonlight before Jerlayne finished her tale. "I was so certain. I let her become between Aulaudin and me. Yet I was wrong. How could I have been so wrong?"

Elmeene rose from the floor, no trace of stiffness in her joints—but that was Elmeene. She lit a lamp and set it beside an iron-sealed chest. "I'm to blame," she said as shaping flared between her hands and the metal. "When you didn't come, I thought you'd guessed for yourself. Some women do. None of your sisters ever asked. Maialene came to me afterward, to confirm her own suspicions. The others . . . well, they made no mistakes. I thought you were too proud, too angry, and I left the matter lie. You have a fine stubborn temper, Jerlayne. You take after me."

"Never asked *what*, Elmeene? Never guessed *what*? What did Maialene know that I've never suspected?" Jerlayne exploded as bitterness overcame despair. "A siren, Elmeene! I gave my husband a daughter. I told him she was an elf, that he should love her as an elf, take her into his heart as I did. I taught her *everything* I knew, mother; everything you'd taught me She was *good,* mother; better than I could dream of being, but she was a siren. *A siren!* Could I have known? *Should* I have known? What should I have done different? Strangled her before she first opened her eyes?"

No answer. Jerlayne heard iron clatter to the floor as Elmeene rummaged through the now-opened chest.

"Tell me, Mother. Tell me what Aulaudin and I did wrong . . . what did *I* do wrong, and what I could have done to prevent it?"

Elmeene dumped an armload of silk-wrapped parcels onto the seat of another chair, then dragged the chair close by Jerlayne's. "Nothing," she said, sorting through the parcels. "There is no curse, no failure, no shame. Sirens must be born. Sirens, dragons, and griffins; Fairie must have its guardians. Count yourself blessed not cursed: doubly blessed—you bore a guardian and you survived.

"We shape more than metal, wood, and flesh, my daughter; I *thought* you understood: We're the strength. We shape Fairie itself through the children we bear."

Jerlayne stared at the incongruously bright silks on her mother's lap. "I'm not strong. Sometimes I want to run away from Sunrise—even before Evoni. I can't face saying goodbye to Aulaudin time after time. I want my own children, sons and daughters. Pieces of Aulaudin around me." Tears made their way down her cheeks; they marked the silks. "You knew. I always knew my own name. Jereige believed you, trusted you . . . because you knew. How do you know the scyldrin from the elves?"

"It's really very simple." The edge was gone from Elmeene's voice as she settled on a red-wrapped parcel. Unknotted, the cloth revealed a wooden plaque which she placed in Jerlayne's hand. "I know your father. Turn it over."

Jerlayne refused. She had questions whose answers couldn't be found on a piece of wood. "I—"

"Turn it over. Then I'll tell you everything I know."

The plaque held a portrait; a man's portrait painted in Elmeene's quick-stroke style. But the man wasn't her father— wasn't an elf at all, nor a gnome or dwarf, nor even a goblin; which left only the mortals beyond the veil, the mortal men whose faces Jerlayne had never seen.

"Hear me well, daughter. There is only way to secure yourself an elfin child: part the Veil and mate with the mortal men you find beyond it."

Beyond words, Jerlayne could only shake her head as Elmeene unwrapped the other parcels. This had to be a nightmare, a part of her herb-dreams, but she wasn't asleep. It had to be a deceitful jest, but there was no mockery in Elmeene's voice or in her hands as she exposed portrait after portrait; one for every elfin child she'd born until the last, which was only a charcoal sketch on raw wood.

"You have a brother coming."

"No." Jerlayne poured her soul into the denial. There was magic in her hands. She had the power to shape the wood, to change the portrait into the face she knew and cherished; she lacked the will. The stranger in her hands was her father. "Why?" she asked, a wealth of questions in a single word.

"No reason that I know, only the truth as you've heard it at every wedding feast. When elves join, scyldrin are born. If you want an elfin child, you must part the Veil."

Jerlayne traced the portrait with her fingertip. "Jereige—" her voice caught. She cleared her throat and continued: "Father knows."

Jereige would always be Jerlayne's father, the man who been part of her life from its beginning. The other would never be more than a painted image. She couldn't know him, even if she'd wanted to. Though she was young for an elf, she was older than any mortal.

"Father parted the Veil for you at a pass-through; he took you with him. Together you foraged a mortal as my father." It was easier to speak each thought as it came to her than to consider its implications. "I asked Aulaudin once. He said *no*. I'll ask again. I'll tell him—"

Elmeene seized Jerlayne's wrist and pinched it hard. "You will say nothing! No man has ever known this; no man shall! You must *never* speak of it to them. The truth of our children has been a women's secret for too long to ever be shared." Elmeene shook her head vigorously.

Jerlayne had come from Sunrise in search of one answer and gotten them all. There was an awful symmetry to Elmeene's revelations that, combined with the plaques and Jerlayne's own failure to bear an elfin child, shaped a single truth. "Is there no other way? Must there be secrets at the heart of everything? Do I have to deceive Aulaudin?"

She let the plaque drop. "I won't. I've done too much wrong already. I can't—" Her spirits lifted: the whole notion was impossible. "I don't know where the Veil is."

"The Veil is everywhere, Jerlayne, just as men say. It's in the forest and in this very room. You need only to think about it to find it. Shaping must be taught, and the subtleties of thought that are passed from father to son must be taught, but any elf can find and part the Veil."

To prove her point, Elmeene opened her arms. A mist not unlike the mist beyond Sunrise flowed into the workroom and, with it, the discordant sounds of the mortal realm.

"Come. I'll show you the rest. That's the easiest way; the way I couldn't learn from my own mother. I'll show you what to do and how to do it. You'll have your elfin child by morning."

Jerlayne balked and the mist vanished. She had a thousand questions and twice that many objections, but Elmeene was clearly prepared. She rewrapped the portrait plaques in their silken squares, returned them to the chest which she refortified with shaping, then proceeded to calmly counter everything that her daughter said until, in despair, Jerlayne confessed her darkest, most shameful secret:

"Aulaudin and I are *estranged*. We have been since Evoni was born. We haven't joined . . . it's been over a year now—"

Elmeene's eyebrows arched.

"You understand, then . . . what you're suggesting. Men may not know where we get our elfin children, but they understand the rest. Aulaudin will *know* this secret that must never be shared. It's unthinkable; undoable, if no one is to ever guess the truth. And it will take time to heal the breach that's grown between us. Years."

"Nonsense," Elmeene said with a scowl. "Aulaudin confessed to Jereige that he joined with you while you lay in your bed after the rising. He apoligized of course; he's certain you despise him. Jereige worries that he may do something foolish and swears he won't let him part the Veil alone, but Aglaidia—bless her, she's known hardship, too— guessed correctly from the start and told him exactly what to do. You see, there's nothing to worry about. No excuses. You want an elfin child: what better way to heal this breach between you?"

Before Jerlayne could object, mist once again clouded the workroom and, with it, the smells and sounds of mortality. Elmeene took her daughter's hand.

"They're not so bad. Not like joining with your husband, of course, but they're not without their charms. Like trysting— you meet at a festival, you go off together, and you come back, as simple as that, except you've gotten yourself an elf-in child. You're fortunately, too, that it's scarcely any time since I went hunting. I have a bolthole, with clothes and the like. They are so changeable, these mortals, and it's best that they suspect nothing. Though sometimes . . . well, that's another tale."

Jerlayne clamped her free hand around the wooden arm of her chair. "I can't. We can't. Suppose someone came into the workroom—"

"Into *my* workroom? When I've closed the door and shaped the bolt? Who would do such a thing? Not even you, at your most rebellious; not even Jereige if ogres set fire to the roof."

That was true enough, though the reason had always been that a woman was vulnerable while she was shaping. "So it's all been for secrets, ever and always. Women locking their workrooms to deceive their husbands—"

"Don't think of it as a betrayal, Jerlayne. It's an act of love and survival. It must be done, must be faced—like shaping iron. Do it and be done with it. Remember, you're my daughter. There's nothing you're not strong enough to face."

Jerlayne stayed where she was.

"Whatever are you afraid of, Jerlayne? Iron is deadly, yet you embraced it. You fought me every day you lived here, and

I swear to you, daughter, I am more dangerous than any *ten* mortals. Have you lost your courage?"

Jerlayne shook her head even as she loosened her grip on the chair. Elmeene was right: she was dangerous. She knew exactly which words would compel her daughter to walk through the mist.

Chapter 14

When the mist faded, Jerlayne and her mother were in a box—a sharp-cornered box lined with huge red-and-purple flowers such as bloomed nowhere in Fairie. The ghastly flowers were visible because of harsh light flowing from a fist-sized globe suspended from the ceiling. Everything smelled faintly rotten and the air itself was alive with shrill, angry sounds. Jerlayne freed her hand and covered her ears.

"Think of a wall filled with feathers and covered with moss," Elmeene suggested. "Imagine it shaped around you."

Desperate enough to obey, Jerlayne imagined feathers and moss. The din became bearable.

"What was it?" she asked, cautiously lowering her hands.

"They've learned to share their thoughts the same way they've learned to shape, with brute force and *science*. It wasn't always like this," Elmeene admitted, regret and something akin to worry. "When I came the first time, for Jermeen, there were places here that could pass for Fairie. Even when I came for you. But now . . . I listened silently while Jereige complained about how this realm had changed. I didn't think it could be the way he described, then I came myself and found it was even worse. I said to myself, No, I will not learn their ways again, not like this. I went home; but without us and our children, Fairie will die as surely as through blooddeath. I'd borne gnomes and dwarves since you left with Aulaudin; your father had begun to ask when our own house would be brightened again."

There was a heap of clothing in the center of the box which Jerlayne had beleatedly recognized as a closet. She understood that they would have to shed their Fairie garments; Aulaudin wore mortal-realm clothes most of the time. Jerlayne liked their bright silks and satins, but only as uncut fabric. A shiny red sleeve snaked out from the pile; nothing that Jerlayne

wanted to imagine against her skin, but she yanked it free
rather than look for something else.

Elmeene approved the selection; it was, she said, the gown
she'd worn the night she'd conceived Jerlayne's unborn
brother—though *gown* seemed overly generous for a tunic
which, when Jerlayne held up, stopped at her knees. She
looked for a skirt.

"Don't bother. You won't need it."

"I'll be cold."

"You won't wear it long enough to be cold."

Jerlanye's gut soured. She took a step backward, steadying
herself against the perfectly smooth walls. *Mate with the mortal men you find there,* Elmeene had said at sundown. Not joining, nor even trysting, but mating. Jerlayne thought of cats
yowling through a hot, summer night, mares hobbled before a
stallion was loosened in their paddock.

"I can't do this, Elmeene."

For a moment it seemed that Elmeene understood. She
brought mist into the closet and beckoned Jerlayne to enter it,
which Jerlayne gratefully did. But it was only another lesson: a
single stride back to the Stonewell workroom followed by:
"Now, you try. You remember what it looked like, felt like.
Shape yourself through the Veil, let that red cloth in your hands
be your guide."

As little as Jerlayne wanted to return to that particular
flower-walled room for that particularly unpleasant purpose,
the notion that she could part the Veil was irresistible. She
wrung the slick red cloth between her fists, thinking of the
closet, and, to her astonishment, there was a palpable attraction between the cloth in her hands and the garish wallflowers
vibrating in her mind's eye.

Suddenly there was mist. Jerlayne strode forward, with
Elmeene beside her, and they were back in the mortal realm
with its foul odors and piercing air.

"Now, close it behind you!"

"How?" Jerlayne asked, but the question came with its own
answer: let go of Fairie. The mist evaporated. She examined
the red cloth with a shaper's sense: no plant had grown it, no
animal had shed it; yet it was, on the whole, a very ordinary
piece of cloth. "Will anything from the mortal realm shape the
attraction?"

"Very nearly, if it's been made or handled by mortals. When

you're ready again, ask Aulaudin to bring you a present—some garment that he's seen mortal women wearing, that gives you warning of what to expect. I found *your* father with a shovel."

That brought a smile to Jerlayne's heart, her first in recent memory. "Almost as good as a fishing pole . . ."

Elmeene's voice, which had been all lessons and commands, softened. "There were good men to be found here."

"Where?" Jerlayne seized the implications. "You didn't find a good man when you wore this, this—*gown!*"

"We don't need good men. I could have looked further; you could, but for what end? All any of us need is a sire. If he's wretched, so much the better: there's no regret."

By which remark Jerlayne understood why some of the silk-wrapped portraits were more detailed than others and why the portrait of her unborn brother's father was a crude sketch on raw wood. Uncomforted by these insights, she asked herself if she truly needed an elfin child. Her sister, Maialene had chosen to live without daughters; perhaps it was possible to live without sons as well.

Elmeene interrupted. "Now, practice opening and closing until it's familiar. I've never needed to hurry home, but you should know how. Never doubt your ability to part the Veil. It's like iron: you must be precisely confident."

So Jerlayne practiced. She'd always been a quick study: three passages and she was confident of her confidence.

"There. I've learned it. That's enough for one night. I can learn the rest some other time."

Elmeene scowled. "I'm not taking that chance, Jerlayne. I'll not have you accusing me again *or* putting yourself in danger. I don't care if you mate with him or not—though you'll be more the fool than I can imagine if you don't—but we won't be done here until I've shown you how to find the mortal you need, and you *will* pay attention. This time we'll leave our Fairie clothes in the workroom. Like as not, no mortal would know the difference, but we abide the men's traditions while we're here and leave nothing of our own behind, not even for a moment."

Secrets everywhere, secrets and deception for the best of reasons: to keep Fairie safe from mortal greed. And for the worst: so their husbands might never where their sons and daughters came from. In her mother's shape-locked workroom, Jerlayne unlaced her gown and cast her linen shift on the floor beside it. She wriggled into the shiny red garment. It clung to her like something wet, like something alive.

"You'll do fine."

Jerlayne stopped tugging on the hem. She looked at her mother and couldn't restrain a gasp. Elmeene's garment was made from the same breathless cloth. It was black and longer, but it had no sleeves and very, very little across the bodice.

"We look like cats in heat," she grumbled; it was an ever-so-slightly more palatable image than hobbled mares. "This can't be done. It shames us, mother. It shames our husbands. It shames *me*."

"There is no other way," Elmeene insisted. "Let it be cats-in-heat, let it be whatever it needs to be, if you want an elfin child. Let down your hair and take off your shoes."

Jerlayne obeyed. In the end she knew she had to know, had to learn everything her mother was willing to teach, the same as it had been with iron. She'd survive—short of actually *mating* with a mortal tomcat. She'd make her own decisions later, when Elmeene wasn't watching. Still, a bitter complaint, "Barefoot, too?" slipped out as she shucked off her comfortable dwarf-made boots.

"No, my daughter. Mortal women wear shoes with their gowns, but you won't like them."

That, at least, was the simple truth. Back in the closet, Jerlayne winced as she crammed her feet into lethal-looking shoes and nearly fell when she tried to walk.

"Forget you're shod," Elmeene advised. "Stride on your toes, as if you're dancing barefoot."

"I'd rather *be* barefoot." But the advice was sound. Jerlayne followed her mother out of the closet and down a dark corridor without misadventure. "We'd better not have far to walk," she muttered as Elmeene touched the metal lock on another, more substantial door.

"Not far at all."

The flower-walled closet had been a place like nothing Jerlayne had ever imagined, but what she saw beyond the second door could have been lifted from any of the fragmentary mortal-realm memories that seeped from Aulaudin's memory when they joined. It was twilight in this place; Jerlayne remembered that time cycled differently in the mortal realm. The strange, sharp scents which Aulaudin hadn't shared with her were muted by a still-falling cold, autumn rain. She was grateful for that, but a drizzly rain in autumn was still cold wherever it fell. And she knew the mortal realm was crowded and cluttered with buildings that dwarfed the largest Fairie homestead. She wasn't, however, prepared for the *closeness* of them or the way everything reflected the bright, many-colored lights.

Though both Aulaudin and Maun had told Jerlayne about *cars,* she'd imagined them no larger than ponies. When the first hulking, glare-eyed device swished closer on the slick, black roadway beyond the stairway where she stood, Jerlayne yelped and closed her eyes. When she reopened them Elmeene was glowering.

"Don't do that! This realm is iron. You must pay attention to its every move."

Another *car* came by, larger than the first and open in back, like a dwarf's cart. Jerlayne clung to the railing beside her—it was tingling iron beneath its shiny, black skin—and forced herself to watch the reeking thing roll by.

"Don't stare, either. You'll attract the wrong sort of attention. They have their own guardians."

Jerlayne had never heard that before. She tried to imagine what sort of guardians mortals would need when they, themselves, were so numerous and unnerving, walking fast through the rain, darting among the *cars,* and sheltering in doorways. She tried to absorb everything without screaming, staring, or being overwhelmed by strangeness, and didn't see the man at the bottom of their stairway until after he'd begun gaping at her.

It wasn't merely that the mortal was *old*—Jerlayne had seen *old*—he was decrepit. There was no symmetry to his body: one shoulder slumped lower than the other, one leg was both rigid and withered. He leaned on a metal rod; gripped it in gnarled flesh scarcely recognizable as a hand. Disease and neglect hovered around him like a cloud fed by his exhaled breath.

Swine waiting for slaughter did not suffer so in Fairie—yet Jerlayne wasn't moved to shape away his pain: when their eyes met, she saw herself and Elmeene naked, worse than cats in heat.

"Begone!" Elmeene hissed and placed herself between them. "There is nothing here for you!"

The man stiffened as if struck, then shambled away.

"Conceal yourself!" Elmeene directed the same command-ing tone at Jerlayne.

"How? Dressed like this, how?" she replied, as angry as she was stunned and confused.

"Think of shadows. Imagine a drab, heavy cloak over your shoulders. Do *not* think of why we are here. This is not one of Jereige's streams where you toss out your hook and never worry about what it attracts. You must shape their thoughts. They're not Fairie-born. *We* can beguile them. *Women* can be-guile them when we need them."

Jerlayne thought of amorous cats again and insects that de-voured their mates while Elmeene easily got herself and her treacherous shoes down the four stone steps to the place where the mortal had stood gaping. Amber eyes stared up, waiting for Jerlayne to do the same. Step by unsteady step and hand by hand along the black-painted iron, Jerlayne made her palm-tingling way to Elmeene's side.

"Then why not beguile them with visions of sylphs and wear our own clothes? At least our own shoes!"

"Why? Why? Why? Is there only one thought in your head? I don't know why, Jerlayne. This is what I know: dress as they dress, however they dress, and beguile the ones who notice."

"They don't all notice?" Jerlayne asked, curiosity instantly getting the upper hand against anger.

She followed Elmeene along the hard, yet uneven path; hop-ing that, truly, no one did notice her mincing awkwardness. Her toes spasmed in their narrow, sloping shoes; she'd walked through discomfort and was approaching agony.

Elmeene pursed her lips. "This isn't Fairie—no scyldrin or goblins, but, no, they aren't all alike. You want one who *notices*."

"So, it's not just a find a mortal man and . . ." Jerlayne let her words trail off in distaste. "How easy is it to find one that *no-tices?* The one at the foot of the steps, did I want him? He *no-ticed,* but you sent him away. Did he understand you, or was that beguilement? Aulaudin says mortals don't always under-stand one another. He says he's had to learn another language: Spanish. What languages do you know? Where did you learn them?"

"Languages!" Elmeene sputtered. "I speak, they listen; they speak, I listen. I assure you, I know nothing about *languages*—" She stopped, thought a moment before adding slowly, "This last time, in this very place, the ones who *noticed* understood me, but I didn't always understand them." Elmeene was many difficult and head-strong things, but not stupid. "If there is another language, if they've become like goblins, speaking a language we can't understand—well, getting what we need will become a little more difficult, but we can still beguile them."

"Would you—I—*we* ever have to mate with the creature at the stair bottom?"

Elmeene grimaced. "Don't be ridiculous. His ballocks were as withered as the rest of him."

"You said *when I had questions.* I have questions: I'm trying to learn."

"You don't need questions to learn. Just pay attention. Do what you're told. You always want your own way, Jerlayne. There is no alternative here. The mortal realm isn't a place for questions."

"How else am I supposed to know which mortal is the right mortal? Which one is a right-for-elves mortal and not a withered, useless one? He *noticed.* You can't deny that he noticed us."

Elmeene spun around. In her strange clothes and lethal shoes, she might well have been a guardian. "If you'll be quiet . . . if you'll watch and listen instead of asking questions, I'll find you one of the right sort. You can take his measure as you would a lump of wood, clay, or metal, and answer all your questions yourself."

"I'm sorry."

"And I am, too. This place . . . no matter what I do, it gives me a headache. It didn't used to. It was a pleasant place once."

"I am sorry," Jerlayne apologized again. She developed a headache herself. The mortal realm was fascinating in a strange, unpleasant way. It hurled the answers to lifelong questions at her senses: the smells of food rotting in the gutters, the sounds and smells of machinery, the many-colored lights that were almost beautiful. There was so much to remember; in her heart Jerlayne couldn't imagine returning. The mortals she glimpsed, men and women alike, repelled her as she strove to keep up with her mother.

How many times had Elmeene parted the Veil in search of a mortal sire for her son? She'd said everything had changed; Elmeene hadn't worn lethal shoes to find a father for her. She couldn't have mastered the art of walking on tiny metal bits that hit the ground like hammers in a single visit.

Jerlayne walked on her toes, never letting the long, metal-tipped heels touch the ground. Her toes screamed. They fueled a quick-fire hatred of the realm she'd wondered about all her life. There was no way—no way at all—she'd mate with a mortal man; no way she'd let one touch her. She saw one standing in a doorway, staring, with fire in his hand and foul smoke gushing from his nose and mouth. It was like having bryony in her mind rather than her stomach.

Weak at the knees, Jerlayne could go no farther. "Wait! Elmeene . . . Mother. Please!"

Jerlayne steadied herself against one of the many pillars that grew instead of trees in this realm and marked the boundary between the cracked, gray stones where mortals walked and the smooth, black stone where the machines of metal and oil rolled by. Moistening her fingers from the rain-slicked metal, she pressed them against the hollow of her throat. The queasiness passed; Elmeene touched her arm.

"You'll learn to endure it. It's unpleasant, but it's not 'death,'" she said, as gently as she'd said anything since leaving the Stonewell workroom.

Staring into the night, Jerlayne lied with a nod of her head.

One of the cars veered toward them, blinding Jerlayne with its too-bright lights. Cold water splashed her bare legs as it came to a stop a few paces—if she were wearing comfortable shoes—ahead. Elmeene's hand tightened.

"Turn around. Start walking. I don't like the feel of that one."

Quite an admission from the Mistress of Stonewell, but Jerlayne was transfixed by the huge, black car as its shiny shell cracked, revealed a door and a glimpse into a dark, smoky interior. Elmeene tugged hard. Jerlayne had taken an awkward retreating step when another door opened, in the nearest building, at its bottom, like a cold-cellar below a kitchen. She heard fast-scuffling feet, saw a silhouette, and sensed—almost the way she sensed Aulaudin's moods—an anxiety as dense as her own.

Then there was a face: a man, perhaps a boy. She couldn't be sure, but could mortal age matter to an elf in her second century? The cold-cellar mortal was pale-skinned, pale-haired, and garbed in leather, but once their eyes met, Jerlayne lost interest in the rest of him. They were large and dark as any goblin's, though ringed with white. They pierced her like an iron sword.

Him, she would touch, if he *noticed,* and, by the way he was staring, he did *notice*. His hand rose to cover his mouth. She'd swear she could feel the warmth of his breath on her cheeks and whatever she saw, Jerlayne imagined him against her, their clothes melted away by the rain.

"You coming or not?" a gruff, masculine voice boomed from the car's depths. Jerlayne understood the words; they were rooted in a language men had already brought home to Fairie. "We don't have all night."

The pale mortal said something Jerlayne didn't hear, didn't understand: they were locked in something as potent as joining, but wilder and dangerous: cats in heat haunted her. The mortal grinned behind his hand; she grinned back before she could stop herself.

"Move your high-price ass in here!" the gruff mortal demanded.

The mortal obeyed, but his eyes didn't leave hers until he had to lower his head. The car sealed itself with a *bang!* then lurched forward with a liquid squeal and another spray of cold water. Elmeene cursed and stamped a metal-heeled foot.

"Him," Jerlayne whispered.

"Don't waste your time. He's the last place to go for what we need."

"You said I'd know. I took his measure, like iron." She felt her face grow warm and was grateful for the weird mortal-realm lights that made lies out of every color. "I could get my child from him."

"Never."

"He *noticed!* And his ballocks aren't withered, I'm sure of that." She amazed herself with her crudity.

"His ballocks won't do you a bit of good, Jerlayne. That one's a sport. He trysts with other men." Elmeene spoke with a bitterness that suggested personal experience and cautioned against further questions.

Jerlayne was in no mood for caution. "So do half the dwarves. You said beguile them, didn't you? Make them see what they want to see. A sylph or a boy, what's the difference when neither's real?"

"Don't be a reckless, stubborn fool. There are easier ways. *Safer* ways."

"But he *noticed*. You admit he noticed; you *noticed* that he noticed. He's the right kind of mortal. He's an elf-mortal who could give me my child?"

"Yes, Jerlayne. Yes. Yes, he noticed. Like ice in summer, he noticed and you'll wash and wash and never be clean of him or anyone like him. It's not good for them if they notice us. The ones who don't notice often savage the ones who do. You don't want a mortal who's been savaged, especially one who's been savaged and survived. I'll show you how to find the ones you can wash away."

Jerlayne had first thought Elmeene's bitterness was rooted in the young man, but it went deeper than that. She recalled her mother saying that she hadn't learned these secrets from Alseyne. "It must have been very hard for you. Hard, dangerous, and painful." Jerlayne tried to imagine her sister, Maialene, here, alone, for the first time.

"Mind your voice," Elmeene said, clearly wanting no sympathy. She glanced about nervously. "Don't fight me, not where we don't belong."

The night was watching; Jerlayne could feel what she couldn't see. "I'm sorry. I'll be quiet now. Show me what we came to see. Show me a mortal you'd pick for your child." She was already planning her return to this precise place: remembering the textures and angles as if they were a piece of iron. The pale-haired mortal had come out of the cellar; he'd return eventually. She wait for him; mate with him, get her child, and be gone. She wouldn't make her mother's mistakes, whatever they'd been.

Jerlayne learned as she had learned all her life once they entered a dimly lit, smoky room where thudding music shook the walls. She watched and listened from a chair almost as uncomfortable as her steep shoes. In short order she was able to distinguish suitable mortals from the other sort, and, among suitable mortals, those who could be safely forgotten and those whose faces would haunt a woman for centuries. She learned according to her mother's rules and by comparing them to the tidal attraction she'd felt toward the pale-haired man on the sidewalk.

She'd learned that word, sidewalk, and a hundred others that mortals used to describe themselves and their realm. It wasn't difficult: mortals spoke loudly though their mouths and with their thoughts, at least the minds of suitable mortals echoed loudly. No wonder her mother considered their spoken language an afterthought. With suitable mortals, words weren't necessary, though not all suitable mortals were men. Women, too, *noticed* Jerlayne and her mother sitting at their little table in their steep shoes and clinging dresses. They glowered. Elmeene glowered back.

Cats in heat.

"What about them?" Jerlayne whispered to her mother who was sipping a frothy, yet potent, drink that she'd beguiled from a mortal she called a *bartender*.

Elmeene scowled deeply. "What about who?"

"Them. The women. What if they . . ." The notion was clear in Jerlayne's mind, but difficult to say aloud. "What if a mortal woman who *noticed* beguiled a man." She meant an elf.

With a wrinkled nose, Elmeene appeared to understand. "What interest would a man have in one of them? What can they give a man? They can't join."

True enough, Jerlayne supposed. But men came regularly into the mortal realm and many of them, like her bachelor brothers— like Aulaudin for more than three hundred years—weren't joined. None of the *noticing* women were half as compelling as the pale-haired man had been; but, then, none of the men she'd seen in this, Elmeene's chosen place, were particularly interesting, either.

"Men have no need to be noticed," Elmeene continued, toying with her empty glass. "They don't need to display themselves. Women keep the secret so men can believe in their children. They don't suspect our secret and they never will."

Jerlayne stared at her scarcely diminished drink, ignoring the threat in her mother's words but not quite able to keep herself from wondering, aloud: "Suppose something terrible happened, right now. Suppose this roof crashed down and crushed us—"

"How do you sleep at night, daughter?" Elmeene answered on question with another. "If I were plagued with your notions, I think I should have run off to the forest long before I met Jereige."

Jerlayne sipped her drink: it was sweet and burning together and left a thick, bitter taste on her tongue, like cream mixed with copper. She'd rather take a few drops home to her workroom than drink another. She pushed it away and thought about running off to the forest.

Maialene had lived in the forest.

Maialene had known where to get elfin sons . . . had gotten Ombrio before or, more likely, *after* her unbeloved husband's death.

And what of Redis, whose body had never been found? What if a man had suspected the secret his wife and mother kept from him? What if, some night as he foraged, he caught the eye of a *noticing* mortal woman?

Jerlayne thought about her estrangement from Aulaudin and all the time he'd spent these last years beyond the Veil. No man could have spent all that time foraging. If he'd seen a pale-haired mortal and *he* had been *she* instead? Jerlayne suppressed a shiver.

A lithe, long-limbed man had come into the dark and smoky bar where Elmeene claimed to have found the father of her unborn son. He was dark-skinned, wood-colored, not blue like a goblin. Jerlayne knew before their eyes snagged, that he *noticed*.

She learned all she needed and nothing she wanted to know. It was time to put an end to this. With a sigh, she shoved her feet back into the step shoes and pushed her chair away from the table.

"Oh, yes, he'll do," Elmeene agreed softly—eagerly—as Jerlayne walked by.

He wouldn't, but Elmeene didn't have to know that: women could lie to one another without risk of exposure. Jerlayne held his attention, let him stare, and see her as he would dream of her. He strolled to their table and they talked while Elmeene pretended to be lost in other thoughts. Jerlayne almost didn't catch his name; he shaped his words differently than the others Jerlayne had overheard during the long night, and names were different than other words: they had no underlying meaning. she understood Tayo—his name might have been Tayo— because his thoughts were so lustily clear.

Conversation required more effort than she was willing to concede—except to say, as Elmeene had told her to say, "I hear there's a quieter room . . . in the back," and beguile him with her intentions.

Tayo seemed surprised by her boldness. For a moment he said nothing and Jerlayne feared she'd failed. Then his eyes brightened, narrowed. He suggested another place, his place.

Jerlayne, naturally, declined. Elmeene had said their thoughts could be shaped, so she tried, moving with instinct rather than insight, until he said, "Let's go," and eased away from the high table where they'd been sitting.

Jerlayne caught a glimpse of Elmeene's tight, satisfied smile before she started down the dark corridor, Tayo a half step behind her. His hands were on her as soon as they were both in shadow. It was cats in heat, nothing like joining, nothing she could, or would, enjoy.

Maybe men didn't either. Maybe Aulaudin had never met a *noticing* woman in his bachelor days or more recently. Maybe he didn't suspect and, without suspicion or need, as Elmeene insisted, had never been tempted.

They came to a locked door. Jerlayne tightened her hand on the knob and shaped it free. Elmeene had spoken of a room; Jerlayne had imagined something at least at large as the closet where they'd begun this misbegotten adventure. What she found on the far side was midnight dark; impossibly cramped; and treacherous with poles, buckets, and bottles. Taking a deep breath—her *suitable* mortal smelled heavily, improbably, of spices and metal—Jerlayne laid her palms against his temples.

It was not vastly different from numbing a mind to the agonies of an injury, although Jerlayne couldn't completely stifle the movements of his arms or keep him from pressing her against the wall. The steep shoes were nearly her undoing: She lost her balance and her concentration, regaining both as he hitched the too-short, too-tight red gown up over her hips.

Sometimes, when an injury was truly severe, it wasn't enough to numb a mind. For mercy's sake, women had to learn the paths of oblivion. Anything, once learned, could be put to different uses. Jerlayne shaped soft darkness and let it flow through her fingers. The mortal man sighed and sagged. Suddenly, she was holding up upright, grimly aware that loud noises would attract the worst sort of attention. She withdrew her oblivion and felt his awareness return.

"What are you?"

His mind seethed with notions that weren't her or Fairie. Jerlayne understood, as she'd never guessed, why mortals feared elves and why they wished to destroy Fairie. It was a dangerous game men and women played when they foraged in the mortal realm.

"What are you?" Tayo asked again, a clear accusation.

Jerlayne was frightened, but fear was a familiar enemy for a woman who shaped iron. She calmed herself in a heartbeat and took his measure as if he were a lump of metal.

"Satisfied," she replied, holding him much tighter than she wanted to. "Aren't you?" She shaped the ecstasies of joining, the peaks of passion, and beguiled him with them. He shuddered and wrested free.

"We're finished here," Jerlayne told him.

He stayed behind when she left the room. She didn't want to be near when he found the courage to leave. Without sitting, she told her mother. "It's done."

With a faint smile still playing on her lips, Elmeene led the way to the street where rain fell in earnest. By the way she was striding down the wet sidewalk, Elmeene intended to march back to the clothes closet—much farther than Jerlayne intended.

Opposite a dark-shadowed crevasse between two quiet building she announced, "I'm going home."

One step into the space, Jerlayne's steep shoes were deep in a cold, loathsome puddle. Even so, she found the Veil and opened it before Elmeene clattered back.

"Not here!" her mother protested as light began to flicker through the mist Jerlayne had summoned.

"Too late. I'm leaving . . . and never coming back!"

Jerlayne expected an argument; biting sarcasm at the very least. Instead, Elmeene entered the mist with her and then embraced her when the familiar shadows of Stonewell's workroom fell about them.

"It was hard. I know it was hard for you, Jerlayne, but you've got your child! An *elfin* child. It will all seem worthwhile come summer, when he's born."

Chapter 15

The problem with lies, Jerlayne decided, was their consequences, their endless consequences. When she stuck to the truth, the consequences, however unpleasant, were also the truth. But once she began telling lies, each lie produced an explosion of new lies, and with each lie the consequences became more difficult to predict. Having allowed her mother to believe she'd mated with Tayo, she'd had a heartbeat, perhaps ten, in which to create another lie in response to her mother's enthusiasm.

A hundred heartbeats weren't enough; a lifetime wouldn't have been enough. She simply said: "Thank you. Thank you for everything. It's all clear to me now."

In all her life, Jerlayne had never seen her mother so happy, so eager for friendship. They cast their tawdry mortal garments, steep shoes and all, into the hearth and shared a bowl of pudding while the slippery cloth burnt malodorously. Then, dressed in the soft, comfortable clothes of Fairie, they sipped tea while Elmeene talked of the mortal realm as it had been when she was young. Jerlayne yearned to be alone.

Dawn brightened before Jerlayne got her wish. Her old bedroom was long-since given over to different furniture and new purposes. She climbed the stairs to a guest room where her husband's clothes—but not her husband—were laid across a plumped-up bed. Aulaudin was with her father—Jereige— beyond the Veil. They departed together while she and Elmeene were also in the mortal realm, or so Elmeene had said when they'd boiled water for their tea.

If Jerlayne believed anything Elmeene said.

Fairie was limned in shades of gray when Jerlayne slipped out the guest room window and, after closing it carefully behind her, made her way across the roof, down the eaves, and into the deserted fields. There, amid the hayricks and unobserved by her mother, she parted the Veil.

She emerged in the damp, stinking crevasse where she'd last been. Rain had become fog. The glaring lights had softened into pleasant lamp-glow, and the street was nearly quiet. Jerlayne had realized the angular, unnatural patterns of the mortal realm would confuse her and had taken care to notice precise details, all of which were hidden by the fog. A wise woman—a wiser one, at least—would have returned to Fairie: there was nothing to say she couldn't come looking for her pale-haired mortal some other day.

Jerlayne didn't expect either her curiosity or her courage to last that long.

She struck out through the fog, matching what she saw against her remembered shapes until she came to the end of them: stone stars rising to a door that could be any door, wrought-iron railings whose tips and swirls were like the ones she remembered, and identical to ones she'd passed four times already. Her pale-haired and suitable mortal had appeared behind an iron gate, beneath stone stairs. There was a such a gate here, sealed with a cunning bolt devised from a variety of metals that might deter a mortal or a man, but was nothing to an elfin woman.

Jerlayne put her face between the iron bars that served for shutters in front of the flawless glass windows. Like wool or silk on a cold, dry winter night, stinging sparks jumped from the iron to her bare cheeks. Sparks of 'death, they brought tears of frustration, but she didn't flinch until she was certain the pale-haired mortal wasn't in the cellar.

She could, she thought, wait for him. Other mortals waited. She'd passed them, awake and asleep, as she'd searched through the fog. What was it that the second, faceless voice had said: we don't have all night?

Jerlayne didn't have a good instinct for the time difference between Fairie and this part of the mortal realm but she'd gone to bed at Fairie's dawn and thought she could wait until the mortal realm's dawn before anyone would look for her. There'd be an uproar at Stonewell if she were wrong, but Elmeene would keep her secret; she'd have no choice.

Jerlayne tucked down in the triangular space between a brick wall, an iron fence, and a row of huge, reeking buckets.

Noisy and foul as it was, there was a kind of peace within the mortal realm's fog. Her hiding spot became a suitable place for sorting through her memories since that warm afternoon when she'd watched her daughter dive into the millpond. Jerlayne shed the tears she'd never shed in Fairie when engine sounds and paired light beams pierced the pre-dawn fog.

Other cars had rolled by during her contemplation, some of them traveling just as slowly. But the hair on her arms and at the base of her neck hadn't risen in fright and anticipation. As she'd once hidden from her teasing brothers, she kept her head down, ready to bolt—ready to part the Veil, if necessary—as the car came to a quiet stop at the foot of the concrete stairs.

It spread its wing-like doors and disgorged the pale-haired mortal, who, standing with his hands braced against the car's top, one foot on the sidewalk and the other in the street, exchanged words Jerlayne couldn't hear over her heart's pounding. She heard him laugh: a surprisingly deep and bitter sound that made her reconsider his *suitability*. Still laughing, he backed away from the car, which sealed itself and sped off.

Mortal laughter stopped as soon as the car was gone. The pale-haired man spun on his toes—an elegant, practiced gesture that reminded Jerlayne of Goro moving about silently in his considerable armor. He took a stride toward the locked gate and paused. Pale hair became a pale, tense face with eyes that stared through the fog, directly into hers.

Jerlayne held very still. Her brothers had seldom found her hiding places and of all the tales told by men, none hinted that mortal eyes were keener than an elf's. He *couldn't* see her, no more than she could have seen him were their places reversed, yet he squinted and came closer. With all the care and control a shaping woman could command, Jerlayne sank closer to the ground.

She heard another step, almost certainly in her direction, and another after that.

"Who's hiding there?"

How did he know? Jerlayne demanded frantically of her conscience. What had she failed to do properly? Most important, how could she save herself when he couldn't be more than one long stride in front of the buckets and the Veil mist would surround him as well as her, if she could have parted it. Which, at that moment, she couldn't have.

"I know you're there."

His speaking voice had none of the harshness of his laughter. Jerlayne would have judged him tired, but friendly, and just a bit impatient, if she'd been willing to trust her judgment.

"I can't help you if I can't see you."

That remark jangled Jerlayne's understanding, but before she could make sense of it, he'd come closer. The buckets sighed as he leaned on them. Completely numbed between fear and recriminations, Jerlayne raised her head, reminding herself as she did that she wasn't defenseless, she could beguile him as she'd beguiled Tayo, and shape any threats out of his mind.

They studied each other—or the mortal scowled and studied Jerlayne. She used the beguiling tricks she'd first practiced on Tayo. She willed him away; he leaned closer. The now-burnt red dress shimmered in *her* mind's eye, so real she could feel it clinging to her skin.

"You," he said on a long, exhaled breath. "I saw you before. You were here when I left. You looked at me. You were unhappy; you didn't want to be here. What brought you back?" He retreated, plainly inviting Jerlayne to stand up and fully reveal herself, which she refused to do. "That can't be comfortable," he chided and held out a hand.

There was beguiling and there was being beguiled. Jerlayne sensed the difference and tried to imagine what Aulaudin would do from her position, or Jereige, or her brothers, or even Elmeene. It was futile: none of them would *be* in her position. There was no going backward, so she stood.

"What happened to you?" His scowl deepened and she didn't like the violent notions that seethed in his thoughts. "Your clothes. You're a mess. Your face—"

Belately Jerlayne recalled the iron-borne sparks.

"That other woman who was with you . . . were you both hurt?"

"I'm not hurt and she's gone. It's nothing for you to think about."

Jerlayne tried beguiling him again. Her efforts transformed a mistake into a disaster as he touched her arm. She threw up a mind-wall that blocked his awkward, yet powerful, attempt to share her thoughts. The wall was sufficient, but not at all reassuring. This mortal, this suitable and noticing mortal, not only had a spark of men's magic, and a bit of practice using it, but he'd challenged the exclusivity of joining as well!

It was a terrifying notion. Jerlayne didn't want to face its implications and might not have to, at least not until she was alone again. She'd learn to lie to her husband; Aulaudin had more than a spark of men's magic and much more than a bit of practice using it.

"There's nothing for you to think about," she informed him with all the intensity and respect she'd give Aulaudin, if he'd been the man she'd been trying to deceive. "My *friend* went home. I'm going to go home now."

The gambit seemed to have worked. He took a backward step. Jerlayne measured the distances between the mortal, the buckets, the stone stairs, and the empty sidewalk; asking herself if she had the strength to charge past him or the confidence to part the Veil.

"So you came back here, 'cuz you recognized me, and thought I could help?"

He radiated come-hither trust as surely as if he'd been her father—Jereige—on a stream bank with a fishing pole in his hands. The notion was not reassuring. No one, not the sages, not her parents, her brothers, nor Aulaudin had ever hinted that there were mortals who shared elfin talents. Had she learned something no other elf knew or—more likely—had she stumbled across another well-kept secret?

And whose secret was it?

A mortal-realm street wasn't the place for questions or answers, not with the pale-haired man coming closer and reaching for her arm again.

"I was foraging." Jerlayne dodged his hand and found herself flat against a solid, damp wall.

"Foraging?" The word came out different when he said it. "You're not from around here, are you?"

He was measuring her, as she'd measured the *suitable* men from the table beside Elmeene and there was no guessing what he learned. Deception seemed a safer course than outright lies . . . until he'd retreated another step and given Jerlayne the path to freedom she desperately needed.

"No, I'm not."

Instead of retreating, he scuffed forward. Jerlayne stiffened and he did likewise, convincing her that he was a hunter and she resembled his prey. Yet a voice at the back of her own stubborn mind insisted that his mortal was more than *suitable:* if she wanted an elfin child, she should stay where she was and let this man become the father.

"What are you foraging?" he asked and retreated.

A path appeared between them, but surely he knew what he'd created. Surely it was a hunter's trap.

He recast his question. "What did you hope to find?"

"Metal," she answered, which could have been the truth. "Iron and the white metal, aluminium."

"You don't sound English," he replied, a remark that befuddled her. "I've got cans inside. You take 'em to Raoul, two blocks over; he'll give you the best price around here. You can do better across the river, but you lose what you gain if you have to take the bus, and if you walk, you get hungry. Right?"

Jerlayne nodded, not knowing in the least what he was talking about. Elmeene had taught her that nodding was a generally wise gesture on both sides of the Veil. Her mortal finger-raked his pale hair and took another step backward. He shoved his hands into pants pockets: Jerlayne could get by him, maybe, if she tried.

She didn't.

Beyond doubt, she'd been beguiled.

"Hungry, maybe?"

"No." Jerlayne shook her head: the opposite of nodding here as in Fairie.

"I've got ice cream, rocky road. Sure you're not hungry?"

She shook her head again, vigorously: frozen cream and roadway dirt wasn't an appetizing combination. The notion of frozen cream by itself was enough to leave her feeling ill.

"I'll just get the cans, then. You can come inside and get warm . . . if you want."

He pulled bits of metal strung together from one pocket. Keys, she guessed after a heartbeat: small, sharp, pointed, and harder than anything she could shape. Keys meant for the lock in the gate behind him.

"Don't run away," he warned, sliding a key into the lock and turning it. "I'll come back."

He pulled the gate shut behind him, disappeared in the shadows beneath the stone stairs, used a key on another lock and opened another door, which he didn't pull shut. There was yet another lock, another door, then light glowed behind window-linen.

Empty sidewalk beckoned. Jerlayne could run, hide, and escape to Fairie; she *should* run, hide, and escape. But he'd told her not to run away. When Jerlayne was out from behind the buckets, she went to the iron gate. Her confidence had been improbably restored: she was calm and he was *suitable*. The risks could be no greater than they were every time she touched iron. The gate was shut tight and, having seen the sort of key that unlocked it, she knew the lock's secrets were beyond her. But not the gate itself. Jerlayne merely wrapped her hands around the iron grillwork and compressed it until the bolt pulled out of the frame.

The gate swung open silently on well-oiled hinges, just as had when the mortal had opened it. Jerlayne entered the shadows beneath the stone steps. She tried to reshape the gate behind her, but the iron was rust-riddled and some of it crumbled in her hands. When she'd done the best she could the gate appeared closed, but the lock was loose and the least touch would reveal the truth.

The door beneath the stairs was solid wood with a simple lock that yielded readily. Once opened, it revealed a corridor not unlike the one beyond Elmeene's closet. Another light-spilling door opened on the left. Jerlayne and the pale-haired mortal faced each other across its threshold. He dropped a clattering, loud armload of metal.

"How'd you get in?" he demanded, backtracking and no longer the subtle hunter: fear billowed around him.

"You said I could come inside and get warm."

"I—yeah. But . . . the gate?"

"It opened when I touched it." Jerlayne shrugged, using the truth to make a lie.

She sidestepped, remaining in the room while he rushed past. She heard a *clunk* as the gate swung wide and another afterward, as the tempered lock hit the ground. The pale-haired mortal swore an oath as she might have sworn if she'd come face to face with an ogre in the Sunrise pantry. He was definitely not the hunter she'd taken him for and, despite her mistakes, Jerlayne began to feel as she'd felt with Tayo: in command of an exhilarating situation.

When he returned, he showed her a shaped-out, rusted-out

section of the gate. "Shit—the whole thing's busted . . . rotten through. It'll have to be replaced." He shook his head repeatedly while, with practiced, yet anxious, moves he shut the inmost door and cranked three separate knobs that set three separate bolts. "I don't know where I'll get the money," he muttered, then sighed. "Yeah, I know. I know."

His pale face was bleak and bloodless when he turned around. Jerlayne wanted to tell him she'd lied about the gate and that, with a little time and a few of the metal cans still scattered across the floor she could shape it back as strong as it had been. She wasn't, however, quite that thoroughly and foolishly beguiled.

"Is *money* hard to forage?" she asked instead.

Another deep, bitter laugh began his reply: "Yeah, lately it is. I'm getting too old to do what I do best."

How could any mortal be too old for anything? Jerlayne wondered, then thought of the decrepit creature who'd first noticed her from the foot of the stairs. The pale mortal was surely much, much younger than that. She was about to ask his age when he volunteered his name: "As long as you're here, you can call me Cuz, 'cuz when I was a kid, I talked too much and asked too many questions. Who're you?"

"Jerlayne," she answered, seeing no harm in the truth. She couldn't judge whether Cuz talked too much, but he certainly talked fast and slurred his words together. She had to listen to the notions beneath his words to be sure of their meaning, and then, the notions that clung to Cuz were dark and slippery as soot. *Sharing* them filled her with an inexplicable sense of shame. "Why aren't you a *kid* anymore?"

Cuz gathered the metal bits. His hands shook; he dropped them as quickly as he grasped them. After a second attempt, he kicked the nearest ones at the wall and left the rest where they lay. "Why aren't I? I grew up, that's why. It took a long time, but it finally happened." He stared at the floor. "Never really was a kid. Never had the time. Maybe you'd understand—?" His head came up with one of his penetrating, measuring stares. "No, you wouldn't. Say your prayers and be glad."

Their eyes locked. It wasn't joining, not even a trysting invitation. It was more like hunger and without Elmeene or the sleek, black car to separate them, Jerlayne found herself taking a step closer.

"This is all wrong," Cuz protested. "This isn't me."

It wasn't Jerlayne, either. She had Aulaudin, back in Fairie, whom she loved more than life itself. For a moment her husband's face was in her mind's eye, then Aulaudin faded, turned pale, became Cuz: a *suitable* father for the elfin child she and Aulaudin desired.

Cats in heat.

What did the yowling she-cat care for her tom and what did the tom care for her? Or her kittens?

Nothing. Nothing at all.

And a man, a mortal man who would die young no matter when he died?

Jerlayne shaped her curiosity smaller, cooler. She'd guessed correctly at the start, if she hadn't moved swiftly—before she'd had a chance to think—she'd never have returned to the mortal realm. What she wanted *was* wrong, for both of them.

She looked everywhere except at Cuz, drawing the textures of his cellar into her memory. There were so many differences, so many objects whose names she didn't know, whose purposes she couldn't begin to guess. And similarities, too: a huge purple cushion, the twin to one on her workroom floor; a patterned carpet, not as fine as the one Aulaudin had lugged through the Veil, but otherwise the same colors, the same design; a mural painting, no better than her own efforts, of a sunset or, maybe, a sunrise.

Jerlayne was thinking about Sunrise when Cuz touched her arm. She jumped; he jumped. They confronted each other from opposite sides of the triple-locked room.

"I don't bring anyone here. I don't talk to them and I don't do *this,*" he said. "Not for myself. Not with women."

A sport then, as Elmeene claimed; a dwarf among mortals. Jerlayne caught notions through the faint joining of their thoughts: passion and helplessness combined with tangled cloth and crowded rooms. The disturbing images threatened to become more vivid. Jerlayne threw up a wall, as she'd thrown up a wall before around her own secrets, but outward-facing, to keep Cuz's secrets from invading her mind.

"I'll leave," she said, but Cuz blocked her path to the door.

He put his hand around her arm, not gently. "I don't want you to."

What was the harm? Jerlayne asked herself again. The answer was endless, and irresistible.

"Now," he whispered, echoing her own thoughts. "Now, before I think about it and change my mind."

The tension on Jerlayne's arm urged her toward an unmade bed: a small, rickety thing compared to the bed she and Aulaudin shared—*had* shared before Evoni. It was clean and vastly preferable to a dark and cluttered closet, even so, she hesitated long enough for Cuz to wrap himself around her and whisper: "I *know* what you're thinking."

They were suitable because they noticed; that was enough. And if Elmeene knew what they noticed—an admittedly unlikely notion—she'd forgotten to pass that tidbit along to her youngest daughter.

There was a subtle violence in the caressess and kisses that Cuz bestowed on Jerlayne's neck while she wrestled with her doubts and her conscience. Not at all like her husband; not entirely unpleasant, either, knowing, as she did, that she could shape Cuz numb or unconscious if she needed . . . or wanted to.

She didn't.

Not yet.

They tumbled onto the bed. Springs creaked in protest. Listening to the metal, Jerlayne sensed they'd both be safer and more comfortable on top of the great purple pillow, but she kept her reservations to herself. The bed held together until they were sated, which was long after Jerlayne had gotten what she'd needed from her tomcat.

Dawn seeped through the dingy, tattered curtains. It was late afternoon, at least, in Fairie and time to leave. Someone—Elmeene for a start—would be looking for her. Cuz's eyes were closed. His limbs were lax. She thought he was asleep, thought she could slip away silently, shape her way through his locks and out of his life. If he didn't see her leave, he might think she'd been a dream.

Cuz was a dreamer, she'd learned that much. What had passed between them wasn't joining but it was much more than a festival tryst. She knew him as she knew no other man, short of Aulaudin. Cuz's dreams protected him from his memories, to the extent that anything could. Elmeene was half right about Cuz: He didn't tryst with anyone. Jerlayne had learned a new notion in his bed, one she wouldn't soon forget:

rape. Rape was the soot that darkened his every thought and gesture.

Jerlayne had gotten what she'd wanted from the mortal realm and to balance what she'd taken, to ease the guilt already corroding her heart, she hoped to leave one small, bright dream behind.

She touched his arm; it tightened like an iron vise around her ribs.

"No." His hand wove through her hair, clutched the nape of her neck.

Jerlayne's hopes shattered. She knew what had to be done; the notions had come from him. She stroked his arm. Her fingers came to rest above the elbow, where nerves ran close to the surface. "I must."

"You were hiding behind the garbage! Your *friend* took your clothes and left you behind. You're gonna go back? Don't be a fucking ass. You're better off here."

"It's time to leave." She tried one last gentle time to loosen his grip. "I can't explain."

"Won't," Cuz countered as his grip tightened.

He was strong for a slight-boned, light-muscled man, but elves were stronger.

"Don't be a *fucking ass* yourself."

Cuz threw himself over her. There were teeth in his kisses, fingernails leading his caresses. Jerlayne shaped pain and let it flow from her. When Cuz went rigid from the shock, Jerlayne shoved him off the bed. While he whimpered on the floor, Jerlayne gathered her clothing and got dressed.

You don't want one who's been savaged and survived, Elmeene had said. *You'll wash and wash and never be clean of him.*

Elmeene, as usual, was right.

The knobbed locks on Cuz's door opened with a twist, no shaping required. Jerlayne turned the first and the second.

"Don't go. Don't leave. Don't leave me behind."

Cuz sat naked, cross-legged, with his back to the wall. Jerlayne left the third knob unturned.

"I can't stay."

"Because of me? What I did?"

Cuz writhed his arms together, waiting for the answer. Head down, he raked jagged fingernails along the tender skin inside his forearm. Jerlayne watched in morbid fascination; she'd never seen anyone hurt himself deliberately. The first pass raised red scratches. The second drew blood.

"Stop that!" she demanded when Cuz dug in for the third time.

He gave no sign that he heard her voice, just opened another set of shallow gashes along each forearm. In frustration that verged on anger, Jerlayne knelt in front of him and seized his wrists. Cuz struggled half-heartedly, carefully keeping his chin tucked against his breastbone and his face hidden. Jerlayne didn't need to see his face; she remembered not looking at her husband not long ago.

"It's not anything you did. You tried to hurt me; you shouldn't have done that, but I couldn't stay, can't stay, no matter what you did. This isn't . . ." She didn't want to lie. "You're right, Cuz, I'm not from this realm and I've got to go back where I belong."

"Some big, rich house up in the 'burbs." Cuz sat back with a jolt, slamming his head against the wall. It *had* to have hurt, but he merely closed his eyes and smiled through his tears. He had, at least, stopped ripping at his arms. "Rich clothes, rich cars, rich boyfriends . . . little rich girl with a dark secret. Why'd you come here, little rich girl? Were you and your friend slumming? Were you looking for something to pick up for a night and throw away in the morning?"

Jerlayne sat back on her heels, releasing his wrists. She shook her head, but Cuz's eyes were closed. He went on talking.

"Did you want something to make yourself feel better? Something to make you feel all rich again? That scene . . . it was all an act, wasn't it? Who put you up to it? You and your black-dress friend. Don't talk about *me* trying to hurt you!"

Another head-slam. When his eyes reopened, they were bright and feral.

"You *will* get hurt, you'll get yourself dead-hurt. You're careless, little rich girl. You don't ask the questions you should. You don't take *precautions*. Where do you think I've been? Waiting for *you* like some damned prince in a fairy tale? Everyone I knew ten years ago is dead; I should be, too. I didn't try to live, but I have. They tell me I got nothing, that I'm lucky. But I've never been lucky, not really, and you're a fucking fool."

As with so much of what Cuz said, though Jerlayne understood each word, the strung-together meaning escaped. But when Cuz struck his head a third time, she regrasped his hands, shaping a soft, numbing darkness, and let it flow. He clung to his desolation and pain, building a wall against the relief she offered. That surprised her, but Cuz was no match for a woman who could shape iron.

"Your hands . . . your hands are so warm. Oh, God—Oh, God, it's all true. Everything she said. You're one of them."

His face came up. Jerlayne saw the helpless dread she'd felt in that moment when she'd looked into the storm her daughter had become. For her, *them* had been a guardian. For Cuz . . . ? There was always warmth when a woman shaped. Suddenly, and as unwelcome as the notion of rape, there was another— better—explanation for her mother's reaction to the young man who lived not far from her mortal realm closet.

Jerlayne didn't, for even a heartbeat, think her mother was deliberately responsible for Cuz's many nightmares—at her worst, Elmeene was callous, not cruel—but callous was cruel enough.

"We're elves," Jerlayne said and took a breath, half-expecting Elmeene and all the sages to burst through the Veil around her. "We live in the realm called Fairie. We don't grow old, but we can die, and if we want to have children we have to come here, to this realm, the mortal realm."

Cuz didn't react so Jerlayne kept going. She told him about suitable men and joining, about Fairie and the Veil between the realms, about Sunrise and the scyldrin who were her children but who weren't elves, and about Evoni, Aulaudin, and Elmeene—

"My mother finally told me the truth, some of it. Elves keep secrets from each other, Cuz. We lie and we deceive and my mother is the elf of elves. She was the woman in the black dress. Right after she told me I had a mortal father, she brought me here—"

"What if you didn't?" Cuz asked without warning. "You come here. Your mother comes here. But what about the man you call your father? Or Aulaudin? What was *he* doing nine-and-a-half months before I got born?"

Cuz's question cut close to the bone. Jerlayne stammered, "I don't know. My mother said—" before his laugh shamed her into silence.

"Your mother, the elf of elves, she lies and deceives, but you don't. Oh, no, *you're* gonna tell your Aulaudin what you've done with me, aren't you? *My* mother did. She told everyone. Not quite the immaculate conception—just a demon lover who stuck it to her one night when she was stoned and promised to come back. Funny thing—he never did. He had warm hands, that's what my mother said to me, oh God, did she tell me about him and his hands. She waited for him, when she was straight. The rest of the time—most of the time—she hit drugs . . . or me. When she needed money she took me to visit my uncle. *That* was fucking fun."

Fueled by rage and memory, the notions seething around Cuz were enough to make Jerlayne nauseous. She released his wrists and pressed a hand over her mouth.

"You feel that? You see *that* when I think about it? When I remember? Nothing like that in Fairyland?" Cuz sneered and, with his strength restored, took advantage of his freedom to stand and walk across the room. He rifled through a cardboard box. "She died. OD'd. Heroin and alcohol. Finally got enough in her blood to kill her. I called the cops, then I called my uncle." Cuz found what he was looking for: a handful of ragged paper which he held close as he sat down again. "I figured it out later. A human—I guess that's *mortal* to you— needs about two-hundred-and-eighty days to get himself born. I was born on November twenty-ninth and she OD'd on the twenty-third of February: that's two-hundred-and-seventy-nine days' difference. I looked it up. It took her ten fucking years to figure out her demon wasn't coming back and when she did, she killed herself. Figure your Aulaudin was busy all that time?"

He held out the ragged papers. It was Elmeene in the Stonewell workroom again, with pictures of fathers wrapped in silk. Jerlayne folded her hands into fists and refused to touch them, refused to look at them when Cuz turned them over, one by one, on the floor between them.

"Tell me!" he demanded. "*Lie* to me! She was an artist, when she could hold a pen. She drew this picture every goddamn day, now you look at them and you tell me about him. You *owe* me that much, Jerlayne-the-elf. You got what *you* wanted and you *owe me!*"

Snared on the battered remnants of her honor, Jerlayne

glanced down and nearly laughed with relief before she caught herself. What Cuz's mother had drawn wasn't Aulaudin or Jereige or any elf. What she'd drawn was a dark-skinned, dark-toothed, dark-eyed goblin.

Chapter 16

"Go ahead," Cuz snarled. "Go ahead and laugh. She was drunk and stoned and she fucked a blue-skinned demon. She was out of her head. It couldn't've happened. Everybody knows there aren't any blue-skinned demons, just like everyone knows that there aren't no elves or fairy tales—'cept, I just fucked an elf, didn't I? An' everyone knows that lightning never strikes the same place."

His voice was thick, though it was impossible for Jerlayne to guess whether Cuz was on the verge of tears or rage. Perhaps it didn't matter. Drunk, drugged, or stoned—whatever that meant—Cuz's mother had drawn a goblin.

Elmeene had drawn portraits of mortal men who *noticed*, as Cuz had *noticed*.

"I am an elf," Jerlayne said, more to calm the questions storming her own thoughts than to answer Cuz.

"So, what's that make my father?"

"A goblin."

"Don't *lie* to me! Damn you, don't lie to me!"

Like a wolf, Cuz lunged at Jerlayne from a naked crouch. She staggered backward, shaping pain without thought. He lost consciousness instantly. His body went limp and collapsed. His head hit the floor with an awful sound and there were two perfectly formed handprints glowing on his pale chest.

Sputtering apologies and shame, Jerlayne knelt quickly beside him. Cuz hadn't stopped breathing and his pulse, though rapid, was stronger than hers at that moment. She hadn't come close to killing him, which was troubling relief: surely, if Cuz weren't a goblin's son, he'd be dead. He'd said something about others dying, about how he should have died with them. Jerlayne hadn't grasped his meaning then and couldn't resurrect it when he began to awaken in her arms.

Cuz struggled and fell into spasms. Jerlayne hugged him tighter. He was a child in her mind, a child like Evoni—exactly like Evoni—who might explode and destroy her. But when Cuz opened his eyes again, he knew himself and her precisely. His lips were open against hers before she had the wit to recoil. The taste of him filled her mouth.

Sex was the last thing Jerlayne wanted, but Cuz radiated sex as both weapon and armor. Unless she wanted to batter him again with pain, the most Jerlayne could do was counter his rape-stained dreams with what she hoped was a cleaner passion. Cats in heat, they swept the goblin drawings aside and trysted on the bare-wood floor.

It was no more comfortable than the rickety bed. Jerlayne nursed scrapes and bruises when they were finished and noticed, with horror, that the sun no longer cast shadows through the curtained windows. She thought it must be nearly sunset in Fairie and resolutely refused to think further than that.

"You have to leave," Cuz said flatly, a tone short of accusation.

Jerlayne said nothing. Perhaps he'd plucked the notion from her mind. She didn't know how or why he could get inside her thoughts. Maybe any man—elf, mortal, or goblin—could have; since she'd first joined with Aulaudin, she'd trysted with no one else. Maybe it had something to do with the portraits scattered across the floor. She didn't want to know.

There was no resistance when she stood and shook out her clothes. If he'd accepted that she did have to leave, she'd let her questions go unanswered. Would that she could have left them unasked.

She stepped into her skirt and look about for her tunic.

"Take me with you?"

If Cuz had asked when or if she'd return to him, Jerlayne was ready to answer honestly that she wouldn't, ever. But he'd asked a question she'd never imagined possible. It left her speechless.

"If it's one of those 'you can't ever come back' deals, that's not a problem. If I'm too old to be a changeling or whatever, I'd be a slave—*your* slave, in bed and all. I'm good at that."

He wasn't. Sweaty, feral sex had limited appeal and though Cuz could batter his imagination against hers, he had no aptitude for the shared illusions and passions of joining. She knew; she'd tried. And as for slavery, though Jerlayne understood the word, the folk of Fairie, not even the ogres or the goblins, had no use for slaves. Changelings, on the other hand, were a mystery and would remain so.

She shook her head slowly.

"Honest—I got no one here who'll notice I'm gone, 'cept maybe to say good riddance, and it's not like I got plans, or anything. Take me with you. Anywhere's got to be better than here."

There were no mortals in Fairie, except for animals and ogres. If a mortal blundered into the mist-shrouded borderlands the guardians did their duty. But to bring a mortal directly through the Veil and into Fairie's heart? Jerlayne didn't know if it could be done.

"I'm beggin'. Say *something* for God's sake."

"I don't know—"

"You don't know one helluva lot, Jerlayne. It's kinda hard to believe you're some high-and-mighty elf. How come you get to be immortal? No, wait—you don't know that, either, do you?"

Cuz had a knack for shaming Jerlayne the way she tried, and usually failed, to shame her mother. He made himself difficult to refuse, despite the problems—the outright catastrophes—she suspected she was inviting into her life, and into Fairie, when she said: "I'll try. Get dressed. Get what you need—not more than you can carry."

"Got nothin' worth carrying," Cuz countered as he pulled on the same clothes he'd worn before.

Parting the Veil proved harder this time, not because she was in Cuz's sparcely furnished room, but because he was watching her, radiating notions of a fairyland that had nothing to do with the Fairie she knew.

Though he'd grown sharply impatient while she composed herself, Cuz fell silent when mist began to flow in a lazy spiral from the ceiling to the floor.

"I'll go first," she told him.

"And leave me here."

"No, for your sake. I don't know what might happen."

"Yeah. Right. Whatever."

"I've never done this before."

"And you call yourself an elf."

Jerlayne didn't understand, though he'd clearly insulted her. She compromised, saying she'd go backward into the mist, then reach back for him. But part-way in, part-way out of the

Veil mist proved to be an uncomfortable and instinctively dangerous place to be. "Now!" she commanded. "Take my hands. Don't let go!"

Sparks flew between them, when Cuz seized Jerlayne's wrists. He grimaced as Jerlayne pulled him in up to his elbows. The sparks congealed into lace-work threads of blue and white fire, as hot as half-shaped iron, but he'd survived worse when she'd flooded him with pain. She kept pulling. A finger's breadth before the mist would have touched his chin, Cuz wrested free.

"I'm not ready to die," he said retreating until his back was against the wall.

Jerlayne strode forward. The Veil sealed behind her.

"You weren't dying; I could feel your heart. You've been hurt worse and been more frightened.

"Yeah, but those times, they just happened, I wasn't responsible. Maybe if you did that thing to me, that thing you did before, when everything just faded out."

"I could try," Jerlayne agreed. She touched his arms and let oblivion flow. Again, he wrested away. Jerlayne let him go.

"Can't do it." he said sadly. "Can't give up control. What if I closed my eyes and never woke up again? Shit. I don't care whether I live or die, but I can't make the choice. I always thought I could. Maybe it's good to know I can't. Maybe. 'Snot your fault." He shook his head several times and chafed his hands along the sleeves now covering his scratched forearms. "Give me something to remember?"

Perhaps he was a changeling. Jerlayne had never met anyone whose moods shifted so suddenly or unpredictably. Perhaps it was part of being mortal. She wasn't wearing jewelry: Aulaudin's gifts were all in boxes at Sunrise. And her garments were Fairie-made; Jerlayne had broken so many rules already it seemed absurd to balk at leaving Fairie-stuff in the mortal realm, but she did. Then she though of the hair she'd wheedled from Aulaudin so long ago and spotted one of the sharp-edged metal bits. She quickly-braided several long strands together and hacked them off. Holding the fresh-cut ends between her thumb and forefinger, Jerlayne shaped a bead to keep them together.

"This is the best I can do."

Cuz took her gift gingerly. "Magic?"

Jerlayne hesitated, then nodded. There wasn't time for an explanation or a lie. She had to get home.

"Real magic . . . shit, it's more than I asked for . . . I could take this to a lab, or someplace, they'd scope it out and I'd be rich—"

She didn't know precisely what *lab* meant, but his thoughts were of *science,* and *science* was a word to strike terror in any elf. Jerlayne wrung her hands, wanting to reclaim her gift, but not quite daring to.

"Hey, just kidding! Nobody gets rich donating a body to science . . . an' I wouldn't give this up anyway. Not for a bazillion." And, as if to demonstrate his honor, Cuz made a tight bracelet of her hair around his wrist.

Jerlayne had never heard of a *bazillion,* but it must have been quite valuable. She reopened the Veil.

"You're really immortal? You're gonna live forever?"

She let the Veil go with a sigh. "A long time, I hope."

Cuz rummaged frantically through the box where he'd found his mother's goblin drawings. He came up with a single piece of paper. "Take this. I want you to remember me, too."

As if she'd be able to forget him. He wouldn't wash away. Another victory for Elmeene.

The paper was much-folded and soft as suede. Jerlayne opened it carefully into an odd, dangling shape. Her fingers confirmed what her eyes had guessed: it was old and so near decay that a single drop of water could be its doom, but neither her eye nor her fingers could make sense of the tight, regular black lines drawn across both sides. A gray, blurry splotch covered the center of one side. Another moment of examination and she realized that the splotch was a crude picture of a grinning, dark-haired boy.

"It was a contest," Cuz explained. " 'Summer in the City.' Every kid in the second grade had to draw a picture. Mine won. It was everywhere, on all the buses and trains. I met the mayor an' stuff, and did stuff all summer long. Then it was over. There was a trophy, too; don't know what happened to it. Hocked off, probably; if it was worth anything. Everybody forgot, 'cept me. An' now you. You'll make me immortal."

The blurry boy's hair was dark; Cuz's hair was strikingly pale. Nothing else was clear enough for comparison, but elves were raised to cherish inexplicable gifts.

"I'll treasure it," she assured him, carefully recreating each fold.

"You didn't read it."

Reading. Reading and writing. Aulaudin mentioned both words occasionally. Mortals shared their knowledge through writing and she'd wondered if writing wouldn't be useful for women. She'd thought the paper might be covered with writing, but it was covered with reading instead. The mortal realm was a confusing place.

"I'll treasure it," she repeated, then surprised herself by adding, "but I'd remember you better if I had a lock of your hair."

"So you can find me again, if I'm not here when you come back?"

She wasn't coming back, not in this lifetime, maybe not ever. But if she did come back for another child, she'd collect another lock of hair. It would be better than a portrait. "Don't wait for me. Don't look for me."

"Yeah, I shoulda figured that," Cuz grumbled, taking up the sharp-edged metal and attacking his hair. "A day in the real world is, what? A month or a year in fairyland. That's your immortality, isn't it. You live like dog years."

His words' meaning, if there was any, started in contradictions and wound up far beyond Jerlayne's imagination. She took the finger-length lock he offered her and shaped another bead at the cut end.

"Fuck," Cuz mused aloud. "You can't read and you don't really understand half of what I say. Maybe it's all tricks, but maybe you really *are* an elf."

"Elf is a mortal word. We borrowed it; stole it. All our words come from here. Only the goblins have their own words."

"His people?" Cuz pointed at the drawings on the floor.

The question reined in Jerlayne's wandering thoughts. It hadn't happened, couldn't have happened. Goblins couldn't part the Veil and no woman would be attracted, mortal or not . . . She remembered Goro, that first winter at Sunrise, fighting the ogres. Until yesterday, she'd believed that women couldn't part the Veil. Her world had become riddled with holes that couldn't be filled on Cuz's side of the Veil.

"I must go home," she told him and caught the Veil firmly with her mind. Mist furled around her.

"Yeah, you go home," Cuz replied, changeable and bitter again. "When you see him, you tell him he can go fuck himself."

Jerlayne let the mist pour between then until it was fog that swallowed her half-hearted *goodbye*. Heartbeats later, she hugged herself in the Fairie moonlight and filled her lungs with Fairie air.

"I got what I went for."

Though it was too soon, even for a shaping woman, to know for certain that she'd conceived a child. The moon, rising among countless stars, was at its last quarter. Jerlayne couldn't be certain of her pregnancy until it came full.

"It will be all right. I've always known from the first moment. I've never been wrong."

Hearing her own foolishness, Jerlayne began to shiver. A clear autumn night had sucked the warmth from the ground and she'd left her warm cloak on the peg beside the guestroom rood. She stuffed Cuz's hair and folded paper into the hem of her sleeve then, rewrapping her arms in her light shawl, Jerlayne set out for home—for Stonewell, where Elmeene would be waiting.

Praying mortal gods that her path be clear of goblins and ogres alike Jerlayne forgot that there might be others roaming the forest.

"Jerlayne! Beloved!"

Aulaudin's voice nailed Jerlayne's feet to the ground. A golden spot of lantern light bobbed through the trees.

"Here," she called, worrying what she would say and how she would keep her secrets, now that she possessed so very many.

Not that Aulaudin needed to hear her voice to guide him. His mind tugged at hers, growing stronger with each breath. So much had happened, so much that Jerlayne couldn't share with her husband. She stopped again, dizzy and disoriented, and steadied herself with a hand on the bark of the nearest tree. Jerlayne's eyes were closed and she was shaping each breath as Aulaudin's footfalls grew nearer and finally ceased.

"Beloved? Beloved, I couldn't find you."

He was close, but not touching close. And why would he touch her, considering how she'd treated him these last— Jerlanye's head came up as she measured the years of empty memories—thirty-odd years. In shame, she didn't turn toward his voice, nor open her eyes.

"My mind was empty," Aulaudin continued. "I feared you were lost forever, then suddenly, I knew you were near—"

Your mind was empty because I'd parted the Veil, Jerlayne thought, behind the strongest, thickest walls she could imagine. *I was in the mortal realm, mating with the mortal man who has given us, I hope, a son.* It was very simple, and she couldn't say a word or think a shared thought, not even to reassure him.

"Beloved, will you . . . can you walk back to Stonewell with me? The night will get very cold before dawn comes."

Jerlayne opened her eyes then and saw him differently, now that she'd seen the portrait of her own father and looked upon mortals with her own eyes. There was none of the edge about him as there was about Cuz, no sense of danger or deception at all. Only a warm concern and a lesser hope that she would not turn away from him again. She had a sense of waking up after a long night of turbulent dreams and embraced her husband, but gently, without jostling the lantern he carried at the end of a pole.

"I'm all right. I needed to be alone—" There were lies now that could never be completely disentangled even from the most heartfelt truth. "I've found myself again. I love you, Aulaudin; I love you forever."

Aulaudin said nothing, thought nothing that he shared, but his free arm tightened around her and she heard him sigh before they kissed. They separated once, so he could prop the lantern pole against a tree, and again when they were both breathless.

"Are you ready to go back?" Aulaudin asked.

Jerlayne thought of Sunrise. Her last images of it, storm-wracked and ruined were truly the scattered visions of a nightmare. "Yes. Yes, there's so much to do . . . and undo. But we have time, Aulaudin." She touched his cheek and turned his face toward her. "We have time, don't we? We can repair what was damaged?"

"If we think of it as damage, we'll never repair it. If we think of it as something new, then we can build something new around it, but before we go back to Sunrise, we have to go back to Stonewell. Do you remember, beloved, I brought you to Stonewell? Elmeene has half the homestead poised to clear this forest if I don't return before dawn."

Secure within her walls of lies and deception, Jerlayne

didn't believe that any trees were in danger, but, on reflection, it was a miracle that Elmeene hadn't come looking for her in the mortal realm. Or perhaps the miracle was that her mother hadn't found her and Cuz.

Aulaudin's arms tightened around her again. "Your father is with her, keeping her calm. There's nothing to fret about."

She'd thought about Aulaudin, about Elmeene, about Cuz, and about Sunrise which was, almost, a thought about Evoni. There was a place for them all within her fast-growing tangle of lies. But a thought of Jereige, grappling with worries that had nothing to do with the truth, nearly brought the whole brittle structure down. A woman couldn't shape a child out of nothing, but a single uncompromising notion could guarantee that one never took root within her womb.

"You're shivering," Aulaudin observed, shedding a mortal-realm coat, with all its machine-made seams and buttons, and draping it around her. "You'll be warmer if we start walking."

It wasn't the cold, of course, that fueled Jerlayne's shivering. Another lie, another deception. For sanity's sake, she'd have to stop counting. She took up the lantern pole and led the way while Aulaudin walked silently beside her. The lights of Stonewell were farther away then Jerlayne remembered and in a different direction. She thought she'd come back to the same grove she'd left, but she hadn't. If Aulaudin hadn't been there to find her, she'd have walked herself lost.

Thinking about that made the lantern quake as if it hung in a gale. Aulaudin took the pole and all was calm again.

"We will have time, beloved."

Shaking her head, Jerlayne disagreed: "There's so much I can't tell you. So much I have to hide . . . *want* to hide. There shouldn't be secrets between us."

Mindful of the lantern pole, Aulaudin slid his arm around her waist. "There have to be secrets."

"There shouldn't be."

Aulaudin laughed. His arm dropped from her waist. "Two realms are filled with things that shouldn't be, but most of them are necessary and the rest can be ignored . . . should be ignored."

The first words to form in Jerlayne's mind, *That sounds like something a mortal man might say,* were unspeakable and, fortunately, she caught them before they escaped, but she failed to catch her second thought: "Men have nothing to hide. You don't have to keep secrets!"

Her husband's smile vanished. "Do you think Vigilance is the end of secrets?"

Jerlayne nodded, not knowing where his inquiry was headed, but confident it couldn't be worse than anything she might say.

"Sharing has to be taught and learned. It's always easier to defend a notion than to share it."

"I wasn't taught. Our wedding day, when we first joined—" Despite all the intervening years Jerlayne blushed.

Aulaudin's face softened. "Another secret? You don't want me to know how you felt, what you remember? I promise you: your secrets are safe, yours especially."

Curiosity, as always, proved irresistible. "Why mine, *especially?*"

"Because you're fierce, beloved. All that shaping iron, I guess, though you were fierce when I first met you, years before Elmeene taught you how to shape iron—unless that's one of your secrets: your mother didn't teach you anything you hadn't already taught yourself."

Jerlayne blushed deeper and Aulaudin spread his arms, nearly losing the lantern off the pole.

"A guess," he insisted. "A good guess, perhaps: I know you well, beloved, but I can't go where I'm not wanted. No man can. It can't be done."

"Can't be or shouldn't be? Is that something your father—" Jerlayne caught for a heartbeat on the realization that Maun wasn't Aulaudin's father, no more than Jereige was hers. "Is that something Maun told you?"

"Do you mean, was I ever bull-angry enough to try to take what wasn't being shared?" Aulaudin cocked his head and grinned. "No, but Boraudin was once and the next thing he knew, he was out cold on one side of the room and I wasn't doing much better on the other. It *can't* be done. Oh, maybe I can catch something if someone's sleeping or careless, but nothing, ever, that's defended. Not that I didn't try. When I was ten, he was fifteen—those are five large years. The only advantages I had were unfair."

Aulaudin rarely spoke of his older brother and never, to Jerlayne's memory, so openly. Suddenly, it was as if Boraudin was there, shimmering in the moonlight just behind Aulaudin's shoulder. Sharing her husband's deepest memories, Jerlayne couldn't keep from thinking that Aglaidia must have been dangerously beguiled by their father.

"That one time, when he struck back—scared us both, but not half so much as the thought of what Maun would do if he found out. Not our first secret, but our best-kept one." Aulaudin's grin and Boraudin's ghost faded altogether. "He never shared it; now I've told you."

"Shared it."

"No, not shared it. I don't share it, even with myself."

That, Jerlayne thought, was a lie, but she saw, for the first time, that there were necessary secrets, necessary lies.

Where Boraudin's ghost had hovered, two bright lights appeared moving quickly from the Stonewell walls.

"Elmeene's coming," she warned.

"We'd better hurry." Aulaudin grasped Jerlayne's hand, squeezed it. "For luck."

"My mother's very fierce," Jerlayne agreed with a laugh, matching her husband's strides.

"Unpredictable, like Maun, but not nearly as fierce as you, beloved."

They met where the inner gardens of flowers, herbs, and vegetables abutted the meadows and harvested fields. Jereige carried one of the lantern poles. Arhon in his full armor carried the other. Jerlayne hadn't seen him since her marriage, hadn't seen any goblin since she'd met Cuz. She found herself looking for similarities.

Elmeene embraced Aulaudin first. "You found our wanderer." She kissed him chastely on the cheek.

Then when all the other gracious pleasantries had been exchanged, Elmeene hugged Jerlayne tight and whispered in her ear: "I need you in the workroom. Without delay."

Foolishly, Jerlayne thought there was some other problem, a different emergency, which required the skills of two elfin women. Elmeene shattered that illusion when she closed the workroom door, threw the bolt, and shaped it solid.

"You went back." An accusation rather than a question.

Elmeene pointed at the wooden chair where she wanted Jerlayne to sit. Jerlayne chose a different, more comfortable chair, between the hearth and door.

"Always pushing," Elmeene complained. She dragged her own chair closer. "Nearly two centuries on your own and you haven't changed a whit: You treat me as if I were some blood-spilling ogre! I'm your mother, Jerlayne: give me some respect, if you can't give me your love."

"Stop judging me."

Elmeene opened her mouth and shut it again. "You went back," she repeated calmly. "You might at least have told me before you left. I had no idea. I was worried sick . . . and then Jereige and Aulaudin returned. You left me with nothing to tell them! You're so quick, Jerlayne, with some things, but with others, you can't see past your own nose. What could I tell them? I said you'd wandered off in your sleep. I wailed and tore my hair and behaved as a woman with no sense at all."

"I'm sorry you had to lie. I didn't think about Jereige and Aulaudin. I should have; I won't make that mistake again . . . if I ever go back again."

"Don't give me that. You'll go back again and again, and not just for a child! You can't resist danger, Jerlayne, whether it's iron or the mortal realm."

"Stop judging me! You don't know me, Elmeene. You just admitted it: sometimes I'm quick, sometimes I'm slow. I never guessed the little secret we've been keeping since the beginning of Fairie, but you thought I had and you were wrong. Whatever you think about me, it's probably wrong."

Elmeene smoothed her skirt, worried the tassles on the arm of her chair and knotted her hands together before conceding, "Very well, I'm wrong. You won't go back again, but you went back. And, since I don't know what you may have guessed for yourself, I must ask you: did you seek out another mortal?"

"I did—the pale one." Jerlayne watched for any tell-tale reaction in her mother's eyes. There was none. "You remember him, don't you? On the steps, getting into the car. The one you called a sport who wouldn't tryst with women. You were wrong about that, too."

"I am wrong about a great many things, Jerlayne. I do my best; it's all I can do. I did my best when I sought your father." Elmeene untangled her hands and stared at the hearth.

There was an invitation in that last remark: an offer to speak about that unknown, long-dead man. Another time, if another time came when she weren't quite so angry, Jerlayne might take that invitation, but for now she ignored it. "All right: why do you need me here? To tell me I'd made you lie?" She stood up, strode toward the shape-locked door.

"Don't join with your husband tonight, Jerlayne. Don't join with him at all until after you're certain. I meant to tell you last night, but I forgot. When I came to your room, that's when I realized you'd gone back."

"Why not join with him?" Jerlayne asked.

"It's bad enough you sought two men. You won't know the father, of course. What was that phrase you used: cats in heat? But they were both mortal. Any child you conceive will grow to be an elf, but join with Aulaudin tonight and you're asking for trouble. Unless that's what you want: complete uncertainty, again. I couldn't face that, but I'm wrong about so many things these days."

Jerlayne had figured it out for herself while Elmeene was talking. And though it was tempting to answer sarcasm with sarcasm, the truth was that she would have joined with her husband if it hadn't been so cold in the forest and joining with him was precisely what she'd had on her mind when she'd grasped workroom bolt.

"As a matter of truth," Jerlayne said, unable to resist all temptation, "there was only one mortal, so I will know precisely who my child's father is, thanks to your warning. I hadn't thought about waiting . . . there's never been a reason. You're right about this much: I want an elfin child—a son for Aulaudin—and I want to be certain."

"A son's wise. You're not ready for a daughter."

Jerlayne let that remark pass. She'd done well enough with Evoni, to a point, but any child of Cuz, and her, would do better with Aulaudin for a teacher. The bolt warmed in her hand and hissed as she undid her mother's shaping.

"We will come to Sunrise this time, all of us: your father and I, Aglaidia and Maun."

"It's not necessary."

"Aglaidia's worried about her son; I can't say as I blame her. She and I will vouch for your judgment. Maun and your father will reassure Aulaudin."

"How?" Jerlayne asked, walking away from the door. "It's supposed to be the blood-bond between fathers and sons, but there are no fathers and sons. How can their sharing happen?"

Elmeene shrugged. "Iron shouldn't shape itself in our hands, but it does. Men believe they are more sensitive to their close-kin, so they are. Sooner ask why it's cold in winter or why the rain is wet. It is; it always is. Think how much more difficult our lives would be if it weren't, and be grateful."

Jerlayne envied her mother's blithe and brutal outlook. "I'll try."

"Try to come up with a reason for all of us to come to Sunrise next summer; that, too, will make lives less difficult."

Jerlayne nodded. She cracked the door, thinking of summer and a baby son with pale, pale hair and dark eyes. Then, as it so often did, a contrary thought crossed her mine and she shut the door again.

"One last question?"

"A *last* question. Not from you."

"For tonight. Do goblins part the Veil?"

"Goblins! By stars, of course not. You know that."

"I know what I've been told, but so much of what I thought I knew has changed in the last few days, I thought, maybe that had changed, too."

"You *are* tired. Goblins are and have always been completely dependent on us. They have no magic. They don't shape, they don't share, and they don't part the Veil. And just as well! If they could forage their own metals, then where would we be? No, it works for the best: Men forage, we shape, and goblins protect us in exchange for a bit of both."

"Good," Jerlayne said, opening the door. "It's good that some things don't change."

Chapter 17

"Will it ever get better?" Ombrio asked.

Aulaudin gave his nephew a backward glance. They rode, single-file with a pack-horse between them and a second pack-horse behind Ombrio, from a new resting place back to Sunrise. Three months had passed since he and Jerlayne had returned from Stonewell, at peace with each other and ready for rebuilding their homestead. In many ways, it was already better, much better, for him.

Twenty scyldrin, dwarves and gnomes together, had trekked up from Wavehome, Fairie's only other sea coast homestead. They'd declared their intention to work the sea as others worked the land. The Wavehomers had balked a bit when they'd learned that Sunrise's siren made her home on an island easily visible from the shore—Wavehome's guardian had never been seen and was heard only in the thickest fogs, the wildest storms—but they'd decided to stay. Their first boat was cobbled together with timber salvaged from the destruction and now, a scant season after Evoni's transformation, they were hoisting a great bucket of sea creatures up from the stony beach each day.

Aulaudin, who'd developed a fondness for seafood in the mortal realm centuries ago, had no complaints with the new menu, but he was, perhaps, the only Sunrise elf or scyld who didn't. Still, it wasn't fish-head chowder that had hollowed Ombrio's cheeks or put bruises beneath his eyes.

After sharing the alarm that had sent Aglaun looking for Aulaudin, Ombrio, in a self-confessed panic, had parted the Veil and made himself small in the mortal realm. He'd had no notion of the destruction he'd escaped until he'd tried to return and found himself in every man's nightmare: all his resting places had changed. He couldn't find his way home.

Worse, no one had been looking for him. At Sunrise, Aulaudin had been preoccupied with Jerlayne. Maialene's cottage had vanished completely in the siren's sea-shaping. Not a piece of lumber, a branch, or a root washed up on the shore to memoralize it and, when the young man's brothers, Medis and Relene—not to mention the four men sages—said that Ombrio and his mother had vanished with their cottage, Aulaudin had perceived no reason to question their judgement.

Then, one sunset about a month ago, Cendranis, a man from the west, a man Aulaudin scarcely knew, pierced his Vigilance thoughts, sharing the notion of a guilt-ridden, emaciated Ombrio living like an ogre in a mortal-realm cave.

«He calls your name,» Cendranis had shared. «He tells me he won't return to Fairie unless you're the man who comes for him.»

Aulaudin had reached the cave before midnight. He'd brought Ombrio home to the much-transformed Sunrise and with Jerlayne's help had tried to ease the young man's despair. If there was guilt, Aulaudin had insisted, it all fell on his shoulders for having assumed the worst and never once questioning his assumptions.

Ombrio ate the food Jerlayne prepared because he was starving, he bathed because he itched from filth, and he slept because he was exhausted; but he didn't believe a word Aulaudin said. Even now the notions seeping into Aulaudin's mind were grief for the mother and scyldrin Ombrio hadn't rescued; and aching for a woman whose face he tried not to remember and whose name he wouldn't allow himself to mention, certainly not to her father.

For Ombrio, nothing had gotten better.

«You don't have to stay here,» Aulaudin shared, one mind to another.

He'd shaped the notion as carefully as any woman shaped her twenty-link chain. It had all the complexity it needed, including a hint of regret that he, Aulaudin, didn't—couldn't— mourn Evoni as Ombrio mourned her. Even so, Aulaudin instantly sensed emptiness at his back as Ombrio retreated behind walls that were as strong as they were unsubtle.

Aulaudin reined the horse he rode and the pack animal he led off the trail. Ombrio called his to a halt. They were no closer together than a moment earlier, but Aulaudin could face his companion without getting a stiff neck.

"Spit it out, Ombrio," Aulaudin urged using a phrase he'd picked up on the mortal middens and which seemed appropriate for the situation: if the younger man pressed his lips together any harder, he'd swallow them.

Ombrio adjusted his grasp on the reins of the horse he rode and the one he led. Aulaudin suffered images of careening blindly down the trail, not caring whether he lived or died. They hadn't come from his imagination. He held out his hand.

"Leave the pack horse with me, if that's your choice. Sunrise needs that flour."

That was the simple truth. This winter, Sunrise dodged famine. They'd gotten the harvest in before Evoni reshaped the land. They had grain, but no mill for grinding it. Olleta's pond hadn't refilled before the ground froze and most likely wouldn't refill in the spring: every stream within a half mile of the great house had gone dry as the watertable sank. The dwarves were talking about building a new mill, a windmill that would take advantage of the winds that blew off the water. They talked about deeper wells, too, or a system of pumps and pipes that would bring water from where it flowed naturally to where it was needed. In the meantime, the gnomes hauled barrels of water every day and Aulaudin was foraging food as he hadn't foraged it in over a century.

He waggled his fingers impatiently. "One or the other, Ombrio: talk or go."

Ombrio walked his horses close enough to pass the pack animals' rein to Aulaudin, but changed his mind before his hand moved. "How can you be so calm?" he demanded. "I loved your daughter. I dreamt of her and a homestead like Sunrise. I hated you because you were cruel to her; I hated myself because I stayed here not just because she was here but because you were here and I wanted to learn the men's trade from you. You're a better forager than my brothers are because they learned from Redis. Then she rose up. I saw her face in the clouds. She looked down at me—I think she knew me; I know she didn't care. She would have killed me the same as she killed everyone else."

While Ombrio paused for breath, Aulaudin said, "Evoni would have killed me, too, if I'd been here. She nearly killed her mother." He remembered the hours after his return, as Evoni's storms raged and Jerlayne lay nearly lifeless on their bed. He remembered defacing his daughter's portraits and ripping apart his wife's tapestries. There wasn't a calm fiber in his being, then or now, but he saw nothing to be gained by reliving that rage and for Ombrio's sake, Aulaudin forced himself to *appear* calm.

"Nearly killed her mother!" Ombrio mimicked Aulaudin sarcastically. "Viljuen's tears, Aulaudin, Evoni did kill *my* mother! You were right all along. Evoni wasn't an elf! Her mother and I, we made fools of ourselves loving Evoni and she nearly killed us all when, if we'd listened to you, she would have gone off like the Wavehome siren did and never harmed anyone!"

"We don't know that."

"*I* do! I know Evoni stayed here and destroyed everything because of Jerlayne and me, and you—you just start picking up the pieces. You never blink, you never say anything. Why won't *you* spit it out? Get angry with me! Tell me the truth. Tell me that it's my fault! Viljuen's tears, every time you start to say something I think: *This is it. This is it. It's going to hurt, but then it's going to be over, too.* But then it's just more of you being calm, and I think: *I haven't suffered enough. He wants me to suffer more. He wants me to think about what I did and how many died because of it.* I can't take it any longer, Aulaudin. Punish me, hurt me, do what you want, but do it *now.*"

It had been a long time since Aulaudin had opened his mind completely to another man. Too long. He couldn't lower all the barriers, and not merely because four horses demanded attention. He and Boraudin had lived so close together that they'd known just about everything there was to know about each other, with or without sharing. Aulaudin wouldn't have that kind of familiarity in his life again, not with Jerlayne, certainly not with young Ombrio who needed the privacy, and freedom, to learn from his own experiences.

Ombrio had no such reluctance. He seemed not so much to accept Aulaudin's invitation as to explode with pent-up doubt and grief. Aulaudin learned more about life in Maialene's vanished cottage than he wanted to know: Jerlayne's sister had surely been iron-touched. And whatever Evoni had become, whatever Aulaudin had seen in her storm-gray eyes from the beginning, she'd never given Ombrio any reason to doubt her affection until the very end.

Aulaudin shared a memory he'd thought he'd keep hidden forever: the muddy banks of the emptied millpond where Evoni's battered, mutilated body lay, arms reaching toward the grass, discarded by the siren she'd become.

«She was trying to escape, trying to get away from the water that was changing her?» the young man sighed.

Aulaudin guided his horse closer and put his arm around Ombrio's shoulder, letting his nephew sob on his shoulder as his memories rearranged themselves into an easier shape. In the end, Aulaudin was half-persuaded himself. Sharing was like that, sometimes, and no matter what any man remembered or shared, no one would ever know the truth. His siren daughter sang endlessly, but her songs had no words.

"Let's go home," he suggested when Ombrio's grief subsided.

Ombrio composed himself quickly. Aulaudin was careful not to notice Ombrio blotting his face with his sleeve. When dry, Ombrio's cheeks seemed less hollow, his eyes less shadowed but Aulaudin, remembering Tatterfall, knew the healing had only begun. They rode in silence a while before Ombrio said: "I need to talk to Jerlayne."

Aulaudin nodded. A man with six centuries behind him could sometimes glimpse notions in a younger man's thoughts before they were fully formed. "She needs to talk to you. I'll see to the horses when we get back and to what we've foraged." He seen his daughter as someone else had seen her, and he was glad of that, but insight hadn't changed him and he wanted no part of the conversation his wife and nephew needed to have.

The barn had been damaged in Evoni's rising. One wall remained open to the weather. But the homestead's livestock had suffered worse winters. Scyldrin had seen him coming and were waiting for him; gnomes to take possession of the sacks of flour, dwarves for everything else except a coil of pale green rope.

"You won't be keeping that snake-stuff here, will you?" Funder, one of the dwarves who'd come to Sunrise with Olleta, complained. "The cows'll throw their calves early if they see it." Funder and Grezel had stayed at Sunrise, but the sylph's death weighed heavily on them—her death and all the changes that came with it.

Aulaudin slung the odd-colored rope over one shoulder. It was stiff and would never grow supple, and it had a slippery, greasy texture that was quite unlike a snake's skin. As far as he knew, cattle, pigs, goats, and horses were blind to color, but scyldrin weren't. They were blind to the Veil, though, and had no notion how the differences between the mortal realm and Fairie had grown during their lifetimes. Mostly, Aulaudin foraged to protect their blindness, bringing home only those objects that mortal themselves had taken to calling "natural."

"It's for the 'Homers," he explained, and grimaced as he caught himself lumping the newcomers together. Sunrise needed those sea-wise scyldrin if it was going to thrive again. The scyldrin who'd known Sunrise when it was all hills and forests were going to have to swallow the newcomers as part of their community, if he and Jerlayne were to preside over a peaceful homestead.

So far, the swallowing hadn't happened. Funder walked away without another word.

Aulaudin left the barn in a bleak mood. A gusty, frigid wind blew off the bluffs. He buttoned the top button of his mortal-realm jacket, raised its collar to his ears, and stuffed his hands into his foraging gloves which were proof against iron but less effective against cold.

A man who lived in Fairie—a gnome or dwarf or even a goblin—expected snow when the weather turned cold enough to make his eyes sting when he blinked or freeze his nose with every breath. But Aulaudin, who'd spent a good part of his life beyond the Veil, knew that no place was colder or less likely to be blanketed by snow than the oceanfront on a clear day, two weeks past midwinter.

Glancing to his right as he walked the path that would take him to the beach, Aulaudin saw activity in the great house kitchen and in the solar where Jerlayne passed winter afternoons mending clothes. Last winter his wife and daughter had stitched by themselves. This winter, Jerlayne usually had the company of gnomes and dwarves. Today, framed by heavy draperies, she stood at the largest window with Ombrio beside her. Eyes met through glass and cold; Aulaudin shrank into his jacket and kept walking.

A few strides further and there was music in gusty wind, haunting wordless music, beautiful in its own wild way. Within days of Evoni's rise, the five sages had come to Sunrise to witness her transformation. They still came. There were only two sirens guarding Fairie. The other, whose rise had led to the founding of Wavehome, was never seen, seldom heard. Fairie's dragons weren't seen either, nor its griffins. Fairie's guardians dwelt within the mists or on the far side of them, where no sane man or woman was fool enough wander.

But Evoni's island was on Fairie's side of the mists. When no scyld would row their boat across the channel that first time, the sages had rowed themselves. Returning, the swarthy sage Ertinel had said the siren appeared much like her former self, albeit some twenty feet tall . . . or long: her legs had fused in the transformation and on land she dragged herself across the rocks with her arms. In the water, the siren—Aulaudin's daughter—was all grace and speed, circling the boat twice for each beat of the oars.

«Did she recognize you?» Aulaudin had asked Gudwal when he returned from that first visit.

«She recognized us well enough to leave us alive, but more than that?» the elder had smiled and shrugged. «Yet, I think you need not worry about the sea storms that plague Wavehome. She guards the border she's made, but I had a sense that island is still very much attached to this homestead.»

When the light was right, which it was, and if he strained his eyes, which he did, Aulaudin could see the siren on her island. Her hair, the same color as his, was unmistakable against the nearly black rocks. He could see a small boat, too, moving among a score of bright colored specks floating on the waves: traps for the crabs and lobsters that swarmed in what had become, by default, Sunrise Bay. The crabs were as big as his two palms together, the lobsters as long as his forearm.

"Where did they come from?" he and Jerlayne had asked their sage guests. Aulaudin could believe—almost—that the bay was part of the same sea that crashed at Wavehome and that Wavehome fish could have swum beneath the mists, but shellfish weren't school fish and it took more than three months to grow a lobster to any recognizable size.

"They were always here. The sea was always here," Ertinel had replied.

"Trees grew here, apple trees and wild trees. The air smelled of trees, not salt."

"Then the sea was not here. The siren made it and all the crawling creatures within it as she transformed. You're young, still, both of you; you live in the present. It doesn't matter what you believe about the past or the future."

There was no point in arguing with a sage: the longer a man argued with them, the more confused he got. Aulaudin supposed it didn't matter where or how the huge lobsters had grown. Thrown into a pot of boiling water, they made a horrid racket then turned into a bright red delicacy that brought Sunrisers and Wavehomers together for a feast. When lobsters were piled on the table even the goblins came down from their new camp in the hills above the great house.

Alone by the foundation stone—now moved to the bluff between the great house and the sea—Aulaudin recalled the first lobster feast two months ago and smiled at the memory. Goro had come to the trestle with his sword drawn, expecting trouble from his supper. Aulaudin was still grinning when footsteps crunched the dry grass behind him.

"It's not right."

Aulaudin recognized the mournful voice of Petrin. He wasn't surprised that the gnome had come looking for him; he'd been home for almost a half-hour; sometimes Petrin caught him before he'd dismounted. The gnome had lost everything he cherished when Evoni rose: his wife had been crushed by a tree, his cottage had been damaged beyond repair, and the hills where his apple trees had once blossomed had become shifting ocean waves. His daughter—Aulaudin's daughter, too—had been one of those who left. They'd heard she'd gone to Stonybrook, an old, established homestead in the western heartland. Aulaudin had suggested Petrin follow her, but shaking and sobbing, Petrin had insisted that Sunrise was his home, his only home until fate reunited him with his beloved Banda.

In his darker moments, Aulaudin hoped for a speedy reunion. If it had been possible, Petrin would have drained the ocean and mounded up new hills for his orchards. As that wasn't possible, Petrin had become the voice for everyone who ached from change.

"What's not right?" Aulaudin asked, although he had a pretty good idea. The way Petrin stared at the green rope, it might well have been a serpent.

"It's that boat they're working on. The big one. They mean to sail it, too, and use the nets."

As long as there had been scyldrin living on elfin homesteads, gnomes had been responsible for food while dwarves took care of just about everything else. The tradition wasn't written in stone; nothing much in Fairie was *written* and as far as enforcement went, well, Petrin had come to Aulaudin with his complaint.

"A sailboat's not a rowboat," he said, reminding himself of Maun; his father had never been a patient tutor. "The Wavehomers say it takes two sets of hands to catch fish from a sailboat, one set to handle the boat, the other for the nets and lines. At Wavehome, a dwarf and a gnome work together."

Petrin pruned his face; they'd come closer to the heart of his problem. "This is *Sunrise.* We meet at the crossings, but we keep to our own paths. We do what suits us and we don't go meddle in another scyld's life."

"Are the Wavehome scyldrin meddling?"

Despite his question, Aulaudin thought the opposite was nearer the root of Petrin's sourness. It was unusual for so many scyldrin from one homestead to trek together to another. The dwarves and gnomes from Wavehome got all the friendship they needed from each other; they weren't lonely and didn't look for friends among the Sunrise scyldrin, perhaps because they weren't mourning or grieving. They didn't see, as Petrin saw, a rippling, blue-gray emptiness where his orchards had grown.

When the gnome wouldn't answer his question, Aulaudin cleared his throat and tried again. "Petrin, what do you want? Do you want to sail one of their boats? I think it would be a good idea to pair Sunrise scyldrin with the Wavehomers. Would you go first?"

"Sail a boat? Fling a net? I want my trees! I asked for saplings and you brought back rope! What next, Aulaudin: a smoke-engine?"

The snarled question caught Aulaudin off guard. "No, not at all." But the Wavehomers had repeatedly asked for an engine, for emergencies, for when a storm blew the winds out of the wrong quarter, when sails were no help, and oars wouldn't be enough. At Wavehome, Helvert had foraged five engines for Wavehome and kept one of his sons foraging nothing but gaso-

ine. Aulaudin had said no, without giving any of his reasons
that ranged from an aversion to engines that went deeper than
anything Petrin could imagine to a lack of any sons to help
him. But he had forgotten Petrin's saplings . . . again.

"When will I get my orchard?"

"When there's a place to plant it!"

"And when will that be?"

"I don't know!" Aulaudin shot back, ashamed that he was
losing his temper, yet unwilling to restrain it. "It's not like the
first time, when it was just you and Banda, Jerlayne and me,
and a handful of dwarves. We could turn the animals loose and
feed ourselves. There are over three-score scyldrin here at
Sunrise. That's less than we had . . . less than we had *before,*
but everyone still needs to eat, Petrin. We didn't get our grain
milled. We lost half our flocks. We're going to have to trade to
survive. Trade. Petrin, do you understand *trade?*"

Men did, elfin men. Theirs wasn't a formal trade with coins
and paper, such as mortals practiced, but spending so much
time beyond Fairie, men had learned how to mark their favors
with one another. Thanks to thirty years' leaping at any excuse
to avoid Sunrise, Aulaudin owed no one; he'd called in favors
since autumn. As he waited for Petrin, Aulaudin was deciding
whom he'd ask, not for fruit-tree saplings—he could forage
those, if he remembered—but for dwarves to clear the land to
plant them.

"Trade," Petrin declared, "means I give you something I
don't need and you give me something I do. I used to trade my
fruits and ciders."

"And you'll trade them again, Petrin, I promise you. We'll
clear land for your orchards, a day's walk from the sea, if that's
what it takes, but not this year or next. This year what Sunrise
has is the sea and what we can trade is fish—"

"And salt," Petrin interrupted. "That sea's put salt in our water. The rain's salted. The dew's salted. Put a pot on to boil and
what you've got left is *salt.* Scrape it out and trade it away before it rots all the metal. Every morning Jerlayne's got to scour
salt from the skillets."

Aulaudin's breath caught in his throat. As the water table
had dropped, their wells had gone brackish. The air itself
smelled and tasted of salt when the wind was right. He didn't
mind, but he wasn't bound to Sunrise every day. "We could,"

he said as possibilities opened in his mind's eye. "We could trade salt. There's not a homestead that wouldn't rather trade salt rather than bargain with goblins or forage it from mortals. We could bring water up from the sea and boil it. Or build fires on the beach, that would be easier."

"Easier still: let the sun and the wind do the work; dig pits in the sand, they'll fill with the tides—"

"And empty with them, too."

"Then line the pits with clay, the way we do with the grain pits. Keep rats out; keep the sea in 'til it's turned to salt."

Aulaudin shook his head. "It's a good idea, but it won't work: line a pit where the tide can fill it, and the tide'll keep it filled."

"Then we'll cover our pits," Petrin countered, as grim as ever, but facing the future, instead of the past. "It can be done, Aulaudin. We can trade salt. You just said it: no one has enough salt. We should grow salt."

The gnome had a point. Not even Maun at his most cantankerous turned his back on extra hives of goblin salt. It was the first thing Aulaudin had learned to forage and he never passed up an opportunity to bring some home. Salt was *that* necessary, that precious, and nearly impossible to find in Fairie.

A prickly thought slipped into Aulaudin's enthusiasm: Wavehome didn't trade salt. No insult to the gnome, but if Petrin could imagine making salt from seawater, surely some Wavehome scyld had had the same notion years ago. Or perhaps not: Wavehome had been founded after the southern mists had revealed the salt sea. They'd had fields and fishing boats from their beginning, unlike Sunrise which, at the moment, didn't have enough of either.

Mortals said necessity was the mother of invention. At Wavehome, as at every other Fairie homestead, tradition kept necessity at bay and very little was ever invented.

Aulaudin clapped Petrin on the shoulder, a familiarity he'd learned from his father and used freely among dwarves, but only rarely among gnomes. "We'll trade salt, Petrin, and you can be in charge of the pits, but there'll be boats, too. There's no avoiding that: we cannot *eat* salt and we'll have little enough meat until we've rebuilt our stock."

The gnome's face soured.

"*Before* is gone, Petrin. Whether you stay at Sunrise or go somewhere else, there's only tomorrow. You'll have your saplings, you'll have salt, too, and fish."

Petrin warned, "There'll be trouble, Aulaudin."

And Aulaudin nodded his agreement. "We'll be as prepared as we can be, and we'll deal with it as best we can when it comes."

The gnome walked away without farewell. Privately, Aulaudin didn't think the trouble would come from the fish. Petrin's idea was sound, though, and heading down the exposed and rickety wooden scaffold that served as a stairway between the bluff and the beach, he planned to ask the Wavehomers if their homestead had ever harvested salt from the sea.

The 'Homers were hard at work on the ribs of their boat-to-be. They were a scruffy lot; from a distance they could pass for the derelicts Aulaudin so carefully avoided on the mortal middens. Their faces were seamed from sunlight and shiny with the grease they slathered against the cold, gritty wind. He wished for another pair of gloves and a heavier coat, though the 'Homers had a better answer: oiled-wool sweaters, worn long and in layers. The sweaters were proof against wind and sea spray; they moved with a man, not against him, but left him smelling like a rain-drenched sheep. Aulaudin supposed he'd succumb eventually and ask Jerlayne to knit him a few, but not before the dwarves got the homestead's water-house repaired so he could wash away the stench.

A gnome spotted him and left the others to meet him.

"Beautiful!" she said of the rope when he handed it to her. "Just what we wanted. Now, we need caulking compound."

"Tar?"

"There's better than tar to be found in the mortal realm. We'll show you."

Aulaudin kept his rueful thoughts about necessity and invention to himself as the gnome led him toward the wooden skeleton that was the ribs and keel of Sunrise's first fishing boat. He didn't ask questions; Mergatta would tell more than he needed or wished to know before he escaped the beach. The Wavehomers lived for their boats.

If Petrin had wanted to know anything about boats or the sea, all he needed to do was offer Mergatta a mug of his cider, then sit back and listen.

If ignorance had been Petrin's problem.

Work stopped when Aulaudin and Mergatta got close. It had been three days, after all, since he'd last visited the beach and much, in Wavehomer minds, had been accomplished. He was master of Sunrise and they insisted he inspect their work before he praised it. With his knees on the damp sand, Aulaudin got a lesson in how ribs were properly set on the keel and how the siding planks were pegged to the ribs.

"The pegs must be greenwood," Drast, a dwarf with hair as red as Aulaudin's, explained proudly. "They'll never come out."

Aulaudin admired everything they showed him then, carefully casual, asked about salt. "I suppose you'll be digging salt pits here on the beach once you've begun to bring in fish."

The Wavehomers stared at him.

"Whether you get it from a lake or a sea," Aulaudin explained himself, using the argument he'd thought up on the stairs, "fish reeks after a day. What do you do plan to do with it, if you don't salt it out?"

The 'Homers exchanged questioning glances before Mergatta cleared her throat. "We'll smoke it, Aulaudin. There's wood enough nearby." She noticed Aulaudin's puzzled frown. "Unless you've got a stash of charcoal somewhere we haven't seen. We smoked our catch at Wavehome, downwind, of course. Salt wouldn't do, Aulaudin. The mistress traded for six hives, and that wasn't near enough. Word is, your wife trades for less, and you're all alone, no sons to help you forage. If it stays cold and bitter like this, we'll air dry some, too."

Aulaudin had his answers, but disdaining comments about Jerlayne's salt bargain and their lack of sons cut deep. At moments like this, he could understand exactly how Petrin felt. So he asked, for Petrin and himself, "What about the sea? It's full of salt!"

The cocked their heads again. "It's easier to smoke fish than be boiling water day in and out," Mergatta said patiently. "Less wood, less time, less smoke, less smell, less all around. You'll see, Aulaudin. Drast, here, and I—we've been doing this since we were younger than you."

The gnome didn't add, *So be quiet, young elf, and let the scyldrin do as they know how to do.* Scyldrin needed elves, but not to tell them what to do around a homestead. She seemed genuinely surprised when Aulaudin continued the discussion.

"If there were pits—clay-lined pits—dug in the beach sand, then the sea tide could fill them."

"You'd still get a stench enough to shrivel your toenails where you stood," Drast interrupted. The other Wavehomers went back to their work. "The smoke won't be so bad and the smell . . . you'll get used to it. Too bad you lost your orchards. Fruitwood makes a sweeter charcoal."

Drast turned away. Aulaudin moved quickly to block his escape.

"I didn't propose putting fish in the pits, Drast. I think there's enough salt in the sea to preserve all the fish you can haul into this boat; the trick is to separate it from the water."

"Waste of time."

"Why? Was salt harvesting tried at Wavehome?"

The dwarf shrugged. "Maybe. Maybe before my time."

"What happened?"

Another shrug. "We've done well enough with smoking our catch, air-drying a bit in the winter. It's the way we've always done it; that makes it the safest way, the best way. No cause to be different here."

Drast sidestepped and Aulaudin let him go. Aulaudin was walking back to the wooden steps thinking about changes, scyldrin, and the salt in the sea, when he spotted a dark finger pointing out of the sand far down the beach, where the sand should have been bare. Curious, he walked past the steps. Halfway there he knew it was a goblin, wrapped in his black cloak and staring at Evoni's island. A bit closer, he recognized Goro. The thoughts stewing in his head nudged him toward suspicion and hostility: if they could harvest salt from the sea, goblins would only have their protection for bargaining.

He didn't imagine they'd like that.

"Looking for something, Goro?" he called when he was certain he could be heard over the wind.

Clearly startled, the goblin spun around, drawing his sword. Aulaudin was equal parts pleased with himself and disturbed: elves didn't usually take their protectors by surprise.

Goro re-sheathed his weapon. "Inspiration, Aulaudin, and you."

It was Aulaudin's turn for surprise: goblins bargained with women, they didn't usually pay attention to men. He and Goro hadn't exchanged a word since Goro walked away from the great house door.

"You're lucky to find me here. I don't come down to the beach except to inspect the boat. What did you want me for?"

The goblin sheathed his sword and faced the sea again. "So much water, Aulaudin. In my life, I never imagined so much water. She brought it all."

She . . . Evoni . . . Aulaudin followed the goblin's eyes. He saw a red-capped shadow that might have been his daughter, but mostly he heard her song.

"Is that what you wanted—to talk to me about Evoni? What about salt, Goro? Would you talk to a man about salt?"

A sound that might have been a chuckle blew on the wind between them. "It is very salty, isn't it. Strange thing, salt. We have a death for traitors. We give him a feast of salt and water. We give him a knife, too: a very little knife with a ragged blade. He always chooses the knife."

"Is that a warning, Goro? Beware the goblins and their salt?"

"A warning that too much of anything is death. I don't care what you do with our salt, and an elf cannot *be* a traitor."

The black haze that was a goblin's presence in a man's mind hardened, then shattered. For an instant Aulaudin felt himself surrounded by giants. There was noise: one man screaming as others shouted . . . cheered. He was angry and afraid, of what he couldn't guess, though his right hand throbbed all the way to his elbow. The senses weren't his. Someone—*Goro?*—was sharing thoughts with him.

Aulaudin was rallying his thoughts when a light blinded his mind's eye. A heartbeat later, wherever Aulaudin looked, all he could see was a face—a goblin face—a detached face—a severed, dripping goblin's head that one of the giants had hurled at him. And though he knew it was sharing, Aulaudin dove out of the way.

A strong, leather-gloved hand caught him, kept him on his feet, and broke the sharing spell.

"What did you see?" Goro demanded, giving Aulaudin's arm a violent shake before releasing it.

Aulaudin didn't bother to answer, or dare to ask a question of his own: since when had goblins shared with men? They glared at each other while Evoni sang on the wind. Goro looked away first.

"He was my father. He chose the knife."

The whisper was nearly lost on the wind. As unprecedented

and unexpected as the sharing had been, the admission was more so. A man could share an utter lie; Maun, in particular, was a master of deceit. One glance at Goro's rigid profile and Aulaudin was ready to swear that the goblin had shared truth as painful as Tatterfall.

Aulaudin didn't want to know why Goro had shared the memory, or how he'd shared it, or—above all else—what the goblin's father had done to merit a traitor's death. As soon as his legs were his again, he took a long backward step.

"If you wanted to harvest salt from the sea," Goro said, no louder than before, "a pool would be more useful than a pit. Dig it shallow and broad. Up there, where the sun warms the sand—" he swept a mail-sheathed arm toward the widest, highest portion of the beach. "It will be harder than you imagine. You must skim the good salt out at just the right moment or it will turn bitter and poisonous, but, with help, it can be done. We will help."

"Why? Why?" Aulaudin stammered. "Why help me?"

"Because I can, Aulaudin." Goro smiled, gleaming back teeth in a dark, dangerous mouth. "I said I was looking for inspiration. I must ask Jerlayne for a favor. I didn't know how I would persuade her. I thought you might inspire me and you have."

The goblin walked away from the steps to Sunrise and the boat-building scyldrin. Aulaudin needed a moment to get his mind around the goblin's implications. He ran after Goro and laid his hand on the black-cloaked shoulder.

The next thing Aulaudin knew, he was on his back, looking up the length of Goro's naked sword. He rose on one elbow; Goro pressed the sword's tip against the hollow of his neck.

"You haven't a chance, Aulaudin."

"Maun is right," Aulaudin snarled defiantly even as he dropped back to the sand.

"Right isn't enough." Goro raised the sword. "My father was right, and he faced salt."

"I want you gone from Sunrise, Goro, you and your band. I'd sooner have ogres."

Goro scabbarded his sword with a much-practiced gesture that ended with a loud, metallic *snap*. "You might get your wish, Aulaudin, and you would regret it, but not today. Not while I live."

The goblin walked away, his cloak wild behind him, his

boots kicking up sand with every stride. Aulaudin didn't get up until Goro was gone. He made his way to the high, wide portion of the beach. Pools were a better notion than pits, now that he thought about it, but he'd be damned before he'd accept any goblin's help.

Chapter 18

Jerlayne swiped several swift charcoal lines across a paper scrap. After smudging them slightly with her thumb, she straightened on her stool and peered one-eyed at her artwork. She'd learned the basics of memory-inspired portraiture in Elmeene's workroom where she'd been taught so many other things. Looking back, Jerlayne knew why her mother had wanted her to know how; at the time, there'd been no magic, no *shaping,* in the exercise and she'd resented every wasted lesson.

Elmeene sketched the way Jereige fished: regularly and for relaxation, and as a result, there was no shortage of paper in Stonewell's workroom. Jerlayne hadn't drawn before Evoni when she'd made sketches for her tapestries, now conspicuous by their absence. She'd wanted hard pencils then and large sheets of paper, which Aulaudin, grim-faced and silent, had dutifully brought her from the mortal realm.

Paper was, oddly, one of the most difficult shapings; far more difficult than iron. It was easier to shape bread from flour than wring a usable sheet of paper from sticks or rags. Water shapings were always difficult.

If she'd asked, Aulaudin would have foraged all the paper Jerlayne desired, plus whatever charcoal, chalk, and pigments in water or oil he could find. They'd repaired their estrangement, forgiven each other with love and laughter, but there remained tender spots, like the empty walls where her tapestries no longer hung.

Aulaudin had confessed, without apology, to destroying them while Evoni shaped the sea. Since that night, he'd never once mentioned their daughter's name. When conversation required it, he'd just say *the siren,* as if they'd known all along.

But the truth was in Aulaudin's eyes each morning when he studied the sea. He'd think of their daughter, if Jerlayne had

asked for paper or a proper stick of charcoal rather than a lump
scavenged from the workroom brazier. To deny the hurt Evoni
still evoked in their hearts, Aulaudin would have willed himself to *appreciate*—using the mortal-realm world—whatever
Jerlayne had drawn.

The last thing Jerlayne would ever show her husband was a
portrait of mortal Cuz, assuming she ever drew one she liked.
Her paper, stolen from Stonewell before they left, was pale, as
he had been, and charcoal was just another form of the soot that
tainted his imagination. Jerlayne had the fragile remembrance
Cuz had entrusted to her. Blurred through it was, she could see
Cuz in the dark-haired boy's face now; she didn't have to rely
on one night's memory. But the eyes were never right and his
mouth was either too hard or too soft, never the quicksilver
mix of both.

Perhaps when her son was born. . . .

Three months into her pregnancy, Jerlayne wasn't yet aware
of her unborn son, not the way she'd be in another three
months. The twinge that shot along her spine was entirely
rooted in her mind, though in what part of her mind Jerlayne
couldn't quite say, except today's time for sketching had
passed and she'd failed again to capture the mortal's haunted,
angry expression. Sighing, she returned the remembrance to
a burnished wood box where it rested with the lock of his
pale hair.

She closed the box and sealed with a bit of shaping. The
flawed portrait she left on the table.

Steel-colored clouds smeared the eastern horizon, the main
force of a winter storm that already shook the bare-branched
trees and rattled the windows. Waves like snowdrifts raced
across the bay. They struck the hidden beach with such force
that spray was hurled higher than the bluff. They struck the
rocks where Evoni dwelt, too. The black stones disappeared in
each violent swell. A mother's heart reflexively feared for her
daughter, even while her ears listened to the wild song riding
the wind.

The last time Gudwal had visited Sunrise—the sage had
been here three times since Evoni rose—he'd assured Jerlayne
that a siren had nothing to fear from the stormiest sea, and neither did Sunrise. They'd spoken with her in the indescribable
way that sages communicated with guardians. They'd reminded her of the homestead she'd left behind, the homestead

whose fertile land she'd shaped into an arm of the sea and
whose great house perched a short, windy walk from the raw
bluff that separated the stony beach from the grassy fields. Before that conversation, every high tide had seen a little more
land fall down to the beach; since it, the bluff had held and was,
in the opinion of those scyldrin who examined it, slowly trans-
forming from dirt to clay.

I'm going to shape the world.

Jerlayne heard her own voice, right after she'd shaped her
twenty-link chain, echo out of memory. The scene was fresh;
she hadn't thought of that night since it happened. She hadn't
shaped the world, either, but her daughter had shaped Fairie.
The immortal realm had an eastern shore now and a red-haired
siren guarding it.

A tear slid down Jerlayne's cheek. She'd been so caught up
in thought and memory that she hadn't noticed her eyes had
blurred with sadness. The thirty years during which she'd believed Evoni was an elf had been a time of obsession and delu-
sion. Jerlayne did not regret that the time had ended, but locked
within that madness were some of her happiest moments: the
undoing of her own childhood.

In the eye of memory, Jerlayne could see her mother standing in the workroom doorway, a fresh-made chain draped over
one hand and a lamp in the other. Elmeene's mouth moved, but
try as she might, Jerlayne couldn't remember what Elmeene
had said, only that the door shut and the light disappeared.

Another tear tracked Jerlayne's cheek, and another: tears for
Evoni, herself, and even Elmeene. She blotted them with her
sleeve. It was a futile gesture. The tears were immediately replenished; Jerlayne didn't know why. The grief, she'd thought,
was largely behind her, along with the pain. These weren't
noisy tears; her heart didn't ache. She thought of Evoni in the
water—not the siren in the sea; but a child splashing beside a
sylph—and something that felt like a smile formed on her face.

"I loved her," Jerlayne whispered. "I miss her. I'll always
love and miss the child she was."

She'd made those statements three days earlier when her
nephew Ombrio had stood in this room and she'd made them
again each afternoon since when the young man had come to
her workroom. Behind the closed, heavy door, they shared the
sorrows and joy no one else at Sunrise wanted to remember.
Jerlayne had been embarrassed the first time, when Ombrio's

heart-wrenching confession that he'd loved Evoni and continued to dream about her had wrung tears from her mother's
eyes. But those were the first tears that healed more than they
hurt. She and Ombrio had quickly come to trust each other.

Soon, perhaps, they'd talk about Maialene, too. The sad,
lonely woman's disappearance had gone largely unnoticed,
even by her sister and son. Jerlayne didn't wish to admit that
she mainly missed Maialene because, without her, there was
no one with whom she could discuss the mortal realm nor share
her other secret: the face of her unborn child's father. She'd
tried, for Ombrio's sake, to stir up a deeper sort of mourning,
but Ombrio withdrew into himself whenever she mentioned
M'lene's name.

Gentle rapping at the closed, but not bolted, workroom door
broke Jerlayne's concentration. A quick glance at the grandfather clock, a recent gift from Aulaudin, confirmed what her
eyes and stomach told her: it wasn't noontime yet. Other days,
Ombrio hadn't knocked on her workroom door before mid-
afternoon; but three days didn't make a tradition, and she'd
told her nephew to visit whenever he wished.

"A moment," Jerlayne called, drying her tears for a second,
more effective time.

On her way to the door, Jerlayne slid a blank sheet of paper
over her failed portrait, then heaped her shawl over both as the
rapping continued.

"I'm coming!"

Jerlayne opened the door, expecting to look into Ombrio's
still-hollow face and looked down at gnome instead. Gelma,
who struggled to take Banda's place and hadn't yet succeeded,
was pale as her hair in the winter light.

"Mistress—Mistress Jerlayne, the goblin's come to see you."

"Goro?" Jerlayne asked aloud.

The gnome wrung her hands together and nodded. "No one
knew he was there until Rem headed out to get wood from the
pile. No one saw him come up the path."

It was one thing to see the goblins going about the homestead's business, doing the dirty, heavy chores the scyldrin left
for last. They were neither invisible nor silent, at least among
themselves. The newcomers from Wavehome and elsewhere
complained that light and noise from the goblin camp—a new
goblin camp higher on the hill than the great house—kept them

awake at night. Especially the noise of conversation in the goblins' native tongue which made no sense to elf or scyld ears.

But catch sight of a goblin who didn't want to be seen? The scyldrin of Sunrise might sooner chase the rain back into a cloud or the incoming tide off the beach. Goro could have been waiting for hours or moments.

Still, Jerlayne wasn't entirely surprised to hear Goro had come looking for her. Aulaudin had told her about their beach conversation, a conversation which, in Aulaudin's retelling, had ended with the goblin drawing his sword. As hard as it was to imagine a goblin seeking out a man for conversation, it was harder to imagine what Aulaudin might have done to merit such a response. Hard, but not impossible: she had heard from the dwarves about how the goblins had rescued her from drowning after Evoni rose and how her husband had challenged the lot of them with a broken tree branch.

She'd worried a bit when time had come for the midwinter exchange: one overlong mail shirt, slit front and back for comfortable, protected horseback riding, swapped for five hives of salt. The entire bargain tradition was based on the notion that goblins were a homestead's sole defense against ogres. There was nothing about goblins defending themselves from a homestead's elves. Goro might have refused the trade altogether.

But he hadn't. Jerlayne and Aulaudin had hauled the mail, carefully wrapped in oiled canvas, out to the foundation stone at sunset. Come morning the armor bundle was gone and five tall hives stood in its place. Jerlayne had thought that was the end of the matter; she should have guessed better. Goro, Aulaudin had said, wanted a *favor.* Favors weren't part of any seasonal bargain.

Don't settle for salt, Aulaudin had warned when he'd finished telling his tale. *Petrin and I had it mostly figured out. We'd have gotten the rest after a few false tries, even without his help.*

Husbandly advice with regard to goblins and trade, however wise or well-intentioned, wasn't part of any bargain either. Between her daughter, her husband, and Goro himself, Jerlayne hadn't reshaped Fairie, she'd simply watched it change all around her.

For years now the Sunrise bargain had been for a mail shirt at midwinter and a barrel of iron scrap at the summer festival. Jerlayne calculated that she'd already made enough mail to

outfit every Sunrise goblin twice over. She had assumed Goro
was hoarding armor for the next outbreak of war on the plains:
he seemed the plan-ahead sort. Assumptions were necessary
with goblins, but after the unraveling of her assumptions about
elfin sons and daughters, Jerlayne suspected everything, including the obvious. And goblins were rarely obvious.

Though Goro, when he showed up for conversation, was invariably polite, Jerlayne was never eager to see him. She didn't
have a single word for the feelings her blue-skinned trading protector roused. Apprehension—a sense that everything around
her had become unstable and was apt to change—was perhaps
the best word, though within the apprehension there was an odd
exhilaration. Jerlayne's heart raced as she turned away from
Gelma and stared out the workroom windows.

She could see the ocean, the foundation stone, the path
Aulaudin walked when he went down to the beach to inspect
the Wavehome boat. Aulaudin, of course, was nowhere to be
seen; he'd left after dawn for the mortal realm. Goro had an exquisite sense of timing where Aulaudin was concerned.

Suddenly cold, Jerlayne grabbed her shawl from the worktable and whirled it tightly around her shoulders. The papers
shifted, but Cuz's portrait was not revealed and, more to the
point, Ombrio hadn't been the one knocking on her door.

"Mistress," Gelma pleaded.

Though not from Wavehome, Gelma hadn't been at Sunrise
long enough to feel comfortable using Jerlayne's name. She
wanted Banda's place, but she wasn't ready to claim it. "Please,
Mistress. He's come *through* the door!"

Jerlayne swore at mortal gods: goblins did *not* come through
doors, stand under roofs, or between walls. She tried to imagine the circumstances that could plant Goro *inside* her home
and quickly decided no reality could be worse.

"All right! I'll attend to him!"

With a frustrated sigh, Jerlayne quickly folded the portrait
papers into a narrow fan which she tucked above the cuff of her
sleeve. Gelma had achieved a twisting of fingers that had to be
painful before Jerlayne was finished.

"Hurry, Mistress. I'll lead you to him, Mistress."

Jerlayne shook her head. "I know my own house, thank you.
Just tell me which is the unfortunate door he's come through—"

"The high door, Mistress, the one with all the new glass!"

Maybe Goro didn't think a glass-paneled door was a proper

door, Jerlayne thought as she hurried through the maze of corridors, rooms, and reconstruction that was Sunrise this winter. She was relieved to find he wasn't *inside* at all, but precisely *at* the threshold with the door open outward behind and cold air streaming into the great house around him.

"I disturbed you?" Goro said in the lilting goblin way that made questions into statements and stood statements on their heads.

"I wasn't expecting you."

"You expect me on other days?"

Goro unnerved her the precisely the same way that Cuz had unnerved her and *that* was a revelation which turned Jerlayne's blood to cold water. She drew a ragged breath and pushed the thought out of her mind. Since the goblin wouldn't enter the great house, she'd have to leave it. Her shawl wasn't warm enough for a winter day but a short, gnomish cloak hung on a peg above a cold brazier. Jerlayne draped it over her shawl and struggled to close its unfamiliar clasp.

"I suppose we could walk to the foundation stone," she said, imitating his lilt.

"I suppose we could."

Goro stepped back from the threshold, giving her room to pass, but barely: their cloaks furled against each other. The long, silky fringe of Jerlayne's shawl caught on a trailing ring of Goro's sword scabbard. Grappling with two layers of cloth, the inner one slippery, the outer heavy, Jerlayne tugged the fringe loose and caught a glimpse of a goblin smile as she did.

Cuz had measured her with a similar look. Cuz had been awash in dark thoughts of sex and passion at the time. Sunrise's goblins, she thought, lived without women.

An elf, Jerlayne told herself as Goro fell in step beside here—an elfin woman who could shape iron, or pain, had nothing to fear from any mortal, or any goblin. But Jerlayne's efforts at self-reassurance failed and she clutched her billowing garments around her like armor.

"Did you find flaw with the mail?" she asked as they neared the relocated stone. The rings had been as perfect as a Stonewell daughter could make them, as good as any she'd delivered in the past, and she'd defend her workmanship if he dared challenge them.

In the back of her mind, Jerlayne realized she was hoping for an argument, which was a foolish attitude for a woman to take into a bargaining. But the way her heart pounded, an argument would give focus to her anxiety and settle her nerves.

"There were no complaints."

"What, then ?"

Jerlayne hadn't accustomed herself to the new, strong winds that blew off the bluffs. The shawls and cloaks she'd worn all her life were cumbersome, even dangerous, especially wearing layers of them. She'd promised herself a coat with sleeves, such as Aulaudin wore; she could make it herself, or ask him to forage one for her. And she'd have to learn not to leave the great house unless her hair was bound. The wind made short work of a loose braid. Jerlayne's hip-length hair whirled a hundred fingers around her face and reached for Goro, too. When she freed a hand to gather her hair, her borrowed cloak's clasp popped open. It and the shawl flapped like wings.

She needed an extra set of hands to control the layers and got them, sheathed in black leather.

Without thought, Jerlayne lowered her eyes and refused to look at Goro's face as he tucked locks of wild hair beneath the heavy cloak. He closed the metal clasp firmly, then a dozen heartbeats passed before he released it. They were in clear view of half the homestead, if anyone had thought to look. Jerlayne began to blush. Only the cold wind stemmed her embarrassment.

"We could talk beneath the trees?" Goro said.

A helpful suggestion or something else? Jerlayne chose not to find out. "We're here now. Why did you come looking for me? What do you want?" She made her voice firm, even sharp; the way women had to speak when dealing with goblins.

Goro sighed. His arms dropped against his sides and Jerlayne felt her confidence returning.

"I wish your help. I have an object, how it came to me and why is of no concern to you or Fairie. I've been told what it does, but I need to know how it succeeds, how it's made and, of course, if an elfin woman—you—could shape its substance from scratch into a tunic."

Jerlayne thought immediately of the mortal realm. If he'd come to her a year earlier, perhaps she would have had the same thoughts, but she wouldn't have illustrated them with the goblin portraits Cuz's mother had drawn.

Even so, the reality of Goro's request, after days of dreading it brought a sudden sense of relief: all Goro wanted was a shaping. Though shapings might be difficult, even unwise or impossible given her pregnancy, they were never frightening. And if she could get more salt for Sunrise, so much the better, no matter what Aulaudin thought.

"We can always make a new bargain," she offered with a smile.

"Ah," Goro sighed, his hair as still and shining as the blueblack mail beneath his cloak. "Perhaps, but perhaps not? Perhaps it would be best if you examined my object carefully before committing yourself to any bargain that surrounded it?"

Jerlayne bridled: did he think he'd found something she couldn't shape? She, who could bend aluminum without destroying its strange, fragile temper? She thought of the garish green rope Aulaudin brought back for the Wavehomer boat, and the unlamented red gown she'd worn in the mortal realm. There were objects in the mortal realm whose structures might challenge her, but never defeat her.

"A bargain, then, for this coming midsummer. Instead of iron, I'll take your object in my hands and tell you what I learn from it."

The goblin frowned. "There can be no compromises this year, Jerlayne. Scrap iron is the least I can accept for myself and my companions. I suggest a separate bargain: salt?"

Jerlayne pretended to be surprised. "Salt? Your object would be worth an additional hive of salt?" Jerlayne wondered aloud. "An extra hive or two would be welcome. The newcomers threaten to overwhelm us with fish once they get their boat built."

The corners of Goro's mouth twitched, his chin dipped and rose and dipped again; it was as much reaction as she'd gotten from him in years. Jerlayne wished Aulaudin were nearby to share the sight.

"It would depend on this object of yours," she continued, quite pleased with herself.

"The salt I had in mind comes from the sea. I described the digging of harvest pools to your husband, and I'm sure he described them to you."

"Aulaudin and Petrin were planning to dig pools before you spoke to anyone. Living by the sea, it's an idea that's bound to occur. I waste my time shaping salt out of our cooking pots. I'd have imagined pools myself, sooner or later."

Goro was nearly as tall as Aulaudin and, therefore, considerably taller than Jerlayne. He contrived to stand very straight and to stare down at her with fatherly disapproval. "Then you should know that the salt clinging to your pots is not pure like the salt we bring in hides. But, perhaps, you plan to sift your sea salt through your fingers, separating the bitter, *poison* grains from the pure. A woman of your talents could do it without wasting her time. Or I could show your scyldrin how and when to draw the ripe water off and pry the pure salt from its grasp."

Jerlayne did know that the salt she shaped from the pots had a different taste and, more importantly, a different texture than the salt the goblins brought. Aulaudin had said salt was salt and not to worry. "Perhaps if I could see this object?"

From within his own wind-rippled cloak Goro produced a bulky slab of drab green color and lumpy, cloth-covered contours. By the way he held it out to her, it was lightweight for its size. Jerlayne accepted it reluctantly. She determined immediately, and to her considerable surprise, that it was more similar in substance to wood or oil than to either pottery or metal. Irregularly circular in shape, nearly two-thirds of its edge had been burnt. The material between the cloth layers resembled matted moss, but was wiry in texture. The unburnt remainder was finished with a smooth, thick ridge.

"Armor?" she guessed; it wasn't a weapon. "For your wars?" A casual, shaping touch had failed to recognize the material from which it had been made. With every passing heartbeat, Jerlayne thought of the mortal realm and the pictures Cuz had shown her.

"It came from the plains. Armor is my guess, too."

Weapons came before armor: Women had made swords while the blooddeath ravaged Fairie; they didn't begin to make mail links until her mother showed them how to handle iron. Jerlayne tried to imagine the weapon that the slab was meant to defeat. Not a sword, she guessed; mail was good enough against a sword; but something more powerful, something mortal. With her eyes closed, she ran sensitive fingers along the burnt edge. Burning itself was a form of shaping that went beyond a woman's ability. Jerlayne couldn't be certain what the springy stuff had been before, but what brushed her fingertips was as complex as living flesh though as dense and repetitive as any metal. And there were elements within that she judged it dangerous as well.

"Our bargaining will have to wait. I cannot help you just now."

"Cannot?"

Another twitch at the corners of the goblin's mouth, the beginnings of a scowl. The moss-filled slab must be very important. Jerlayne wanted to take it to her workroom, but her reservations about shaping it were real.

"I'm carrying a child and I've never touched anything like this before. I'd be unwise to meddle deeply before I'm delivered. I can examine its surfaces, but the surfaces are damaged. To learn what it *was* I'd have to change its shape, and I dare not do that now."

"It isn't mine, Jerlayne, it must not be damaged or changed in any way. Our hope—the hope of Uylma who gave it to me—is that you can duplicate it."

"Then I definitely cannot help you until I'm delivered. It will be that long before the Wavehomers have built their boat and I know if we need your help with the sea salt after all."

Goro stared at her belly, "You will birth your child in autumn?"

"Sooner. A month beyond midsummer." Her unborn son was hale and whole, but a hair's breadth different from her other children . . . from Aulaudin's children.

"I can't wait that long. Uylma wants tunics made from this brittle, springy stuff and wants them quickly."

Jerlayne took a backward step so she could look the goblin very nearly in the eye. "I will not risk my child for this." She brandished the slab but did not attempt to return it. "Sunrise has enough salt for now, even if we harvest nothing from the sea. Aulaudin and I have waited for—suffered for—an elfin child."

Goro's whole face moved, first with eyebrows rising in surprise, then sinking into an unrestrained scowl.

"You may mock me," Jerlayne snarled back with a courage she did not truly feel, "but you will not change my mind."

Cuz had taught her how to shape pain. Goblins affected an impassive demeanor, but she'd shaped their wounded flesh and knew their nerves were lively. It would be difficult; she couldn't hope to touch the exposed skin of Goro's face, but his gloves would melt beneath her fingers if she willed.

"I have told Aulaudin where salt comes from," the gobli
said with icy calm. "Should I tell him about elves?"

Jerlayne reeled backward. The goblin might well hav
clouted her with a closed fist. She caught her balance again:
the foundation stone and though her mind filled with denials,
was too late to pretend she hadn't felt his threat in her heart.

"You wouldn't," she sputtered. "It would . . . it would te:
Fairie apart! There'd be nothing left. You *need* us. You nee
elves!"

"We need guardians and the Veil, Jerlayne. *I* need as man
tunics made like that slab as you can shape."

The foundation stone supported Jerlayne's back as she san
slowly to the dry, brittle grass. Everything around her ha
become very bright, very calm, very slow. She could hea
Evoni's singing, see each scratch on the buckles of Goro'
well-worn boots. Fairie was as good as dead, not from iron an
blooddeath, but from her foolish bargaining.

The black leather creaked and flexed; she was looking int
Goro's all-black eyes as he knelt in front of her.

"Help me, Jerlayne."

She shook her head, fumbled with the slab that reste
against her knees. "I can't. I've undone everything. There'
nothing left. I should have died in the mud."

Goro studied the dry grass between them. "Nothing? If ther
was nothing left, Jerlayne, I would not ask for your help."

Jerlayne raised a hand to her face. Her cheeks were dry; sh
had only imagined her tears. "If you tell Aulaudin—"

"Is that the 'nothing left' that frightens you so much? Ver
well, I will not tell your husband."

"You say that today, but what about tomorrow, or nex
midwinter?"

"I could have told your husband the truths we both knov
yesterday, or any day, Jerlayne. I could have told him when I wa
a boy on the plains. My grandfathers and great-grandfather
could have told Gudwal's father the day he was born. How muc
better would it be for all of us, if I'd told *you* before Evoni wa
born?"

Words failed; tears flowed. They tickled Jerlayne's nose
She sniffed and life, inexorably, continued.

"My life has been a dream. I've dreamt that I'm awake; bu
I'm not. There are secrets in my dreams, and I never suspecte
them until now, when it's too late."

"A bargain, Jerlayne. A bargain none of my kind has offered to yours: Help me and I will tell you what I know about Fairie."

She looked at the slab, thought of her child. "I'm afraid."

"So am I—and I know I'm awake. Will you help me?" When she didn't answer, Goro stood, leaving the armor in her hands. "Come here to the stone when you're ready. If it is not too late, we'll trade knowledge."

The grass crackled as the goblin walked away. Jerlayne followed him with her eyes until he was past the great house and headed down the hill. Hours later, with the slab hidden beneath her borrowed cloak, she stood and walked to the great house herself.

Chapter 19

Springtime had come to Fairie. There'd been rain yesterday and there'd be rain again tomorrow or the next day, but tonight, at sundown, the air had been crystal clear and full of life. Goro—he remembered his birth name but never used it, even in his most private thoughts—had fallen soundly asleep on a straw-filled pallet with his face pointed upward. He slept soundly, as befitted a man who practiced daily with his weapons and labored hard as well, and when he awoke from unremembered dreams, there was a knife in his hand before there was any wit in his thoughts.

Faint starshine told him there were no other lights in the in goblin camp. His ears, catching only the occasional snore or owlish hoot, told him there'd been no alarm raised among his men or across the way among the varied scyldrin. Yet something untoward had awakened him and he kept a wary grip on his knife, waiting for the shadows to move and his wits to sharpen.

A handful of moments, then, had passed before he heard a *thunking* echo of the sound that had awakened him and remembered a swift, chill wind against his cheek. Reaching across his body, Goro swept his off-weapon hand through the darkness beside his pallet. His heart skipped a beat when his fingertips adhered to a bitterly cold arrow shaft.

Whichever herald had shot the arrow could have—would have—slain Goro as he slept, had assassination been his orders. A pent-up breath forced its way out of Goro's chest as the tension in his muscles gave way to a subtler tension in his mind. He was a sworn protector: it was his right to receive a herald's summons, his duty to respond, and countless reasons for Fairie's protectors to assemble that didn't directly involve Sunrise—though Goro's gut discarded all of them in a heartbeat.

After returning the knife to a wrist sheath, Goro clothed himself in the rolled-up garments he tucked beneath his pallet every night. The sounds, though slight, were enough to bring his second, who slept unsheltered in all but the worst of weather, to the chime-weighted tent-flap.

"Goro?"

"Coming," Goro replied as he wrenched the chilly arrow from the dirt.

The camp was moving before Goro lifted the flap. Threaded pebbles jostled one another, a deafening sound, like the light tread of a man through fallen leaves which echoed as other flaps were lifted. Goro and his second joined the score of men gathering around the dark hearth pit.

"First," Goro announced in a soft, yet carrying, tone.

"Second," came from his immediate right, followed by "Third" and "Fourth" and so on, familiar voices in an uninterrupted sequence.

Goro asked for light when the assembly was complete. Two men struck flint and steel to spark the lamps they carried, a third man flashed a cold, white, mortal-realm light to show he'd come prepared. Goro nodded once, though he'd expected nothing less than perfection. His men were well trained and reliable for all that they were bound to him by oaths, not blood. The best of them should have pieced together that a herald had come and gone; the least and youngest had the wit to keep their questions to themselves.

Goro brandished the arrow and carefully broke its shaft. A slender tube rose from the fletched end. His men waited motionless while he unrolled the parchment, scanned the scattered symbols, and interpreted them.

"A summoning," he told them, the demands of leadership keeping his own apprehensions in check. He turned to his second: "Saddle two horses. We leave at once." He then turned to his third man. "Hold this place for four days. If neither of us has returned, send word to the plains."

His third man showed a fist and nodded. Goro returned the gestures as he had many times before. In and of themselves, summonings were not uncommon. Fairie's protectors lacked the notion-sharing magic of the elfin male scyldrin; they relied on summonings to keep one another informed. Last autumn there'd been a dozen summonings right here in Sunrise as the protectors took the measure of Fairie's newest guardian.

But the heralds had not used cold arrows to announce them.

"How many? How far?" the third man asked, presumptuous, but justified: They were oath-bound men who'd known from the start that Sunrise was a dangerous place.

Goro repeated what he'd gleaned from the parchment: "The northern reach. At once. That's all I'm told." He crushed the parchment and tossed it on the ashes before adding, "It could be anything. Here or from the plains. Wait four days."

Another fist, another nod, this time echoed by all the men who'd remain behind protecting Sunrise from ogres and their fellow goblins.

Goro returned to his tent with one of the lamps. Unassisted, he laced on his armor and collected his weapons: knives, sword, bow, and a quiver of iron-tipped arrows. When he finished one of his youngest men waited with the reins of two horses.

"This can't be good," the youngster said nervously.

Away from formal and ritualized gatherings, goblins talked among themselves, little different from the scyldrin they protected. Goro's goblins conversed rather more than other bands, partly because they were oath-bound and less familiar with one another, and partly because Goro had deliberately set their camp among the scyldrin where they were constantly exposed to habits that would get them in serious, even fatal trouble if they returned to the plains.

Another protector could have punished the youngster for his impertinence. But Goro who was not as old as his peers. In fact, he wasn't much older than the man in front of him and compromised regularly with goblin tradition.

He had nothing to lose and no reason not to try new ways.

"We're all alive and not under attack. It could be much worse."

"If it gets worse and we are attacked, what then?"

Goro shrugged. "You do what you're sworn to do until you can't do it any more, then you die."

His second emerged from the larger tent where he and the other watchmen stowed their limited possessions. Without further words or farewells, the two travelers mounted up and guided their horses into the forest.

"The northern reach? That's all it showed, nothing more?"

"That's enough, isn't it, Joff?" Goro replied.

He knew his companion's birth and lineage names—which

was not true for all the men sworn to him—but rarely used it, especially when he wasn't using the language of the plains. In Fairie, men succumbed to the fast, flexible language the elves cobbled together from words of their foraging.

"Enough," Joff agreed, "but I don't like it. I don't like it for one step of the way. You should go back, Goro, and let me go alone."

Goro reined his horse toward the darkest shadow and drove it forward by tightening his legs against its ribs. "That wouldn't keep me—or you—alive even one day longer."

Unspeakably cold air slapped Goro's face and sucked the air from his lungs. No matter how many times he rode the shadows, he was never prepared for that first bitter breath. With the next stride his horse had returned to warmth, and another part of the Fairie forest. The animal tossed its head and threatened to bolt. Goro hauled in on the reins until its nose nearly touched its chest and it stood quiet, but quivering, beside Joff's equally unnerved mount.

"You waste valuable time," the older goblin commented as Goro patted his horse's neck and spoke to it softly, in the language of the plains, the language it had been trained to obey.

"You'd waste valuable animals."

Joff's muttered retort was lost to the cold. Shadowing was no place for conversation. Whether walking or riding, a creature quickly learned to breathe on the warmth strides or feel his lungs turning to ice. Clothes, or fur, would keep a man, or horse, warm enough, if he kept moving. Nothing could keep his skin, his eyes, his nails, and even his teeth from darkening. A goblin's hair was black from birth, but the rest of him was stained by shadow.

Cloud-covered, moonless nights brought the best, easiest shadowing: walk or ride a straight line, right foot in shadow, left in Fairie. On such a night and with a long-strided horse beneath him, a man could ride from the forest all the way to the plains. It wasn't magic—at least it wasn't Aulaudin's sort of magic that let him move from any one place in Fairie to any other in the mortal realm without moving a muscle—but it served the goblins well enough.

Joff and Goro had half of what they needed for easy shadowing. The moon had set shortly after sundown, but the night air was exceptionally clear and the starshine bright enough that Goro, riding in the lead, had to choose each shadow and guide

his horse into its depth. And though it was possible to go shad
owing beneath the midday sun, he called a halt as soon as daw
brought color back to the trees.

"We're alone," Joff said once he'd chafed the feeling bac
into his gloved hands.

"You noticed that, too?"

The older man nodded. "We could turn back. There's noth
ing waiting for us but a trap."

Goro shook his head. "There's a bigger trap waiting for us a
Sunrise, if we don't go to the northern reach."

He lowered his hand and the horse began to walk forward
Joff should have followed. Though older men normally com
manded the obedience of their juniors, Goro was a protector
the Protector of Sunrise, and Joff was his second. After severa
empty moments Goro stopped his horse.

When they'd branded Goro's father a traitor, they hadn'
stopped with condemning one patriarch to a salt-feast death
They'd purged the entire lineage. Sisters, daughters, nieces
and every woman whose blood was held to be tainted had he
eyes put out with hot coals before being parceled out to what
ever other lineage would take her. Brothers, nephews, and es
pecially sons were bound and trampled by the herds. The
lineage had been extinguished, forgotten, except for one boy
whose mother was Uylma, one of the sacred women. Uylma
challenged tradition and refused to renounce him.

She'd kept Goro alive. Of all the men who'd ever lived o
the plains he was the only one to grow up surrounded by
women. Once he'd grown, she'd sent him off to claim his heri
tage: the rights and duties of a protector in Fairie. She'd be
lieved he'd be safer in Fairie, further away from the men whc
remembered his father and considered their victory incomplete
while even one son survived. And to strengthen her beliefs
she'd arranged for Joff to be his second.

If Goro himself believed in anything it was in his mother'
wisdom and Joff's loyalty—but the man had been a herald, anc
who better to shoot a cold arrow past a man's cheek or put an
other weapon in his back when they were utterly alone?

"Are you coming?" Goro asked without turning around o
slipping his wrist knife from its sheath.

Hooves beat softly on the dewy ground. "Just making peace
We could circle around; come in from the west."

"And let the others know we suspect their honor?"

"Well, we do."

Goro grimaced. "From the east, Joff. I'm not going to make it easy for my father's murderers."

"You're just like him."

"I take that as a compliment."

They rode through the morning: the main reason Goro had called for the horses. A man or a horse walked through shadows at roughly the same pace, but in the forest the horse was faster. And if the horse was tired when it arrived at the northern reach, it could rest while Goro confronted this day's fate.

The northern reach was a steep hill, carved by two streams that came together at its base. Recent floods had swept away seasons of forest debris, leaving a wide expanse of untracked mud in their wake. Songbirds filled the air with nesting songs while a pair of squirrels raced beneath Goro's horse. The animal snorted in loud indignation; Joff's mount answered in kind, but no sounds came down from the hilltop.

Joff pointed upstream. Goro shook his head, saying, "If they're up there, they know we're down here," and reined his horse into the mud. After another peace-making moment, Joff followed.

Once, a very long time ago, the reach had been a scyldrin homestead. It bred several hundred scyldrin before fading away, then the protectors had made it their own. Stone huts that echoed the black tents of the plains marched in ordered, tree-shaded lines along the hill's long ridges. All that Goro and Joff passed were empty; none of them had been swept clean of winter debris.

If he'd believed he'd been staying any time on the reach, Goro could have claimed any one of them as his own for the duration.

If he'd believed that.

Goro noticed when Joff slipped the knotting on his scabbard to free the sword for immediate use, but said nothing: the hilt of his wrist knife was already resting against his palm. A gravid fox, flushed from one of the empty stone tents, brought both men to alarm, but she was, if anything, only further proof that the reach was empty. Tents and trees both stopped at a clearing some forty paces across where hearth pits and meeting stones were scattered exactly as they'd been for Goro's last visit in the fall.

"Pointless to ask, but you are certain the cold arrow pointed toward here?"

Joff knew the answer to his own question. Goro put his fist lightly into the base of his horse's mane. It responded by lowering its head, allowing Goro to swing his leg forward and over the animal's neck. He dismounted with his back against his horse.

A hawk circled overhead. A second glance saw that it was one of a handful. A third and Goro realized the birds were vultures, not hawks. On any given day, in any given part of the forest, there was a good chance that something lay dead beneath the branches. Spring, for all its beauty, was a deadly season.

"You ride among the trees. I'm going to poke around the stones and pits. Maybe there's another message. Give a call every few moments. I want to know you're still alive."

Joff answered with a raven's caw.

A raven cried five times while Goro searched the sodden pits and barren stones. He was expecting a sixth cry when Joff called him by name.

"There's a message, all right."

Goro followed Joff's voice, leading his horse among the trees. He was ten paces off when the older man raised his arm and pointed at a particular tree.

At first Goro's mind rejected what his eyes grasped: something hung from a treetop bough. Even after he saw the rope and the corpse together, his first thought was to question how anyone had gotten it to the top of one of the tallest trees in the reach. And why when so many other trees and branches would have done the same job. But it was a message, just as Joff had proclaimed, meant for him.

Goto retrieved his bow and fitted it with a notched arrow.

"Mind the wind," Joff said, ever his teacher.

"There's no wind."

"Aye, that's what I meant."

He chose a shot that would impel the rope against the branch that held it, increasing his chance for severing it with a single shot—not that the hanged man would complain if it took two arrows to bring him down for burying. By then, there was a slight breeze stirring the treetops. Goro took it into account and let fly.

"Sharply done," Joff said as the arrow found its mark.

The corpse struck the ground feet-first and snapped before

toppling sideways like an axe-struck log. Goro who had seen enough violence in his time, felt his heart sicken with the sound, but that was only the start. He hadn't taken two steps toward the mangled body when he realized it wasn't a goblin— or rather, it wasn't a man, but a woman.

"Vachan," he swore by the name of the men's god, unaware that he'd spoken aloud.

Joff seized his arm, held him back. "I'll look."

"My message," Goro countered and shook free.

He could wish he hadn't. Whoever hanged her hadn't set the noose right, or had meant for her to die from suffocation, not a broken neck. She'd been trussed hands and feet together, so she hadn't had a chance to save herself. Her face was swollen, hideous, and blue as any shadowing man; that was why Goro hadn't known at once that the corpse belonged to a woman.

Women didn't leave the plains and though they could walk the shadows, they did it rarely enough that their skins remained pale. Except for her hair, which was an iridescent black, Goro's mother could pass for an elf.

Goro didn't recognize the dead woman and hoped against hope that he didn't know her. Her eyes weren't scarred over; at least she wasn't kin. Once again, as he started to kneel, Joff caught his arm. Once again he shook free.

Removing the glove from his left hand, Goro attempted to straighten her rigor-stiffened limbs. He loosened the rope and wrested it from her bruised, bloody neck. He would have closed her mouth and eyes, if that had been possible. Then, with his breath exhaled and his teeth gritted, he slid his fingers inside her tunic until he snared another rope, this one of pebbles, beads, and copper nuggets. The beads were marked with symbols similar to those on the herald's message and sealed beneath a blue-green glaze.

He knew her, maybe not by name, but she'd dwelt in the nafoga'ar, the maze of caverns and mysteries where Goro had been raised, and was sworn to his mother's service. Joff saw the same truths.

"Uylma—" he meant Goro's mother—"will be wroth."

That was no truer than saying a blizzard brought snow: one of her acolytes attacked, stolen, and cruelly killed . . . Uylma would go on a rampage. Men had surrendered their magic ages ago, except for the shadowing, and most of their women, including this acolyte, were similarly bereft. But Goro's mother was Uylma, a woman of the goddess. She and maybe a dozen other women could still command the ancient magic.

For a moment, Goro imagined her vengeance. It looked very much like the vengeance he'd held in his own heart since the day his father died. For that reason, if no other, Goro knew he wasn't thinking clearly. Vengeance was important on the plains, but his enemies—his father's enemies—however much he despised them, weren't foolish enough to risk Uylma's wrath. There had to be more to the message.

Sitting back on his heels, Goro looked up at Joff. "Take the horses into the clearing and keep them between you and me until I call for you again."

Joff folded his arms across his chest and refused to move.

"You cannot do this, Joff. I'm already exiled; I can't go back, but you must. She cannot remain here. Go. Stay where you can see nothing and wait for me to call you."

The older man didn't move.

"That was a command, Joff. A protector's command to his second. Was it in any way unclear?"

"In no way unclear, but in no way necessary. You would send me away so you can examine her closely, open her clothes, read the lineage-mark over her heart. You would spare my honor, but it's too late for my honor, Goro. I know this woman. We were chosen."

Men and women did not live together on the plains. Men had herds to tend, wars to wage, scyldrin to protect. They stayed on the move. Women stayed in their cave homes, harvesting salt, placating the gods . . . and their uylma. Yet they were not completely separate or the race, despite its immortality, would have been extinguished long, long ago. Their uylma—Goro's mother was uylma of the nafoga'ar and the only one who used her title as her name—chose men for her women. The men and women had no say in this, of course, and sometimes, perhaps most of the time, there was no affection among the chosen ones and the children they brought into the world.

Joff had never mentioned a woman; it wasn't something men discussed, so few of them were ever chosen. But to look at his face was to know that love did blossom in the harsh soil of the plains and with love came grief. Goro eased the necklace free and held it out for Joff, who broke his stance to take it.

"Do you know why?" Goro asked after a moment's silence.

"I can guess. That slab of *gennern* forage I gave you for the elf? She gave it to me; Uylma's command."

Not a message for him, then, but for his mother. Possibilities exploded in Goro's mind, all of them unprecedented and unpleasant. He stood, unclasped his cloak and covered the woman with it. There were customs for most things on the plains, but nothing that told two goblins in Fairie how to console each other.

"We will bind her to my horse and you will take her home and tell my mother what happened, what we found."

"What has she told you about the slab? I think it's armor; I don't want to know if it's weapon," Joff said, flat emotionless, and already adjusting the saddle girth and stirrups to accommodate an awkward burden.

"We said everything before I left. I dream, sometimes, but there's never another dreamer. I'm one of the men who serve— less than one of the men. I'm accustomed to my place."

That got a wide-eyed, flared-nostril reaction of disbelief from the older man. "I will tell Uylma that we left before the arrow had warmed and that we were already too late then."

Goro dipped his chin.

They worked together to bind the stiff, cloak-wrapped corpse to the horse's back. It would be secure so long as Joff didn't have to set their pace above a walk. Even with shadowing, a walk to the plains could take days and nights. The border between the grass and the forest wasn't defined by mist or defended by guardians. A man without faith couldn't carry enough food and water to survive the passage.

Joff had faith, determination, one of Jerlayne's swords, and the bow Goro had carried.

With two horses and a dead woman, Joff needed large shadows and deep ones for his journey. He didn't expect to leave the reach until sunset. Goro could have left immediately, except—

"I'll get no farther in the whole afternoon than I'll get in one hour of twilight. Better to rest here until you leave."

Joff didn't argue with the truth and neither man said anything at all for several hours. On the plains boys learned early how to let their minds lie empty and quiet. Then, as the sun passed high overhead, a few clouds drifted down from the north. More followed on a stiffening wind. The sun disappeared behind a gray mountain of clouds. A man could make good time shadowing a storm, if he didn't mind taking risks. Joff readied the horses.

"I will speak with my sister, Goro," he said when he was remounted and ready to ride home. "It is not right that she's forgotten you."

He'd suspected, but until that moment not known for certain, that there was blood between his mother and his second. He doubted anyone could change her mind.

"Shadows watch you," the older man said, facing north, into the storm.

"And you watch the shadows," Goro replied.

"You sound like one of them, sometimes."

Goro shrugged. "The elves aren't animals, Joff. They're as wise as we are, maybe wiser."

"Aye, and that's the problem isn't it?"

This time it was Goro who didn't argue with the truth. He watched the trees until Joff found a shadow and vanished, then he set off himself. Any shadowing path would lead to the plains if a man followed it long enough, but Sunrise was a specific place. Alone and afoot, Goro zigzagged across the path he and Joff had traveled the previous night. He ran and he walked, but rarely rested: a shadowing man was an elusive target, even for an enemy who'd know where he was going.

Sunset, midnight, and dawn each found him on the move, drawing closer to home. Twice he'd hidden himself in ordinary shadow. Twice the danger—if there'd been any danger— passed him by. By noon he was a day-and-a-half without food or rest and within sight of familiar black tents.

A protector who commanded his men with blood might have been able to postpone explanations until he'd slept and eaten. Goro told his tale to the five men waiting at the tents and told it again as the others came in from their work around the homestead. Oath-bound men in Fairie's forest had little chance of being chosen. Most of them had put all thoughts of women from their minds, though several had known what Goro had not: their second was a chosen man with a woman and two children on the plains, one of them a daughter in Uylma's own tent.

To a man they had just one question: "Will Uylma claim vengeance?"

Goro couldn't give them the answer they wanted to hear and fell asleep to the monotonous sounds of men whetting steel.

Days passed, beautiful springtime days and dreary ones, ideal for shadowing. Traveling by night and with no other storms to aid him, Joff should have reached the plains in five or six days. Another two or three—by far the most dangerous of the journey—to reach the nafoga'ar. Another day, or less, for his return, if Uylma put the shadow-wings at Joff's back. Every man in the camp knew the way; the eleventh day and every day thereafter made the men warier. Breaking ancient tradition, Goro had set his camp in sight of the great house. He counted on another tradition to keep it safe: men did not attack men in front of elves and scyldrin.

There were stories—true stories—of attacks that exterminated all witnesses, men and scyldrin alike. Goro doubled his night watch and ordered his men to sleep only when the sun was shining. He contemplated the great house with its thick stone walls, far more defensible than any tent.

Once traditions began to fall, were any worth keeping?

Twenty days, the protector told himself. If twenty days passed without word from the plains, he'd tell Jerlayne everything and settle his men under a fixed roof.

Goro didn't sleep well on his decision, but he slept and was asleep when a plains wind—a wind that sighed of bending grass, not branches and leaves—brushed over him. Awake, but strangely unalarmed, he attempted to rise and found the task impossible.

"You're not awake," a stern, yet unmistakably feminine voice chided him. "While you sleep, you cling to the ground. Let go of the ground and you will rise."

She'd come. After all the years of Goro's exile, his mother was visiting him. Goro wasn't aware of holding onto the ground, but when Uylma spoke, it was wisest—safest—to obey. He loosened his mind's fingers and drifted upward, another thought and he was standing, a third and he was facing her, looking as he imagined he looked when he went up to the great house to meet with Jerlayne.

As a protector but more importantly as an exile from the plains, Goro did not have to lower his eyes. He looked directly at his mother's face—at the face she chose to reveal in this dream. Goro wouldn't have been surprised if he hadn't recognized her. He'd forgotten his father's face, except at the very end, and nearly two centuries had passed since he'd seen his mother. But she was—or had decided to be—very much as he remembered, except wearier and, oddly, kinder.

"I have sent Joff back to you. He'll arrive tomorrow, toward evening, I think. I've given him a cloak for you to wear."

Goro lowered his eyes, thinking both of why he needed another cloak and that since she'd given him his life, she'd given him no other gifts. Joff had kept his word. "I expected nothing in return," he replied. There was a dose of defiance stirred into his humility: a sharp warning that when he was asleep a man was apt to be braver and more honest than when he was awake.

"Wise," Uylma said coldly as the hints of kindness vanished. "Joff will tell you that there is war again. Or there was. I was driven from the nafoga'ar—"

Goro's head came up with such vigor that, on the pallet, his body thrashed. "That can't be!"

"It can. It is. A month ago, by the moon. They could not control me. The daughters they sent to me would not serve them any longer, so, in the end, they unsheathed their swords and swept down as if we were scyldrin to be culled."

"I'm grateful you survived, even away from the nafoga'ar." In truth, Goro couldn't imagine his mother anywhere but in that place which was the center of the plains. "Had I known—"

"Be grateful you did not; enough men died covering our escape."

"And the woman we found in the reach, Joff's chosen?"

"Women died, too. I thought she was among them." Regret touched Uylma's pale face. The plains were harsh, with no room for sentiment, and Goro's mother was the harshest of all, but she'd defied the lineages to save his life and her acolytes were unswervingly loyal to her because she was loyal to them. "There will be a reckoning."

"Forgive me, but how—if you are no longer in the nafoga'ar?"

There were other sacred places on the plains where an uylma could settle her community of women, but the nafoga'ar was the most sacred space and the uylma of the nafoga'ar spoke for all the others. Goro's mother could not have saved him if she'd been the uylma of some other place.

"That is the question they will be asking themselves before long."

When he was young, it had seemed to Goro that on those rare occasions that his mother smiled, her eyes sparkled like

wildfire smoke and embers. As a sleeping man he could feel
their heat as well. Suddenly, but of his own will, he was an
arm's length farther away.

"I am free now, my son. An uylma who rides a horse and
sleeps in a tent: no rites to perform, no gods to placate, nothing
at all to stand between her and her vengeance. I should thank
them, but I won't. Not until all their heads are piled at my feet."

Goro thought of his father, and that the *gennern* had finally
made their fatal mistake. "How may I serve you, Uylma?"

"There is blood, now, on that armor slab I sent you. What
has the scyld learned about it?"

Goro swallowed hard; his body began to gag, but he felt
nothing except the fear of his mother's displeasure.

Chapter 20

Summer had come to Sunrise homestead and, like the spring and winter before, it was a different kind of summer than anyone remembered. Even the Wavehomers, plying the bay in their new boat and learning its lessons, admitted that Sunrise Bay was no more like Fairie's southern sea than a gnome was like a dwarf.

It seemed to Jerlayne that summer hadn't come at all. A week before the midsummer festival and she was still wrapping herself in shawls or a fleecy sweater Aulaudin had foraged for her—surely not on one of his infamous middens. She didn't complain, though; hot weather would have made these last weeks of her pregnancy more uncomfortable than they'd already been.

The son she'd conceived with a pale-haired mortal promised to be both willful and large, if the way he assaulted her ribs and back each night were any measure of personality. He'd be born early, too. Jerlayne had marked the first subtle changes three days ago. Reluctantly, she'd kept the word she'd given at Stonewell and told Aulaudin that this time—in light of all that had happened—she wanted their mothers, both Aglaidia and Elmeene, at Sunrise for her lying-in. Aulaudin, to her surprise and dismay, had embraced her request wholeheartedly.

We haven't had guests—ordinary guests—since the sea came to us, he'd said as he headed off for sunset Vigilance. *We'll have a celebration.*

But keeping secrets herself had sharpened Jerlayne's awareness of secrets kept by others. Aulaudin honestly wanted to celebrate his son's birth, and just as honestly feared another disaster.

Stonewell arrived first. A solitary peal of midmorning thunder heralded Jereige, Elmeene, Matereige—her four-month-old son—and a small caravan of nursemaids and food.

"You've been close-mouthed," Elmeene had whispered when Jerlayne had asked about the size of her retinue. "Jereige didn't know how the land lay between you and Aulaudin. We don't want to be any trouble."

Finding room for a passel of unexpected scyldrin was, *of course,* no trouble at all in a great house still under repair from Evoni's transformation, and *exactly* what Jerlayne had hoped to be doing as her body prepared for birth. She expected better from Aglaidia and thought she'd gotten it when the view from the front porch revealed just three riders and a single pack-horse. Then she caught a clearer sight of the third rider.

"Claideris! Who invited *Claideris* to *my* home?"

Elmeene, who stood on the porch beside Jerlayne, shielded her eyes from the sun and muttered. "I knew she was worried, but I didn't think she was *that* worried."

"That worried about what, Elmeene?"

"I couldn't very well ask your father for details, could I?"

Elmeene set her teacup down hard enough that Jerlayne feared for the patched saucer beneath it; and, though she'd had ample reason to distrust her mother's pronouncements, Jerlayne suspected she was telling the truth, or close to it, this time. The great house that could shelter the likes of Elmeene *and* Claideris hadn't yet been built.

"Do you suppose you could find out why she's come or, better still, convince Father to escort her somewhere else?" When her mother didn't spring immediately into action, Jerlayne made wings of her mismatched shawl and sweater, "I'm hardly dressed for greeting sages and I don't intend to change."

Elmeene rolled her eyes; they'd stopped discussing clothes and proper appearances not long after Jerlayne had learned to dress herself. "I'll do what I can. I'll tell her you've secluded yourself but, Jerlayne, I may only make things worse."

A familiar twinge of betrayal seized Jerlayne's stomach. She eased herself into the nearest chair. "Mother, what do you know that you haven't told me?"

"Nothing. Only that, well—I hadn't considered it myself, but no one, no one at all, recalls a woman bearing a child *after* she's borne a guardian. There was my aunt, of course, and her dragon; she died in the rising. And Belsalen. She survived because her daughter left before she transformed into Fairie's first siren. Everyone at Scattergood survived but it wasn't long after that Kreelon was lost beyond the Veil and Belsalen chose the forest.

"Before that . . . most of our guardians are older than our sages. It's all been passed along in feast-stories, and you know how the wine flows at them. But the few women who didn't die because of the guardian they'd given birth to don't seem to have had children at all afterwards, neither elves nor scyldrin. I suppose it *could* seem odd . . . or worrisome, if you were inclined to worry. Not that I'm that sort myself."

Jerlayne let out a held breath. "Not at all," she agreed. "You showed me the way. You saw the one I chose. If there were secrets left, you'd have shared them with me, wouldn't you?"

"Let's not talk about that again, Jerlayne. I didn't keep *anything* from you; I *assumed* you'd figured it out for yourself—" Elmeene paused, looked at the ocean. "Poor Maialene. Poor, unhappy M'lene. Even she figured it out by herself."

"Assume nothing. What else is there?"

"Nothing. I've taught all my daughters—and tried to teach you—everything I know."

And with that, Elmeene left to meet their guests.

Jerlayne stayed where she was. The spasms hadn't let go of her gut. She picked up her mother's teacup and sipped from it. It was bitter; Elmeene shunned sweetness in any form. Worse than that, she'd probably believed everything she'd said, especially that last part about teaching her daughters.

As Jerlayne herself did not believe what she'd said about changing from her comfortable, but raggedy, attire into something slightly more presentable. She hadn't gone into seclusion, and wouldn't—not when seclusion meant giving the likes of Claideris free rein in her home.

After a final sip of cool, bitter tea, Jerlayne started to stand, and fell back into the chair with such force—and surprise—that the teacup tumbled from the table and shattered against the floor. The thought of Claideris roaming Sunrise was all her body needed to decide that the time had come to speed her elfin son into Fairie.

Jerlayne caught her breath and managed to stand. Her first step was awkward; her second was stronger and by the third she thought she'd be able to walk the corridors to her bedroom where she'd set up her birthing stool. Walking would be good for her; Banda always said it was a good idea to walk until walking became impossible—which it did before Jerlayne reached her workroom door. On hands and knees, she crawled to the mound of pillows where on other days she worked her most subtle shapings. She grasped one to her mouth and stifled a moan in its tassels.

«Aulaudin!» Jerlayne opened her mind to her husband. Once her parents had arrived, he'd promised to remain in Fairie until their son was born.

It wasn't the first time—she'd given birth before. But not without Banda beside her. Not to a son who would remain hers. «I need you!»

He was nearby. Her thoughts found him, joined with him. She felt his pulse—almost as rapid as her own—but his mind was shuttered tightly. Jerlayne could only pound imaginary fists against that man's ability to isolate himself and hope that, somehow, her frantic efforts were noticed.

A second contraction shrank Jerlayne's world to the pillow mound. With thoughts that were scarcely conscious, she re-arranged the pillows until Aulaudin's presence announced it-self her mind. She had the sense that he was upset, angry, but his moods were of no importance.

«Now!» she shouted from the trough of another contraction.

Aulaudin was in the workroom before the next contraction faded. When he took her hand, the need to shape her thoughts into words faded, too. He knew what she felt, where she wanted to be, and lifted her up in his arms.

"Don't be ridiculous," a woman commanded from the doorway.

Jerlayne thought she recognized the voice, but until she stretched her neck, until she saw Claideris with a reeking, fum-ing pipe clamped in her teeth, she refused to believe her ears.

"Put her down!" Claideris said through a cloud of smoke. "There's more space in here and the light's better. Bring her stool, if it suits her; water too, and rags. Then go down the hall. We'll call you."

«Put me down, indeed!» Jerlayne agreed. «On my feet, thank you!» She wriggled her feet to the floor and stayed up-right by keeping both hands grasped tightly around Aulaudin's arm. "Claideris," she said, letting birth-pain put an edge on her voice. "You're the one who can go down the hall. Down the hall and through the door. I asked our mothers to be here—" that was a lie, too, but angry as Elmeene could make her, it fell short of the rage that contracted every muscle in her body the moment she saw the sage's sour, sallow face. "I didn't invite strangers."

"I'm no stranger, child. I'm kin to you. Closer kin than old Gudwal, and I'm here to make sure nothing more goes wrong."

Color drained from Jerlayne's vision as headstrong anger warred with her son's need to be born. She squeezed Aulaudin's arm so hard she could feel his pain. Elmeene walked into the workroom, and Jerlayne tried to catch her mother's eyes. If this was another of Elmeene's oversights, if Claideris were an aunt or grandmother! Elmeene was staring knives at the sage's back, which meant: «Why haven't you ever told me that woman—that creature—was among your grandmothers!» Jerlayne turned her pain and rage on her husband.

«I didn't know,» Aulaudin replied, and Jerlayne recognized the anger she'd dismissed earlier. «Aglaidia swears *she* didn't know, but she *is* the one who asked for a sage. Maun agreed and shared with Arlesken, but Claideris showed up instead.»

To no one's surprise, or at least not to Jerlayne's surprise, a strong wind sprang up, carrying a siren song and the promise of a storm.

"Close the shutters," Claideris ordered and Jereige—her father, the man her heart called Father—hurried to the open windows.

"Don't touch them!" Jerlayne countered. "If I'm going to lie in here, I want fresh air." And she wanted, above all else, not to smell the smoke of Claideris' pipe while her every nerve was raw.

Jereige's mouth hung open as if he'd been struck in the stomach, but he stopped short of closing the shutters. There was something in his expression that demanded more attention, attention that Jerlayne couldn't spare just then. There was too much happening, too many angry looks and subtle gestures, especially for the eyes of a woman needing to give birth. Jerlayne lost her balance and sagged against Aulaudin's shoulder.

«Do you want to lie down again? Do you want to go to the bedroom? I'll take you there and lock the door behind us. I've been with you every other time.»

«I want her *out* of here. Get her out, whatever you have to do, and keep her out. I want you with me, but I want her gone more. Leave my mother behind, and yours, too. It's not Aglaidia's fault.»

Aulaudin agreed. He helped Jerlayne recline among the pillows before approaching Claideris.

"My wife wants privacy and the care of her mothers. The rest of us will leave until my son is born."

He reached for the sage's arm which she clamped against her side.

"No husband knows," Claideris sniped, narrowing her black-eyed gaze on Jerlayne, who didn't trust herself to answer.

"Joining tells," Aulaudin said, drawing, Jerlayne noticed, a slight nod from Maun, who stood with his hands resting on Aglaidia's shoulder. Elmeene was looking at Jereige; he was looking at the floor.

"What did joining tell you last time, when a siren was born? What did joining tell you this time that was different? Your wife has shown that she does not know the difference between a siren and an elf. That's why I've come to witness the birth of this *elfin* son she claims to bear, why I was *invited*."

Grinding her teeth with another contraction, Jerlayne wished there was something she could say or do to make the smoke-blowing old woman disappear. She remembered her mother's warning that she might make matters worse and wondered—while Elmeene stared resolutely elsewhere—if that wasn't what had happened. There couldn't be any other excuse for a woman—a *widow* who must have parted the Veil herself—to stir the sort of doubts she was stirring. Unless there were, despite her pleas and direct questions, secrets Elmeene hadn't revealed.

When no one else spoke up, Claideris continued, "Your wife can't *know*. She knows her own blood, of course, but fathers are a mystery. There's only so much a mother can know about them. Isn't that true, my dear child?"

When those black eyes bored down on her, Jerlayne found her voice. "I know my husband!" she shot back, not truly an answer, but she was confident that all the women in the room shared a secret and defied the sage to expose it.

"But do you know enough about your child's father to trust him? Do you know what lurks in his ancestry? A dark shadow or two?"

"Worse!" Jerlayne snarled back, "I hear he's related to *you!*"

That brought a satisfying gasp from the sage and everyone else in the workroom, except Aulaudin who was trying hard not to laugh. Jerlayne felt his mind trying to join hers and brutally shut it out. Her thoughts swam with secrets: mortal men and charcoal sketches. It was difficult—no, it was impossible—to believe that Claideris knew anything about the young mortal or the portraits his mother had drawn. Then dawn broke in Jerlayne's mind: Claideris wasn't talking about mortals . . . Claideris had just accused her of trysting with her goblin!

As if she—or any woman—could tryst with a goblin!

Then Jerlayne's indignation shattered like ice on a cold, windy night and she sank, shivering, into her pillows. Aulaudin was beside her in an instant, but she turned away from him, with mind and body together. She said the pain was too great to share, and it was, but it had nothing to do with her body. Thoughts of Cuz clamored inside her head: violent, pale-haired Cuz, whose touch had been so different than the mortal Elmeene picked out, but not so different from Aulaudin's. Elmeene had warned her away from Cuz, so she'd *had* to pursue him, but who was Cuz? More importantly: Was his mother touched by madness, or had Cuz's mother trysted with a goblin?

And had she, herself, trysted with a goblin's mortal son?

While Jerlayne contemplated questions she should have asked months earlier, Aulaudin took matters into his own hands.

"This has gone too far. Yes, Sunrise raised a siren, and Sunrise survived. We will raise this child, too. Jerlayne says he will be an elf, and I cherish the thought, but if she's wrong, then she and I will face the consequences together, without interference and without witnesses. This is Fairie. We're elves, and no one tells us what to do in our own homesteads!"

Jerlayne couldn't see Aulaudin's face, but his voice was enough to wrest her attention away from her private obsessions. She was proud of the way he defended Sunrise, and shamed too, because he didn't know how much of what he defended was built upon deception. Like the others, she hung in silence, waiting for someone else to speak first.

"That's not true, Aulaudin," Jereige grumbled. "There's a sea out that window that wasn't there the last time I was here. All Fairie faces the consequences of that: in the south and now the east, there's a limit to our realm. Our sages are concerned, and we need to listen to what they have to say."

"When the *sages*—" Aulaudin emphasized the plural, "have something to say, I will listen. Until then, my wife, your daughter, needs the attention of her mothers and *only* her mothers!"

"I've brought beer," Maun added quickly, slipping past Aglaidia to take his old friend's stiff arm. "Brewed it up myself. Barley beer so thick it scarcely needs a mug—"

Jerlayne closed her eyes and tried not to imagine the taste. When she opened them again, her father was walking through the door with Maun and Aulaudin was herding Claideris after them. He pulled the door shut. Jerlayne glanced at her mother first, looking for clues. With the men and Claideris gone, she was more aware of the wind coming through the open windows and Evoni's singing.

"Do you want us here, or was that just Aulaudin's notion?"

"My notion," Jerlayne said, but her relief was short-lived.

She wanted to ask—to shout and scream—if giving birth to an elf was always so much more painful and difficult than bearing a scyld, and she would have, if she'd been alone with Elmeene. But Aglaidia, though she was kind and gentle and quick to make useful suggestions, had brought the sages into this—even if she hadn't bargained for Claideris.

"I never knew she was kin to us," Aulaudin's mother whispered, as she held Jerlayne's hand.

Elmeene had opened the door, calling for gnomes and linen and buckets of clean water.

"My mother never told me about her. Maybe her mother didn't have a chance to tell her."

Who could blame either of them?

Elfin infants were not, Elmeene volunteered before the gnomes arrived with water and cloth, any more troublesome than scyldrin. From the strength and frequency of Jerlayne's labor pains, both older women thought she'd be delivered before noon. They were wrong. The wind died; Evoni fell silent; and the midday heat, the worst yet of the season, turned the workroom into a fever den.

Elmeene sent for the birthing stool, hoping its rungs and grips would help, but Jerlayne was exhausted by then, too spent to respond to her womb's increasingly weak contractions. With thirteen elfin births and uncounted scyldrin to her credit, Elmeene took Banda's place: on her knees before the stool.

"What do you see?" Aglaidia asked.

Elmeene scowled, then stood up, shaking her head. Elfi
women were experts at giving birth, but not at assisting one an
other. Furrows of sincere concern aged Elmeene's face as sh
laid hands on Jerlayne's belly.

"I brought a nurse for Mati," she berated herself. "I shoul
have brought a midwife for you. You said you'd lost Banda."

The elves consulted with the gnomes, who'd clumped to
gether on the porch where teacup shards still littered the floo
The gnomes suggested the dwarves who tended the livestoc
each spring.

"They've got wooden tongs," Gelma said, "and they *pull* ou
those that won't fall on their own."

Jerlayne rallied long enough to say she wasn't *that* desperat
yet. Aglaidia thought aloud that cool water would be welcome
ice from the ice cellar, if Sunrise still had that amenity, woul
be even more welcome.

Sunrise did have an ice cellar dug into a hill, but getting
bucket through the kitchen meant they got the men an
Claideris again, too.

"What's gone wrong?" Aulaudin demanded as he shoul
dered his way to Jerlayne's side.

They joined immediately. Jerlayne knew he was concerne
about her, and her alone; there wasn't a thought in his head fo
their son at that moment. But what Jerlayne knew wasn't wha
the others heard.

"Is something wrong?" Jereige repeated. "Is it misshapen
Discolored?"

"Larger," Elmeene replied quickly. "The boy's just large
than we expected—than Jerlayne expected."

"Larger!" Claideris cackled. She blew two streams o
smoke from her nostrils; Jerlayne closed her eyes and felt faint
"Larger and earlier, too. Not paying close enough attention
were you, my dear?"

If she'd had any strength left, Jerlayne would have hurle
something across the room, something harder and sharper tha
a pillow. But the accusation cut deep. She'd been so please
that her son was thriving before his birth that she hadn't pause
to measure the consequences.

A gnome handed Aulaudin a dripping towel. He draped i
around her neck and shoulders. The cold took her breath away

then invigorated her. She gathered her strength to prove them all wrong.

"Rest a bit longer, beloved," Aulaudin advised. "You'll waste your strength if you bear down now."

When it had been just the three of them: her, Banda, and Aulaudin, his attention had always been on her while Banda's was on their child. She'd been foolish to think she could get through this with neither of them nearby.

"Aulaudin and my mothers can stay," she decided. "The rest of you can leave." When everyone, even Aulaudin continued bickering with one another and ignoring her, she raised her voice. "Go! Leave! All of you! Leave me alone!"

The workroom fell silent until her father spoke: "There's no need to shout. We came because we were worried about you and wanted to support you. But, if that disturbs you so much—" He held out his hand toward Elmeene. "Shall we leave?"

Elmeene stood firm.

"Our daughter has told us—all of us—to leave," he explained. "It's not for me, or you, to argue with her."

"I wouldn't think of it," Elmeene said pleasantly, always her most dangerous tone. "I never argue with weak, fevered women—and I'm not going to leave her, either. We'll be done when we're done, and have a cold supper afterward."

Jereige surged forward. He seized Elmeene's arm with sufficient force that she winced and nearly lost her balance. Watching her mother go wide-eyed and gape-mouthed, Jerlayne forgot about labor pains and waited for an explosion that never came.

"We can eat our supper warm at Stonewell," Jereige said firmly, implying that a meal at his own table was suddenly important enough that he'd skirt the Veil recklessly to enjoy it.

Or, that he wanted to put a great deal of distance between himself and Sunrise, and quickly, too. Jerlayne asked herself if she were dreaming or delirious; the answer, both times, was no. Her father had insulted her homestead and, incredibly, laid rough hands on her mother. She could imagine only one explanation for such unseemly behavior: Claideris.

What had the malingering sage said to the men while they'd waited in the kitchen?

Elmeene had freed her arm. She rubbed the place where Jereige had clutched it but said nothing, because there was nothing that any well-mannered elf *could* say, which meant breaking the silence fell to Maun.

"You had more courage in the old days," the blue-eyed elf said softly, yet sharply. "No sage could have put you off your heart then."

The barb struck deep. Jereige paled and Elmeene quivered—leaving Jerlayne to wonder what parts of her parents' story remained secret. Her father, at least, had the decency to lower his head and seem embarrassed.

"We'll stay, of course," he muttered, "and you'll stay here with Jerlayne. I'll see to *our* son. I was only thinking of Matereige."

That was a comment which, considering where they were and why, served only to thicken the air. Tension remained even after Maun, Jereige, and Claideris had left.

«I'll go keep an eye on them, beloved,» Aulaudin suggested, making it clear, as only joining could, that he thought more than an eye might be necessary.

«No, stay.» Jerlayne wrapped her hand around his. «Your father has eyes for everyone.»

Jerlayne had had one too many thoughts about fathers by then, about fathers who raised sons—and daughters—who didn't belong to them, about men who, suddenly, weren't the fathers their daughters thought they should have been. She threw up a wall, quick, thick, and unfair, between herself and Aulaudin. Then, before he could ask any questions, Jerlayne gathered all her strength to shape a single, all-consuming contraction.

Everything turned shades of gray and pain after that. Jerlayne had no idea who held her hand or who entered the room, and had no interest, either. As a thoroughly unpleasant day drew to a close, she willed her son—the son who would be Aulaudin's son—into Fairie.

"Ten and ten," Aglaidia warbled as she washed him and wrapped him in new linen. "Five fingers on each hand, five toes on each little foot."

Banda would have said the same words, the same exact words, the same sing-song melody. Exhausted and in the grip of a natural and irresistible reshaping to heal her birth-battered womb, Jerlayne found the memory of Banda's face more than she could bear. Sliding off the stool, she curled into a tight ball

and purged three seasons of anguish with violent sobs that
ended as suddenly as they'd begun.

"Your son," Aulaudin said when she'd sat up again and
wrapped herself in the clean robe Elmeene had offered her.
"Our son."

He held the boy—a good omen in itself; he'd never wanted
to hold Evoni. The infant was larger than her other children
had been and bruised by his arduous birthing. He had a cap of
wild, dark hair. Jerlayne had expected pale hair; she'd planned
to blame the color on Maun. His eyes, when he looked at her
for the first time, were dark in the dying light.

"Is he . . ." Aulaudin began. "Is he all that you hoped for?"

Jerlayne answered yes without hesitation though, in truth,
beyond his sturdy size, there was nothing extraordinary or
elfin about him. Evoni had been the one who'd sent shivers
down her spine.

"He is the image of his father," Aglaidia purred.

It was an absurd, almost insulting remark. Aulaudin had a
somewhat narrow face, a rugged nose, red-brown hair, and amber eyes, and prolonged labor had not been kind to the little
boy's nose or chin. But Aulaudin accepted the compliment
with blushing pride, as men, perhaps, had done since Fairie's
founding.

"Have you chosen a name?" he asked.

She shook her head; she hadn't dared.

"What about Laydin?"

Before Jerlayne could agree, Claideris opened the door with
sufficient vigor to slam it against the inside wall. Jereige was
a half-stride behind the sage; Maun two steps further back
with Ombrio and Aglaun—*Ombrio and Aglaun!*—at his side.
The bachelors stayed in the doorway and, by the sounds, the
household scyldrin were behind them. Jerlayne was beside
herself with anger as the sage demanded to see the infant in
Aulaudin's arms.

Claideris wasn't satisfied with a glimpse of the boy's face.
"Strip him down! From top to bottom, nave to chops! Let me
see him whole."

Jereige produced one of the big bull's-eye lanterns that
properly hung outside the high door. He set it on Jerlayne's
worktable and lit the wick with flint and steel. It was glaring
bright and much too hot for a summertime room. Aulaudin

retreated, their son in his arms, but habits ran deep. Elves didn't fight and he didn't resist when Claideris took Laydin away.

The sage stripped his linen and held him above the lantern like an egg in candlelight. "Ten and ten," she said, but without Aglaidia's gentleness. Laydin began to cry—the gasping mewls of a frightened newborn—and Jerlayne used the birthing stool to haul herself to her feet.

"Give my son to me!"

Instead, Claideris gave him to Jereige, who held the infant at arm's length, as if Laydin were a poisonous snake, while the sage snapped her fingers and cast menacing shadows over his face. Laydin began to squall. His face darkened in the ruddy lamplight; his eyes scrunched and disappeared.

Jerlayne got her right foot in front of her left, but Elmeene was quicker.

"This is unnecessary!" She plucked her grandson from Jereige's grasp, wrapped him swiftly in his discarded linen, and cradled him beneath her breasts. "He's perfectly formed. Aglaidia and I examined him ourselves. There was never any *doubt.*"

Elmeene cast a glance at Claideris which Jerlayne remembered from her lesson days, then she took Laydin from her mother's arms.

"Perfect on the outside," the sage retorted, though she didn't try to reach past Elmeene. "But what about its eyes and ears? Did you examine them?"

Jerlayne held her son close, shielding him from her anger. "Laydin hears and sees *perfectly,*" she snarled, but one statement didn't vent her anger, she needed another. "All our children have seen and heard perfectly, including Evoni—"

"Your daughter—" Claideris smiled with honeyed malice, "was not destined to become a dragon. Dragons are born blind and deaf."

That was nothing Jerlayne had heard before. "My son is—"

Jerlayne strove to match the sage's venom, but Claideris cut her short.

"Your son is what, my dear? What do you know about *this* one that you did not know before?"

"*Our* son is surely an elf," Aulaudin interjected.

"*Surely?*" Claideris mocked. "Your hopes have gotten the better of you. You were more cautious last time, I think."

She paused and appeared to reconsider. "Ah, but that was a daughter and this is a son. Perhaps you've already shared a notion or two with him?"

With a reluctant shake of his head, Aulaudin admitted he hadn't. Bones had to strengthen before any child could walk; minds had to strengthen before an elfin child could shape or share. Laydin would be five or six before he shared a thought with his father.

Jerlayne had no sense of her husband's thoughts. Claideris' hostility had isolated each of them. She imagined that none of the men were joined to their wives or sharing thoughts with each other.

"I believe," Aulaudin said slowly, "that fate would not be so cruel to us."

Claideris savored his discomfort with a sigh: only gnomes and dwarves believed in fate; elves, supposedly, knew better. "Fate doesn't care, Aulaudin. Fate doesn't care about Fairie. We care about Fairie. *I* care about Fairie. Your wife was wrong before. You can believe, but I don't, I *can't*. I'll take this child of yours—"

"No!" Jerlayne interrupted.

They locked eyes with each other. Silently, Jerlayne vowed she'd fight to protect Laydin from Claideris, she'd shape pain the way she'd learned to shape it in the mortal realm and stop the sage's heart, if she had to. Her vow was scarcely finished when she realized the black-haired sage knew the same secrets—about pain, about fathers and sons, about women parting the Veil—and wasn't threatened by any of them.

Claideris, for reasons Jerlayne hadn't begun to guess, wanted Laydin and even if Jerlayne were willing to expose every elfin secret she knew, the sage wouldn't likely back down.

Aulaudin was beside her. She hadn't noticed him moving: they were that isolated. The air began to tingle against her face: He was parting the Veil around her, around her and Laydin.

"There's a better way, son," Maun said. "Safer, too."

Jerlayne felt Aulaudin shudder and the tingling stopped.

"You can't be serious!" Jereige sputtered.

The men were sharing thoughts and the women, including Claideris, were left out. In less than a heartbeat, Jerlayne's rage grew to include her husband.

«Trust me, please, beloved. Trust him; trust my father.»

"The boy'll have no mind left when you're done—if he is the elf you think he is. You'll ruin him!" Jereige, her father, shouted. "I'll take no part in this!"

"Take no part in what? What, Jereige? What are you men talking about?" Elmeene was frantic.

Whatever happened tonight at Sunrise, Jerlayne thought that Stonewell would never be the same.

"A modest experiment," Maun explained. "I noticed, when I was trying to raise two sons at the same time, that months before I shared a thought with the older of them, I was aware of the two of them sharing thoughts with each other—"

Jerlayne shared her husband's cringe.

"It was very faint, less than a whisper across a room much larger than this, but once I became aware of it, I remained aware of it until the oldest began to share his thoughts with me: the moment he learned privacy; they both learned privacy and *I* got mine back." Maun wasn't going speak Boraudin's name, no more than Aulaudin would speak Evoni's. Like father, like son went deeper than blood. "The little one, Laydin, he cries, he twists, he turns, he has thoughts, and if we listen, if we put ourselves together the way we do at midsummer, but right here beside him, perhaps we can hear him babbling, the way I heard my sons."

"Can't be done!" Jereige retorted. "A boy so young, what thoughts could he have? It's a waste of time. Let Claideris take him somewhere where what he becomes—if it's not an elf— won't harm anyone. And no harm to him, either, if he is."

«He's *not* my father!» Jerlayne thought while Jereige dismissed Maun's plan, then panicked behind mental walls as she realized what she'd shared and what Aulaudin could infer.

«Don't be so harsh with him,» Aulaudin advised. «He's anxious. He was worried about you when he got here, now, thanks be to Claideris, he's worried about everything. Will you let us try to listen? There's no harm to it, I'm the proof of that . . .»

Jerlayne freed one hand to take Aulaudin's hand. They held their son and each other. «Do whatever you can.»

Aulaudin's thoughts became quiet. Maun, Aglaun, and Ombrio—Jerlayne could guess, now, why they were present— closed their eyes. Jereige, after a moment's grumbling, joined in, while Claideris' face tightened into a scowl as if she were determined to counter the men's efforts and didn't care who knew it.

So Jerlayne thought, «Find him! Hear him!» with all the intensity she could muster, which wasn't much and was less wise. Her knees weakened and the room grew dimmer, but she didn't relent, not even when Aulaudin's arms tightened around her.

There was joy and excitement in the wordless thoughts Aulaudin shared; Jerlayne knew they'd succeeded before he said: "There's no doubt! My son won't change!"

"An elf," Jereige agreed. "I would never have believed it, if I had not heard myself. The boy will not change."

In the hallway, the scyldrin actually cheered.

Jereige looked across the room at his wife. That, and whatever thoughts he shared, was enough for Elmeene, who fairly threw herself in Jereige's open arms. Jerlayne was grateful her father didn't look her way; she wouldn't forgive so easily—

«Try, beloved. He's your father.»

She closed her eyes and tried to lose herself in Aulaudin's joy.

Claideris didn't surrender quickly or easily. She wanted Laydin, for Fairie's sake, but without Jereige, the sage had no allies.

"I know my son," Aulaudin insisted. "A father knows his own son."

Claideris sputtered, but Aulaudin had won the argument. The sage left amid threats that when Sunrise next needed a sage's presence, it would find itself alone. Jerlayne didn't believe that: Gudwal would come, if they ever needed a sage, because Gudwal truly was kin.

But she worried, when all the excitement had ebbed and she was alone with her dark-haired son. Among all the lies, deceptions, and secrets, one truth stood out: Laydin was her son, not Aulaudin's. What had he and the other men sensed that so reassured them? And, remembering the portraits Cuz's mother had drawn, could she ever share their confidence?

Chapter 21

Summer—the first weekend of July—in the big city. The sky was hazy, no-color bright. The air hung like hot honey and it smelled rancid, from the empty two-gallon, handle-topped cans of olive oil taking in their second day of summer beside the overflowing dumpster behind JoJo's Pizzeria. Each can was bright yellow, except for a stripe of red letters saying, "100% Extra Virgin."

Like anything to do with JoJo's was virgin, even 10 percent.

Cuz flattened his back against bricks hot enough to ease the cramps in his back, but not as hot as the kitchen he'd escaped for his second ten-minute break of the afternoon. Business was lousy; with the Fourth coming tomorrow everybody who had a Get-Out-of-the-City ticket card had punched it hard. He could hear a few cars a block over on the Avenue; they weren't even honking.

So, of course, JoJo had him scrubbing out the ovens.

"You're little. Just lie on your belly and crawl in. I won't turn anything on or nothin'."

JoJo jokes. Employees were supposed to laugh, so Cuz had laughed and stuck his head inside the flat, steel ovens: his head, his arms, his shoulders, and a wad of steel wool drenched in something so green and foul it had to be illegal. Maybe, if it'd gotten him wrecked instead of nauseated, he wouldn't have minded.

"Hey! Faggit! Time's up."

Cuz knew ten minutes better than that. He blew out green crud, breathed in dead-sour oil and closed his eyes. No, if he'd been wrecked, he wouldn't have minded at all. Everything on his mind would've melted and run out his ears. He'd've been nicely buzzed. With a bit of concentration, he could fake a pretty good buzz without chemistry: *Practice, practice, practice!*

Wills' voice came back to him: Wills, like the bloody, fucking prince of England, not Will or Bill or anything but Wills. Wills' face came back, too. Not what Cuz wanted to remember in JoJo's alley.

"Get your squeaky butt in here, Faggit."

Wills had been the good times, such as they'd been.

"What you thinkin' about? You thinkin' about me?"

The Mouth belonged to one of JoJo's innumerable nephews or cousins. JoJo was forty-five, single, and had never come close to having a son. You had to wonder if his walking-shit family could add two and two. The Mouth had come outside. It was five years younger than Cuz, a head-and-a-half taller, and at least forty pounds heavier. Too much pizza, too much olive oil, not enough extra virgin.

"You thinkin' about me, Faggit? You want what I got, right? You want me 'cuz I'm the man. You want to suck what I got. You want to get on your hands and knees and beg like a dog."

The Mouth had delusions. Cuz was desperate enough that he was crawling inside pizza ovens; he was *not* desperate enough to do any kind of crawling, whatsoever, with the Mouth. And he wasn't a faggot, a queer, gay, or anything else. It was just what he did, and he'd done it so much he didn't think about what he'd done or who he'd done it with.

Except Wills.

So, maybe he was gay, or queer. For Cuz, even with Wills, queer made more sense than gay.

The Mouth seized Cuz's shoulder and shook him. "You listenin' to me when I'm talking' to you, Faggit? I'm tellin' you, stop thinkin' your slime-ball, ass-sucking thoughts about me. You understand?" Another shake and a shove that landed Cuz against the dumpster.

There was a rule—Cuz's Street Rule number 434 or maybe 433—that said the assholes who hassled you worst were the ones who couldn't get laid on a bet with some other guy's money.

"I wasn't thinking about you."

Cuz wasn't tough-looking; he traded on that, even with Wills. Most of the time, they let him off with verbal abuse or maybe he'd have to give them what they wanted. No big deal. In fourteen years, he'd been beaten up three times, by assholes who'd probably killed their kid brothers.

"Sez you. I'm gonna believe you? I seen the way you was lookin' at me before. You want me."

Fourteen years on the street and you learned things nobody taught outright. The Mouth was straight, but not as straight as he wanted to be, or thought he should be. He'd sleep better knowing he humiliated some faggot-boy behind JoJo's. The problem was, on a hot, miserable day like this, Cuz wasn't in the mood for being kind to assholes.

"Between you and nothing, fat boy, nothing wins every time."

The Mouth swung on him, a sloppy, ham-fisted punch that started somewhere beyond his ear—beyond the orbit of Saturn. Mouth had seen too many Hong Kong rip-off movies. Cuz waited, and waited, then leaned. Mouth rammed his fist into the dumpster.

"Fuck you, Faggit!"

Mouth was hurting and making less sense than usual.

"Not a chance."

Cuz would have been at a disadvantage in a fair fight, but to make a fair fight between him and Mouth they'd have to put a tube in his head and suck his brains out. Still, Mouth was so stupid, he actually pulled himself together when he got angry. There was a bit of heft behind his second punch. Cuz leaned the other way and Mouth dinged the dumpster again.

More curses and another solar system punch. Cuz scooped up one of the extra virgin cans. Full, it could have killed a man; empty, it was mostly noise, like Mouth himself. Cuz waited, got under the Mouth's guard—no trouble there—and popped him across the face.

Just Cuz's luck: the Mouth had a delicate nose which spurted like a fire hydrant and which, naturally, the dumb-shit thought was broken. Mouth was truly panicked, truly berserk, and in the heartbeat Cuz had before the bawling ape tried to squash him against the dumpster, he cursed himself thoroughly for getting suckered into a fight with a moron.

Cuz's lungs were full of humid, rancid air when Mouth slammed into him. He took one good clout along the ribs before he got his legs braced and shoved back. The alley was six feet wide, eight at the most. Mouth was still trying to catch his balance when his back collided with the opposite wall. He went ass-first into a scum puddle. Cuz whiffed something dead as Mouth wheezed and cursed.

You could almost feel sorry for him: a big, brainless ox who truly couldn't comprehend that a little guy had thrown him against a wall. Then Mouth spotted a lump of loose concrete the size of a softball. He put his paw around it and Cuz stopped feeling any kind of sorry for him.

Cuz was small and slight and he didn't have the luxury of fighting fair. Using his head as a battering-ram, he ran at Mouth, spearing his gut, slamming him against the bricks. Then Cuz straightened up along the Mouth's sternum. The top of his head clipped Mouth beneath the jaw. It hurt, but Cuz kept going and the back of Mouth's skull cracked against the wall.

The guy who'd taught Cuz that trick had said, done right, it could kill a man. The guy was dead himself now—AIDS, what else?—and since Mouth didn't have anything vital above his waist, Cuz kneed him one for good measure. Then he let go to catch his breath.

"You better come inside, Cuz," JoJo said from the doorway.

Yeah, his ten minute break seemed about over, but Cuz had a feeling his break wasn't the only thing that was over.

JoJo and Mouth went at it for a few minutes. This was Mouth's third day at the ovens and JoJo had already admitted to Cuz that he had sauce sitting on the shelf that could make a better pizza. When JoJo started reaming Mouth out in Italian, Cuz thought there was a chance he wasn't going to lose this lousy job, but one look at JoJo coming through the door again and fried that hope.

"You can't go beatin' up on my sister's kid like that. He don't know better yet."

"Then he can pay me for the lesson. I *need* money, JoJo. I told you that."

"Yeah, yeah, I know. And you was working out okay, too. You're smart, Cuz. I always said you was smarter than the rest of us, but then you go beatin' up on my sister's kid. Jesus, Cuz—I can't fuckin' fire him—"

"So? You fuckin' fire me instead!" Cuz had known it was coming, but that didn't cut the sting. "I didn't *start* it. Your sister's fuckin' *homophobic* kid started it."

"So, I *can't* fire him."

JoJo was trapped; his family didn't know, and Cuz couldn't blame him for not telling them. Mouth would keep his job and Cuz was scrambling again, trapped again. JoJo had been the bottom of his list. He pounded the stainless steel table, not

loud, but hard enough to make the knives at the far end jump.
Another mistake: JoJo looked at the knifes and JoJo looked
nervous.

"I gotta pay my rent the day after tomorrow."

JoJo reached into his pocket, pulled out a roll, and peeled a
bill out of the middle. "Here's twenty."

"Shit. Twenty won't cover it."

"What I'm paying you won't cover it. You got expensive
tastes, Cuz."

"Not any more, JoJo. Not for a long time."

"Get yourself another sugar daddy like Wills."

Cuz shook his head. JoJo was as close to a friend as he had
anymore; it wouldn't help to pound snot out of him for bringing Wills into this. He took the twenty, stuffed it in the front
pocket of his jeans. "Yeah, well, be seein' ya."

"Look," JoJo whispered. "Come back in a few weeks, if you
still need the job. He ain't gonna last that long."

A few weeks was an eternity the way Cuz's life had been going lately. He kept a lid on his temper until he cleared the corner, then, as he settled in for the long, steamy walk—there
wasn't a bus in sight and he couldn't afford a cab—he let it go.
No can or bottle was safe.

If he was so damn smart, why did Mouth have his job?
Why was he working off the books for below minimum wage?
Double or nothing, Mouth didn't even know what minimum
wage was.

Wills had gotten Cuz reading again while they were together. Before Wills died, Cuz had sworn he'd use the legacy
to get off the streets and go back to school. He'd meant to keep
his promise; he'd really meant to, but it hadn't happened. The
legacy was gone and Cuz needed rent money by Tuesday, or
he'd be truly on the streets, like he hadn't been in too long.

The streets had changed while he'd squatted safe in a basement room. Cuz wasn't sharp the way he'd used to be; mostly
because he wasn't as young. There was a whole new generation of boys prowling the places he'd called his.

He took aim at a beer can and kicked it without bothering to
see what, or who, might be in way. It missed a baby stroller by
inches. Cuz hadn't meant to hassle anyone. He'd've apologized to the woman pushing the stroller, if she'd given him a
chance. Shit, he *had* manners. And maybe that was why she
reamed him out as he slouched past.

A bus rumbled by. Cuz caught the driver's eye and sprinted for the corner. The bus waited until he was ten steps short, then slapped its doors shut and popped its air brakes. A belch of diesel fumes caught Cuz face-on. Crud coated his already-sweat-sticky skin. It was like being cooked in dirt. If he could have remembered how, Cuz might have wept, just to clear his eyes. Instead, he picked up a broken bottle and hurled it after the bus.

His aim was good enough, but it didn't make any difference. Glass shattered without making a sound.

Home, when Cuz finally got there, was hotter than the streets. 'Til Tuesday, he had a squeaky fan to move the air around and a bottle of tap water in the refrigerator. When he'd spat and swallowed the street-taste out of his mouth, Cuz climbed into the shower—a concrete stall backed against the kitchen sink. He had ten minutes, maybe, before the hot water ran out, ten minutes to come up with a way to come up with the rent.

It wasn't much time and it wasn't much of a plan: haul his lost-boy gear out of the closet, head uptown again, cruise the big hotels south of the park. Cuz didn't shave and his hair was back to its natural color. In an oversize soccer jersey, baggy jeans, and sloppy shoes he could still pass for thirteen. These days, *acting* thirteen was the challenge. He was making an practiced mess of his damp hair when someone knocked on the door.

"You said Tuesday, George," he shouted, making no move to open it.

"I talked to JoJo. He's worried about you."

Cuz mouthed an obscenity at the mirror. JoJo's good intentions were going to get him hurt.

"He told me what happened today."

"So? It's Sunday, not Tuesday."

"So, I got an address for you, Cuz. Go there and forget about Tuesday."

Cuz mouthed another obscenity, but he put the brush down and headed for the door. "You don't own me, George." He spun the locks and cracked the door.

"Thank God for small favors."

In his county-club shirt and designer khakis, George could pass for the kind of fish Cuz hoped to hook south of the park the same way Cuz could pass for thirteen. He had a straight place somewhere uptown with a straight wife, a straight dog, and two better-be-straight sons he watched like a hawk; because George lived another life upstairs, over the basement, and George knew what happened to lost boys.

He flashed a business card between the first and second fingers of his right hand. "You interested? I give you another week?"

Cuz seized the card, memorized the address. "Two."

"Yeah, and wear your own clothes."

Cuz returned the card. "These are my own clothes. Don't you remember buying them for me?"

"Must've been somebody else. And, another thing, Cuz—don't go pulling something; it won't work. You don't show up and tonight's Tuesday. Don't even bother coming back. I'll have the locks changed before you do. Understand?"

"What's to understand?"

"Wise up, sonny boy. You're on the way down."

"Thanks for the warning."

Cuz leaned on the door to close it and stayed leaning until he heard George's feet on the stairs. Then he stripped off the lost-boy look and eased into black leather and silk.

JoJo had a point: Cuz did have expensive tastes.

He broke JoJo's twenty taking a cab to an address one block short of the business card. The building was new; fancy, but discreet; with a neon-lit glass awning and a moonlighting cop for a night doorman. Cuz felt the moonlighter target him before he crossed the street and rattled off the apartment number as soon as he hit the neon light.

"You expected?" the moonlighter asked.

"Yeah."

"Name?"

"Don't have a name. Surprise, surprise: I'm the entertainment. Just call and tell them George sends his regrets . . . his regards."

George was a brass-plated bastard, but he didn't play games, not where money was involved, and neither would his "friends." The moonlighter wasn't happy, but he punched the numbers into the house phone. Throbbing music muscled out of the intercom grille and the moonlighter had to shout to make himself heard. But the electric lock buzzed louder than the cheap speaker and Cuz headed for the elevator.

Seventeenth floor, one down from the penthouse. Too bad

the night was hazy. With clear skies, the view might be worth the rest. Cuz studied his reflection in the elevator mirrors and shook his head, just once, just slightly. The view was *never* worth the rest.

Digging into a pocket, Cuz pulled out a flat, flexible coin-catcher that held pills rather than dimes. He selected two purplish ovals and a powder blue tablet, then hawked enough saliva to gag them down before the elevator coasted to a stop at seventeen.

The floor lobby was stone quiet. An old building then, with thick walls and neighbors who probably had no idea what went on in what proved to be the last apartment off the right-side corridor. Cuz hesitated before he punched the door buzzer. The pills were cutting in. He was starting not to care, not to feel. The door swung open.

"Cuz! Lookin' good."

Cuz slipped under the bridge a man's arm made between his shoulder and the door jamb. Heavy music hit him like a wall, and the smell: booze, smokes, and through it all, sex. Heads in the hall and next room swivelled his way, smiled, showed teeth. Cuz hadn't recognized the address, hadn't figured on knowing anyone in the room. Should've known better: the address came from George. Three pills wouldn't be enough. Cuz wished for a pair of V's; he hadn't had a V since winter.

A presence loomed behind. An arm made a noose around his waist. A spread-fingered hand pressed against his thigh, probed the nerve below his hip bone until he gasped and sighed and leaned back to see a face he'd known too long looking down at him.

The phone rang and the man who picked it up, an older gent with a trimmed beard and snake eyes, looked straight at Cuz before saying: "Yeah, he showed."

It would be a long, long night for a two-week reprieve.

*   *   *

Cuz left the seventeenth floor in the quiet hours between three AM and dawn. He was a little drunk, a little sore, and willingly in the arms of a soft, gray man who smelt of limes and spice. His name was Ralph and he swore parties weren't his thing. Ralph was lying about the parties, and maybe about his name, but his wallet was thick and shiny; and his clothes had all the right labels.

Ralph directed a cab crosstown to a building that had been grand for a hundred years. The ceilings were higher than they needed to be and the view from Ralph's windows was postcard-perfect. Once upon a time, Wills had promised them a window view like this; that was before they knew how sick Wills was, how quick he'd wither away.

The jewel-lights were blurring together when a cough caught Cuz's attention.

"What do you want to do tomorrow?" Ralph asked from another doorway. He'd changed into a shiny satin robe that hung wrong over his gut. When he sat down, it was pretty obvious what Ralph wanted to do.

What Cuz wanted was to get paid and go home. He knew the drill, though, better than Ralph who moaned sloppily when Cuz climbed into his lap and slid his hands beneath the satin.

They were inseparable through dawn and an itchy morning. Ralph snored and kept his soft, hairy leg crooked over Cuz's thighs. When Ralph finally awoke, Cuz wanted food and got a home-cooked breakfast, which should have served as a warning that Ralph didn't know the drill at all, that Ralph thought he'd gotten lucky, that Ralph thought when you brought the entertainment home there wouldn't be anything due and owing.

Cuz broke that bubble around four.

"I gotta go. Give me three bills and we'll call it even."

Ralph's mouth had worked like a fish's. He never *paid,* he said, never brought party-boys into his home. This was real. He'd opened his heart, not his wallet.

Cuz folded his arms and shook his head. Nobody went to that seventeenth floor for the first time. "Three bills," he repeated, not adding that it was a bargain: he *was* out of practice and the window view was better by day than by night.

Ralph got pissed, made threats, but finally paid up.

Feeling flush, Cuz took another cab back downtown—as far downtown as the cabbie would drive.

"Time's money, kid, and there ain't no fares coming out of your neighborhood," the face in the mirror said bluntly.

Cuz couldn't argue, not dressed as he was. He walked the rest of the way, ignoring the stares as he'd ignored them most of his life, and was halfway through a shower when George let himself in with the master keys.

The row began with, "You punk piece-of-shit," and devolved from there. Lawyer that he was, George knew how to throw a punch that Cuz couldn't dodge. Cuz was wedged in a corner, nursing a busted lip, when the truth came out: "I send you up there to do something *nice* for you—to help you out of a tight spot—and you hustle my best friend!"

George and Ralph? Cuz didn't buy it, but his opinion didn't count, especially when he spat, "I put in my time with your best friends," and got his blood on George's blindingly white T-shirt.

Never mind that he was bleeding because George had belted him. The red stain crossed the line.

"You're outta here," George sputterd, his uptown enunciation gone. "Now. Through that door. I don't want to see your sorry face around here again. I don't want to hear your piss-ant name again. Understand?"

They always had to ask, as if there were some magic in understanding.

"I'm gone," Cuz agreed, wiping his face on his hand then shaking his hand, spattering blood on the floor.

He dressed quickly, with George watching him. Modesty was nothing Cuz had ever understood, except as an act, and, in a deeper sense, he and George were too much alike to notice or care. Cuz had a backpack in the closet, a sturdy souvenir from earlier days. When push came to shove, he could live out of it for while, once he'd shoved his leather pants into the bottom: the leather pants that held his entire three-bill life savings in their right-side pocket.

After money, the most important things were memories, the dregs of life with his mother and Wills: a few packs of paper, wrapped in plastic and bound with rubber bands. Cuz was transferring them from a box to the pack when an ash-brown-hair bracelet caught his eye. The girl-woman-elf-whatever; her name had been Jerlayne, he remembered that. Come to think of it, life, which hadn't been great before her one-night intrusion, had really turned sour afterward, when George spotted the damage she'd done to his precious wrought-iron gate.

Still, if Cuz only kept the good memories, there'd be, maybe, three sheets of paper going into his backpack. He tugged Jerlayne's bracelet over his hand and tucked it under the cuff of a long street shirt. Even in this summer weather, long sleeves, long pants, and solid shoes were best on the street. Another five minutes, with George ranting at him the whole time, and Cuz left the basement he'd called home for the last five years.

Panic set in around dawn the next day, when a kid—a maybe-twelve-year-old kid—pulled a gun on him, just for getting too close in the open cesspool their neighborhood called a park. The good places, the real parks, the subway stations, bus terminals, and arcades, were taken and defended. Cuz could have taken the kid, his gun, and his lair betweeen the handball court wall and the big green dumpsters . . . and by Wednesday every street rat in the city would be laying for him. He knew; he'd been one of them, a long time ago.

They'd accepted him then as one of their own, the smallest predators in the jungle. Now they looked at him and saw the enemy.

Cuz walked twenty miles that day, if he walked one, and rode the trains all night, staying one station ahead of the transit cops. He broke his bills before he started looking too seedy and stashed them in a train-station locker. The locker was scarcely shut before a suit suggested a rendezvous. His allure wasn't completely shot. But when Cuz looked in the suit's eyes, he didn't like what he saw and blew him off.

Sundown and fireworks got him two hot dogs, rancid fries, flat Coke, and a quarter-sized blister on the bottom of his foot. By Tuesday afternoon, Cuz saw the abyss looming ahead. JoJo still had the Mouth working for him and George was out of the question. That left the last hellhole in the universe: a glass-walled office on the forty-fifth floor of a corporate hard-on tower.

After washing in the bus station's men's room, resisting another dubious advance, and putting on his last clean shirt; Cuz presented himself to his uncle's secretary, a no-nonsense woman who gasped when she looked up from her computer.

"He said you'd died a year ago."

"And you believed him? How many times has he told you that about me? He here?"

She nodded, a quarter-inch in each direction. "I don't imagine he's expecting you?"

Cuz shook his head and sat where she told him to wait. She was smart enough not to use the intercom to deliver her bad news. Not that it mattered: good ol' Uncle Ted swore loud enough to wake the dead when he heard who was sweating on the office furniture. She returned to her desk as if nothing had happened, but that was what she did every rare time Cuz came calling. It was enough to make him wonder how his god-damned uncle treated her the rest of the time.

Five more excruciating minutes spun off the wall clock, then he was there: Uncle Ted in a suit, tie, and contempt.

"Theodore?" Uncle Ted said, as if there were anyone else sitting in the plushly uncomfortable chairs. "You should have called." He stuck out his hand.

"Don't have a phone," Cuz replied, standing, ignoring the hand, stalking into the wood-paneled office with his shoulders up and his head down.

Uncle Ted closed the door behind them. "Don't sit," he warned. "You stink. Where've you been living? Back on the streets?"

"Yeah, your prophecies finally came true."

Their eyes locked for the first time. Identical names, Theodore Alfred Kennicut, were all they had in common, and Cuz had left the name behind years ago. Maybe if he'd been tall and blond and muscular like the pure-American Kennicuts, but Cuz took after his mother and grandmother, both slight and artistic, both dead before they turned thirty-five—not to mention whatever he'd inherited from his missing-link father. Maybe life would have gone differently. Maybe they wouldn't have shunted him off to a boarding school after she died. Maybe they wouldn't have locked their doors after he busted out of school, leaving him no place to come except here, where Uncle Ted managed very old, very sound investments for the very best families, including his own.

"And now what, Theodore?" No one else called him Theodore; these days, no one else even knew the name his mother had given him.

Uncle Ted stood behind his leather chair, behind his sleek desk. More than enough power to keep anyone named Cuz at arm's length. Cuz couldn't meet his uncle's eyes so he read the paper strewn across his desk. Upside down or sideways, it didn't matter: Cuz could read fast and remember every word he read, but the meanings—the keys to the code—slipped away.

"If you've come for money, Theodore, there's none. I told

you that the last time and the time before that: it's gone. You
knew what you had to do, and you didn't do it."

A million. That's what Wills left behind when he died: an in-
surance policy with Theodore Alfred Kennicut typed in, all
formal, as the beneficiary. A million wasn't a million any
more; that's what Uncle Ted said when he read off a list of
taxes and fees. Cuz had asked to see the paper. He could remember every word, every number. But what did he know
about estate taxes or executors? A million wasn't a million;
that much he believed.

"I need a job," he confessed. "Messenger, maybe. Something like that. Anything."

"Anything, Theodore?"

Cuz dropped his eyes, even if it blew what little chance he'd
had. No, he'd blown that already himself, saying "anything" to
Uncle Ted. Uncle Ted had taught him the meaning of *anything*
while his mother was still alive, when he'd visit wherever they
were living—the great big brother who worked miracles with
landlords and telephone companies and never failed to "take
care" of his namesake nephew. By the time he hit the streets,
Cuz knew all the tricks, all the cruelties.

Uncle Ted came around the desk. He laid his hand alongside
Cuz's ear. Despite himself, despite the years and everything
that filled them, Cuz raised his head and found himself on the
losing end of a stare war.

"Still got your health?"

Cuz swallowed air and admitted he did. It was an old question and no one asked it more often than Cuz asked it himself.
What he'd done, where he'd done it, he should have been dead
before Wills came along. Wills said he was charmed, too good
to die, but that was Wills. Wills' doctors said it was only a matter of time and he should get himself tested. That was doctors,
and Cuz trusted doctors less than he trusted Uncle Ted.

He did get sick—when he ate something rotten, an occupa-
tional hazard the way he'd lived. And he'd had so many sore
throats when he was little they'd taken his tonsils out. But
since then, nothing, really; not even a cold in the worst winter.

Uncle Ted wanted Cuz dead. He'd told him so, right after his
mother's funeral: "You're an embarrassment to this entire
family. A mistake that should have been corrected before you
were born. A branch of the family tree that needs pruning."
There'd been money, afterward, when Cuz had needed it, like

rope for a noose. Except it hadn't worked. No matter how many times Uncle Ted told his secretary otherwise, Cuz didn't die.

Year after year, he didn't die until he—and Uncle Ted—began to wonder if there weren't something *wrong* with him.

Cuz sucked in his gut. "No doctors. No experiments." He'd seen what they'd done to Wills.

"They'll pay you, Theodore. Enough that you can have an address and a shower, if you're serious about getting a job."

The hand fell; Cuz looked out the window. Whatever it was, it wasn't charm. Nobody else outgrew the streets. He could kill himself: jump off a bridge or in front of a train, but that was just another kind of planning for the future.

"I know some people, Theodore. Genetic research: immunology and DNA. We're investing in them. They're scientists: chemists, not doctors. I've told them about you. They'd like to meet you—"

Cuz shook his head, but it was too late. It was as if he were standing on the window ledge instead of inside it. The wind was blowing in his face and a voice was saying *Jump. Jump!*

Uncle Ted made a few calls: to his chemist-guys, to a restaurant ("You like Italian, right? There's a new place, five stars: their osso buco can't be touched." Cuz had nodded, betrayed by his stomach, by the life he'd tasted with Wills), to a nearby hotel.

"Take a shower, Theodore, a long one. I'll have Marta send over some clothes. Be in the lobby at eight."

The shower, with unlimited hot water, numbed Cuz's nerves. Reminding himself that he hadn't actually promised to do anything except eat a good meal, Cuz hit the lobby at seven-thirty. The doormen didn't notice him in a high-price get-up that blended with the carpet. Uncle Ted introduced him as Theodore, no last name to confuse matters, certainly no kin to the Kennicuts. The chemists—three of them, all older than Cuz had expected and different kinds of foreign—pumped his hand and asked blunt questions during the walk to the restaurant.

More important, they listened to Cuz's answers and answered his questions, even the testy ones where he already knew the answers. It stood to reason, they said, and Cuz agreed, that somebody out of five billion people had to be immune to AIDS. The first problem was finding that someone; the second was figuring out why. Between the departure of the proscuitto-wrapped melon and the arrival of the osso buco, Cuz began thinking he'd let them have a shot at his blood.

One shot. That's what they said they'd need. Their chemistry could do the rest.

It was too late to save Wills, but not for his memory. The money—they tossed out ten thousand for a start with royalties, if they found something they could patent—wasn't a million, but Cuz promised himself, as Uncle Ted poured Chianti, that he wouldn't waste another legacy.

The chemists raised their glasses. Cuz raised his, too, and even dared a glance at Uncle Ted who wore a contented smile beneath his rat-shiny eyes.

The food was good, better—richer—than Cuz had eaten in months, so he wasn't exactly surprised when he got gut pains halfway through. No one seemed to notice when he stopped eating—Wills had taught him how to do that—and, anyway, he'd had more than enough. But the pain got worse, like hot metal, like nothing he'd known before, even when he'd been dumpster diving. Saying nothing, Cuz pushed his chair from the table. Standing happened, walking didn't . . . couldn't. Cuz didn't know if he was swaying or if the restaurant was.

Then the lights started getting dim.

Uncle Ted caught him before he fell, shoved him back in his chair. The lights came back; the pain just got worse.

"When did you eat last?" he asked, as if starving were a crime.

Cuz shook his head. He didn't dare open his mouth, not the way he felt inside.

Waiters fluttered. Someone suggested a cab and an emergency room. By then, Cuz felt bad enough that he liked the idea. One of the chemists had his cell phone out.

"Don't worry, kid," Uncle Ted said. "We're getting you an ambulance. Everything's working out just fine."

Cuz knew then that he'd been poisoned. He didn't know how, but, shit, those three *chemists* were still sitting, absolutely rock-solid calm, across the table and they were in on it from the start. Pain or no pain, Cuz had to get away, and he tried—oh, God, he tried—but Uncle Ted had him trapped by the shoulder and when he tried to shout and tell the waiters, the other diners, anyone who'd look or listen, what was really happening, his stomach betrayed him and everyone looked away.

Two waiters hustled him to the sidewalk where the last thing

Cuz remembered was an ambulance jolting to a stop at the end of the awning. It had the right shape, the right colors, all the right flashing lights, but Cuz knew the name of every hospital in the city and Metropolitan General wasn't one of them. He tried screaming as the med-techs hoisted him into the back. Then they slapped a plastic mask over his nose and a needle in his arm.

The gas that flowed wasn't oxygen and the lights went out for good.

Chapter 22

Jerlayne took her four-month-old son from Gelma's arms, settled him against her shoulder, and walked the length of the workroom, tapping him gently between the shoulders until a froggy burp escaped. She wasn't nursing him. It weighed heavily around her heart, but Goro had bargained for a favor and nursing interfered.

So, Gelma had moved into the great house and Laydin recognized the gnome better than he recognized his mother. Gelma took Laydin when he began to fuss and whisked him away to the nursery. They'd be together again before supper. Jerlayne never missed his feedings. She loved Laydin with all her heart, but it wasn't the same as it had been with Evoni.

That probably was better for everyone.

Jerlayne went to the window, stared out toward the sea. It was a foggy day; she could barely see the grass where it ended at the bluff, but she could hear her daughter singing from the rocks.

Nothing odd had happened since Laydin's birth. Nothing odd, truly, had happened then, either. He was an elf, just as he was supposed to be. Aulaudin hadn't tried to share Laydin's thoughts again. There wasn't any need. Even Jereige had been persuaded before he left with Elmeene for Stonewell; and Jerlayne had reconciled with him.

Fear, as Aulaudin had said, could shape a man's thoughts into a stranger's.

Ombrio had decided to move himself to Briary, to improve his foraging skills, he said. That was certainly possible, though Jerlayne thought it more likely that her sister's last son was finally ready to leave the homestead that held so few good memories him. Whatever his reason, he was gone, along with all their other guests, including Claideris, who'd never had the simple decency to apologize.

Sunrise belonged to her and Aulaudin again and, despite everything that had happened in the last year, Jerlayne had begun to think there was order in her life again—except for Goro's favor sitting on her worktable.

Thus far, it had defeated her every attempt to unravel its secrets. If the goblin had been willing to let her change it a bit, Jerlayne thought she could have gotten farther. Her understanding of aluminum, after all, had been built on a ruinous heap of slag and dross. Jerlayne had gone so far as to seek Goro out less than a week after Laydin's birth. She'd stood on the far side of the ditch surrounding the goblin camp until they fetched him out for her.

He hadn't been pleased to see her standing with the dark green slab in her hands and he wouldn't give her permission to change it in any way.

"If it is beyond you, then I'll take it back. It was only a hope."

Jerlayne had her pride. "Another month," she'd bargained. "It's tempered—I know that much—and held together with heat. I'd wanted to remove the heat, to make it easier, but I don't have to make it easier."

"A month then," Goro had agreed.

She'd gone back twice more, losing the summer to frustration. The last time, Goro had said one more month was the last month. Three of those four weeks were gone and Jerlayne had nothing to show for hours upon days of futile shaping. Gelma knew of her frustration, and Aulaudin, of course. They offered encouragement; Aulaudin offered to escort Jerlayne to Stonewell and her mother. Thus far, Jerlayne had resisted *that* suggestion, and would continue to resist it, for another day, perhaps two, then her choices would narrow: admit defeat or ask Elmeene for help, with no assurance that her mother could untangle the puzzle.

It sat on the worktable, an accusing slab of cloth and mystery. Staring at it, Jerlayne thought of all the other chores and shapings she'd left undone: from chipped plates to an ominous crack in one of millstones. Every one a good excuse to walk out of her workroom without touching Goro's maddening challenge.

A seditious voice in Jerlayne's imagination reminded her that she'd gotten no farther yesterday than she'd gotten a week ago, or a month. The wiry interior was a mass of contradictions: not an alloy, as bronze was part copper, part tin; or steel was iron steeped in charcoal; and not a mixture, like sand or fruitcake, or layers of paint on a wall. It was solid, yet slippery; it moved away when she tried to shape it, then flowed back like Evoni's sea.

Jerlayne had run out of tricks and, though she knew it was an illusion, the puzzle mocked her as she picked it up. A force, like heat shimmering around a fire, flowed through her arms and became a vile-tasting presence in her throat. In proud stubbornness, she gripped it tighter, pushed back, and recalled— for no good reason—the red dress, the horrible, dense, and slippery red dress in the flower-walled room where she'd prepared for her first exposure to the mortal realm.

She'd thought about the dress together with the puzzle before: there were similarities in their tangled structures, similarities that had led nowhere. But the dress by itself had been the key to parting the Veil. When Jerlayne let it permeate her thoughts, it had pulled her to its own place in the mortal realm.

The puzzle had been shaped in the mortal realm. Aulaudin, though he'd never seen anything quite like it, agreed with that conclusion. Why not let it pull her to its own place?

Jerlayne's silent question produced a score of cautionary answers, all of which paled compared to her need to solve the puzzle before Goro lost faith in her.

Swiftly Jerlayne shaped the bolts, closed the shutters and drew the curtains, lest the parting light betray her. Then she settled among her favorite cushions and clutched the object against her breasts. She imagined joining with it, as she might have joined with Aulaudin—

«Pull me to your proper place!»

With the red dress in her hands, Fairie had seemed to melt away as the mortal realm took shape. With the slab, there was no such gradual transition. One moment Jerlayne was comfortable in her workroom, the next she was in darkness: endless, frigid darkness. Her breath froze in her throat and though that sensation faded after a moment, a moment was long enough for Jerlayne to reconsider and regret her confidence. She thought *home* and *Sunrise* and *workroom* and regretted those thoughts, too: no elf, man or woman, could part the Veil from Fairie to Fairie without pausing in the mortal realm.

No great surprise, then, when Jerlayne found herself in no

proper place at all, but grateful she could exhale, swallow, open her eyes to darkness, and breathe in rancid, musty air. An ogre's lair? No, ogres were part of Fairie and, by rights, she wasn't—couldn't be—in Fairie. Another closet-room such as the place where she and Elmeene had changed their clothes? Or where she'd come face-to-face with her first mortal man?

Once a woman knew a place, she could return, just as men could; it was the infrequency of women's mortal-realm trysts that, according to Elmeene, made object-guides necessary.

In her panic, Jerlayne could believe she'd blown herself back to one of those closets, but she sat on dirt, not wood or stone, and the first wall she touched, if it were a wall, had the feel of coarse, woolen draperies. Warily, quietly, she rose to her feet, still clutching the slab, one-armed, against her breast; it wouldn't do to lose that. She saw light then, seeping through cracks in the walls, and waited for her eyes to make out everything that might be seen.

The place Jerlayne had come to wasn't a closet, wasn't a room at all, and though she'd never come closer than twenty paces to a goblin tent, every nerve said she was inside one. And surrounded by heaps of dense, layered cloth like what she held in her arms, only complete tunics; the tunics Goro wanted her to shape.

As in a dream, Jerlayne exchanged Goro's torn, burnt slab for a larger one, definitely meant to protect a man's heart. She noticed others that seemed meant for arms and legs. The tent was too dark for an accurate count, but she guessed it held enough armor for a dozen men . . . a dozen mortal men who erected tents uncannily similar to the tents goblins raised in Fairie?

It seemed unlikely, yet Aulaudin—and other elfin men— said the mortal realm was vast beyond Fairie's measure and that all the elves together had not yet seen the whole of it. Could the goblin plains be part of the mortal realm? Also unlikely: goblins swore they couldn't part the Veil—unless you listened to and believed Maun.

Jerlayne didn't believe Maun because Aulaudin didn't believe his father, but when she realized that the patterns of light seeping through the wall formed a door, she knew she'd have to open it before she made her way back to Sunrise. Retrieving Goro's slab, clutching it together with the whole tunic she'd found, Jerlayne made her way to the bright-line arch. She felt the blankety wall up and down until she touched the leather thongs her memory matched with the flaps of Goro's tents.

Her heart was pounding, with excitement, not fear, as she slipped the knot, lifted the flap—

A blue-skinned, black-eyed goblin stood not an arm's length away. Behind him, there were tents everywhere, more than Jerlayne could count without moving her eyes. And goblins, goblins like elves and scyldrin at a wedding.

His mouth dropped open, but the scream Jerlayne heard clearest was her own. He reached toward her; she shaped pain, as much pain as she could imagine, blinding pain, burning pain, and let it flow down her arm when he touched her. Flames leapt through her sleeve to engulf his hand. They were both afire, both screaming. The goblin fell to the ground; Jerlayne thought of escape.

To the right and ahead she saw tents and goblins who'd begun to move in her direction. Directly behind was the tent where she'd emerged out of Fairie. Her panicky mind dismissed it as any sort of safe haven. Jerlayne turned to the left where a great, grassy meadow loomed beyond a pair of tents. Without further thought, she ran toward the horizon.

Jerlayne had no sense of where she was, no escape plan, other than the fervent wish to be *home*. It could be done. In the aftermath of Evoni's rise and her reconciliation with Aulaudin, he'd told her how he'd exploded through the Veil.

Aulaudin had been parting the Veil for centuries. He knew how to think solid, familiar thoughts despite rising panic—and Jerlayne's panic rose fast. Fanned by her own desperation, flames had spread from her sleeve to her skirt and hair, but fire didn't frighten her half as much as the goblins whose shouts she heard through her own screams.

They were Goro's ilk: hard and powerful. Jerlayne couldn't hope to outrun them, but she had to try, just as she had to try to shape Sunrise within her mind and leap from horrors of *here* to the safety of *there*.

If she'd had to wit to think, she might have thought her plight couldn't have worsened—then something struck her thigh. Healer and shaper that she was, Jerlayne knew a hole had been punched through her flesh. She felt the pain, like nothing she'd experienced before, and felt nothing, too, as if the rest of her leg no longer belonged to her but ran with its own mind, its own panic.

After two strides Jerlayne no long knew where her foot was or how her knee bent. Her balance faded. She staggered, headed for the grass and worse. As terror overwhelmed her, Jerlayne forgot about Sunrise; there was only one safe-haven when she was this frightened—

"Mother! Mothermothermother—"

She was swimming through air, drowning as she'd nearly drowned trying to stop Evoni's transformation. But this time, the hands that grabbed her weren't blue.

"I'm here," Elmeene shouted, "I'm here! Let go. Let go of the Veil! I can't hold you!"

Jerlayne let go of everything she held: two pieces of strange goblin armor, one whole, one broken, and the Veil. The sinking, drowning sensation ended, replaced by slaps and swats as her mother beat out the fire she'd brought with her. When all was quiet—safe—again, Jerlayne looked up into dark amber eyes and sobbed: "I didn't know. I didn't know what would happen . . ."

They were on the floor of Elmeene's workroom. Blood trickled from the wound in Jerlayne's thigh, which had begun to throb and swell. The air was already bitter with the stench of burnt cloth, singed hair, and stupidity.

"I thought I would be drawn to the mortal realm."

Elmeene blew air through her teeth: "*Sssshh* . . . tell me later. Tell me *everything* later. Now, try to relax and help me set this right. You're bleeding, daughter, and burnt."

From the floor and through a haze of blood loss and pain, Jerlayne caught the sour look on her mother's face as she collected the armor and set it on the old table beneath the wall of twenty-link chains. She wondered if she could hold the line on everything or if she'd have to confess the revelation that her goblin knew where elfin women went to secure their elfin children and had sworn all other goblins knew it, too.

Jerlayne could imagine how that would sour her mother's expression.

Still she thought she could keep the secret, then Elmeene exposed the wound in her leg.

"You've been *shot*, Jerlayne. *Shot!*"

Jerlayne didn't argue, though nothing protruded from her flesh. There should have an arrow.

The wound was messy, Elmeene said. Jerlayne didn't argue

with that either. Whatever had struck her had spun and tumbled as it passed through her flesh.

"Be grateful it didn't strike a bone or something vital."

That, too, was beyond argument, though Jerlayne thought—between white moments of agony as Elmeene broke down the flesh that couldn't be healed and stretched the flesh that could—about the tunic she'd been carrying. She asked herself if one of the leg pieces she'd left behind could have protected her. Another moment and she guessed why Goro wanted as much of the stuff as she could make.

The sun set while Elmeene labored over the blistered flesh of Jerlayne's arm. An elfin woman healed with her hands, not her eyes. Elmeene worked in darkness before she pronounced herself finished and in darkness they sat, mother and daughter together when the Stonewell chimes were struck to summon the homestead to supper.

"I will bring you something to eat later."

It went without saying that a daughter couldn't suddenly appear at her mother's side for supper, not without the man—the husband, father, or brother—who'd escorted her along the pass-throughs.

"We'll talk, Jerlayne; we must talk. I'll make some excuse to your father, if he's back. Send him off foraging again, and with your brothers, too. There must be something we desperately need . . ."

Elmeene's voice trailed, leaving Jerlayne to wonder, in the midst of her own confusion, how joining ran between her parents in the wake of Laydin's birth.

"I must tend Mati before I come back here. He's an easy infant; it won't take long." Elmeene's skirt rustled as she stood and started toward the door. "There's some fruit in the bowl and bits of sweet cake, if hunger takes you before I get back. Close the drapes, if you make a light. Wait for me, Jerlayne," her voice took on a warning tone. "I deserve to know what happened . . . I *need* to know."

Jerlayne was grateful for the darkness: With her wounds mostly healed and her own workroom standing empty at Sunrise, she'd intended to part the Veil to the mortal realm closet—she'd never forget that closet, especially getting there from *this* room—and from the closet to Sunrise before Elmeene's soup cooled. She still would have preferred to vanish, but Elmeene's request was both fair and undeniable. Whatever chaos her absence from Sunrise wrought, her mother had earned the few answers Jerlayne could provide.

She closed the drapes, made a light, and ate every bit of fruit and cake she could find: a healed body craved food after a healing. It wasn't nearly enough. Jerlayne had paced herself sore by the time the latch on the workroom door freed the bolt.

"Meat pie," Elmeene explained, setting a cloth-covered plate down. "I know it's not your favorite, but I'm known to like it when I'm working late. Your father hadn't returned; we can hope he's gone until tomorrow. And your brothers, except Nereige, set off in the morning. Where is Aulaudin?"

"Foraging. I expected him home—"

"We'll lie. We'll find a lie. What were you doing? You have a son—" Elmeene stared at the objects Jerlayne had brought with her as if she were seeing them for the first time. "You shaped those?"

Jerlayne broke the pie crust. A puff of steam escaped, but she put a forkful in her mouth and swallowed. Her eyes watered as her throat burned. "No." She reached for the water pitcher. "Goro gave the smaller, broken slab to me. He wanted me to shape more . . . More for what, I wanted to know." She forced a simple, foolish smile and filled her fork again.

Elmeene fondled the dense stuff as any shaping woman would. Jerlayne watched questions and frustrations weave through her mother's expression.

"Your *goblin* gave you this?"

"He did."

"None of us made it," Elmeene said, a cat with her eye on a mouse. "It must have been foraged."

"So I thought," Jerlayne agreed, in no great hurry to expose her secrets. "I remembered the red dress and what you'd told me about letting something mortal-made pull me through the Veil."

"I believe I had something different, less dangerous in mind."

"I promised Goro I'd unlock the wretched thing by midsummer. When I couldn't, I bargained for another month, and another and another. I'm on my last month. I've bargained myself into a corner and I'm no closer than I was at the beginning: I was desperate. I thought no harm could come from following it through."

"You don't think, Jerlayne," Elmeene said sadly. "You have a notion and you give into it; that's not thinking."

"I found a tent filled with what I was looking for," Jerlayne retorted, then paid close attention to her fork.

"A tent, Jerlayne? What sort of tent?" The cat was suspicious.

"A black, half-round tent surrounded by other tents. A goblin tent, Elmeene, and more goblins than I could count. There's *another* Veil; I *saw* the plains. I don't know how or why, but when I followed that small slab you're holding, it took me to the goblin plains."

Elmeene frowned. She dropped the armor on her worktable as though it were suddenly more dangerous than iron, but she didn't claim that her thoughtless daughter must have been mistaken.

"You were shot through by a gun, Jerlayne, by a bullet, not an arrow. Mortals have guns and shoot one another with bullets. Think again about what you saw: not all mortals are fair skinned."

Jerlayne had thought about that already, remembering the wood-colored mortal she'd lured into a back room. "Their skin was *blue,* Elmeene. You aren't going to tell me that there are mortal ilks with dark blue skin?"

"No, I'm not; I can't. This is serious, very serious. You think the worst that's happened to you is raising a siren, but this, I tell you, could be much worse. Mortals have had guns since before you were born. Your father—your mortal father—collected them. They hung from his walls like my chains. He let me handle them, never guessing why I would be interested in them, of course. They are made from steel, many pieces of heat-hard steel such as I could never shape, nor you. Guns are what they use now, instead of swords.

"I won't permit a gun at Stonewell. I'd never give one to a goblin, even though it might kill ten ogres for every one that died of a sword thrust. I have asked Jereige subtly and discreetly, while we were joined, what he knew about guns. He will not admit that they exist. By that I know we agree that they must not be brought into Fairie. I can't think of any man or woman who'd feel differently."

"Mother, I didn't mean to imply that you or father were giving *guns* to goblins. Aulaudin's mentioned them, but never shared them, and I didn't see the gun or bullet that shot me. I didn't know."

Elmeene picked up the armor tunic. "I believe you. "I wish—I truly wish—that I didn't. I don't want to know the name of the homestead that's given guns and bullets to their goblins and *this,* too. When I trysted with your father—your mortal father—he said guns were so powerful that a man would have to wear steel armor as thick as his thumb to protect himself from a bullet the way mail had once protected him from a sword. You can imagine how heavy and useless that would be! So there's been no armor against bullets, until now."

She held the tunic against her shoulders. It was mail, all right, with dangling strips of sticky cloth—men called it *velcro,* everyone loved it, and women couldn't shape it—instead of leather laces to make it fit.

"If your goblin gave you the torn slab and you found a tent filled will shirts like this, then, some goblins have armor, certainly, and weapons, perhaps, which other goblins do not—"

Jerlayne interrupted: "When the goblins have been at war with each other, I have seen wounded men outside Goro's tent. I offered to heal them, but Goro wouldn't let me. I thought it was men's pride. Maybe he didn't want me to see their wounds."

"Men?" Elmeene asked with her eyebrows flying high. "Since when do you refer to goblins as *men?*"

"They camp so close to the great house," Jerlayne stammered, "because we're so close to the Veil. They work in the fields and do the work no one else wants to do—"

"Because they aren't like us! They see cock-eyed. They are not *men.*"

It seemed to Jerlayne, as she chewed a mouthful of cooling meat pie, that Elmeene had, however, inelegantly, put words to the discomfort she'd felt around Goro—her goblin—from the beginning. Arhon was just as interesting and just as dangerous as a boar or bull; he was a goblin, not a man. Goro was different. He made himself interesting, so she thought of him as a man.

That, however, was a revelation Jerlayne intended to keep to herself. Besides, the chunks of meat and thick, brown gravy from the meat pie weighed in her stomach. As hungry as she'd been, her appetite had been prelude to exhaustion. She yawned not once but three times in quick succession.

"I've got to get back to Sunrise," she insisted, rising unsteadily to her feet. "I've told you everything."

"You don't think! Even now, you're not thinking!" Elmeene complained. "You're here and here you'll remain until you're rested. I shudder to think where you'd wind up if you parted the Veil now!"

Jerlayne was not unaware of the danger but said, "I've got to get back. Laydin, the scyldrin, even Goro. It's one thing for me to miss dinner—they know I've been wrestling with that armor—but they'll worry twice as much for the same reason if they don't see me at all."

Elmeene began to pace. "You've lost blood, Jerlayne. You need rest; you know you do—*I* taught you how to heal!" Her shoes squealed as she spun sharply, one stride short of the closed draperies. "I don't like it, not one bit, but there is a way . . ." She marched over to Jerlayne and without warning pressed her palms over her daughter's face. "I know I'm going to regret this, Jerlayne. I don't know how or why or when, but I'm sure that I will."

Jerlayne jerked away as soon as she felt the warmth of shaping and healing, but it was already too late: she watched in slack-jawed astonishment as her mother's face began to look like a reflection.

"Viljuen weeps, Mother!"

"It was a trick we played a long time ago—after we found the cure for blooddeath. We'd pretend to be someone else and—well, never mind that. It's more than the glamour you can weave around a mortal, less than real shaping. Have a hope that your husband's delayed beyond the Veil. There's no deceiving a joined man, but the scyldrin will think you're simply tired and gone to bed early."

"You pretended to be someone else?" Jerlayne asked the image of herself. "You trysted with other men after you were joined to Jereige?"

"There'd been so much death, so much mourning, so many hasty weddings afterward to bring Fairie back. We were never young, Jerlayne." Then Elmeene sighed. "You were never young either. You knew nothing of gaiety when you joined with Au-laudin, but that was your choice. It was never mine."

Jerlayne let that invitation to argument pass and yawned in-stead. "No matter how close together we stand, Elmeene, we never see the same things. You astonish me."

"*I* astonish *you?* You're the one who wanted to change Fairie, as I recall. Now, quick, before you fall asleep, where you're sitting, let me borrow your jewelry. Between fire and blood, your dress was a ruin, but no one will notice if the jewelry's right."

"Forget jewelry. Our hair—"

Jerlayne's was dark blonde and nearly straight; her mother's was an intricately arranged jungle of ginger that fell past her shoulders. It made an odd contrast with Jerlayne's pale complexion. But Elmeene had planned ahead. She swept the mass of locks and braids atop her head and confined it in a fringed table-scarf.

"I never wear my hair like that!"

"You will when you get home. Your hair was burning when I grabbed you. You've lost a bit on the right side. Sunrise or Stonewell, you're quite a sight this evening, Jerlayne. Aulaudin himself might not recognize you."

Jerlayne raised her hands to her scalp and felt the truth of her mother's observations. She wasn't a particularly vain woman, and hair would always grow back, but the brittle strands that broke when she touched them were the final blow in a long, brutal day.

Even if she'd gotten herself back to Sunrise she'd be weaving lies and deceptions. Worse: if she had gotten back to her own workroom, there would have been no one there to put out the flames or heal her wounds.

"Don't fret so," Elmeene advised, unclasping the first of her daughter's necklaces and fastening it around her own neck. "If only your son were older or Maialene's lad hadn't taken up with Maun! I could prevail upon one of them to escort me—as you, of course—to Stonewell tonight. Using pass-throughs, you could be here properly by tomorrow morning and our problems would be solved."

"Our problems aren't pass-throughs and deceiving our homesteads; our problems are that there's a second Veil, Elmeene: another Veil between Fairie and the plains where the goblins are fighting. And I parted that Veil. *That's* our problem!" Jerlayne had passed exhaustion. Her hands were shaking; she was more asleep than awake.

Elmeene stroked Jerlayne's fragile hair and soothed her temples with warm, gentle hands. "If it pleases you, yes, that is a problem. I suppose it makes sense; there have never been grass plains in Fairie, but I'd never thought about it. Truly, I'd never spared a single thought about where goblins lived.

They're goblins. I bargain with Arhon, I don't *talk* to him. You're the first, I think, to *talk* to a goblin.

"Even now, I can't quite hold the idea in my mind: another realm, not mortal or Fairie, where goblins live . . . with guns. It can't be true. I want to shake my head and say it's all a bad dream and I would, if I thought you'd let me."

Jerlayne freed herself from Elmeene's healing touch and broke a bit more hair in the process. "It's not a matter of me *letting* you! Look at me. Look at my hair. I didn't have a dream this afternoon!"

"I know," Elmeene replied, very quietly. "And I mustn't let myself forget, must I? But there's nothing I can do about goblins with guns and armor in a realm that isn't Fairie, isn't mortal. I can go to Sunrise. I can barely go to Sunrise . . . a woman, without her husband, parting the Veil to visit another homestead. I get chills just thinking about it!" She held out her arm which Jerlayne could see was covered with goose-flesh.

"Then don't go! Maybe no one will notice. Maybe Aulaudin's not there. Maybe he's already been there and is coming here. Maybe he'll share thoughts with Jereige and we'll all have to face one another and the truth, the truth about everything. I'm tired of lies, Mother. I was tired of lies when I lived here. I thought I'd be free of lies when I joined with Aulaudin, but I've only sunk deeper. Don't go to Sunrise and pretend to be me. Let there be one less lie in Fairie."

Elmeene wouldn't hear of that. After promising that she'd shape everything right, like a twenty-link chain, Elmeene parted the Veil and vanished from the workroom. Jerlayne fought and lost her battle to stay awake.

Chapter 23

A body didn't know why it ached or how it had been healed, only that after healing it needed dreamless sleep. Jerlayne was rested and refreshed when she opened her eyes the next morning. She was also alone in a shadowy room that was not immediately familiar. There was a dull ache from the deep, but fading, bruise around her thigh and no chance at all of drifting back to sleep.

In the time it took to rise from the pillows where she'd slept, Jerlayne's thoughts raced from empty contentment to panic: having done something she shouldn't have done, and hadn't intended to do, she found herself in a room she didn't dare leave waiting for her mother to return from Sunrise, where she should have been.

And she was ravenous to the point of moistening her fingertip to collect stale crumbs from her meat pie dinner. Jerlayne savored each tiny morsel, with the hope of blunting her appetite and, more importantly, distracting her from her helplessness. Both hopes were dashed. The bits of crust and gravy only set her stomach churning and as for helplessness . . . twice she set her mind to parting the Veil for a two-step journey to Sunrise. Each time—whether she thought about Elmeene's closet with its flower wall or the alley where she'd begun her search for Cuz—lights failed to flash, mists failed to swirl, and her mother's workroom remained solid around her.

Both mortal realm places could have changed. Men made a point of visiting their haunts frequently, lest their memories fade or the haunt change beyond the precise recognition that parting the Veil demanded. It had been a year, an eventful year, for Jerlayne, and perhaps the awful flowers had been more orange than pink . . .

It was easier—less humiliating, at least—to believe that the mortal realm had changed than to accept her other suspicion:

she'd lost her nerve. Her unwelcome discovery of a second Veil, not to mention having a hole ripped through her thigh, had thrown Jerlayne's desires into conflict. However much she wanted to return to Sunrise, she feared the possibility of that screaming goblin even more.

His face, haunting her as a bright morning fought its way through the curtains and shutters, broke Jerlayne's appetite. She picked up the smaller piece of armor and played with it in her hands as she paced the workroom's perimeter.

Goro had come to her because he wanted her to make more of the dense fiber that formed the armor, which implied that he was in no way the owner of the stacks Jerlayne had stumbled upon. Surely he'd be pleased to have what she'd found as a gift and not begrudge her a bit of tampering with the burnt and torn piece he'd given her. But that, as Elmeene might say, was thinking of Goro as a man and forgetting that he was a goblin. Forgetting, too, that he might wonder where she had gotten an entire tunic, when he had only a piece of one, and had claimed not to know what, exactly, it was.

Jerlayne stopped halfway to the door, turned and contemplated the dark green heap on her mother's worktable. Better to vent her curiosity on the piece she'd found for herself? There'd be fewer questions, fewer lies.

Assuming she found any structure at all. Taking risks she hadn't dared take at Sunrise, Jerlayne wasn't encouraged by her initial probes. Although she recognized and had shaped many of the armor's ingredients before, there were several she'd never encountered before. She had more success tearing through the wiry fiber with her teeth than she had with her shaper's skills.

She was seated at her mother's table, eyes closed and entranced with her mystery, when changes in sound and light shattered her concentration. There were good reasons women demanded privacy when they shaped: Jerlayne's fingertips were bleeding when she saw her mother, with the Veil closing behind her and wearing her own face.

"I'm sorry," they said together.

"There was nothing else to do," Jerlayne added, massaging her fingers to stanch the blood flow.

"I should have guessed and made a noise, several." Elmeene unbound her hair, heaping the cloth carelessly atop the table where it formerly lay smooth, leaving Jerlayne with the sense that her mother's journey had been exhausting and perhaps eventful, a suspicion Elmeene confirmed when she said: "I wouldn't want to make a habit of that."

"Goblins?" Jerlayne asked anxiously as the thought *They know. They followed me. They went to Sunrise!* raced through her mind.

"No. Nothing. No difficulties once I got to Sunrise. I'm out of practice plunging through the Veil. When you came here after . . . well, it had been scarcely a month since I'd gone after Mati. I knew the shapes of things. That little room I showed you? It's gone, the whole building's gone! No wonder men rely on rocks to mark their resting places! I tried five times before I found a way, and that wasn't quite right. I felt terrible when I slipped into Sunrise—I didn't look like myself or you, I'm sure—" Elmeene paused and continued on a different thought: "Your homestead cherishes you, Jerlayne. Thank the dust and stars, Aulaudin wasn't there. They let me retreat to your bedroom, but they'd have sent your husband in after me, if they'd had a way to find him."

"They worry; they've been through a lot on my account," and might endure more from her latest blunder.

Elmeene shrugged. "They weren't about to let me go without two cups of tea and sympathy. I told them to let me—you—sleep the day through, but Viljuen's ghost knows if they listened. You've got to hurry home. I'd hoped to be clever and send myself off on a journey from there to here, but they simply wouldn't hear of me traveling alone! Your scyldrin take liberties, Jerlayne; they expect you to listen to them."

"They think they're my mother. They think they're *you*."

Elmeene's brows rose in a half-hearted arch. "I had promises of dwarves to escort me and dwarves to ring the bell outside the goblin camp. Your scyldrin treat them as if they, too, were scyldrin."

"Or they treat us as if we were goblins," Jerlayne said quickly, and falsely, if what she'd glimpsed on the plains were any true measure, but she was mostly gathering her courage to admit that she'd already tried, and failed, to return home with the Veil's aid.

Elmeene noticed the broken armor on her worktable and, since it was *her* worktable, picked it up. She was running her hands across it, as women often did when their minds were laboring, when she responded to her daughter's provocation.

"Viljuen weeps if we should find ourselves becoming like goblins! Cold as fish. I'd sooner be mortal—and where *are* their
women? There are always more goblins; there must be goblin
women somewhere." She closed her eyes suddenly and twisted
her face into a supremely puzzled frown. "Will you leave this
with me? I have some notions—"

"No, it's not quite mine."

"But you have the big one now. Wave that in front of your
goblin and whatever he said he wanted, he'll fall at your feet in
thanks."

Jerlayne shook her head. "There's a problem—"

"Your leg?"

Another shake of her head. "I couldn't wait. I knew you'd
be upset, but I tried going home, through the Veil, before you
got here. I couldn't find the little room; I didn't guess that
it had disappeared, but there was another place, too, and I
couldn't find it, either. I—I don't think I can do it. Not alone."

She expected arch sarcasm and got an embrace instead.
"Poor child, I'm not surprised. It's shaping, of a different sort,
but you must believe before you do, and your confidence has
been hard-struck, quite absolutely hard-struck. It will come
back," Elmeene paused and her eyes glazed with unshared
thoughts. She blinked and was looking at Jerlayne again. "It
will, or you're not the daughter I know you to be, but, until
then, we'll go together, as far as the last pass-through. You can
ride home from there, yes?"

Jerlayne nodded as she said, "Pass-through? Yes, I could
ride home from the last pass-through, if I were *at* the last
pass-through."

"I'd had so much trouble remembering the mortal realm on
my way to Sunrise, I tried a different way home. Your father and
I, we were out of sorts coming home last month. It was especially awkward at the pass-throughs. I don't think I could forget
them if I tried." Elmeene shrugged dramatically. "Yesterday's
loss, today's fortune."

"You used the pass-throughs to come here from Sunrise, this
morning?" Jerlayne couldn't keep astonishment from coloring
her words: the notion was so simple, so hitherto unimaginable.

Elmeene's warm hands on Jerlayne's shoulders flexed then
tightened. "I was accounted a wild child in my early years.
There was very little that frightened me, nothing that stopped

me. If Fairie hadn't been dwindled in those days, I'm sure I would have borne a guardian myself."

Breaking her mother's embrace, Jerlayne went to the window and stared at the closed drapes. Her mother followed her.

"You ask so many questions, Jerlayne, but never the ones I was expecting, not even after Evoni."

"I was stunned by the answers to the questions I *had* asked, Mother. If I should have asked more questions . . . I was already overwhelmed; I still am. It simply never occurred to me that I would have to part it, that I'd have to betray Aulaudin to . . . to . . ." Words came and went in Jerlayne's mind, none of them took the shape of her thoughts. "I didn't want to believe we had to do *that*."

"Neither did I. I was outraged when I found out, and ashamed that I—the woman who'd bested iron—had been so blind, so naive, that I hadn't guessed the truth for myself."

Jerlayne's heart skipped a beat and she was speechless. It made sense, like a rainbow after a storm; Elmeene explained it anyway.

"My mother was dead of blooddeath before I joined with Jereige. I knew nothing. I suppose I wasn't alone, but I neither guessed nor gossiped. We'd had scyldrin, your father and I, and wondered when our time would come—as you must have wondered—but I was young, I didn't worry; I was sure Jereige and I would have our own children to raise. I was caught by complete surprise when Claideris—*that woman!*—appeared here to tell me that Fairie had enough scyldrin—they hadn't been 'death depleted—and it was my duty—*duty!*—to bear elfin children, to *continue the blood that conquered 'death.* That was how she put it. It could have been a compliment, but it wasn't. Then she told me how I must perform my duty. I swore I'd tell my husband; she swore she'd keep personal watch over me and she'd kill us all, if I so much as hinted the truth about or failed to raise my sons and daughters properly."

Claideris, the widow-sage, the only woman among the sages, the sage who'd questioned her and Aulaudin before they joined and the one who'd intruded into Laydin's birth. Was she truly related to Aglaidia? There was some resonance to their names. Or had she woven a lie to get herself inside the Sunrise great house?

Forgive your mother, Jereige had said, a long time ago. *She's suffered enough.* Two thousand years under Claideris' threats. Jerlayne, at last, returned her mother's embrace.

"Claideris is a hateful woman. If any elf could kill, I believe she'd be the one who did."

"If not her, then me," Elmeene continued her confession. "I imagined it many, many times, not counting last summer in Sunrise, but one day to the next, I began to live cautiously, for your father. I've not been unhappy, Jerlayne; don't feel sorry for me, but when I was at Sunrise last night, I asked myself, how does *that woman* get around Fairie? Does she always part the Veil? And it came to me, she had to use the pass-throughs, and if *that woman* could make them open for her, then so could I. I expected to see her waiting for me here, black hair, black eyes and puffing on that horrid pipe and, I tell you, only one of us would have walked away."

"It would have been you. But all these secrets, Mother— how many more are there?" Jerlayne guiltily counted the ones she kept from Aulaudin and her mother, as well. Her throat hurt, but she swallowed her guilt and continued: "We need to put an end to them. If we told the truth about *everything*—you and I together—Claideris would lose her power."

Elmeene jerked free of her daughter's embrace. "No. Never. It's not Claideris, Jerlayne. I could do anything to *that woman,* but not to your father. To all the men of Fairie. Or the scyldrin. I cringe, but Claideris was right: Fairie cannot survive without all of us: we *need* our husbands, Jerlayne, need them in countless ways. And we need the scyldrin, too. And we need to provide for the future: we're immortal, but somehow, none of us live forever. We have to grow, so we have to venture into the mortal realm. It's the only way. We must be strong—strong enough to carry our secrets."

"Maybe that's why we give up and die," Jerlayne whispered. "We get tired of being strong."

Her mother said nothing for a long moment, then: "Are you ready to go back to Sunrise?"

They hadn't quite argued, weren't truly at odds with each other; they'd simply come to the moment where there was one word left to say: "Yes."

It wasn't as simple as walking out of the great house. Jerlayne needed to borrow clothes; her own were beyond wearing. They were challenged to find something in Elmeene's vast closets that wouldn't betray where Jerlayne had been for the past day. By the time they'd settled that, they were both hungry and, knowing that it would be nightfall before they'd eat again, Elmeene stole from her own larder. Then there was the matter of horses.

"I took one from Sunrise, from the pasture, not the stable. Less chance it will be missed," Elmeene explained as they scurried from the great house.

Jerlayne had difficulty imagining Elmeene of Stonewell saddling a horse by herself, much less when it was loose in a field, but horse theft was apparently another of her mother's hidden talents: She recognized a bay gelding grazing with the Stonewell animals.

"Someone will notice," she warned as the horse shied away from her. "The gnomes are diligent."

"Someone *might* notice," her mother corrected. "And, if someone does, you'll lie."

Elmeene filled a bucket with grain, poured molasses over it, then stirred it into a sticky mess. All the horses, including the Sunrise gelding, came eagerly to the gate.

"This smacks of cheating," Jerlayne muttered as she slipped a rope around the bay's neck.

"Nonsense. I'll ride the black-necked gray. Put a halter on her, too."

Jerlayne obliged, Elmeene threw the last handfuls of sweet grain into the grass, and shortly thereafter, mother and daughter were on their way. They passed a few dwarves, a few gnomes, all of whom could have noticed their elfin mistress riding off with a daughter who shouldn't have been visiting. But if the Stonewell scyldrin noticed, they hid it well.

Secrets.

Everyone had them and protected their own by not exposing— not noticing—the secrets of others.

Elmeene tried to share the secrets of Fairie's pass-throughs, but they remained beyond Jerlayne's grasp. They blamed it on her thigh, which began to throb as soon as she'd settled in the bay's saddle and grew worse with each skirting.

"The Veil undoes my healing," Elmeene observed as she laid her hands on Jerlayne's thigh after they'd gone through their third pass-through. "It's worse now than it was before. I think it would be better if you could endure the pain until we're as far as we can go together."

Jerlayne had already reached the same conclusion, nodding grimly when Elmeene said there were two more to endure. But there was more to negotiating the pass-throughs than Elmeene had suspected. They weren't simple doorways between two unchanging places; and passing out of Fairie's heartland wasn't quite the same as passing into it. Two passages later, though Elmeene insisted they weren't lost, they weren't anywhere that Jerlayne remembered from her journeys with Aulaudin.

"We've got to go all the way into the mortal realm," Jerlayne whispered. "Then we can come out again at Sunrise, or Stonewell, or anywhere."

"Not with the horses, Jerlayne. It takes ten men, working together, to steal a horse without killing it."

"Then we abandon the horses."

"Nonsense. *That* would get noticed! One more, Jerlayne. I can feel it up ahead. I will question Jereige about this, I swear I will. When he's doing this, it's the same coming and going. There must be a trick to it, a men's trick."

"Tell him the truth, while you're at it," Jerlayne grumbled, too softly for her mother to hear.

Not one, but three, pass-throughs remained before the women came to a place in the forest the Jerlayne recognized through the pain-haze fogging her mind. The journey had taken longer than they'd expected. Neither of them would be home before supper and Jerlayne, clinging to consciousness and the bay's mane, doubted she'd find her way home at all. She blamed herself.

"More nonsense," Elmeene countered sharply. "We didn't know the pass-throughs would undo healing. And we didn't know how far we were from Sunrise or from Stonewell once we did. We misjudged, we may have made mistakes, but we weren't *wrong* and no one's to blame. And, anyway, you'll feel better in a moment."

Elmeene, who had dismounted, stood beside Jerlayne, who hadn't, and pressed her hands firmly on her daughter's swollen, throbbing thigh. The healing wasn't difficult. Jerlayne could have done it easily herself, if she weren't the one who needed the healing. She'd have greater sympathy, though, for those who came to her in the future. When the heat of her mother's healing met the fever brewing in her Veil-damaged flesh, Jerlayne would have sworn her leg had burst into blue-white flames. Tears streamed down her cheeks even after Elmeene relented and stepped away.

"Deep breaths. The worst is over."

Jerlayne didn't argue; she couldn't. Several moments passed before she could unclench her jaw.

"You knew that would hurt."

"And if I'd warned you, you'd have tensed and made it worse. Now it's done. There's swelling, but you can tend that yourself. The inside bleeding's stopped, that's what matters, isn't it?"

"That's what matters."

As the shock faded, so did the pain. Jerlayne felt bruised, but not wounded. She knew where she was, how far she had to travel and, though she agreed aloud with her mother's assessment, inwardly, Jerlayne was already planning to catch a night's sleep under the stars before returning home. The night would be warm for autumn. She wouldn't suffer without a blanket and the saddle pad would suffice for a pillow. It wouldn't be difficult; she'd camped countless times with Aulaudin—

"Ride steady, and you'll be home not long after dark. There's a moon tonight, I think. I didn't notice yesterday."

—But never without him.

"Jerlayne? Are you listening to me? I could ride with you a while longer . . . to the roofs of Sunrise, if you think you need me."

Elmeene's offer seemed sincere, but it was also a goad, a prick to Jerlayne's pride.

"I'm fine. I'll ride steady and be home just after dark, just as you say. You do the same."

"Depend on it. And, when you talk to Aulaudin, tell him Sunrise needs new cooking pots."

Jerlayne shook her head. "Cooking pots! What were you doing in our kitchen? We have all the pots we need. We've had problems with salt, but I'm ahead of that now."

"New ones. They make odd pots and pans now. Cook an egg in one of their new skillets and it slips around as if it's on ice. Some of the gnomes won't touch them; the others won't use anything else. I didn't pay much attention when Jereige first brought them back but, as we've been riding, it's occurred to me that the armor you're trying to unlock . . . it reminds me of nothing so much as the slippery layer on those skillets. If you're having trouble with salt pitting the metal, all the more reason to get new pots."

"Slippery skillets, I'll try to remember that."

"Don't just try, Jerlayne. I'll shape one apart when I get home and, somehow, I'll let you know if I learn anything, but you've got both pieces—" Elmeene eyed the bulky pack behind the bay's saddle, clearly another request for the smaller slab.

A request which Jerlayne ignored. "I promise I'll lay hands on a slippery skillet. We could meet right here in ten days' time to share what we've learned?"

Elmeene backed away from her daughter and her daughter's suggestion. "I don't want to get into the habit of this. It's good to know what can be done. Otherwise, I leave well enough alone."

From the distant, worried look on her mother's face, Jerlayne imagined she was thinking of Claideris and let the subject drop, which had been what she wanted, anyway. They said good-bye a bit differently than before, with more affection and anxiety, at least from Jerlayne's side, though Elmeene, too, seemed subdued and glanced over her shoulder once as she rode back toward Stonewell . . . twice . . . and then she was gone.

There'd been neither a mist nor a flicker of light to mark Elmeene's entrance into the pass-through: one moment there was ginger hair swaying above a gray horse's back; the next, there wasn't.

"Interesting," Jerlayne mused aloud, thinking about goblins.

The trail to Sunrise was clearly marked, a far cry from the rain-soaked blazes of Jerlayne's first journey through these woods. Dwarves had hauled gravel from pits and streambeds to fill the low spots and built wooden bridges over the streams. If luck were with her—or, perhaps, if luck weren't—she might encounter an eastbound cart hauling grain or a westbound one with barrels of salted fish.

"I needed to get away," Jerlayne rehearsed her excuses. "The armor is so strange—I was afraid to study it further under our roofs. I thought it might explode or ooze poison gas. And it did! Just look at my hair! Wasn't I wise to get away?"

And if anyone asked what she'd learned? Was there anything she could tell Aulaudin or the scyldrin?

"Slippery skillets . . ." No, she couldn't know about slippery skillets because they were at Stonewell and she hadn't been there. She'd have to ask Aulaudin for new pots, new skillets, and hope he brought home the necessary inspiration.

"Lies. Lies and secrets! Viljuen weeps."

Her thigh had begun to ache again, and her back and her rump. Jerlayne wasn't used to riding all day. She could soothe some of the discomfort from within, but short of reshaping her hips, there was little she could do except dismount and walk the kinks out. At the next bridge, where a stone wall and pillars anchoring the wooden planks would give her a leg-up if she needed one to remount, Jerlayne eased herself down to the ground.

Walking didn't help and sitting proved a disaster when she tried to stand again. She'd need every finger's breadth of the highest pillar to remount. Her legs, anticipating their fate, knotted up. Gracelessly, Jerlayne kneaded her muscles through the folds of her borrowed skirt. Maybe she *could* spend a night in the forest. It couldn't be worse.

Then Jerlayne heard a rhythmic echo through the eastern trees. A single horse, she guessed, moving with considerable speed. Dwarf legs were ill-suited to horse flanks and stirrups. Gnomes could ride, but like dwarves, usually preferred to ride in a cart. That left elves and goblins. Jerlayne wracked her imagination for a reason Aulaudin or Goro would be galloping west from Sunrise—a reason that didn't revolve around her and, coming up with none, made haste to the pillar.

Jerlayne's haste wasn't fast enough. The horse—the coal-black horse and its black-cloaked rider—hove into sight before she'd clambered up the stone. Her gelding wanted no part of the impending adventure. It shied toward the stream and threatened to rear when the black horse threw up a spray of dirt and gravel coming to an abrupt stop.

Jerlayne knew all the theory and much of the practice of horsemanship. If she hadn't been weak in the legs, she might have had the strength to keep the bay's head down and its feet grounded. But she was aching and the bay spooked thoroughly when its hind hooves slid into the stream. It was bolting and she was—foolishly—still clinging to the reins when there was another, stronger, black-gloved hand above hers.

Nothing shaped from muscle and bone could have moved so quickly—unless it knew a different Veil, a different sort of pass-through.

Instincts no different than those which panicked the gelding sprang Jerlayne's fingers from the reins and sent her scrambling for shelter between the pillars and the bridge.

Goblins weren't gentle with animals, not like the gnomes, not like Aulaudin when he handled the bay. They weren't cruel, either. Goro—Jerlayne had glimpsed and recognized his face by then—never struck the animal or raised his voice, and by sheer muscle, the bay was surely the stronger of the two, yet beyond doubt Goro dominated the animal. Once he'd made the gelding see his eyes, the rebellion as over. The bay quivered and blew, but its hooves were rooted on the ground until the goblin gave it leave to follow him to the bridge where Jerlayne had taken shelter.

"I was looking for you."

Jerlayne recited the lines she'd memorized. The bay reacted more than the goblin.

"I thought you might have gone to Stonewell."

"Not without an escort," Jerlayne lied. "A man to pass me through."

She stood up, wincing, and hoped Goro would assume it was nothing more than saddle-strain.

"Did his hooves strike you?"

For a heartbeat Jerlayne had visions of her goblin slaughtering her horse—Aulaudin's horse, if the truth were told—on the spot. "No, I rode too long. I'm not used to it."

"Then you should rest."

"I should go home. I've been gone too long already."

"Have you, now?"

Their eyes met. Jerlayne wasn't a gelding. She wasn't about to be dominated by Sunrise's oath-bound protector, but there was no one who could unnerve her as Goro did.

"They told me, when I asked where you were, that you'd disappeared from your bedroom. They said you'd talked about going to Stonewell. I asked about a messenger. I'd seen none, and neither had they, but I might have missed him, if he were one of your brothers and he had not lingered to escort you."

He was baiting her, but she'd lose more, she thought, if she failed to take what he offered.

"Nereige came before dawn."

"You were riding from the west."

"I parted the Veil." He already knew *that* secret. "It was nothing serious. My mother had shaped something she wanted to show me."

"A remarkable woman, your mother."

"Very."

Jerlayne wanted the bay, whose reins the goblin still held. She wanted to be gone from the bridge and the goblin, too. She reached toward him; he offered the braided leather.

"You rode this horse through the Veil to the mortal realm? Remarkable. And back again, but to here, not Sunrise?"

Her hand closed around the leather. They were necessarily close, close enough that Jerlayne could smell Goro's sweat, his amusement. He let go of the reins.

"Of course not directly to Sunrise, or the mortal realm. It would take ten men, working together, to get this horse from here to there and back again. I used the pass-throughs."

The bay snorted, but followed Jerlayne to the stone wall. She couldn't lengthen her leg bones, but she'd tear her hamstrings, if she had to, to mount and be on her way, though surely Goro would insist on escorting her and the bay couldn't outrun his black.

"Think a moment; if you hurry back, someone might become suspicious. With neither parting nor pass-throughs your journey should have taken, what? Three days to reach Stonewell, three more to return? If you return now, you won't have been gone too long, Jerlayne; you won't have been gone long enough."

Jerlayne sighed. "I'll think of something to tell them: I changed my mind. I realized how foolish I'd been to head off on my own. I took your armor out to work with it and my hair caught fire."

There was a pattern to lying; a seductive rhythm. It distracted Jerlayne from the more important task of raising her stiff, sore leg. She lost her balance. This time Goro did not move fast enough and she crumpled to the ground.

"Rest a while," the goblin repeated his initial suggestion.

For a man—he *was* a man; Jerlayne had healed others of his ilk, seen them naked, knew goblins were in all essential ways manly—shorter than her husband, Goro was broader across the shoulders and considerably stronger. Not because he could lift her up and carry her—Aulaudin could do that; Jerlayne was neither tall nor heavy—but because when she attempted to free herself, he merely stiffened his fingers and she was effectively imprisoned. Jerlayne could have resorted to shaping. With a little effort she could have leaked pain through any pore where he touched her, but for all his insistence, Goro offered no threat.

He set her down on a mossy boulder some paces from the bridge.

"Wait here. I will bring you water and anything else you need until you're rested."

Jerlayne watched with some apprehension as Goro tied both horses to the bridge rail and dug through his saddle packs for a small bowl. The torn armor slab he had given her and the complete piece that she stolen from the plains were wrapped in coarse cloth and lashed to her bay's saddle—loosely, even carelessly wrapped: Jerlayne could see one of the sticky-cloth straps from where she sat.

Would Goro see it, too? Would he recognize it? Would he believe she'd gotten it at Stonewell? From the mortal realm? Or would she have to tell him the truth—with all the truth's unforeseen consequences?

Goro filled the bowl and brought it to her. Jerlayne thanked him. She thought she'd dodged a danger, until he began a straight-line walk to the bay's rump.

"Goro!"

The goblin ignored her. Tearing first at the lash knots, then at the cloth, he freed the dark green tunic and hauled it to the boulder, dropping it on the dirt between them.

"Am I to believe you shaped this with your mother at Stonewell?"

Jerlayne could have answered him accurately with the single word, yes. Somehow, pure accuracy seemed unwise. She prepared to unfold the truth.

"No, I didn't shape it at all."

"But you got it from Stonewell? You have been at Stonewell, haven't you, Jerlayne? You went to Stonewell. You took what I gave you to your mother. You showed it to her and you've brought this back."

Goro was angry, but anger wasn't the dominant tone in his voice. He sounded like a man whose life was falling away from him. Jerlayne knew the sound because she'd felt it the day Evoni changed.

"I was at Stonewell this morning and I did show Elmeene both pieces, the one you gave me and that one, but I didn't get that at Stonewell. I had it in my arms when I arrived."

"Arrived from Sunrise?" Goro folded his arms as if he'd guessed the answer she'd have to give.

"I couldn't unlock its secrets, not if I couldn't change its shape. I was failing, until I remembered Elmeene showing me how to part the Veil. I used a red dress the first time, but Elmeene said anything would do, if it had been made and handled by mortals—"

"*I* gave you that first piece; I'm not mortal."

She nodded, swallowed hard. "But you didn't make it, and you were in Fairie. I didn't think there'd be any harm to trying. I didn't know there was another Veil—" Jerlayne's guilt was oppressive, but when she looked up at Goro's utterly impassive face, some of it became anger: "How could I have known that? I believed you when you said you had no magic and you couldn't part the Veil—"

"I can't. Not the Veil between here and the mortal realm."

"But there's another Veil! There's always been another Veil, hasn't there, since the Ten. Viljuen didn't have to go looking for the goblin priestess; she was right there. But we never knew, we never found out. No one stumbled into your world until I did, trying to do what you'd asked me to do, so you'd tell me the truth. The truth! Were you going to tell me that there's another Veil between goblins and us?"

Goro had sufficient decency, or sense, to purse his lips and look uncomfortable. "I hadn't decided."

"I was *shot,* Goro! I was in a round, black tent, surrounded by heaps of this—" she pointed at the tunic lying on the ground between them. "I didn't know I wasn't where I thought I was— I only thought I was in the mortal realm, I didn't expect that I would recognize the place. I was going to shape my way back to Sunrise when a man surprised me—a *goblin,* Goro. He could have been your brother—"

"Not a brother," Goro interjected, as if, of all she'd said, that were all that mattered.

Jerlayne set her jaw, "I shaped pain to get past him. I set us both afire." She hoped he was paying attention because that would be her only warning. "I was on the plains—*your* plains. There were tents everywhere, and goblins with *guns!* They shot me as I was running away. A *bullet* went clear through my leg." She almost lifted her skirt to show him the remains of the wound. "I didn't know it. I just knew I had to get somewhere safe, and safety—true safety—was Stonewell. I couldn't heal

myself so I pulled myself through that other Veil to my
mother's workroom. She healed me—" Her throat tightened
and words nearly failed, but she got them out, little more than
a whisper: "I would have died, Goro. On your plains or even at
Sunrise, I would have died."

They stared at each other. Jerlayne relived her fear. Goro—
she had no notion what went on in the goblin's mind. He made
three sounds: words, she supposed, in his noisy language. His
fingers contracted into black leather fists and his eyes, never
easy to interpret, became cold, deadly. Jerlayne braced herself
to shape pain and held her breath, hoping pain would be
enough, when he wrapped his arms around her.

Chapter 24

"Without you, I would have no life."

Pressed as she was against the goblin's chest, Jerlayne wasn't certain she'd heard Goro correctly. She didn't doubt his sincerity. Despite the discomfort of chain-mail links biting into her cheek, Jerlayne understood that the goblin didn't mean for his embrace to hurt her. Relaxing as best she could, forgetting the pain she'd been prepared to unleash, she waited for the moment to end and the opportunity for explanations to begin.

There would be explanations. She wasn't going anywhere, and neither was Goro, until they'd laid some secrets to rest.

"I want to know the truth," Jerlayne said firmly when she could see his face again. "What is this thing?" She pointed at the dark green tunic on the ground. "What, exactly, is it for? Where did it come from, other than the mortal realm. Who gave it to you? And why? And when you're done with those questions, I want you to tell me *everything* about goblins . . . and about elves."

"I can't."

"Why not? What more does a women—an elfin woman— have to do to get the goblin who's sworn to protect her to tell her the truth?"

"Because you have asked me to tell you the truth, Jerlayne." With a deadly calm voice and a cold stare, Goro erased the advantage Jerlayne thought she'd had over him. "I have never lied to you. Never. I can't tell you *everything* because I don't know everything. I didn't know the—" he spat out a word; at least Jerlayne assumed it was a word. She couldn't have repeated it. Fairie's language, for all its variety, simply didn't have the clicks, chirps, and whistles that passed for goblin communication. The best she could have done was *gennern.* "Had guns. I didn't know for certain the gennern were involved."

"We can start with words. Who are these gennern? What are they? The men I saw looked a lot like you. Are you gennern, too? Is that your word for men?"

Goro shook his head. "You wouldn't understand."

He started to walk away. Jerlayne scooped up the armor and threw it at him.

The goblin turned around, with a look on his face that promised something rash and regrettable, but Jerlayne was quicker.

"Don't you *dare* tell me what I can or can't understand. Tell me the truth, and keep telling me the truth until I tell you that I do understand it!"

"Gennern is them, the foul and unclean, those who will kill you if you don't kill them first. Gennern is—is the opposite of men. No man is gennern, except to those he calls gennern. It is enemies, but what do you know about enemies?"

"I know I was shot."

"You were stealing from them, Jerlayne. I do not defend them, as Uylma holds my honor, I do not. But, by what you described, you might just as well have been an ogre. I would shoot an ogre, if I had a gun, but ogres aren't gennern. You see, you don't understand." He picked up the armor and continued toward the horses.

"Ogres are beasts; they can't understand. Gennern are men, except they choose not to understand what you understand. It's the choosing that makes them gennern. Am I a beast, Goro? Do you believe I can't understand, or will you give me a choice?"

Thongs snapped as Goro lashed the armor to the bay's saddle. Jerlayne thought she'd been handed her choice in the form of an unwelcome, unpleasant morsel of truth, then Goro hobbled both horses, slipped their bits, and, after unlashing the small pack which had held his drinking bowl, turned them loose.

He'd made a circular hearth in the dirt before he said, without looking up. "You're all beasts. Ogres are the wild beasts. Elves and scyldrin are the tamed beasts—herded beasts. All the children of the Ten are beasts."

"You could say all the men and women in Fairie are scyldrin," Jerlayne corrected, "or you can call us elves, gnomes, dwarves and all the ilks. But the Ten were elves; gnomes, dwarves and the rest are our children. We're not beasts."

"Elves, scyldrin, ogres, beasts, Jerlayne: it's all the same. Fairie is filled with beasts and only beasts."

She was horrified. "You've sworn your life to us. You can't believe that."

Goro quickly and silently finished laying the fire. "No, I don't, not for a long time," he conceded as he stood. "But it is what I was taught, and much of it is true."

"It's nonsense, Goro. Don't ask me to believe nonsense."

"You wanted a choice. Very well, I'll give you that choice: There is another way to tell the tale of the Ten, the way it is told on the plains. Come; sit." He unclasped his cloak and spread it over the dirt. "To my knowledge, no elf has heard it before."

Curiosity drew Jerlayne to the furled back cloth. She settled near the hem, leaving ample room for Goro, who chose to sit in the dirt.

"Our tale begins with Grandfather Death who visits a *karg*— no, I will use your words. He visits a homestead; Disease, his daughter, is with him. The master invites them in—

"This is pointless, Jerlayne. Our tale of the Ten a long story, many days and nights long, and much of it is not interesting, even if I could remember it all. I'll make it shorter, much shorter, but I'll leave nothing out. I give you my word."

Jerlayne nodded.

"It comes to pass that ten children are hidden in a mist-filled cave by their parents. They don't come out until the people of another homestead come searching. At first, everyone is excited: Grandfather Death and his daughter have been outwitted and the children are welcomed into a new homestead. But Grandfather Death is a proud spirit. He's ashamed that he missed the youngest and weakest of the homestead. He vows revenge, and his revenge is very clever: since the children hid from him, he and his daughter will never have anything to do with them. The ten children had become immortal."

"I always wondered where the Ten might have come from."

"Ah, but these Ten aren't elves," Goro reminded her. "Our Ten are like ourselves. Elves come later. But to mortals, in either tale, it's the immortality that enraged them. When the Ten didn't die, the families who once welcomed them drove them out in jealousy and hatred. The Ten retreated to the misty cave where their parents had first hidden them. They went deeper and deeper through the cave until they emerged onto plains where they lived in peace and immortality.

"There is a misty place on the plains. We call it the *nafoga'ar,* the navel where our realm was attached to the mother realm. In our tale of the Ten, Viljuen and his immortal kin could enter the nafoga'ar and return to the realm of their birth, as the ten elves in your tale could enter the mortal realm. And, as in your tale, mortals never forgot their hatred. They threatened to destroy the nafoga'ar, so the Ten made it stronger by drawing the mist out into the mother realm.

"But when the mists of the cave mingled with the air of the mortal realm, the air itself quickened with immortality. When mortal mothers gave birth in the mist, their children lived. Grandfather Death and his daughter starved. Together, they appealed to the God-of-all saying that the way of life is death and therefore the Ten and their mist were abominations. Their curse couldn't be allowed to spread through the mother realm. Grandfather Death and his daughter demanded that the Ten be given to them for punishment.

"The God-of-all determined that Grandfather Death and his daughter spoke the truth, but the God-of-all refused to punish the Ten by giving them to Grandfather Death, because Grandfather Death had caused the problem when he and his daughter rejected them. The God-of-all said the Ten could remain immortal, so long as they stayed out of the mother realm. If they entered the mother realm, then Grandfather Death could have them—"

Jerlayne saw a pattern emerging. "The Veil mists, the mists beyond Sunrise, they're what remain of the mists that came out of the cave?"

Goro nodded. "Fairie became the halfway realm, not through the nafoga'ar, not part of the mother realm. Grandfather Death was enraged by the God-of-all's judgement. He sought to destroy Fairie. His weapons were mortals, but mortals didn't want to *destroy* Fairie and the immortality it could bestow on their children; they simply wanted it. The longest and least interesting parts of our story tell how Grandfather Death and his mortal allies waged war against each other, a little; and against us, a lot. The important part, unless you like dirges, is that we abandoned peaceful ways and have never returned to them, yet as hard as we fought, we couldn't win because mortals could always retreat into the mother realm where we couldn't follow.

"We were desperate. We turned to our gods—how we found our gods is not interesting, I promise you—and our gods told us to lure the mortal warriors into the Fairie mists, let our women seduce them, and then the mongrels—the *elves*—would hold Fairie for us—"

"Viljuen wept."

"Ah, as I said: Viljuen is one of *our* names."

"How can you stand there at our weddings and listen to our sages?"

"How not? *We* taught you the story. You are lesser creatures—imperfect copies of us—mortal-bred and born in Fairie to keep the nafoga'ar safe."

"But we don't," Jerlayne protested. "If anything is true, you protect us!"

"We protect our horses, also, because we need them and because they—and you—are the measure of our wealth and prestige, the strong backs that carry us from one place to the next. We've fought among ourselves on the plains and here in Fairie to possess this or that homestead, this or that elfin woman and her daughters—only her daughters. We know how you breed; men do not pass their blood along and, anyway, *elves* aren't what matter. Homesteads matter, because the size of Fairie determines the size of the plains. We didn't concern ourselves with ogres, until they started overrunning homesteads, and the plains have yet to recover from the way they shrank when blooddeath ravaged Fairie. And *guardians* matter. The guardians keep Fairie safe from mortal invasion, and Fairie, of course, keeps the nafoga'ar safe.

"When Sunrise pushed back the mists of Fairie, it increased the horizons on the plain. That was a glorious day near the nafoga'ar. Then you and Aulaudin whelped a *guardian* and survived. I could consider myself a fortunate man."

There was nothing in Goro's tone to indicate whether or not he considered himself fortunate. When he'd finished his most provocative of statements, he folded his hands and said nothing more.

Outrage and shock fought for Jerlayne's thoughts. She could

swallow her words, but she couldn't keep her face as rigid and mask-like as Goro kept his, so she turned away. Let him think she was ashamed, let him think she was a coward—as, perhaps, she was. Once she'd turned away, Jerlayne couldn't turn back. She bolted into the woods and hid behind a tree, sobbing because a picture long in shadow had been brought into the harshest, least forgiving light.

But there remained questions in her mind. Jerlayne had paid a terrible price for letting her questions go unanswered—she paid it still—and wouldn't let the debt grow deeper. Drying her tears, she headed back to the road. Afternoon had become evening. Goro had brought out his food: coarse, brown bread in thick slices, a pot of something that might have been scraped from the bottom of a pickling barrel, windfall apples, and water from the stream. If Goro were a fortunate man, it didn't show in his meals or clothing.

The food was untouched, as though he'd been waiting for her to return. He'd go hungry a while longer, then; Jerlayne had no appetite.

She sat down exactly where she'd sat before. "I wouldn't believe anything you've said, if I hadn't parted the Veil between Fairie and the plains yesterday and been shot as well."

"I might not have told you so much without yesterday. Are you hungry?"

"No."

To Jerlayne's moderate surprise, Goro used one of his knives to spread the pickling paste on the bread. His mouth was full when she asked:

"Aulaudin's father, Maun, thinks goblins don't value us at all and would just as soon we were all dead."

Goro slowly chewed and swallowed a second mouthful. "Not all of us, but some, yes. When the blooddeath ravaged Fairie, there were fewer elves, fewer homesteads. Whole lineages were diminished. The balance was lost among us, and hasn't been recovered. War is endless now. Those who have nothing left to lose say the time for Fairie and elves has passed and it's time to protect the nafoga'ar ourselves. Some even say that gods no longer matter and Grandfather Death no longer watches for us to enter his realm. They also think we're better than elves and mortals together."

"What do you think?"

He finished his slathered bread. "I think Grandfather Death is no more real today than he was when the tale was first told to wide-eyed children, but it will never be safe for immortals to walk in the mortal realm."

"And elves? Do you think you're better than us?"

She was angry and anger filled her voice. Goro heard it; his eyes widened and for a moment his knife was frozen in the air above the pickling pot, then he slathered another slice of bread and offered it to her.

"It's very good. Berries and nuts ground together and simmered in a pot—"

"I want to know, Goro: Is Maun right? I've listened to him and to you and I think he is right."

"Considering that he started thinking for the wrong reason— Tatterfall *was* destroyed by ogres—Maun has seen a good many things quite clearly. If he weren't regarded as a fool, I'm certain he would have been culled, and all Briary with him."

For a moment Jerlayne couldn't breathe, then she found the air for one word: "Culled?"

"You know the word, Jerlayne; I do not misuse it. Sunrise culls its lambs and calves. You cull the weak ones, the deformed ones, and the ones that are too hard to handle. There's been little culling since the blooddeath. On the plains, many think Fairie's overdue for a severe culling."

"Goblins . . . goblins like you would destroy the homesteads they've sworn to protect?" Jerlayne turned away from the food. She felt sick and as if she were sinking through water.

"It has happened. Not in your lifetime, or mine, but it happened frequently before blooddeath; ask your sages. These days, it happens more often that one lineage challenges another lineage's right to protect a homestead. If they're successful—a quick, decisive raid here in Fairie—another lineage takes over the homestead's protection. We *do* look very much alike. No mortals fouling our lineages."

Jerlayne plucked threads out of her sleeve, shaped them idly into a tiny flower, then tossed the flower into the fire. "I'd know if another goblin tried to take your place . . . I'd know before I saw him. Your tents are so close. We'd know if other goblins attacked you . . ."

"That has always been my hope. We protect each other, Jerlayne. I do not like it at all when I don't know where you are. Neither one of us is safe then."

And when they were together on the cart road from Sunrise? Was that a safe place to be alone with the goblin sworn to protect her?

"Do we have many enemies? Do you? Or I?"

"I did not think we'd live this long."

Evening had become twilight. They needed the fire, not for heat but to see each other beneath the branches. Goro's eyes, so inscrutable by day, were livelier in firelight: black pupils, irises, and sclera each reflected the flames differently. Jerlayne could watch his pupils widen as she remembered other conversations and considered her response.

"You've been waiting a long time to tell me all this. Why?"

"Have I waited so long?" Goro gave one of his small, ironic laughs. "Did you not just say that today is the first day when you would believe what I've told you?"

"You've been pushing me toward this moment since you stepped out of the shadows at my wedding to Aulaudin."

"Oh, longer than that, Jerlayne. Much longer. My father and grandfather were waiting for you."

"They're alive? Watching?"

"No." Goro blinked. His goblin detachment failed him and for once, he was the one who looked away. "They are gone. Dead. All of them. There are none of my lineage left." When he faced Jerlayne again his eyes were as bright as the flames they reflected. "I was given a heritage, my grandfather's vision from the day when we first learned of iron and of blooddeath. He saw, somehow, what would happen, how elves would die, Fairie would shrink, and the plains would suffer. He said the culling must stop, and for a while, because elves were dying, all the lineages listened to him. Everyone agreed that if there would be a cure for the 'death, elves would have to find it for themselves, and that meant leaving them alone to learn and explore. After your mother learned the secrets of iron, some lineages wanted to go backward, to rigorous culling. Others wanted many elves, many new homesteads, so they could regain what they'd lost. But everyone wanted to be rid of curious and troublesome elves. We fought for Stonewell . . . many times.

"They killed my grandfather in an honor duel; my father was ready to take his place. But, the price of not-culling is, sometimes, foolishness."

Goro stopped speaking. He ate bread while Jerlayne absorbed what he'd said. He ate an apple down to the seeds before she thought through the implications of her mother, his father, and foolishness.

"Maialene?"

"I was not yet born when your sister joined with Redis—"

So, her goblin was older than she was, but not as old as her husband. Jerlayne had often wondered. His coldness when M'lene came to Sunrise was also explained.

"I knew no reasons for what happened, and I have no reason to trust those who've told me their side afterward, and she is—was—your sister, so I will say nothing about causes. Only that there was a challenge made: a charge of treason against our lineage. It was not enough to slaughter the men overseeing Brightwings: a whole generation of grudges and accusations was brought to bear against my father. There was a war, bloodier and shorter than most, and my father lost.

"He was brought to the nafoga'ar, where, as it happened, I dwelt with my mother—I was still a boy under six. My education hadn't begun. I was surprised to see him of course, doubly surprised that he was wounded and in chains and that all my uncles and elder brothers and cousins were with him, my aunts and sisters, too. He was a patriarch, and so far as I knew, patriarchs were untouchable; I didn't know what I was seeing until it was too late: he was confined in an arena of salt, with only salt to eat unless he took his own life. He did of course, and then our lineage had no patriarch. The carnage began. My brothers and uncles were hacked apart; my sisters and aunts were blinded with blazing sticks, then given to whatever men would take them."

Jerlayne was glad she hadn't eaten anything. She emptied the water bowl and placed what food remained inside it, then put the bowl closer to the hearth, where she wouldn't see it when she looked at Goro or thought about the life that had produced him and the goblin who'd shot her.

"Except my mother. My mother stood behind me, her hands dug into my shoulders, so I couldn't shame myself by running. She warned me that if I made a noise, she'd let them kill me, so I was very quiet until there was no one of my lineage standing and a man with a sword whose clothes dripped blood stood before us. He held out his hand and my mother released me. I wanted to ask her what I'd done—but that would have been making a noise. I was taken into the arena where my father's body—some of it—still lay. They told me to spread my hand on a block of salt that was lying there. When I did, the bloody man raised his sword and struck off a part of my finger.

"The wound took up salt. I remember nothing until later, when I was in my mother's tent. She told me I no longer had a name or a family. I was no longer to think of myself as her son, but as her servant—if I forgot, she would no longer be able to protect me from my father's enemies. Everything he'd believed in would be lost; everything he feared would come to pass.

"I lived with her another ten years, until I was grown and could no longer live among the women. After that I lived wherever I could until she came to me in a dream. She said it was time to challenge the gennern for my right to over-see a homestead: the elf who'd shaped iron had had another daughter—"

"Me, when I married Aulaudin?"

"You, when you were born. I was not optimistic, but even if I'd still been her son, a man does not argue with Uylma. I challenged them eleven times before I left the plains; I stopped counting challenges after I came to Stonewell. The goblin you call Arhon is the blood-dripping gennern who cut off my finger, he is not the Arhon who swore to protect your mother. It was not a healthy time for any of us."

And Stonewell had never guessed. As Goro had said, all goblins did look very much alike and Elmeene, whose opinion of goblins matched goblins' opinion of elves, would never have bothered to look for a change. But Goro had been watching her all her life. A hundred moments when she'd thought she was alone flooded Jerlayne's memory and flushed her cheeks.

"It wasn't all bad. We looked forward to Maun's visits—"

Jerlayne shouted, "Stop!"

Goro did, and once again they were reduced to staring at each other.

"You're no different than Arhon, or whatever his name is: you *do* think you're better than us. You're not, not you personally or you as all the goblins who ever were. If we seem foolish and make you laugh, it's because you've made us seem foolish with your lies."

"That is almost exactly what my grandfather said when he decided the culling must stop, but I didn't look forward to Maun's visits to laugh at him. Maun stirred up arguments in the shadows, and it pleased me to watch the gennern fight among themselves instead of with me. And he brought Aulaudin with him. I hated Aulaudin for his freedom, but he was your freedom and your freedom would become my freedom: you let nothing stand between you and your heart's desire."

How could any one, even a goblin, *hate* Aulaudin? Jerlayne asked herself, then she repeated to herself exactly what Goro had said. She framed her next question carefully.

"Will your sons become my daughters' protectors? My elfin daughters, after they've shaped their twenty-link chains."

"I have no sons."

"We have no daughters, but we will, someday, I hope, and your sons—"

"Your daughters go to the gennern!" Goro shouted; Jerlayne had never heard a goblin shout, never seen one not in complete control of his passions. "What my grandfather began ends with me . . . with you. I'm no patriarch. I'm not a man; the gennern saw to that."

Jerlayne had thought—guessed, assumed, and presumed— from what he'd said about Aulaudin, that her goblin protector was infatuated with her. She'd thought that would explain so many of the odd looks and skewed reactions that had confounded her over the years and that by exposing the truth she could gently—but firmly—redirect an unrequited passion. She hadn't begun to guess how hopeless a passion it was if Arhon— the only other goblin Jerlayne knew by name and sight—hadn't stopped with Goro's finger, which, once she'd thought about it, she'd never noticed was missing.

Embarrassed, Jerlayne looked quickly at the fire—though not before she'd stolen a glance at Goro's black-gloved hands. Goro responded—the sounds were unmistakable—by pulling off his gloves. Irresistible curiosity pulled Jerlayne's eyes away from the flames toward . . . what? Despite expectation and futile attempts to deny expectation, there was nothing grotesque about the hand Goro flaunted in front of her. Jerlayne needed a second look before she saw that the middle finger of his right hand was shorter than it might have been and the nail curled sideways as it grew. No wonder Jerlayne hadn't noticed: The twisted nail might be painful, cramped inside a tight leather glove all the time, but if Arhon hadn't cut off anything else . . .

"I can heal that," she said, touching his hand, as she would have touched any other injury, to take its measure before healing it. "No one will ever know—" Shaping magic began to flow.

"It was the price of my life: a man without a father, a man no woman would accept. There was no need to kill me; I am beneath notice, beneath contempt. The gennern know, even if I am right—if my grandfather was right—they will reap the rewards."

"That's wrong," Jerlayne whispered, though she could see the brutal logic that had shaped Goro's life.

She inhaled her healing thoughts, let her fingers slip. Goro's scarred hand squeezed shut around hers.

"It's past. Over. Nothing clouds my vision. I see only you."

Jerlayne could have shaped pain to free herself. She could have simply remained motionless, her fingers limp within his, waiting for him to see the foolishness of his words, his gesture. There were choices; Goro had promised she'd make her own choices. Elves married for life. They were joined, their minds and memories were linked, despite the secrets they learned to keep from each other. Though her daughter had blinded her for thirty years, no *man* endangered Jerlayne's love for Aulaudin.

Including the man—the goblin—who claimed no life except through his devotion to hers?

She could have resisted pity. It was danger—the thrill of danger that lured her time after time into iron and through the Veil—that led Jerlayne to bend her arm and bring Goro's blue-skinned hand toward her lips.

They'd been sitting more than an arm's length apart; Goro had either to lean forward or release Jerlayne's hand. When his hand remained clasped around hers, she wasn't surprised that the rest of him moved closer, too. The chain mail might have been a problem, if Jerlayne hadn't been the woman who'd shaped it and who knew precisely which laces to loosen, which links to open. It slipped from his back like a snake's shed skin. His tunic followed, and the gown Jerlayne had borrowed from her mother, both shoved aside into darkness.

Once—only once—after they'd kissed for the first time, Jerlayne almost spoke aloud, but any word would have hauled them both back to their senses, their right-and-wrong senses. Goro, too, said nothing.

It was trysting: plain physical passion, satisfying yet restrained, and without the union of thoughts that made joining incomparable and which, in a primitive form, had flowed between Jerlayne and her son's mortal father. When it had ended and she lay quiet within his arms, away from the firelight, Jerlayne was mildly disappointed and greatly relieved that it had been nothing more than trysting. The attraction—Jerlayne admitted to herself there had always been attraction, now that it was history—had been rooted in her own imagination, not, as it had been with Cuz, somewhere that she could not control.

The night was clear and warm, almost too warm for the layer of woolen cloak Goro had, with some last coherent thought, drawn over her. Jerlayne thought of the comfortable cotton and linen, just beyond reach, and rejected the thought. Best to stay where she was, right where she was, until dawn, when she would pretend this had been a dream . . . and hope that Goro had the sense to do likewise.

Jerlayne fell asleep and awoke in darkness. The fire had burnt out, the sky hadn't brightened. She forgot where she was, what she'd done. She'd moved and awakened her lover before she remembered. Guiltily—her curiosity was sated; there was nothing more that she was tempted to learn—Jerlayne pretended she wasn't awake. But Goro knew better, or didn't care; *his* curiosity was not nearly sated and, after a few caresses, hers had reawakened, too.

In time Jerlayne saw his silhouette beside her. The sky was brightening. She closed her eyes, as if she could keep the sun from rising, and hid herself against his chest.

"Open your eyes," he said when he was braced on his arms above her.

She did, carefully: The sky was filled with golden clouds.

"Look at me."

She did that too, which was a mistake. Black goblin eyes pulled Jerlayne away from the safety of trysting and simple passions. It was mid-morning before she was within herself again.

Goro spoke first: "We have been perilous. I have no regrets."

Jerlayne held him with all her strength and said nothing.

Chapter 25

Jerlayne bathed in the stream, cold and modestly alone, but unashamed. She hadn't finished wet-braiding her hair (it would be a challenge until the burnt locks grew out) when Goro finished his morning rituals. He offered her the last of his bread. The nut-and-berry paste wasn't *good,* but it was edible and put an end to the empty churning in Jerlayne's stomach.

Her notion to pretend that nothing had happened seemed well on its way to becoming reality. When Goro offered to boost her into the bay's saddle there was no trace of familiarity in his voice. Still, she refused the offer. A night of passion didn't leave her weary or aching. If anything, it had faded all memory of her leg wound. Then, when he was mounted and they were ready to ride toward Sunrise, Jerlayne caught Goro staring at her.

"No regrets," she reminded him.

"None at all," he agreed, looking nowhere except Jerlayne's face.

Jerlayne wasn't a vain woman. Comfort was her watchword when it came to appearances. She liked her clothing plain and sturdy; and she'd never developed an interest in cosmetics, either the herbals of Fairie or the ever-changing confections produced in the mortal realm. Still, there were days when she looked better than others. With her flame-frizzed hair in tight, damp braids and her mother's gown hanging loose around her shoulders, Jerlayne would have been the first to agree that she was not having one of her better days.

"I don't travel well," she conceded and commanded the bay to start walking.

Goblin horses were trained to heed subtle signals from their silent riders. Tossing its head and altogether more spirited than her bay gelding, Goro's horse wanted to race, not walk. The bridge was well behind them before Goro had it behaving well enough to say: "You are all so different. It is easy to be blinded by the variety and never see that a face which is like no others can also be beautiful."

Jerlayne laughed, more nervous than offhand, "Especially if it's not dark blue."

"We are not dark blue."

It became Jerlayne's turn to stare silently at her companion. Goro didn't flinch. "We are naturally quite pale, on the plains. The nafoga'ar marks us when we leave and here in Fairie, the shadows deepen the stain. If I went back to the plains—if I could return there—and stayed there, it would fade."

"You move through shadows?" The rest was interesting, but that might be important. "That's how you come and go so mysteriously? For you, the shadows are like parting the Veil."

"Perhaps. I have never parted a Veil, not to the mortal realm or back to the plains, but I can enter one shadow and emerge from another one, never farther than my eyes can see. Or I can hide in a shadow, if it's dark enough and I do nothing to draw attention."

The bay had stopped, a horse's usual response to inattention from its rider, and usually Jerlayne would be hard-pressed to get it going again. This time she was content to let the bay stand while she considered Goro's remarkable admission.

"If you can do that, how can you say that you have no magic?"

"Lies. Convenience. Habit. Is shaping simply what you do, like walking or eating? Or is it magic? You can do things that we can't. It suited us to let you believe that there was nothing—other than killing—that we did that you couldn't. And killing is the main reason we culled: we don't want violent elves. You are half of us, half goblin, but you're also half mortal. We don't trust you; right below the surface, most of us are afraid of you. We *need* the guardians to protect the nafoga'ar. But to have twenty guardians, we need thousands of elves. We've done our best to make you docile."

Jerlayne was ready to lose herself in comparative thoughts. Everything Goro had said was shocking, not surprising. Surprising was how much he sounded like Elmeene talking about goblins.

She tapped the bay with her heels and reminded it that they were supposed to be walking. Horse-stubborn, it ignored her. When it came to riding, Jerlayne realized, she'd learned how to sit in a saddle . . . docilely. Incensed, she slammed her heels against the bay's ribs and slapped it with the knotted reins. With a saddle-shaking snort it ambled forward.

Goro and the black caught up effortlessly.

"I want to *hate* you and all goblins for what you've done."

"Another reason never to tell you. Secrets breed secrets. I've heard *you* say that."

"If goblins had been honest at the beginning . . . we're not fools, Goro, and we're all the same to the mortals. Elves and goblins together could have shaped something better than this."

"Perhaps. I don't know the truth; no one does. We may be immortal, but no one is left who remembers the Ten. My mother said that ogres caught us by surprise. Ogres and the discovery that two elves together might raise a guardian, but they'd never raise another elf. The two together . . . ? By the time anyone stopped to think what had been done, it must have been late for the truth. The ogres brought us out of the shadows, but you discovered mortal fathers on your own."

"As far as you know. You can't know what every goblin might have said to every woman when they were alone." Jerlayne said caustically, not liking the way the conversation had drifted: elves treating scyldrin the way goblins treated elves, the secret women kept from men.

Goro laughed. "I yield. I have too easily assumed we are the first man and elf who talk to each other."

"I didn't mean *that*," Jerlayne muttered hastily, fighting a losing battle against the warmth in her cheeks. Goblins couldn't blush, or couldn't be seen blushing.

"Then what, Jerlayne?" Goro replied, grimly serious: "Do you think that because *you* had to be told, no woman could have uncovered the truth by herself? By what I have seen and heard, more women learn for themselves than are told by their mothers, and none of you has told her husband. Think of it, Jerlayne: all that has happened to you in the last several days has happened because you're desperate to keep Aulaudin from learning that he is not Laydin's father. You worry what he'll do when he finds out. There's a lot of goblin in you, Jerlayne. It's not that we're different, it's that we're the same."

Jerlayne shook her head but it was true and it included mortals. She had only to make herself think of Aulaudin, Cuz, and Goro together to know that, immortality notwithstanding, they were all the same.

"My head hurts," she complained, and recalled Elmeene's similar complaints.

"You'll recover. Will you be ready next week? Have you learned how shape those tunics?"

"Not yet. It's like nothing I've held before. Even the bits I recognize are out of place. Elmeene suggested I ask Aulaudin for slippery skillets."

"Slippery skillets? Do what you must. If the gennern have a tent filled with it, and guns as well . . ." he let his voice trail off suggestively. "I don't think you can plan to steal their hoard."

When it came to pretending that nothing had happened, Jerlayne found herself firmly in the goblin's shadow. She considered several replies, including, *Haven't you already fulfilled your end of the bargain by telling me everything?* and left them unsaid. If Goro had more shattering revelations, she wanted a day or so before she had to absorb them.

The goblin was content to ride in silence, watching her as carefully as he watched the road. Knowing now that goblins did hide and travel through shadows, wondered if they were truly alone, or if his men were fanned out around them. She didn't ask; after the previous night, she didn't want to know.

They came to the ridge above Sunrise at midafternoon, the same ridge from which Jerlayne had gotten her first glimpse of her homestead. The Wavehome boat was under sail in the bay, smoke plumes rose from the great house kitchen and from a ring of tiny houses downwind of everything else. All the dwarves were at work on the windmill that would, they hoped, be ready to grind their grain by harvest time. Gnomes, made obvious by their distinctive silvery hair, were scattered about, doing chores. A breeze blew off the water, carrying the siren's song with it.

Jerlayne could listen to the faint, wild sounds and think, not of her daughter, but that all was as it should be at Sunrise. The homestead wasn't in a turmoil looking for her. Halfway down the ridge, Goro veered onto the narrow track to the goblin camp, saying that he'd be at the foundation stone in a week's time. She watched his back a moment, perhaps the shadows weren't deep enough, or he couldn't take a horse through them.

Then she thought about the armor and the days she had left to examine it. Headed for the stable, Jerlayne was concentrating on the armor as if she were already in her workroom.

"I was worried, beloved." Aulaudin emerged from the shadows, almost like a goblin, except he'd simply been worried and waiting. "I looked for you all night."

Sheer and sudden terror froze Jerlayne's heart. "I'm sorry . . ."

He offered his arms to help her down from the saddle. When Jerlayne shook her head, he reached for the cloth-wrapped bundle on the bay's rump. She slid to the ground and embraced her husband quickly.

"I thought you'd be gone longer."

The truth, on occasion could sound worse than a lie.

"I came across an unbroken sheet of glass as large as a table and brought it straight through the Veil."

Jerlayne nodded. Everyone wanted clear windows and every Sunrise window had broken when Evoni rose. They'd salvaged as much as they could. Jerlayne had spent a good portion of the winter shaping shards together. A large, unbroken sheet was a treasure she could understand.

"I'm sorry I wasn't here to welcome you. I needed to be alone . . . with Goro's challenge. There's not much time left."

Jerlayne unlashed the bundle. Aulaudin knew the size of the armor slab she'd had. He had to see there was something more wrapped within the cloth. She waited for the questions.

"Gelma said you'd gone off alone in a dither, headed for Stonewell and your mother. She said the goblin rode after you, to bring you back."

Was that to be the lie they all lived with?

Jerlayne nodded.

"He must have found you during the night?"

"Before. We camped on the ground rather than ride through the dark." She swallowed hard. "He talked me out of going to Stonewell. There's no need to involve Elmeene; I can untangle it myself."

"You're sure?" Aulaudin asked. "He might have discouraged you from talking to Elmeene because he might not want you to succeed. You say he's honorable, but he's still a goblin, Jerlayne. I'll take you to Stonewell this moment, if you thought it would help hold him off. We're doing better with the salt pools. Each day there's less and less reason for you to do his bidding." There was suspicion in her husband's voice, all directed toward Goro.

"It's not Goro any more. *I* want to know what it is and how it's made. It's become my challenge, not his."

They started walking toward the great house. The bundle wasn't heavy. Aulaudin didn't offer to carry it for her; he knew how it was when she was enrapt in a shaping challenge.

"If I knew what it had been before the goblins broke it, I could look beyond the Veil for a whole one for you."

Slippery skillets. If there were a way to ask for Elmeene's pots, without unraveling a score of half-told stories . . .

Aulaudin stopped, touched her arm. Joining flowed between them, stronger than all their secrets combined. If Jerlayne couldn't trust Aulaudin with the truth, could she trust anyone?

A year hadn't been enough time to repair the damage of three decades' estrangement. Now that Laydin was sleeping in his own cradle, Aulaudin wanted to return to their early years together, when their love could blind them to everything else. He resented, in a quiet, half-formed way, the time she spent in her workroom and, more sharply, he resented Goro's intrusion into their lives.

Swiftly, Jerlayne threw up distractions.

"After sunset," she promised, thinking that would be enough time to gather her wits. "We'll have our supper beneath the trees, with just the two of us, a basket of food, moonlight and breezes for company." She would shape a story that would include slippery skillets and as much of the truth as could be told without mentioning goblins.

Jerlayne was getting quite good at shaping stories.

There'd be no sunset that evening. A late afternoon sea-storm burst through the mists, engulfing the homestead with wind and rain. As Sunrise measured storms—and the past year had given them ample opportunity to make comparisons—it was merely an inconvenience, a squall of a few hours' duration, bright and loud, but scarcely dangerous. The trees would be dripping until midnight, but the rain would end long before then. Jerlayne and Aulaudin could salvage their supper on a porch that faced away from the sea.

By thunder and siren song, Jerlayne set the table, then, with lightning flashes to guide her, she went to the nursery to settle Laydin for the night. The door was open. She heard voices: Aulaudin talking to Gelma about toys. Their conversation was nothing Jerlayne shouldn't have heard, couldn't have interrupted, but she lingered in the corridor, listening to her husband pace and chatter. He spoke as if there'd never been another son born in Fairie.

Jerlayne had already decided to tell Aulaudin the truth. The box with Cuz's hair, remembrance paper, and the best of her sketches waited on her worktable, the lid wide open. They'd part the Veil together, her way; she'd show Aulaudin where she'd been. And the consequences, whatever they turned out to be, would also be the truth.

"He has his mother's eyes, her nose and mouth—"

Aulaudin's pacing brought him across Jerlayne's line of vision. He didn't notice her standing outside the door; his attention was on the lightly swaddled infant resting quietly in his arms.

In his father's arms.

"I think he has my hands. Long fingers. A forager needs long, strong fingers."

Jerlayne's imagined explaining to Aulaudin that Cuz's hands were short-fingered, like her own and that the son he adored was less a part of him than Evoni had been. Aulaudin might turn against her as Maun had turned against his mother, but that would be better than another possibility: Aulaudin might part the Veil and never return. Her heart sank.

She could live with lies, a whole realm of lies, before she could live with that silence and emptiness.

They ate their dinner on the bedroom porch then retreated to the room itself, shutting the doors and draperies behind them. Joining was exquisite, but Jerlayne remained wide awake after Aulaudin had fallen into a restless sleep. Men didn't share dreams. The sleeping mind dwelt alone in a realm of its own shaping, or so Jerlayne hoped.

Aulaudin stirred and mumbled her name when she swung her legs off the mattress. He was accustomed to a wife beside him, as neither Cuz nor Goro had been, and rolled onto his side without awakening. His breathing never wavered as Jerlayne searched for her robe and slippers. She left the door open behind her.

Lights flickered in the kitchen where a few itinerant scyldrin sat around the table comparing impressions of the homesteads they'd visited and rejected. One, a dwarf by the depth of his voice, said he thought he'd stay at Sunrise because it reminded him of the homestead where he'd been born.

Jerlayne remembered when a scyld's birthplace had been the greatest secret she'd imagined. Now, she didn't bother to linger at the top of the stairs to hear if he was, indeed, from Wavehome, but went softly on her way. The nursery was quiet, except for Gelma's snoring. Leaving her slippers behind, Jerlayne tiptoed across the carpet to see her son . . . Cuz's son . . . Aulaudin's son.

Laydin had escaped his swaddling and slept curled up in moonlight at the foot of his cradle. Autumn nights were cool and damp by the sea. Jerlayne tucked the blanket around him, kissed her fingertips, then stroked his wispy dark hair with a light touch.

Her workroom was quiet and empty. Jerlayne hadn't told Aulaudin the truth and didn't know if she'd ever have the courage to tell him outright, but she was past lying to direct questions. So, just as she'd left the bedroom door open, she left the workroom's lock unshaped: tempting fate, just a little.

Moonlight danced on the bay and through the many-paned windows onto the worktable where Cuz's portrait stared back at her. She'd never gotten the eyes quite right, or the corners of his mouth. The eyes were lost forever, but she could fix the mouth: Laydin had his father's mouth.

"I never saw him smile, except in anger or bitterness."

Taking up her charcoal, Jerlayne gave Cuz his son's wide grin. Then she redrew his eyes.

Jerlayne shaped a circle on the table, outside the portrait. The wood grain shifted and, with a fingertip's pressure on the edge, the circle lifted to reveal a hollow within the planks. She laid the portrait where it wouldn't likely be found, even by another woman, and was about to seal when she noticed her remembrance box. There was no need, now that she'd tested her courage and found it lacking, to leave it out and open. The fragile paper with its blurry portrait and reading on both sides would be safe with the portrait, anyway, and the hair . . .

She plucked the pale snippet out of the box and spun the bead she'd shaped to seal its ends between fingers. Perhaps Laydin's hair would fade, like a gnome's, as he grew, although she hoped it didn't. If her son's hair couldn't be rusty like Aulaudin's, then Jerlayne preferred that it remain dark.

Fairie kept time by seasons, deliberately ignoring the named months and numbered days of the mortal realm. They counted years haphazardly, accurately at the start of something—a life or a homestead—then became careless. Jerlayne had known her exact age when she shaped her twenty-link chain, but she was less certain now: one-hundred and sixty? one-hundred and sixty-five? It had been about a year since Evoni rose and brought the sea to Sunrise. A year, then, since she'd let herself be beguiled by a mortal.

Jerlayne had told Cuz more truth, more quickly and more easily, than she'd told to anyone else. There might be a lesson in that, if she had the courage to learn it. Staring out the window at the bay, his hair twirling idly through her fingers, Jerlayne tried to summon Cuz into her mind's eye.

Start with Cuz, Jerlayne thought. Tell him about *his* father and all else she'd learned since she'd left him in his basement room, a lock of her hair clutched in his hand. Imagine Cuz's reaction and maybe she could shape a little iron back into her spine.

Her mind drifted . . . Cuz . . . Aulaudin . . . Goro . . . Aulaudin, again . . . Laydin, their son, her son . . . Cuz . . . without a smile . . . with dark hair grown shaggy around his face . . . bruises around his eyes . . . a glass snake (a pipe? a *tube?*) wound around his face and into his nose.

«Jerlayne . . .»

Thoughts of Cuz clung to Jerlayne's mind. They surrounded her with despair so bleak and thick that the Veil remained dark when she parted it to a room that was not the basement room she remembered.

But it was her mortal lover, the father of her son, who lay in a contrapted bed—gaunt and dark-haired. He was bound by slender threads of metal and hollow tubes shaped from substances Jerlayne could not name by sight alone. The threads attached themselves to boxes with glowing faces. Their ominous light fell on Cuz's bruise-mottled skin. The tubes led to hanging pouches of varying sizes and colors, mostly crimson dark, like blood. The boxes made her arm tingle violently when she touched the nearest one. She thought of feathers and moss, as Elmeene had once suggested, and added a sea fog for good measure. The pain subsided—her pain, not the despair radiating from the bed.

"Cuz?" she whispered.

They were alone in the room, which had no windows and one closed door. She thought of her mother's closet, but this room was larger than that, much larger than it had first seemed to be. The bed was larger and all the ominous boxes.

Jerlayne whispered his name a second time and and—careful to avoid the dark, serpentine tubes extending from his forearm—took his hand in hers.

Cuz's eyes fluttered, reminding Jerlayne of Maialene's son, Dalan, as he lay dying.

His first words, "Am I dead yet?" did nothing to ease her apprehension.

She told him "No," and watched in horror as more of his life ebbed through her fingers.

"Take me away. Make this all end." Cuz rallied enough to squeeze her fingers. "I'm ready now. Please?"

The crude pressure of thought and feeling that had been so much a part of Jerlayne's first mortal encounter had vanished. Cuz was purely mortal now, without any semblance of immortal vitality. His hand in hers felt no different from an animal's paw. Most often she failed to heal animals because, by the time she tried, their injuries were unhealable or they had sunk so deep into age that her slightest touch was enough to push them into oblivion. When she knelt beside a horse or dog, it was usually to end suffering.

Cuz suffered, though he had no obvious wounds, aside from the tiny slits where the tubes pierced his flesh; and he wasn't old, even by mortal measure.

"Please?"

Jerlayne peeled away the white cloth covering his chest: more slit wounds, more wires. She couldn't place her hand over his heart without encountering metal wires. The wires sparked when she touched them, like silk on a dry, winter's morning. She pulled her hand back quickly. The sparks had bitten Cuz as well; he moaned and swept his hand across his body, trying, Jerlayne guessed, to yank the wires loose, though his strength failed. His hand fell limp on his ribs.

Unlike the tubes, the wires did not appear to pierce his skin. By eye, Jerlayne traced the two most inconvenient ones to a box that spat out a tongue of slick, black-scratched paper. Keeping a close eye on the paper tongue, she cautiously reached for the wires. Before her fingers closed around them, another box let out a series of insect chirps and the faces of several others came to life. A clear fluid flowed through one tube into Cuz's right arm. His whole body went rigid then began to shake.

She had neither words to describe nor guesses to explain what was happening to Cuz, except that in some primal way his suffering was *wrong* and had to stop. Death would stop Cuz's suffering, but only because the dead couldn't suffer. There had to be a better way.

Jerlayne seized all the wires circling Cuz's heart and pulled. The box crashed to the floor; she dropped the loose ends on top of it. Then Jerlayne attacked the tube flowing into his right arm. It burrowed a finger's length beneath Cuz's flesh and dribbled venom onto the bed linen one she worked it loose. Dark blood flowed from the wound it left behind. She pressed her thumb over the puncture to seal it.

The room, formerly quiet, erupted with loud noise. Red light flashed through the cracks above and below the closed door. It came to Jerlayne then, out of a century's accumulation of Aulaudin's unexplained, mortal-realm memories, that this room was *science,* that Cuz had fallen afoul of *science,* and that *science* had just become her personal enemy, her gennern.

Jerlayne's first thought, which she did not indulge, was to part the Veil and take herself back to Sunrise before she got hurt again. Her second was to lay her shaping hands on the door—which proved to be made from metal, not wood—and fuse it, lock and hinges both, into its equally metallic frame. Then she tore all the wires, all the tubes from Cuz's flesh.

She had Cuz, unconscious and slowly bleeding, in her arms when the *science* mortals threw themselves against her shape-sealed door. Before Jerlayne could take any satisfaction from her handiwork, there was a familiar, frightening sound—a *shot.* The door didn't fly open, but one of the boxes exploded with bitter smoke and, a heartbeat later, flames.

Jerlayne told herself to stay calm, to sit on the cold, hard floor with Cuz in her arms, and think of Fairie, of her workroom in Sunrise where *science* couldn't harm her. A second shot broke her concentration. A third brought her to the edge of panic when it blasted one of the hanging pouches and blood sprayed her face. She would have panicked, if she'd been alone, but Cuz was still alive in her arms. Her determination to keep him alive kept her calm. More shots punctured the metal door, but a door wasn't flesh and holes wouldn't undo *her* shaping.

She built her workroom in her mind's eye, from the carpet pattern, to the pillows, to the wood grain of her table. When it seemed real enough to touch, she thought of the Veil.

Mist swirled around her. Jerlayne felt the carpet beneath her, smelled the sea breeze. But her lap was filled with burning light; and when Jerlayne tried to lift Cuz from his realm to hers, the burning light spread up her arms. Frantic and enraged, Jerlayne willed hands that had gone numb to grasp the mortal man she could no longer see, then she struggled to her knees and pulled, as if he were some deep-rooted weed.

The harder she pulled, the heavier Cuz became. When she mistakenly relaxed, Jerlayne toppled forward. Her chin struck the floor of her workroom and her arms stretched through the floor to the mortal realm.

"Viljuen weeps! What are you doing?" a sleep-disheveled Aulaudin called from the doorway.

"Help me! Help me bring him through the Veil."

Aulaudin blinked and shook his head, but asked no time-wasting questions. He didn't even move away from the doorway. His arms opened, releasing the Veil mist, and a heartbeat later, Cuz was feathers in Jerlayne's arms. She lifted—

«Slowly!» Aulaudin shouted inside her skull. «Life comes through *slowly!*»

But slowly was more difficult. He became heavy again. Jerlayne withdrew her arms to the elbows and could go no farther.

«My hands! He's falling away. I can't hold on! I'm losing him!»

«That's me, beloved. I have him. Let go, now.»

She obeyed without a thought, as soon as the notion was in her mind. The rebound was such that she sat hard on her heels. Aulaudin grunted and staggered backward. He collided hard with the doorway and lost his balance, but there were extra limbs around him as he collapsed: Cuz was in Fairie.

Jerlayne never remembered if she ran across her workroom or crawled, but she was beside both men. She couldn't hear Cuz breathing and he wasn't moving on his own. She tried to find his pulse, but her hands were swollen and she had to heal herself before she could begin to heal the mortal.

"A light, please," she said to her husband. "And blankets. He's near frozen."

She prayed to Cuz's mortal gods that Aulaudin would ask no questions, and he didn't. He set a worktable lamp on the floor beside her, then headed off for blankets and, perhaps, clothing: both men were naked.

Beyond shock and frostbite, Cuz's apparent injuries were minor—old bruises and the slit wounds left by the tubes she'd yanked from his flesh, but serious, and contradictory, poisons flowed in his blood.

«Like blooddeath,» she answered, belatedly realizing that Aulaudin had returned with blankets and had asked what was wrong.

«Bryony?»

"No." She relied with her voice, which was easier than sharing when she was trying to vanquish poisons she couldn't name. "He's filled with *things* that aren't part of him!"

«He's sick, then—*diseased*.»

Aulaudin shared a cascade of memories: mortals coughing, mortals heaving, mortals in their beds and in their graves. There was a coldness to the images, hostility and distrust. Her husband knew what she'd done and it had shaken him, but the images taught Jerlayne about the ways mortals died and the ways they might be healed. Aulaudin stayed beside her while she countered one *disease* after another until dawn, when she'd beaten back the worst.

"He'll live," she announced, sitting back on her heels. "He'll live until I've got the strength to root out the rest."

Jerlayne's fingernails were black as any goblin's. Her forearms had blistered. The skin sloughed away in disgusting tatters. She remembered Goro saying that goblins weren't born blue but were stained by the shadows. She remembered that a day hadn't passed since she'd had that conversation. Weariness caught up with her and she began to shiver.

Aulaudin sat bent forward in a chair, his elbows resting on his knees. He'd watched everything and had only one question. "Why?"

She slumped forward, shaking her head. "Not yet. I'll tell you everything, I swear it, just . . . not yet."

"He's mortal. You know that, don't you? You've brought a mortal into Fairie."

There was no anger in Aulaudin's voice, which only made it harder to bear. Jerlayne lacked the courage to stifle her tears. Her shivering got worse. Aulaudin abandoned his perch and wrapped another blanket around her shoulders, but he didn't come close to joining.

"I swear—I'll tell you everything, but the words—I'm too tired now."

"Best sleep here, then, where I can keep an eye on you both."

Chapter 26

Jerlayne awoke hours later. Without reprieve, she knew instantly where she was, what she'd done, and what she'd promised to do. She also knew, before she opened her eyes, that Aulaudin wasn't in the workroom. Sitting up, she saw that he'd shuttered the windows, drawn the drapes, and also opened the rooftop louvers, to keep the air fresh. The door was locked—bolted from the inside. Aulaudin couldn't shape metal as she would have; he'd left the workroom by parting the Veil.

She thought that was a good sign, a prudent but not hostile sign: he didn't want the scyldrin blundering across a mortal man, but he hadn't—even symbolically—tried to confine her. Or Cuz.

The battered mortal lay on the floor. He didn't appear to have moved much at all while Jerlayne had slept and didn't rouse when she flattened her hands against his neck. To her surprise, Cuz's fever had dropped and his pulse, which had been rapid, was steady. Yet more surprising, many of the *diseases* Jerlayne had expected to battle were weakened; several, she thought, had vanished altogether.

Cuz remained thoroughly exhausted. Jerlayne needed only the slightest pressure at the base of his neck to send him into another cycle of deep sleep. Ever curious, she decided against healing any of his lingering diseases. Perhaps mortals were more resilient than she'd imagined, or perhaps Cuz, who'd *noticed* her and whose father might have been a goblin, was not a typical mortal.

If Jerlayne believed Goro's version of the tale of the Ten, the first elves were the children of goblins and mortals.

Aulaudin had left bowls of water, fruit, and crusty rolls on her worktable. Her hairbrush and a change of clothes waited

there, too. They were all neatly arranged around the shaped circle. Her portrait of Cuz was missing.

Jerlayne splashed water on her face. Her stomach was busy
churning against itself; she left the food untouched. After she'd
dressed and twisted her hair into a knot to match her stomach,
Jerlayne laid hands on the shutters and sealed the door behind
her—lest Cuz awaken and make a bad situation worse.

The great house was as quiet as it had been in the middle of
the night. Idly, Jerlayne wondered what her husband had already told the scyldrin. It hardly mattered. Whatever he'd told
them, it couldn't have been the truth.

She headed for the nursery. Gelma intercepted her.

"What's wrong, Mistress? The master's sent everyone out."
The gnome wrung her hands. "Has he got the 'death? Nothing's
done for supper. I'm worried sick for the boy. The master let me
in at noon for nursing Laydin, but that's all. He's told me to wait
out here until he calls me."

"Here's too close," Jerlayne said grimly. "You'd best go
over to the cottages and wait. One of us will come for you."

"But what's wrong?"

"Ghosts," Jerlayne replied, plucking the word from the
depths of her memory: spirits from the past, secrets that should
have died generations ago.

Gelma's lips were set in a bloodless scowl before she scurried off. The homestead would be buzzing with worry and
ghosts by sundown. They'd probably lose scyldrin. A small
loss, considering what else was at stake.

Aulaudin sat in the nursery much as he'd sat in the workroom while Jerlayne had healed Cuz: tipped forward in a rocking chair, his elbows on his knees, staring at Laydin through
the lathe-work at the foot of his cradle. Jerlayne surveyed the
room quickly as she entered: Her charcoal portrait lay atop the
washstand, unharmed. There was, she thought, still hope.

"I've come to tell you everything. To answer every question."

Aulaudin sat back in the rocking chair, said nothing.

Jerlayne got another chair and made a triangle opposite both
the cradle and her husband.

"I'm not sure where to start . . ."

"He's the mortal's son, isn't he? Not mine at all."

"No, not yours," Jerlayne confessed as silent tears fell. She
hadn't wanted to cry and should have been able to stop, but

sometimes the simplest shapings were the hardest. "I'm sorry. I'm so sorry. It's the only way . . . the only way for elves. Our children will change. All of them. I didn't know. Truly. When Evoni—"

"No more. I believe you. I have eyes."

She raised her head, not far enough to meet them. "It's been a secret. Daughters aren't told . . . aren't told until they can keep a secret. Elmeene said my sisters all guessed, but I'm the blind one. Evoni nearly destroyed us. Now I've done this. I don't know which is worse."

"Evoni. Evoni was worse. The night after she rose, when you were lost inside yourself, I found my father and told him I wanted to bring you to Briary. My father shared that Aglaidia didn't know you well enough and that I should take you to Stonewell. But first, she said, I should join with you. *That* was the worst."

"I'm sorry," Jerlayne looked down at her hands again.

"Maun's not my father."

His voice told her nothing. She couldn't see his face. Wouldn't. "No, he's not."

Aulaudin began to pace. When his path brought him near her chair, Jerlayne shrank away from him.

"I tried being angry, Jerlayne. All morning I tried to be angry with you. I'm not very good at it. I feel cheated and betrayed, but it's not as if you singled me out. My mother deceives my father. Your mother deceives your father. Every wife has deceived her husband since the Ten. Who am I to complain? I could wish you hadn't dragged him back here, but could I wish you'd left Laydin's father to *die* like that? Would I want to think that I loved someone who didn't care enough about her son's father to save his life? I'd lose the most precious parts of myself if I let myself become angry for that."

Jerlayne curled deeper into herself. Her tears flowed more freely after he said the word *loved*. "It happened so suddenly. I couldn't sleep; I'd gone to the workroom—" She was lying again, not telling the whole truth. Lying proved to be an insidious habit, one she couldn't break, not yet. Jerlayne sniffed gracelessly and continued, "When I looked at his portrait . . . *I heard him through the Veil*."

"Does that often happen? Hearing him through the Veil."

"No! Of course not—"

"I don't know 'of course,' Jerlayne, when it comes to women and the Veil. I'm still trying to get used to the idea."

Determined to stop lying, Jerlayne took a deep breath and said, "There's a second one."

"A second mortal?"

"A second Veil, between Fairie and the plains where the goblins live. I went there by mistake. I was trying to find a larger piece of what Goro had given me. That's how women do it—how *I* do it . . . part the Veil. I hold something that belongs to the mortal realm and let it pull me through. But I went to the plains by mistake. I found what I wanted, but I got *shot,* by a goblin with a *gun,* and I—I got so frightened I pulled myself to Stonewell rather than here. Elmeene took care of me, but I was in the wrong place. We tried to smooth everything right again. We used the pass-throughs. Elmeene turned back. Goro met me. I told him what had happened. He told me *things* . . . what the goblins believe about the Ten, about Fairie and elves."

Aulaudin sat down heavily in the rocking chair. "Viljuen weeps. The goblin told you *things.* Goblins have guns. There's another Veil between here and the plains and the goblins. Viljuen weeps tears of blood. I'll have to visit Briary to share this. I have to see Maun's face. Tell me quickly, what do goblins believe?"

Jerlayne cleared her throat, wiped her tears. "To start, Viljuen is a goblin name and they tell a different version of the tale of the Ten . . ."

She repeated it, as closely as she could remember, and everything else. They didn't join; the thought of joining was painful and, anyway, joining was best for images and impressions, not words. Jerlayne hoped, even as she related goblin myths, their Veil, their deadly rivalries, and how they moved through shadows, that there might be a few secrets she didn't have to share. Aulaudin stopped her a few times, when he'd missed a word, but he said nothing of substance until she'd come to an end.

Late afternoon shadows had darkened the nursery. Laydin awoke, fussing and hungry, wanting Gelma. Jerlayne placated him with apple juice while Aulaudin stared out a window that faced the tree-hidden goblin camp. She had Laydin back in his cradle before Aulaudin asked his first question.

"Did you tryst with him?"

Shock made Jerlayne stand straight and look directly at her

husband. She could lie, but not quickly, not after her body had betrayed her and shaped her mind into a fortress. "What a thought!" she babbled, sounding like Elmeene when Elmeene got caught. "Goro's a goblin."

"I've seen him look at you."

"I'm his life," Jerlayne said. The damage was done; the panic had passed. "That's what he said: without me, he has no life. The goblins divide us up, as if our homesteads were flocks of sheep and they're the shepherds. We get passed along, elfin daughters to goblin sons. Something happened to Goro's father. He lost a war and his enemies killed him and all his family, except for Goro. Goro's mother's some sort of priestess—I can't remember her name—but she bargained for his life, then she sent him to Stonewell. The men who killed his father, they cut off a part of his finger—"

Aulaudin turned. Wrapped tightly in her guilt, Jerlayne didn't know if his thoughts reached toward her and couldn't make sense of his expression.

"I wouldn't have noticed, if he hadn't shown me, but among goblins, losing a bit of finger like that must be very serious. A man with a missing finger can't be a father. Our daughters won't be protected by his sons," she heard the error, *our* daughters, but let it pass uncorrected. "He said Sunrise is the only way he can prove that his father was right about us, about elves. He wouldn't harm any of us, me or you or any of the scyldrin."

"Did the goblin tell you how his father died?"

Jerlayne rummaged through her memories. "Salt, they made him eat salt— No, wait—he killed himself rather than eat salt. I think. I didn't listen too closely to that part, I'm sorry. Goro said he was there when it happened. When I thought about what he might have seen, my mind went blank—"

"They threw his father's head at him."

She grabbed the back of the chair where she'd sat earlier. "Goro didn't say that. I wouldn't be able to forget that."

"He *shared* it with me, on the beach that day when he told me about salt, before he came to you. I don't know if he meant to or not, but he knew it had happened. As long as we're exposing secrets, that's one of mine: I got sucked into a goblin's memories. I thought it was deceit; some goblin trick to confuse me. I felt pain in my finger—" Aulaudin raised his left hand, his second finger.

"Not that one. The middle finger, of his other hand."

Aulaudin sighed. "Yes, just so. He was very young, not grown, a boy about this high—" he held his palm level with his waist. "Very frightened, and very angry. I think it was a mistake—the sharing. He drew his sword on me moments later, wanted to kill me because I'd seen past his mask."

"He's not your enemy, Aulaudin."

"That's what he told me himself, when the siren had risen and he'd dragged you out of the mud before I got here. 'I am not your enemy, Aulaudin.' "

He captured that strange, ambiguous goblin accent perfectly.

"Goro's alone. He envies you."

"Did you tryst with him? With a goblin?"

"Yes." Jerlayne held her breath, waiting for Aulaudin's response. When, after several moments, none came, she added: "I shape iron, Aulaudin. I heal wounds that would kill—"

"You let nothing stand in your way."

Jerlayne could have said that she'd heard almost the same words from Goro, but decided to say, instead. "You're my husband, Aulaudin. What I've done, I've done because it could be done, like shaping iron. No man stands between us, not Goro, not Cuz."

"Cuz? Who's *Cuz?*"

"The mortal—"

Who might—have awakened; they'd been in the nursery for several hours. She glanced in the direction of her workroom. Cuz would have found the food on the worktable and eaten all of it—healing created an appetite that couldn't be denied. After that? The shutters and door were shaped shut. Maybe he would fall back to sleep. Maybe he'd try to escape through the louvers.

"I need to go back to my workroom. Cuz doesn't know what's happened to him. He was unconscious when I found him in *science.*"

"Cuz isn't a name, Jerlayne, and science isn't a place."

"He was alone in a terrible place, and *science* seemed the right word for it. There were wires attached to him and tubes—bloody tubes—piercing him. When he saw me, he wanted me to kill him, but I brought him here. He might hurt himself, or worse."

"Go to him. He needs you," Aulaudin said, then smiled, as if moving each muscle had required a deliberate decision.

Jerlayne released the chair she'd been holding. Blood rushed back to whitened fingers. She started for the door, thinking she'd weathered the worst.

"Would you love me more if I were weary or injured, frightened or alone?"

The hardest blow was struck when and where Jerlayne had least expected it. She sobbed once, behind her hands. A choice loomed before her: run away from the man who stood at the center of her life, or run to him, and the risk that he would turn away.

As she had all her life, Jerlayne chose risk. Her arms were around her husband's shoulders. She pressed her tear-damp cheek to his heart before he could fend her away. She sought his mind for joining, and he did not shut her out, though he'd made himself into a cavernous room with no furnishings. Jerlayne had nothing left for her own defense. He could have plundered every memory, every secret, but that was not Aulaudin; he did not pry.

«Beloved, you cannot be rid of me so easily.»

«I don't ever want to be rid of you!»

«Then we will find each other on the other side of this darkness, just as we did the first time.»

In the empty room of Aulaudin's mind, Jerlayne caught a breeze of departure and absence. She loosened her hold until she could see his face. His eyes were quiet as he shook his head.

"I won't be gone long, a few days. No, I *will* come back, right here, to you. I love no other woman, Jerlayne. If you change, then I must change. But I need time—"

"Don't leave. Please, don't leave."

"The mortal, Cuz—"

They were still joined and in joining, a small act of will could unleash a torrent of memory. Jerlayne wanted Aulaudin to know that Cuz wasn't a threat. In a heartbeat, she unleashed everything . . . and had no idea what he perceived. Yesterday, Jerlayne had told Elmeene that two women standing beside each other did not see the same thing. When the sharing flowed so quickly, details were lost, forgotten, never remembered.

"His name is *not* Cuz," Aulaudin repeated, kissing Jerlayne lightly, chastely on the forehead. "And we must hope Laydin does not take after him."

"Laydin . . . you won't—you won't turn your back on Laydin?"

"I will come back, beloved, when I know what I must do and how to do it."

Aulaudin gently pushed Jerlayne away and walked out the nursery door. She knew the only way to ensure that he never came back to her was to pursue him. A door opened, then closed. Moments later, before Jerlayne was ready to face anyone, Gelma hurried into the nursery.

"He didn't see me. The master took a red goblet from the shelf over the door. He looked straight at me without seeing me, Mistress. If it's not the 'death, Mistress, what is it ails him so? He left as if he weren't coming back."

"Laydin," Jerlayne answered quickly. There'd never truly be an end to lies. "Some fathers need time to accept fatherhood."

"But he was doing so well . . ."

"He changed. He thought about the future. He'll be back, Gelma. Aulaudin said he would be back. That's the important thing, isn't it?"

"If you say it is, Mistress, if it's not the 'death or something worse."

"Nothing worse," Jerlayne assured the gnome. "You'll tend to Laydin, please? With Aulaudin gone, I'm retreating to my workroom. I have work to do."

"He'll be safe with me!"

Safer, Jerlayne thought putting her own words to Gelma's silent, sober expression, perhaps than with either of his parents . . . *any* of his parents.

She filled a good-sized basket in the larder: more fruit and bread, plus cheese, sweet cakes, and a generous slab of smoked fish. When she had enough to feed two dwarves after a hard day's work, Jerlayne went to her workroom. The lock opened to her touch. The shuttered room was night-dark and silent; Cuz was, possibly, still asleep. Jerlayne closed the door and shaped its lock without making a sound. Normally, Jerlayne knew her workroom thoughtlessly, the way she knew herself, but the workroom didn't belong to her today. She advanced slowly, one hand in front, scouting the darkness and scuffing her feet across the carpet, lest she trip over a mortal asleep.

There should have been an oil lamp on the worktable . . .

Jerlayne remembered Aulaudin had brought it to her while

she healed Cuz. She found it on a smaller table by the door. It was light, almost empty. She lit the wick with a match from the drawer in its base—less effort than shaping a flame—then turned around, wondering where she'd put the oil jug.

Cuz was right behind her, his arm above his head and jagged scrap iron clenched in his fist.

They were both startled and they both jumped backward, Jerlayne colliding with the smaller table. The lamp rocked precipitously until Jerlayne steadied it with both hands.

"Shit!" Cuz exclaimed, lowering his arm. "It's *you*. I wasn't taking chances. So, it really happened . . . You came to that damned lab an' busted me out. Where are we? New Jersey?"

Jerlayne's heart beat again. "I brought you to Fairie. You were very weak—dying. I brought you here to heal you."

"No shit."

"Shit. No shit. I don't understand." She didn't. The beguiling magic that had helped Jerlayne understand mortals didn't work in Fairie.

"Yeah, I forgot—you do magic-stuff, but you don't understand. So, *this* is fairyland?"

"Fairie." The difference was subtle; Jerlayne didn't expect him to hear it. She'd forgotten how strange he was, or perhaps he only seemed stranger because this time they were face-to-face in her home, not his. "You must be hungry. I brought food—" she pointed to the basket on the worktable.

Cuz tore into the sweet cakes.

"Go easy," she warned. "I didn't finish healing you. There were so many poisons! I got the worst, but I didn't get them all."

He dropped the cake on the table and examined the tiny red mark on the back of his hand where one of the tubes had plunged beneath his skin. "Poisons, too? Shit. I thought they were just pumping me full of viruses and bacteria to see how much I could take before I croaked." He extended his arm across the worktable. "Thanks. Big-time thanks for getting me out of there."

"You called me," Jerlayne explained, cautiously matching his gesture and keeping her thoughts to herself when he clasped her hand with his and pumped it vigorously up and down. "I had that lock of your hair. It led me to you, to that place, what was that place, Cuz?"

"Call it an underground lab for hi-tech drugs—"

Jerlayne committed the words to memory; Aulaudin might know their meaning.

"My fucking uncle set me up. I don't get sick, see? When everybody else was dyin' of AIDS, I was still goin' strong and doin' all the same fucking stupid shit. Nothing bad was happening to me . . . well, nothing like AIDS was happening to me. My uncle, he's been holding that over me, like he's the lion tamer an' I'm the lion: jump through the flaming hoop and get some raw meat. I wasn't ever gonna jump, then I got into a jam— Shit! Fuckin' shit—my stuff's gone. Didn't have much, but the locker's been confiscated. Fuck. Like it matters, right? My uncle set me up with these science-guys—"

Ah! *Science* . . . Jerlayne had been sure *science* had something to do with Cuz's misery, not that she understood much else. Cuz didn't need anyone to understand him once he'd started talking.

"They put some shit in my food. Fuck! Maybe the restaurant was in on the scam? Nah. Uncle Ted poured the wine; that'll teach me to drink Chianti, right? So, they hauled my ass out to an ambulance—the ambulance was definitely in on the scam—an' stuck a needle in my arm. End of story. Shit, I tried to bust out a couple times, when I got ahead of the meds, but they got black dudes with guns hangin' around the doors, so I didn't get too far. When they weren't takin' blood out, they were shootin' shit into me." Cuz paused and made a point of catching her eye. "I wasn't gettin' outta there, Jerlayne. I saw that. Whenever they were done with me alive, they were gonna start on me again when I was dead. I don't get sick, but, hey, I can die the old-fashioned way, right?"

"Probably."

"But nobody figured I knew an elf. So, how did you get me out? Lightning bolts? Fireballs?"

Cuz pawed through the basket. He found one of the soft cheeses and smeared it on one of the rolls. Jerlayne reminded herself that she'd dug deep to heal him, and that healed men were known to chew wood afterward.

"I heard you, then I followed your remembrance to that room with all the boxes. There were tubes and wires all around you and you said you wanted to die. I tried to heal you there. When that didn't work, I brought you here."

"You couldn't heal me in that lab?"

She shook her head. He finished the cheese-slathered bread and went rummaging again.

"The boxes made noise when I pulled the wires from you. And there were flashing lights and louder noises outside the room. The door was metal; I shaped it so it wouldn't open—even when mortals shot at it—the *dudes?*"

"That's what gets me about you, Jerlayne. You don't know an EEG from an EKG, but you touch a door an' the lock falls out—or it won't open. What's this?"

"Smoked fish, and I don't know what kind."

"Figures." The golden-brown slab fell from Cuz's hand. "You eat that shit? *Elves* eat smoked fish?"

"We're getting used to it."

"Shit. I could figure no cheeseburgers or pizza; they're not very fairy. And, I can see you've got no electricity, so I know you don't have cable, but isn't there supposed to be, well, fairy feasts with food that keeps you from knowing seven years have passed in a single night, and tall, thin guys wearing fancy clothes, and deadly guys on wild horses?"

Jerlayne shook her head again. She didn't think he meant the goblins.

"You're shittin' me, right? This place—this place right here with the curtains that don't match, the worn-out carpet, and everything else glued back together—*this* is fairyland?"

"Fairie. This is my home: Sunrise. What do you mean the curtains don't match? There are two on each window."

"Well, *look* at them Jerlayne. There's blue flowers on white on one of them, red flowers on white on the one in the middle, and white flowers on *purple* on the third. And the fucking carpet's mostly *green*. It was worse before the sun went down."

Aulaudin had said he'd be trouble.

"Is Cuz your true name?"

"My true name? What do you need my true name for? Some kind of black magic? I know all about not giving witches or leprechauns my true name."

Jerlayne's jaw tightened. Black magic? Like black dudes with guns? Witches were mortals mistaken for elves, at least that's what men said. But what was a leprechaun? And where was the charm, the beguiling charm that had kept her trysting with Cuz much longer than was necessary?

"So, Jerlayne, what's on the other side of that door? I tried it, you know. You'd done your metal-magic thing with it. Is there anything else to eat, beside this fish stuff? The cheese was good, and the bread. I'm not much for fruit. It's okay, but it's just fruit, right?"

"I *like* fruit," she snapped.

Cuz fell silent . . . for a moment. "Sorry," he muttered, sounding more hostile than apologetic. "I'm new here. I don't know the rules."

"Enough! You're talking so much I can't think! This is all wrong."

" 'Cuz of me? Hey, you saved my life. Anywhere's got to be better than where I was, right? You tell me what I'm supposed to do, and I'll do it. I'm all yours. Shit, isn't that how it works: you save my life and I belong to you until I can return the favor? You got a seraglio someplace, just send me there."

"A *what?*" Jeralyne rubbed her fingers against her temples. Beyond the Veil she'd been able to hear mortal thoughts more than mortal words. "Talk slower, please." Though she didn't believe that would truly help.

"A . . . seraglio. . . . the . . . place . . . where . . . you keep . . . your . . . changeling . . . lovers."

"No!"

"Then where are you going to keep me?"

"I don't know." She spread her fingers until they covered her face and raked through her hair. "I don't know."

"What happened to your hair? It's all short and frizzed on one side."

"I caught fire." Jerlayne tried to sound like her mother when Elmeene answered a question in a way that ended a discussion.

"When you were rescuing me from the lab!?"

She'd failed; she wasn't Elmeene.

"Before." Jerlayne counted the days in her memory. There were only two; she'd have sworn she'd lived an entire lifetime. "The day before yesterday. I got shot and I caught fire."

"Shit."

Cuz stopped chattering. Jerlayne didn't ask why, didn't dare say anything, lest he start up again. She stood beside the table—her own worktable in her own workroom—with her eyes closed and her hands over her face. She wondered if things could get worse, and called herself a damned fool for tempting fate.

Then there were hands, mortal hands, resting on her shoulders, seeking the tightest muscles and kneading with gentle strength.

"Poor kid. Sounds like you've been living my life."

A bit of Cuz's charm awakened when he touched Jerlayne, nothing like the feral, cats-in-heat passion of his basement room—and for that she was most heartily grateful. But her mood lightened and she stopped regretting that she'd rescued him.

"With wires and tubes all over me and poison inside me? No, it hasn't been that bad."

"But bad enough? I can make myself scarce. Honest. Just hand me a book, point me at a corner, and I'll chill till you need me for something."

"No books."

Redis and Maialene had collected books at Brightwings. The *library,* they called it, the only one in Fairie and another of Redis' inexplicable habits. It had burnt with the rest of their homestead.

"Shit."

Chapter 27

There was little left to say where the great house of Tatterfall had once stood. If he'd swept down through a decade's worth of autumn leaves, Aulaudin could have traced the foundation stones of his brother's homestead. Could have, but didn't. Memory was enough, memory and the odd realization that Sunrise was older and, despite the siren and the sea, larger than Tatterfall had ever been.

A newer ruin rose beneath the quiet trees, close by what had been the kitchen hearth: a one-room cottage with a sprung door and a broken roof. He'd built it during the bad years, when Sunrise had belonged to Jerlayne and their daughter. Now it held the habits of a lifetime: Fairie clothes, mortal-realm clothes, gifts not yet given, and enough iron to turn a goblin's eyes white, just in case they drove Jerlayne to an impossible bargain.

Aulaudin didn't trust the goblins and hadn't trusted them long before Tatterfall. The way they came and went and always seemed to be thinking something they weren't saying—as if elves were lesser creatures. The way mortals were? Maybe that was why he didn't trust goblins: he'd been tempted too many times to treat mortals as beasts.

In Aulaudin's most private thoughts, it rankled more that Jerlayne had succumbed to a goblin's charms—wasn't that a contradiction?—than that she'd gone to the mortal realm to find a father for their son. Mortals *were* charming. Every boy learned that midway through his lessons. Fairie had its festivals and feasts every season. There were times when no one opened a door without knocking loudly, but two or even three feasts a season weren't nearly enough for an unmarried man, especially when it was with a rare woman who trysted with a man younger than herself.

A frustrated bachelor eventually lost interest in the finer

points of foraging. Maun had dealt the problem with his usual
directness on a hillside outside a city that was, then and now,
proud of its beautiful women.

You may marry someday—Maun had said to him and Boraudin together—*and a fine day it will be when you do, but it's a
simple fact that there are more men than women and so the
women do the picking and choosing. Now, you could follow the
dwarves—be damned, maybe you already do, it's no matter to
me—but beyond the Veil's not such a bad place on a cold,
lonely night. It's riskier than foraging, in a good many ways—
though if you're clever, you can do your finest foraging in a
bedroom. And—not to put too fine a point on it, sons—we're
better at it than their men are.*

*I'm not about to give either of you lessons on the courting
side, just one piece of warning: never forget they're mortal.
Oh, it's not just for lack of joining, though if you marry, like as
not you'll lose interest in mortal women; 'til then, well, you
can't miss what you haven't had. But they age and you don't,
and age falls hard on a mortal woman. Don't linger. A year, at
most, less is better, then move on. Don't look back; you won't
like what you see, and neither will they.*

Aulaudin and his brother took Maun's advice about never
looking back, not because they'd found it wise, but because
even when the mortal realm had been much smaller, men kept
moving. A season was a long time; a week was more common;
a single night not unheard of. The brothers had been young,
handsome, and vigorous rivals.

Sitting in the Tatterfall twilight, Aulaudin shook his head as
he remembered those days—nights—with his brother. Though
Aulaudin was still considered young by the other men of
Fairie, at least a dozen mortal generations had ebbed and
flowed since those wild years. The resting places where he and
his brother had parted the Veil were as forgotten as any children they might have left behind.

They'd never thought about children. They were elves and the
women they courted beyond the Veil were *mortal*. Though there
were no differences that their eyes could see, they called that fortune and thought no further. An elf with mortal offspring? Might
as well mate a stallion to a cow. The notion had been unthinkable until Jerlayne had enlightened him two days ago.

Stallions didn't mate with cows, but the men of Tenwoods
homestead had an easy life trading mules for lumber and brick.

Unthinkable.

Blind.

Domesticated.

Jerlayne hadn't used the word. Probably the goblin hadn't either. It was one of the thousands of words and notions Aulaudin had foraged but never shared, because—

Aulaudin shook his head again in mid-thought. He believed his wife and what she'd shared with him, her astonishment as she'd shared her memories of a city so confusing that he hadn't recognized it. Jerlayne had tried to tell him she wouldn't go back. He'd told her not to make promises she couldn't keep, and she'd dissolved in tears again.

She'd have to go back. Laydin wasn't enough. Not for either of them. He had no problem forgiving Jerlayne—for Cuz. The goblin was different.

Aulaudin wasn't ready to think about the goblin. Maybe he'd just forget. Elves were very good at forgetting.

Domesticated.

That's what the goblins had done to Fairie: domesticated it. Aulaudin worked beside the scyldrin each fall, culling the Sunrise flocks. Culling. Jerlayne made it clear she'd gotten that word from the goblin. When Sunrise culled, they didn't remove just the weak or undersized; they got rid of the ornery and the troublesome. *Too clever for his own good,* Aulaudin could hear himself saying those exact words, year in, year out. The words were always a lie: the culled animals weren't too clever for themselves; they were too clever for the scyldrin who took care of them.

They scyldrin who protected Fairie's domesticated flocks . . . the way the goblins protected everything else.

Aulaudin leaned back against the fallen trunk of a tree that had grown and died since the goblins failed to protect Tatterfall against its, or their, enemies. He hadn't come here to contemplate goblins. He'd come to answer the question that had burst into his thoughts the moment he'd realized what—who— Jerlayne had hauled through the Veil.

It was a question he should have asked and answered long ago: Why were some mortals aware of a man?

Already Aulaudin had spent a day and a night wrestling with that question. He'd started with the places he'd haunted when the one-room cottage behind him was his Fairie home, when loneliness, frustration, and anger had gotten the better of his affections. It had only been a year, but a year was a long time in the mortal realm, and thirty years was an eternity. A good many of his trysting places were gone or changed beyond recognition.

So, Aulaudin was back at Tatterfall, sitting on ground that cooled quickly after sunset, staring at a goblet made from etched red glass, one of five that sat on a shelf in the room where he and Jerlayne ate when they ate alone. He couldn't remember the mortal woman's name or the precise shape of the farmhouse where she'd lived, not that names or shapes mattered. In the way of the mortal realm, it was likely that the woman and her home had both been gone for decades.

Life had been different then, *his* life before Jerlayne had ended her childhood, their friendship. When Aulaudin had taken the mortal woman to her bed, he'd intended to return for the following year. He'd joined with his wife instead and never gone back at all.

Aulaudin didn't need Jerlayne battering his mind with Cuz's memories to know what life could be like for a child who didn't know his father's name. He knew it for himself: mortals who noticed men—noticed them as bees noticed honeysuckle flowers—couldn't keep their thoughts to themselves.

The red-glass woman hadn't been one of those. If Aulaudin had pieced it together correctly, her father hadn't been an elfin man. True, she'd had an eye for him from the moment their paths crossed—and he for her—but nothing they couldn't resist. He had resisted for four years. If he'd held out another year, his conscience wouldn't have bothered him so much that he couldn't concentrate on the glass.

There were many ways to follow an object through the Veil—he'd have to teach them to Jerlayne. If those seven goblets Aulaudin hadn't claimed still existed, he could find them, easily. If they were all together and near the place where he'd last seen them, and if he convinced himself he did, truly, want to find them. Twilight deepened quickly at Tatterfall. If he couldn't master his idle thoughts in another few moments, it would be too dark and he'd have to live with his conscience until dawn.

Aulaudin adjusted the many straps of a backpack and let the goblet fill his mind.

*   *   *

The most important and useful lesson regarding objects and the Veil—and another which Aulaudin would have to teach Jerlayne—was not emerging on top of them. Aulaudin entered the mortal realm in an open field a good walk away from the white-trimmed house his senses had told him held a few red goblets. Breezy, dappled sunlight obscured the flash and wind of the Veil as it closed behind him. Nothing was familiar. Aulaudin could have been anywhere that wasn't city or wilderness. Once the Veil closed, he had only an image of the house and a fast-fading hint of direction to guide him.

But with six centuries of experience helping him, that image was sufficient. The sun was still high when Aulaudin stood in front of the white-trimmed house, the largest on its street. A sign stood in the front yard, another in a window pane: a store, then, rather than a house. Stores weren't much use to a foraging man, but when their doors were unlocked, anyone, including an elf, could enter.

"May I help you?"

A woman, neither old nor young, noticed Aulaudin before he'd shut the door, but not in the way he'd hoped. His clothes were clean and, he thought, *respectable,* but a man couldn't always be sure what a mortal considered *respectable.* The woman regarded him with undisguised suspicion.

Aulaudin grinned, that sometimes helped, and added, "Just looking."

She smiled too, tight and thin-lipped. "If you're looking for something specific, I know everything we have in the store and who owned before it came here."

Reflected in this woman's eyes, Aulaudin found himself not quite respectable. Another time, he would have retreated, but if she were telling the truth . . .

"I'm looking for seven wine goblets. They're red, with etched patterns. Stags."

She narrowed her eyes. "I don't have seven, but I've got three Czech-glass goblets. The etchings might be stags."

The etchings were stags and because he could be very charming, even with thin-lipped mortals who didn't notice elves at all, Aulaudin soon traced the goblets to another woman behind the information desk at the town library. She was definitely older. Her hair was a faded, rusty color, streaked with gray, but she *noticed.* And he'd seen her eyes before.

"May I help you?"

"There are three red glass wine goblets in the antique shop on Decatur Street. I was told you knew where they came from."

Her eyes widened. "They were my grandmother's, from her first husband." The woman didn't blink, didn't glance away from Aulaudin's face. "He was German. My father—" She looked down at her desk. "Excuse me, but you look so much like the pictures of my father when he was young. It's uncanny."

Aulaudin told her that the similarities were coincidence and she believed him without hesitation. Once they'd noticed, an elf could make a mortal believe almost anything.

The librarian's father had died years earlier. "He said he remembered everything from horse-drawn buggies to men on the moon. I don't think he was sick a day in his life. One day he said, 'Peggy, I'm tired.' Two weeks later he was gone, in his sleep. It's almost trite to say a whole town turned out for a man's funeral, but they did here, for my father, Auden McCormack."

Auden. Aulaudin used that name more than once. He must have used it here. He'd forgotten.

Peggy showed Aulaudin the obituary printed on fragile, yellowed paper. Aulaudin pretended to read the words, but the pictures, six of them, showed him what he might look like, if elves aged. They were images to send a chill down a man's spine but they laid another worry to rest: Not every mortal elf went wild like Cuz.

Auden McCormack had lived ninety-four years, raised eight children, buried two wives and, according to his daughter, had no enemies, only friends. As for Auden's mother, Peggy said her name was Kate, which roused no memories for Aulaudin. There'd been four sons from Kate's first marriage, about which Peggy knew nothing, not even the man's name; three daughters from her second. She'd died of a fever after giving birth to the third.

"Folks died easily before antiseptics and antibiotics," Peggy explained, an older woman talking to a presumed younger man. "These days, if you've got good genes, you can live to be a hundred."

"Hard to believe."

A hundred years were better than forty, and Aulaudin remembered when forty had been old for a mortal. He stayed

in the library a while longer and left with directions to the
cemetery where all the McCormacks were buried. Auden's
grave was marked by an upright slab of polished granite, not
unlike the foundation stone at Sunrise. Another chill shook
Aulaudin's spine as he stood looking at it, then he was calm
again.

It was, to borrow Peggy's word, uncanny: men with mortal
children they'd never suspected, their wives trysting with
those children, then coming home to give birth to immortal
sons and daughters. But almost anything became uncanny if a
man thought about it for too long.

Aulaudin climbed a fence at the back of the cemetery, wandered into a small woods. He didn't bother memorizing trees
or rocks. There was no reason to come back. Clearing his mind
of everything except Tatterfall where he'd left the goblet sitting in the leaves, Aulaudin parted the Veil.

Tatterfall was dark, quiet, quickly replenished with mists
from the Veil: not a place where a wise men lingered after midnight. Aulaudin pulled a flashlight from his backpack and was
grateful for its unnaturally steady light. He bundled the goblet
in cloth, dried leaves, and a paper box that had seen better
days. Then, with it in the backpack and the flashlight in his lap,
Aulaudin cleared his mind a second time.

He'd made the journey from Tatterfall to Sunrise so many
times that it was more like habit than thought. Take a deep
breath. Imagine a rocky landscape so unchanging that men had
been using it since before Gudwal's time, so desolate that
Aulaudin never lingered there longer than it took to imagine
the textures of home and shift back into Fairie.

When the last shift failed and Aulaudin found himself adrift
in the Veil, his reaction was embarrassment, not panic. Those
grainy pictures of his own wrinkled face must have unsettled
him more than he'd noticed or admitted to him. Aulaudin rallied his concentration, imagining each tree and rock with exquisite detail. The Veil flexed around him, the scene in his
mind eye became the scene for his senses . . . almost. A wind
was blowing out of Sunrise, not the salty breeze that he'd
grown accustomed to, but something different, something he'd
never felt or heard before.

The siren was singing in the Veil.

His daughter sang more often than not. When he imagined
Sunrise, Aulaudin imagined her voice the same way he imag-

ined the sky: always present, never precise. And she'd given him no trouble . . . until now. Did she object to where he'd been and what he'd been doing? Or, as a guardian, did she object to what her mother had done: bringing a mortal into Fairie? Guardians kept mortals out of Fairie.

She hadn't done anything when they brought the youngster through, nor the day after, while Aulaudin had waited for Jerlayne's explanations. Had she waited until he was gone? Had she decided her father was to blame? Aulaudin and Evoni had never made peace between themselves; merely achieved a tolerance somewhere between distrust and disinterest. The sages, even Gudwal, to whom Aulaudin had once confessed his misgivings, had told Aulaudin not to worry; but the sages weren't as reassuring as they'd once been.

With the trees and rocks of Sunrise visible around him like shadows on a wall, Aulaudin loosed his daughter's name into the wind.

Shadows deepened into to storm-gray eyes he couldn't forget. Aulaudin felt his daughter surround him. Whatever the sages had spoken to out in the bay, *this* was a siren, a guardian. He didn't waste effort on words, simply thought of Jerlayne, in the mud, and of the great house where he expected—Aulaudin made his expectations clear—to find his wife alive and safe. The wind reversed, drawing Aulaudin into its eyes. He felt as Olleta must have felt when the rising siren absorbed her essence, then all was quiet.

Three voices, all of them Evoni's, sang together: «Be careful . . . take shelter . . . set me free . . .»

Aulaudin bowed his head. He'd do the first, but the last? Could a man free a guardian? Could a father free his daughter?

If a father could walk away from his son's grave without regret . . .

«Be free. Be a siren.» He could accept her as a siren. It was Evoni as an elf whom he'd never accepted. «Be what you are.»

He fell, head over heels, losing the flashlight. Chance, nothing more, set him feet-first on the ground.

The wind and song within the Veil were nothing compared to chaos whipping through Sunrise. Whole trees swayed and groaned; Aulaudin saw them because the cloudy sky seethed with lightning. A tree fell nearby. He saw it fall, taking a dozen others with it, in a sequence of frozen paintings. Evoni wove the crash into her song.

There was no moving with the wind; it gusted from every quarter and straight down from the clouds, pelting Aulaudin with leaves and twigs. Not rain. It took him a moment to realize there was no rain. This wasn't an ordinary gale; this was a siren, a guardian.

What did a guardian remember? In the tale of the Ten—the version that the sages told at elfin weddings—the guardians forgot where they'd been born and what they'd been; they'd let ogres rampage through Fairie's heart. But Evoni remembered her past. The rest of Fairie was quiet, none of the other guardians were active. His daughter was guarding her home, defending it—against what?

Aulaudin hadn't fallen to his usual resting place. Barely keeping his balance against the wind, he sought landmarks in the now-dark, now-bright forest. He saw nothing familiar, but there was movement to his left: billowing cloth, rearing horses, men among the trees with their arms raised and flailing. The lightning bleached the colors but Aulaudin had no doubt that the men weren't gnomes or dwarves.

He thought of Tatterfall. Take shelter, his daughter had told him, be careful. Be damned instead. Aulaudin fought his way toward the flailing goblins. He might not be able to stop their treachery, but he'd witness it and he'd share it, when he could, after the storm.

But the only treachery in the goblin camp came from its tents which had ripped their ground ropes. Though goblins possessed little—greed was not their vice—that small amount was in ruins. While he watched, a metal-sheathed tent-pole snapped. It flew with the wind and embedded in a goblin's mail-protected flank.

Lightning rippled overhead. When Aulaudin's vision cleared again, two goblins knelt beside the fallen one, wrestling with him and the pole. Goblins did not abandon their own. That came as a surprise, but not as much a surprise as the fist locked around his elbow.

Goro, of course, his mouth working uselessly, his free arm extended, pointing the way to the great house. The goblin gave Aulaudin a shove in that direction. His lips formed the words *take shelter.*

The two kneeling goblins had removed the pole. The third goblin wasn't moving. Goro released Aulaudin's arm with a harder shove.

Take shelter.

The guardian's storm grew more intense with each moment. Aulaudin had told his daughter to be free and herself. Then she'd spat him out here, by the goblins. No matter what else Aulaudin believed, goblins were part of Fairie, part of what the guardians protected.

He took the hand that pointed toward shelter and pulled it hard.

"You, too." Aulaudin swung his arm to include the camp. "And them. Forget this. It's already gone. Let the horses run. Come to the great house."

Goro pulled against him, but Aulaudin held on.

"Now, Goro! The great house or death. Your choice."

Aulaudin thought the goblin had heard him, but he couldn't make anyone listen. Goro freed himself with quick strength that left Aulaudin's hand aching and his thoughts wound tight with hate.

"Be da—"

The goblin surged through the wind, seizing his men and spinning them toward Aulaudin who raised his arm and pointed the way to safety.

"Be quick."

Goro led the last goblins forward, the three of them bearing the fourth between them. Aulaudin got his arm beneath a limp leg and walked with them.

Their walk, less than a quarter mile, was brutal, seemingly endless, and worst when they reached open ground surrounding the great house. The wind assaulted them with all its fury. Aulaudin lost his grip on the injured man's leg. He cursed himself for clumsiness and carelessness, but he fared no worse than the others. Even Goro had staggered and gone down on his knees before they reached the eaves.

"Inside!" Aulaudin roared, as the goblins clumped together at an interior corner that offered some, but not enough protection.

In lightning glow, Goro shook his head. "How?"

Sunrise had seen trouble coming. The homestead had done what it could to keep itself safe. Every shutter had been closed and cross-tied. Young trees had been felled, stripped, and angled against the largest shutters. The storm was locked out; so were Aulaudin and the goblins. Aulaudin cast his thoughts out for his wife. In calm weather he could have found her anywhere within the boundary stones, but with Evoni raging through the Veil as well as the sky, Aulaudin's sharing reached no further than his fingertips.

And Evoni's song grew ever stronger.

They had to get inside. Aulaudin expected to labor alone when he put his shoulder under one of the wedged-in trees, but there were four goblins lined up with him before he felt the strain. A fifth had his knife in the ropes. Moments later they were in the deserted kitchen.

Goro barked a few incomprehensible commands in the relative quiet and goblins scrambled to secure the window, get the injured goblin onto a table, and build a fire in the middle of the floor. Aulaudin stopped that immediately. He got a lantern lit before the shutters slammed closed, cutting off the light.

"What happened?" he asked; less than a shout, but not by much. "There was warning?"

Goro nodded, his greater attention on the table where the injured man had yet to move. "Yesterday, the clouds were down and she was gone from the rocks. Jerlayne called the scyldrin in. It started last night, after sundown."

"You've seen Jerlayne?"

Another nod.

"She's here then? Safe?"

The goblin faced Aulaudin, but only for a moment: the injured man had groaned. "She goes where she wills. We can only hope she's here and safe. I must see her—"

Aulaudin couldn't keep his eyes from narrowing.

"For *Joff,* Aulaudin." Goro gestured helplessly toward the table, then looked around the scarcely illuminated kitchen. "I do not know my way in here, Aulaudin. Have you led us inside to watch Joff die?"

"No." Aulaudin lit another lantern. "They'll all be toward the center. Near Laydin's nursery. Follow me."

Goro had words for his men, and the boldest of them had words for him. Aulaudin didn't need a translator to know what had been said. Swords and armor notwithstanding, none of the goblins had stood between walls, beneath a roof. They'd followed Goro through the window because Goro commanded the kind of obedience no homestead master presumed. Without him they were frightened, even rebellious, though not for long. Goro growled more words and made a fist.

If he hadn't been standing so close, Aulaudin would never have guessed that Goro himself was afraid.

The Sunrise great house sprawled across a hillside. There were no great staircases connecting layers of rooms, but three steps here, four there, every set a different height and width. And doors. Doors everywhere, and all of them closed. Between the doors, which Goro couldn't pass without flinching, and the steps, which invariably caught him off-stride, the goblin became a desperate man. Aulaudin, who knew each plank and carried the lantern, kept his pace up and made the route long; Jerlayne *might,* after all, be in any of the rooms.

"Enough!" Goro gasped.

Evoni's storm howled above them and beat the shutters of the rooms beyond the doors. The goblin flattened against the wall outside Jerlayne's workroom. His eyes were closed and his jaw was set in a tight-lipped grimace.

"Joff has done nothing against you," Goro said through clenched teeth. "And he will lead those men against me, if you tell him what I have done. Now, I ask you: find your wife and plead with her to save him."

"Why?" Aulaudin demanded. "Why did you touch Jerlayne? What do you want from her?"

"What does it matter? Jerlayne loves only you. She doesn't care about me."

"I know my—" Something crashed onto the roof directly above them. Plaster and wood dust rained down "I know my wife, what she did and why. Why did *you* put yourself in my place?"

"To feel what you feel every night."

Aulaudin had told Jerlayne he wasn't good at anger; he was worse at hate. "Come on." He prodded the goblin's arm.

Goro shook his head. "Your walls are too close. Too many shadows." He shook his head again, muttered something in his own language. "I will leave."

"Joff and everyone else down in the kitchen will die if you go outside now."

"I will give myself to the siren."

"You're a fool, Goro. I don't know what's happening above the clouds, but it's got nothing to do with you . . . or me."

Goro contradicted him. "This began after you left. Rumors fly, Aulaudin; we hear them. She told you what happened between us. I said I have no regrets, and I have none for myself, but you and she are strangers again, and this guardian remembers."

"Maybe, but the notion I brought out of the Veil was that Evoni was holding back until you—all of you—were out of the woods. Just listen to her now that we're all in the same place."

Goro stood away from the wall. He blew out a breath and said, calmly, "*Something* happened to arouse her. What else happened before you left?"

"Cuz."

"Cuz?"

"A mortal man. He was dying, so Jerlayne brought him through the Veil."

"A mortal man?!"

"Laydin's father."

The goblin barked something in his own language.

"I said the same thing."

"We've got to find Jerlayne. For Joff and this—this *Cuz*." Goro signaled his determination by staring down the corridor ahead of Aulaudin and the lantern. "No mortal should ever be in Fairie. The guardians and the Veil are meant to keep them out. If they fail, it falls to us to set Fairie right again. That's why Evoni wanted us beneath this roof!"

The two men turned onto the corridor that led to Laydin's nursery and the common room where the household weaving and sewing was done. Ruddy lantern light spilled out of the common room. They were spotted and the racket beneath the homestead roof was, momentarily, as loud as Evoni's roar above it.

Chapter 28

Cuz listened until he could hear no more, then eased the door to Jerlayne's workroom shut and released the latch. The bolt fell gently, not that anyone could have heard a hundred bolts clunking into place in the noisy hell of fairyland. He'd have a new test for nightmares, if he got out.

Jerlayne hadn't precisely imprisoned Cuz. He'd seen what she could do to locks, this lock in particular. If she'd wanted to keep him from opening the door, she could have done it easily.

And maybe she should have, then Cuz wouldn't have been out in the hall, spying on Jerlayne and her friends down the hall. Or trying to spy on them. The outside noise was a problem, mostly, though, Cuz couldn't understand half of what they said. They spoke English. Cuz figured he wouldn't have understood anything, if they weren't speaking English, but it was foreign English, like being in a roomful of exchange students and needing five minutes to realize they were speaking his language not theirs.

Anyway, Cuz had been spying when he'd spotted light that wasn't blasting in from the outside. Jerlayne had told him all the scyldrin were inside. That's why he had to stay hidden (not locked up): The scyldrin would ask questions when they saw him and she wasn't ready to answer those questions, not until Aulaudin got back.

Now he'd seen Aulaudin and a goblin. Goblins weren't supposed to come between walls or under roofs; that's what Jerlayne had told Cuz yesterday. Which had maybe meant that his mother had been lying about where she'd met his supposedly goblin father (surprise, surprise) or that goblins knew something about interior decorating. God knew Jerlayne didn't.

Back inside the workroom with lightning coming through the shutters, making everything look like a bad and not-very-silent movie, Cuz had the sense that he'd been trapped in the mother of all attics. Fairyland wasn't gold, silver, and cob-webs. It wasn't even houses made of mushrooms or sugar plums. Fairyland was the largest thrift store that Cuz could imagine made ten times, no—a thousand times larger. Any-thing that wasn't patched or stuck together was weird or just plain ugly.

Except Jerlayne. Jerlayne was the most beautiful woman Cuz had ever seen. If she'd lose the droopy clothes and farmer's-daughter braids, Cuz could think of at least twenty men who'd fall all over themselves to keep her happy, and some of them were gay. Even with her rag-picker look, Cuz didn't need to see her mess with metal or heal his bones to know she really was an elf. (And all that fairytale shit about elves dying when they touched iron! Yeah, smoke might rise from Jerlayne's hands when she touched the stuff, but she sure wasn't dying.)

Aulaudin was an elf, too. He'd been the one carrying the light that got Cuz's attention and sent him scurrying. Tall, lean, graceful, but not at all delicate, with one of those chiseled-out, survivor faces; Cuz could think of a hundred men who'd make fools of themselves for Aulaudin. He included himself in that number. Cuz didn't usually go for the anguished-romantic type and hadn't been drop-everything attracted to anyone since Wills. Cuz had wanted to see that hair when the light wasn't flashing cold and almost blue, until he'd seen what Aulaudin was talking to.

All his life Cuz had been of two minds about his father. One mind despised his mother for sinking into madness and believ-ing her own lies about a dark-skinned, dark-eyed, dark-toothed lover who'd promised to come back. The other mind believed at least enough to want to back the demon up against a wall and ream him out for what he'd done to her and him. Cuz had so much experience brooding about his missing father that he could think with both minds together and not suffer a pang of illogic. He'd rehearsed countless acid comments, each meant to ease the pain of decades of neglect.

Somehow Cuz had thought that his father would be a man like his mother and himself: that was, a man who could be in-jured with words.

Jerlayne had told him about elves and gnomes and dwarves and a dozen other weird creatures she said were collectively known as *scyldrin*. She hadn't said much of anything about

goblins, except to give him the name and the notion that they
hung around elves but wouldn't come inside. Until a few moments ago, Cuz hadn't seen any elves other than Jerlayne. She
was on the short side of average for humans; everyone else
he'd glimpsed through curtains and around corners was shorter
than her. He'd figured goblins for short, ugly dudes, not a
black, long-haired, muscled biker in chains and leather with a
sword—a fucking *sword!*—strung from his belt.

Cuz hadn't gotten a long look at Goro; the biker had chosen
to lean against the workroom wall while he and Aulaudin had
their eye-opening conversation. Just as well. If Cuz had been
looking at Goro, he might not have been listening and
he wouldn't have learned that Jerlayne—beautiful, clueless
Jerlayne—had fucked the goblin.

Aulaudin was pissed about the goblin-dude fucking his
wife; Cuz read that in the elf's body language more than his
words. But Aulaudin rolled over without taking the goblin on.
Aulaudin had a backpack, not a sword, and unless he was some
kind of martial arts wizard, he didn't have the weight to push
Goro around. For that matter, neither did Cuz and he'd learned
just about everything he knew about martial arts from Hong
Kong movies.

Then the two men started talking about him, about Cuz himself. How he was mortal. How he was the father of Jerlayne's
kid down the hall. How the goblins had come inside to kill him.

Cuz knew—because he'd been down betrayal's path too
many times before—that there was no way Jerlayne or Aulaudin weren't going to turn him over to the goblins. Oh, he
fantasized a moment, after they were gone and he was trying
to breathe: he'd tell Goro he was half a goblin and Goro would
tell him how goblins had been looking for him. His father—his
late father—had been prince of goblins and now it was time for
him to become the heir.

Cuz liked his fantasies; they got him to sleep each night, but
he wasn't fucking fool enough to believe them, not at home,
not in fairyland.

Once he was breathing regular again, Cuz thought about escape. He'd been a world of hurt before Jerlayne pulled him out
of Uncle Ted's lab-hell. He'd been going to die there, and he'd
go back to dying if he went back, but Jerlayne had sort of
said—Jerlayne wasn't real good at explaining what she did or
what went on around her—that she could go from fairyland to

anywhere in the real world through something she called the Veil.

Elves, Jerlayne had said, could use the Veil anywhere. He'd seen her call the Veil just by raising her arms in his basement and she'd obviously gotten past all Uncle Ted's super-high-tech security. She'd said that goblins couldn't use it, never mind that his father was a fucking goblin and his mother sure as hell hadn't invaded fairyland to screw him. At least his mother had always said they'd done their screwing at home— Cuz's grandparents' house—while the Kennicuts, mére and pére, were away in the Alps, or the Bahamas, or wherever the hell they'd been that winter.

Well, shit—Cuz just had to hope he'd inherited something useful from his father.

He locked the bolt into place. (Fat lot of good that was going to do. Locks only kept honest people out, not thieves, elves, or halfway goblins!) By storm light he looked around for something worth stealing; if he did make it back to the real world he'd arrive with nothing but the clothes on his back. (Aulaudin's clothes, sturdy clothes, good for blending in and not being seen.) Fairyland didn't have money; Jerlayne hadn't grasped the concept at all, but some of the stuff Aulaudin had stolen wasn't half worthless.

Aulaudin was a thief and scrounger, no doubt why he was wearing a backpack. According to Jerlayne, Aulaudin had gone to the real world right after she'd fessed up to infidelity and he'd just returned when he and Goro had their conversation outside the workroom. It stood to reason—Cuz's reason, based on what he'd heard—that Aulaudin had come back to fairyland to spy on his rival, which meant—with a real stretch of the old imagination—that if Cuz could find the spot where Aulaudin had arrived in fairyland from the real world, then, maybe, he'd have found a place where he could go the other way.

A lot of ifs and maybes, but Cuz didn't have anything better and he did know where the goblin camp was. Oddly enough, or maybe not—she had committed elfin adultery with both him and the goblin, so maybe they did pop up in same part of her head—Jerlayne had stood beside him on a porch and pointed out the trees, behind which, she'd said, Sunrise's goblins made camp in black, half-round tents.

Dwarves had sealed up the porch as the storm worsened.

When they'd gotten to the workroom windows, Jerlayne had hidden him in the nursery. Shit, she'd hidden him in the room with his goddamned son—*his* goddamned *son*—and never peeped a word. Cuz didn't expect to get out through anything those dwarves had tied down. There were a few other choices: louvers in the ceiling, if he wanted to risk the roof in this wind, or a tiny window in the closet that passed for a john.

They kept the john cleaned and drained and all; it smelled better than half the real-world johns he'd seen, but it was still a fucking shit-hole dug in the ground. When he'd asked, Jerlayne said they built and rebuilt the house to give the ground a chance to recover.

Cuz wanted civilization—the streets of the real world—and he wanted it bad.

Jerlayne had tied the tiny window shut. Cuz got a knife from Jerlayne's work table—probably not a bad idea to take one anyway—and hacked his way through the knots. There wasn't any point to trying to untie them, not *her* knots.

He'd been listening to the storm since late afternoon, watching it through cracks since the sun went down. Cuz thought he knew what was happening, but he wasn't prepared for the noise, which had a fist-in-the-belly force, or the light show. Thick clouds boiled with lightning and hung so low that the tallest trees had vanished. Sliding out the window, standing on the ground, Cuz was frozen by the unreal power and beauty. A lightning serpent rippled and bulged through the cloud directly overhead. He hadn't thought of danger until it crashed into the trees near the goblin camp, near where he was headed.

And the noise!

Jerlayne had called it singing and said the siren who sang was her daughter. Cuz thought it sounded like a dozen cats yowling, only louder, a lot louder. He put his hands over his ears, but that made no difference. The noise was physical; it passed right through his fingers.

Cuz didn't think of the wind until he'd taken his third step toward the trees. It took him by surprise and sent him reeling backward. Another wall caught him. Wiser, warier, and bent over to make himself small, Cuz ventured out again. Wind caught him from the opposite direction, but he was ready and held his balance with only a sideways stagger. Thank God. If the second gust had come first, he'd could have tumbled all the way to the cliff and the sea.

Cuz could balance against the chaotic wind, but not walk against it. To move toward the trees, he had to get down on hands and knees to crawl. There were moments, as the storm's fury hammered him, when Cuz lay flat with his fists full of rooted grass and was grateful to stay on the ground. He covered the distance slowly, no more than a quarter mile, but he did cover it, including a stream whose existence he hadn't suspected until he was elbow-deep in cold water.

The trees offered as much danger as protection. Their leaves were gone, but branches, from twigs to limbs, rained down steadily. The twigs were dangerous. In a constant swirl just above the ground, sharp twigs no longer than Cuz's fingers pierced his clothes. If one struck his eyes, he'd be blind. Cuz stood up; that was possible again beneath the trees. Using his hands to shield his eyes, he looked around and knew he'd never find what remained of the goblin camp, much less the spot where Aulaudin had split into the Veil.

Cuz had turned around to look back at the low, angular great house and the wild sea, when something inspired him to look straight up—

There was a tree in the trees right over head: a fucking tree trunk balanced thirty or forty feet above the ground. Sure as hell, it wasn't going to stay there! Cuz bolted blindly and never heard the tree trunk hit: his foot got tangled in something else. Cuz didn't stumble or stagger, just pivoted around his trapped ankle, too fast for him to get his arms out. His face took the fall.

The pain was bad for an instant, got worse, then nothing.

*   *   *

"Easy, kid. You're not going anywhere."

Cuz tried to prove her wrong . . . her. He was looking at a woman with wild, ink-black hair, steel studs along her cheekbones and above her eyebrows, rings in her nose and eyebrows, and chains around her neck and wrists. Cuz recognized the type: goths, people-in-black. If he hadn't seen Jerlayne first, he could have believed this strange woman was an elf. But he had seen Jerlayne, and compared to the rest of fairyland, this woman had to be an hallucination.

While Cuz scrambled to separate the real from the not-real, the goth leaned back. Behind her, the sky was filled with low, funky clouds and a tree in a tree.

"Fuck."

No hallucinations, no drugs: everything was real. And she wasn't a goth; she *was* an elf. When Cuz tried to lever himself onto an elbow, she stopped him with a warm touch. He tried to catch his balance and failed because his wrists and feet were bound. Walls of panic and rage closed in.

"You're lucky I've healed your kind before," she said. "You smashed your chin up pretty good."

This time she let him move his arms, together, of course. His chin was exquisitely tender, but intact. It was probably just as well there were no mirrors nearby. Cuz got a look at the cord around his wrists: nylon, with a shiny knob—just like Jerlayne had made from his hair—instead of a knot. He got a handle on his panic; the rage continued to build. Bondage wasn't his game, not at all.

"My sister couldn't have fixed you better," the black-haired elf continued. "And you were running away from her."

Sister? Jerlayne was this pierced woman's sister? That put all Cuz's emotions on hold. No kid who'd grown up with Ted Kennicut for an uncle took sibling rivalry for granted. He flexed his wrists cautiously. Nylon cord stretched sometimes. He felt a bit of play as he said, "Not a chance."

"The hell you weren't. I watched you come out her workroom window. Did Jerlayne bring you through the Veil?"

His gut said this was a woman who'd been around, who wasn't uselessly innocent. She commanded his respect . . . and suspicion. "What Veil?" he stalled, hoping she'd lay a few more cards on the proverbial table before he had to come up with answers.

"You're mortal. Healing you was like healing mud. You didn't come here by yourself. So who brought you through—if not my sister?" She crossed her legs as she sat on the ground, twisted them tight, all knees, ankles, black lycra, and high boots.

Cuz tried silence, tried working his feet. She didn't seem to notice.

"Look, I don't care why you were running. Hell, I'd run, too, if I had to be cooped up in one of those again."

She gestured to her right, but she'd moved Cuz after she'd found him and they were tucked behind boulders, not hiding, but hidden from the house he'd escaped. The house she'd escaped, too? No, that wasn't what she'd said. Cuz forced himself to breathe and stay calm. He couldn't listen, couldn't think or plan, if the panic got loose.

"Someone must have finally told my little sister where elves come from. I wouldn't have figured her for a punk like you, but you've got the buzz. If she was looking, and she decided she wanted you . . . Elmeene always said Jerlayne's like water; you think you've got her stopped and the next thing you know, you're knee-deep. I always thought she could do anything but lie, and then you pop out her workroom window. To tell the truth, I didn't think it could be done: bringing a man through. I've thought about it, but never dared try. Redis couldn't bring home a chicken without killing it . . ."

The elf-goth looked right through him, a cold, cold, calculating look in her eyes: a predator thinking about her next meal, and sure-as-shit, it wasn't going to be chicken.

"Aulaudin helped," Cuz volunteered quickly; she didn't look like she fell for the anguished-romantic type. "Jerlayne was losing me. I would've died if he hadn't joined with her."

"Joined? So that's it. She must've told him. Kinky. Didn't think either of them had the imagination."

"They don't," he said firmly, defending both of them, and not quite knowing why. Except he'd defended the new kids the same way, when they first hit the streets. There wasn't any honor among thieves, or predators, but he gave everyone a second chance, the chance no one had given him. "I wanted to come here and Jerlayne brought me. Call it a trade. End of story."

Cuz didn't flinch from her eyes or her black-enameled fingernail when she ran it under his chin. "So why run away—if that's the end of the story?"

He told her about hiding from the scyldrin, that seemed safe enough, and overhearing someone say that the guardians were angry because there was a mortal loose in fairyland. "I didn't want anyone to get hurt because of me."

"Gnomes. The dark lining in every silver cloud. They're wrong, though, just so you know. Evoni—she's the guardian around here, in case you didn't know her name. Jerlayne's daughter, Aulaudin's, too, in case they didn't tell you that, either. Evoni's not after you. She and the other guardians are defending the Veil itself from a mortal-realm threat."

"Aulaudin said no, it's just here. Just Sunrise."

The elf sat back again. She cast her calculating glance at the low, dense clouds overhead. The storm had ended while Cuz was unconscious and a new day had begun, but if the clouds were part of Evoni's defense—Jerlayne had told Cuz the guardian's name and parentage—then the siren hadn't stood down. The leafless trees were washed in twilight darkness made eerie by its lack of shadows.

Cuz wiggled around until he was sitting up. "Want to let me go now?" He held out his hands.

She shrugged, then wrapped a hand around the cord. Cuz felt heat, but the nylon didn't actually melt, just separated. When she let go, he shook the coils off easily and put forward his feet which she freed as well. He wadded up the dead cords and threw them into the woods.

"Mind telling me why you did that?" he asked, keeping a lid on his anger. He'd learned not to panic, not to fight when he didn't have a chance. The lessons hadn't been easy and afterward, sometimes, he'd lose it.

"Nothing personal. Thought I might need a peace offering if the storm got much worse and I had to get inside." She drew patterns in the dirt and studied them intently. "Jerlayne thinks I'm dead."

"And you're not?"

She raised her eyebrows, staring at him through black fringe without raising her head; he felt like a goddamned idiot.

"Yeah, I get it: elves, not vampires. Yeah. You're the black sheep of the family. Jerlayne didn't tell me her dead sister's name."

"M'lene."

She unwound some after admitting her name. Through the ebbing rage and panic, Cuz once again sensed that they were the same, even though she said she was nearly four hundred years old. Aulaudin was even older, and Jerlayne *was* young— for an elf—having been born "a hundred-and-seventy or -eighty years ago. We don't keep close track. You know who's older, who's younger, that's about it."

M'lene was a widow and glad of it. She told Cuz about joining, which Jerlayne had failed to describe.

"The sex part of joining's what made it worthwhile, the only part. Mortals are intense on the surface, empty underneath. It's the sound of one hand clapping. Scratching the itch you can reach when you can't reach the one that's really making you crazy. The rest of joining, though . . . imagine you've got a stranger trashing your mind, bent on making changes. After a few years with Redis, I didn't know who I was. Fairie isn't a bad place, kid, if you're good at what we do. If you're not, it's hell."

"My name's Cuz, not kid." He said nothing about joining, but he'd been in Jerlayne's mind when they'd fucked in his basement apartment, and she'd been inside his. If that was joining, he'd been through the good and the bad already.

M'lene had food: thick, gooey candy bars. Cuz wasn't big on candy, too many bad memories, but she'd healed him and he needed to eat.

The candy bars were fresh, so he asked: "Can you get me back to the real world? Part the Veil, do whatever you do? Fairyland—this isn't *me*. I've gotta get home."

"No can do. Evoni's got the Veil tied up in knots. I wouldn't want to try parting it for me right now, and I'd probably just kill you. Your best bet's to go back to Jerlayne—"

The singing started up again, along with the thunder rumbling and the wind. With the first gusts, the tree in a tree came crashing down. A moment later, everything was quiet again. No damage done, except for some dust spread across the candy, but they weren't fooled. Cuz looked at M'lene.

"It's starting earlier today," he said.

"Yeah, and louder. I'm not going through another night like last night. C'mon, let's go knock on the front door and see if they'll take us in."

M'lene stood up. No hips, no breasts: she could pass for a man, if she'd wanted to, if she never opened her mouth. Cuz stayed where he was.

"Viljuen weeps, Cuz—what was she doing to you in there? This is *not* going to be a safe place in another hour and it was the best I could find yesterday."

"Can't go down there again, that's all. Goblins."

"Damn—you're right." M'lene sat down quickly. "I thought they'd all gone in last night. Damn strangest thing I've ever seen: goblins going *inside*. They'd lost their tents, but I thought they'd cling to the trees like bats. I'm not much for goblins: shifty bastards, always spying on us. They spied on me when I lived out there—" M'lene gestured toward the water, "back when it was still forest. We'll lay low here until they're done checking out their old camp. I wouldn't worry about them once we're inside."

"They'll kill me, cuz I'm mortal; I heard one of them say so."

M'lene didn't think her sister would let that happen. Cuz replied why he thought Jerlayne would: all of it, from Jerlayne getting shot in a place she called the plains, to Aulaudin accusing Goro of sleeping with his wife, all the way to the pictures Cuz's own mother had drawn night after night. It felt good to finally tell someone.

"I thought something stank," M'lene said when he'd finished; Cuz started to stiffen. "No, not you, kid. The goblins. Around here, everything's built on the idea that we need goblins to protect us from ogres and they need us because they can't shape or shift—that's parting the Veil. But, Efan—there's one head goblin for every homestead. Jerlayne got Goro; I got Efan. It's not real important, except, maybe two hundred years ago, Efan *changed*. I got suspicious and started following him. I couldn't prove that he parted the Veil for the mortal realm— to tell you the honest truth, I couldn't figure out *where* he went; I'm not one of the *good* elves. But Efan was going somewhere that wasn't Fairie. Guns, that's almost logical, but I never thought they'd chase mortal women."

"You believe that I had a goblin for a father?"

She shrugged. "Why not? The rest makes a depressing sort of sense. Goblins as sheep-herders . . . elf-herders. I despised Efan, before and after he changed, but no more than he despised me. The one you should really talk to is Maun— Aulaudin's father."

Evoni had started singing—shrieking—again. The clouds were starting to churn with lightning and the wind blew straight down. M'lene stuck her head cautiously above the rocks.

"What do we do now?" Cuz shouted.

"Told you before: go down to the house. C'mon. We'll take our chances with the goblins."

He balked and M'lene grabbed his hand.

"They can't *tell* whether you're mortal or elf or half-goblin. I knew you were mortal because I healed you—it tells in the blood—but even I couldn't tell about the goblin part. If they bother us, I'll tell 'em you're my son, Ombrio. You don't look much like him, but hell, Cuz, I don't look much like me any more, and they all think I'm dead."

Cuz didn't like trusting a woman who'd tied him up, even if

she was easier to talk to than Jerlayne, but the wind was getting stronger by the second. The clouds were getting darker and weirder. The singing would make him crazy, and it wasn't like he had a better plan.

With M'lene still holding his wrist, they started toward the great house like the air was calm, the sun was shining, and they had all the time in the world. Cuz thought they were going to get away with it. They were past the stream and a hundred feet from the end of the trees when, through the wind and the siren singing, he heard a gunshot. M'lene heard it, too; they both looked over their left shoulders.

"Run!" the elf advised and let go of his hand. Cuz was right behind her for a couple of strides, until there were goblins in front of them and on either side.

A numbed part of Cuz's brain said it couldn't be happening. There were too many of them and they were moving too fast to be real. Then, at the worst possible moment, lightning grounded beside him. He ran blind, got a few strides before he got grabbed. Instinct kept him fighting until a fist hit his jaw, then instinct let him go.

Chapter 29

No one could have been more surprised to see Aulaudin and Goro walk into a room together than Jerlayne, though she couldn't have said which surprised her more: that Goro was between walls or that Aulaudin was the man who'd led him there. She'd been relieved to see her husband under any circumstance. Evoni had sealed the Veil, at least against the parting skills of a woman, when she started singing after noon yesterday. Jerlayne had tried to be optimistic, assuming her husband would find his way back to Fairie once the crisis had ended, mostly, though, she'd been too busy getting Sunrise through the disaster to worry about anything that might happen *after* the crisis.

Before surprise had worn off, they told her about the man on the kitchen table.

The tent stake, sheathed in metal and sitting in the ground year in, year out, had left a nasty, dirty wound in the goblin's side. A leaking wound as well. By the time she laid hands on him, he'd lost a frightening amount of blood and Jerlayne's mind filled with memories of Dalan. Jerlayne had relived that failed healing many times. She could have used her sister's help to save the goblin's life, but she didn't need it.

Dawn came and went, taking the furor of Evoni's storm with it. Jerlayne didn't notice until the goblin was breathing steading on his own.

"Watch him closely," she told the assembled goblins. "Give him water when he awakens and keep him quiet. I've done what I can; he's got to do the rest."

A handful of dwarves had been outside by then. They said all the trees had been stripped and battered, but were mostly still standing. Everything with weak roots or rotten heartwood had fallen the previous year when Evoni rose. The roofs had held on the great house and all save one of the cottages, but the clouds were still as thick as they'd been at sundown and Evoni hadn't reappeared on her rocks.

Warnings were taken without being given: A half dozen scyldrin headed off for the barns and stables to relieve a similar number who had spent the night with the livestock. The weary returnees reported that five chickens and a calf had died during the storm, apparently of fright, but everything else was secure—for the moment. Those who were hungry stayed in the kitchen to eat a cold breakfast; the rest straggled off to sleep while sleep was possible.

Jerlayne left the kitchen with a well-piled plate. While Aulaudin kept watch, she opened the bolt on her workroom door. Cuz didn't immediately assault her with questions. Asleep, she thought, and set the plate just inside the door.

Aulaudin caught her in an embrace as she stood up again.

"I made my peace with everything. I know what's important: Sunrise, my children, and, most of all, you."

She molded herself against him and said nothing. They slept, fully clothed, in each other's arms until Evoni shook the walls again.

"The goblin and I think this is to do with the mortal you brought through . . . Cuz," Aulaudin told her as they rolled out of bed. "He shouldn't be here. Can't stay."

Jerlayne finished splashing water on her face and cleaning her teeth. "I thought of that. He's healed now, and he'd leave without a backward glance. Cuz isn't happy here. He pretends to be grateful, or tries to, but he's trapped in my workroom. When I'm there, he tells me everything that he finds strange or unpleasant about Fairie and I'm trapped as well. Cuz *is* grateful to be alive, but he's angry too. Yesterday morning, after he called me a 'queen bee in a scyldrin hive.' I tried to part the Veil to send him back right then. *I* was very angry.

"I thought my anger was the reason I couldn't part it, but I've tried since then, when I was calmer. I can sense the Veil— barely—and Evoni everywhere within it. I was so glad to see you! I thought—feared—well, never mind, but surely we can't shift Cuz through the Veil now. He'd die. He's very hardy for a mortal, but he'd die, and I can't be part of that. You can't either."

"The goblin can," Aulaudin said without looking at her. "To him, Cuz is no different than an ogre."

"But he is, Aulaudin, Cuz is—"

"The father of Laydin? The mortal you chose to be the father of our son? I understand. I've made peace with it, with all of it."

The boot Jerlayne was pulling onto her foot slipped to the floor. "More than that: Cuz's own father . . ." she paused, remembering the tense, horrible day when Laydin had been born: This was the secret whose uncovering she dreaded most.

"His own father was an elf," Aulaudin finished for her.

"Not an elf—"

In one stride, Aulaudin was in front of Jerlayne as she sat, half-shod, beside the bed. He grasped her shoulders, then released them. With the Veil in turmoil, joining was in turmoil, too.

"An elf, Jerlayne. A man like myself. Viljuen weeps, I don't believe he could be my son, but I *did* leave sons behind me, sons, daughters, and grandchildren that I never suspected. I found the grave of one of them, beloved: that's where I made my peace."

"*Mortal* children?" The implications, though they could have nothing to do with Cuz, raced through Jerlayne's thoughts and she was glad they were not joined. "You?"

"Me and every other man who's ever foraged beyond the Veil. Think of Briary or Stonewell: brothers and sons who will never marry. We're not goblins, beloved . . . I wasn't. When I was young, Maun told my brother and me that mortal women would *notice*. They did, and we noticed them back. Viljuen weeps, I had been a bachelor for three hundred years before you were born, Jerlayne. I knew only some mortals would notice, but I never asked myself, why? And, if I had, I would have guessed wrong: they're mortals, we couldn't really be the same!"

Aulaudin shook his head ruefully and walked away from Jerlayne's chair. A desperate, and destructive, voice in her mind wanted to know if he'd stopped *noticing* after they were married but he'd answered that question, in a way, when he'd said he didn't believe Cuz was his son. A wiser voice within suggested that Aulaudin, for her sake, should keep some secrets forever.

"That boy in your workroom," Aulaudin said to the walls of their bedroom, "he's as much an elf as Laydin is, except he was born to a mortal mother in the mortal realm."

It was easier not having to move or face her husband as

Jerlayne said: "Cuz showed me portraits his mother had drawn of his father. His father wasn't an elf."

"That could be," Aulaudin conceded with a sigh. "The noticing trait lingers. I found a granddaughter. Cuz's elf could have been a grandfather. We are bound to mortals on both sides of the Veil. I'm sure of that. It's our children—our abandoned, mortal children—who *notice*."

"And goblins," Jerlayne said. "Cuz's father was a goblin."

Aulaudin didn't move. Evoni's singing wasn't loud—not compared to the previous night—but he might not have heard. Jerlayne repeated her revelation: "The portraits Cuz had were pencils drawings of a dark man with no white to his eyes or teeth. His mother had drawn a goblin, Aulaudin."

"And I saw myself in pictures of the man buried in my son's grave. Mortals imagine much, beloved; they gave us the words for elf and goblin. Somewhere, sometime, an elf could have told his mortal lover what goblins look like. Unless Goro lied and goblins *can* part the Veil."

Jerlayne felt her husband's accusation close around her heart. For Laydin and his own conscience, Aulaudin might forgive her for Cuz and perhaps forgive Cuz, too, but not Goro. It would be a sore point between them for a very long time.

"Before last year, if you had asked me whether women could part the Veil, I would have said no and not been lying. I didn't know how to do it, so I thought it couldn't be done. I was wrong. Goro could be wrong. Wrong isn't the same as a lie."

Another silence while Aulaudin thought and Evoni sang. Shuttered and lashed, the bedroom grew gloomier with each of Jerlayne's shallow breaths. Aulaudin was a shadow among shadows until the day's first lightning flashed through the cracks. Jerlayne left her chair, slipped her arms around her husband, and felt emptiness, turmoil.

"We're alone, beloved. We face this alone. Evoni has the Veil in her teeth. I sought the sages and they're beyond me. I can find no other man's mind, not my brothers' nor my father's . . ."

Aulaudin's voice faded into thoughts that Jerlayne couldn't share. The louder Evoni sang, the fainter joining became. It was disconcerting to touch him and feel nothing but cloth or flesh. Jerlayne wanted to hold him tighter, but released him instead.

"We are not alone," she reminded him and herself as well.

"We have each other, Cuz, Goro, and all the scyldrin of Sunrise—even Evoni."

"Shall we go outside?" Aulaudin asked, his voice rich with irony, "and ask the wind what we should do with a mortal elf—or is that a mortal goblin? Or about goblins who visit the mortal realm, taking guns away and leaving sons behind?"

Jerlayne shook her head without anger. "No, though the sages *did* talk to her that once, and we should try, sometime, when she isn't singing. But, you said yourself: she put you down near the goblins, to lead the goblins inside. That brought us all together, Aulaudin: elves, scyldrin, goblins, and a mortal, all under one roof. We haven't begun to share what we know."

"I don't think that has ever happened before. Elves, mortals, and goblins. The sages should be here—"

"If you think about it, Aulaudin, when the sages are here, we don't talk, we listen. Maybe they don't know any more than we do right now, or maybe they're the ones who've been keeping our secrets for us: Claideris told Elmeene how to part the Veil—because Fairie needed elves to grow after the 'death—and when Elmeene wanted to tell Jereige, Claideris threatened to kill her."

"Claideris." A wealth of memory and dislike in a single word. "Perhaps you're right and we're better off without sages, at least for now."

They agreed to assemble everyone in the kitchen. It wasn't the largest room in the great house, but the goblins were already there—Jerlayne and Aulaudin assumed they were still there. With Evoni singing overhead Goro would have been a fool to lead his men anywhere else. Aulaudin would comb through the rest of the house, gathering the scyldrin, while Jerlayne headed first for the workroom, to prepare Cuz for what might be a difficult afternoon, then to the nursery, to check on Laydin.

The workroom door was closed, just the way she'd left it, and bolted on the inside, also the way she'd left it and no challenge for the shaping woman who'd designed the lock.

Jerlayne called his name, "Cuz?" as she drew the bolt back.

No answer. He might have been sleeping, or sulking. Jerlayne hadn't lied when she'd said he wasn't happy in Fairie or that she'd found herself, after only a taste of his company, avoiding her own workroom. After what he'd been through in the mortal realm, she could understand that Cuz was suspicious, even frightened by Evoni's eerie singing and her own insistence that he stay out of sight. But he had only two ways of expressing himself: bitter, acid comments, half of which she, fortunately, couldn't understand; or trysting hints which simply—perhaps, cruelly—fell on her deaf ears.

"Cuz?"

With its windows boarded over, this part of the great house was particularly dark. Jerlayne carried a flashlight and shined it at empty chairs. Blankets were heaped and rumpled over her mound of pillows. She approached them cautiously, but there was no mortal huddled beneath them. Perplexed, she cast light quickly across her worktable and along the walls; the food she'd left at dawn sat untouched.

He could have gotten out the door, but it took shaping to lock it from the outside. And he couldn't have gotten out through the windows. They'd all been shuttered and lashed from the outside and the largest were braced with timber and tree trunks.

"There's no need for this, Cuz. No need at all. Aulaudin's back and we've agreed to tell everyone everything. I'd like you to come to the kitchen with us."

Nothing. Between early evening, when Jerlayne had last visited him, and dawn when she'd left food beside the door, the mortal had run away. She pointed a flashlight beam at the ceiling. The louvers were untouched. It was a mystery, and for a heartbeat Jerlayne wondered if Evoni had reached down from the clouds to seize him, then she remembered the privy. On tiptoe, Jerlayne couldn't reach the room's one tiny window without a stool, but Cuz had found a way to open it and escape.

The goblins were in the kitchen when Jerlayne raced breathless down the three stone steps. Goro was on his feet immediately, asking what the trouble was and where. The other goblins stayed where they were, sitting or standing with their backs to the walls, waiting out the storm like statues.

"No trouble," Jerlayne replied, not wanting to tell her story twice; not, in truth, wanting to tell it at all. The thought of Cuz alone in the windstorm filled her with a dozen kinds of guilt.

Goro, clearly, was not persuaded, but he didn't challenge her, just returned to his place beside the hearth, beside the goblin she'd healed. Walls diminished the goblins. Their swords and armor, which they continued to wear, seemed woefully out of place beneath the hanging racks of pots and pans. They were meant to fight ogres and each other, not idle in a noisy kitchen.

Jerlayne was pondering the notion that different enemies demanded different warriors using different weapons when Aulaudin came down the steps, leading all the scyldrin he'd found.

"Where's Cuz?" he asked, not thinking, perhaps, of the consequences.

"He ran away," Jerlayne replied and they were into the thick of it, sixty voices strong.

At times that long afternoon, Jerlayne was certain that there was more noise and rancor beneath the Sunrise roof than above it. If someone wasn't shouting, someone was crying, or running from the room—including Jerlayne herself when she realized she hadn't visited the nursery after discovering that Cuz was gone.

She needn't have worried. Gelma sat in the rocking chair beside the cradle, knitting lace by lightning light.

"You should be down in the kitchen." Jerlayne told her.

Gelma set her needles aside but kept her place beside Laydin's cradle, benignly defying the infant's mother to disturb his sleep. "Listening to goblins and such? Not for me, thank you. My faith's in Evoni. She'll take care of us. The sages said she wouldn't let any harm come to Sunrise. That's enough for me."

Ashamed, then, as well as guilty—because it was easier not to tell Gelma that she might be very wrong, and convenient to leave the gnome with her knitting and Laydin—Jerlayne touched her son's forehead lightly with a kiss. When she got back to the kitchen they'd gotten as far as Goro's version of the tale of the Ten. To the last gnome and dwarf, the scyldrin refused to consider the notion that they were ultimately the children of blue-skinned goblins.

Jerlayne would never have predicted that a contrary version of the tale of the Ten would rile the scyldrin so much more than the revelation that every elf had a mortal father.

She was silently relieved when, after the hour when the sun should have set, Evoni's singing finally grew loud enough to end the pointless discussion. None of the scyldrin would remain in the kitchen to eat another cold meal. They took their share from the larder and headed off, grumbling, for the dormitories where the itinerant scyldrin kept their cots.

Jerlayne, suddenly seeing disaster in their stubbornness, wanted to follow them. Aulaudin caught her arm and said to let them go.

"But what they're upset about," she shouted, "it makes no sense! The tale of the Ten is just a story. What we told them about us, about elves right now, that's what they should be talking about."

"The scyldrin don't care about elves." Goro interrupted, also shouting. "At least not about you or Aulaudin or any elf whose name they know. They don't want to know about their parents, because they can never be parents themselves. With neither children nor parents, the scyldrin have only the tale of the Ten to tell them who they are."

Aulaudin scowled and Jerlayne foresaw more disasters, but he conceded: "The goblin's right," as a fist of wind pounded the roof, shaking dust and soot out of the rafters.

The larder and pantry were full—they'd gotten the harvest in before Evoni sang up the wind—but the bread bins were almost empty and the loaves Jerlayne brought out were hard, better suited to pudding than a cold supper. Not that the goblins complained, at least not about food. Jerlayne had a sense, despite the racket and the flashing light, that their black-eyed guests weren't happy about eating in the company of elves. Or, they weren't happy that Goro ate his meal standing at a table, opposite two elves, rather than huddled against the wall with them.

There was no conversation. Between thunder and wind, Jerlayne's throat strained at the thought of conversation. Thought, alone, was an effort. She was eating with an empty mind when Joff—the goblin she'd healed before dawn; Jerlayne recognized him by the tied-together hole in his mail—plunked his plate down silently between Goro and Aulaudin.

She cleared her throat and shouted at Goro: "Ask him how the wound is."

Joff clapped his hand over his flank. "Much better."

For a heartbeat, Jerlayne thought she hadn't heard right, that with all the noise, her ears were playing tricks on her mind. But Goro hadn't said anything; Goro was staring so intently at his food that Jerlayne couldn't see his face. And Aulaudin's wide-eyed face was surely a mirror of her own.

"Ears hurt now." Joff pointed at the roof and added a few words in his own language before nudging Goro with his fist.

The surprise wasn't that Joff understood, or that he could make himself understood to elves. Sunrise's goblins had been living closer to the great house than many of the scyldrin for a century; a dog could have picked up another language in that time. The surprise was that he'd acknowledged familiarity with not only Fairie's language, but done it in front a tongue-tied Goro. Then, one by one, the rest of Goro's goblins made their way to the middle of the room to stand beside their leaders and beside elves.

Jerlayne would have liked nothing more than to pull Goro aside and ask what had happened to lure them away from the walls. But, Goro, who chewed his bread with the slow determination of a thoroughly speechless man, probably didn't know.

She would have liked to share a few thoughts with Aulaudin; that, too, would have to wait. Maun's son was rigid, surrounded by men—goblins—he neither liked nor trusted. He ignored the rest of his plate even after the goblins reclaimed their places along the wall. Aulaudin mouthed a single word, *Later*, when Jerlayne touched his arm while collecting the plates.

Later didn't arrive.

Evoni's fury went on for hours. Jerlayne thought the shrill winds were louder than they'd been the night before. No one could have said for certain. Wandering through the great house, she saw gnomes with bits of fleece wadded into their ears. She followed their example. The fleece didn't so much lessen the noise as push it away, leaving a little space for private thought.

Jerlayne was in the nursery with Gelma and Laydin, thinking about the scyldrin in the barn and about Cuz, outside, alone when Evoni struck a note of purest rage overhead. The sound shook the great house to its foundations. Shelves and pictures crashed to the quaking floor. Window panes exploded, shooting glass across the room. Gelma and Jerlayne both lunged for Laydin's cradle, protecting him with their bodies while Sunrise shuddered again and again.

The moment lasted an eternity and ended in silence. Jerlayne stood up, assessing the damage. Half the carpet sparkled with broken glass, but not the half where the cradle stood. Laydin had awakened. His arms and leg thrashed, his little mouth was wide open. With or without the fleece in her ears, Jerlayne couldn't hear her son. Gelma had the same problem, or seemed to: She rubbed her ears furiously before picking Laydin up.

"Stay here!" Jerlayne told the gnome, mouthing the words deliberately as she said them.

Gelma nodded.

There was a pattern of broken glass on the floor in front of nearly every window and no few of Aulaudin's foraging treasures were smashed beyond repair, but aside from deafened ears and minor cuts, none of the scyldrin Jerlayne encountered had been injured. By the time she got to the itinerant dormitories, Jerlayne could hear a little, as if her head were under water—enough to realize that Evoni had fallen silent. Winds were fading, and lightning flashed less frequently through the now-naked shutters.

Aulaudin was one of those who'd been cut by flying glass. His feet, in particular, were a bleeding mess. He'd been in bed when the din began and lept out without a thought for his shoes.

"I caught the rose," he proclaimed, still a bit stunned and punchy. "It didn't break!"

Jerlayne had run her hands over his feet before she realized he meant the musical rose that had given their homestead its name. They celebrated his small triumph with a kiss. When Aulaudin realized that the windows were all broken again, he might decide that Sunrise could make do without glass of any sort.

There was only the faintest hint of water in Jerlayne's ears when she came to the kitchen. The heavy racks of pots and pans were on the floor and the goblins were outside again. No doubt, they felt safer there than beneath treacherous roofbeams.

Jerlayne and Aulaudin followed them through the open door, down the path that would take them to the bluff, if they went that far. A breeze still blew across the homestead: a steady gale, if they all hadn't just survived Evoni's storm. The thick cloud blanket had already begun to disperse. Stars twinkled in the west, casting gentle light on the wind-torn landscape.

Standing behind Jerlayne, Aulaudin rested his hands on her shoulders. "Not as bad as last time."

Joining flowed between them, weaker than it should be, but enough that Jerlayne could see what Aulaudin remembered: Sunrise the night their daughter rose.

«You can find our fathers and brothers and tell them we're all right.»

«Soon,» he agreed.

Ahead of them, a goblin pointed out to sea. Jerlayne heard it, too: Evoni singing her customary song from the rock. She'd defeated her enemy—Fairie's enemy, Sunrise's enemy. And none of them had the least notion who, or what, that enemy had been.

If it hadn't been the mortal, missing man, Cuz.

Jerlayne shouted his name and begged him to come back to the great house if he could hear her voice.

Suddenly, Goro was beside her. "We'll look for him after dawn."

He'd confessed to everyone at Sunrise that goblins moved through shadows. Jerlayne supposed she shouldn't have been surprised by his appearance. Between the stars, the wind, and the dispersing clouds there were shadows everywhere. Maybe it was just as well she'd been surprised: it served to remind her that goblins saw everything differently.

"We'll *all* look for him."

Lightning flashed in the west. Jerlayne thought it was the storm.

Aulaudin said, no «The Veil. Parting or skirting—I couldn't tell which. Odd. Very odd. Must be Evoni's aftermath.»

He released Jerlayne and walked away toward the place where they'd seen the flash. Goro followed Aulaudin, Jerlayne followed Goro and the rest of the goblins followed her. She heard some of them draw their swords.

The ground was littered with windfall branches. Neither Jerlayne nor Aulaudin had thought to bring a flashlight, but the goblins had. A dozen steady beams marked their progress toward the west ridge. An old, thick-trunk oak blocked the path. Aulaudin had fallen back to help Jerlayne climb over it when they heard a woman scream.

"Elmeene!" Jerlayne seized her husband's shirt and vaulted over the trunk. "Mother!"

Elmeene was nailed in the beams of several flashlights.

"Mother?"

Her gown was torn and filthy. Her curls were a wild, wild tangle around a face that seemed both swollen and discolored. She clutched a torn blanket to her breast. Behind her, clinging to her gown and each other, cowered at least a score of hollow-eyed scyldrin, dwarves and gnomes together, most of them bleeding.

Jerlayne raced through the goblins. The relief on her mother's face once Jerlayne was in the flashlight beams rather than behind them nearly broke her heart. She took the blanketed child in her arms. Aulaudin was right behind her to catch Elmeene before she collapsed.

Goro wasn't far behind Aulaudin, but when Elmeene saw him she became hysterical. Screaming curses, she fought like a cat for the privilege of scratching out his goblin eyes. Aulaudin took an elbow across the nose and lost his grip.

Jerlayne shouted "No!" as Elmeene threw herself at Goro.

The goblin protected himself, nothing more. He fended off Elmeene's teeth and nails until he gained a firm hold on her wrists, holding her at arm's length until futility reduced her anger to sobs. Released, Elmeene sank joint by joint to the ground where she curled on her side, covering her face with her crossed arms.

Jerlayne, whose attention had been fixed on her mother, looked at Goro and realized he was coldly unsurprised. She passed Mati, who'd begun to cry—he was alive, Jerlayne hadn't been sure at first—to the nearest gnome and knelt beside her mother.

"What's going on? Mother, what happened?"

"They came. *They* came." She raised her head to wail at Goro. "Hundreds of them!"

"Ogres? Jerlayne asked urgently. "Did ogres attack Stonewell?"

Elmeene shook her head, her shoulders, her entire body.

"Goblins," Goro said as he got down on his knees. "Elmeene. Elmeene—where was Arhon? Did you see Arhon among those who attacked you?"

"No." Elmeene raised her head again, calmer than before. "I didn't see him. There were so many goblins. I'd never seen so many. Fighting each other. Blood and guns. *Guns* in Fairie. Arhon had no guns. Never. I wouldn't allow it."

Goro's lips were set in a thin line. He'd gotten the answers he wanted; Jerlayne swore to herself that she'd get her answers, too. First, she had to get her mother and the Stonewell scyldrin—the surviving Stonewell scyldrin—into Sunrise. She helped her mother stand and take a few hesitant steps. Elmeene didn't appear to be physically wounded, merely exhausted and in shock.

Merely.

What Jerlayne had just lived through at Sunrise was a picnic compared to whatever her mother and the Stonewell scyldrin had endured.

"Faster!" Goro demanded.

"Are you blind?" Jerlayne shouted back. "She can't go any faster! None of them can."

Without warning, Goro swept Elmeene into his arms. He barked commands at his men who swarmed the Stonewell scyldrin, lifting them up, regardless of their protests. "Now, *run!*" he told Jerlayne. "The men who culled Stonewell cannot part the Veil, but they will follow her through shadow and they will come here. *Run!*"

The burdened goblins were already running and Aulaudin needed no additional persuasion. He caught Jerlayne's wrist and pulled her along beside him.

Once again there was chaos in the Sunrise kitchen. Jerlayne's obligation was to the battered scyldrin and her mother. She tried to put everything else out of her mind as she tended their injuries, but snippets of conversation forced their way into her awareness: Her father had been in the mortal realm when the goblin attack began. Her bachelor brother Nereige was dead. Elmeene had gathered her youngest son and all the scyldrin she could find and hidden them beneath a stairwell until flames drove them out. She'd led them across Fairie, skirting the Veil toward Sunrise: the one place she'd thought they would be safe. But Evoni had the Veil in her teeth and they'd gotten lost.

"It was dark. I couldn't see my hand in front of my face," Elmeene said, staring blankly at her daughter, seeing, perhaps, the darkness she'd barely escaped. "I lost them. I lost half of those I brought out of Stonewell. They were there, and then they were gone."

There was nothing Jerlayne could do for her mother except offer her tea laced with garden herbs and spirits from the mortal realm. "You're alive," she said while Elmeene sipped. "Mati's alive and sleeping beside Laydin."

Elmeene tried to smile, but sobbed instead. Jerlayne took the cup from her trembling fingers. She couldn't imagine what Elmeene had suffered. As she stroked her mother's tangled hair, Jerlayne gave thanks for her ignorance.

"We'll tell everyone. Aulaudin will."

Aulaudin stood by the bread oven in animated conversation with Goro. So much had happened and so quickly, that Jerlayne scarcely marveled at the sight before catching her husband's eye. They both came toward her: not the response she wanted—Elmeene didn't want to be near a goblin, and who could blame her?

Jerlayne left her mother with the potent tea and met the men by the table where they'd eaten supper a lifetime ago.

"Have you awakened Maun yet?"

"Not yet. The Veil was there for Elmeene to skirt, but only, I think, because she was already moving through it. I can't pierce it with my thoughts and I wouldn't want to try parting it right now. If I were beyond the boundary stones I'm sure it would be easier. Come dawn, if the Veil hasn't settled, I'll saddle a horse and ride out toward Briary—"

"Talk to him, Jerlayne! Explain to him that leaving is the most foolish thing he can do!" Goro complained. "Aulaudin, if you leave Sunrise, we are truly alone."

"We're alone now!" Aulaudin countered. "We've been alone for days. We don't know how many other homesteads were culled. I've got to go to Briary! I've got to find out what may have happened there."

"And if it is the worst, as you fear? If the gennern are waiting there . . . what then, Aulaudin? Do you want to die alone? Stay here, wait for Vigilance, if you can't communicate with you lineage before then. Share everything with your lineage, with every man your mind can touch. Stonewell and Evoni's storms, everything your wife has told you, everything I've told you." Goro turned to Jerlayne again. "Tell him to listen to me."

Jerlayne had had a long, hard day. She was weary and confused, but not nearly enough to plunge between Goro and Aulaudin, especially when she agreed with the goblin. She tried to change the subject.

"If Arhon is your enemy, Goro—if he's gennern—and he's been killed, why aren't you rejoicing? Why is Sunrise in a panic?"

"I would rejoice if I were the man who killed, or if I knew who had. It is possible Arhon's lineage has been destroyed as mine was; then I would rejoice. Yes, that would please me, though the price of that in Fairie would be very high. Stonewell would not be the only homestead culled—"

"Briary?"

"No, not Briary. The lineage of Briary lost many homesteads during the 'death. They play a small part on the plains. They wouldn't challenge Arhon's lineage, not without my knowledge: I have three of their blood sworn to me. I can think of no one who would challenge Arhon's lineage, but that lineage would devour Arhon if they thought he'd been careless."

"Careless, how?" Jerlayne asked.

"Arhon's lineage are the gennern with the guns and armor. When you stole from them, you escaped to Stonewell. I know elves can be followed as they skirt the Veil through Fairie; it's possible that you could have been followed to Stonewell and possible that they thought your mother was the one who stole from them. Arhon would have denied it. The patriarch and elders would judge him a liar and traitor. If he was a lucky man, they killed him at Stonewell."

Jerlayne leaned heavily on the table. "I did that to Stonewell? I caused all this?" She looked around the room, but not at her mother.

"Better Stonewell than Sunrise," the goblin said with brutal honesty. "My men are on the roof keeping watch. We lost our bows to the storm, but bows would be little use against guns. My hope is that gennern will see us together with you and think twice before attacking . . . and that Evoni remembers."

"You don't think her storms were to protect us from your enemies?"

Both men frowned and shook their heads. Jerlayne hadn't thought it was such a foolish or simple question.

"I can forage guns," Aulaudin suggested in the silence.

"You can stay *here* until after the next Vigilance. You can try to rouse Maun before then. Get one of your brothers to come here, or Ombrio. Any elfin man. No one else here can do what you do, Aulaudin. You *can't* leave."

It occurred to Jerlayne that she could part the Veil and forage guns from the mortal realm—if she'd known what one looked like. Aulaudin was the only elf at Sunrise who could share his thoughts through Vigilance, but not the only one who could part the Veil.

Goro said, "Your hands are shaking."

Jerlayne looked at Aulaudin's hands, but the goblin meant hers. She folded them into fists, but the damage was done: the shaking spread up her arms, down her spine. It stopped, then started again.

"You need to rest, beloved. You've tried to heal everyone today."

Her mind wanted no part of their bedroom where doubts and

memories would be her only company, but her body was going to win this battle. "You won't leave?"

"I'll keep trying to awaken Maun. I won't leave until after Vigilance."

"Reason, at last!"

Jerlayne plodded up the stairs, a lantern in one hand, headed for the bedroom. If Goro pushed too hard, he and Aulaudin might start brawling in the middle of the kitchen. The goblin might be surprised. Aulaudin wasn't a *docile* elf. He'd brawled with his brother and enjoyed it, or so he'd implied. They both might be surprised.

Someone was pounding on the high door.

Jerlayne veered right instead of left of the next landing. A tired gnome got to the door ahead of her, what was left of the door. All the glass had shattered when the storm ended, but the dwarves had nailed boards over the glass before the first siren-storm broke, then they'd braced the boards with angled timber. Jerlayne crunched through broken glass and thumped her fist against the wood.

"You can't come in this way. Go around to the kitchen!"

"Jery? Jery—I've got to talk to you."

Jerlayne was more tired than she'd thought: the voice had sounded like Maialene's. "Go away!" she grumbled. She was asleep on her feet and dreaming that her sister had returned now that her bachelor brothers were dead. "You're a ghost!" Rubbing her eyes with her free hand and muttering that her life had gotten too strange, too fast, Jerlayne turned around, walked away.

There was a *thud* and a groan and a sound no shaping woman could fail to recognize: wood crumbling to sawdust.

"Jery!"

A ghost, definitely a ghost and not her sister. Maialene's hair was black, but never short and stiff, and Maialene's face never had shiny metal bits growing out of it. Jerlayne guessed she must have caught the 'death while she was healing the goblin, or the Sunrise scyldrin, or her husband's feet. There was bryony in the bedroom . . .

"Jery!" The ghost grabbed Jerlayne's arms "Migod, what's wrong with you?"

So Jerlayne told her, "Stonewell's been culled. Nereige is dead, Jereige and our bachelor brothers are missing. Mother's here; she rescued Mati and a few of the scyldrin. Goro thinks we're next."

The ghost's arms dropped to her sides, "Well, there's one more disaster to add to the list: There were goblins out there today, before Evoni raised hell again. They had guns. You know what a gun is? They had guns and they got your mortal, Cuz—"

M'lene continued to say things that Jerlayne couldn't hear. Her hands had started shaking again. The lantern fell from her hands. More glass shattered across the floor, followed quickly by flames and shouts. Colors faded and dimmed. Jerlayne was fainting; she knew it and was embarrassed by her frailty, but staying on her feet had become impossible.

Chapter 30

Jerlayne vaguely remembered the gnome and her sister—her back-from-the-dead sister—swatting out flames and trundling her to bed like a weanling child. She remembered her dreams better: a crazed patchwork of memory and fantasy that fell mercifully short of nightmare. They lingered in her mind as she awakened: a sense, however fragile, that life would return to reason, if she were patient.

If there were no more surprises.

That hope died with a crash. Jerlayne sat bolt-upright in a swatch of sudden sunlight.

"Sorry! Your pardon, Jerlayne! Our mistake! We were just opening the shutters all around!"

The dwarves were as embarrassed as Jerlayne and ran off before she found a loose corner among the blankets. She'd have to find them later and assure them that they'd done more good than harm. Broken windows hadn't figured in her dreams and, but for them, she would have walked barefoot across a sparkling carpet.

Jerlayne's nearest shoes sat on the floor of her closet. She stood on the footboard and leapt to the seat of a chair and from there to the closet where, thinking about what she'd just done, she succumbed to laughter. Laughter, even if it were sometimes hysterical, might be more useful than patience in the coming days.

The dwarves must have confided their embarrassment with other scyldrin. Jerlayne hadn't finished braiding her hair when a gnome appeared in the doorway, dust-pan and broom in hand.

"Am I the only one who slept past dawn?" she asked as the silver-haired woman put her broom to work.

"You were very tired, Jerlayne. Vartel and Olvan didn't mean to awaken you."

The broom never missed a stroke.

Jerlayne knotted a ribbon around her hair. The plaits didn't match. "I *am* the only one who slept late."

"Not the only one." The gnome slowed her broom. "But Aulaudin, the goblin—They're all in the sun room waiting for you. Petrin's there, for us. I'm glad I'm not him."

All in the sun room: the thought struck terror in Jerlayne's heart. She fled the bedroom without another word, wondering who *all* might include beyond her husband, her goblin, and Petrin.

The answer was a dwarf and two elves: Mergatta, a Wave-homer who looked more uncomfortable amid cushions and draperies than Goro; Maialene, a study in black and steel who looked more dangerous than Goro; and Elmeene, sallow with grief and clearly in command. Jerlayne stopped at the doorway. She took a deep breath, stood tall, and crossed the threshold.

"Did you know his father was a goblin?" Elmeene asked.

Jerlayne understood the question, but it wasn't not an easy question to answer, not with six pairs of eyes and ears waiting to weigh her words. "Cuz didn't know what his father was. He had drawings his mother had made before she was stoned."

Maialene laughed. Aulaudin shook his head. The other four sat back in shock.

"Stoned. Oh-deed. Dead. Cuz scorned her. I didn't know what to believe. He was mortal." Jerlayne forced herself to look at her mother who, after all, had asked the question. "He *noticed.* You agreed that he noticed and you said that I wanted a man who noticed."

"I said he wasn't suitable."

"Viljuen weeps!" Jerlayne protested. "You *said* he was a sport who trysted with other men, not women. I didn't take that to mean his father was a goblin!"

That brought another laugh from her sister, silence from everyone else. Jerlayne studied the walls. Each one was covered with a different printed paper that Aulaudin had brought back from the mortal realm. Individually, Jerlayne was fond of each, but together—Well, Cuz had had a point: together the patterns and colors were not at all restful. She lowered her eyes and, one by one, met the eyes of the six others in the sun room.

"Laydin is an elf—a child born in Fairie of mortal father and an immortal elfin mother. We settled this when he was born. Aulaudin?" Jerlayne met her husband's eyes last.

He agreed, "We did. And whoever my son's grandfather was, I'm content that his grandmother bore elfin blood. Wives aren't the only elves who prowl beyond the Veil. Bachelor sons have done the same." He turned to Elmeene. "*That's* what we notice, what makes some mortals notice us: the elfin blood men leave behind."

"The truth at last!" Maialene clapped her hands three times.

Jerlayne's sister had changed, reshaping herself with more than bits of metal. She sheathed her legs in tight leather boots and black cloth that molded and stretched like her own skin. Elmeene was outraged and so was Jerlayne—a bit. Watching Maialene dangle her legs over the arm of her chair, well, Maialene looked *comfortable*. Her weak-willed sister looked not merely comfortable, but confident and relaxed.

"You've been beyond the Veil since Evoni rose, haven't you?" she asked her sister. "You've become happy."

"She's become a disgrace," Elmeene corrected before Maialene could speak. It was easier, perhaps, to berate a daughter returned from death than to face the loss of her sons. "Pretending to be one of them for no good reason, putting men at risk. If anything had happened to you . . . If you and Redis had worked harder you would—you would—" She covered her face, unable to complete her complaint.

"I would have what, Mother? Followed my husband into the forest? Starved? Waited for ogres to find me . . . or goblins?" Maialene dipped her chin in Goro's direction. "Is that what *you* intend to do now, Elmeene? Migod, do you think I'm the only elf who discovered life *after* homesteads?"

"I do," Goro said softly. "You were fortunate, M'lene. Efan paid for his carelessness and if you'd come anywhere but here, I would not have given you a month's life in your little cottage. I'd still be careful, if I were you."

"Threat?" Maialene asked, metal-trimmed brows arching high above her eyes. Elmeene's daughters couldn't help but take after her.

"Fact. There's no place in Fairie for an elf who, as you said, discovers life after the homesteads."

If the goblin's warning worried Maialene, she hid it well. "I'll keep a closer eye on shadows . . . when I'm here in Fairie, which, frankly, I'm not very often."

Jerlayne cut in, "But you came last night."

"No," Maialene said. "I came back to Fairie when Evoni

seized the Veil. We crossed in the Veil when she was halfway to becoming a guardian. It's not joining—thank god—but I knew there was going to be trouble."

Goro asked, "What kind of trouble?" Aulaudin asked, "Trouble in Fairie or outside it?" And Jerlayne asked, "Did I cause it by bringing Cuz through the Veil?"

Maialene slouched in her chair, swinging her legs and grinning: a black-haired counterpart of Cuz at his most annoying.

"Evoni doesn't *talk* to me," she explained with exaggerated patience. "There's not really any *Evoni* left to talk with. The attack came from the mortal realm, that much was clear, and she fought it with her voice and with that storm. With sound and light. If you've been in the mortal realm, you know how noisy it is. She fought noise with noise. Cuz was a street punk, Jery; he had nothing to do with the siren storms, and neither did you, so stop blaming yourself."

While Jerlayne tried to take her sister's advice, Goro, Aulaudin, and the two scyldrin peppered Maialene with questions about Evoni and the attack. She answered most of them with shrugs and blithe ignorance: "Who knows what makes mortals do what they do? They don't know themselves!"

The discussion had flagged and Jerlayne was thinking about breakfast and an overdue visit to the nursery when Elmeene broke an uncharacteristically long silence.

"What about the sages? After homesteading, what sort of elf becomes a sage?"

They all turned toward Goro.

"One who never causes trouble for us and is admired by all of you. You'd know more than me; except for Jerlayne, you're all older than I am. I know only that troublesome elves are always considered a threat." The goblin didn't say that Elmeene would never become a sage. He didn't need to, that conclusion was woven into his answer, exactly as Elmeene's will to become a sage—to somehow *replace* Claideris—had been woven into the question.

Outrage brought color back to Elmeene's grief-sallowed face. "I am more troublesome than *that woman?*" She rose to her feet. "What trouble have *I* or my daughters ever caused you?"

Jerlayne froze: Whatever revelations had been shared in this room while she slept late, they apparently hadn't included the fate of Goro's family. She didn't dare look directly at the goblin who sat, unnaturally still and quiet on the hardest, least-comfortable chair in the room. She looked at the floor instead, at carpet and feet and the worn tip of a scabbard. Elves got angry and shouted; goblins waged war and killed.

"You have caused me no trouble," Goro finally replied.

They were back to telling lies to preserve secrets, and Jerlayne had rarely been so happy. She tried to catch the goblin's eye, to thank him with a smile, but he continued to look only at her mother.

"Another man might not say the same."

"I will confront *that woman*. My home, my life, my love— I've lost it all. I have nothing left to lose."

Goro's smile was narrowed, black eyes and large black teeth. "Then you will most certainly become troublesome."

Jerlayne couldn't see her mother's face. It was obvious that the goblin and her mother had found a common ground.

"Sooner or later," Elmeene agreed.

"Sooner," Aulaudin, the only elfin man in the sun room, seized attention with a quiet voice and a lifted finger. "They're coming."

"The sages? Jerlayne asked quickly. "Gudwal, I hope, and the other men. Claideris is *not* welcome here."

"I share only with men," her husband reminded her unnecessarily. "Gudwal is on his way . . . slowly. The Veil near Sunrise is still—" he searched for a word, "tangled. Last night my thoughts seemed trapped in brambles, but some man must have heard."

"A grieving mother, her daughters—the dutiful one and the not-so-dutiful one, a goblin refugee, a man whose mind is trapped in brambles, and now—our *sages* are coming to visit!" Maialene clapped her hands again. "Be grateful, sister dear, that your precious windows are already broken, because they'd never last till sundown."

Silently, Jerlayne was inclined to agree, but she said nothing, except that she was going to spend a moment with her son and would meet them all again in the kitchen for a late breakfast. Aulaudin led the way to the nursery. If he had any thoughts in his mind that weren't revolving around Laydin, he kept them well hidden.

Mati, Elmeene's son, slept in a cradle improvised from a dresser drawer, but Gelma had their son in her lap. The carpet, she said straight off, would never again be clean enough, safe enough for Laydin. She wanted this one removed and a new one foraged from the mortal realm. Soon.

"Soon," Aulaudin agreed.

By the tone of his voice, if the sages weren't coming or the Veil weren't tangled, he'd have left that instant. Jerlayne eased aside, letting her husband take Laydin from the gnome's arms. She loved her son. His every move fascinated her; she could watch him all day, every day, so long as Gelma did the dirty work. Gelma or Aulaudin. When he was in the nursery with his son, Aulaudin became a stranger, a fool for giggly smiles.

She was taken aback when he abruptly handed Laydin to Gelma.

He said "Maun's on the ridge," and shared the notion of his father, the goblin-hater, catching his first sight of the Sunrise great house with goblins perched on its roof.

«You knew he was coming?» she asked as they hurried from the nursery.

«No,» he replied and shared a sense of the tangled Veil that left Jerlayne scratching itchy arms.

Maun had traveled from Briary by skirting the Veil rather than parting it. His horse, which he cantered to the high door steps, was lathered over, and he was too. Jerlayne suggested a bath and a change of clothes, but Maun wasn't concerned about horse sweat or her furniture.

"Another night ruined!" he complained, taking the steps two at a time. "Next time have mercy on your weary father's mind and keep a rein on your worries until Vigilance. I need my sleep!"

Jerlayne hoped he was joking. She was never quite certain when to take her husband's father seriously. Aulaudin dodged the inevitable back-slapping embrace; she was less agile, less lucky, and wound up with elf sweat and horse sweat staining her gown.

"Good to see you alive, daughter. Where's your mother?"

"Eating or asleep . . . trying to—"

Maun bellowed Elmeene's name and started down the nearest corridor.

"This way." Aulaudin insisted, catching Maun's sleeve and guiding him to the kitchen.

Scyldrin scurried. They needed no directions from Jerlayne to search for Elmeene before Maun broke loose again. But

Elmeene was in the kitchen, not-eating an apple. The uproar hadn't pierced her solitude: she caught her breath with a sob when she saw Maun at the top of the kitchen steps.

Elmeene and Jereige had opened their home to Jereige's unruly friend after blooddeath left so many orphans behind. Jerlayne hadn't thought about it until she saw Maun on his knees beside her mother's chair, but he was, in some ways, Stonewell's oldest son and, right now, Elmeene's truest friend. He took her trembling hands between his.

"I found him. I found him, Elmeene. As soon as I heard, I went looking for him. He wouldn't come here. He had to go *there* first. But I've sent my son, Aglaun to be with him, and Ombrio, too. He's safe, Elmeene. He'll be here long before sundown."

No need to ask who *he* was. Elmeene freed her hands which trembled as they slowly rose to touch Maun's face

"Safe, Elmeene. Alive and safe."

She slumped forward into his arms.

For the first time, Jerlayne imagined Stonewell with tumbled, blackened walls. She didn't know if the image came from her mind or Aulaudin. Nereige, her brother, was dead. Brel and Joren too. They'd never missed a chance to tease her mercilessly and she'd never thought she loved them. While everyone else watched Maun and Elmeene, Jerlayne shed tears of relief for her father and sorrow for her bachelor brothers.

Then Maun stood up. He looked around the kitchen until he found Goro, leaning against a wall, not far from the open door. The goblin could have left; no one would have noticed or, perhaps, blamed him.

"So you're what passes for an honest goblin."

It wasn't a question and Maun, though he was nearly a head shorter than the goblin, managed to seem much larger. Goro stood away from the wall.

"My son filled my mind with such stories last night that I didn't know whether I was awake or asleep. I woke my wife—she says it's all lies and nonsense. She's never parted the Veil, never seen a mortal man much less made a father out of one. But we did as we were asked: we rang the gong—in the middle of the night, no less. I tell you, waking everyone up like that . . . never have I felt so beloved of the Briary scyldrin. I told them about goblins, about Stonewell, and left Aglaidia to deal with them, since they all know *I'm* a madman. Then I prepared to part the Veil, to find my friend, only to have my dear wife burst in on me. Goblins, she said. *Our* goblins, as if I would ever lay claim to one, were at the door, wanting to come in . . . come into *our* home for our protection and for theirs.

"Now *that's* madness, I thought, and said they could stay in the barn. But here you are, and another dozen on the roof. So, I ask Sunrise's honest goblin: What brought *our* goblins to our door?"

Goro grinned; Jerlayne recalled the goblin saying that he'd looked forward to Maun's visits. "Unlike your wife and scyldrin, *we* know you're not a madman."

Silence grew thick. Jerlayne had a profile view of Maun: His mouth was open. He didn't blink for a long time, then he threw his head back and laughed.

"I thought so!" Maun turned to his son. "You hear that? Your honest goblin agrees with me his brothers, cousins and uncles are going to kill us all! I've been right all along!"

The goblin cut Maun's celebration short: "*Except* about Tatterfall."

This time the silence was dangerous.

"Ogres, Maun. It was ogres. They breed in the mist. Tatterfall was one of the first new foundations since blooddeath. Seven men were sworn to Tatterfall. Seven would have been enough in the heartland, but at Tatterfall, against the mist, they were overwhelmed. I've seen hordes two hundred-strong with my own eyes a half-day's walk from Sunrise. I have thirty men sworn to me; I'd feel better with three times that number."

"So you say," Maun countered, unimpressed.

"Come, walk the mist with me whenever you want. You *do* need your goblins, Maun. The question has always been, do they need you? This morning, you got your answer. Any man can have two enemies. Yours and mine and Stonewell's turn out to be the same: ogres and other goblins."

Maun frowned. "Two enemies is it? So goblins bring their wars to Fairie. You fight over us like dogs over a bone. Damn! I should've guessed. You're a proper bastard. Give me your name."

"Goro."

"Tell me, Goro: Who's stronger, us or them?"

"Them, Maun. Definitely them. There'd be no need for 'us' otherwise."

"Viljuen weeps, he is an honest goblin. Stay where I can see you, and we'll get along fine."

Goro laughed. He strode toward Maun and disappeared. There were gasps and cries until Maialene got their attention with a two-fingered whistle:

"In the shadows, by the hearth!"

Jerlayne opened her eyes wide, then squinted. She hadn't been entirely surprised when Goro vanished. Against all expectation, he had a Maun-ish sense of humor. Still, she couldn't see anything in those shadows—until she noticed that Maialene wasn't looking directly into the shadow. Angling her head to match her sister's, she noticed a blur within the shadow, like a film across her eye, but she didn't actually see Goro until he moved.

A fast-fading mist surrounded him when he returned to sunlight. His breath came out in a cloud.

"I'll tell you who should be culled from Fairie!" Maun complained, pounding the goblin's shoulder. "I'm going to put my fist in every bedroom shadow before I lay my head down at night."

Goro pointed at the open door. "Your bedroom's safe. If the shadows aren't made directly by the sun, moon, or stars, no glass in the way, they're too thin to use."

Maun would have no peace until he'd tried and preferably mastered the shadow-shifting deception. Never mind that Goro insisted that too much time spent in shadows would turn him into a blue-skinned, silver-haired man who was neither elf nor goblin. His first attempts were complete failures, but when, after the sixth try, Maun pronounced the shadows unnaturally cold, Aulaudin and Maialene decided they couldn't be left out.

Jerlayne thought it all a waste of time, but Sunrise had a bit of time to waste while waiting for their other guests to arrive. There was no point in discussing anything serious before then. It would only have to be repeated.

The scyldrin wanted the kitchen back. On an ordinary day it belonged to them and they all wanted their ordinariness back, too. The shadow-shifters eagerly moved outside where the shadows had more heft. That left Jerlayne with Elmeene.

How ironic to think that she'd become the dutiful daughter, one arm around her mother's waist, leading her toward the nursery where Mati was still asleep.

Elmeene held him close, but without evident joy. "He has no home," she explained to Jerlayne. What she meant was that *her* home had been destroyed.

Jerlayne began to say that they were still rebuilding Sunrise, then stopped herself. There was no comparison. Sunrise had acquired an ocean and a guardian. Stonewell had been destroyed with its goblin protectors, possibly *by* its protectors.

"You should try to rest before Father arrives. I can make you a drowsy tea?"

"I'm not tired. I don't need to rest."

"Then, come to my workroom. The armor's there. I've scarcely touched it."

Elmeene agreed and fell asleep in an upholstered chair, the unbroken armor balanced in her lap. Jerlayne was on the floor, enjoying a cool breeze through the unglazed windows and shaping glass silvers out of the carpet when Evoni shattered the late afternoon calm. Clouds had gathered by the time she poked her head out the window. She grabbed the latches and pulled the shutters inward.

There wasn't time to lash them or replace the angled trees.

They'd all been fools to think the siren wouldn't sing again.

When she'd secured her workroom as best she could, Jerlayne moved on to another room, leaving her mother behind. Elmeene hadn't roused to the first notes of Evoni's shrill, piercing song. If she could sleep through those, she'd won the right to sleep as long as she could. The storm would almost certainly delay Jereige's return from ruined Stonewell. And the sages, too.

Jerlayne grabbed another pair of shutters and pulled them closed. The assembly gong was clanging—as if anyone in earshot needed a metal slab to tell them what was happening. She fastened the room's other shutters and collided with Maialene in the doorway on her way out.

"We've got to leave now," Maialene informed her.

"Leave? Are you deaf? Viljuen weeps, M'lene. You can't run away now. We're not prepared this time. Scyldrin are going to get hurt—*we're* going to get hurt. *I* need you." Jerlayne tried to shoulder past her sister but Maialene spread her arms across the doorway.

"You're coming through the Veil with me, Jery, if I have to hit you over the head first—"

"Maialene!" Jerlayne wrapped a warm, shaping hand around her sister's wrist.

"We're not running away. It's not just us who could get hurt: Evoni's hurting. She can't keep this up."

Jerlayne loosened her grip. "You're serious about this."

"I told you: it's a little like being joined. Listen to her, can't you hear the difference? She's a guardian, but she can't hold off the whole mortal realm."

"And we can? You and I can do what a guardian can't?"

Jerlayne wanted to dismiss her sister as an iron-touched madwoman, but there was a difference in the siren's singing. Weariness? Desperation? She couldn't say, but she couldn't call M'lene a madwoman, either. Releasing her sister, she retreated into the shuttered room.

"What could we possibly do, here or in the mortal realm?"

M'lene followed Jerlayne and closed the door behind her. "Find the machine that she's fighting and unshape it."

"You can't do that!"

"I can find it, if we part the Veil right now. And you can unshape it. There's no one better than you."

"I don't know anything about how mortal machines work. I've taken a flashlight's guts apart, but I can't put them back together again, not so they make light . . ."

"You don't have to put this machine back together, Jery. Just take it apart so no one can put it back together." Maialene took Jerlayne's arm. "We're losing time. The Veil's not gonna be there much longer. In and out, Jery. We chase it down, you unshape it, we come back—no one even knows we've been gone."

"No, we have to tell someone." She'd made up her mind. The risk was huge, the challenge greater. She couldn't resist. "I'll find Aulaudin."

"There's no time! Leave him a message."

Jerlayne tried. She closed her eyes and sought her husband's mind. A piercing, pulsing whine drove her back within herself. "I can't—"

Maialene had wrenched a colored candle from its holder and was using it to mark up the wall. "A *written* message, Jery!"

Writing, then, became reading, "But—none of us understands writing or reading."

"Aulaudin must know some, and Maun's here. Maun can

read." Maialene threw the candle to the floor. "Now, c'mon.
We're out of here."

The machine, if Evoni were fighting a machine, was evident
from the moment Maialene parted the Veil. It was dangerous,
as iron was dangerous, and rooted in another realm, like
Elmeene's red dress or Goro's armor slab. Maialene proposed
to follow the root. The passage was dizzying, but quick. Evoni
spat them out on a partly wooded hillside that could have been
Fairie, except for the noise. M'lene said they might be in the
Catskills or New Jersey.

"What do we do?" Jerlayne shouted.

"Unshape that house!" M'lene replied, also shouting.

House? Jerlayne thought. Squinting through the cloudy
moonlight, there was nothing she'd name *house* or *homestead,*
just a huge box, larger than any Fairie barn and a pair of shiny
metal cars. The huge box seemed to be the source of the shrill,
relentless noise that pierced her ears. She imagined fleece and
feathers in vast quantity. The noise retreated. Jerlayne perceived it in her stomach rather than her ears. Thinking became
less painful, but the Veil remained out of reach.

Night ruled the Catskills or New Jersey. The sisters circled
the huge box, counting windows—none—and looking for
doors. Jerlayne had guessed wrong about the noise. Another
car, many times larger than the other two, sat on the far side of
the huge box. This third car—M'lene called it a *bus*—bristled
with spikes, wire. Three shallow bowls perched atop the bus.
The smallest of the bowls could hide a dog; the largest, a man.

"How does it make that noise?" Jerlayne asked when they'd
completed their circle.

"Beats the hell outta me, Jery." M'lene confessed with a
laugh. "It says it's from a *television station.*"

"You hear words in the air and they have meaning? I only
hear noise; it makes me sick to my stomach."

"Writing, Jery. The writing on the side of the bus. It says
which station it comes from. I don't recognize the letters,
though; it's not from around here—or maybe we're not in Jersey. All I know is: that's the source. That's what's making the
noise Evoni sings against: her song against its song. We unshape it, and there's peace in Fairie. That's all I need to know.
You want more answers, or better answers, then you're going
to have to get them yourself.

"At least it's not very big . . . not as big as I expected," Maialene mused as they started down the hill. "We should be able to unshape this in no time. You should."

Jerlayne didn't share her sister's optimism. The bus was ringed with dark windows, all of them, so far as she could guess, sealed shut. There wasn't a door, at least not one that Jerlayne recognized until they'd crept close to one end the metal-sheathed bus and Maialene did something that made the wheeled box sigh. A big panel swung open, narrowly missing Jerlayne's shoulder.

M'lene led the way up three uneven steps.

Five mortals looked up from cluttered tables midway down the bus. By their gape-jawed expressions, they were as surprised to see Jerlayne and her sister as Jerlayne, at least, was to see them. Machines, Maialene had said, and unshaping. Jerlayne had expected metal, not four mortal men and a woman.

There was metal: the walls of the bus were lined with cabinets that stared back at Jerlayne with the same sort of ominously glow she'd seen in the *lab* where she'd found Cuz. There was another similarity between the bus and the lab: wire, wire everywhere like threads in her thread box.

One of the mortals told them to leave. Another threatened to call the *police*.

The sole woman screamed: "It's her! It's the one from the surveillance tapes!" She reached inside her clothes and brought out an angled piece of metal not much larger than her hand. "Don't move," she warned.

"A gun, Jery!" Maialene surged toward the mortal woman. "Quick! She's got a gun."

So that's what a gun looked like; Jerlayne had expected something bigger. When the mortal woman used her gun, Jerlayne recognized the sound and feared for her sister, but Maialene was unharmed. M'lene collided with the mortal, pushing her into the cabinets. Light flickered within the bus—the windows had appeared dark from the outside because the cabinets blocked them.

The gun shot again and punctured the ceiling.

Two of the men attacked Maialene's back. The other two rushed Jerlayne. She shaped pain, all the pain she could imagine. If the two men had been made from iron, they would have melted. Made from flesh, they stiffened the instant they touched her, then collapsed. They twitched and stank on the floor.

The gun shot a third time and there was blood on Maialene's shoulder. Jerlayne seized one of the mortals grappling with M'lene at the base of his neck. She shaped more pain. He let go of M'lene but Jerlayne kept her hold on him until, horrified, she realized smoke was swirling up from his face. He, too, collapsed when she released him, but did not twitch on the floor.

The fourth man had released Maialene by then. With his back against the cabinets and pleading for his life, he sidestepped the bodies on the floor until he could make a straightline run for the door. Jerlayne could have stopped him. She'd killed three men. She—an elf, a *docile* elf—had shaped the life from three mortals! So far, she'd done her killing not quite by accident, but not quite deliberately, either. That would change if she pursued the fourth mortal. For her own sake, more than his, she let him escape.

Within heartbeats she heard the roar and squeal of a car rolling off at high speed.

Maialene removed her hands from the mortal woman's neck. Her face was almost goblin blue and she was quite dead. "Well, that could have gone better," M'lene said, one hand on her bloody shoulder. She prodded the third mortal, the man Jerlayne had pulled from her back, with her foot and gasped when she saw what remained of his face. "You don't do anything by halves, do you?"

Jerlayne stumbled down the steps and collapsed in the grass. She retched until her stomach was empty, then retched some more, until Maialene hauled her to her feet.

"C'mon, kid. We've got to finish what we came to do before the last one comes back with company."

"They're dead!" Jerlayne broke free of her sister. "I *killed* them."

M'lene caught her wrist again. "I *killed* one," she said, leading Jerlayne inside. "I think the word for what you did is *nuked*. You *nuked* three mortals."

Once again, Jerlayne broke free. Her hands shook and she couldn't stop crying as she attacked the nearest cabinet. Jerlayne hammered it with her fists, then unshaped it into chunks she could hurl through the windows. She paused when it was rubble, caught sight of the corpses she'd shaped, and became a trembling statue.

Maialene grabbed Jerlayne's wrists. "It was us or them," she shouted. "Five of them and a *gun* against the two of us. Dammit, Jery, you made the right choice!"

Jerlayne wrested free. "The *right* choice would have been to stay in Fairie! We're not supposed to kill, M'lene. I never wanted to change *that!*" She ripped wires from the walls and wadded them together. Stinking globs of metal and oily filth dripped from her fingers.

"The hell. Give a listen to your ears: that noise has stopped."

Jerlayne stopped her vengeful shaping. Maialene was right: the night had fallen quiet. She went back to squeezing the wires. Her sister tried to help, but Maialene had needed four tries to shape her chain. Her clumsiness showed, even in destruction.

"Wait outside," Jerlayne commanded her sister.

M'lene retreated only as far as the cluttered tables where she began examining sheets of writing—or reading—covered paper.

"Just stay out of my way," Jerlayne snarled. "You wanted this and you've gotten it, but stay out of my way!"

Maialene kept her head down and her mouth shut, while Jerlayne unleashed her anger and remorse.

"It's finished," she said when every cabinet was unrecognizable and the air within the bus reeked of oil and poison. "Until the next time. All the men say there's always a next time with mortals."

"And the men would know," her sister responded.

Jerlayne was too distraught to wonder what her sister meant. She took M'lene's arm. "Let's go home."

Maialene's feet stayed where they were. "Look at this first." She held out a piece of paper. "They recognized you, Jery. The woman did, anyway."

At first Jerlayne made no sense of the shades-of-gray image on the paper, then she saw a woman's face and a necklace; her necklace, her face. A pale blur of flame or fog surrounded her portrait and whatever bulky, awkward object she'd carried in her arms. She didn't recognize Cuz, at least not until she'd recognized the lab bed where she'd found him.

"We were alone!" she protested. "There was no one to draw this picture!"

Maialene explained: "It wasn't drawn, Jery. It's from a surveillance tape. Mortals have *cameras* everywhere, Jery. They caught you rescuing Cuz on tape. Better believe they caught you parting the Veil."

The paper slipped through Jerlayne's fingers. She didn't under stand half of what her sister had just told her, but half was enough to leave her speechless with shock and shame.

"So, what's the connection between Cuz and the attacks?" M'lene asked. "He and I didn't have a lot of talk-time."

Jerlayne shook her head. "His uncle. His uncle had put in him the room with all the boxes and tubes; that room," she pointed at the picture. "He's different, M'lene. He's mortal, but he doesn't get sick; that's what he says. His uncle was suspicious—"

"Better believe that uncle's more than suspicious now."

Jerlayne worried the fringe of her shawl. It was damp and reddened her fingers. She cast it aside. She'd ruined more than a shawl. Her clothes were stained and pocked with burns from her unshaping frenzy.

"We've got to leave . . . ."

M'lene nodded slowly, then, just as slowly, scanned the walls and ceiling. "There could be surveillance here. It's quiet now, but maybe that uncle of his could wake it up, unless . . . unless you can make it burn."

Jerlayne stared at her sister. "I can try."

There was a limit to shaping and Jerlayne was closer to it than she'd ever been before. The table around which the mortals had been crowded when she and M'lene had arrived was made of wood, with considerable effort, Jerlayne lured fire to its corners. Flame spread to the poisons she'd melted away from the wires. The air turned dark and foul.

"Let's go!"

Jerlayne fled the bus ahead of her sister. Maialene had healed herself. She'd claimed the gun that shot her for her own and had it tucked into the waistband of her clingy pants. She offered Jerlayne jewelry she'd taken from the mortal woman's neck, calling the metal-and-bead strands a *souvenir.*

Jerlayne wore mortal jewelry; every piece Aulaudin had ever given her had been made in the mortal realm and worn first by mortal women. Of course, she'd never seen those women, and the knotted cord with its lumpish, blue-green beads and animal claws was nothing she'd ordinarily wear, but she was past arguing with her sister.

"Get us home. Everything's quiet now: just get us home" she pleaded. "I couldn't open the Veil if it fell on me."

"I'll get us out of here," Maialene replied, "but Sunrise is out of reach. We'll take one of the cars."

Jerlayne didn't ask where M'lene had found the key she used to start the machine, or where she'd learned to control it. Simply opening the door and stuffing herself inside had taken the last of her courage. With her fists clenched together and her eyes tightly closed Jerlayne tried to think of pretty flowers while her sister cursed and drove the car down a rutted, miserable road.

Chapter 31

When he got hit in the jaw, right where M'lene had put him back together, Cuz thought he'd come to the end. He'd felt himself going down. There hadn't been any of that fairytale watch-your-life-like-a-movie stuff. Then again, fairyland wasn't a fairytale sort of place.

Or maybe Cuz should have known he'd come back up.

In a worse place, the way he usually did.

The worse place was a creepy forest with cold, November rain, no food worth eating, and four goblin guys who didn't speak any kind of English holding him prisoner. They got their messages across with fists and growls and—oh, yeah—they'd chopped off half of his right middle finger the first—and only—time he'd tried to run away.

For two days now—at least Cuz thought it was two days. The forest was so damn gloomy and the goblins stuck to the darkest parts of it. He hadn't seen the sun or moon since they'd captured him. For two days, then, Cuz had been trying to work up the nerve to do something so bad they'd kill him before they got wherever the hell they were going. If he could kill one of them, Cuz figured that would be bad enough.

But, shit, if Cuz could have killed a goblin, he'd have gotten away before they cut off his finger. And he really didn't want to know what they'd cut off next if he didn't piss them off enough to get himself killed.

His hand hurt in an odd way. Cuz had known a guy on the streets who, every time he got beat up, would say: No problem. It's a long way from my heart. The guy had gotten killed by a taxi cab. But a finger was a long way from Cuz's heart. He wasn't in agony and it wasn't going to kill him—though he hadn't untied the scrap of cloth they'd tied tight around his hand while it was still bleeding.

Cuz got sick every time he thought about his missing finger;

not because of the pain. He'd run. When he didn't get away he'd expected a few broken bones. Two of the goblins had wrestled him to the ground. A third had knelt on his arm. Then, *whack!* He'd known immediately what had happened. He should've passed out, but he'd been too damned scared to faint. The goblin guy who'd chopped him kept Cuz's fingertip in a pouch. He'd take it out and shove it right into Cuz's face, saying things Cuz hadn't a prayer of understanding.

That's what really made him sick.

At least, Cuz assumed the goblin who'd chopped him was the one who taunted him. The blue-skinned men might have all been twins for all the luck he'd had telling them apart. And any of them could have been Goro's twin, too, or his father's, which left Cuz asking himself stupid questions about clones and penguins. He could have used a bit of whatever sense God had given penguins for telling themselves apart.

Maybe it would have been easier if he'd been able to unscramble their conversations. Cuz had decoded the sounds for *rest time's over, get up,* and *start walking.* They weren't anything he could have repeated on a bet. With its clicks and whistles, goblin language sounded like something out of a bad science-fiction movie.

He heard the sounds he recognized and got to his feet.

The Ghoul—the name Cuz had give to the goblin hauling his fingertip and the one who seemed to give the most orders—clicked and buzzed some more. One of the nameless goblin guys grabbed Cuz's wrist. Cuz hadn't decoded the Ghoul's final words, but he knew what it meant when they held onto him when they walked, and it scared him more than losing all his fingertips.

They didn't seem to care if he screamed, so Cuz screamed at every other step, when indescribable cold closed in around him and the only other sensation was a goblin hand yanking him forward, back into the forest for one lousy stride. With the next, they'd be back in the cold and dark again.

This time the two-stride nightmare didn't end. The cold got to his bad hand, like a needle in a nerve—Cuz knew what that felt like. Eventually, he stopped screaming. His throat was raw, his nose was frozen, and it was too damn much effort.

Cuz didn't know whether he tripped over something on a forest stride or lost it in the cold-dark, but suddenly he was hanging by his bad hand and the Ghoul called a halt. He started shivering and sweating, both at the same time. A bell rang in his mind: he had a fever. Just when Cuz thought he'd hit the bottom, he'd gone and gotten sick.

Even the goblins seemed to know something was wrong. They poked, prodded, and went after his bandage. Cuz hit the wall of fainting pain.

He was gone only a few minutes, barely long enough to miss them stripping off the last layer of clotted cloth. The goblin who'd been dragging him all day produced a leather flask of liquid fire, which he poured on the open wound. If two other goblins hadn't been holding him down, Cuz would have wound up in the trees. But the liquid numbed his nerves and when the goblin offered him a drink, Cuz took the biggest pull he dared. If there were such a thing as three-hundred-proof booze, then that's what goblins drank.

The goblin plugged his flask, threw Cuz over his shoulder, and the nightmare resumed. A headful of blood and alcohol didn't improve the cold-dark. Cuz went from wanting to die to hallucinating that he'd gone straight to hell. He didn't pass out, but he didn't remember leaving the forest. Suddenly there was sunlight and grass, and his fever got worse.

After the longest upside-down walk of his life, the Ghoul led them over a hill crest and into what appeared to be a fairly permanent goblin camp with more goblins that Cuz could count in his current condition, and maybe twice that many horses. The horses were as blackly identical as the goblins and the whole scene left Cuz wondering if he'd gone delirious.

Wills had a ferocious fever when he died. Between the fever and the drugs, he was delirious for days.

The Ghoul and one of the new goblins engaged in the longest conversation Cuz had yet overheard. They clicked and barked and pointed at him several times. Cuz got the distinct feeling that the new goblin—a guy with a shiny hubcap thing on his chest—didn't think he owed the Ghoul a favor.

Hubcap lost the argument. The Ghoul—and Cuz's fingertip—vanished while Hubcap made noises at goblins who didn't argue with him.

Fevered, weary, and propped against a post like baggage, Cuz nodded off while Hubcap's guys ran around. He awoke with a foot prodding his thigh. A one-eyed goblin—the wound looked recent; Cuz wondered how he'd gotten hurt, then decided he really didn't need to know—wanted him to climb onto one of the black horses. Cuz remembered riding a pony at a birthday party; he couldn't have been more than six at the time. He'd fallen off then, and expected to do no better now.

One-eye barked something unpleasant; Cuz wobbled to his feet. He tried to get his foot into the stirrup but, all things considered, the horse was a lot larger than the pony. Cuz didn't get close to the saddle until One-eye hoisted him up by the seat of his pants. Then, before Cuz or the horse had recovered from the shock, One-eye tied a rope around Cuz's left ankle, fed it through the stirrup and under the horse's belly before pulling it through the right stirrup and, finally, knotting it off around Cuz's right ankle.

Cuz protested. If he fell off—make that *when* he fell off, he'd be upside down among horse legs. One-eye, though, couldn't understand Cuz any better than Cuz understood him. He put the reins in Cuz's good hands, like Cuz had any damn idea what to do with them.

At first, riding wasn't too bad. Cuz wound the reins around his good hand—he'd heard somewhere that he shouldn't tie them—while the black horse did what it wanted. Fortunately, the horse wanted to be in the middle of a herd of ten mounted goblins and twelve unsaddled horses. Then without warning— naturally—Hubcap shouted something that must have meant *They're off!* and what had been a bored horse became an uncontrolled monster with a death wish.

Bounding like a rabbit—like Cuz imagined a rabbit would bound if it weighed over a ton—his horse surged past the unsaddled horses and the mounted goblins until only Hubcap raced in front of them.

Fear trumped pain. The reins went flying as Cuz clung to the saddle with both hands. They were gaining on Hubcap when One-eye galloped alongside, got a grip on the reins near the bit, and brought Cuz's horse to a second-place finish.

There was a lot of goblin yelling and goblin shouting. Hubcap brought his horse around. He yelled at One-eye who never blinked, then Hubcap came face to face, knee against knee, with Cuz.

"Do you want to die?"

English. Hubcap spoke English. That was a puzzling shock.

Hubcap had a knife, too, and prodded Cuz beneath the jaw with its cold, sharp tip. That was a thoroughly unpleasant shock.

"Do you?"

Cuz wanted to say no. Never mind that he'd been plotting his own death for days, when the opportunity arose, he wasn't—never had been—suicidal. But Hubcap's knife would have pierced Cuz's tongue if he'd opened his mouth; and shaking his head could have severed something vital, too. Cuz gulped hard until Hubcap lowered his knife; then he blurted out, "No fuckin' way," as if he were back on the streets and cornered by cops.

Hubcap pricked him; Cuz was sure there was his blood on the blade.

"Talk plain, elf."

Cuz realized then that Hubcap hadn't spoken *English.* Hubcap had spoken the same almost-English that Jerlayne and everyone else in fairyland spoke because Hubcap had assumed that Cuz was an elf. M'lene—dear ol' M'lene—had said that she'd known he was mortal because she'd healed him, but that the goblins wouldn't know the difference between him and her son. M'lene had bailed out on him, so Cuz had figured she'd been lying from the start.

He felt like a damned fool: The Ghoul hadn't kidnapped him because he was a mortal trespassing in Fairyland. Goblins killed mortals right where they found them; he'd heard Goro say so. The Ghoul had kidnapped an elf. Cuz couldn't imagine why the Ghoul had kidnapped an elf. Goblins, from what little he knew were supposed to protect elves. And they might kill him anyway; they'd proven they didn't need him intact or unharmed. But there was a chance they'd keep an elf alive another hour, another day and, even though in his experience, tomorrow was never better than today, Cuz wanted that chance.

"No, I don't want to die," Cuz said, as plainly as he could. In the depths of his heart, he wished that he'd spent a little more time listening to Jerlayne's odd accent, not that he was any good at accents even when he paid attention to them.

"Remember it. Try escaping again and you die. Ride beside Diras." Hubcap returned his knife to a boot sheath.

Diras—One-eye's name was Diras, or something that sounded like Diras with a cricket chirping between the *Dir* and the *As*—held out the reins Cuz had lost when the race began. Inspiration struck: Cuz was sweating out a fever and after that last bone-jolting ride, his hand hurt worse than it had when the Ghoul whacked his finger off. Cuz held up a dramatically shaky bandaged hand and shook his head.

Diras and the other goblins saw something funny in Cuz's gesture. They shared a good laugh at his expense. Cuz was duly embarrassed and with fever already heating up his blood, he blushed spectacularly, but he'd been embarrassed before. It wasn't fatal and, anyway, Cuz had gotten what he wanted: Diras looped the extra reins with his own.

With Diras firmly in charge of both horses, they walked and raced, raced and walked until after sunset. More than once Cuz had gone one way when the damned horse went the other. He'd lurched and bounced and seen stars he hoped never to see again, but the damned rope between his ankles had kept his feet in the stirrups long enough for him to get his ass down on the unforgiving saddle again. By the time Hubcap barked a halt, Cuz's ass had to be bruised as blue as a goblin's face.

He waited quietly until Diras had the ankle rope untied, then made a valiant attempt to move his leaden right leg before Diras wrapped him up at the waist and dragged him free. His arms fell naturally around the goblin's neck and remained there even after Cuz had gotten his feet underneath him. In all his miserable life, no matter how bad it had gotten, he'd never gone victim, never succumbed to the allure of an oppressor. The realization that he'd held on to Diras was the worst shock of a bad day. Cuz crumpled to his knees when Diras released him.

Diras barked and Hubcap appeared, a dark silhouette in twilight.

Elves were immortal. Elves didn't get sick. Hell, Cuz didn't get sick, that's what brought him to fairyland in the first place. But he was sick in the grass between the goblins: a gut-retching, shivering, and shaking sick that might prove fatal, if it left Hubcap thinking he wasn't an elf.

Hubcap produced some of that three-hundred-proof alcohol. Cuz didn't think he kept enough in his gut to make any difference in his pain or perception, but he lost track of himself until morning when the horse-walking and horse-racing began again. After a few hours of Cuz flopping around, unable to keep himself upright in the saddle, they'd set him down behind Diras' and lashed his arms cross-wise around the goblin's shoulders. Cuz drifted in and out of consciousness to the beat of the goblin's heart.

He didn't remember stopping for the day or eating dinner, though he remembered vomiting afterward. That was the last moment Cuz remembered clearly for a long time—until he looked up and saw the ribs of a black-cloth tent above him. His head hurt, his back and his shoulder; he didn't want to be awake. When he tried to roll over, Cuz discovered that his arms were stretched wide and shackled to the ends of a log that dug into his back. The fever wasn't gone. He didn't have the strength to sit, but he could—and did—scream.

Hubcap and another goblin came to see their prisoner. They each took an end of the log and carried him, dangling, into the sunlight. Between black tents and red rocks, the plains had disappeared. While the second goblin kept Cuz upright, Hubcap fussed with a second rope which he looped over Cuz's wrists and the log together. Cuz had a feeling something bad was about to happen, and it did: When the second rope tightened, he began to rise. The rising stopped when his toes barely touched the ground.

"What happened at Sunrise?" Hubcap asked.

Cuz shook his head and got clouted for his insolence.

"What happened at Sunrise?" the goblin repeated.

"I don't know."

"What is your name?"

He'd seen a hundred movies with interrogation scenes: only the star kept his secrets. Cuz wasn't a star. The way his ribs and arms hurt, he didn't know if this was his first interrogation scene, or if he'd already spilled his guts.

"Cuz."

"Cuz?" Hubcap mused. "Try harder, Cuz. What happened at Sunrise?"

"I don't know."

Hubcap struck Cuz again, snapping his head against the log. The impact made the log spin. His toes lost contact with the ground. There was an awful, moaning noise; Cuz realized he'd made it.

"It's very simple, Cuz," Hubcap explained, stretching his arm against the log; Cuz hung with one arm higher than the other. "Tell us what happened at the homestead. Why have the gennern gone under the roof? Why is the siren singing a storm over their heads? Don't imagine you can lie—or that you can save them.

They're dead already, Cuz. You can save yourself with the truth. We'll always need a few of your kind—a few elves, male and female. You can be one of the few who survive . . . if you answer the questions. What happened at Sunrise?"

In the movies, when the prisoner spilled his guts, the interrogation ended. Maybe he got killed or maybe he got set free to squirm in his conscience, but his torture—his physical torture—ended. Of course, in the movies, the prisoner knew something worth spilling. Cuz didn't know shit about what had happened at Sunrise. He could barely remember Sunrise through his fever.

Hubcap kept Cuz hanging for what felt like eternity but was probably more like an hour before dragging him and his log back to the black tent where Diras smeared goo on his rope burns and spoon-fed him as much food as he could keep down. Cuz spilled his guts to Diras, too, in every imaginable way, and when they thought he'd regained enough strength to keep things interesting, they dragged him out of the tent again.

Sometimes they asked him the same questions, other times they ignored him, leaving Cuz to dangle in the sunlight until he passed out. Cuz learned to fear the slightest breeze. He cursed Jerlayne and all other elves. He told them he was a mortal and about Uncle Ted and the drawings of his father, his goblin father. Hubcap called him a liar: goblins couldn't pass into the mortal realm and mortal couldn't pass from the mortal realm into Fairie, much less into the plains. Cuz was alive so Cuz was an elf: the son of a mortal man and an elfin mother.

"What happened at Sunrise?"

Cuz told lies, hoping that would put an end to the pain. They unwound the cloth from his hand, reopened the wound, and stanched the blood with salt. Diras waited in the tent after that, too. The one-eyed goblin begged Cuz to tell the truth.

"You'll lose more than a finger," Diras warned as he gently bathed the bloody streaks from Cuz's arm.

So, Cuz returned to the truth and Diras walked away. Night came and went without Diras, Hubcap, or any other goblin entering the tent. He heard them—goblins generally, not individuals—walk close. The tent flap rippled, but never opened. His fever worsened. Whatever Cuz's sickness was, it spread to his eyes which swelled shut and wept until all his tears were gone.

How long did it take to die of thirst, pain, or simple misery?

The irony was, Cuz wouldn't know. Between nightmares and hallucinations, he'd lost all sense of time.

When Cuz first heard the shouting and clang of metal, he took it for another hallucination. When he smelled smoke, a new truth penetrated his private haze: death would come by fire. He'd read in the paper that death by fire was painless because flames burnt out a person's pain nerves before it killed him. But what did the paper-people know? They hadn't died, had they?

Cuz tried to stand. He hadn't had the strength for sitting since his ordeal began. All he did was breathe more smoke. Smoke made him cough. Coughing made him scream. Screaming pulled more smoke into his lungs.

There was movement in the tent. Someone tripped over his log-bound arm and came crashing down on his chest. He barely managed a groan. Death had arrived and death wasn't going to be painless. Death handled Cuz roughly, slashing the ropes, folding him into an awkward ball—bouncing him, jolting and dragging him out of the tent until he begged for an end to life.

"Bear your pain quietly," a man suggested with Hubcap's accent but not his tone. "It will end soon."

Cuz took that as both threat and promise until he heard the sounds horses made. The voice lifted him up like a sack of stones and set him down the same way, with a ridge of saddle leather pressing the length of his breastbone. Then came a blanket, thoroughly but not cruelly tucked around him, and an arm, not ropes, to keep him in place. Cuz warned himself against trust: Diras had been kind—kinder—and had left him to starve.

"We must run through the shadows. You won't feel anything."

The voice spoke the truth. After the first shadow, Cuz was unconscious.

He came to with a bandage wrapped over his eyes and nothing else to restrain him—nothing except a pair of hands racing over his face. Cuz batted them aside. He heard two gasps. The first was his own; his fever had broken, but the aches were far from gone, though his eyes had ceased burning. The second was softer and followed by footsteps. A moment later a woman was calling out in the noisy goblin language.

Wasting no time—there'd only be one chance to escape, if there was going to be any chance at all—Cuz tore the cloth from his eyes. He was, as he'd expected, in a black-domed tent with daylight seeping through the seams. Against expectation, he lay on a plush carpet and was warmed by a fleece blanket. Beyond the blanket, Cuz saw no ropes, no log, only a low stool where his keeper, presumably, had sat, and a basket of prunish fruits. His circumstances had clearly changed, and the wiser portion of Cuz's nature advised him to not to bolt, but he'd never counted himself among the wise.

Cuz threw back the fleece and froze. His hand . . . his maimed hand wasn't merely missing part of a finger, it was dark . . . dark blue . . . bruised, midnight blue, like a goblin's.

"I'm blue!" Cuz would have shouted if he'd had any air in his chest. As it was, he could barely hear himself.

When the tent flap swung away and sunlight revealed his transformation in all its glory, Cuz's voice failed entirely.

"I imagine it's a shock."

Cuz recognized the voice of the goblin who'd freed him from the log and gotten him out of Hubcap's tent. "I'm *fucking* blue!" he exclaimed as his own voice returned. "I've turned into a fucking goblin!"

"The Uylma agrees," the goblin said as he sat. His weight left the stool creaking and sinking into the ground.

"What the fuck happened to me?"

"We can only guess. You must have been hurt when you were brought through shadow. That finger, most likely. Jerlayne said you claimed a man—one of us—as your father; Aulaudin said you must have had an elf for a grandfather. Though you were born mortal, there was immortality in your blood. When she healed you, she may have awakened your father's blood. When you passed through shadow, shadow knew you and marked you as it marks all men who pass through it. When Uylma regains the nafoga'ar she will ask the gods. Perhaps this has happened before; I doubt it."

Cuz made a dark blue fist and brought his other hand into the light. It was blue, as were his arms and what he could see of his chest. His fingernails—those he had left—were black. He was just as glad there were no mirrors lying around; he didn't want to see his teeth or eyes.

He didn't want to think about what had happened to him at all and asked, "You know Jerlayne and Aulaudin?" instead.

"I am sworn to Goro at Sunrise. After Jerlayne healed me . . . after we learned of you and that you had disappeared, he sent me to tell Uylma. Uylma guessed where you were and sent me to bring you here to her."

"Why?"

"I'm sworn to the Uylma. We're all sworn to her. We do what she tells us to do—or she'll send us to join our ancestors. You'll learn."

"No! Why this?" Cuz held out his hand. "Why am I a goblin? Why do I look like you?"

The seated goblin shrugged. "The shadows have marked us that way from the beginning." Another shrug. "It sears some more quickly than others. You were as you are when we arrived here at dawn."

"Dawn? I've been here less than a day?"

"The gennern gave you *pokorshi*. It dulls pain—among other things. A man lives fast on pokorshi. Perhaps that is why you were seared so quickly. I will ask Uylma."

"Will it go away?"

The goblin laughed. "In a hundred years—if you never enter the shadows again!"

Cuz folded his arms, tucking his hands beneath them. He could see nothing of himself then, but the deepest changes—if the goblin were telling him the truth—weren't the obvious ones: he'd lost his mortality, his humanity. Uncle Ted would bust a gut. Ol' Uncle Ted had been looking for a cure for AIDS but he'd wound up shoving his worthless nephew down the path to immortality instead.

No, that couldn't be right . . . Theodore Alfred Kennicut wasn't interested in curing AIDS, wasn't interested in doing any damn thing for *humanity*. Theodore Alfred Kennicut had known about immortality. Maybe he'd tried to steal it from Cuz's goblin father. Maybe that was the real reason Cuz's father had never returned. And that left Uncle Ted with a half-breed nephew. He'd had to wait and see just how much immortality Cuz had inherited . . .

Now *that,* knowing Uncle Ted the way Cuz did, made sense.

"When can I leave?" Cuz asked. He unfolded his arms, threw aside the fleece. It wouldn't be easy to go home and have it out with Uncle Ted. For starters, Cuz looked like he'd escaped from a low-budget movie. "I've got some business to take care of back home in the so-called mortal realm."

Before the seated goblin could answer, a woman entered the tent: a goblin woman.

She had the same features as the seated man, Hubcap, Goro, and every other goblin. Her hair was the same glossy black, but her skin was normal, even pale; ditto her eyes, teeth, and fingernails. The seated man stood instantly and chattered in goblin-speak, repeating everything he and Cuz had said, no doubt.

While that was going on, a third goblin entered the tent. Another woman, she looked liked all the rest, except for her eyes. Diras had usually worn a patch over his no-good eye, like a pirate. This woman's eyes were scarred, empty pits in her face. When she came toward him, Cuz flinched, then steeled himself to be touched. The way he'd changed, he'd lost the right to cringe. Her fingers read his face gently, lingering over his eyes.

The other two had finished their conversation.

"Uylma wishes to question you. Uylma doesn't speak the languages of Fairie or the mortal realm; she is Uylma and it would not be fitting. She tells me to speak to you for her, and to her for you. But before we begin, she asks if you are comfortable and offers to answer any question you may have. We are not gennern."

Whatever the hell gennern was.

Cuz had a million questions. He asked the first, "When can I go home?"

The simple, five-word question produced several exchanges of goblin noise before the man said: "Uylma answers that you are home. She saved your life; it belongs to her. You are one of us now. She understands that you do not know what this means and she will make allowances while you learn. I add, speaking for myself, with her permission, that among us, no man serves himself. This may prove difficult for you—elves say mortals have no notion of service, and elves are troublesome enough—but it is a lesson you must master. And you cannot 'take care of business' in the mortal realm. Your former home is lost to you, not because Uylma commands it, but because you will wither and die if you part the Veil beyond Fairie. You are one of us now, and death waits for you beyond the mist."

"You're saying there's some kind of goblin curse and I've got it?"

The man didn't answer, not aloud, but his chin dipped a notch or two and Cuz had been pretty sure of the answer before he'd opened his mouth. Another possibility with his father: maybe the guy had gotten trapped in the real world and died there. If Cuz's father was dead, Cuz bet his Uncle Ted knew about that, too.

There'd be justice or vengeance. Goblin curses or no, there would have to be.

Uylma was talking. The man translated: "What do you know of your father?"

Chapter 32

Evoni's third siren storm in as many days had caught Sunrise by surprise. With the siren sitting on her rocks after the end of the second storm, Aulaudin had gone down to the beach assessing damage to the boat with the Wavehomers and to the salt pits with Petrin. He'd sensed the wind change and had sent the scyldrin running for high ground, but he'd lingered on the sand. The tide went from nearly high to dead low between two waves. Black water leapt around the rocks where moments earlier his daughter had been swimming.

Aulaudin watched in awe as the water became a soaring pillar that spewed clouds. Within moments, the entire sky was dark, the tide roared back to the shore, and Aulaudin raced up the swaying stairway. Evoni's wind blew Aulaudin toward the great house, or he'd surely have been pushed over the bluff and killed.

In a handful of frantic moments Aulaudin watched his home take more damage than it had taken in the two previous storms combined. He threw himself in with a pair of dwarves and a goblin who struggled to close and lash as many shutters as they could reach. The were wrestling with one of the bracing timbers when a spinning wind tore it free. Aulaudin landed on his back, stunned but otherwise unharmed. The goblin and one of the dwarves were standing before he was; the second dwarf hadn't been so lucky. Conscious, but not coherent, he rolled on the grass, screaming and bleeding from a head wound.

While one dwarf tended the other, Aulaudin cast his thoughts out for Jerlayne and wrapped his arms around the bracing timber again. There was no sense in carrying the injured dwarf inside if inside were no safer than outside. The goblin, though, probably could have done the job alone. He certainly had no trouble carrying the injured dwarf.

Jerlayne hadn't answered Aulaudin's call, nor was she wait-

ing in the kitchen where they brought the dwarf. He'd have
been more surprised if she had been. The effects of Evoni's last
song storm hadn't entirely disappeared before this one began.

From the way the injured dwarf fought free of the goblin—
both of the dwarves he'd tried to help had come from
Stonewell with Jerlayne's mother; Aulaudin didn't know their
names—he was healthier than the timber that fell on him.
Aulaudin didn't know the goblins' name either. He pointed at
the blue-skinned man then toward the door. The goblin nodded
and started moving.

Goblins weren't friendly and Aulaudin still didn't like them
much, individually or as a group, but since the crisis had begun, he couldn't fault their efforts on Sunrise's behalf.

They were in the howling wind when Gelma attached herself to Aulaudin's arm. The gnome's place was in Laydin's
nursery. Her appearance anywhere else always got Aulaudin's
attention.

"The Mistress *left* with the other one!" Gelma shouted over
Evoni's shrieks.

"Inside!" Aulaudin shouted to her and the goblin together.

Gelma was only too glad to obey, but the goblin shook his
head. He pointed at three other goblins already headed toward
the barn which surely needed all the help it could get. Aulaudin
clapped the goblin on the shoulder, as he would have encouraged a scyld or another elf. His hand struck mail, not cloth—a
reminder that they were never unarmed, never unarmored, and
he could be making the biggest mistake of his life in letting
them into his home.

Inside the kitchen, Gelma told him that she'd heard Jerlayne
and her sister arguing as the storm began. There'd been a loud
crash in their room, which she'd taken for a shutter slamming
into the walls. Then, once she'd seen to Laydin and Mati—and
left Laydin in the *temporary* care of Mati's nurse, Gelma gone
to check on her mistress.

"The shutters were closed tight—shaped!—but the room
was empty. She and that sister of hers were gone—gone
through the Veil, if you ask me. I never liked that Maialene, not
a bit. Fate be kind to us all, but Banda warned me about her.
She's drug the mistress off someplace. There's blood marks all
over the wall."

Aulaudin couldn't say that he liked Maialene either, especially since her return from the mortal realm where she'd

obviously been living since the sea came to Sunrise, but he
hadn't suspected her of violence—at least not violence toward
Jerlayne. Perhaps he should have paid more attention to those
bits of shiny steel she'd shaped into her face. Dreading bloodstains, Aulaudin followed Gelma to the darkened room where
Elmeene was waiting for them, flashlight beam weaving
wildly from her hand.

"What do they mean?" Jerlayne's mother demanded before
Aulaudin got a clear look at the marked walls. "What made
them? Goblins moving through shadows? The enemy that the
siren is fighting?"

The marks, though not hard to see between the flashlight and
lightning flashes, were beyond Aulaudin's skill as a reader.

"Find my father," he told Gelma.

"What are they? What do they mean?" Elmeene repeated.
She waved it around the room. "What do they have to do with
my daughters?"

Aulaudin reminded himself that his wife's mother had lost
her homestead, her bachelor sons, and that her husband was
still somewhere between Stonewell and Sunrise. "The marks
are writing, such as mortals make—"

"Mortals! I knew it! I warned her that young man wasn't
suitable! If he's harmed her or Maialene—"

"If he has, we'll *all* see him punished—"

"Punished! I want him killed!"

Privately, Aulaudin didn't think Cuz had anything to do with
the wall markings. Elmeene's wild handling of the flashlight's
beam had revealed a red candle lying on the floor, the same
dark red as the marks on the wall. Though the candle's wick
was unburnt, the wax had been partially melted. That bespoke
shaping to Aulaudin and since Jerlayne, so far as he knew,
could neither read nor write, that meant Maialene had written
the message.

But what had Maialene written?

Aulaudin waited until Gelma led Maun and a crowd that included Goro and several scyldrin into the room. Elmeene surrendered the flashlight.

"Can you read it?" Aulaudin asked. "I think Maialene
wrote it."

Maun made light circles around a small portion of the message. "If she didn't, then someone signed her name for her."

"What's written, Maun?" Elmeene asked. "What's happened to my daughters?"

"They've gone to the mortal realm. Maialene says here," he circled another part, "that she knows where the mortal end of Evoni's fight is and that she and Jerlayne have gone to finish it."

Elmeene took the flashlight from Maun's hand. "Impossible. Jerlayne would never be so foolish."

"Jerlayne takes risks," Goro said. "She'd go with her sister if she thought there was any chance that sister was right."

Reluctantly, Aulaudin agreed with the goblin. "Is there anything written about where in the mortal realm they went?" Not that he or any man could follow them until the storm ended.

"Nothing at all. I'd call the whole thing a compromise: Jerlayne wanted to leave a message but couldn't write it. M'lene wanted her sister's cooperation and no interference from us. She's not fond of men, you know."

"So we wait," Aulaudin concluded.

"We wait," Maun agreed. "We wait while the siren shrieks, while women finish fights in the mortal realm, and for our guests to arrive. I've always found that waiting's best with wine or beer. What have you got in that cellar of yours, son?"

"Cider," Aulaudin replied, as bald a lie as he'd told in many months. When Maun's indignation flooded his mind, he shot back, «I'd like you sober when the sages get here, otherwise I'm going to have to rely on the goblin for good sense.»

They'd barely gotten the bung out of the cider barrel when an ear-numbing peal of thunder rattled the walls. Maun made another silent plea for beer. Aulaudin stood firm. A night alone with Maun, Elmeene, Goro, and two-score anxious scyldrin was bound to be a long night, but Aulaudin would have faced it more calmly if his inner senses weren't wound tight, waiting for trouble from the Veil as well.

Midnight found the barrel nearly empty and most everyone still awake. The sky was black as a goblins' eyes between lightning bolts. The storm had subsided, but not completely. Evoni wasn't taking any chances, this time. Goro fretted that it was too windy still to post his goblins on the rooftops, but calm enough for a man to walk the shadows. The gennern, as he called his enemies, wouldn't have been content with a mortal.

"If they knew he was a mortal," Maun interrupted. "Would they know that, goblin? I'd know the moment I hailed him and got nothing in reply, not even the hollow I get from the likes of you. But *how* would a goblin know a pale-faced man wasn't an orphan elf?"

When he was sober, there wasn't a sharper man in Fairie than Aulaudin's father, but he gave some credit to the goblin. Goro listened to Maun's questions, but never seized his bait.

"Only by mistake," the goblin conceded after a moment's thought. "Right now, right here, even the shadows are disturbed. If a mortal man were quick-witted enough to pretend to be an elf, I would be hard-pressed to prove he wasn't. Though, on a night like this, I might mistake an immortal elf who couldn't part the Veil for a mortal and kill him anyway."

Well, Goro *almost* never took Maun's bait.

"Would goblins kidnap an elf?" Aulaudin asked before the tension thickened further.

"If I saw men like myself between walls and an elf wandering loose, I would take him and question him. A little *pokorshi* would loosen his tongue and keep him from escaping through the Veil."

"*Pokorshi?*" Aulaudin, Maun, and Elmeene asked together.

"You call it goblin wine. We use it for many things, the least of which is getting drunk."

"I like you less each time you open your mouth," Maun complained.

"I can tell you the truth no other way," Goro said with a broad, black smile. He seemed to understand that Maun's complaints were not the best way to judge Maun.

"Another thing: I can think of no way to prove that Cuz's father was a goblin. I'm not sure I *can* be convinced. Whenever men like myself have found a path through the shadows that leads to the mortal realm, they've died for their efforts. Even if they lived long enough to return to the plains, they still died; there's no healing what the mortal realm does to a man marked by shadow—"

Aulaudin's breath caught in his throat. He asked himself if he'd heard correctly and decided that he had. For generations, elves had asked the wrong question: Can goblins part the Veil? They'd gotten honest answers, but not the truth. The important questions were: How often did goblins visit the mortal realm and what did they do while they were there? Someday, he'd get those answers from Goro, but possibly not today as the goblin followed another thought.

"We made elves to keep track of our mortal enemies," Goro explained. "But there have always been men—goblins—who would rather there were no elves. Men who would like to forage iron for themselves. The death we fear is not blooddeath.

"If the gennern came to believe that a man—a goblin— fathered Cuz, they'd be very interested and if they learn that Cuz himself has an immortal son, they will want to know what kind of son he is: goblin or elf? Can he walk the shadows, or does he part the Veil?"

The goblin's question was one more provocation than Aulaudin could bear. He took a meaningful stride in Goro's direction. "My son is an elf! My fathers and brothers and I listened the night he was born. We shared his thoughts, his joy of life. No goblin can do that."

Goro didn't argue, except to say: "The first elves, Aulaudin, the *true* elves were the immortal children borne of mortal women and men like myself. Their true children were gnomes, dwarves, and everything else that is born in Fairie. You don't breed true. You are not the son of *elves*. You are the child of an immortal woman and a mortal father, and you call yourself an elf. But if Cuz's father was a shadow-walking man, then he is more elf than you, for all that he was born a mortal. If his son with Jerlayne is an elf, then that is the first time two elves have bred true."

Aulaudin was still groping for words when his mind resounded with sharing. Gudwal, Ertinel, Arlesken, and Rintidas had broken through Evoni's chaos.

"They're here," Maun announced. "Our sages have arrived."

Gelma and the scyldrin had begun leaving before Maun finished his announcement. They raised their voices as they hurried through the corridors, summoning one and all to the foundation stone. Elves respected the five sages as their living history, but the scyldrin cherished them. And the sages cherished the scyldrin, too. Even Gudwal would hardly be pleased by the disorder Sunrise had brought to sensible scyldrin lives.

It was a small insight, a small disillusion, but it kept Aulaudin in the dark room long enough to see Elmeene tug on Maun's sleeve and hear her whisper: "Jereige?"

Maun shook his head, then took her hand between his and led her from the room. The way they looked at each other as they walked out, another man could almost believe they were joined—but some truths remained beyond challenge. At least Aulaudin hoped they did. He was on his way out when he noticed Goro from the corner of his eye. The goblin was, as goblins could so easily be, barely visible in the shadows.

"Have *you* been to the mortal realm?" Aulaudin demanded.

Goro shrugged and confessed. "If, when I was younger, my mother had believed the path could be found, she would have sent me to the mortal realm, I think, not here."

"But goblins do visit the mortal realm, even if it kills them?"

Another shrug. "If we do not visit the mortal realm, then the gennern get their guns and armor from elves. Which do *you* prefer to believe, Aulaudin? As for the other—I could be wrong about that, too. But I have seen the death of a man who got lost in the shadows. He seemed glad enough to be alive when we found him. Less than a day later, he burst open like rotten fruit." Goro smiled and added: "I'll never forget the smell."

"You can't scare me off, Goro," Aulaudin countered. "We're going to finish this conversation. You're going to tell me everything you goblins have kept to yourselves. You owe me that much. You owe Jerlayne."

"I can try, Aulaudin, but I wonder if we can finish anything. Together, we don't have all the questions. We could share everything we know and still be at the beginning."

Not for the first time, the goblin's words echoed Aulaudin's private thoughts. "But I'd know more than I know right now. Come on, I agree with my father: I feel better when you're standing where I can see you."

The goblin became indignant. "I am not your enemy, Aulaudin. We should not be gennern to each other."

"It's a sad day, isn't it, when a man trusts the goblin who betrayed him more than he trusts his own living ancestors." Aulaudin swept an arm forward, to indicate that he wanted Goro to go first.

Goro hesitated. "My kind made two great mistakes: we forgot that all of us were mortal once and we've let ourselves believe that men are unimportant."

"We can finish *that* conversation later, too."

"There is nothing to finish," Goro countered, but he walked ahead and, despite Aulaudin's best efforts, disappeared into shadow.

Sunrise was awash with shadows. Evoni kept the clouds

simmering like a soup pot. Conversation was possible and—obviously—the sages had parted the Veil, but she wasn't making the mistake she'd made the other night when she'd returned to her rocks and let the stars shine. Aulaudin wondered how long she could sing, how long any of them could abide the anger overhead.

The sages were on the path to the foundation stone, escorted by a handful of the eldest scyldrin. Aulaudin was surprised that there were only four of them. He hadn't expected to sense Claideris parting the Veil—he'd never sensed her before or he and every other man would have suspected what women could do—but he'd expected to see her noxious pipe and black hair.

Maun and Elmeene were already at the foundation stone. They stood politely and properly to one side, leaving ample space for Aulaudin to greet the sages as master of Sunrise. He'd have loved to know what his father made of Claideris' absence, but it was considered improper for men to exchange private thoughts before the sages had been welcomed.

Aulaudin asked Goro instead. The goblin had emerged from behind the foundation stone well just as Aulaudin arrived in front of it.

"My men are prepared for anything."

That was probably as good an answer as any, though not one to set any man's heart at ease.

Nor was Aulaudin heartened when Gudwal wouldn't meet his eyes as they exchanged the traditional embrace.

"There has been much turmoil here at Sunrise," Gudwal said sternly, keeping his grip on Aulaudin's elbows. "You have forgotten who you are and what it means to be an elf in Fairie."

Chastisement and shame swirled in the notions Gudwal and the other sages spun around Aulaudin. If he'd doubted his wife's fidelity or his son's paternity, he should have come to them. They, not goblins, nor wives, were the keepers of Fairie's truth.

Aulaudin broke free and laughed his father's snorting, disdainful laugh. He'd begun with dread, which had turned to disappointment, and ended in contempt. "I have never doubted my wife's fidelity." He had never *doubted* it. Cuz and Goro had been utter surprises. "And I know exactly who the father of my son is." The mortal man, part goblin and part elf, named Cuz. "If you've come to Sunrise to set my mind at ease on those matters, then you've come a long way for a cold supper. But if you want to settle my mind about the second Veil, the Veil between Fairie and the goblin plains, I'm ready to listen. Or if you want to tell us what happened at Stonewell and why, there are those here who desperately need answers."

He almost felt sorry for Gudwal. The sage's discomfort was a palpable pressure against Aulaudin's mind. But the old elf pulled himself together; he looked Aulaudin straight in the eye and clasped his hand with the promise of truth.

"Your grief is understandable. This has happened before, and close to you. It is hard to accept, but Stonewell fell to ogres."

"My hind foot!" Elmeene exclaimed with a roar that Evoni might envy. "I was there. I survived! I watched my sons and scyldrin die. It wasn't *ogres* that killed them. It was *goblins*. *Goblins!* Do you hear me, Grandfather? There were no ogres at Stonewell!"

Rintidas intervened to grab Elmeene's arms as she lunged for Gudwal's throat. On any other day, Aulaudin would have been appalled by her behavior—and a good many of the scyldrin plainly were. This day, he waited to hear how Rintidas answered.

"Your eyes were seared by blood and confusion," Rintidas soothed, all compassion and lies. "You think you remember, Elmeene, but you don't. Not truly. Ogres overwhelmed your homestead. You feel pain, because you should have died. You blame your protectors, because it is natural to blame someone."

Aulaudin's heart skipped a beat. He didn't like the implications of that statement. It was bad enough when Maun said goblins wanted them dead, but to hear a sage say almost the same thing. If he'd been holding onto Elmeene, she would have broken free.

Rintidas continued: "That you saved yourself, your son, and a portion of your scyldrin is beyond belief, but for your heart's peace, you must face the awful truth: Ogres—the scourge of Fairie—are to blame."

Carnage loomed in Aulaudin's mind: Stonewell in flames, bodies everywhere, hacked apart and mutilated, and with the carnage, a single word whispered endlessly: *ogres, ogres, ogres*. He had no doubt that the same images battered Elmeene, though she, a woman, might not sense their source. Beside himself with disgust, Aulaudin seized two fistfuls of Rintidas' bleached-white tunic and spun him away from Jerlayne's mother, toward the bluff and the sea.

A dwarf caught the sage before he fell. Everyone was staring, glowering, at someone, mostly at Aulaudin. He might well have been on a mortal midden for all the distrust and threat in the air. Except, on a midden Aulaudin would have been alone. On the bluff beside the Sunrise foundation stone, he had allies: his father, Jerlayne's mother, an unknown number of goblins, and— Viljuen wept tears of joy—Jereige coming through the Veil with Aglaun, Ombrio, and what felt like half the men of Fairie behind him.

They'd broken through Evoni's simmering storm. The forests were alive with bursting light, and if the scyldrin didn't know what was happening around them, the sages surely did. Rintidas was as pale as his tunic. Gudwal's mouth was moving silently. Ertinel and Arlesken had the look of men who'd swallowed wasps. The moment fell just one image short of perfection: Jerlayne wasn't beside him to share it.

"You've embraced lies, Aulaudin." Gudwal made one last attempt to change Aulaudin's perceptions. "For Fairie's sake, embrace the truth."

The truth, according to Gudwal was ogres, not goblins, and the oddest part of the truth was that as hard as Gudwal clung to it and as fervently as he preached it, the sage didn't quite believe it himself, though he seemed to believe that terrible things would happen to Fairie if homestead elves and scyldrin believed anything else.

Aulaudin shared the assault and his conclusions with his father and Aglaun. Maun's presence had become wintry silence. Aglaun shared a livid memory: two dead goblins, each with his sword in the other.

«A mistake. An accident.» Gudwal's retort was more an explosion than sharing. «Embrace the truth before it's too late.»

Thoughts with edges weighed against Aulaudin's mind and the minds of his companions outside the Sunrise great house. Jereige and the mass of elfin men had stopped walking toward the foundation stone. Even the scyldrin were wide-eyed and breathing shallowly through their mouths. Like Evoni's song-storms, the sages had isolated Aulaudin within himself. They exerted subtle, yet potent pressure on the shapes in his memory. The two dead goblins in his mind's eye shimmered and grew pale.

Ogres . . . ogres . . . ogres . . .

"Lies!"

Maun shouted because sharing was impossible, unless it was the sharing of lies. He came forward from his place of polite respect and planted his hands on either side of Aulaudin's neck. Together they were stronger, not strong enough to fight back, but strong enough to stand.

"Too late for what, Gudwal?" Aulaudin demanded. "What happens if we don't *embrace* these *truths* you're forcing on us?"

Gudwal wouldn't answer, but Rintidas broke off the assault. "Fairie dies. For the love of everything you cherish, believe what we tell you is the truth. It's the only way: the bargain we all must keep. We must be careful, always careful. Our closest neighbors are out greatest enemies. We are surrounded by enemies."

"What enemies?" Maun asked.

"Ogres," Rintidas replied.

"Ogres are nonsense!" Maun thundered back. "Ogres never hurt anyone! Bring them out of the forests. Geld them, if that's the only way—we do it with the scyldrin. Put an end to this nonsense. Ogres never . . ."

Aulaudin let his thoughts drift away from Maun's blind arguments. He could do that now that Rintidas had withdrawn from the other sages. Jereige, too, was free and walking purposely toward the foundation stone; Elmeene ran toward him. Four sages was a battle. Three sages weren't nearly enough. Five sages . . .

If all five sages had come to Sunrise, he'd be a changed man, either believing in ogres or as mad and mocked as his father.

He interrupted Maun's tirade: "Where is Claideris?"

Maun wasn't listening to anyone but himself and everyone else listened to Maun, except for Rintidas, a sage who, like Claideris, circled mostly in the west and rarely came east. Rintidas heard Aulaudin's question and Rintidas' suddenly pale face hinted that the answer would be more than interesting.

"Where is she? Why isn't she here with you."

Rintidas glanced over his shoulder: the scyldrin remained transfixed, Jereige wasn't yet in earshot, but he would be very quickly, and all the elfin men behind him.

"You're not strong enough without her," Aulaudin reminded Rintidas. To think that he owed his mind's freedom to

Claideris! It was enough to make a man question everything he knew . . . and Aulaudin was doing just that. "Where is she?"

"Claideris abandoned us when the siren began her battle against the mortal realm. She entered the mist and has not returned."

Something in Rintidas' statement was sufficient to induce Gudwal, Arlesken, and Ertinel to inhale their assault. Their rigid faces bespoke betrayal and immense shame. Aulaudin sensed a subtle sharing among the sages. Its substance eluded him and there was no time to ask another question as Jereige thrust himself between Arlesken and Gudwal.

"There were no ogres at Stonewell," he said with evident disgust. "We were destroyed by our protectors, by *goblins!*"

Behind Aulaudin, Maun couldn't resist saying, "I tried to warn you. I tried to warn everyone: We're animals to them and they'll kill us all. It has taken an honest goblin and a courageous woman to prove me right. Elmeene of Stonewell has saved us before; her resourceful courage is no surprise. The goblin? An honest goblin is a traitor to his own kind. We were lucky. If any of you had listened, we could have been spared this."

Ertinel—tall and furious—turned on Maun. "Because of you, the peace of ages has been ruined. For your *proof* Fairie will never be the same . . . if it survives. You and your questions. You've spread doubt whenever you've open your mouth. No matter what we do, you will not believe us. You've brought a plague worse than blooddeath into Fairie."

"I was right! Right is right!"

"Right about what?" Ertinel shouted back. "When we went to the mists to hear the truth about this rising here at Sunrise and the destruction at Stonewell, the voices were silent. Our own dead turned away from us because you have offended our protectors. Goblins fight among themselves now, because of you."

A chill wind passed in front of Aulaudin; Goro appeared beside him, sword drawn and pointed at Ertinel's naked throat.

"What ghost told you that, Ertinel? We fought everyone and ourselves before you were born and we'll keep fighting after you're dead. An elf—you, Maun, or anyone—can no more offend us than a flea offends the dog. When a flea offends a dog, the dog doesn't fight with other dogs, the dog kills the flea! You are chattel! All of you—sages, elves, and scyldrin alike.

We protect you because out of your sorry loins come the guardians, and we *need* the guardians because the mortals were *our* enemies long before the first elf was born.

"I swear by my god: that is what I was taught and if I had never listened to Maun—if I thought you were the cleverest elf in Fairie, then I would never have doubted what I'd learned."

Aulaudin wasn't surprised that the goblin knew Ertinel's name; he wouldn't have been surprised, either, if Goro plunged his sword into the sage's neck. He'd had that view of Goro's extended arm before. Ertinel was plainly terrified beyond speech and the other sages weren't much calmer. Whatever they knew of goblins fighting, it didn't include personal confrontation. Aulaudin could have put a restraining hand on Goro's steady arm; he thought he could presume as much with a man who wasn't his enemy, but he got a coldly satisfying pleasure from watching the sages squirm and, anyway, there were elves clamoring for his attention.

«Does he speak the truth?» Jereige wanted to know. A score of men echoed that question while others asked, «Who is he?» and «Can he be trusted?» Aulaudin answered «Yes,» to the first and the last and, after a moment's hesitation, «A friend of Sunrise,» to the middle.

That opened the floodgates. With voice and thought, every elf wanted his questions answered immediately. Aulaudin remembered their confusion, their outrage; he'd endured it only a few days ago. But so much had happened since then, and he quickly lost patience with everyone.

It was just the opposite with his father. After centuries of mockery, Maun was the man everyone wanted to hear. And he had something to say to everyone, though he listened, too, and had a knack for rephrasing both questions and answers that gradually convinced the majority of elves and scyldrin that they agreed with one another.

The sun set. Vigilance spread images of the unprecedented gathering to the farthest homestead. No man wanted to be left out. No woman, either, if the echoes were any measure of exchanges that could not be directly shared. Aulaudin withdrew, wishing for and worried about his wife. The scyldrin of Sunrise demanded a voice in the otherwise silent debate. They wanted everything to stop until the scyldrin of every homestead were represented on the Sunrise bluff.

Elfin men could always retire through the Veil to their own

homesteads at the end of the day, but feeding and sheltering that many scyldrin would be a major undertaking for any homestead. For Sunrise, in its storm-wracked disarray, Aulaudin judged it impossible, though he'd been raised to do—or try to do—whatever the scyldrin wanted. It fell to Maun, the man who raised him, to thrash out a compromise: a circuit of bachelors escorting scyldrin across Fairie. Sunrise today, Wavehome—where the other siren was the nearest guardian—tomorrow, Tenwoods, the day after.

"Be patient," Maun counseled as lightning chased its tail through the night clouds. "We've never done anything like this before. It will take time—but it won't be as bad as iron was."

Aulaudin couldn't help but notice that his father didn't suggest that *Briary* stand host to a horde of debating scyldrin. "My father's become a politician," he mused aloud.

From the middle of shadow, Goro said, "I do not know that word."

"Keep watching, you'll learn," Aulaudin replied when his heart was beating again. He hadn't noticed the goblin lower or sheathe his sword. With Maun holding everyone's attention, Goro had simply disappeared.

"Can you see each other when you're hiding like that, in plain sight?"

The goblin grinned, which apparently made him visible to others in the crowd. Suddenly there was agitation: pointed fingers, murmurs, and a few shouted accusations.

"Yes, I know there's a goblin behind me!" Maun shouted back. "There are two beside that tree and three more halfway up the hill."

Maun was right, of course. Once Aulaudin looked where his father pointed, he could see what his father saw.

"Politician, you say. I won't let him out of *my* sight." Goro grinned wider. "The answer is: We all see what we expect to see. You're a very trusting man. Maun hasn't trusted anything since Tatterfall."

As night deepened, the sometimes rowdy debate made its way back to already-asked questions: Why had the sages—men they trusted and cherished—twisted the truth in their own minds and asked them to believe lies? And where was Claideris? The sages had no answers, at least not that they were willing to admit.

Standing near them, listening more than he'd been talking,

Aulaudin was aware that the four elfin elders had seldom been out of one another's minds. He thought they were divided among themselves, but canny enough to keep their disagreements hidden. And he supposed he didn't blame them: they weren't accustomed to disobedience, much less revolt.

Aulaudin had a new question: How many times had five sages together contrived to shape Fairie's collective thoughts? He shared it quickly with his father.

«Let that one rest a while, son. The answer to that will only break our hearts when we hear it and we've already stirred up enough trouble for one night. Let me send them back to their homes and off to bed. What we sow tonight we reap tomorrow.»

Aulaudin couldn't dispute that. The elves and scyldrin gathered at Sunrise's foundation stone would be talking throughout the night, but not at Sunrise. At least not the elves. They all departed, punching their way through the Veil in groups of five or more.

«Wavehome!» Maun shared after them. «High sun. Bring food.»

«You did get Helvert's permission?»

«Did anyone ask yours, son?»

Short of binding him to a tree or knocking him unconscious, it was difficult to stop a man from parting the Veil. The air around the foundation stone shimmered as the four sages prepared to part the Veil together.

"Go now and it's over," Maun said. "By tomorrow morning, every homestead in Fairie will have its own notion of what had already happened and what should happen next."

"You wanted this, Maun," the sage Arlesken countered bitterly. "You put yourself above everyone else. You're the one who has shattered Fairie with a single blow. We offered you truth and you refused it."

The shimmering stopped. The shadows were deep enough that anyone could have disappeared and the autumn breeze off the sea felt like winter to anyone not accustomed to it.

"You offered lies," Jereige said, more bitter than the sage. He'd stood quiet while Maun rode the ebb and flow of debate, joined with his wife, if their hands were any measure of their thoughts. "Elmeene *saw* the truth."

"A truth," Gudwal suggested, still the kind, calm grandfather they all thought they knew.

Jereige didn't want to follow Maun's path into the future. He'd shown that clearly the night Laydin was born. He'd risked Elmeene's love then; he'd lose it forever now, if he let the sages call her mistaken or a liar. Aulaudin didn't know Jereige well enough to guess what was most important to his life. He hoped it was Elmeene and he worried about his own wife. The Veil was roiled. It took at least two men to part it. Jerlayne had departed with her sister. Maialene had shaped all the foolery at Brightwings; Aulaudin didn't think she'd be as useful with the Veil.

Elmeene's voice, gravelly from grief and exhaustion, pulled Aulaudin out of his thoughts. "There's only one truth, Gudwal: goblins destroyed Stonewell. I don't understand why. My daughter's goblin here has tried to explain it to me, and I've tried not to listen. After what I saw—what I remember— I couldn't—didn't want to—believe anything he said. I've waited for you, all of you, because you're elves, you're like me, and I've always trusted you, especially you, Gudwal. And by the dust of the Veil, I've been as wrong as I could be, but if you'd *all* come to Sunrise trust wouldn't matter. By now I'd believe I'd seen an ogre cut down Nereige and I'd never know you'd blown your lies through my memories, would I? *Would I?*"

Elmeene was magnificent in her outrage and for what she'd done with iron, there were already those in Fairie who considered the mistress of Stonewell the sixth sage. Aulaudin didn't see how the four sages could deny her, but he didn't know—no one knew—how many times Fairie's sages had bent their memories around a false truth.

"Your son would still be dead, Elmeene," Gudwal countered, soft-spoken, yet intense. "Your homestead would still be a burnt-out ruin. Those are the truths and nothing can change that. But think about it—think *honestly* about it: wouldn't the truth lie more easily in your heart if you remembered ogres? Look at him," Gudwal kept his eyes on Elmeene while he pointed at Goro. "Fleas and chattel he calls us, tolerated because once in a very great while an elfin man and woman make a guardian between them. That's all they care about; all they've ever cared about: we are the breeding stock for the guardians of the plains, *their* plains. Fairie is nothing to them, we're nothing, except for the guardians . . . and the ogres. They don't want us fighting; we might rise up against them! So they fight the ogres for us; and they fight each other for the privilege."

Gudwal turned to face Goro. He wagged his finger derisively. "Don't swear by your god at us, Goro! We know who you are. We know what happened to your father . . . and to your mother. We watch and listen to you. The nafoga'ar mists are home to the elfin dead! We cannot defeat you, but we, we sages, we know your secrets. We keep one small step ahead of you."

"Viljuen wept, Elmeene." Gudwal turned back to face Elmeene, but his voice was loud enough that the farthest scyld could hear him. "Viljuen wept for shame when he saw what he'd done to his children. Since that first priestess appeared to him, we have been at their mercy, but they have no mercy. He was the first to enter the mists, to find the plains where goblins dwelt and when he'd found them, he summoned sages. He's told us the truth, and what we must do to keep Fairie. We never failed. For thirty thousand mortal years we never failed . . . until now, when Claideris did not return from the mist with Viljuen's instructions."

As he absorbed what Gudwal had said, the topmost thought in Aulaudin's mind was Goro's insistence that Viljuen was a goblin name.

Chapter 33

As the sages described their predicament, goblins had taken advantage of Viljuen's desperate invitation from the very beginning. Fairie's sages had no love for the goblins but, because they loved Fairie, they did what the goblins asked, or—better—they relied on ghostly spies. They staggered under unimaginable guilt—or so they said from comfortable chairs in Sunrise's best-preserved sun room. They'd never wanted to impose their will on other elves or the poor scyldrin; they'd had no choice.

"If every elf or scyld knew how the goblins regard us as little more than animals, that they trade us about like coins in a mortal market," Ertinel explained, "then the goblins would kill every elf and scyld. We propagated ignorance because the goblins wouldn't harm a homestead where everyone believed our own grandchildren were the enemy."

"In the mortal realm they have words for you, Ertinel," Maun said. "They'd call you collaborator because you did your enemy's dirty work and called yourself a hero. If you were lucky, they'd execute you cleanly. If you weren't lucky, you'd live longer than you wanted to."

"Nonsense, no one's a collaborator until the enemy is defeated! We're not fighters, Maun. If we walked out of here determined to get rid of the goblins, you know what would happen. You more than anyone else! When your enemy is beyond defeat . . ." Jereige's voice faded.

Jereige wanted to be on the familiar side—with the sages, not against them. But it was his homestead that the goblins had destroyed, his sons who had died. The master of Stonewell wasn't the most courageous man in Fairie, but he wasn't craven, either. The conflict in his mind was eating his heart.

Aulaudin rose from his chair, the chair nearest the door: he'd left the room before and left it again. His heart wasn't in another endless recitation and comparison of deeply held, partial truths. Gudwal had been a sage for three millennia, a forager for an earlier two, and Fairie had been old when Gudwal was born. They'd never untangle the past and shouldn't waste time trying to. They had better things to do; better things to worry about.

Jerlayne hadn't returned.

It was nearly dawn and the sky was golden. A six-year-old boy could part the Veil now, but Jerlayne hadn't. Evoni had returned to Sunrise Bay. Her song was a low murmur, like the waves. Aulaudin had to pay attention to hear it. Mostly he listened to other things, to the emptiness of the Veil. He hoped to hear Jerlayne calling him. She had to be in trouble somewhere in the vast mortal realm. And there was nothing he could do for her.

He entered the nursery, the darkest room in Sunrise. Priorities were different in the nursery. Goblins, sages, and Fairie's fate didn't matter here. Evandi, the Stonewell gnome who cared for Elmeene's son, didn't like the smell of the sea, especially at night. She'd decided it was wasn't healthy and in the midst of everything, she'd persuaded some dwarves to hammer thick blankets over the gaping windows.

An oil lamp glowed between the infants, between the nurses. Evandi slept on a pallet beside Mati's cradle. Gelma slept in a rocking chair, her ever-present knitting heaped in her lap. She'd be mortified if Aulaudin caught her sleeping, so he turned away and paced the corridor to Jerlayne's workroom.

"Now you know what Jerlayne went through when Sunrise was founded."

Aulaudin leapt backward from the unexpected sound, striking his elbow on the door's edge. His nerves overreacted, and the rest of him, too.

"Viljuen weeps—this is *her* room! What are you doing here?"

He heard soft footfalls. Once a man knew goblins walked through shadows, it *was* possible to hear them and see them.

"Waiting. You need a familiar place, yes? when you part the Veil. For Jerlayne, this must be her most familiar place."

Aulaudin had wanted to believe the same thing but, "She went to Stonewell when she got shot on the plains. There is no Stonewell now. She hasn't parted the Veil often. It's easy to get lost when your resting place isn't there. Think back to Ombrio."

Goro said nothing, which wasn't to say he hadn't listened or wasn't worried. Aulaudin wanted to hate the goblin; he had every reason, but lacked the will. No one else understood that there was a bleeding hole in his heart. He'd had to plead with Elmeene before she'd take him to the mortal-realm boltholes she'd and Jerlayne had used when Jerlayne found Cuz. It had been the first time an elfin man and woman had parted the Veil together.

Or maybe not. Now that he'd seen the sages fail to change the texture of memory, Aulaudin had freed himself from trust. He could see a goblin's moods. But he hadn't found Jerlayne. There'd been no trace of her at any of the boltholes.

"There's no point in standing here in the dark," he told Goro.

"There's no point in standing—or sitting—anywhere else. The dark is quiet. It doesn't chatter."

"You've given up on them, too?"

Goro made a soft noise, between a sigh and a laugh. "No, I could ask no better revenge against the gennern. Elves talking to each other, truly *talking* to each other . . . The sages exposed as our servants— No wonder the nafoga'ar is so important to my mother! The Uylma who controls the nafoga'ar controls Fairie! Word will spread. In a month, nothing will be the same, not here in Fairie nor among the men on the plains. But, I'm not a man and I'm not an elf. I'm an oath; the oath I swore to your wife. . ."

"If I had any notion where Jerlayne was, Goro, I'd part the Veil in a heartbeat."

"She left with her sister."

Aulaudin rubbed an elbow that no longer tingled. "That's not a reassuring thought."

"It wasn't intended—"

Aulaudin's attention fled from the goblin before he finished speaking as Maun's presence shouldered its way into his mind. «You'll be pleased to know we've made a decision. Rather than visit Wavehome, the sages are going to take us to the mists where they speak with the dead and where Claideris vanished. I knew they'd see reason. If you want to come, come quick.»

"Jerlayne?" Goro asked hopefully when Aulaudin brought his thoughts back to the workroom.

He shook his head. "Maun. The sages don't want to go to Wavehome. They're taking my father to the 'mists' to speak to the dead and find Claideris. I'm invited—"

"You'd be with all five sages? Don't go, Aulaudin. Men who meddle with your memory . . . not even the gennern can do that. They would, I'm sure, but meddling with memories seems to be something else only elves can do."

He would *not* defend the sages to a goblin, to this goblin. "We'll leave one or two behind, if Maun hasn't thought of it already. My father's far ahead of me in distrust and suspicion; he could see you standing behind a tree. Can I trust that you'll keep them here?"

"I'd give much for a jug of pokorshi, but a boot to the head will do just as well. Leave your brother behind, too."

"You don't trust Aglaun?" Aulaudin bristled. Whenever he began to forget who stood beside him, Goro would remind him why he'd never liked goblins.

Goro held out his hands. "If something happens here—if you're needed, he would find you quickly, wherever these 'mists' are. You elves don't appreciate what you've got. Sharing each other's thoughts, using the Veil the way you can; if you wanted to fight. . ."

"But we don't, do we? Jerlayne told me about goblins 'culling' their flocks of elves."

"Yes, we culled, Aulaudin, but we've given ourselves false glory. I didn't know what your sages could do, what they've been doing—and I would have. I was well-born, once. I grew up in the nafoga'ar."

"What does that—?" Aulaudin began, then stopped. "No, this is another discussion for later." He took a step across the workroom threshold. "I'm going with my father—if he hasn't already left. I'll suggest we leave every sage but Gudwal behind. And I'll ask Aglaun to stay behind."

Aulaudin felt a chill, subtle breeze. He knew the goblin had passed beside him, but that wasn't enough to keep his feet on the ground when Goro was suddenly *there* in front of his face.

"Be careful. If you find Claideris in the mist, don't let your guard down for a heartbeat."

"If you know something, Goro, tell me, otherwise, don't talk to me about beating hearts." His own wasn't beating regularly at that moment.

The goblin flattened against the corridor wall. "Call it a distrust of black-haired women. There's something about Claideris that makes me uneasy every time I've seen her. And now the mist where she's supposed to gone to speak with

Viljuen and not returned. I don't believe in ghosts, Aulaudin. Whoever the sages talk to, it's not Viljuen. And as for what happened to Claideris—" Goro sighed, as he often did before yielding up some new secret. "Yesterday, the sages said they knew what happened to my mother. Perhaps they lied, perhaps not. I will tell you: she was driven out of the nafoga'ar by the gennern—"

"I knew that much, Goro."

Another sigh. "She should not have been driven *out*. When one uylma deposes another at the nafoga'ar, the loser is driven *into* the mist. Even my mother, who fears nothing else, fears the mist. I don't believe in legends, Aulaudin, any more than I believe in ghosts, but by our legends, the land of Fairie was born when the nafoga'ar mist flowed into the mortal realm. I can imagine—I can just imagine that mist still flows from the plains to the mortal realm, with Fairie in between.

"If Joff were here, I'd send him through shadows to tell my mother what her son begins to suspect. But I sent Joff home the day Cuz was kidnapped, so I tell you instead: if Claideris is in the mist, then Claideris was once an uylma—*the* Uylma, as my mother was. Such women, Aulaudin, are not to be crossed by men. I might be wrong—I pray to Vachan that I am, but be careful."

"Do you want to come with us?" Aulaudin scarcely believed he'd made the offer.

"No, I want you to come back unharmed. Sunrise needs you as much as it needs Jerlayne."

In silence, Aulaudin eased past the goblin. He anticipated another subtle breeze, another nerve-jolting appearance, but none came. It wasn't that Aulaudin couldn't understand Goro. He had only to remember his brother and the larger pieces fell into place, but it was too early to think of Boraudin and the goblin together. Headed toward the mists where the sages hoped to find Claideris, probably, it was no time to be thinking about his slain brother.

Maun didn't need his tardy son to tell him five sages were two, perhaps three, too many, though he appreciated Goro's comment about pokorshi when Aulaudin shared it privately with him.

«If he weren't a damn goblin, I could grow fond of that Goro. I'd invite him to Briary and give him some of my best ale, but I'd never turn my back on him, son. Don't you, either. If push comes to shove, he'll side with his own ilk.»

«Absolutely,» Aulaudin agreed and kept the rest of his thoughts about the nature of men, elfin, goblin, and mortal alike, to himself.

There were five of them going to the mists: him and Maun, Gudwal and Arlesken, and Elmeene, who had decided that Claideris was responsible for all her grief and rage. Aglaun would have come and wasn't happy to be left behind, but bachelors did what their fathers and homesteading brothers told them to do. Ombrio, with no father, a renegade mother, and two brothers who wanted no part of him, stuck close to Aglaun. Jereige, who should have come, begged off. He'd been in the Veil too much; he was bone tired.

«I forget, sometimes,» Maun shared with Aulaudin as they filed out of the great house to begin their journey, «because I don't want to remember, that my friend was born before the blooddeath began. With Stonewell gone, I fear he'll wander into the forest and not come back out.»

Gudwal and Arlesken linked arms. Maun took Arlesken's free hand and Aulaudin took Maun's. There was an awkward moment when Elmeene reached for Gudwal's hand and he held it back. To a man, the four sages at Sunrise had insisted they'd never suspected that women could part the Veil. They were *shocked* to hear that elfin children had mortal fathers.

That had been the first time Aulaudin had walked out.

The air around them shimmered. Aulaudin's mind filled with the harsh touchstones of the mortal-realm Barrens. Though he strove to keep his own notions of the place to himself, Aulaudin was out of practice in the skills of parting the Veil with companions. The temptation to envision the ruddy rocks from his preferred angle proved irresistible and at the last moment he lost contact with his father's hand. Aulaudin's only consolation, as he picked himself up off the dusty ground, was that Maun had landed both harder and farther from the sages.

They regrouped and new touchstones flooded Aulaudin's mind: giant trees, luminous moss, and five starlit stones set in a rough circle: another man's touchstones and a part of Fairie that moved to different time!

Aulaudin made each touchstone image his own; he might want to come back. Aulaudin carefully remembered his initial impressions as they arrived, also. It was an old place, like the mortal-realm Barrens they'd just left. Very much alive and very much dead, the scents of decay pervaded the damp air. The ground was soft. He scooped up some of the dark, loose dirt. When he felt insects crawling across his palm, Aulaudin threw the compost down and swiped his hand rapidly against his trousers.

Maun laughed, though he'd done the same thing.

There wasn't any·mist, but parting the Veil dispelled mist; Aulaudin knew that from Tatterfall. And despite the presumed effect of five elves arriving together, mist returned quickly. It sank through the giant trees like midwinter snow: fine and glittering. Aulaudin committed it all to his memory until, standing at one end of the line of five, he couldn't see Elmeene on Gudwal's other side.

"What do we do now?" Maun asked aloud, so Elmeene wouldn't have to.

Gudwal answered: "We ask our questions, we call her name, and then we wait."

"Where is *that woman?*" Elmeene demanded.

"Silently! The dead don't have ears."

They did, though: ears, eyes, noses, and mouths. At least the dead man Aulaudin saw had ordinary and achingly familiar features. He told himself that what he saw was an illusion, one of the five upright stones tricked out in the mist. But faith was stronger than distrust when the face was Boraudin's.

*   *   *

Jerlayne had earned her splitting headache. Exhausted as she'd been after setting the bus ablaze, she'd have been better off hurling herself into the Veil than sitting beside her sister in a mortal realm car. She'd have been better off driving the car herself!

At least they had been somewhere in a place called New Jersey, although by the time M'lene figured out *where* in New Jersey, the car had sputtered and died like an oilless lamp. Bloodstained and ragged as they were, M'lene had said they could walk the rest of the way. By then the sun had risen behind charcoal clouds and the skies were shedding a fine, cold, late-autumn rain on their heads.

Shivering and miserable, Jerlayne had tried to part the Veil, but she was past exhaustion and there was nothing she could do except trudge behind her long-legged sister. Night had fallen before they'd entered a noxious, car-filled tunnel and it had been past midnight before Maialene fumbled her way through a trio of locks on a street-side door.

"Five flights up. Can you make it, kid? Dry clothes, a bed, blankets, the whole nine yards."

Jerlayne hadn't known what a mortal-realm flight was until she'd climbed up two of them. If she hadn't found a bed with nine yards of blankets, she sworn to herself that she'd have found the strength to *nuke* her sister. But the bed had been there, as promised, and Jerlayne had collapsed on it, wet clothes and all. She vaguely remembered M'lene asking if she wanted something to eat or drink, then oblivion had called Jerlayne's name and she'd answered it eagerly.

The room where she awakened reminded Jerlayne of Cuz's below-groundhome, though it was a dizzying height above the street and sidewalk. It reminded her of Brightwings, too, with a jumble of furniture and color. She could almost hear Cuz complaining about M'lene's "taste."

Cuz.

She had to return to Fairie where other crises awaited. She'd been gone a full day, at least, maybe more. M'lene's wall-writing would have created chaos long before now. Once her headache subsided, she'd leave. The Veil was calm, but her aching head kept her from parting it safely. Jerlayne couldn't heal herself, she'd tried. The merest shaping thought had sent her back to the rumpled bed where Maialene still sprawled in a thrashing, pallid sleep.

A water room opened near the bed. After a few false starts, Jerlayne got the bathtub filled with hot water. The steam soothed her aching head. She shed her bloody, singed clothes and put distance between who she was and what she'd done at the hillside bus.

Three mortals had died. She'd *nuked* them, or so M'lene said. *Nuked* was easier to say or think than killed, but changing the word didn't change what Jerlayne had done. Elves didn't kill; she'd never imagined that truth would prove to be as much a lie as the notion that women couldn't part the Veil.

Jerlayne left her clothes heaped on the water room floor where, except for their faded-flower colors, they were scarcely noticeable amid her sister's castoffs. Brightwings had been cluttered, but within her mortal-realm home, M'lene had achieved an astonishing level of disorder . . . and had completely abandoned Fairie's skirts and gowns. Clean or dirty, heaped on the floor or in a closet, every garment her sister owned was black, stretchy, and meant to fit over a woman's arms and legs like one of Gelma's knitted stockings.

The black sweaters weren't too bad. Living by the sea taught Jerlayne the virtues of sweaters. But the trousers—M'lene's clingy trousers reminded Jerlayne of Elmeene's skimpy red dress. She pulled them on with great hesitation and, in the end, pleasant surprise. She added the blue-green-bead-and-animal-claw necklace Maialene had foraged from the little house—unrelieved black left Jerlayne feeling a bit like a goblin—and beheld a stranger in the water room's mirror.

"Welcome to the twentieth century."

Red eyed and wild haired, M'lene had watched her dress from the doorway.

"You don't mind, do you? Mine were . . . I didn't want to wear them again."

"No. Go ahead. Take what you want; take everything. Cut off all that *hair* and get something pierced, an ear, at least. Poor Aulaudin won't know what hit him."

Jerlayne lost a battle with a blush. "I like my hair and a hole in my skin is something to be healed, but I'll keep the stockings."

"We'll scrounge up a pair that fits."

"Some other time. I had a headache when I awoke, but it's gone away since I bathed. I can part the Veil now and I have to go back to Sunrise. You don't have to come with me—I can see that you're happier here."

"You going to look for that punk father you found for Laydin? I really hadn't figured you for the boy-toy type."

Another blush followed by a sigh. "I'll talk to Goro when the dust settles. I don't suppose you recognized the goblins?"

Maialene brayed sarcastically. "Recognize goblins. I'd sooner recognize cockroaches. Watch out, your goblin's in love with you."

"Whatever made you think that?"

"How about you, just now, sounding like our mother? Or Cuz telling me about a conversation he overheard between your husband and your goblin? Or the way he looks at you when he's wrapped up in shadow and thinks he can't be seen?"

"It's not love. He can't go back to the plains, can't marry, can't have children, and doesn't have any family so he's put me at the center of his life. Did you ever raise orphan ducks or geese at Brightwings?"

"Jery, listen carefully: a goblin is not a duck."

"I have to go back," Jerlayne replied quickly. She wouldn't think about Goro. "Are you coming?"

"Yeah, give me a moment here. I'll help you search for Cuz. Fucking kid's more screwed up than I am."

"Now who's in love?"

"Sometimes, when you heal them, you get a sense of them that goes beyond words. Cuz . . . It's not love; I'm not interested in love, Jery. He could be a friend, a good friend, but he's mortal, Jery. I can handle them growing old and dying; it's they way they look at us when we don't that beats me down."

Jerlayne had no answer for that.

M'lene pushed buttons on a tiny box and a brown-skinned woman's head appeared in the window side of another, larger, box. *Television.* Maialene had used the word before to describe what the bus had told her about itself and Aulaudin had told her about the picture-window boxes mortals kept in almost every room of their homes. Her sister pressed more buttons and the pictures changed in dizzying succession, until the brown-skinned woman once again filled the window.

"Local news," M'lene explained. "Maybe they'll say something about what we did last night."

Jerlayne nodded and, with thoughts of fleece and feathers to dull the noise, sat transfixed by the flickering images. She scarcely noticed when Maialene sat down beside her.

"You'll get used to it—well, you probably will. Some mortals never turn it off."

They waited until Jerlayne was more than ready to chase the talking woman and all her strange companions away. She was ready to part the Veil and leave her sister behind when a dreadfully recognizable picture flashed in the window.

"Ha!" M'lene shouted as Jeralyne struggled to hear the window words. "I told you it was from a television station. The thing's been missing since last week. Missing—not reported stolen. Good for us!"

"Good for us?" Jerlayne repeated, mystified, as usual, by the ways of the mortal realm.

"Look whatever that bus was doing in the woods where we

found it, it didn't belong there. Whoever owns it, though, didn't tell the police it was missing—"

"Cuz's uncle?"

M'lene wrinkled her nose, "The mortal realm's a strange place, but they'd probably get upset if they thought close-kin were locking each other up. 'Course, they'd be more interested if they thought one of them was immortal—or, almost immortal. And that surveillance tape of you—it could get nasty. But, this place is *strange*. All kinds of mortals believe in aliens and angels—"

"What are *aliens* and *angels?*"

"Not us. That's the important thing. Nobody believes in elves. Nobody would believe anyone who said they'd stolen a television station bus to search for Fairie and elves. And look at that thing! Burnt right down to the ground. They'll never figure it out. We're safe. Fairie's safe. Cuz is safe—if we can get him back from the damned goblins."

Jerlayne was less optimistic. "Are there many television station buses like that one? If Cuz's uncle owned one, maybe he owns more—"

"Then we'll come back and unshape it. Better, we'll talk to Maun. If anyone on *our* side of the Veil knows what's inside a television station bus and how it could rile Evoni, Maun will."

M'lene pushed buttons, the window darkened with a *snap!* and a flash that left Jerlayne blinking.

"Well, are you coming? You've been saying how much you want to go home."

Jerlayne swallowed a sigh and stood up.

Aulaudin had explained the inherent dangers of parting the Veil in or out of a closed space to Jerlayne. He'd promised to show her the safer ways that men used, but they hadn't had an opportunity for lessons and Maialene insisted they were less exposed in her one-room home than they'd be in any alley or park. So Maialene got them out of the mortal-realm city and Jerlayne brought them into Fairie at the Sunrise foundation stone—the only outdoor place she could imagine with sufficient detail.

It was the middle of the night in Fairie and though she knew their arrival would have been preceded by a flash of light, Jerlayne hoped she and M'lene could slip unnoticed into the great house. They hadn't taken a dozen steps away from the stone when a pair of sword-bearing goblins blocked their path.

M'lene shouted, "Run!" and took her own advice.

The goblins hesitated a moment longer before sheathing their weapons. "Didn't recognize you, Jerlayne. Sorry," one of them said, gesturing awkwardly at her borrowed clothing. "The house will be relieved to know you're home safe."

Another goblin had wrestled M'lene to the ground. Maialene got the last word, and shin kick, before identities got properly sorted out.

"Bastards," M'lene muttered as the two women continued along the path. "Who do they think they are?"

"The protectors of Sunrise. Dressed like this, you can't blame them for not knowing who we are."

"That's no excuse. They should've asked before attacking."

"You ran, M'lene. It's quiet. Do you notice how quiet it is? I can scarcely hear Evoni singing. We did it—you did it, actually: you were right about the source of the attack, and right about how to stop it."

"Yeah, well, no one's perfect. Even I've got to be right sometimes."

The high door was still battened shut and a corner of the porch had collapsed. The last attack—the attack she and Maialene had stopped—had done the most damage. Their goblin escort led the sisters to an open window where Goro, but no Aulaudin, waited for them. Mindful of her sister's all-too-accurate observations, Jerlayne was careful not to get too close to her goblin or look up into his eyes. It was easy to do: Once Jerlayne saw her father she saw nothing else.

While M'lene told the others what they had done, Jerlayne knelt beside her father's chair. The loss of their home had, understandably, changed both her parents. Elmeene's grief burned; it hurt everyone she touched and would, in the end, make them all stronger. Beyond doubt, Jerlayne foresaw her mother's life continuing. Her father's grief was a smaller, quieter thing that seemed trapped within his heart. It was devouring him from the inside. Already Jereige had shrunken. His eyes faded and his skin had a translucent glow.

Elves did die, not of age or disease, nor usually through accident. Elves died when they lost the will to live. The Fairie saying was that they went into the forest . . . where the dead were said to dwell. Elmeene had explained it long ago, before Jerlayne's shaping lessons had truly begun. As a child, she'd imagined a festival, with the elder elves dressed in their finest traveling clothes, embarking on an endless journey with music and goblin wine to see them off. Like so many of her childhood fantasies, it had completely missed the truth.

She took Jereige's hands between her own. There was nothing that shaping or healing could do for him.

"Father—Father, I love you." Those were the only words she found worth uttering.

Elmeene should be here beside her husband, anchoring him and filling his empty thoughts with hope. But her mother, Jerlayne overheard Goro tell Maialene, was at the misty place with Gudwal, another sage, Aulaudin, and Maun. They were, for reasons Jerlayne didn't overhear or the goblin didn't relate, looking for Claideris. They'd been gone two days and everyone was frantic. Jerlayne didn't want to ask how long she and M'lene had been gone and adding to the worry. Goro said that Aglaun and Ombrio, who'd stayed behind, were lying at Vigilance.

Jerlayne could believe that Elmeene had left her father at Sunrise. Fragile as he was, Jereige might have vanished altogether in any mist. Still, Jereige needed someone. Never mind that Jerlayne had tried to wall him out of her heart when Laydin was born, only a few months ago. Memories of that night belonged to a different lifetime. As she knelt beside him, Jerlayne put her arms around Jereige. She held his head tight against her heart and curled around him, resting her cheek on his hair, dampening it with silent tears.

Jereige touched her arm, squeezed it lightly.

Considerable time passed before any part of Jerlayne's awareness spun back to the Sunrise room where other sleep-disheveled elves had assembled: two sages, Ertinel and a man whose name she'd forgotten; Aulaudin's brother, Aglaun; and Ombrio. The reunion of mother and son, the first since Evoni had risen over a year ago, took place at arm's length and in stony silence. It broke the spell between Jerlayne and her father. She slipped away from him and stood up.

"When will Aulaudin and the others return?"

No one answered. They were staring at her as if she'd grown another head. Her borrowed clothes! It was a wonder Jereige had recognized her. Jerlayne suffered a wild urge to run to her closet and drape herself in her customary shawls and skirts. She fought the urge, but it wouldn't go away, not completely, not while Goro led the stare.

"I *borrowed* clothes from my sister," she told him angrily.

"That necklace. Did you borrow that too?"

The goblin wasn't staring at her, his attention was glued to the haphazard collection of beads, claws, and bones she wore around her neck.

"No, not exactly. Last night . . . the night before . . . whenever . . . while we were in the mortal realm—it belonged to one of the mortals I *nuked*—killed. I killed three mortals when we broke the *science* that made Evoni sing."

Goro had no reaction to Jerlayne's murderous confessions. He held out his hand. "Let me see it."

There was something in his voice that made disobedience unthinkable. Jerlayne undid the clasp—a crude affair of blackened steel wire and hardened leather. The closest goblins came to wearing jewelry was the hammered rivets on their weapon hilts and sheathes. Goro's were plain, even the bosses that held his cloak around his shoulders were unadorned metal disks.

"If you want it," Jerlayne told him, "Keep it."

"You found this in the *mortal* realm?"

"Took it off the neck of a woman who tried to shoot us with a gun," Maialene interjected.

Goro shook his head slowly. "These could not have belonged to a woman."

"Are you calling me a liar?"

More head shaking. "No." A long pause. Something had rocked Goro to his core. "But women mark their lineage differently."

"Are you trying to say that necklace we found in the mortal realm once belonged to a goblin man?" Jerlayne watched for any reaction and thought she saw one in Goro's wide, black eyes. "Once belonged to someone you knew?"

"A man, yes, but no one I know. I've been gone so long, I've forgotten what little I knew about reading the beads. If Joff were here, he could read it, but he hasn't returned either. I must think about this carefully. I may need to leave—"

"Aulaudin says, don't leave without him."

Aglaun surprised them, Goro most of all.

"I—" he stammered and fell silent.

"That's why I stayed behind: to tell my brother if something happened. As soon as I walked in and saw Jerlayne I cast my mind after him. I don't know where those mists are, but they're not close. It's like listening at the top of a well.

Aulaudin shared that he can't leave before dawn and you—Goro, the goblin—aren't to leave without him. I didn't share the necklace. I couldn't—he faded away. He shared the rest straight-off; he knows something. He's seen something."

Gogo tucked the necklace inside his shirt. "I will wait, then."

Chapter 34

The longest hours of any day were the hours before dawn. The longest hours of Jerlayne's life were the hours before Aulaudin returned from the misty place. Goro was outside somewhere, hidden in shadows. They had his word that he wouldn't leave without seeing Aulaudin, but in some critical way, he'd left the moment he'd seen Jerlayne's necklace.

He'd seen something in those beads and though Jerlayne believed Goro when he said he didn't know to whom it had belonged or what its patterns meant, she also knew she hadn't asked the right questions.

Her father was another man who hovered on the brink of leaving.

"They had two thousand years at Stonewell and they've lost everything," M'lene mused when the three of them—the sisters and their father—were alone. "That's a long time, maybe too long for starting over after everything's changed."

The two sages had gone back to bed, the younger men, also. For them and all of Fairie it was the middle of the night while Jerlayne's stomach was churning for breakfast. She brought dried berries and dry toast up from the kitchen. Jereige wouldn't eat enough to feed a mouse.

"You can rebuild Stonewell," Jerlayne assured him. "Or stay here, the way Maialene did—"

"Damn, you're hopeless and blind together, Jery. Let him go."

Jerlayne folded her arms beneath her breasts. "Maybe you should go, instead." She wasn't blind and, as for hope— "It's too easy to be hopeless right now. We haven't lost just windows and shingles, our lives have been blown inside out. Giving up now, it would be like giving up after mother made her chain but before they'd found the cure for 'death.'"

"That's when they did give up," Jereige whispered.

He stood and walked slowly from the room. Maialene

followed him out the door, but turned the other way in the corridor. Jerlayne was left alone.

The scyldrin had been through with their brushes and brooms, but broken glass still glinted everywhere. Months, even years, might pass before Sunrise could forget the moment when all its windows shattered. Jerlayne picked up one splinter, then another on moistened fingertips. As she pressed her fingers together and rolled the splinters between them, they fused into a single, translucent bead. She picked up other splinters, adding them together.

It was what a shaping woman did when she had nothing but worries to occupy her mind.

By the time Aulaudin entered the room with Elmeene and two sages behind him (Maun had gone home to Briary), Jerlayne had shaped a shallow, fluted bowl the size of her palm.

The returning quartet was exhausted and disheartened. They hadn't, Gudwal told her, found Claideris or any answers to any questions, and he was more interested in sleep than he was in any goblin necklace. He and Arlesken asked to be shown to guest rooms. Jerlayne would have done her duty as Sunrise mistress, but there were scyldrin in the doorway whose desire to see the old elves sleeping comfortably in their bed was more sincere than hers. Elmeene had another place to be as well.

"I'm worried about Father," Jerlayne said before she left. "He's drifting away."

Elmeene's eyes glazed with tears. "It's not Stonewell; it's everything. The Fairie he loves is drifting—*whirling*—away. He doesn't want to see what comes next."

"You won't let him go. Please, don't let him go."

Her mother made an odd little gesture, midway between a shrug and a frown. "I can't tell him that he's wrong, Jerlayne. I can't hold his hand. Stonewell. *That woman*—"

"I killed three mortals, Mother. I touched them and they died. Let me confront Claideris and you hold Father's hand."

A tear tracked down Elmeene's cheek. "You've changed Fairie, Jerlayne. You've changed everything." She pulled Jerlayne into a quick, rib-snapping embrace, then hurried down the hall.

«You killed *three* mortals?»

Jerlayne daubed a few tears of her own before facing her husband. «I didn't mean to . . . the first time.»

She released her memories to joining. When she was finished, they stood as one in the morning light with their arms wrapped around each other.

«No wonder you look different.»

Jerlayne teased him: «I've borrowed M'lene's clothes!»

«That, too.» Aulaudin relaxed his embrace. «Where is Goro? Did he leave?»

He was scruffy with a two-day beard. Jerlayne caressed his chin with a healer's touch; the stubble fell away in her hands.

"The necklace disturbed him. I think he wants to take it to the plains." When the subject was Goro, Jerlayne preferred spoken words to shared thoughts. "Aglaun told you?"

"No, my brother and I had only a few moments . . . my youngest brother. The mists were a strange place, Jerlayne. Time ran different there. We were there for one night, but we've been gone for two. I'll take you there when this is over—" Aulaudin stopped, ran his fingers through his hair. He needed more grooming than a shaper's fingers could provide. "I didn't see Viljuen or Claideris but I saw my brother . . . Boraudin."

"But Gudwal said—?"

"I didn't tell anyone. Not even Maun; I didn't want to know what my father saw. Don't want to. He was different. Our dead are *different*. They don't care about us; I guess that much, at least, is the truth. But our dead return to the mist; *we'll* go to the mist, I guess, when our time comes.

"He was still Boraudin. Still my brother. I knew him. After all these years, I knew him . . . I knew him better than I'd know you, beloved." Aulaudin raked his hair again. "He told me to let go. Then he told me Goro would die if he left Sunrise without me. He was my brother, but my brother never knew anyone named Goro."

There were a few berries left in the bowl Jerlayne had brought up from the kitchen. Aulaudin ate them slowly. Jerlayne waited.

"I thought about it: why should I leave Sunrise with a goblin? I didn't know about your necklace, but, even now: Why should I care if Goro lives or dies? Or, put it another way— why shouldn't I let him leave without me? What do I owe him . . . or Boraudin, for that matter? Let my brother go! I let him go when he died; he didn't give me any choice."

Jerlayne stood silent before her husband's anger, waiting for it to pass.

"We were going to share everything," Aulaudin said softly when it had. "Everything. Nothing was supposed to come between us. Not Tatterfall. Not Diera. What we had, it was more than joining; different than joining, but more, too. Then he died, and last night—what felt like last night—he tells me that Goro will die, as if it's going to be *my* fault if I let a damned goblin walk out of my life."

"Aglaun didn't say anything about death," Jerlayne said quickly. She'd think about what her husband had just said, but not until she was alone. "He said only that Goro shouldn't leave without you . . . without seeing you or talking to you."

"I didn't share everything with Aglaun . . . I've shared it with you. You would let Goro leave alone?"

"Rather than risk both you." Jerlayne turned away. "I didn't ask Goro to love me. It's not something I chose."

"I have to go with him, Jerlayne, if he's going to leave Sunrise."

"There'll be trouble that's got nothing to do with the necklace. Goro's not allowed to go back to the plains. I don't understand entirely; I didn't ask questions. If he goes back, he's going back to die. I saw it in his eyes when he told me how he'd come to Fairie and again when he saw the necklace."

"I wouldn't believe anything I saw in a goblin's eyes, beloved."

She faced Aulaudin again. "Then why go with him? Why do that to yourself . . . to me? I don't want you to go anywhere with Goro. You despise him for what he and I did. Blame me instead—I'm the one who chose the trysting. Goro would never have touched me otherwise."

"That's the point, beloved," Aulaudin said, not unkindly. "I know he loves you and I know he didn't want you—or me—to suspect that goblins have any emotions at all, much less love for elves. That's what my brother was telling me. I can't let him die for us."

In her heart of hearts, Jerlayne didn't think Goro would agree. But when the goblin returned to the great house, Aulaudin took him outside the kitchen for a short conversation that Jerlayne couldn't overhear. When it was over, *they* considered the matter settled. *They* would take the necklace to the plains together, and she stormed to her workroom alone.

They were gone when she came out again.

* * *

Aulaudin told Goro the unadorned truth when they spoke together outside the Sunrise kitchen: he'd seen his own brother in the mists and Boraudin had made him responsible for another man's life.

It's my conscience, Goro, and I'm the one who's got to live with it. My mind's made up.

I'll trust your brother, Aulaudin. I'm not eager to die. We can ride together, if it will keep me alive.

Aulaudin had hoped for a bit more of an argument, but for all the doom implied in Boraudin's words, he did trust his brother, and there'd been no sense in the mist last night that he and Boraudin were going to be reunited any time soon.

Little more than an hour later Aulaudin was riding a plains-bred stallion, avoiding the roads, but headed due west toward the Fairie heartland. His mettlesome horse, which had survived the siren storms quite nicely, was trained to different signals than elfin men gave their lightly muscled mounts. The animal took umbrage to Aulaudin's initial, innocent miscues and tested him repeatedly thereafter.

From the start, Aulaudin would have preferred a Sunrise gelding beneath him, but Goro insisted that riding through shadows was nothing like skirting the Veil at a pass-through. For Goro's sake, Aulaudin hoped Goro was right, because his whole body ached from the effort of keeping the black horse—whose name he couldn't hope to pronounce properly—in hand. They hadn't come to shadows yet, but if the shadows didn't live up to Goro's claims, or if Aulaudin decided his own horse would have been equal to the challenge, there would have to be retribution.

The way he'd had to respond to his brother's challenges, and Boraudin had been compelled to answer his?

They stopped to rest the horses, but not make camp, at sunset.

"Are you ready to ride the shadows?" Goro asked.

Aulaudin could almost hear the goblin grinning with anticipation. He realized he was headed into a second sleepless night. "As ready as you are."

"Good! We'll start at a jog trot. Stay close behind, less than a length or we'll get separated. If it's too much, shout out. If you get the knack for exhaling, but never inhaling, when you're in shadow, we'll try a canter. The shadows are easiest at a canter."

"I'll master breathing," Aulaudin promised. He'd toyed with shadows a few days ago outside the Sunrise kitchen. They were eerie. He hadn't mastered them and didn't intend to, but he wasn't intimidated by them, either. How hard could breathing be?

Aulaudin found out moments later, when Goro led him to a realm that had nothing to do with shadow and everything to do with freezing to death. After that first blood-curdling encounter, Aulaudin's instinct was to hold his breath as they entered the cold. At a jog Aulaudin could barely complete exhaling and inhaling on the Fairie stride. The stallion's spring-legged gaits didn't help. He'd have been gasping and unconsciousness at a canter.

Pride cut in; the same pride that had drive Aulaudin to keep up with Boraudin when the five-year difference in their ages had passed him the short end of every stick. The stallion knew how to inhale and exhale at the proper time, so Aulaudin put his cheek against the horse's neck and breathed with it. The first time he lost his rhythm completely and filled his lungs with shadow, he thought he was going to freeze solid. Goro, like Boraudin, expressed his sympathy with unrestrained laughter. But there was still a lot of night left when Aulaudin called out that he was ready for a faster gait.

The risen moon was squarely behind them; they were still traveling west, but beyond that, Aulaudin didn't know where they were. The shadows were featureless and the Fairie strides came and went so quickly he'd lost his bearings. When Goro called another rest—for the horses—Aulaudin was among tall, moss-hung trees the likes of which he'd never seen before. He wouldn't have guessed he was in Fairie, if he hadn't spent a mysteriously long night in the mists outside a stone circle.

Although the forest was neither too quiet nor too noisy, Aulaudin couldn't escape the sense that he was being watched. It could have been nerves. With his red hair and fair skin, he felt like a bonfire in the night.

"You ride the shadows well," Goro complimented.

"Just staying close behind. The skill, I imagine, is parting the shadows up front."

"It doesn't take skill to leap off a cliff. Landing on your feet, though—that's a skill."

Aulaudin laughed honestly, and glanced over his shoulder. Nothing was there. "Must have been quite a shock the first time."

"I learned to walk the shadows by myself before I tried riding them. Joff taught me. I sat in front of him and his saddle—a painful lesson. A boy learns quick or he doesn't grow to be a man. But when I'd learned to ride the shadows alone . . ."

"You got used to the cold?" Aulaudin asked when it became clear that Goro wasn't going to finish the statement.

"Never. We'll have to see if the shadows turn you blue, or if elves go untainted."

"Blue! Viljuen weeps—you might have warned me I could turn into a goblin." Aulaudin tried to be outraged, but found himself laughing instead. He truly *had* gone too long without sleep.

Goro laughed, too, but was serious again when he said, "It takes more than shadow to make a goblin, or less. If you meet Uylma, you'll find her as pale as Jerlayne's sister M'lene. We *do* look alike; maybe there is some truth to our tale of the Ten. We're definitely not like you, sending our women out to the mortal realm."

"How would you know?"

"They don't turn blue!"

Aulaudin sat back, chuckling. "I think of Cuz: maybe a bit of elf, maybe a goblin father, born mortal. Or my son: a lot of elf, a bit of goblin, mortal in there someplace, but born in Fairie, born immortal. I start wondering what makes the difference? Except—they die."

"We die."

Aulaudin let the discussion die, too. His wife had said Goro would die if he went back to the plains. Boraudin said Goro would die if he left Sunrise alone. There was a sense of death in the air around them. Death and malice.

"We're not alone," he said, thinking he'd changed the subject and, on hearing his own words, realizing that he hadn't. "I mean, I feel that we're being watched."

"I thought that was you, sharing every stride with half the elfin men of Fairie. I thought I could hear the debate: Do the goblins have magic or don't they? Have they been lying all along? Magic is what someone else has that you don't."

"You'll have to talk to some other elf about magic; I've

never thought about it very much. And I'm not sharing with anyone. It's a tickle at the back of my neck, as if someone were staring at me, at both of us."

Goro fussed with his boot in the dark and handed Aulaudin a sheathed knife.

"I carry a knife," Aulaudin grumbled, though his was a tool less than half the size of Goro's weapon.

"Now you carry two. Why aren't you sharing everything with your brothers and father? Are they all asleep?

"I shared everything with one brother, now I keep my thoughts to myself. I'm out of the habit." He strangled a laugh. "Got to change that if I'm going to raise a son. I've shared more talking to you these last few days than I have in years with anyone except Jerlayne." Aulaudin hadn't realized that until he'd said it.

The goblin stood up and stretched. "You'll be a good father, like Maun."

"Viljuen weeps! I hope to do better than that." Without thought, Aulaudin took the hand that Goro offered, and pulled himself upright.

Perhaps Goro had offered his hand without thought, too. Face to face, they both froze and let go at the same moment. Neither man spoke as they remounted and resumed their journey.

Aulaudin made peace with his goblin stallion. It did what he wanted in Fairie and he accepted its wisdom as they charged through shadows, dangerously close to the streaming tail of Goro's horse. He wasn't about to abandon any of the horses in the Sunrise stable, but he could thump the lathered, black neck with sincerity when dawn slowed their pace. He still had the sense that they were followed.

"Do you know where you are?" Goro asked.

They rode abreast in trailless forest.

"Fairie. Some part of Fairie I never knew existed—but until recently I've stuck to the roads and trails."

Aulaudin expected a laugh and was concerned when he didn't get one.

"You could get back to Sunrise from here?"

"Going home is rarely a problem."

"Then go. The next shadows take me to the plains." The goblin looked out between his horse's ears, not at Aulaudin.

"I can get home from the plains; Jerlayne did—with a bullet through her leg."

"I don't know what lies ahead. We don't share, but we dream. I dreamt. My mother, Uylma—you'd call her one of the goblin priestesses—abides in dreams, when it pleases her. I dreamt that I was bringing someone's lineage home. I don't know if she dreamt my dream with me."

"That's important?"

A black-cloaked shrug. "It's been a long time since I've seen the plains. Jerlayne was a child. And, anyway, my mother's on the run, driven from the nafoga'ar. I don't know where she is, so I dreamt for a guide. We are not close, my mother and I—"

Aulaudin remembered a windy day on the beach last winter and a severed head—Goro's father, slain for treason—hurtling toward him. He remembered the hurt and pride in Goro's voice then, and wasn't surprised that there were difficulties between the goblin and his mother now.

"She might not send anyone, even if she'd dreamt my dream. Or another Uylma—the one who rules in the nafoga'ar now—might have dreamt it instead. When I come out of shadows next, I might live long enough to get the beads to my mother, or I might not. I don't want you beside me when I find out. Last night, I did not want to ride the shadows alone. It was good to talk, but now: you must leave. Go back to Sunrise."

"Before I see the goblin plains with my own eyes?" Aulaudin shot back, though his indignation was feigned. He didn't know what to say to a man riding toward his own death. "I should have guessed you'd never let an elf through your Veil."

Goro wasn't fooled. "Jerlayne shaped my knife, but the sheath was tanned on the plains. It will get you where you want to go, as the armor moved Jerlayne. Go home. They will send someone and he will say his name is Goro. I can't tell you what lineage he will be, except it won't be mine. He might not be gennern. There have been changes on the plains; we saw that when the goblins came down to Briary. Talk to him, you and Jerlayne; judge him. If he is gennern, then you will have to fight. You *can* fight, Aulaudin. You were ready to fight me with a stick. We could never cull the fierceness out of you and your sages haven't meddled with your hearts, only your memories."

"Maybe this priestess-mother of yours will be grateful for those beads."

"If I thought otherwise, I wouldn't bring them to her. But death is the only answer to a broken oath."

"A salt supper?"

Goro took a one-handed grasp on the reins. His free hand was shaking. "No."

"I'm not leaving, Goro."

The goblin pulled the necklace out and thrust it into Aulaudin's face. "Once I wore beads like this. Once I was an uylma's son. Then the gennern claimed my father for a traitor and I had nothing. Before Jerlayne was born, perhaps long before she was born or you were born, the gennern were trading with mortals! My father suspected it, but he had no proof, and so he became the traitor. This is the proof my father never had: Some other uylma cast her son into the darkest shadow and he found a path to the farthest side. With this in her hand, my mother will rally the lesser uylmas and lesser lineages against the gennern. She'll take back the nafoga'ar and the nafoga'ar will embrace her again. With this necklace in her hand, she'll stalk the mist like a panther. She'll make the plains safe for us, because that is what she does, but she'll make Fairie safe, too.

"I've told Jerlayne, and you, all that you need to know about us, but you've got to be alive to make use of it. Sunrise has to survive. It doesn't need me; it needs you. *Go home!*"

"Can't do it, Goro. Won't."

A man had to credit the goblins as superb horsemen, better on the whole than elves, as were their black horses. He never saw Goro twitch as he and the horse moved as one, from a dead stop to a dead run. Fortunately for Aulaudin, he'd been expecting Goro to bolt and his horse had gotten used to the idea of being in a tight second place.

There was a bad moment when Goro got an extra stride on them and Aulaudin felt the shadow shifting in front of him. He didn't know how to manipulate the shadow, but he knew Goro's back and his horse's tail as if he held them in his hands. So, he closed his eyes and thought of chain mail and horsehair. They fell; Aulaudin's ears said they'd leapt off a cliff, but they landed a half-stride behind Goro in a place of distance horizons and endless, green-gold grass.

"Damn you!" the goblin shouted.

It would be hard to get to the plains. Maybe that's why no one had ever stumbled across them. There were no rocks, not even any trees to say *this* place rather than *that* place. Nothing but a half-dozen black tents nearby to breakup the landscape. But Aulaudin could go home, an elf could leave the plains the

same way he left the mortal realm. The Veil was all around
him, ripe for parting. All Aulaudin had to do was dismount and
think of Sunrise. For the moment, as a lone rider raced away
from the tents, Aulaudin remained in the saddle.

"Our guide?" he asked.

Goro wasn't talking. The vague gloom floating above them
both since they'd left Sunrise had settled around the goblin like
a shroud and the sense that they'd been followed through
Fairie was gone. For Aulaudin, this much was clear: Goro
might expect to die, might even think he'd done something to
deserve it, but he didn't *want* to die, and he was mortally afraid.

"Goro! If Jerlayne could haul Cuz out of the mortal realm, I
can haul you back to Sunrise. Leave the necklace. Give me
your hands!"

He extended his own hands. The goblin, though, didn't
budge and Aulaudin wasn't confident enough to grab Goro's
wrists without some gesture—any gesture—that his offer
would be accepted. The lone rider cantered up. Aulaudin lowered his hands, but stayed close. He summoned the textures of
his Sunrise resting place and kept them in mind as the rider
brought his horse to a flying stop. He thought he recognized
Joff, the goblin Jerlayne had healed a few days ago in the
kitchen, but the man jabbered in goblin clicks and whistles and
never glanced his way.

Goro surrendered the necklace without a word. The stranger
held it up briefly in the sunlight before tucking it into a pouch
attached to his saddle. The stranger jabbered some more; Goro
dismounted and began disarming himself. He dropped a knife
and fumbled with the leather laces of his mail shirt. When he
was finished, Goro walked toward the tents.

The remaining goblin, the stranger with the necklace, met
Aulaudin's eyes for the first time, then quickly glanced down
at the weapons and armor Goro had heaped on the grass. When
the goblin took the reins of Goro's horse and started after Goro,
Aulaudin left the iron, steel, and leather where it lay.

He got a good look at the riding goblin's mail. It had lost a
few links recently and was still patched with string Aulaudin
was sure he'd foraged. He had to be Joff.

"Stop him," Aulaudin demanded; not (he hoped) loudly
enough for Goro, walking several paces ahead of them, to hear.
"Let him come back to Sunrise with me. Don't let him throw
his life away for *beads!*"

The riding goblin wasn't deaf and wasn't ignorant of Fairie's language; his body language proclaimed that clearly enough, but he didn't answer.

Aulaudin counted nineteen goblins milling around the tents, all of them staring at his very out-of-place rusty hair and not-blue face. A few of them fingered knives or swords. He wished he had a woman's talent for shaping; he would have *nuked* them all.

The goblin who'd understood, but wouldn't speak, Fairie's language dismounted, exchanged a few words with the others. A goblin came forward—young, Aulaudin thought, truly young, not out of his teens but blue as the rest of them—claimed two sets of reins and held out his hand for a third. Joff walked toward one of the tents. Goro had entered a different tent. He caught Aulaudin's eye and took hold of the flap.

Inside the tent Goro had entered, Aulaudin heard a woman's voice making the noises that passed for goblin language. No one had laid a hand on him, no one told him what to do—except by holding the tent that flap. Goblin language, by its nature, always sounded harsh and angry to Aulaudin's ears, but the woman sounded harsher and angrier than most. He thought of rushing into her tent, tackling Goro the way he would have tackled Boraudin and shifting them both back to Fairie.

But Aulaudin entered the tent where Joff held the flap. He was blinking, adjusting to the dark, when someone called his name.

"Aulaudin. Jesus-H-mother-fucking-Christ! It's good to see you!"

A man threw a hearty embrace around him, almost a woman's embrace in its full-body closeness and intensity. Aulaudin put an arm's length between them and got even more confused. He didn't recognize the voice. The man's accent could have been mortal-realm, but his face, Viljuen wept, in the tent's shadowy light, the man had the face of a goblin. No, the coloring of a goblin. The face was animated as no goblin face he'd seen, going from elation to despair in the blink of an eye.

"Shit! I knew it—I'm a fucking freak!"

Definitely mortal, which suggested one possibility, though the last time Aulaudin had seen Cuz he certainly hadn't looked like a goblin. "Who are you? What's your name?"

"Cuz. Shit. Theodore Albert Kennicut. Dammit, Aulaudin I

don't know what they did to me, but I gotta get outta here.
You're gonna get me out, right? Shit. You're here to get me out,
right?"

"I didn't know you were here," Aulaudin said slowly. Cuz . . .
kidnapped by goblins serving Goro's mother? None of it made
sense, unless he was willing to consider treachery and betrayal
on a grand scale. "I came with Goro, to deliver a necklace Jerlayne and her sister, M'lene, found in the mortal realm—and
probably get him killed."

"Shit. Fucking shit." Cuz backed away from him. "Look,
Jerlayne an' me— Shit. I don't— It was, like, an accident,
okay? I just want to get back home, if I can. These freaking
aliens tell me I'm one of them now an' I'm gonna fuckin' die if
I go home. Look, just get me outta here. Do that lightning thing
you do an' dump me back in the City. Shit—why're they gonna
kill Goro? You brought him here to get him killed?"

"I didn't bring him here, Cuz. I followed him. He's broken
some sort of oath by coming back." He paused and said, with a
close thought for Cuz's reaction, "Cuz, I think this is Goro's
mother's camp—"

"Damn!" Cuz interrupted. So much for betrayal; the mortal
couldn't keep a secret if his life had depended on it, and he'd
been honestly surprised. "An' I thought *I* had a shit-rotten
family. She's some sort of queen here. She sneezes, they blow
their noses; she squats, they all strain—you know what I
mean? She's killed two guys just since I got here. One guy with
her own hand, just made a fist an' blood started coming outta
his ears and nose. The other goblin-guy, they tied him up in the
grass and ran their goddamned *horses* over him. He looked like
fucking *road-kill!* Damn. I wouldn't want her for a moth—"

Aulaudin took a breath because his companion clearly
didn't need to and he now had most of the information he
needed. "Cuz! Shut up!"

"Yeah, whatever you say, but—"

"Shut up! Listen to me. Were you kidnapped or did you just
run away? Did you get here on your own or did Goro's goblins
kidnap you and bring you here, to his mother?"

"Shit, no— No, yes—"

Aulaudin groaned. "Jerlayne said you could talk sensibly
when you tried. Please, *try!*"

The mortal youth—goblin—*whatever* he'd become on the
plains—made an effort. "I got kidnapped. Yeah, I ran away—I

saw you and Goro an' he was talking about killing mortals, so I ran out into the storm like the stupid shit I am. I found M'lene; well, she found me an' things were going better. She'd talked me into coming back into the house, when we spotted goblins. I guess she thought they were just goblins, Goro's goblins, an' nothing to worry about, but when we started for the house, they came after us. They had guns—like the guys who shot Jerlayne, okay? M'lene, she did the lightning thing and got away, but not me.

"Man—these guys are *crazy*. I tried to get away. Like, every prisoner's supposed to try to get away." Cuz held up a bandaged hand. Aulaudin could see where one finger was partly missing. "They cut off my fucking finger—so, yeah, Aulaudin, I got kidnapped. The guys that snatched me and chopped off my finger, they passed me off to another bunch, who tied me to a log and let me hang a while, while they asked me questions about Sunrise—so, they had something to do with fairyland cuz they spoke funny, the way you do. But I got kidnapped from *them* by these guys here the day before yesterday, at night—I think, maybe. Everything's kinda blurred, 'cuz they gave me something wild to drink an' 'cuz I was turnin' blue like this. These guys, well the alien queen in there, what she wants to know about is my father, 'cuz he was one of them. I kinda told Jerlayne that, but I don't think she believed me. Shit, I didn't *really* believe until I saw you talking to Goro.

"I can't tell them shit about my old man. My mother was a drug addict. She was whacked outta her head; you'd have to be some special kind of stupid to believe her. You got any idea what I'm talkin' about?"

Aulaudin nodded.

"Good, 'cuz Jerlayne, she's a neat lady in a lot of ways, but she hasn't got a clue about how the world works. So, you gonna get me outta here now?"

"You and Goro," Aulaudin agreed and wondered how he'd manage it. "Once I fit all these pieces together in my mind."

"Man, you can't wait that long. These alien-goblins, they're crazy, I told you that. The queen, Goro's mother—she's the craziest one of all. Men here, Aulaudin, men don't count for nothing. You know, like bees or ants? It's not sex, it's not like the queen has a guy-harem or anything, it's like she's playing a big game, and men are just . . . just . . . you know . . ."

"Pawns," Aulaudin suggested. He'd played chess most of

his life; it was one of the few mortal-realm pastimes that hadn't changed much in his lifetime.

"Yeah, *pawns*. Use 'em up an' toss 'em aside; kill 'em." Cuz took a breath and got serious. "Maybe you could come back for Goro? I got a feeling—I don't understand what they say, except what the interpreter-dude says—but I got a bad feeling that I'm not gonna be interesting to them much longer."

Noises came through the tent's felt walls: base-metal chimes and goblin conversation. Aulaudin made a move to peek beyond the tent flap. Cuz warned him off. He didn't want to lose a finger, so he resisted his curiosity. And just as well; the noise flowed toward them, then stopped, and the goblin who'd met him and Goro outside the camp ordered them into the sun.

Aulaudin blinked a few times from the light and in surprise. Goro had warned him that his mother would prove pale-skinned. She was as tall as Goro, too, every bit as solid, and black-haired as well. Her face was a goblin face: smooth, hard, without discernable emotion. Aulaudin knew the word *alien* from beyond the Veil and, having now met Goro's priestess-mother, he didn't begrudge Cuz the use of it.

She wore a black gown, trimmed with golden plaques and beads in lightning patterns that flashed in the sun. Several necklaces hung around her neck. One was green beads and copper, similar to the necklace Goro had brought from Fairie, although considerably more ornate. Another was strung with bones that might have been collected from several dozen chicken dinners but were more likely the tips of men's fingers. Even so, it wasn't any part of the woman's appearance that held Aulaudin transfixed.

When she looked at him, Aulaudin felt the air grow cold in his lungs. She pulled his hair, hard, from the opposite side of the tent. He winced and when he reopened his eyes, a rust-red lock dangled from her fingers.

It took strength to look past her, to see Goro with his shirt hanging lopsidedly from his shoulders and blood trickling from an ugly cut on his lower lip. His gloves were gone and his right hand was shiny in the sunlight. Aulaudin had spent his life not caring much about the fate of men not born in Fairie. He'd learned not to see the thousands of cruelties of the mortal realm. He told himself that Goro was responsible for his fate and that Boraudin was wrong in death as he'd sometimes been wrong in life.

He did a lousy job of persuading himself.

The priestess spoke in chirps and whistles, then Joff translated.

"Uylma asks why you have come here, where you don't belong. She wishes to hear why she should not have you killed."

Aulaudin took a deep breath. The Veil was all around him, yes, but he'd experienced Uylma's power. He judged that she could cut his throat as easily as she'd cut his hair, and faster than he could part the Veil. Aulaudin judged, too, that he should have expected her question and should have come up with an answer rather than listening to Cuz ramble about aliens and queens.

"Tell her," Aulaudin began without any notion of where he would end. "Tell Uylma that the elfin sage Claideris isn't really an elf. She's a goblin, a priestess, just like Uylma herself—"

Joff frowned as he translated. No great surprise. Those were Goro's conclusions and Goro was dripping blood into the packed dirt floor. But the from moment Aulaudin had laid his own eyes on Goro's mother, they'd taken on the force of truth.

It was easy to say all goblins were blue and that they all looked alike, but what, actually, did they look like? Blue-skinned Joff and Goro shared the same broad, high forehead, the same wide-set eyes, arching cheeks, and somewhat shallow jaws, and they shared those bony features with Goro's mother.

Jerlayne could shape away a scar with a single touch, but bones, she said, were a greater challenge and faces the greatest challenge of all. She could restore a nose's shape after it had been broken and blunt ears that never stopped growing, but there was an absolute limit to what she could do to reshape a skull.

No wonder Claideris always kept a fuming pipe clenched between her teeth. The stem distorted her jaw and the smoke obscured everything else.

Aulaudin could scarcely wait to share his realization with Jerlayne, but first he had to leave the plains alive. The goblin had finished rendering Aulaudin's statement into clicks and pops. Uylma replied quickly.

"Ulyma says she knew this."

"Then tell her that I know where Claideris hides. I know the

place—the *exact* place—where the nafoga'ar mist flows into
Fairie. I can take her there and show her where to wait."

And again, after the clicks and squeals had ended, Joff said:
"Uylma says she knew this and needs no elfin guide."

Aulaudin wasn't a gambling man; he left risky games to his
father. But he had nothing else to offer the priestess, so he took
the greatest chance of his life: "Tell her she lies." That thickened the tension. "If she knew where Claideris was, or how to
get there, she'd be gone. She wouldn't waste precious time tor-
turing her son."

"Shit, Aulaudin—you're going to get all of us killed!"

But Joff translated and the tension dropped as the goblin
woman spat out a few words then threw her head back laughing and sputtering.

"She says you are wrong, but bold, and you may live."

The priestess sobered quickly. She pulled the necklace from
a pocket in her robe and folded it over her hand so that only a
few of the larger beads were displayed. She'd begun to jabber
when Cuz interrupted:

"Hey! Where'd you get that? Is that the fucking necklace
you were talking about, Aulaudin? The one Jerlayne found?
That's my mother's necklace, damn it. Shit, she always wore
it. She was wearin' it the night she died, but it disappeared. I
want to know what the fucking alien's doing with my fucking
mother's necklace?"

"I think he's got a good question," Aulaudin added. "The
first time I saw him, he was pale as Uylma."

Joff presumably did his best to turn Cuz's profanity-laced
English into proper goblin squawking. Again the priestess answered rapidly.

"Uylma says that the boy can be forgiven, but the beads do
not record a woman's lineage. They belonged to a man, the son
a woman a banished into the nafoga'ar mist a long time ago."

"And the boy's mother *was* a mortal," Aulaudin countered,
putting a hand on Cuz's arm in the faint hope of keeping him
quiet. "She may have worn the necklace, but it was his *father*
who put the goblin blood in this youngster's veins. You're Joff,
right? You remember the siren storm at Sunrise? You were
there; Jerlayne healed the wound a tent pole put in your side.
Well, after you left, she went to the mortal realm to put a stop to
the attacks. She killed three mortals before she succeeded—"

Aulaudin knew that was a risky confession, but he wanted this woman with the finger-bone necklace to know that elves didn't necessarily want, or need, goblin protection. "—She took that necklace off one of the mortals she killed."

"No shit? *Jerlayne* nuked three bad-guys? She get their ID? Anyone named Theodore Albert Kennicut? I'll bet he's in this. I'll bet he is. If she didn't nuke him, she should've."

While the goblin translated, Aulaudin asked Cuz, "Theodore? Isn't that the name you gave me in the tent?"

"Yeah, but it's my uncle's name, too. Man, he was always riding me 'cuz I didn't get sick. An' takin' of my mother. Shit for sure, he knew where she got that necklace. He had it all figured it out somehow. If you ask me, him and my uncle were in it together."

Aulaudin couldn't guess if Joff heard or translated that, too, but Uylma took longer to reply.

"Uylma says you must return to Sunrise and protect your son. The one who calls herself Claideris will come for him."

He'd hoped for an opportunity to plead for Goro's life; he hadn't hoped it would be this clear-cut. "Goro is responsible for my son's protection. I need to take him back with me."

Frowning, the goblin translated; there was no reaction from Goro, but his mother became enraged. Her shrill jabbering could have melted iron.

"Uylma says Goro cannot protect anything. He has disavowed his oaths to her. Uylma has already chosen the time and place of his death—Aulaudin, listen to me, there's nothing you or I can do about it. Uylma has decided to use him to regain the nafoga'ar. He knows; it's his idea, his *fucking* idea. He's determined to redeem his father's honor—*Don't* look at him, Aulaudin. Get him killed now and it's all for nothing. If you're right—and you probably are—you *want* Uylma to regain the nafoga'ar. If she does, she'll finish with your sage. But if she doesn't—if she can't bribe her way back to the mist, then if the gennern find out who, and what, Claideris is, they'd sacrifice their own uylma to serve her instead."

"What kind of father's honor demands a son's life?" the son of Maun asked, ignoring the rest. "If I'm going back to Sunrise, I'm taking Goro with me."

Aulaudin tried to get to Goro past Joff. He hadn't completed his first stride when Uylma seized him with her power and hurled him into shadows. The last thing Aulaudin heard was Cuz shouting: "This sucks. This bloody, fuckin' *sucks!*"

After that, Aulaudin had all he could to do find his way back to Sunrise. Whatever Jerlayne and her sister had done to get the necklace, they hadn't permanently destroyed the *science* behind the mortal-realm attacks: Evoni was singing again and the homestead by the sea was awash in her fury.

In absolute terms, this was not the worse storm the siren had thrown up in her defense of Sunrise, but coming on the heels of the victory Jerlayne and her sister had claimed in the mortal realm, it was the most disheartening. Most of the windows were shuttered, but no one scurried to close those that weren't.

Aulaudin climbed easily across the sill of one such neglected window and into an abandoned, empty room.

«Jerlayne! Beloved!»

The met in the corridor. Jerlayne was once again the wife of Aulaudin's memories and dreams. He saw enough of mortal realm fashions and preferred a woman dressed in layers of soft cloth who wrapped him in her shawl as they embraced. She wanted to know what had happened, if he'd ridden the shadows all the way to the goblin plains, and where was Goro. Aulaudin sealed his memory and deflected her curiosity with questions of his own.

«When did the singing start again?»

«Not long after you left. M'lene and I failed. I killed three mortals for nothing. Maun says the machine we destroyed is called a *mobile television satellite uplink,*» Jerlayne relayed the words so carefully that Aulaudin could hear his father's voice within the sharing. «He says there are hundreds of them—thousands—and that they can be aimed like an arrow at any tiny place in the mortal realm. Or at Fairie. I don't understand—»

Aulaudin held her tight. «We share the sun and moon. When you look up at night, you see the same stars year after year, and the same stars that a mortal sees. We are, somehow, attached to their realm. They have become very good at finding things with their *science,* even things they cannot see with their eyes. If they had a notion where to aim their machines, I'm not surprised that they've found us.»

He was going to add that finding Fairie was not the same as invading or destroying it, but Jerlayne overwhelmed him with a wave of anguish first.

«When I rescued Cuz, there was another machine. It drew my picture as I parted the Veil. It's all my fault, Aulaudin: they got their notion from *me*.»

Aulaudin rocked his wife gently in his arms. He shared nothing, said nothing. There was nothing to share or say. The storm overhead wasn't Jerlayne's fault, not in any deliberate way, but if she had been seen—and seen by *science*—then perhaps much could be explained.

«I should have left him there. I should have made myself forget him once our son was born—before he was born. My mother warned me away from him, but I didn't listen. She said he'd be trouble—»

«*Sssh,*» Aulaudin whispered through Jerlayne's mind. «It's done. They have so much science, so much that we don't understand—not even Maun. We were going to be seen sooner or later. Better to be seen saving Cuz's life than foraging a sack of bricks. Fairie survived iron and steel; we'll survive this . . . somehow.»

They made their way to their bedroom and the solace of their bed where Aulaudin kept his secrets about Goro, Cuz, and the plains until sunrise.

Chapter 35

Cuz was back inside the black tent, with two goblins standing guard and Goro, rather than Aulaudin, for a companion. After she'd vanished Aulaudin, the goblin queen had yelled some stuff that nobody had bothered to translate for Cuz. He didn't think it had been a dinner menu, though, or an order to get her son and his formerly mortal tent-mate some clothes that weren't covered with holes and bloodstains.

By the way Goro just sat in the dirt, leaking blood from a half-dozen places and staring at nothing like he was seriously spaced, Cuz guessed that the goblin noises for *Off with their heads!* had played a major part in his mother's speech.

"Look, I know you speak English—kind of. I *heard* you talking to Aulaudin. And I know you've got to speak goblin. So, could you, like, wake up long enough to tell me what's gonna happen? Just once, so I know. I'd like to know."

Goro didn't turn his head or blink, but something got through, because he finally said, "You don't."

"Is it gonna take a long time and hurt a lot?"

"I have to live until sundown tomorrow."

He made one day sound very ominous. "What about me? How long do I *have* to live?"

"As long as you're alive when we get to the nafoga'ar, what happens to you afterward doesn't concern Uylma. The gennern might decide to let you live. They might feel Claideris' grandson is more useful to them alive."

"Is that who I am? The grandson of some woman that neither your mother or the elves like?"

"Yes."

"Shit."

"Yes."

The tent was quiet while Cuz absorbed the ironies of his existence. There was only one bright spot: if Uncle Ted were

involved—and Cuz would bet his last imaginary dollar that his
uncle had been involved from the moment of his conception, if
not before—then Uncle Ted was going to find himself in a
black tent some day. These goblins . . . these *aliens* were nas-
tier than ten Uncle Teds. Their queen wasn't interested in ty-
ing up little boys, but maybe she'd make an exception for
ol' Uncle Ted. She'd done quite a number on Goro's back
already—nothing kinky, just a slow peeling away of skin with
an invisible knife and a liberal application of salt.

The damp marks on Goro's shirt turned white as they dried.

A goblin entered the tent with a jug of water and a straw platter heaped with pale stuff that looked like a cross between
mashed potatoes and maggots. A day and a half had passed
since Cuz's last meal. He prodded the mass with his finger and,
after licking it clean, asked: "You gonna eat your half?"

"No."

"Mind if I eat it?"

"No."

"Maybe I shouldn't, huh? Like, if it's your last meal, an' you
get hungry later."

"Eat it all, if you want, but if you have pride, it's better to
face death with an empty gut. Everything lets go."

"Shit," Cuz said, staring at the platter.

"Yes."

The image Goro had conjured left Cuz sick in the mind, but
didn't dent his appetite. Jerlayne had said something about
healing and eating. Turning into a goblin must have been some
sort of healing. His fingers hovered a scant inch above the platter mound.

"These gennern, they might want to keep me alive, right?"

"They might, but Cuz—if I live until sundown, they'll be
dead by starlight. You're bait. If Aulaudin is right—and I, too,
think he is—whoever holds the nafoga'ar will use you as bait
to lure Claideris back to the plains. The gennern will want to
know how she trades with the mortal realm. Uylma . . . ." Goro
shrugged, a gesture that had to be painful. "In the past, a uylma
vanquished at the nafoga'ar was driven into the mist—it was
like giving a man a knife before he was surrounded by salt. My
mother never makes the same mistake twice. She'll destroy her
present rival, and hunt down anyone who survives from the
past, especially your grandmother."

Cuz made a fist, a dark blue fist. He didn't know who to hate anymore. Goblins, elves, Uncle Ted and everyone else he'd left behind: they all lived in their narrow us-and-them worlds. Elves were terminally naive. Goblins thought they could solve problems by killing and dying. Humans? No, make that mortals, because they were all human. There was no way he could have been born or become a father if goblins, elves, and mortals weren't all human.

And Cuz was the most human: a fucking mess of elf, goblin, and mortal mixed together. He didn't fit anywhere without hating a part of himself. Unmaking his fist, finger by finger, he set the conflicts aside. What did any of it matter, if he was only bait?

"What about water?" he asked. "Am I going to piss myself if I drink water?"

"I wouldn't mind a drink of water."

Cuz offered the pitcher to Goro who drank deeply before returning it.

"What happens tomorrow at sundown?" Cuz asked before putting the rim to his lips.

"My mother will pray for the power to defeat her rivals for the nafoga'ar. The gods will reply and, if the reply is favorable, she will claim vengeance. If not, we all die, except, possibly, you."

"She can't do that tonight? And why should you have to die? It doesn't seem fair to me."

"Uylma has to be in the nafoga'ar to receive the power. The gennern aren't fools, they wouldn't let her near the nafoga'ar unless she offered them something they wanted very much."

Cuz set the jug in the dirt. "You? Me?"

"Together, we are an irresistible gift. She will say that I have broken my oath to her, which I have, and whatever else she thinks necessary to convince the gennern that peace with them is a small price to pay for the satisfaction and pleasure of punishing me. The gennern aren't fools, but they are predictable."

"The satisfaction? The *pleasure?* You people are sick, you know. You'll all sick."

Goro cradled his maimed hand. "If she succeeds— If I succeed in living until sundown when she can call the gods, then she will be *the* Uylma again. She'll crush the gennern and make a pyre of their severed heads."

"Jesus. Fuckin' Jesus," Cuz muttered, wanting it to be lies but being pretty certain that Goro told the truth. "An' what do you get out of this, besides the satisfaction and pleasure of being dead?"

"My father's honor is restored; a man judged traitor by traitors becomes a hero. Uylma will not suffer her rivals to live; she will pursue Claideris to the brink of mortal realm. She'll kill her in combat or keep her in the mortal air until she dies—"

"This shit about dying if I go home . . . that's really true? That's not boogey-man stories? You'd die, if you went where I was born?"

Another shrug. "That's what I've been told. It could be lies; so much is lies, but if not lies, then I'd find myself dying in a place where I didn't belong, wouldn't I?"

As opposed to hanging on until sunset tomorrow? But an even more disturbing thought rose out of Goro's question: "My father's dead, dead in a place where he didn't belong."

"Unless Claideris took that necklace from him and gave it to your mother, it is hard to imagine it around her neck unless your father, Claideris's son, was dead and haddied in the mortal realm. Perhaps he gave it to her; so his mother wouldn't know that he was dead, that he'd failed to do whatever she'd wanted him to do. It's not an easy thing to be an uylma's son. But to face her again without the tokens of her lineage . . . that would be to deny that she had given him his life. . . . *I* would not do that . . . if the choice had been mine to make."

Could a dead man abandon his son? Had Cuz's mother always had the necklace, or had Uncle Ted given it to her? Cuz couldn't remember. Had his father been his uncle's willing partner, or had he been a man like Goro with an alien-queen for a mother?

"Why are you doing this?" Cuz demanded of his companion. "Why are you going to let your mother kill you?"

"I told you: to redeem my father's honor. The Uylma will avenge the loss of her husband once he is no longer without honor. She'll rid herself of Claideris; that will rid Fairie of its own treachery and betrayal. And afterward . . . My father believed Fairie should not be culled."

"What do you believe?"

"The elves and scyldrin of Fairie are clever enough to find their own path. We are certainly not wise enough to find it for them—"

"Fuck fairyland!" Cuz shouted loud enough that a guard poked his head into the tent and glowered a moment before retreating. "You're not doing this to liberate fairyland from its goblin oppressors." Cuz continued in a softer tone, "you're doing this for Jerlayne. You fucking love Jerlayne, but she loves Aulaudin, so you're sacrificing yourself for them, and you won't even admit it to yourself! It's so damn noble, Goro, it's *stupid*. You're stupid. Stupid and sick. An' come three o'clock tomorrow afternoon, you're gonna realize I'm right, but it's gonna be fuckin' too late."

Goro gave Cuz a look that hurt. "Shadows may have touched you, but you're still mortal inside," Goro said, as polite and deadly an insult as Cuz had ever heard. "I swore to protect Jerlayne and her homestead. I will survive until sunset, then I will die knowing that I kept my oath."

"Yeah? Suppose the gods don't think as highly of your mother as you do? Suppose they think it's too fucking cruel and squash her like a bug? Suppose she decides this Claideris isn't so bad after all and that they should do business together? You can't go sacrificing yourself so somebody else can be the fuckin' hero! Man, if you can't take care of it yourself, don't fuckin' do it at all."

It was the best wisdom Cuz had to offer, and Goro just closed his eyes and sat there in the dirt, ignoring him.

Sundown came and had almost gone when the translator-goblin came into the tent. He tossed Cuz a heavy shirt and a heavier cloak.

"Get dressed. We're riding out. Through shadow, prepare yourself."

Then he made goblin noises at Goro, who'd stiffened from his wounds while he sat and couldn't stand without help. Cuz had been with too many men not to realize when two men knew each other well, maybe not as lovers, but well enough to hold on just a bit longer than necessary.

There'd be no extra shirt for Goro. He had to look like the genuine article—a beaten man, a tortured prisoner—if the harebrained scheme he, or his alien mother, had concocted was to have a prayer of success. While Cuz pulled his shirt over his head and wrestled with the unfamiliar cloak, Goro loosened up: stretching, flexing, sucking his teeth as the salt-crusted wounds reopened.

Cuz ran from the tent and fell to his knees. He retched gut-acid onto the grass. Some goblin laid hands on Cuz's shoulders, not violently, but to get him up on his feet and pointed toward the horse they expected him to ride. It was the last fucking straw. Cuz panicked, lashed out with his elbows, and started running through the twilight. He didn't have a hope of escape; he was back to hoping they'd kill him dead on the spot. But, no luck—he was the ass-end of the queen's Trojan Horse and he went wherever Goro went.

When he balked at riding by himself, they plopped him down behind Goro, where the heat of their bodies together had to make the salted cuts on the goblin's back sting like bloody hell. That was, the heat of their bodies when they weren't plunging through the cold-dark.

Dawn found them on a plain that looked absolutely no different than the one they'd left, except that they were ringed by twice as many goblins: some with spears, some with swords, and some with long-barreled guns propped in front of them. It was a scene from countless movies. Silent, inscrutable, and tribal bad-guys flashing the latest weapons. Except, of course, it wasn't a movie and the alien queen was bartering with their lives.

Cuz started vomiting again, right there on the horse's back behind Goro. There wasn't anything left in his gut, not even acid, but he couldn't stop. The goblin reached down and held his hand until one of the bad guys—one of the gennern—prodded Goro in the leg with his rifle.

"Can you walk?" Goro asked. "It's not far. I can carry you."

"I can walk."

Cuz didn't want to walk, he didn't want to be here, he didn't want to be anyone's martyr, but he'd be fucking damned before he let *Goro* carry him.

Not far was at least two miles, to the top of a rolling hill and down to a bunch of bleached rocks that didn't look like they belonged in the middle of a grassy nowhere, but didn't look like Stonehenge, either.

The translator goblin and all the other goblin-guys who'd ridden with them and the queen gave up their weapons outside the rocks. They stayed out there, too. Of their "friendly" escort, only Goro's mother, the alien queen, accompanied Goro and Cuz along a rather narrow path among the rocks.

They'd entered a maze, Cuz decided when they'd been walking inside the rocks longer than they'd walked outside them and far too long to be anywhere but on the other side of the rocks he'd seen from the hilltop. That got his terror fired up again, though there was nothing he could do except keep walking. His eyes were as dry and empty as his gut.

The nafoga'ar—assuming that's where they'd come— proved to be a stone yard about the size of a city street inter- section. The ground had been leveled, but not paved or tiled, and the rough-hewn walls were, maybe, thirty or forty feet high. It wasn't the size of the Grand Canyon or anything, but still, Cuz knew he damn-well should have seen the nafoga'ar from the hilltop. He had better things to worry about, though, than optical illusions, mirages, or magic.

There were three smallish stone buildings in the stone yard, and a pillar that Cuz uncomfortably recognized from his day and night of hanging from a log while Hubcap asked questions he couldn't answer. But the main thing had to be the cave pretty much opposite the maze-end where he and Goro stepped into the stone yard. The cave seemed to be a little less than man-high and surrounded by symbols that were the closest thing to writing that Cuz had seen since Jerlayne pulled him out of the lab.

A goblin shoved a spear between Cuz and Goro as they stood together on the edge of the stone yard. A second goblin appeared to lead Goro away. Cuz was starting to have trouble with air and breathing when a third goblin yanked him side- ways. He stumbled, caught his balance, and glanced back quickly, but Goro was gone.

Without thinking, Cuz shouted Goro's name and got a fist in the gut for his foolishness—*there* was some real pain to take his mind off dread. Then his captor shoved and spun him through a narrow doorway into one of the three buildings. In- side, there was one elevator-sized room, completely empty, and open to the sky. The sun was straight up, a long way from sundown. But, shit—at least it was autumn, not the middle of June. Autumn back in the city Cuz had left behind. Shit, for all he knew, this weird-ass place didn't have anything to do with the Earth or June or autumn. It could be the land of the fucking midnight sun.

Cuz rubbed his gut and his yanked shoulder. He was alone; the goblin hadn't followed him through the doorway. Nothing stopped Cuz from pacing, or weeping, or peeking out to the stone yard.

Two scary women stood out there: Goro's mother and an- other one who actually had a crown on her head and carried what had to be a magic wand. She waved the wand in front of Goro's mother. Nothing happened, except they both walked out of Cuz's sight. Somewhere, big drums started pounding out a two-beat rhythm: thump, *thump;* thump, *thump;* slow at first, growing faster. Cuz knew the tricks that drums could play, but he was unable to keep his heart from pounding in synch with the drums.

Then the wailing started. Back against a corner and standing on his toes, Cuz saw goblins lining the top of the nafoga'ar walls. He figured they'd have to stop after a few minutes, but they kept it up—a blanket of eerie sound that sank into the nafoga'ar, echoing off the stone, worse than the goddamned siren storm at Sunrise and enough to drive a man mad. Cuz slid down the wall till his butt touched the ground. He covered his ears with his hands, not that it helped.

When the wailing and the drumming stopped, the silence was even worse. Cuz crept to the narrow doorway. He got there in time to see Goro paraded by. The goblin had been stripped to a loincloth. A log balanced along his shoulders, and his hands were lashed to the ends of the log. Cuz knew what that meant, though he imagined Goro faced something more than Hubcap asking questions about Sunrise.

Cuz wondered if Goro would scream or if the goblin was one of those hero types who never cracked. He was immediately ashamed of himself for even thinking such a question, but got an answer almost as quickly when every rock echoed agony.

The sun hadn't moved far. There was a whole lot of time until sundown. Squatted in the corner again, with his fingers pressed as far into his ears as they would go, Cuz put another piece into the puzzle: The gennern had let Goro's mother come to the nafoga'ar—where she'd once ruled and where she expected to regain her power—because they assumed there was no way in hell Goro would survive long enough for her to snooker them.

Goro's mother—out there on the other side of the wall, ripping her son to little pieces—was next to go, if Goro didn't last until sundown.

Damn, but goblins played dangerous, deadly games; with no net, no retreat, no margin for error.

Cuz curled up tighter. He started saying prayers he'd learned before he went to school, before Uncle Ted started in on him, back when he still believed in God-with-a-capital-G.

"Now I lay me down to sleep . . ."

He didn't know any other prayers, and he hadn't started believing in God again, but he needed something to wall himself
away from what was happening to Goro.

"Now I lay me down to sleep . . . now I lay me down to
sleep . . ."

Cuz was mindless in futile prayer when they came to get
him. There were shadows across the stone yard—not quite
sunset shadows, but getting there. They—goblins, two of
them, with spears—prodded Cuz toward the cave mouth. He
looked at his feet as he walked. Cuz was determined not to look
at the pillar, but it was like not thinking about an elephant, and
his eyes cranked up by themselves—

Not good. Not good. Goro's toes weren't touching the
ground; and Cuz knew how bad that, just by itself, was. All the
goblin's weight hung from his wrists; and he weighed a lot more
than Cuz. That blue skin didn't show the wounds like other colors would, but there was a big red splotch on the stone beneath
him, and his head just hung there against his breastbone.

As far as Cuz could see, there wasn't any part of Goro that
was moving, but his alien-queen mother was still on her feet,
so maybe he was still alive.

Maybe they'd dragged him out for the last rites. It sure
seemed that way when Cuz's two goblins veered to the right.
They were pointed at the pillar, then, not the cave.

The drums started beating again, and the wailing—which
was almost a relief, because Goro was still alive. Cuz watch his
head snap up and all his muscles bulge when his mother started
making her hand movements. But he was weak enough and his
vocal cords were torn enough that, even though they had Cuz
standing no more than ten feet from the pillar, he couldn't hear
anything coming out of Goro's wide-open mouth.

On the other hand, the shadows were getting longer by the
heartbeat. It was closer to sunset than Cuz had imagined it was.
The other goblin woman, the one with the crown and wand,
looked definitely pissed and the two spear carriers on either
side of Cuz kept changing their grips on their weapons.

He was bait, Cuz reminded himself; he wasn't going to die
before sundown. Two spear carriers, two spears: one for Goro,
one for his mother. Or, maybe, both for his mother, because
Goro wasn't a threat to anyone anymore.

Beyond doubt, these guys cheated.

So Cuz watched the hands of the goblins beside him. *Maybe* he could stop one of them from offing Goro's mother—not that she didn't deserve to die for what she'd done to Goro. Period. It didn't matter whether Goro thought he was getting his father's honor back or keeping Jerlayne safe. Mothers shouldn't ever be allowed to do to their sons what the alien queen had done to hers. But *maybe,* if Cuz could distract one of the spear carriers, he'd succeed in getting himself killed.

Cuz had no sense of time passing. His heart pounded with the drums, faster than the drums. He watched one spear-carrying goblin, then the other, and not the goblin a bit further to his left, the one whose skin was all torn and blistered. The shadows got longer; they were almost at the cave mouth. Belatedly, Cuz realized shadows touching the cave would signal the moment of sunset.

He watched the goblins' hands real close and lucked out. The goblin on his right shifted his grip, tensed up, started to move.

Cuz shouted, "Hey, lady! He's gonna throw a spear at you!" as he threw himself against the goblin's arm.

It didn't really matter if she couldn't figure it out.

Then all hell broke loose. Cuz had forgotten about the damned rifles, forgotten that if *he* could figure out that the gennern goblins were going to cheat, then the alien queen knew it too. And just because her guys had checked their swords, spears, and knives at the proverbial door, that didn't mean they weren't still around or that they'd just been cooling their heels while Goro suffered. Goro's people hadn't had guns when Cuz last saw them, but they'd acquired some during the long afternoon. Bullets and arrows pinged every which way from the walls above the nafoga'ar.

The goblin Cuz hit with his shoulder got hit again by a bullet, went down—on top of Cuz. Another backwards blessing: no one bothered shooting at him. Cuz played dead. He watched the other spear carrier go down, and would have sworn that both of the women had been hit, though neither one of them showed any damage.

Goro *had* to be dead, but he'd gotten his father's honor and everything else: the shadows were in the cave mouth. Goro's mother raised her hands in prayer. Cuz heard bullets. He saw stone jumping all around the alien queen, but she was something special and nothing hit her. Nothing hit the other woman, either. Her hands were up in the air, too.

The drums stopped. The wailing stopped. Finally the bullets stopped. Everything came down to two women and playground battle tactics: My god's stronger than your god. God loves me more than God loves you.

Cuz started wriggling free, trying not to attract too much attention. His sleeve got caught on the goblin's knife. He grabbed the hilt and kept wriggling. He stopped when he noticed the shadows were suddenly going the other way: there was light and mist billowing out of the cave. Cursing, Cuz stopped worrying about attention and kicked free of the dead goblin. He scrambled to his feet in time to see the mist surround Goro's mother.

For a heartbeat or two, Cuz didn't know if that was a good thing or a bad thing, then a dome of light a little like the blast sphere of an atomic bomb, only smaller, spread slowly—a couple of inches with every heartbeat—out from Goro's mother. Nothing happened when it touched Goro or the spear-carrying goblin who'd stood on Cuz's left—but they were both dead before it touched them. Being nobody's fool, Cuz retreated.

The other goblin woman—the one with the crown and the wand—still had her arms up. Cuz wasn't sure about winners and losers until the light dome reached the crowned woman.

She exploded.

Cuz felt the backlash: a fine, hot spray of gritty liquid. For the first time, he was grateful for the magic that had turned him blue, because, though his hand was moist after he wiped it across his face, its color was pretty much unchanged. But he'd let himself get distracted; the light dome caught him and oozed around his arm. Cuz thought it was the end of him and couldn't move. It touched his face; he screamed.

His ears popped and Cuz was inside the light, alive and unharmed.

Bait for the alien queen's next trap.

Goro's mother didn't seem to notice him. Her arms remained upraised; and though she was facing her son, she didn't seem to notice him either. Mist continued to seep out of the cave. A few tendrils rose upward, toward a sky that was obscured by light, but mostly it flowed along the stone like water. Rising water. Whatever the mist touched, it covered and kept covered.

Having survived sunset, Cuz began to worry about his next step. He toyed with the notion of putting his knife between the alien queen's ribs. What she'd done to Goro was, and would always be, unforgivable, and Cuz wasn't nearly close to solving his biggest problem: how to get home, preferably home to the real world, but back to fairyland, at least.

Cuz didn't see himself surviving a long time if he were stuck in this world with these mad, brutal, and cruel aliens. He didn't want to; he'd rather go out in a blaze of glory. But first, Cuz reached down into the misty light. He collected another knife from the goblin who'd fallen on him and a third from the other spear carrier who'd gone down closer to the pillar.

He looked.

"Aw—*shit*."

Goro's head was down, his eyes were closed, but—damn it all—his chest was still moving.

Cuz had a knife and no choice. When it had been him dangling from a log, Hubcap and Diras had hung him and unhung him like a picture on a wall, but there was no way Cuz could lift Goro down. He'd have to cut the rope above the log, which he could do, a few fibers at a time. The rope swayed, the log swayed, Goro swayed, and Goro groaned: not only was he alive, he was sort of conscious.

The goblin let out a long gasp as the last twisted strands of rope frayed loose: Goro's weight swung to one side, he struck the pillar, and then the unhung log drove him down to his knees, to his face. All three happened in the blinking of an eye. Cuz hurried to hack through the ropes holding Goro's wrists to the log.

Incredibly, Goro moved his arm, folding it against his chest, the moment it was free. Cuz worked frantically to cut the other rope and haul the log away, but there was little else he could do, and by then, he'd gotten a good, close look at the damage.

The kindest thing Cuz figured he could do for Goro was slit his throat. There wasn't a square inch of Goro's skin that wasn't burnt or cut—and that was just his skin. Cuz couldn't—wouldn't—try to imagine what Goro's mother had done to his insides. He sat beside him, hip-deep in mist, afraid to touch him; so, naturally, Goro grabbed his arm instead.

"Get away."

It was a voice from the grave, raspy and raw. Cuz could see where Goro had bit his tongue clean through. And his eyes—

Goro opened his eyes. Cuz wouldn't have thought all-black eyes could look different, but they did. He couldn't shake the sense that the goblin was blind.

"You rest," Cuz chided him. Rest was all he could do; rest until he finally did die. "Take it easy and rest, okay?"

"Get away." Goro squeezed the arm he held.

Damned if the goblin weren't still strong enough to wring a wince out of him.

"Can't do it," Cuz replied and stroked Goro's hair. That shouldn't hurt him too much.

"Cave. Get to the cave. Nafoga'ar. Get away."

"Sorry. I'll take my chances right here." Until the goblin was gone. Then Cuz would reconsider putting a knife into his mother.

Goro groaned and got his right arm out from underneath him. He dug his fingers into Cuz's shoulder and tried to pull himself up.

"Get away. Cave. *Sunrise*."

Suddenly, Cuz was paying much closer attention. "Sunrise? That cave goes to Sunrise?" It wasn't any more unbelievable than anything else Cuz had seen or lived through in the last few days.

With considerable strain to Cuz's shoulder, Goro had hauled himself to one knee.

"Look, Goro—you're hurt *real* bad. You can't— You better—" Cuz felt like a traitor, telling Goro he wouldn't live to get back to Sunrise so he shouldn't bother trying. "Just— Lie back and *rest,* Goro. You'll feel better."

"Nothing here to live for," Goro countered, a shout in that ruined voice of his.

He groaned again and had both feet flat on the ground. The goblin was going to stand. Cuz accepted the inevitable and tried help. On his best day Cuz didn't have the strength or size to support a man like Goro, and this had been far short of a good day. They both came within an eyelash of crashing down again. Cuz continued to feel squeamish about touching all that torn and weeping skin.

Goro wasn't beyond pain. He gasped when Cuz wrapped an arm above his waist and he cried out with every step he managed. There had to be broken bones—legs, ribs, everywhere. Cuz had never heard a man make the kinds of noises Goro made. He moved by throwing himself forward.

But he moved toward the cave, with Cuz beneath and beside him.

It was a lost cause, even if they had both been at the peak of health. Though it leaked light and mist, the inside of the cave was pitch black and no where near as smooth on the ground as the stone yard had been. They went down three steps past the entrance and there was no getting up again.

Cuz wasn't sure he'd try to go deeper after Goro died. Without any light, blind faith wasn't going to get him to Sunrise.

Since they fell, Goro hadn't done any more talking. Cuz had wriggled himself upright and sitting, with Goro's head resting in his lap. The goblin's breathing had gone strange the way Wills' breathing went the last hour or so before he died. Chenye-Stokes respiration, the nurse had called it as she disconnected the tubes that had kept Wills alive. She'd looked away when Cuz crawled into the hospital bed to hold his lover one last time.

"You're not alone. I promised you, you wouldn't have to die alone . . . I'm here. You don't know it, but I am."

The cave was utter darkness, utter quiet. They were both breathing mist. Probably it wasn't good for either one of them. Probably it didn't matter. Cuz leaned back against rock. He hadn't chosen a very comfortable spot for his vigil and Goro's weight had cut off the circulation below his knees. He closed his eyes and thought of stories he'd read and preferred to his own life's memories.

A noise roused him, not from Goro. The goblin was quiet, breathing quiet; the shudders and rattles were gone. He seemed to be asleep—or maybe it was Cuz, himself, dreaming that the goblin was asleep. Then the noise repeated: stone bouncing across stone.

Bats or rats? Forgetting his earlier aversion, Cuz patted all the parts of Goro that he could reach: making sure they didn't have company.

But they did. Another stone bounced and was followed by a beam of light. They'd hobbled into the cave from the right. The light came from the left. From Sunrise? Would Aulaudin come looking for them? Aulaudin or Jerlayne. Cuz opened his mouth to shout *Over here!*, then shut it without making a sound. He'd wait, he thought, until the light got a lot closer, or until he thought it might be moving away.

The light came closer: a flashlight by its color and steady

beam. They had flashlights at Sunrise, but still Cuz held his tongue. He began to hear footsteps, and muttering.

"You'll suffer. You haven't begun to suffer. You'll suffer the way my son suffered."

The muttering had a feminine pitch and a not-quite-sane cadence. Goro's mother? God knew, her son had suffered and Cuz, for one, wouldn't pity her if she'd lost her mind. He had no intention of calling *her* over to see her son.

She repeated herself with minor variations. The mist cast the light everywhere. Cuz worried that she'd see them; she seemed headed right their way. But she walked by and she wasn't Goro's mother. Cuz didn't know who she was: her hair was black like a goblin's but she had the upswept, pointy ears of real fairy tales. Jerlayne and Aulaudin had ordinary, rounded ears.

"Betray me!"

In another example of Cuz's usual rotten luck, the woman stopped in front of them to explore some new tangent of her insanity. If she'd looked to her right, surely she would see them, but her attention was thrust downward, at her left hand.

"Betray me, will you? *You'll* see. You'll see betrayal! Kill *my* son! But I'll find the youngster, the baby. I'll find them. They're *mine*. I'm not finished. You wait and see. You *wait and see!*"

She raised her left hand into the light.

Cuz's heart skipped a beat: the madwoman with the cartoon-elf ears was talking to Uncle Ted. Well, talking to his head. The rest of Uncle Ted had gone missing. Cuz didn't think Ol' Ted was listening; then again, maybe Ted really hadn't begun to suffer.

Couldn't happen to a more deserving fellow.

Of course, there were a world of implications in Claideris' mutterings, madwoman or not. Implications and the realization that Cuz was looking at his grandmother, that his father had been his uncle's first victim, and that he was the "youngster" she was looking for and his son—Jerlayne and Aulaudin's son—was the "baby."

"Mine!" the madwoman repeated, shaking some bloody clots out of Uncle Ted's neck. "Did you think I wouldn't find them? Or you?"

Cuz had to breathe. He tried to do it quietly and slid his hand over Goro's nose as well. That was a *huge* mistake: the goblin opened his mouth and moaned. It wasn't a loud moan and it wasn't repeated. If the madwoman had been muttering, she'd never have heard it. But that wasn't the way Cuz's luck ran.

Claideris hoisted her flashlight up as if she was the fucking Statue of Liberty and it was a torch. Old habits, Cuz supposed; it was easy to forget how old these people—his people—were. Then she righted the flashlight and shone it straight toward Cuz and Goro.

The madwoman didn't say anything, and Cuz wasn't about to introduce himself. He wasn't near stupid enough to think he'd have an easy time with the alien queen who'd killed Uncle Ted.

"Look at him," she said, brandishing Uncle Ted's head.

Cuz looked. Something was dangling out of the neck, pointed at the ground. After a numb moment, Cuz realized it was his uncle's tongue. He'd have run, if Goro weren't weighing him down; or vomited, if he hadn't been so shit-terrified.

"He thought he could outwit me," Claideris continued. "Him and my son. I told them to bring the girl to the mist. Her child would be immortal if she bore him in the mist. I told them—"

Without warning, the madwoman lapsed into the clicks, squawks, and whistles that passed for language on the plains. Cuz's luck was running true to form: his one chance to find out who he was and he didn't understand a word she said. Then, just as suddenly, Claideris returned to the almost-English of Fairie.

"They didn't listen. *He* didn't listen!" She shook the head. "My son was already dead. Come back to the mist, I'd told him. Come back at each full moon; I'll shape the death out of you—the mortal death. I've learned it all! The secrets of the plains, the secrets of Fairie, the secrets of science. I can do anything! My children—My son—He stopped coming to the mist. This one—"

Claideris came closer, a lot closer. She thrust her trophy at Cuz's face. He could smell the rot, the fear, and shut his eyes.

"Mortals!" the madwoman shrieked and Cuz's eyes popped open. "No matter what they're given, they want more . . . always more. They destroy what they have to take what they can't hold! He killed my son and hid himself, the girl, and the child. Wait! I told myself. Wait! Be patient. He is mortal;

he'll overreach. He'll want what he can't have and then I'll have him!

"I waited. I was patient. I amused myself. The bride a Sunrise—I had hope for her and her protector, her fool—"

Cuz said a little, grateful prayer that Goro was in no condition to hear *that*.

"I thought they'd trysted. Her son—the son of that elf and that goblin. I kept a close eye on them from the shadows—they never looked!—I thought I might begin again, but I thought too small. *She* had the necklace—my son's lineage—and gave it to her fool. I watched from shadows as he carried it to the plains, to his mother! The dutiful son. The loyal son!

"She'll kill him. She'll kill him, if she hasn't killed him already. Her second son—but worth the price. We'll meet again she and I. She has yet to suffer!"

Hard to believe, but Cuz silently wished Goro's mother wel when she and his own grandmother had their rematch.

"The nafoga'ar will be mine again. Fairie is already mine they think I'm one of them! When I'm done, there'll be no mortals. I'll take it all back and give it to my children—my son—I have a son left. The son of my son, and his son again.

"I'm not finished," she said and dropped her head, Uncle Ted's head.

It struck Goro's breastbone and rolled, nose over dangling tongue, onto the rough stone. Cuz, who'd stopped breathing again, began to gasp. He was fighting for air; Claideris fought for something else. She nearly lost her balance reaching for Uncle Ted's head and her hand—

Cuz hadn't noticed Claideris' hand before, no surprise considering what it had held, but her flesh was rough and pitted like an old sponge. She wasn't well. Maybe she'd spent too much time tracking down Uncle Ted.

Cuz would never know. Claideris locked her fingers in what remained of Uncle Ted's hair and walked unevenly away. He thought about following her and her flashlight, but Goro wasn't dead, wasn't dying. When she'd shone the light on him his skin was scabbed over. His face, which had been a bloody wreck, had healed completely, without even a scar.

And, anyway, Claideris was so mad, there was no reason to think she still knew where she was going. Better to sit in the dark until Goro woke up, or *his* mother came looking for them.

Chapter 36

Four nights had passed since Aulaudin returned from the plains with a warning from a goblin priestess to protect Laydin. Three nights had passed since Evoni returned to her black rocks in the middle of Sunrise Bay. It was the longest the homestead had gone without the siren singing up a storm since she'd sung up the first what seemed like a lifetime ago.

Hints of ordinary life were returning to Sunrise. Gnomes had reclaimed the kitchen from goblins and were baking bread again. The yeasty smells were so thick, so delicious, that Jerlayne yearned for breakfast and her stomach growled so loudly that she'd doubled the lap blanket meant to ward away the night chill. Gelma was in the nursery and Evandi, her brother Mati's nurse, too. The gnomes were both asleep. Their tasks were to take care of the infants; Jerlayne's was to protect them.

She wasn't alone. There were goblins on the roof, a goblin outside the door, and a pair of goblins outside the shuttered and blanketed windows. Sunrise took the threat Claideris posed very seriously. Between thoughts of breakfast, Jerlayne recalled the black-haired sage demanding the right to raise Laydin as her own son, away from homestead life.

She hadn't fully understood the horror and ambition of Claideris' proposal then; maybe Claideris hadn't either. At the time, perhaps the sage—the goblin in disguise—would have been content to steal the son she thought was Goro's. Now though, according to the impressions Aulaudin brought back from the plains, Claideris knew Laydin was her own grandson.

Jerlayne was prepared to *nuke* Claideris with shaped pain, but after Aulaudin described how Goro's mother—the goblin priestess—had stolen a lock of his hair without appearing to touch him, she'd asked Maialene for the gun she'd gotten from the mortal woman she'd killed.

M'lene had promised to fetch it "right away" from her mortal realm bolt-hole. She'd left two days ago and hadn't returned. Jerlayne had some choice words for her sister's notion of fast action. It was just as well that women couldn't share and sharing couldn't pass from one realm to another. If M'lene had gone off searching for Cuz without bringing the gun to Sunrise . . . well, she could forget about another cottage.

Maialene had listened to Aulaudin's description of Cuz's transformation with the attention children reserved for the opening of gifts. No matter that Laydin's father had apparently become a goblin or that M'lene compared goblins unfavorably with insects and vermin.

"He's immortal now."

When Jerlayne had tried, delicately, to explain that, mortal or immortal, Cuz might be a less-than-ideal lover, M'lene had dismissed her concerns.

"I don't want a lover, Jery, and neither does he. That's what makes us perfect for each other."

Jerlayne sincerely wished them both well, whatever they did, wherever they wound up, and whether they were together or apart, so long as Maialene's gun wound up at Sunrise . . . soon.

The latch on the nursery door lifted with a soft, but unmistakable *click*. Jerlayne thought about pain and slipped her hand into a skirt pocket. The knife warmed.

«Jerlayne? Beloved?» Aulaudin's thoughts preceded him into the room.

«Awake. Here,» she replied. The knife cooled.

«The sun's rising. Time for breakfast and bed.»

With its blanketed windows, the nursery was in perpetual darkness. They touched, joined, kissed.

«I want a gun, Aulaudin. I can't wait for M'lene. Will you get me a gun?»

Jerlayne shared the appropriate memories of the bus she had destroyed and the mortal woman with her palm-sized weapon.

Aulaudin had agreed with his father. The bus had contained a *television satellite uplink*: It was part, or all of the cabinets she had destroyed. They agreed, too, that there were thousands of such *communications uplinks* in the mortal realm. *Communications* were part of *science* and the pervasive mortal-realm noise that gave everyone headaches. But neither Aulaudin nor Maun, who prided his knowledge of mortal *science*, could explain how or why a *television satellite uplink* had become a weapon against Fairie.

The how and why weren't as important as the certainty that there weren't enough nights in an immortal woman's life in which to destroy them all. Fairie had to rely on its guardians for a defense against *communications*. They had to rely on Evoni and the siren off the southern coast.

Men still came to Sunrise every day, but using the pass-throughs so the scyldrin could talk face-to-face. As long as they brought their own food, Jerlayne already tended to ignore them. She learned what she needed from Aulaudin. It was as if every night were midsummer; Vigilance might last an hour or more, but they were all learning about one another.

Whether through Vigilance or in conversations beside the foundation stone, elves and scyldrin alike had begun to speculate that more sirens would rise. A few said that Fairie would become an island. Others turned, as they had in the past, to the sages. The sages—the four men, Gudwal, Rintidas, Arlesken, and Ertinel—had no advice. They hadn't known about *communications* and wouldn't speculate about sirens or islands. They hadn't recovered from the revelations about Claideris.

Maun said that if they had any decency, they'd link hands and follow Claideris into the mist. That was Maun. In a week's time, he'd gone from railing against goblins to railing against sages. It was only a matter of time until no one paid attention to him again.

Fairie needed its sages. At a minimum, they were the ones who unlocked the magic of joining at an elfin wedding, and the scyldrin wouldn't hear of Fairie without them.

«We won't do anything about the sages before breakfast,» Aulaudin assured her. «Then, promise me, you'll sleep until tomorrow. Sunrise is not swarming with enemies. There's no need for a gun.»

Jerlayne swallowed her argument that she wasn't worried about nameless, swarming enemies, but a specific woman who, quite possibly, had mastered all the shadowing, shaping, and shifting talents of elves and goblins together.

Instead, she asked, «It was a quiet night?»

Aulaudin could say that Sunrise wasn't swarming with enemies, but like Jerlayne, he was staying awake at night, roof-sitting with the goblins or making a regular circuit of the homestead's great house, outbuildings, scyldrin cottages.

«We surprised a pig,» Aulaudin shared the memories. «I

don't know who was more surprised, me or it, but the goblins know what they're doing.»

With both Joff and Goro still missing—and neither likely to return—the remaining goblins had, improbably, turned to a rust-haired elf for their daily orders. He asked them what would Goro tell them to do, and after they told him, he'd tell them to go ahead and do it.

«The dust will settle,» they assured each other.

Although neither Jerlayne nor Aulaudin had spoken aloud, their presence had awakened Gelma. She'd see to Laydin now; his elfin parents could go on to the kitchen.

They did, arm-in-arm and mindful of the disorder. The Sunrise scyldrin may have been the dwarves and gnomes who'd insisted on their right to be included in the discussions that were sweeping through Fairie, but over the last few days they'd proven that they were more interested in repairing the roofs before winter set in.

The door to the room where Elmeene and Jereige slept was closed. Elmeene had shaped its latch into a tangled mass that said as much about her mood as it did about any need for privacy. Jerlayne's mother wanted to refound Stonewell, to bring it back better than before. Jereige wanted to sit in a chair with his hands folded in his lap. Although no one heard them talk to each other, Jerlayne knew they were waging a sad, desperate war.

«Why not a cottage for them, too?» Aulaudin suggested; he'd already agreed to the new one for Maialene.

«I haven't forgotten why I was in a hurry to leave Stonewell. M'lene I can manage; I'm not convinced Fairie itself is big enough for Elmeene and me.»

They both thought of Cuz, of Goro, and whether Fairie or Sunrise, not to mention their marriage, was big enough for all the mixed loyalties it now contained, if the men who embodied those loyalties were still alive to claim them. By mutual, but unuttered, consent, they retreated into unshared thoughts.

Everything Aulaudin shared at Vigilance and, afterward with Jerlayne, indicated that Goro's mother had reclaimed the nafoga'ar and was the sage-of-sages on the plains. Every sunset, a few more homesteads declared that their goblin protectors had offered new and interesting bargains. The changes in Fairie were being matched, it seemed, by changes on the plains. There'd been blood, but not as much as anyone expected, and now there was peace, peace enforced by a woman who'd sacrificed her son.

Reportedly, goblins were *cheerful* elsewhere in Fairie. At Sunrise, the goblins, like Jerlayne and Aulaudin, were waiting for familiar faces to reappear and growing more apprehensive each day that they didn't.

Aulaudin collected a loaf of bread from the cooling racks by the oven; Jerlayne spooned jam onto a plate. They met outside the kitchen and followed the path until they had a good view of sunlight sparkling on the sea. Steam like the mists at the heart of Fairie rose from the bread when Aulaudin cracked its shiny brown crust.

"When the bread's this good—" Aulaudin began and stopped short.

Aglaun and Ombrio were wintering at Sunrise, which was grateful for the help. Jerlayne thought one of them had seized her husband's attention. She waited impatiently; sharing remained a woman's insurmountable hurdle. Then she heard the shouting. Abandoning their breakfast, Jerlayne raced behind Aulaudin, to the far side of the great house and up the hill.

She saw three goblins fire arrows into shadow—the arrows simply vanished.

Sunrise had traded with Briary and other homesteads to replace the bows their goblins had lost in the storm. They'd salvaged a fair number of arrows; many of the shafts were damaged, but arrowheads could be reused—unless they disappeared.

Jerlayne had cut up an old shawl and given *their* goblins bands of lightly patterned silk to wear on their sleeves in the faint hope of distinguishing one from another. The old goblin campsite might be in complete confusion, but with the fluttering armbands, at least she and Aulaudin knew they hadn't stumbled into an ambush—a serious concern when arrows vanished, though Jerlayne suspected—feared—that there'd only been one target.

"Too late!" Aglaun shouted from further up the hill. "Did you hit her?" he called to the nearest archer.

The question confirmed Jerlayne's fears. She held her breath, waiting for the answer.

"No," the one goblin confessed, a second said, "Wasted shot," and the third said nothing at all.

"But it was her—Claideris," Ombrio said breathlessly. "I saw her face. I'd know that face anywhere, I swear it."

They were all headed downhill again, for the nursery, just in case. Gelma and Evandi flew into a panic when armed goblins traipsed into their domain, but they'd sensed nothing untoward in the moments before the invasion. Over the gnomes' protests, Aulaudin left one of the goblins in the nursery. He and Jerlayne headed out to finish their breakfast.

A flock of seagulls were fighting over their bread. Jerlayne chased them away, but there was no way she or Aulaudin would touch the crumbs that were left. She rescued the jam plate.

"And the day started off so nicely," Aulaudin said.

"She's come once. She'll come again. We haven't been wrong to be on guard for her. I want a gun."

"You saw what happened with the arrows, beloved. Claideris escaped into shadow."

"Bows and arrows won't work inside the great house, but a gun will. I saw what a gun can do. Felt it, too."

"All right. I'll go to the mortal realm today, after I've rested. I'll see what I can find. It's not just a gun. I have to find bullets, too, and they have to be matched to the gun. If they're not, the gun can blow up in your hand."

She hadn't known that bullets were shaped to each individual gun, or that a gun could hurt the person who used it. These were serious disappointments, but she still wanted one of the powerful mortal weapons. Aulaudin's promises were better than M'lene's. He'd part the Veil and bring her back a gun to shoot at Claideris, if she reminded him later on in the day, when they'd both rested.

Even as she yawned and followed Aulaudin through the corridors to their bedroom, Jerlayne was certain she wouldn't fall asleep: the image of those arrows disappearing into shadow without touching Claideris was too disturbing for dreams.

The dwarf who said, "Jerlayne, Jerlayne! Wake up! The goblin's come!" took her by surprise. She was out of the bedroom before she realized she awakened alone.

Through a gaping window, she glimpsed another dwarf leading a black horse toward the stable. She hurried outside where Aulaudin was already talking to a goblin. By the angle of the sun as she came down the high door steps, the day had slipped past midafternoon.

«You shouldn't have let me sleep so long,» she chided her husband. «You should have awakened me the moment you saw a goblin coming!»

There was only one goblin standing in the grass where she wanted to see two. And, before she'd gotten close enough for spoken conversation, Jerlayne knew that the goblin wasn't Goro, either, but Joff, Goro's second whom she hadn't seen since the morning Cuz disappeared.

Neither Joff nor Aulaudin were smiling. Jerlayne slipped her hand around her husband's once she stood beside him.

«Uylma—the priestess, Goro's mother—got everything she wanted,» Aulaudin shared. «As far as we need to know, the goblins have stopped fighting with each other and our side won.» His thoughts were cold and hard-edged.

«Goro? Cuz?»

Aulaudin's presence became an emptiness. Jerlayne couldn't tell if he was angry because she'd asked or because of what Joff was saying.

"She does not approve of men living beneath roofs. The shadows beneath roofs and between walls are thin and will make them weak—but men who have chosen to live in Fairie are not her concern. They may do what they wish, so long as guardians dwell in the mist and the mist does not shrink toward the plains. Elves and scyldrin may do what they wish—"

"Why, thank you," Aulaudin snapped, letting Jerlayne know that his anger flowed toward Joff, not her. "Tell the Uylma the poor elves said thank you."

Joff blinked. "She *knows* the danger, Aulaudin, and accepts it. You *should* give thanks: there will be no more culling, no more fighting among the lineages for the privileges of trade. The Uylma won't allow it. She's taken all Fairie into her hand. Every man who comes here will serve her, no one else, no man or lineage. You're free. Your sages will never hear her speaking in their mists—for that matter, they never did. The Uylma—my sister, Goro's mother—never spoke from the mists. She heeded the wisdom of her consort—Goro's father: Fairie is our defense against the mortal realm, and as the mortal realm changes, so must our defense. When we cull or tell you what to do, we place ourselves at risk.

"My sister thought she was leaving you alone, but the one you call Claideris, has spoken to you, both as Uylma, when she held the nafoga'ar, and afterward, as one of your sages. My sister seeks her, the one you call Claideris, now—"

"That's not good enough!" Jerlayne interrupted, trying to grasp the full extent of Claideris' meddling. "We're waiting for Claideris right here—she wants to steal my son. We'll stop her here, too, with goblin help or without it. We're ready to protect ourselves now. But stopping Claideris isn't enough! She's been a sage since my mother shaped her chain, and she was this . . . this *uylma* for how many years before that? How many others have there been? How many years—how many thousands of years have goblins been twisting our lives around?

"It's over. It has to be over and we have to have proof that it's over. We're not going to be second-class citizens!"

Both men blinked confusion and surprise.

"Cuz told me. He said the scyldrin were second-class citizens to elves because we live in the great house and they're servants. He was wrong about us and the scyldrin, but not about Fairie. You—the goblins, all of you—have treated us as worse than servants. You treat us as cattle or sheep because, you say, Fairie's your defense against the mortal realm. Well, Fairie isn't *your* defense against anything! Fairie is our home—all of us: elves, gnomes, dwarves, all the scyldrin and the guardians, too!

"You can't *decide* to leave us alone because leaving us alone is good for you. You'll leave us alone because if you don't, you can forget about iron or steel or anything else we forage and shape for you. We don't *need* you anymore. You're going to have to do better."

"I am only her herald," Joff said quickly, dismissing Jerlayne's anger and eloquence with a half-step retreat. "I have no part in better or worse. The Uylma has admitted an error. She allowed her predecessor to escape into the mist and die by her own hand. It has always been that way, when one uylma replaces another, but my sister did not roam the mist after she first claimed the nafoga'ar. That was her error and she did not repeat it a few days back when she reclaimed her place. She will roam the mist now, because it serves her. She will slay Claideris and any others she finds there because it serves her. And she will ignore Fairie, except to take the oaths of any man who chooses to dwell here. Is that better?

"In my life," Joff continued, "I have never known any

uylma, but especially my sister, to admit an error. If you consider it, she does you great honor—I would be greatly honored if the Uylma admitted an error to me. And in one day, the Uylma considered two errors: the one which she had admitted and a second, which she still considers: we have let the mortal realm change too much without changing with it. In the beginning, the guardians were giants and trolls, then came the dragons and griffins. We may have misunderstood the sirens when the first one appeared. She watches Sunrise to see what happens next."

"We're honored—" Aulaudin began. His tone contradicted his words completely.

"Very honored," Jerlayne interrupted. She'd purged herself of venom and was ready to think of the future. There was no need to change the tradition that women bargained with goblins, not when men were so quick to make fists at each other. "But the greatest honor would be to have Goro back—" her breath caught, she swallowed hard and continued in a softer voice, "At least to know what happened to him and Cuz. Did they—Have they both died?"

Jerlayne tightened her grip on Aulaudin's hand, determined to not to succumb to any emotion. One was—or had been—the mortal father of her son, the other was a goblin—a man—who had placed her at the center his life without ever asking her permission. She'd never known either of them as well as she'd known Nereige, Brel, and Joren. If the deaths of her bachelor brothers hadn't put a hole in her heart. . . .

"They entered the mist."

"They *died*." Jerlayne corrected. Aulaudin hovered on the verge of her perception. She held him off. "They *died* for the Uylma. She *sacrificed* them to get that place I can't pronounce properly back." M'lene, who'd spent more time in the mortal realm, perhaps, than any other woman, had told Jerlayne the meaning of the word *sacrifice*.

"Goro knew he must survive until sundown to reclaim his father's honor. He was alive then. I saw him move when Uylma called on the gods to confront her first rival. The last I saw, as I put my arrows into the gennern was the young one, Cuz, throwing himself at the gennern beside him. By then the gods had favored my sister and the mist flowing out of the nafoga'ar grew bright. A moment later, I could see nothing. I was first down when the light dimmed. My sister, was alive, flush with her victory. The gennern, except for the uylma she'd destroyed utterly, lay where they'd fallen. But Goro and Cuz were gone. Goro had been cut down and there were bloody footprints leading into the cave itself. There was no mist then and the cave was empty, but we thought—"

Jerlayne shook her head.

"I hoped I'd find them both here. The young one found his honor; he conquered his fears when he attacked the gennern and Goro did not free himself or walk unaided into the cave."

"And Goro's honor?" Jerlayne asked.

Joff shrugged. "It all balanced at the end. He'd broken an oath to Uylma; not even his father did that. He knew what would happen if he ever returned to the plains, but he was the only one who could have gotten her into the nafoga'ar. So it balanced, and when sundown came, he was free. If he lived that long, they were done with each other. Uylma wouldn't care what he did afterward."

"You're cruel." Jerlayne could barely contain her contempt. "You're terrible and cruel and your Uylma is the cruelest, most terrible of all. To kill your own son to have vengeance on your enemies, no true mother could do that. I *am* grateful your Uylma won against her rivals but there's no thanks for whatever she thinks she's doing for Fairie. She should be grateful she doesn't have to face *me!* She's no better than Claideris!"

The goblin examined his fingertips. "We are what we are, Jerlayne. If you think we're cruel, it's no concern to me, but my sister has borne only two sons in all her life and she loves the youngest more, I think, than she loved his father. If there had been another way, she would have taken it. I have never seen her so angry as when she learned he was riding toward the plains; I thought we would all die."

Jerlayne was unimpressed. "It's not just you, Joff, or Uylma. It was Goro, too. He could have sent someone else with the necklace. There were nearly thirty other goblins here. You throw lives away, all of you."

"And you would cling to a life not worth living," Joff shot back. "Only Goro and I were sworn to Uylma. He'd already sent me back. He saw what the necklace meant, what it could do, and he took it back himself. He'd come to believe that Fairie needed to be more than the mist between the plains and the mortal realm. He saw a way to make that happen."

They glowered at each other, Joff and Jerlayne in an empty futile war of wills, until Aulaudin interrupted.

"Before we got to the plains, Goro said someone would come to replace him. Is that still true? Are you the new Sunrise goblin?"

Joff broke away from Jerlayne. "No. She and I hoped Goro was here. This close to the Veil, you need protection. There *are* ogres in those mists. I'll tell Uylma and she'll swear someone. Not me. Too many memories here for me to stay."

He turned from them and walked away, not toward the high door, but around the house, toward the old campground.

"What's the matter with him?" Jerlayne demanded.

She expected Aulaudin to join her condemnation of cold-hearted cruelty, but he slid his hand from hers and said: "He's lost his kinsman and best friend."

Aulaudin started after Joff.

"I don't understand. Where are you going?"

He turned, walking backward. "We look for elves when they're lost. We looked for weeks for Redis. We'll look for Goro . . . and Cuz. Joff and I, if no one else will search with us. I alone, if Joff won't."

Half of Jerlayne was horrified, outraged that her husband thought, for even a moment, about wandering the mist where Claideris was hiding. The rest of her wanted desperately to go with him. Aulaudin knew—by guess or by joining or by the look on her face—he shook his head both wide and slow.

"It's what men do, beloved. Promises we make to each other. It's nothing I planned, but they're part of my family now and I'll bring them back, if I can."

The war between wishing Aulaudin all the luck in all the realms and swearing that she'd never talk to him again if he took another step, ended in a draw. Jerlayne watched until he'd rounded the farthest corner then she turned back toward the high door.

Joff wasn't the only one who'd arrived at Sunrise while Jerlayne was sleeping. Her sister, Maialene, stood silently on the top step. Aulaudin must have seen her.

"Gnomes told me you were here," M'lene said with a nervous smile. "I didn't know I'd be interrupting. Sorry."

"You heard? He's going to look for Goro . . . and Cuz. Alone, if he has to. I think he'd rather go alone."

Maialene came down the steps to embrace Jerlayne. "Just so long as he doesn't run into Claideris—"

Jerlayne shuddered.

"Elmeene's sitting in the nursery. I guess you had some excitement this morning? If Claideris doesn't come back, or if Mother isn't the one who kills her, there'll be no living with her."

If Claideris came to Sunrise, at least she wouldn't be in the mist while Aulaudin was looking for Goro and Cuz.

"Do you have the gun?" Jerlayne asked her sister.

M'lene grinned and shook her head. "Couldn't find it. Not in that mess."

That was M'lene. Jerlayne suppressed her anger and disappointment. They entered the great house together.

*   *   *

Aglaun and Ombrio agreed to search the mist, Ombrio in particular because being included in a search, even for goblins, meant he'd come of age. Joff wanted no part of it, though he reached inside his shirt and offered Aulaudin a knot of beads similar to the ones dangling from the fateful necklace. They'd help, Joff said. Aulaudin declined the offer; he had a knife, the knife Goro had given him before they entered the plains.

Judging by the way the leather was molded and creased, the goblin had worn the knife inside his boot for years. There was a good chance that he could persuade it to lead him to Goro, if anything could lead them through the mist he'd seen with the sages.

But first, Aglaun and Ombrio weren't the only men Aulaudin wanted beside him.

«Father?»

Maun had been in Fairie during last night's Vigilance. He hadn't missed the "fun" since it began. Sunset was only a few hours away.

«Aulaudin?»

«I'm going into the mist to search for Goro and Cuz. I want you to help.» He shared the substance of his conversation with Joff and his confidence in Goro's knife.

Maun shared reservations. «Why? Not why ask me for help, but why are you doing this?» He didn't share his opinions of goblins or Goro. Aulaudin already knew those.

«I told Jerlayne: they've become close-kin.»

«Because of her?»

Aulaudin shook his head. The effect was the same in conversation and sharing. «Me. My pride. My sense of what's right. Dead or alive, I want to bring them home.»

«All right. I've got one thing to do first. I'll meet you there, at the stones in the mist. You *did* pay attention?»

«Absolutely. I had a good teacher.»

* * *

A fifteen-year-old scyld of Amblea homestead who hadn't yet changed and was destined, her father believed, to become a sylph, had run away to the forest ten days ago. With all the excitement in Fairie her father hadn't noted her disappearance in any of his Vigilance conversations. It was an understandable oversight, hardly an oversight at all, but the girl was the only unchanged scyld who'd recently gone missing when Fairie welcomed its third siren, its second new guardian in as many years.

Jereige, the only elfin man at Sunrise since Aulaudin had taken off before Vigilance with Ombrio and Aglaun, came to the nursery hours after dark to tell his wife, daughters, and an uncomfortable-looking goblin who called himself Fifth and sat on the floor beside the largest window. Jereige's son and grandson were sound asleep.

"She's in the south, with the first one," he explained. "Far off shore and no trouble to anyone. No new salt sea. No path of destruction from the heartland to the mist. An altogether considerate guardian."

Jerlayne disregarded the slight to her daughter. Her father had taken the time to groom himself carefully. The wild, wispy hair was clean and combed and the scraggly beard he'd been ignoring since Stonewell burned was gone. He was neatly dressed, albeit in borrowed clothes, but he and Aulaudin were much the same size.

"My friends say we must expect more sirens now that mortals are probing us with *communications*." Jereige continued. "And we need to know more about *science* if we're to understand why noise is a weapon. It's all well and good to have guardians and goblins, but we must take a hand in understanding the threats our enemies make. I'm going to learn how to read."

"I can teach you," M'lene offered.

Jerlayne turned to her sister, "It's too bad your books are all gone."

M'lene rolled her eyes. "Redis foraged books by size and color! I'll teach you, too, so you can leave your own messages for Aulaudin."

Jerlayne still was a bit unclear on the connections between reading and writing, but that was no concern at all as her father continued to talk about his plans for the future and the refounding of Stonewell.

"All this water," he said to Jerlayne, "and fish at every meal, but no fishing except from a boat. I want to go home."

He wanted supper, too, which Jerlayne quickly volunteered to fetch from the kitchen. She grabbed Maialene's hand and fairly pulled her out of her chair.

"What's the matter with you?" M'lene wanted to know.

"Didn't you look at Mother's face? They wanted to be alone for a little bit."

"In a nursery?" M'lene rolled her eyes again, 'With a god-damned *goblin* sitting in the corner."

Jerlayne had forgotten Fifth, but she stood by their need for privacy. "Sometimes, all you need to do is touch one finger together."

Yet more rolled eyes. "I forget, Aulaudin is the perfect husband."

He wasn't, not when he was off endangering himself. There was a lot about M'lene that did remind Jerlayne of Cuz. If he had survived his kidnapping misadventures on the goblin plains, he and her sister might have as much future as Elmeene and Jereige. She pared apples, sliced cold sausage, and arranged pickled vegetables on a plate while M'lene laughed. When she'd rearranged the pickles for the second time, Jerlayne led her sister back to the nursery.

They were walking past her workroom when they heard the first scream.

Food and crockery flew in different directions. Rounding the corner, Jerlayne saw the goblin who'd been standing outside the nursery door all evening stretched across the floor. He wasn't sleeping; as she leapt over him, Jerlayne took note of an ear-to-ear slash on his throat. She was moving too fast for prudence and crossed the nursery threshold at a run.

There was a big scorch-mark in the center of the carpet where Claideris had burst into the room. Fifth had gotten his sword out, but not much more. His face and chest were a bloody ruin, as if a huge rock had been dropped on him. Laydin and Mati's cradles weren't visible from the doorway. Jerlayne had to slow down and turn before she could see them, her mother, and the renegade.

Elmeene was fighting hard and not winning. A woman could shape pain enough to kill anything that lived, but she had to touch an enemy to inflict it. Against elves, scyldrin, and mortals, elfin women could be devastating, but Claideris had been born a goblin. She didn't shape *things*—she shaped nothing—air itself, which she'd used as a bludgeon against Fifth, as a blade against the goblin in the hall, and as a shield to hold Elmeene a long arm's-length away.

From the corner of her eye, Jerlayne caught sight of her father sprawled behind Mati's cradle. She didn't see any blood, but she couldn't look closely. While Elmeene screamed and strained against an invisible wall, Claideris reached into Laydin's cradle. Jerlayne remembered the gun, which M'lene hadn't given her, then she threw herself against Claideris' shield.

If she could feel it, perhaps she could shape her way through it, if it weren't solid around Claideris, if Claideris couldn't part the Veil without collapsing it. Slowly—perhaps too slowly—it began to yield.

Claideris laughed. She had Laydin in her arms, both arms; she held the shield with her mind.

The sound of a gun and its bullets roared behind Jerlayne's back. One . . . two . . . she lost count. Claideris' shield was proof against bullets. The renegade continued to laugh and Jerlayne could think only of the danger to Laydin, if the shield failed. Then the first bullet struck.

A circular mark, no bigger than a fingertip, appeared above Claideris' eyebrow. The laughter stopped, the shield weakened. Jerlayne lunged for her son and closed her eyes. Noise like Evoni's thunder exploded above Jerlayne's head. She hadn't remembered noise from the goblin plains, but she had Laydin in her arms as the shield failed altogether and she struggled to cushion him with her own body. And though she'd seemed to have enough time to move each muscle deliberately, her back was on the floor in a heartbeat.

Jerlayne had a clear view of her sister standing with her feet wide apart and both arms extended straight in front of her, both hands clutching a gun that was considerably larger than the one she'd brought out of the little building in the mortal realm.

"That little gun . . . it couldn't stop *me*!" M'lene said between gasping breaths. "So, I got a bigger gun, and practiced."

Warm liquid moistened Jerlayne's shoulder. She turned and if she hadn't known the bloody ruin was Claideris' skull, she never would have guessed. Worse, as she lay there, the renegade's flesh began to putrefy. The blue skin bubbled and burst like fat flung in a hot pan while the rest of Claideris dissolved into a dark, reeking ooze.

Jerlayne watched in unmoving horror as the ooze became a mist which vanished before it touched the ceiling. Elmeene recovered first. She took Laydin from Jerlayne's arms and returned him to his cradle. Then, she knelt beside her husband.

Jerlayne massaged her shoulder which had been slightly burnt as Claideris's blood boiled away.

She turned to her sister, who hadn't changed her grip on the gun, though it now pointed at the floor between her feet.

"Put it away," she said to her sister. "Thank you. With my life, thank you, but put the gun away."

Maialene did better than that. She wrapped her hands around the weapon and slowly—very, very slowly—shaped it down into a useless lump of metal.

By then Joff was there, whistled down from the ruined goblin camp. Viljuen wept, but Joff looked at the corpses and never once blinked.

*   *   *

Goro had described the nafoga'ar as a mist-filled cave and that was precisely what Aulaudin and his companions found themselves in after they'd linked arms and he'd used the leather-sheathed knife to part the Veil. None of them could say where the Veil had ended and the cave had begun, or if the two were separate at all.

«Damned strangest place I've ever been,» Maun decreed.

They'd unlinked their arms switched on two flashlights, which Ombrio and Aglaun carried and pointed according to their elders' commands. Aulaudin dangled the knife from a bit of string, spun it, and waited to see which way it pointed when it stopped moving. Maun carried a gun—the "one thing he'd had to do first."

They argued about which direction the knife pointed and

where Maun should point his mortal-realm weapon. They argued about making too much noise. They argued until Aglaun thought he heard a sound that they hadn't made and pointed his flashlight at a black-eyed, blue-skinned face.

"Cuz!"

"Aulaudin! Man! I thought I was dreaming."

Cuz climbed to his feet. He was stiff, but mostly he was slow because he'd had Goro laying across his lap and the goblin didn't awaken or move on his own.

«Doesn't look good,» Maun told all the elves.

By flashlight examination, there was nothing obviously amiss with the goblin, except that he was skeletally gaunt. There were a few marks that might have been half-healed contusions, but with goblins, it was hard to judge such things. With his usual profane exuberance, Cuz insisted that Goro had looked very different the last time he'd seen him, in the light of Claideris' flashlight.

"He was dyin'. I fuckin' swear he was dyin'. He couldn't cough and he was breathing all funny, then he'd healed himself and, like he went to sleep. He's been sleepin' since."

Cuz might be telling the truth. It took a lot of healing and a lot of not-eating afterward to wither a man the way Goro had been withered. Aulaudin doubted he'd have the strength to walk if they could have awakened him, which they couldn't.

«How do you plan to get them out?» Maun asked.

«To be honest, I hadn't given it much thought . . . I didn't truly expect to find them alive.»

«We can probably walk the youngster out the way we came; mortal or goblin, he looks feisty enough to survive the Veil, but I not so sure about your goblin, there. Get him back to those five stones and you're still looking at a shift to the Barrens—which is mortal realm and deadly, I hear, to goblins—and another shift to Sunrise.»

"So, we go straight to Sunrise," Aulaudin said aloud.

Maun had his doubts, which he mostly kept to himself for a change, sharing them only with his elder son and not poisoning the minds of Aglaun and Ombrio who had little and no experience bringing living creatures through the Veil.

"You're immortal now," Aulaudin said to Cuz when he balked at letting Maun be his guide and sole companion through the shift. "And, he's my father. He taught all of us the finer points of foraging and he's been parting the Veil longer than we all have together." Aulaudin gave his father the knife. "If it goes bad, come looking for us."

"If it goes bad," Maun replied, "you better all be dead before I find you, because, be damned, you will be afterward."

Maun wrapped Cuz in a bear hug. The mist shimmered and they were gone, though Cuz's screams lingered. Then Aulaudin and the two other elves sat in the mist; Ombrio to Aulaudin's right, Aglaun to his left. They lifted Goro into their laps.

"The more body contact, the better," he explained to them. "When I say so, lean forward and wrap around him, tight as you can, but each leave one hand for me." He offered a hand to each of them. "Think about the hand you're holding, don't think about anything else. This should work. He's not moving and he is immortal. It's not like we're trying to get a goat through."

Aulaudin regretted the words as they came out of his mouth. They were both thinking about goats when Aulaudin began building his Sunrise resting place in his mind. But they leaned when he told them to lean and clung to his hands when the Veil tried to separate them. Aulaudin was sure both shoulders had been dislocated. He could move his fingers but not his arms, and he didn't care: they were at Sunrise and Goro was still breathing.

Aglaun and Ombrio carried the goblin between them. They moved slowly because it was night at Sunrise—the same night, Aulaudin hoped—and they'd lost their flashlights to the Veil. Maun met them halfway to the great house: Maun and Jerlayne and dwarves with a stretcher.

"Laydin's safe and Claideris isn't going to cause any more trouble to us *or* the goblins," Jerlayne whispered when she hugged him. The fact that she had whispered it, rather than shared it through joining, told Aulaudin that there would be more to the story. "You're hurt!" She'd noticed he hadn't hugged her back.

"Take care of Goro," he whispered.

"I will, when we get to the great house," she assured him as, without warning, she put one hand on his right shoulder, the other on his right arm and twisted in opposite directions. "From what Cuz said, I was expecting much worse."

Aulaudin couldn't talk. Tears were streaming down his cheeks, but half the pain was already fading and she was getting a grip on his left side.

"How *is* Cuz?" he gasped when she was done.

"M'lene's taken him off for *healing*."

"Did he need healing?"

"I didn't ask," Jerlayne replied in a tone that promised another story, possibly more interesting than the one about Claideris.

Epilogue

Iron glowed in Jerlayne's steady hands. Her eyes opened and she appraised her handiwork: as close to perfect as she could get. The chain—the twenty-link chain—would be a gift to her mother at midwinter, less than a week away.

Elmeene's workroom wall of chains had been lost when Stonewell burned. Jerlayne had visited the ruins of her childhood home just once, to reclaim enough iron for half the links. The rest were shaped from metal she'd foraged herself in the mortal realm.

The cooling chain wasn't a true replacement for the one Jerlayne had shaped at Stonewell. Obviously, it hadn't been shaped from a single source, nor in an uninterrupted trance. After more than a century on her own, Jerlayne's skill as a shaping woman had progressed beyond such simple challenges.

I want to shape the world.

Jerlayne had never forgotten saying those words to Elmeene. For decades, she'd been unable to remember her mother's response, but Elmeene hadn't.

I've never said it was wrong . . . I said you shouldn't do it . . . unless you have no other choice. . . . You've made yourself blind to all the other choices.

Changing the shape of the world had been as simple as a plunge through an unsuspected Veil to the goblins' realm or a reach into the mortal realm to rescue the father of her elfin son. Problems happened and problems had to be resolved. Jerlayne hadn't worried about choices because she hadn't wasted time looking for them. She did what she could, and dealt with the consequences when they, themselves, became problems.

Mother and daughter argued now more than they had when Stonewell, not Sunrise, had been their home. At least once a day, Jerlayne swore that she couldn't wait until spring when her parents planned to formally refound their homestead. In the midst of Sunrise's own reconstruction, there were now *two* workrooms and *two* nurseries, lest the two women argue all the time.

Yet they were also closer than they'd ever been. Every argument yielded a bit of knowledge, respect, and, above all, honesty. Hence the new chain, shaped slowly, one link at a time, from the ruins of the past and the hopes of the future.

Elmeene never stopped thinking of consequences. With Claideris and her threats no longer hovering overhead, the woman who'd changed Fairie the last time had reshaped herself into Fairie's most outspoken conscience, surpassing even Maun of Briary. While Elmeene lived, Fairie would not repeat its mistakes nor make new ones, at least not without hearing her opinions first.

Weddings and other gathering festivals were meant to be pleasant times, Elmeene said, not times for debate; and Vigilance, though very useful, especially in a time of crisis, left women clinging to their husband's hands, straining for echoes. Her plans for the refounded Stonewell included a new room, large enough for an elf or two from every homestead, where consequences could be considered in advance, now that the sages no longer manipulated Fairie's fate.

Claideris' duplicity had devastated the four remaining sages. Gudwal, in particular, blamed himself for never suspecting that Claideris was anything but a blooddeath widow. He'd tried to lead his peers into the mist and might have succeeded if a score of elves hadn't rallied to stop them at the five-stone circle.

Jerlayne and Aulaudin had both thought the rally had been a mistake: *Let them go; we don't need sages or anyone else telling us what's best.* They were particularly astonished when it became clear that Maun and Elmeene were the elves who'd led the rally.

Consequences, again, or so Elmeene had explained at length afterward. The scyldrin—dwarves, gnomes, and all the rest—were, overall, older than the elves: they hadn't been decimated by blooddeath. Though they lived on elfin homesteads and relied on elfin foraging and shaping for the comforts of their lives, they placed their faith in their living ancestors, the itinerant sages, not their unacknowledged parents.

If we would keep our homesteads and the way of life we cherish, Maun elaborated at one recent Vigilance, *then we need to keep the sages, too, or the scyldrin will grow disgruntled. Besides, the sages are responsible for joining, and what right-thinking elf would want to live—or condemn his children to live—without joining?*

Maialene was an elf who preferred life without joining, though there were those—Elmeene chief among them—who'd question whether Maialene was a right-thinking elf. With her clinging clothes and metal-studded face, M'lene took delight in outraging elf and scyld alike. Elmeene insisted that Maialene trysted with Cuz simply to shock her mother.

That, Jerlayne knew, was an unjust condemnation. Cuz and M'lene didn't tryst and their affection, though built on a shared sense that neither of them belonged in Fairie, was sincere. He and Jerlayne's sister had said good-bye to Sunrise as soon as Cuz had learned to part the Veil.

They'd returned two days later. Some traditions weren't lies: goblins couldn't survive in the mortal realm. Claideris had apparently found some partial way around the limitation— if the ramblings of a madwoman as recounted by a one-time mortal were to be believed. But her secrets had died with her— and Jerlayne would never forget how swiftly and horribly the renegade's corpse had decomposed. She'd healed Cuz's fever and warned him that a day or a night was all the time he dared spend beyond the Veil.

To her surprise, both he and M'lene had accepted her judgement. They were beyond the Veil almost every day, but never for very long. And each time, when they returned, they brought back armloads of books and clutter for their as-yet-unbuilt cottage.

Jereige wasn't the only elf who'd decided the time had come for reading and writing. Less than a season after the changing had begun, every homestead was accumulating a library. Thanks to Cuz and M'lene, Sunrise had not only the largest library in Fairie, it also had the best readers, if not the best reading teachers. With Aulaudin, Cuz, and M'lene all helping her, Jerlayne had learned to read—and write—her name. Her favorite part of reading, though, was sitting at her tapestry loom, weaving pictures while Cuz and Maialene took turns reciting poetry.

Poetry had no fascination for Aulaudin. The books Jerlayne's husband foraged were thick, heavy, and dense with tiny print and incomprehensible diagrams. He pored over them whenever he could seize the opportunity—as Jerlayne would have done with a stubborn shaping. By his own admission, Aulaudin was nowhere near a mastery of *science*, not even the small segment of *science* that might explain why Evoni sang or against what specific threat she guarded Fairie.

Perhaps there is no explanation, she'd said to Aulaudin one evening when his eyes were red and sore from studying. *Perhaps it is enough to know that when mortals aim their noisy machines at Fairie, a siren's song keeps us hidden.*

Aulaudin had come to bed, but he'd been back at his books the next night, as convinced as ever that the explanations lay in an elf's ability to hear the background noise beyond the Veil. Cuz had told them about *radar, sonar, lasers,* and the ways in which mortals tuned that noise the way a musician tuned his instrument, the way Jerlayne shaped iron. He'd said his uncle had *pinged* Fairie hard—"rung it like a bell"—with an *electromagnetic pulse,* but Evoni had used *stealth technology* and *a cloaking device* to counter the attack.

Aulaudin said that Cuz threw a lot of words around and didn't know fact from fiction, but the truth was that neither Evoni nor the other sirens had sung up a storm since the night Cuz's uncle had died, and all of Cuz's words—except for the cloaking device—were included in Aulaudin's heavy books.

We need to know more, Aulaudin insisted. *Maybe there's nothing we can do except wait for the sirens to sing, but maybe there's something we can learn that will help her guard us.*

It was a notion, oddly enough that had been at the center of a message Joff had brought to Sunrise two days ago. The Uylma encouraged the elves to learn all they could about the mortal realm and its *science*. She claimed that the guardians were shaped from elfin knowledge and the more the elves understood about the mortal enemy, the stronger Fairie's defenses—her defenses—would be.

A gift had accompanied the message: a small golden plaque embossed with running horses, a gift given specifically to Jerlayne. Jerlayne's first thought had been to squeeze her hand around the plaque and shape it down into a meaningless lump.

We do not need her advice or gifts! she'd thundered at Joff who hadn't blinked or flinched. *We're not your chattel any longer. We don't stand at the edge of the mist, listening to ghosts and goblins. Fairie belongs to us. We'll learn what we want to learn.*

Joff had turned and walked away.

When Jerlayne had told Elmeene what she'd done, her mother had been beside herself: Didn't she understand that Fairie grew between the goblin plains and the mortal realm, that it was surrounded by untrustworthy neighbors? Couldn't she understand that Fairie needed goodwill from goblins as surely as it needed the sages, if it were to avoid being the battleground in a many-sided conflict?

As Elmeene saw it, consequence by consequence, the Uylma was keeping her promise to leave Fairie alone. Anyone who wanted to visit the five-stone circle, could do so. Elfin ghosts sometimes appeared, sometimes spoke, but Viljuen's voice—most recently Claideris' voice—which had guided the sages for millennia was no longer heard.

Elmeene concluded: *If the Uylma sends us a message, and her advice is at peace with what we have already decided to do for ourselves then, for our own sake, we can say thank you graciously. Fairie loses nothing by being gracious, Jerlayne, and the Uylma is not tempted to break her promises. So, go to the goblin and say thank-you, graciously.*

When Jerlayne had balked, her mother had sent Jereige to plead with her, then Maialene, and even Maun. Aulaudin, though had refused to plead with her. He'd understood that her outrage had had very little to do with Fairie's right to chart its own future and everything to do with the man resting not far from her workroom.

It was easier to understand mortals and *science* than any goblin. The nafoga'ar mist had healed Goro but withered him, as well. The man Aglaun and Ombrio had carried into the Sunrise great house had been little more than a skin-wrapped skeleton trapped between life and death. For weeks, Jerlayne's challenge had been feeding him. She'd begged and pleaded until Joff had agreed to take a message to the plains: Did the Uylma, the priestess of the nafoga'ar, have any suggestions for restoring her son's health?

There'd been no answer until two days ago, no answer other than a golden plaque.

Jerlayne, with suggestion from Cuz, had found a way to feed Goro not long after she'd sent Joff to the plains. She'd inserted a tube similar to the ones she'd pulled out of Cuz down Goro's throat and pumped thick soups into his stomach until he'd regained enough vitality to swallow on his own.

Once the goblin was awake and aware of his surroundings, Goro had expressed his gratitude by rejecting Jerlayne completely. He'd close his eyes if she came into his room and refused to be fed even though his joints had stiffened and he could barely open his mouth, much less control his arm.

Jerlayne had sent her mother to do what she could not. She couldn't imagine the patient that Elmeene couldn't intimidate into good behavior, but Elmeene conceded her match in Goro and, after hearing of their mother's defeat, Maialene refused to try. The scyldrin wanted no part of a goblin's care and neither did the goblins, including Cuz who was at least honest enough to admit that he didn't have sufficient courage to face a proud man reduced to helplessness.

Aulaudin had courage to spare and a hefty knowledge of masculine rivalry. Twice a day he carried a steaming bowl into Goro's room, closed the door, and kept it closed until the bowl was empty.

He was there now. Jerlayne had a sense of Aulaudin laughing as she wrapped the cooled chain in a rag and hid it where Elmeene wouldn't find it before the midwinter feast. She suspected—hoped—that Goro would attend the feast, moving slowly, but without assistance. And her husband would pretend to be as surprised as the rest of Sunrise.

Jerlayne heard a groaning, cursing crash—the loudest one in several days—and hurried down the hall. Her fingers rested on the latch, waiting for an invitation by voice or sharing.

"Had enough?" That was Aulaudin.

"Not yet." That was Goro.

"Need a hand up?"

"Not yours."

She heard the goblin's joints creaking through the door. Her fingers weighed down on the latch. Jerlayne was a healer; with a touch she could soothe his aches, loosen his joints . . . and destroy whatever accord Goro and Aulaudin had built between them. *That* was a consequence even she could see.

Grasping both hands behind her back, Jerlayne continued along the corridor to Laydin's nursery. Gelma acknowledged her with a nod, not breaking the rhythm of her knitting.

Laydin was awake, playing with his toes and a toy Aulaudin had hung above his cradle. The first letters of the alphabet dangled from the toy. Their son would learn to part the Veil, share his thoughts, and forage, all in the traditional way, but he'd grow up with books, too, and never be mystified by the difference between reading and writing. He would know who his fathers were, both of them, and that he was kin to the men and women of the mortal realm, the plains, and Fairie. Laydin and Mati and all the elves yet to be born—all the scyldrin, too—would never remember a Fairie where women didn't part the Veil, where goblins culled entire homesteads, and misguided sages kept the peace by denying the truth.

He'd see the world that his mother had shaped for him, and then the changes would truly begin.

Jerlayne was counting on it.

OWLSIGHT

by MERCEDES LACKEY
& LARRY DIXON

Darian has been living in the temporary encampment of the Tayledras Hawkpeople for nearly four years, working as liaison between them and the survivors of his own ravaged village. But as he is about to return with the Tayledras back to their home Vale to continue his magician's apprenticeship, Darian suddenly learns that his parents, missing for five years, are alive.

☐ **OWLSIGHT (hardcover)**   UE2802-$24.95

And don't miss OWLFLIGHT, the first novel of Darian, now in paperback:

Apprenticed to a venerable wizard when his hunter and trapper parents disappeared into the forest, Darian is difficult and strong-willed—much to the dismay of his kindly master. But a sudden twist of fate will change his life forever, when the ransacking of his village forces him to flee into the great mystical forest. It is here in the dark forest that he meets his destiny, as the terrifying and mysterious Hawkpeople lead him on the path to maturity.

☐ **OWLFLIGHT**   UE2804-$6.99

Prices slightly higher in Canada.   **DAW 172X**

Mercedes Lackey

The Novels of Valdemar

☐ OWLFLIGHT (hardcover)	UE2754—$21.95	
☐ STORM WARNING	UE2661—$6.99	
☐ STORM RISING	UE2712—$5.99	
☐ STORM BREAKING	UE2755—$6.99	
☐ MAGIC'S PAWN	UE2352—$5.99	
☐ MAGIC'S PROMISE	UE2401—$5.99	
☐ MAGIC'S PRICE	UE2426—$5.99	
☐ THE OATHBOUND	UE2285—$5.99	
☐ OATHBREAKERS	UE2319—$5.99	
☐ OATHBLOOD	UE2773—$6.99	
☐ BY THE SWORD	UE2463—$5.99	
☐ SWORD OF ICE: and other tales of Valdemar	UE2720—$5.99	
☐ ARROWS OF THE QUEEN	UE2378—$5.99	
☐ ARROW'S FLIGHT	UE2377—$5.99	
☐ ARROW'S FALL	UE2400—$5.99	
☐ WINDS OF FATE	UE2516—$5.99	
☐ WINDS OF CHANGE	UE2563—$5.99	
☐ WINDS OF FURY	UE2612—$5.99	
☐ THE BLACK GRYPHON*	UE2643—$5.99	
☐ THE WHITE GRYPHON*	UE2682—$5.99	
☐ THE SILVER GRYPHON*	UE2685—$5.99	

*with Larry Dixon

Prices slightly higher in Canada.   **DAW 170X**